KU-648-000

CONTENTS

TEMPEST FROM THE NORTH

THE
WALL
OF
STORMS

BOOK TWO OF THE DANDELION DYNASTY

KEN LIU

HEAD
of
ZEUS

First published in the United States of America in 2016
by Saga Press, an imprint of Simon & Schuster, Inc.

First published in the United Kingdom in 2016
by Head of Zeus Ltd.

This paperback edition first published in the United Kingdom
in 2017 by Head of Zeus Ltd.

9 7 5 3 2 4 6 8

A catalogue record for this book is available
from the British Library.

ISBN (PB) 9781784973278
ISBN (E) 9781784973247

Printed and bound by CPI Group (UK) Ltd,
Croydon, CR0 4YY

Head of Zeus Ltd
First Floor East
5–8 Hardwick Street
London EC1R 4RG

WWW.HEADOFZEUS.COM

For Lisa, Esther, and Miranda, *supra omnia familia*

THE
WALL
OF
STORMS

KEN LIU's short stories have won a Nebula, two Hugos, a World Fantasy Award and a Science Fiction & Fantasy Translation Award. *The Grace of Kings* was his first novel. He is also the translator of Cixin Liu's Hugo winning and Nebula nominated *The Three-Body Problem*.

CLASH OF TYPHOONS

A NOTE ON PRONUNCIATION

Many names in Dara are derived from Classical Ano. The transliteration for Classical Ano in this book does not use vowel digraphs; each vowel is pronounced separately. For example, "Réfiroa" has four distinct syllables: "Ré-fi-ro-a." Similarly, "Na-aroénna" has five syllables: "Na-a-ro-én-na."

The *i* is always pronounced like the *i* in English "mill."

The *o* is always pronounced like the *o* in English "code."

The *ü* is always pronounced like the umlauted form in German or Chinese pinyin.

Other names have different origins and contain sounds that do not appear in Classical Ano, such as the *xa* in "Xana" or the *ha* in "Haan." In such cases, however, each vowel is still pronounced separately. Thus, "Haan" also contains two syllables.

The representation of Lyucu and Agon names and words presents a different problem. As we come to know them through the people and language of Dara, the names given in this work are doubly mediated. Just as English speakers who write down Chinese names and words they hear will achieve only a rough approximation of the original sounds, so with the Dara transliteration of Lyucu and Agon.

LIST OF MAJOR CHARACTERS

KUNI'S CHILDREN

PRINCE TIMU (nursing name: Toto-*tika*): Kuni's firstborn; son of
    Empress Jia.
PRINCESS THÉRA (nursing name: Rata-*tika*): daughter of Empress Jia.
PRINCE PHYRO (nursing name: Hudo-*tika*): son of Consort Risana.
PRINCESS FARA (nursing name: Ada-*tika*): daughter of Consort
    Fina, who died in childbirth.

THE SCHOLARS

LUAN ZYA: Kuni's chief strategist during his rise, who refused all
    titles; Gin Mazoti's lover.
ZATO RUTHI: Imperial Tutor; leading Moralist of the age.
ZOMI KIDOSU: prized student of a mysterious teacher; daughter of
    a farming-fishing family in Dasu (Oga and Aki Kidosu).
KON FIJI: ancient Ano philosopher; founder of the Moralist school.
RA OJI: ancient Ano epigrammatist; founder of the Fluxist school.
NA MOJI: ancient Xana engineer who studied the flights of birds;
    founder of the Patternist school.
GI ANJI: modern philosopher of the Tiro states era; founder of the
    Incentivist school.

THE LYUCU

PÉKYU TENRYO ROATAN: leader of the Lyucu.
PRINCESS VADYU ROATAN (nicknamed "Tanvanaki"): the best
    garinafin pilot; daughter of Tenryo.
PRINCE CUDYU ROATAN: son of Tenryo.

THE GODS OF DARA

KIJI: patron of Xana; Lord of the Air; god of wind, flight, and birds;
    his *pawi* is the Mingén falcon; favors a white traveling cloak.

TUTUTIKA: patron of Amu; youngest of the gods; goddess of agriculture, beauty, and fresh water; her *pawi* is the golden carp.

KANA AND RAPA: twin patrons of Cocru; Kana is the goddess of fire, ash, cremation, and death; Rapa is the goddess of ice, snow, glaciers, and sleep; their *pawi* are twin ravens: one black, one white.

RUFIZO: patron of Faça; Divine Healer; his *pawi* is the dove.

TAZU: patron of Gan; unpredictable, chaotic, delighting in chance; god of sea currents, tsunamis, and sunken treasures; his *pawi* is the shark.

LUTHO: patron of Haan; god of fisherman, divination, mathematics, and knowledge; his *pawi* is the sea turtle.

FITHOWÉO: patron of Rima; god of war, the hunt, and the forge; his *pawi* is the wolf.

Écofi
Island

Arulugi
Island

Lake
Toyemotika

Müning

Canfin

Napi

Dimushi

Amu Strait

PORIN PLAINS

Dimu

GÉFICA

Kiesa

AMU

Tan Adü

Liru River

The
ISLANDS
of
DARA

Zudi

Pan

COCRU

Er-Mé Mountains

Mount Kana

Wisoti Mountains

Mount Ra

Çaruza

Farun

Rana Kida

Tunoa

Gonlogi
Desert

GAN

Sonaru
Desert

Sonaru River

Maji Peninsula

Itanti Peninsula

Nasu

Kishi Channel

Nokida

Toa

0   75   150

Miles

The
LANDS
of
UKYU
and
GONDÉ

Luan Zya's landing site ⚓

Admiral Krita' landing site ⚓

Taten 🏯
(*Pékyu Tenryo Roatan*)

GONDÉ

LURODIA TANTA
(THE ENDLESS DESERT)

Tenryo and Diaman
✗

Sea of Tears

Antler (*Agon*)/
Tail (*Lyucu*)

Wing (*Agon*)/
Foot (*Lyucu*)

WHISPERING BREEZES

CHAPTER ONE

TRUANTS

PAN: THE SECOND MONTH IN THE SIXTH YEAR OF
THE REIGN OF FOUR PLACID SEAS.

Masters and mistresses, lend me your ears.
Let my words sketch for you scenes of faith and courage.
Dukes, generals, ministers, and maids, everyone parades
    through this ethereal stage.
What is the love of a princess? What are a king's fears?

If you loosen my tongue with drink and enliven my heart with
    coin, all will be revealed in due course of time. . . .

The sky was overcast, and the cold wind whipped a few scattered snowflakes through the air. Carriages and pedestrians in thick coats and fur-lined hats hurried through the wide avenues of Pan, the Harmonious City, seeking the warmth of home.

Or the comfort of a homely pub like the Three-Legged Jug.

"Kira, isn't it your turn to buy the drinks this time? Everyone knows your husband turns every copper over to you."

"Look who's talking. Your husband doesn't get to sneeze without your permission! But I think today should be Jizan's turn, sister. I heard a wealthy merchant from Gan tipped her five silver pieces last night!"

"Whatever for?"

"She guided the merchant to his favorite mistress's house through a maze of back alleys and managed to elude the spies the merchant's wife sicced on him!"

"Jizan! I had no idea you had such a lucrative skill—"

"Don't listen to Kira's lies! Do I look like I have five silver pieces?"

"You certainly came in here with a wide enough grin. I'd wager you had been handsomely paid for facilitating a one-night marriage—"

"Oh, shush! You make me sound like I'm the greeter at an indigo house—"

"Ha-ha! Why stop at being the greeter? I rather think you have the skills to manage an indigo house, or . . . a scarlet house! I've certainly drooled over some of those boys. How about a little help for a sister in need—"

"—or a *big* help—"

"Can't the two of you get your minds out of the gutter for a minute? Wait . . . Phiphi, I think I heard the coins jangling in your purse when you came in—did you have good luck at sparrow tiles last night?"

"I don't know what you're talking about."

"Aha, I knew it! Your face gives everything away; it's a wonder you can bluff anyone at that game. Listen, if you want Jizan and me to keep our mouths shut in front of your foolish husband about your gaming habit—"

"You featherless pheasant! Don't you dare tell him!"

"It's hard for us to think about keeping secrets when we're so thirsty. How about some of that 'mind-moisturizer,' as they say in the folk operas?"

"Oh, you rotten . . . Fine, the drinks are on me."

"That's a good sister."

"It's just a harmless hobby, but I can't stand the way he mopes around the house and nags when he thinks I'm going to gamble everything away."

"You do seem to have Lord Tazu's favor, I'll grant you that. But good fortune is better when shared!"

"My parents must not have offered enough incense at the Temple of Tututika before I was born for me to end up with you two as my 'friends.' . . ."

Here, inside the Three-Legged Jug, tucked in an out-of-the-way corner of the city, warm rice wine, cold beer, and coconut arrack flowed as freely as the conversation. The fire in the wood-burning stove in the corner crackled and danced, keeping the pub toasty and bathing everything in a warm light. Condensation froze against the glass windows in refined, complex patterns that blurred the view of the outside. Guests sat by threes and fours around low tables in *géüpa*, relaxed and convivial, enjoying small plates of roasted peanuts dipped in taro sauce that sharpened the taste of alcohol.

Ordinarily, an entertainer in this venue could not expect a cessation in the constant murmur of conversation. But gradually, the buzzing of competing voices died out. For now, at least, there was no distinction between merchants' stable boys from Wolf's Paw, scholars' servant girls from Haan, low-level government clerks sneaking away from the office for the afternoon, laborers resting after a morning's honest work, shopkeepers taking a break while their spouses watched the store, maids and matrons out for errands and meeting friends—all were just members of an audience enthralled by the storyteller standing at the center of the tavern.

He took a sip of foamy beer, put the mug down, slapped his hands a few times against his long, draping sleeves, and continued:

. . . the Hegemon unsheathed Na-aroénna then, and King Mocri stepped back to admire the great sword: the soul-taker, the head-remover, the hope-dasher. Even the moon seemed to lose her luster next to the pure glow of this weapon.

"That is a beautiful blade," said King Mocri, champion of Gan. "It surpasses other swords as Consort Mira excels all other women."

The Hegemon looked at Mocri contemptuously, his double-pupils glinting. "Do you praise the weapon because you think I hold an unfair advantage? Come, let us switch swords, and I have no doubt I will still defeat you."

"Not at all," said Mocri. "I praise the weapon because I believe you know a warrior by his weapon of choice. What is better in life than to meet an opponent truly worthy of your skill?"

The Hegemon's face softened. "I wish you had not rebelled, Mocri. . . ."

In a corner barely illuminated by the glow of the stove, two boys and a girl huddled around a table. Dressed in hempen robes and tunics that were plain but well-made, they appeared to be the children of farmers or perhaps the servants of a well-to-do merchant's family. The older boy was about twelve, fair-skinned and well proportioned. His eyes were gentle and his dark hair, naturally curly, was tied into a single messy bun at the top of his head. Across the table from him was a girl about a year younger, also fair-skinned and curly-haired—though she wore her hair loose and let the strands cascade around her pretty, round face. The corners of her mouth were curled up in a slight smile as she scanned the room with lively eyes shaped like the body of the graceful dyran, taking in everything with avid interest. Next to her was a younger boy about nine, whose complexion was darker and whose hair was straight and black. The older children sat on either side of him, keeping him penned between the table and the wall. The mischievous glint in his roaming eyes and his constant fidgeting offered a hint as to why. The similarity in the shapes of their features suggested they were siblings.

"Isn't this great?" whispered the younger boy. "I bet Master Ruthi still thinks we're imprisoned in our rooms, enduring our punishment."

"Phyro," said the older boy, a slight frown on his face, "you know this is only a temporary reprieve. Tonight, we each still have to write three essays about how Kon Fiji's *Morality* applies to our misbehavior, how youthful energy must be tempered by education, and how—"

"Shhhh—" the girl said. "I'm trying to hear the storyteller! Don't lecture, Timu. You already agreed that there's no difference between playing first and then studying, on the one hand, and studying first and then playing, on the other. It's called 'time-shifting.'"

"I'm beginning to think that this 'time-shifting' idea of yours would be better called 'time-wasting,'" said Timu, the older brother. "You and Phyro were wrong to make jokes about Master Kon Fiji—and I should have been more severe with you. You should accept your punishment gracefully."

"Oh, wait until you find out what Théra and I—*mmf*—"

The girl had clamped a hand over the younger boy's mouth. "Let's not trouble Timu with too much knowledge, right?" Phyro nodded, and Théra let go.

The young boy wiped his mouth. "Your hand is salty! *Ptui!*" Then he turned back to Timu, his older brother. "Since you're so eager to write the essays, Toto-*tika*, I'm happy to yield my share to you so that you can write six instead of three. Your essays are much more to Master Ruthi's taste anyway."

"That's ridiculous! The only reason I agreed to sneak away with you and Théra is because as the eldest, it's my responsibility to look after you, and you promised you would take your punishment later—"

"Elder Brother, I'm shocked!" Phyro put on a serious mien that looked like an exact copy of their strict tutor's when he was about to launch into a scolding lecture. "Is it not written in Sage Kon Fiji's *Tales of Filial Devotion* that the younger brother should offer the choicest specimens in a basket of plums to the elder brother as a token of his respect? Is it also not written that an elder brother should try to protect the younger brother from difficult tasks beyond his ability, since it is the duty of the stronger to defend the weaker? The essays are uncrackable nuts to me, but juicy plums to you. I am trying to live as a good Moralist with my offer. I thought you'd be pleased."

"That is—you cannot—" Timu was not as practiced at this particular subspecies of the art of debate as his younger brother. His face grew red, and he glared at Phyro. "If only you would direct your cleverness to actual schoolwork."

"You should be happy that Hudo-*tika* has done the assigned

reading for once," said Théra, who had been trying to maintain a straight face as the brothers argued. "Now please be quiet, both of you; I want to hear this."

. . . slammed Na-aroénna down, and Mocri met it with his ironwood shield, reinforced with cruben scales. It was as if Fithowéo had clashed his spear against Mount Kiji, or if Kana had slammed her fiery fist against the surface of the sea. Better yet, let me chant for you a portrait of that fight:

> *On this side, the champion of Gan, born and bred on Wolf's Paw;*
> *On that side, the Hegemon of Dara, last scion of Cocru's marshals.*
> *One is the pride of an island's spear-wielding multitudes;*
> *The other is Fithowéo, the God of War, incarnate.*
> *Will the Doubt-Ender end all doubt as to who is master of Dara?*
> *Or will Goremaw finally meet a blood-meal he cannot swallow?*
> *Sword is met with sword, cudgel with shield.*
> *The ground quakes as dual titans leap, smash, clash, and thump.*
> *For nine days and nine nights they fought on that desolate hill,*
> *And the gods of Dara gathered over the whale's way to judge the strength of their will. . . .*

As he chanted, the storyteller banged a coconut husk against a large kitchen spoon to simulate the sounds of sword clanging against shield; he leapt about, whipping his long sleeves this way and that to conjure the martial dance of legendary heroes in the flickering firelight of the pub. As his voice rose and fell, urgent one moment, languorous the next, the audience was transported to another time and place.

. . . After nine days, both the Hegemon and King Mocri were exhausted. After parrying another strike from the Doubt-Ender, Mocri took a step back and stumbled over a rock. He fell, his shield and sword splayed out to the sides. With one more step, the Hegemon would be able to bash in his skull or lop off his head.

"No!" Phyro couldn't help himself. Timu and Théra, equally absorbed by the tale, didn't shush him.

The storyteller nodded appreciatively at the children, and went on.

But the Hegemon stayed where he was and waited until Mocri climbed back up, sword and shield at the ready.

"Why did you not end it just now?" asked Mocri, his breathing labored.

"Because a great man deserves to not have his life end by chance," said the Hegemon, whose breathing was equally labored. "The world may not be fair, but we must strive to make it so."

"Hegemon," said Mocri, "I am both glad and sorry to have met you."

And they rushed at each other again, with lumbering steps and proud hearts. . . .

"Now that is the manner of a real hero," whispered Phyro, his tone full of admiration and longing. "Hey, Timu and Théra, you've actually met the Hegemon, haven't you?"

"Yes . . . but that was a long time ago," Timu whispered back. "I don't really remember much except that he was really tall, and those strange eyes of his looked terribly fierce. I remember wondering how strong he must have been to be able to wield that huge sword on his back."

"He sounds like a great man," said Phyro. "Such honor in every action; such grace to his foes. Too bad he and Da could not—"

"Shhhh!" Théra interrupted. "Hudo-*tika*, not so loud! Do you want everyone here to know who we are?"

Phyro might be a rascal to his older brother, but he respected the authority of his older sister. He lowered his voice. "Sorry. He just seems such a brave man. And Mocri, too. I'll have to tell Ada-*tika* all about this hero from her home island. How come Master Ruthi never taught us anything about Mocri?"

"This is just a story," Théra said. "Fighting nonstop for nine days and nine nights—how can you believe that really happened? Think: The storyteller wasn't there, how would he know what the Hegemon and Mocri said?" But seeing the disappointment on her little brother's face, she softened her tone. "If you want to hear real stories about heroes, I'll tell you later about the time Auntie Soto stopped the Hegemon from hurting Mother and us. I was only three then, but I remember it as though it happened yesterday."

Phyro's eyes brightened and he was about to ask for more, but a rough voice broke in.

"I've had just about enough of this ridiculous tale, you insolent fraud!"

The storyteller stopped in midsentence, shocked at this intrusion into his performance. The tavern patrons turned to look at the speaker. Standing next to the stove, the man was tall, barrel-chested, and as muscular as a stevedore. He was easily the largest person in the pub. A jagged scar that started at his left brow and ended at his right cheek gave his face a fearsome aspect, which was only enhanced by the wolf's-teeth necklace that dangled in front of the thick chest hair that peeked out of the loose lapels of his short robe like a patch of fur. Indeed, the yellow teeth that showed between his sneering lips reminded one of a hungry wolf on the prowl.

"How dare you fabricate such stories about that crook Mata Zyndu? He tried to thwart Emperor Ragin's righteous march to the throne and caused much needless suffering and desolation. By praising the despicable tyrant Zyndu, you're denigrating the victory of our wise emperor and casting aspersions upon the character of the Dandelion Throne. These are words of treason."

"Treason? For telling a few stories?" The storyteller was so furious that he started to laugh. "Will you next claim that all folk opera troupes are rebels for enacting the rise and fall of old Tiro dynasties? Or that the wise Emperor Ragin is jealous of shadow puppet plays about Emperor Mapidéré? What a silly man you are!"

The owners of the Three-Legged Jug, a rotund man of short stature and his equally rotund wife, rushed up between the two to play peacemakers. "Masters! Remember this is a humble venue for entertainment and relaxation! No politics, please! We're all here after a hard day's work to share a few drinks and have some fun."

The husband turned to the man with the scarred face and bowed deeply. "Master, I can tell you are a man of hot passions and strong morals. And if the tale has offended, I apologize first. I know Tino here well. Let me assure you he had no intention of insulting the emperor. Why, before he became a storyteller, he fought for Emperor Ragin during the Chrysanthemum-Dandelion War in Haan, when the emperor was only the King of Dasu."

The wife smiled ingratiatingly. "How about a flask of plum wine on the house? If you and Tino drink together, I'm sure you'll forget about this little misunderstanding."

"What makes you think I want to have a drink with *him*?" asked Tino the storyteller, whipping his sleeves contemptuously at Scarface.

The other patrons in the pub shouted in support of the storyteller.

"Sit down, you ignorant oaf!"

"Get out of here if you don't like the story. No one is forcing you to sit and listen!"

"I'll throw you out myself if you keep this up."

Scarface smiled, stuck one of his hands into the lapel of his robe, under the dangling wolf's-teeth necklace, and retrieved a small metal tablet. He waved it around at the patrons and then held it under the nose of the proprietress of the pub. "Do you recognize this?"

She squinted to get a good look. The tablet was about the size of two palms, and two large logograms were carved into it in relief: One was the logogram for *sight*—a stylized eye with a beam coming out of it—and the other was the logogram for *faraway*—composed of the number logogram for "a thousand" modified by a winding path around it. Shocked, the woman stuttered, "You—you're with the— the, um, the—"

Scarface put the tablet away. The cold, mirthless grin on his face grew wider as he scanned the room, daring anyone to hold his gaze. "That's right. I serve Duke Rin Coda, Imperial Farsight Secretary."

The shouting among the patrons died down, and even Tino lost his confident look. Although Scarface looked more like a highwayman than a government official, Duke Coda, who was in charge of Emperor Ragin's spies, was said to run his department in collaboration with the seedier elements of Dara society. It wouldn't be beyond him to rely on someone like Scarface. Even though no one in the pub had ever heard of a storyteller getting in trouble for an embellished tale about the Hegemon, Duke Coda's duties did include ferreting out traitors and dissatisfied former nobles plotting against the emperor. No one wanted to risk challenging the emperor's own trusted eyes.

"Wait—" Phyro was about to speak when Théra grabbed his hand and squeezed it under the table and shook her head at him slowly.

Seeing the timid reactions from everyone present, Scarface nodded with satisfaction. He pushed the owners of the pub aside and strolled up to Tino. "Crafty, disloyal *entertainers* like you are the worst. Just because you fought for the emperor doesn't give you the right to say whatever you want. Now, normally, I would have to take you to the constables for further interrogation"—Tino shrank back in terror—"but I'm in a generous mood today. If you pay a fine of twenty-five pieces of silver and apologize for your errors, I might just let you off with a warning."

Tino glanced at the few coins in the tip bowl on the table and turned back to Scarface. He bowed repeatedly like a chicken pecking at the ground. "Master Farseer, please! That amounts to two week's earnings even when things are going well. I've got an aged mother at home who is ill—"

"Of course you do," said Scarface. "She'll miss you terribly if you are held at the constable station, won't she? A proper interrogation might take days, weeks even; do you understand?"

Tino's face shifted through rage, humiliation, and utter defeat as he reached into the lapel of his robe for his coin purse. The other patrons looked away carefully, not daring to make a sound.

"Don't think the rest of you are getting off so easily, either," said Scarface. "I heard how many of you cheered when he veiled his criticisms of the emperor with that story full of lies. Each of you will have to pay a fine of one silver as an accessory to the crime."

The men and women in the pub looked unhappy, but a few sighed and began reaching for their purses as well.

"Stop."

Scarface looked around for the source of the voice, which was crisp, sharp, and uninflected by fear. A figure stood up from the shadowy corner of the pub and walked into the firelight of the stove, a slight limp in the gait punctuated by the staccato falls of a walking stick.

Though dressed in a scholar's long flowing robes edged in blue silk, the speaker was a woman. About eighteen years of age, she had fair skin and gray eyes that glinted with a steadfastness that belied her youth. The radiating lines of a faint pink scar, like a sketch of a blooming flower, covered her left cheek, and the stem of this flower continued down her neck like the lateral line of a fish, curiously adding a sense of liveliness to her otherwise wan visage. Her hair, a light brown, was tied atop her head in a tight triple scroll-bun. Tassels and knotted strings dangled from her blue sash—a custom of distant northwestern islands in old Xana. Leaning against a wooden walking stick that came up to her eyebrows, she put her right hand on the sword she wore at her waist, the scabbard and hilt looking worn and shabby.

"What do you want?" asked Scarface. But his tone was no longer as arrogant as before. The woman's scroll-bun and her boldness in openly wearing a sword in Pan indicated that she was a scholar who had achieved the rank of *cashima*, a Classical Ano word meaning "practitioner": She had passed the second level of the Imperial examinations.

Emperor Ragin had restored and expanded the civil service examination system long practiced by the Tiro kings and the Xana Empire, turning it into the sole mode of advancement for those with political ambition while eliminating other time-honored paths to obtain valuable administrative posts, such as patronage, purchase, inheritance, or recommendation by trusted nobles. Competition in the examinations was fierce, and the emperor, who had risen to power with the aid of women in powerful posts, had opened the exams to women as well as men. Though women *toko dawiji*—the rank given to those who had passed the Town Examinations, the first level in the exams—were still rare, and women *cashima* even rarer, they were entitled to all the privileges of the status given to their male counterparts. For instance, all *toko dawiji* were exempt from corvée, and the *cashima* had the additional right to be brought before an Imperial magistrate right away when accused of a crime instead of being interrogated by the constables.

"Stop bothering these people," she said calmly. "And you certainly won't be getting a single copper out of me."

Scarface had not expected to find a person of her rank in a dive like the Three-Legged Jug. "Mistress, you don't have to pay the fine, of course. I'm sure you're not a disloyal scoundrel like the rest of these lowlifes."

She shook her head. "I don't believe you work for Duke Coda at all."

Scarface narrowed his eyes. "You doubt the sign of the farseers?"

The woman smiled. "You put it away so quickly that I didn't get a good look. Why don't you let me examine it?"

Scarface chuckled awkwardly. "A scholar of your erudition surely recognized the logograms in a single glance."

"It's easy enough to forge something like that out of a block of wax and a coat of silver paint, but much harder to forge a believable order from Farsight Secretary Coda."

"What—what are you talking about? This is the time of the Grand Examination, when the cream of Dara's scholars are gathered in the capital. Those who like to stir up trouble would seize the opportunity to harm the talented men, er, and women, here to serve the emperor. It's natural that the emperor would order Duke Coda to increase security."

The woman shook her head and continued in a placid tone, "Emperor Ragin prides himself on being a tolerant lord open to honest counsel. He even honored Zato Ruthi, who once fought against him, with the position of Imperial Tutor out of respect for his scholarship. Charging a storyteller with treason for taking some literary license would chill the hearts of the men and women he is trying to recruit. Duke Coda, who knows the emperor as well as anyone, would never give an order to authorize what you're attempting."

Scarface flushed with anger, and the thick scar twitched like a snake crawling over his face. But he stood rooted to his spot and made no move toward her.

The woman laughed. "In fact, I think I'll send for the constables myself. Impersonating an Imperial officer *is* a crime."

"Oh no," whispered Théra in the corner.

"What?" asked Timu and Phyro together in a low voice.

"You should never corner a rabid dog," moaned Théra.

Scarface's eyes narrowed as fear of the *cashima* turned to desperate resolve. He roared and rushed at the *cashima*. The surprised woman managed to scramble awkwardly out of the way at the last minute, dragging her weak left leg. The lumbering assailant crashed into a table, causing the patrons sitting at it to jump back, cursing and screaming. Soon, he climbed back up, looking even more enraged, swore loudly, and came at her again.

"I hope she fights as well as she talks," said Phyro. He clapped his hands and laughed. "This is the most fun we've ever had sneaking out!"

"Stay behind me!" said Timu, stretching out his arms and moving to shield his brother and sister from the commotion in the center of the pub.

The woman unsheathed the sword with her right hand. Bracing herself against the walking stick, she held the sword in an uncertain manner and pointed its wavering tip at the man. But Scarface seemed to have gone berserk. He continued to rush at her without slowing down and reached out to grab the blade of her sword with his bare hands.

The patrons in the pub either looked away or flinched, waiting for blood to spurt as his fingers closed around the sword.

Crack. The sword snapped in half crisply, and the woman was on the ground, stunned by the impact of the burly man against her body. She was still holding on to half of a sword, and not a drop of blood could be seen.

Scarface laughed and tossed the other half of the sword into the open stove, where the wooden blade, painted to look like the real thing, instantly burst into flames.

"Who's the real swindler here?" Scarface sneered. "It takes one to know one, doesn't it? And now you're going to pay." He strode up to the still stunned woman like a wolf closing in for the kill. Now that the hem of the woman's robe had ridden up, he saw that her left leg was enclosed in a kind of harness, similar to the sort worn by many veterans who had lost limbs during the wars. "So you're a useless cripple, too." He spat at her and lifted his right foot, clad in a massive leather boot, aiming for her head.

"Don't you dare touch her!" shouted Phyro. "I'll make you regret it!"

Scarface stopped and turned to regard the three children in the corner.

Timu and Théra stared at Phyro.

"Master Ruthi always said that a Moralist gentleman must stand up for those in need," Phyro said defensively.

"So you've decided that this is the moment you should start listening to Master Ruthi?" groaned Théra. "Do you think we're in the palace, surrounded by guards who can stop him?"

"Sorry, but she was defending Da's honor!" Phyro whispered fiercely, not backing down.

"Run, both of you!" shouted Timu. "I'll hold him back." He waved his gangly arms about, uncertain how he was going to carry out this plan.

Now that he had gotten a clear look at the three "heroes," Scarface laughed. "I'll take care of you brats after I'm done with her." He turned back and leaned down for the traveling purse attached to the *cashima*'s sash.

Théra's eyes darted around the pub: Some of the patrons were huddled near the walls, trying to stay as far away from the fight as possible; others were slowly inching their way to the door, seeking an escape. Nobody wanted to do anything to stop the robbery—and perhaps worse—in progress. She grabbed Phyro by the ears before he could get away, turned him to face her, and touched her forehead to his.

"Ouch!" Phyro hissed. "Do you have to do that?"

"Timu is brave but he's no good in a fight," she said.

Phyro nodded. "Unless we're talking about a competition on who can write the most obscure logograms."

"Right. So it's up to you and me." And she quickly whispered her plan to him.

Phyro grinned. "You're the best big sister."

Timu, still dancing about uncertainly, pushed at them both ineffectually. "Go, go!"

Over by the stove, Scarface was examining the contents of the purse he had ripped from the woman, who lay at his feet, unmoving. Maybe she was still recovering from the body blow.

Phyro dashed away and disappeared into the crowd of patrons.

Instead of running, Théra jumped onto the table.

"Hey, Auntie Phiphi, Auntie Kira, Auntie Jizan!" she shouted, and pointed at three of the women among those inching toward the door. They stopped to look at her, startled at having their names called by this strange girl.

"Do you know her?" whispered Phiphi.

Jizan and Kira shook their heads. "She was sitting at the table next to ours," Kira whispered back. "I thought she might have been listening in on our talk."

"Haven't you always said that I can't let men push me around if I want a harmonious household after I get married?" Théra continued. "Since the menfolk are all running away with their tails between their legs, aren't you going to help me teach this oaf a lesson?"

Scarface looked from Théra to the three women, uncertain what was going on. But Théra wasn't going to give him time to figure things out. "Oh, Cousin Ro! Practically our whole clan is here. Why are we so afraid of this dolt?"

"I'm certainly not," a voice answered from the crowd. It sounded youthful, almost girlish. Then a bowl flew out of the shadows near the door and smashed into Scarface, drenching him in fragrant, hot tea. "Heck, all of us spitting on him would be enough to drown him! Auntie Phiphi, Auntie Kira, Auntie Jizan, come on!"

The crowd that had been trying to escape the pub stopped moving. The three women whose names had been called gaped at Scarface, who now looked like a chicken caught in a thunderstorm. They looked at each other and grinned.

A moment later, three mugs of beer flew through the air and smashed against Scarface. He roared in rage.

"And here's one from me!" Théra grabbed the flask of rice wine from their table and tossed it at Scarface's head. It just missed and broke against the stove, and the spilled wine hissed in the fire.

Crowds were delicate things. Sometimes all it took was a single example for a loose flock of sheep to turn into a wolfish mob.

Since the women had such success with their first strikes, the men looked at each other and suddenly discovered their courage. Even the storyteller Tino, so obsequious a moment earlier, threw his half-drunk mug of beer at the robber. Bowls, cups, flasks, mugs flew from every direction at Scarface, who wrapped his arms about his head and stumbled about to survive the onslaught, howling in pain. The couple running the pub jumped up and down, begging people not to destroy their property, but it was too late.

"We'll pay you back," shouted Timu over the din, but it was unclear if the pub-keeping couple heard him.

More than a few of the missiles had struck Scarface, and he was bruised all over. Blood flowed from cuts on his face, and he was soaked in tea, wine, and beer. Realizing that he could no longer intimidate the incensed crowd, Scarface spat hatefully at Théra. But he had to get away before the crowd got even bolder and tried to tackle him.

He tossed the purse into the burning stove as a final gesture of pique, and then pushed and shoved his way through the crowd. People, still individually awed by his size and strength, leapt out of his way. He slammed through the pub's front door like a wolf chased away from the flock by a pack of baying hounds, leaving in his wake only a few snowflakes swirling in the eddies near the entrance. Soon, the snowflakes also disappeared, as though he had never been there at all.

Men and women milled about the pub, slapping one another on the back and congratulating all on their bravery while the proprietor and proprietress rushed around with dustpan and broom and bucket and rag to sweep up the broken pottery and china. Phyro pushed through the crowd until he was standing next to Théra.

"Smacked him right in the neck with that first bowl," boasted Phyro.

"Well done, 'Cousin Ro,'" Théra said, smiling.

Tino the storyteller and the proprietors of the pub came up to thank the three children for their heroic intervention—and in the case of the tavern owners, also to make sure they really would pay for the damage. Leaving Timu to handle the flowery language of mutual appreciation and proper humility and promissory notes, Théra and Phyro went to see if the young *cashima* was all right.

She had been stunned by the burly man's blow but wasn't seriously injured. They helped her sit up and fed her sips of warm rice wine.

"What's your name?"

"Zomi Kidosu," she said in a faint, embarrassed voice. "Of Dasu."

"Are you a real *cashima*?" asked Phyro, pointing at the broken wooden sword lying next to her.

"Hudo-*tika*!" Théra was mortified by the rude question from her little brother.

"What? If the sword isn't real, maybe her rank isn't real either."

But the young woman didn't answer. She was staring at the fire in the stove, where the other half of her sword had turned to ashes. "My pass . . . my pass . . ."

"What pass?" asked Phyro.

Zomi continued to mutter as though she couldn't hear Phyro.

Théra surveyed the young woman's worn shoes and patched robe; her gaze lingered for a moment on the intricate harness around her left leg, whose design she had never seen, even from the Imperial doctors who worked with injuries suffered by her father's most trusted guards; she noted the calluses on the pads of her right thumb, index and middle fingers, as well as on the back of her ring finger; she observed the bits of wax and ink stains under her fingernails.

She's a long way from home, and she's been practicing writing, a lot of writing.

"Of course she's a real *cashima*," Théra said. "She's here for the Grand Examination. That fool burned her pass for the Examination Hall!"

CHAPTER TWO

FALLEN KINGS

The swirling snow intensified, and pedestrians and riders in the streets grew scarce as they hurried home or sought shelter in roadside inns and eateries. A few sparrows hiding out under the eaves twittered excitedly, as they seemed to hear a voice in the howling wind.

- *What mischief do you plot, Tazu? Have you come to bring discord to the Harmonious City?*

For a moment, a wild cackling accompanied by the strident noise of a hungry shark gnashing its teeth interrupted the swirling snowstorm, but it faded so quickly that the sparrows sat stunned, uncertain if they had truly heard it.

- *Kiji, my brother, still so humorless after all these years. Like you, I've come to observe Kuni's contest of intellects, a trial of sharp words and stalwart logograms. You have my sympathies for the tribulations of your studious young lady, but I assure you I had nothing to do with the man who ruined her day—doesn't mean that I won't have anything more to do with him, though, now that he's gotten my interest. However, you're acting so* outraged that one wonders who's the girl and who's the patron god.

- I don't trust you. You're always bringing chaos to order, strife to peace.

- I'm hurt! Though I do confess that it always irks me a bit when the mortals reduce the messy truths of history to neat stories. Too smooth and "harmonious."

- Then you're doomed to live in ire all your days. History is the long shadow cast by the past upon the future. Shadows, by nature, lack details.

- You sound like a mortal philosopher.

- Peace has not been easy to earn. Do not stir up ghosts to prey upon the living.

- But we don't want Fithowéo to be bored, do we? What kind of brother are you that you care not for his well-being?

A clanging of metal shot through the storm, like the thundering of shod hooves over the iron bridge spanning the moat of the palace. The sparrows cowered and made no more noise.

- My charge is war, but that does not mean I crave death. That is more Kana's pleasure.

A flash of red behind the clouds, as though a volcano were glowing through mist.

- Tazu and Fithowéo, do not besmirch my name. I rule over the shades on the other shore of the River-on-Which-Nothing-Floats, but do not think that I desire their numbers to increase without good cause.

A chaotic swirl in the snow, like a cyclone roaming over a white sea.

- Tsk-tsk. What happened to doing the most interesting thing? You are all such killjoys. No matter. There is a dark stain at the foundation of the Dandelion Throne, whose empire is born from Kuni's betrayal of the Hegemon. Such a sin at the origin cannot be erased and will haunt him, no matter how much good he thinks he's doing.

The silence of the other gods seemed to acknowledge the truth of Tazu's words.

- The mortals are dissatisfied and will make trouble no matter what you profess to desire. The scent of blood and rot draws the sharks, and I am only doing what comes naturally to me. When the storm comes, I know all of you will do the same.

The chaotic swirl blended with the howling storm, and snow soon covered the footprints of the last pedestrians.

Doru Solofi trudged through the snow, trying to move as fast as he could. Finally, he decided that he had gotten far enough away from the Three-Legged Jug and turned into a small alley, where he leaned against a wall to rest, his heart beating wildly and his breathing labored.

Damn that cashima, *and damn those children!* His little scam had worked well the last few times he'd tried it and earned him a nice bit of money—though he had soon lost it all in gambling parlors and indigo houses. If the *cashima* really reported him to the constables, he might have to hide for a while until things quieted down. In any event, perhaps it was risky to stay in the capital, where security was bound to be tighter than elsewhere, but he was unwilling to leave its bustling streets and thriving markets, where the very air seemed to crackle by proximity to power.

He was like a wolf who had been driven out from his den, and now he yearned for a home that was no longer his.

Thwack. A snowball slammed into the back of his neck, the cold more shocking than the pain. He whipped around and saw a little boy standing a few yards away down in the alley. The boy grinned, revealing a mouth full of yellow teeth that seemed unnaturally sharp, an impression reinforced by the shark's-teeth necklace he wore around his neck.

Who is he? Doru Solofi wondered. *Is he one of the savages from Tan Adü, where the inhabitants file their teeth to points in accordance with their barbaric custom?*

Thwack. The boy lobbed another snowball at him, this one striking him right in the face.

Solofi wiped the snow away from his eyes, struggling to see. Melting snow and ice flowed down the collar of his tunic, drenching his chest and back. He could feel bits of gravel grinding against his skin, especially the tender spots where the hot tea had scalded him. With ice added to the alcohol and tea water that had already soaked his clothes, his teeth started to chatter in the howling wind.

He roared and leapt at the young boy, intent on teaching him a lesson. It was intolerable that even a child now believed that he could torment Doru Solofi, who had once been the most powerful man in this city.

The boy nimbly dodged out of his way, like a sleek shark slithering out of the way of a lumbering fishing boat. Cackling wildly, the boy ran away, and Solofi pursued.

On and on the boy and the man raced through the streets of Pan, careless of the astonished looks of the passersby. Solofi's lungs burned as he panted in the icy air; his legs felt leaden as he stumbled and slipped through the snow. The boy, however, was sure-footed like a goat on the snowbound cliffs of Mount Rapa, and seemed to taunt him by staying just a step ahead, barely out of his grasp. Several times he decided to stop and give up the chase, but each time, as he did so, the boy turned and lobbed another snowball at him. Solofi could not understand how the boy had so much strength and endurance—it seemed unnatural—but rage had driven reason from his mind, and all he could think of was the pleasure he would feel when he crushed the skull of that nasty urchin against some wall.

The boy dashed down another deserted alley, disappearing around the corner. Solofi lumbered right after—and stopped dead in his tracks as he emerged from the alley.

In front of him, as far as the eye could see, was a miniature metropolis constructed of gray-veined marble, rough-hewn granite, and weathered wood, with man-sized pyramids, cylinders, and simple rectangular blocks erected along a grid of snow-covered footpaths. Topped by statues of ravens, the gravestones and mourning tablets were carved with lines of logograms that tried to summarize a life in a few lines of verse.

The boy had led him to the largest cemetery in the city, where many of those who had died in Pan during the rebellion against the Xana Empire, and later, during the Chrysanthemum-Dandelion War, were buried.

The boy was nowhere to be seen.

Solofi took a deep breath to steady his nerves. He was not a super-stitious man and would not be afraid of ghosts. He stepped resolutely into the city of the dead.

At first cautiously, and then frantically, Solofi searched among the gravestones, looking behind each marker for signs of his prey. But the boy had apparently disappeared into thin air like a mirage or dream.

The hairs on Solofi's back stood up. Had he been chasing a ghost? He certainly had been responsible for the deaths of many during the war . . .

"One, two, three, four! Faster! Faster! Can you feel it? Can you sense the power flowing through you? Three, two, three, four!"

Solofi whipped his head around and saw that the cries were coming from a man who stood on the steps of the giant marble mausoleum dedicated to the spirits of the Eight Hundred, the first soldiers who had joined Mata Zyndu, the Hegemon, when he raised the flag of rebellion against Emperor Mapidéré on Tunoa.

"Four, two, three, four! Suadégo, you need to work on your foot-work. Look at your husband: how he dances with dedication! Six, two, three, four!"

The man on the steps was wiry and dark-skinned, and the way he moved—at once deliberate and furtive, like a mouse strolling across the dinner table after the lights had been snuffed out—seemed familiar to Solofi. He headed in the direction of the man to get a better look, taking care to hide himself behind tall gravestones as he did so.

"Seven, two, three, four! Poda, you need to spin faster. You're out of sync with everyone else. I might have to demote you after today if you can't keep up. One, two, three, four!"

Now that Solofi was closer, he saw that about forty men and women stood in four rows in the clearing below the steps of the mausoleum. As far as Solofi could tell, they were performing some kind of dance, though it resembled no dance he had ever seen: The men and women spun like drunken versions of the sword dancers of Cocru; stretched their arms up to the sky and then bent down to touch their toes in some absurd parody of the veiled dancers of Faça; jumped up and down in place while clapping their hands over their heads as though they were fresh recruits in the army being put through an exercise regimen. The only music that accompanied them was a mix of the howling of the winds, the rhythmic, counting chant of the man on the steps of the mausoleum, and their stomping steps against the ground. Though it was still snowing hard, all the dancers were drenched in sweat, and the white mist exhaled from their panting mouths turned into beads of ice in their beards and hair.

Above them, the mousy man continued to pace back and forth, issuing orders to the dancers. Solofi didn't know what to make of this strange drill instructor.

"All right, we'll finish here today," said the man. As the dancers lined up below the steps, he came down and started to chat with them one by one.

"Very good, Suadégo. The spirits are pleased with your progress. Tomorrow you can dance in the second line. Don't you feel all energized? Ah, these are the new envelopes . . . let me count how many blessed faith tokens you and your recruits have sold . . . only two new recruits from this past week? I'm disappointed! You and your husband need to talk to everyone in the family—cousins, second cousins, their children and the children's spouses, and their cousins—everyone! Remember, your faith is evinced by the size of your contribution, and the more people you recruit to spread the faith, the more pleased the spirits will be! Here's your prize—it's a negotiation pill. Hold it under your tongue before you have to talk to a supplier and *visualize* success, you understand? You must *believe* or it won't work!"

He went through a similar speech with every one of the dancers, demoting some, promoting others, but always the chatter centered around the number of new recruits and money.

By the time the man was finished with the last dancer, who departed dejectedly because she hadn't recruited any new members and was thus banished from the next dance session, Solofi finally realized why the man looked so familiar.

He stepped out from behind the gravestone he had been hiding behind. "Noda Mi! I haven't seen you in almost ten years!"

After the success of the rebellion against the Xana Empire, the Hegemon had rewarded those who he thought had made important contributions by creating numerous new Tiro states and naming the men as kings. Noda Mi, who had begun as a supplier of grains to Mata's army before rising to be Mata's quartermaster, ended up as King of Central Géfica. Doru Solofi, who had begun as a foot soldier before being promoted to a scout for valor, ended up as King of South Géfica—where Pan was—largely because he happened to be the first to discover Kuni Garu's ambitions.

During the Chrysanthemum-Dandelion War, Noda and Doru tumbled from their thrones before the might of Gin Mazoti's army and were cast out of the Hegemon's favor. They had then drifted around the Islands as fugitives in subsequent years, making a living as bandits, highwaymen, merchants of rotten meat and spoiled fish, kidnappers, scammers . . . while hiding from Emperor Ragin's constables.

"Look at us," said Solofi. "Two Tiro kings in a graveyard!" He laughed bitterly as he kicked at the snowdrifts on the mausoleum steps. He handed the pipe of happy herbs back to Noda.

Noda waved his hand to indicate that he had smoked enough. Instead, he took a sip from a flask, letting the throat-burning liquor warm him against the bitter cold. "You've certainly put your impressive muscles to good use. That trick with the teahouse storytellers is pretty good. Thanks for sharing the tip; I'll have to give it a try."

"It wouldn't work for you. They wouldn't be scared enough," said Solofi, looking contemptuously at Noda's thin, small figure. "But your pyramid scheme isn't bad either. How were you able to convince so many fools to dance for you and give you money?"

"It's easy! Peace has made many in Pan rich and bored, and they crave some excitement in their lives. I let it be known that I could harness the energy of the dead to give the living good fortune, and many showed up to see if what I promised was true. The thing is: Once people are in a crowd, they lose all sense. If I get everyone to dance around like idiots, no one dares to question me, for whoever behaves differently from the rest would then appear as the foolish one. If I get one of them to say she *feels* energy coursing through her, everyone rushes to say the same, for whoever doesn't would be admitting that the spirits don't favor her. In fact, they compete to tell me just how much better the dance is making them feel so as to appear to be more spiritual in the eyes of their fellow dancers."

"That's hard to believe—"

"Oh, believe it. Never underestimate the power of the need to appear better than their peers to motivate people, a tendency that I'm happy to indulge. I set up little competitions, promoting dancers from the back to the front if they appear more faithful and demoting them if they're not as enthusiastic. I give them prizes based on how fervently they gyrate and strut. I tell them that they're ready to be spiritual teachers on their own, and have them go out to recruit their own magic dance students—and, of course, I collect a portion of the tuition they get. Nothing convinces a fool to believe in a scam better than turning him into a scammer too. I do believe that I could show up naked one of these days and tell them that only the devout can see my spiritual outfit; they would outdo each other in describing the glory of my raiment."

At this, Solofi's eyes dimmed momentarily. "Once we did dress in the finest water silk embroidered in gold, you and I."

"We did," agreed Noda, his tone equally somber. But then his eyes brightened as he examined Solofi. "Perhaps we can again."

"What do you mean?" Solofi asked, the pipe of happy herbs in his hand temporarily forgotten.

"We were once kings, yet now we scrabble for a living among the bones of the dead and the vanities of the living, like so many rats. What sort of life is this? Do you not wish to be a king again?"

Solofi laughed. "The age of Tiro kings is over. Ambitious men now grovel at the feet of Kuni Garu and hope they can pass his tests so that they can serve him."

"Not *all* men," said Noda, holding Solofi's gaze. He lowered his voice. "When Huno Krima and Zopa Shigin met, they started a rebellion that undid Mapidéré's life's work. When Kuni Garu met Mata Zyndu, they tore these islands asunder and knit them back together again. Do you not think it a sign for you and I to meet after ten years in this place, where so many ghosts still cry out for vengeance against Kuni Garu?"

Doru Solofi shivered. The sudden chill he felt seemed to be emanating from the mausoleum behind him. Noda Mi's intense gaze and hypnotic voice were mesmerizing. He could see how such a man could convince crowds to give him money . . . He recalled the shark-toothed boy who had led him here. *Is this truly a sign? Could Noda be right?*

"There are others who think like you and me—disgraced nobles, the Hegemon's veterans, scholars who failed to place in the examinations, merchants who can't make as much profit as they like by cheating at taxes. . . . Dara may be a land at peace, but the hearts of men are never peaceful. I have learned much about fanning the flames of dissatisfaction, and you have a figure that is meant to ride at the head of a crowd. The gods meant for us to meet here today, and we *can* reclaim the glory that is our due from the weed-emperor. Remember, he was once no better than we."

A small cyclone moved through the graveyard just then, whipping the snow into an imitation of the chaotic whirlpool that had once swallowed twenty thousand soldiers of Xana in a single day.

Doru Solofi reached out and grabbed Noda Mi by the arms.

"Let us call each other brother then, and we'll swear an oath to bring down the House of Dandelion."

CHAPTER THREE

PRINCES AND PRINCESSES

THE IMPERIAL PALACE:
THE SECOND MONTH IN THE SIXTH YEAR OF
THE REIGN OF FOUR PLACID SEAS.

"Please, Master Ruthi! Slow down!" the empress shouted as she ran down the long corridor leading from the Imperial family's private quarters to the public areas toward the front of the palace. Ahead of her, an old man with a satchel over his shoulder was marching away at a brisk pace, not even bothering to look back.

Since the emperor wasn't holding court today, Jia was dressed in a simple silk robe and wooden slippers that allowed her to run, instead of the formal court robe bedecked with hundreds of jade and coral dyrans, the heavy, tall crown of silver and bronze, and those three-foot-long court shoes that resembled small boats. She ran so fast that she was having trouble catching her breath, and her flaming red hair matched her flushed face. A retinue of dozens of ladies-in-waiting and courtiers and palace guards ran next to her, keeping pace—they couldn't run ahead of her until she'd given the order to seize the escaping man, and of course she wasn't going to do *that*. The situation was truly awkward for everyone involved.

The empress stopped, and the guards and courtiers and ladies-in-waiting skidded to an abrupt stop as well, some colliding into each other in a jumble of clanging armor and weapons, gasps of surprise, and clinking jewels. Empress Jia caught her breath and shouted, "Kon Fiji said a learned man should not make those craving knowledge run after him!"

Zato Ruthi, Imperial Tutor, slowed down and then stopped, sighing. But he did not turn around.

Jia caught up to him at a dignified pace, still huffing and puffing.

"Your Imperial Majesty," Ruthi said, still not turning around. "I'm afraid that I can't *possibly* be considered a learned man. You'd better seek other able teachers for the princes and princesses. My continued employment would only ruin their education." His voice was so stiff that the words seemed to bounce off the walls like roasted chestnuts.

"I admit that the children can be a bit rowdy and mischievous," said the empress, all smiles. "But that is *precisely* why they need you to discipline their minds with the wisdom of the sages—"

"Discipline!" Ruthi interrupted. The ladies-in-waiting and courtiers winced—nobody interrupted the fiery empress—but Empress Jia's words clearly touched a nerve, and Ruthi was beyond caring. "Indeed, I tried to administer discipline and look what I've gotten for my troubles! All the princes and princesses are nowhere to be found when they're supposed to be in their rooms working on their punishment essays!"

"Well, to be fair, not *all* of them. Fara is still in her room practicing her logo—"

"Fara is four! I'm sure the others would have taken her if they didn't think she'd get in the way of whatever mischief they were planning. And they had the audacity to have their servants rustling paper in their rooms so that if I walked by I'd think they were working!"

"Of course such childish tricks would not be effective against a perspicacious teacher such as—"

"*That* is not the point! Empress, you know that I have tried my best to teach the children, but even the most patient man has limits.

Running away from their punishment essays was bad enough, but look at this. Look!" He dropped the satchel from his shoulder and twisted around to show the empress the back of his robe.

In childish zyndari letters, a couplet was painted on the fabric:

I play the zither for the ruminating cow,
The cow speaks: Moo-moo-moo-moo, why such knitted brow?

The faces of the courtiers and ladies-in-waiting and palace guards twitched as they suppressed the urge to laugh.

Ruthi glared at them. "Do you think it's funny to be compared to the foolish man in Lurusén's poem who played the zither for cows and then complained about not being understood? No wonder learning has such a hard time taking root in such thin soil." Empress Jia's retinue blanched and looked away.

Jia ignored the implied insult. "But another way of looking at this," she offered in a soothing voice, "is to be pleased at the fact that your emphasis on the classics has clearly made an impression. I've never known any of the children to quote Lurusén—except maybe Timu, since he has always been studious—"

"You think I should be pleased?" Ruthi roared, and even Jia flinched. "To think that I once debated Tan Féüji and Lügo Crupo on the proper path of government! I've been reduced to being insulted by impish children—" His voice cracked, and he blinked hard a few times, took a deep breath, and added, "I'm going home to Rima so I can hide in a hut in the woods and continue my scholarship. I'm sorry, Empress, but the emperor's children are unteachable."

A new voice boomed into the scene. "Oh, Master Ruthi, how you wrong the children! My heart breaks to see them so misunderstood."

Ruthi and Jia turned to find the speaker. Coming down the corridor from the other direction was a middle-aged man whose well-cut robe could not quite disguise his beer belly. Wearing a sad expression, he was surrounded by a retinue of his own courtiers and guards: Kuni Garu, now known by the court name of Ragin, Emperor of Dara.

Thank you, Jia mouthed at Dafiro Miro, Captain of the Palace Guards, who was walking at the head of the emperor's retinue and nodded back in silent acknowledgment. Miro had run away to find the emperor as soon as Zato Ruthi started shouting at the empty rooms belonging to Prince Timu, Prince Phyro, and Princess Théra.

Even in his rage, Zato Ruthi couldn't quite ignore the rules of courtly decorum. He bowed deeply. "*Rénga.* I apologize for losing my temper, but it is clear that I have lost the children's respect."

The emperor shook his head like a rattle drum. "No, no, no!" He wrung his hands dramatically to show his distress. "Oh, this reminds me so much of my youth, when I studied under Master Tumo Loing. Why is it that the Garu children are always cursed with being misjudged?"

"What do you mean?" Ruthi asked.

"You have completely misunderstood the couplet composed by my sons and daughters," said the emperor.

"I have?"

"Absolutely. A father knows his children best. The three of them were clearly ashamed by their behavior—whatever it was they did—"

"They made up a silly story about Kon Fiji being tricked by a folk opera troupe instead of practicing—"

"Right! Terrible, just terrible! And so they realized that they had to apologize to you."

Ruthi's face went through a complicated series of contortions as he struggled to phrase the question in respectable language. "How is painting this note on my back an *apology*?"

"You see, they're comparing themselves to cows, dumb beasts who don't understand the beauty of the music played to them. And what they're saying is, to paraphrase a bit, 'Master, we're truly sorry that we have made you angry. We would like to take up the heavy plow under your guidance and labor in the fields of knowledge.'"

Led by Captain Dafiro Miro, the gathered courtiers and ladies-in-waiting nodded vigorously in appreciation and chimed in to support the emperor like a chorus of twittering birds.

"Such humble princes!"

"The princesses are truly contrite!"

"I have never, ever heard a more heartfelt note of contrition!"

"Where's the court historian? He must record this tale of the dyran-wise teacher and falcon-brilliant students!"

"Don't forget the emperor as cruben-astute interpreter!"

Kuni impatiently gestured for them to be silent. The attendants meant well, but there was such a thing as *too much* support.

Jia tried to maintain a straight face. She was recalling the time of their courtship, during which Kuni's unorthodox interpretations of Lurusén had played an important role.

As Ruthi pondered the emperor's words, his face seemed to relax a bit. "Then why did they write this secretly on the back of my robe? I think it happened when Phyro offered to give me a back massage while I continued to lecture the others on rhetoric. That is hardly how you offer a sincere apology."

"As Lügo Crupo once said, 'Words and actions must be read under the guiding light of intent.'" Kuni sighed. "Perspective is everything. My children were trying to enact the Moralist maxim that a sincere apology must come from the heart and not be done for mere show. Apologizing to you right after your angry lecture would hardly show much sincerity. By writing this on the back of your robe, they were hoping you'd see it when you changed for the night and could perceive their true meaning in a moment of quiet contemplation."

"But why have they run away instead of working on their essays in their rooms, as I told them to?"

"That is ... er ..." The emperor seemed to have trouble fitting this piece into the tale he was weaving, but just then the actual culprits arrived: Risana, Imperial Consort, proceeded down the corridor with the three truants in tow.

"Lady Soto and Chatelain Krin caught them trying to sneak back into their rooms," said a smiling Risana. "They were disguised as commoners, and no doubt that was why the guards sent into the city to look for them couldn't locate them right away. Soto and Otho brought them to me, and I've told them how much trouble they're in, so now they're here to explain themselves." She bowed to the emperor and empress in deep *jiri*.

"Da!" shouted Phyro, and he ran up to the emperor and hugged his legs.

"Father," said Théra, grinning as if nothing was wrong. "Have I got a story for you!"

"*Rénga.*" Timu bowed deeply, touching his palms to the ground. "Your loyal but foolish child stands at service."

Kuni nodded at Théra and Timu, and gently but firmly pried Phyro off his legs. "I've been explaining your clumsy apology to Master Ruthi, who's very angry."

Timu looked confused. "What—"

"Yes, your *apology.*" Kuni cut him off and looked at Théra and Phyro severely. The three conversed for a moment with their eyes.

"Oh, yes . . . that was my idea," said Phyro. "I felt so bad after Master Ruthi yelled at us that I had to do something to make it right."

"I thought that looked like your chicken scratch," said Kuni. "And then you decided to run away, no doubt out of shame, am I right?"

"*That* was my idea," said Théra. "I thought we should show how sorry we were with action, not just words. So I suggested that we get some presents for Master Ruthi before we wrote our punishment essays." Keeping her head bowed, she walked up to Zato Ruthi and presented a pair of small plates to him. "I bought these plates from a merchant, who said they were made in Na Thion, your hometown."

"But those are meant as receipts for the prom—" Timu held his tongue as Théra glared at him.

Théra stole a glance at Kuni, and father and daughter exchanged almost undetectable smiles.

Ruthi examined the plates and shook his head. "These look like they're from some cheap tavern—look, there's even a painted sign here for the illiterate. Is this a three-legged *kunikin*? And what are these numbers written on the back?"

"Oh no!" Théra gave a cry of shock, and her face fell. "I did think they looked a bit too coarse, but the merchant made it sound so convincing! He told me the numbers represent the kiln and the artist."

"That's ridiculous! You have to be careful out there in the markets, Théra. They're full of swindlers." Ruthi might be scolding, but his voice was kind. "Still, it's the thought that counts."

"Oh, that reminds me," said Phyro. He patted his robe and retrieved a half-empty bag of sugar-roasted peanuts from a sleeve. "I got these for you because I know you like peanuts." Then he looked embarrassed. "But they smelled so good that I couldn't help but try a few. . . ."

"That's all right," said a mollified Ruthi. "It's hard for a young boy to resist temptation. When I was your age, I spent all my allowance on candied monkeyberries . . . but Phyro, you must learn better self-control over time. You're a prince, not a street urchin." He turned to Timu, his best student. "And what do you have to say for yourself, young man?"

"Uh . . . I didn't really . . . um . . ."

Kuni frowned.

Jia sighed inwardly. Her son had always been proper and kind, but lacked the wit to sense when he needed to play along with a story line. She was about to speak when Risana cut in.

"I'm sure that as the firstborn, Prince Timu felt that he had to find the best gift to express his regrets. But you didn't see anything in the markets that would suit the high regard and honor of your esteemed teacher, did you?"

Ruthi looked at Timu, who nodded with a flushed face.

Risana went on. "So you decided that you have to express your sentiments with a well-written essay later tonight."

Since Risana was known for her ability to intuit the true feelings of those around her, the children had always been more forthright with her than with their other parents. Ruthi was convinced.

"The sentiments were proper and your hearts were in the right place," said Ruthi to the children, sounding more like a grandfather than the Imperial Tutor.

"All credit is due to your diligent teaching, of course," said Jia.

"I'm glad we cleared up this terrible misunderstanding."

"However, since they've made you so angry," said Kuni, putting on a severe mien, "more punishment is in order. The three of them should be made to clean the latrines with the servants for a week, I think."

The children looked dejected.

"But *Rénga*," said a horrified Ruthi. "That seems far out of proportion compared to their offense. This all started because the children were bored while studying Kon Fiji's *Morality*. I think the essays I assigned were punishment enough, and everything else that happened later was just a series of misunderstandings."

"What?" asked Kuni, incredulity straining his voice. "Bored by the One True Sage? That is even worse! Two weeks of latrine duty! Three!"

Ruthi bowed and kept his head lowered. "It is understandable that Kon Fiji's abstract precepts would feel too dense to them. The princes and princesses are so intelligent that I sometimes forget that they're still young and spirited, and it is at least in part my fault for pushing too hard. A teacher who demands too much from his charges is like a farmer yanking up the seedlings, hoping thereby to help them grow while achieving the opposite. If you're going to punish them, then please also punish me."

The three children looked at each other, and all three fell to their knees and bowed to Ruthi, touching their foreheads to the floor. "Master, it is our fault. We're truly sorry and will try to do better."

Kuni reached out and lifted Ruthi by the shoulders until he was standing straight again. "You need not reproach yourself, Master Ruthi. I and the mothers of the children are grateful for the care you've devoted to teaching them. I leave their punishment entirely in your hands then."

Slowly, accompanied by the children, Zato Ruthi headed for his suite back in the family quarters of the palace, his vow of going home to Rima forgotten.

"Oh, Master Ruthi, did you know that the Hegemon yearned for understanding?" Phyro asked as he skipped next to his teacher.

"What are you talking about?"

"We listened to this really great storyteller in—"

"In the markets"—interrupted Théra before Phyro could ruin the hard-earned peace by mentioning the pub—"as we were passing through."

"In the markets, yes," said Phyro. "He was telling us all about the Hegemon and King Mocri and Lady Mira. Teacher, will you tell us more stories about them? You must know a lot about what happened then, just like Auntie Soto, and those stories are much more exciting than . . . um, Kon Fiji."

"Well, what I know is *history*, not fairy tales told by your governess, but maybe there is a way to incorporate more history into your lessons if you're so interested. . . ."

Kuni, Jia, and Risana listened as the voices—Phyro chatting and giggling, Ruthi patiently explaining—faded down the corridor, relieved that another family crisis had been averted. Having the Imperial Tutor resign over "unteachable" princes and princesses would have been quite a scandal, especially coming during the month of the Grand Examination, a celebration of scholarship.

"My apologies, *Rénga*," said Captain Dafiro Miro. "I should have kept a closer eye on the children and not allowed them to sneak out of the palace without protection. This lapse in security is unforgivable."

"It's not your fault," said Risana. "It's hard enough watching regular children. With them, it's ten times worse. I know you feel you're constrained in what you can do because they're your lords, but I give you permission to drag Phyro back by his ear if he tries something like this again that puts their safety at risk."

"I give you permission too, with Timu and Théra," said Jia. "They're certainly getting out of hand, and now I'm wondering if they're even taking the herbs I prescribed them each morning—the recipe is supposed to make them a bit more contemplative and less wild!"

Kuni laughed. "Let's not treat spirited children as though they're in need of medicine! Is it really so bad to have them wander the markets without a bunch of guards and servants by their sides? How else can they learn about the lives of the common people? That was how I grew up."

"But the times are no longer the same," said Jia. "Their status as your children makes them vulnerable to those who would wish you ill. You really shouldn't be so indulgent with their antics."

Kuni nodded in acknowledgment. "Still," he added, "Phyro's antics remind me a lot of myself."

Risana smiled.

A momentary frown flickered across Jia's face, but soon it was again as placid and regal as before.

"Ada-*tika* is very upset to have been left behind," said Phyro as he came into Théra's room and slid the door closed behind himself. "I gave her all the candied monkeyberries I had and she still threw a tantrum. Auntie Soto is telling her a story now, so we have some time to ourselves."

"I'll try to think of some adventure next time that will include her," said Théra.

"I'll go read her a book later tonight," said Timu.

Ada-*tika*, whose formal name was Princess Fara, was Kuni's youngest daughter. As her mother, Consort Fina, had died early, all the other children tried to be extra solicitous of her.

Consort Fina had been a princess from the House of Faça. Kuni Garu had married her to reassure the old nobles of Faça, as that realm had been one of the last to be conquered by the army of Dasu and there were no important figures in Kuni's closest group of advisers and generals from Faça. It was planned as the first of a series of political marriages for the new emperor. However, Fina had died giving birth to Fara, and Kuni had stopped any further discussions of political marriages, arguing that it was a sign that the gods did not favor such unions.

"There's not much time left before dinner if we want to help Zomi," said Phyro.

"I know," said Théra. "I'm thinking." She chewed on her nail as she turned the problem over in her head.

Inspired by the courage of the *cashima*—and, though this wasn't said, also out of a sense of gratitude for her vigorous defense of the honor of their father, the emperor—the children had promised to help Zomi get into the Examination Hall despite the loss of her pass. Zomi had thanked them for their concern, but she clearly had not taken seriously the promise of three children in a pub—even if they sounded like they came from a wealthy family. She gave them the address of her hostel only reluctantly and emphasized that she didn't have time to play games.

"We should have told her who we are," said Phyro.

"Her lack of faith will only make our success more delicious," said a smiling Théra.

"We can't let people know we were out in the streets dressed like commoners!" said Timu. "It's utterly against protocol."

Phyro ignored him. "Why don't we just go directly to Da and ask him to make an exception?"

Théra shook her head. "He can't be seen as intervening on behalf of any candidate to bend the rules for any reason. It would damage the perceptions of fairness."

"Can't we just ask Da to send an airship to take her back to Dasu and get Uncle Kado to write her a new pass?"

"First of all, Uncle Kado isn't in Dasu—he's hunting in Crescent Island," said Théra. "And you know he lets his regent run everything in Dasu for him, so he wouldn't even know who Zomi is."

"Then why don't we just send Zomi to see the regent?"

"Dasu is much too far away. It would take two days to get there, even in the fastest airship. We don't have that kind of time because the Grand Examination is tomorrow. You *do* need to study more, Hudo-*tika*. You have no sense of geography. Besides, such a public gesture would embarrass Zomi and might prejudice her chances in the examinations."

"Then . . . can we talk to Uncle Rin?"

Théra pondered this. "Uncle Rin *is* in charge of security at the Examination Hall and he's always been good about playing along with us, so that's not a bad idea. Problem is, the passes are collected along with the final answers from all the test takers and turned in to the judges in matched sets. Getting Zomi into the hall isn't enough; we also have to give her a real pass. Even the Farsight Secretary has no authority to make examination passes."

"Can't we just forge a pass for her?"

"Do you think Uncle Rin's security procedures are just for show? He cuts the passes out of a single sheet of paper with golden threads embedded at the paper mill so that the pattern on each one is unique, and then he distributes the blank passes to all the provinces and fiefs by the projected numbers of *cashima*. Any passes that are unused are sent back. At the end of the examination, he puts all the used and unused passes together like a big puzzle by matching their golden threads, and any forged pass will stick out like a sore thumb because it won't fit."

"How do you know so much about this?" Timu finally broke into the discussion, his voice full of wonder. "I had no idea you were so interested in the Imperial examinations."

"I used to daydream about taking the examination myself someday," admitted Théra, her face flushed.

"Wh-what?" asked an incredulous Timu. "But that's not—"

"I know that's not possible! You don't have to explain—"

"But why would you even want to?" asked Phyro. "It's a ton of work!"

"As princes, you'll both get to work on something important for Father when you're older," said Théra. "But for me and Fara . . . we'll just be married off."

"I'm sure he'd give you something to do if you asked," said Phyro. "He says you're the smartest of all of us, and there are some women officials too."

Théra shook her head. "They're as rare as cruben horns and dyran scales . . . besides, you don't understand. It's okay for you to work for Father without any qualifications because you're boys and are expected to . . . take over for him some day. But for me—never mind, this isn't important right now. Let's focus on how to help Zomi. We need someone who has the authority to issue passes, and we have to convince them to give Zomi another chance."

"While you're doing that," said Timu, "I'm going to get started on the essays for all of us. I'm no good at plotting, but I can at least free you up. Just remember to save some time later tonight to copy over my drafts in your own handwriting."

Though Timu made it sound easy, Théra knew that ghostwriting for her and Phyro wasn't trivial. Not only did Timu know just the right references to make and the correct moral lessons to draw and the proper structure for assembling the arguments, but he also took care to phrase things so that the essays he wrote for them actually sounded like they were written by Phyro and Théra. Timu really was very intelligent, just not in a way that pleased their father, and Théra could tell Timu sometimes envied her and Phyro, though he tried not to let it show.

"Thank you, Elder Brother," said Théra. "But I don't want you to do that. Phyro and I will write the essays ourselves."

"We will?" asked a surprised Phyro.

"We will," said Théra firmly. "Maybe the 'apology' started as just another prank, but I do feel bad about what we did to Master Ruthi. He really does want the best for us—he didn't even want us punished more than we deserved."

"Well, maybe he's not that bad," Phyro said grudgingly.

"Besides, Phyro, remember the story about the Hegemon and King Mocri. This is a matter of honor."

Phyro's eyes brightened. "Yes! We're like the Tiro kings of old: honorable princes and princesses with the grace of kings."

"I'm very glad to hear that," said a relieved Timu. "Writing an essay with the sort of logical errors Hudo-*tika* habitually makes is *torture*."

The maids and servants hurrying through the halls of the palace did not slow down as crisp peals of laughter and indignant cries of protestation echoed around the Imperial family quarters.

ᔕ ᔕ ᔕ ᔕ

"... we couldn't think of anyone else who could help us," said Phyro.

"No one," affirmed Théra. "This is a task requiring Fithowéo-like courage and Lutho-like wisdom, not to mention Rufizo-like compassion and—"

"And Tazu-like recklessness," interjected Gin Mazoti, Queen of Géjira and Marshal of Dara.

Gin was receiving the children in her bedchamber instead of a formal sitting room. In a lot of ways, the children treated her as family.

She had arrived at the Imperial palace just that day. She didn't visit the capital often, as administering Géjira and overseeing the affairs of the empire's scattered but vast military kept her busy, but the first Grand Examination of the Reign of Four Placid Seas was a special occasion, and she had high hopes for a few of Géjira's scholars to distinguish themselves.

"Er ... I wouldn't *quite* put it that way," said Théra. "I think we should focus on the bravery and wisdom and compassion—"

"Flattery does not become you, Rata-*tika*," said Gin. "You've come to recruit me as your coconspirator because you want me to shield you from your father's rage when your silly scheme blows up."

"Indeed you wrong us, Auntie Gin! Perspective is every—"

"Oh, stop it. Do you think you can outwit me with your tricks? Remember, children, I knew you when you were still making dumplings out of mud and waving willow branches as swords. I understand the way your minds work. As the peasants would say, 'Soon as you loosen your belt, I know the color of your shit.'"

The children giggled. This was one of the reasons they liked Auntie Gin—she never put on airs with them and spoke to them as colorfully as she would to her soldiers.

Now in her thirties, Gin Mazoti still kept her hair closely cropped to the skull, and her compact body, despite her life as a queen, remained muscular and nimble, like a craggy reef standing against the sea, or a coiled snake ready to strike. A sword leaned against the dresser to the side—though no one other than a member of the Imperial family or a palace guard was allowed to carry weapons in the palace, Queen

Gin had been given this singular honor by Emperor Ragin. She was the commander of all of the empire's armed forces, perhaps the most powerful noble in all Dara, and yet now she was being pestered by children to play a dangerous game—breaching the security of the Grand Examination.

Life with Kuni Garu is always interesting.

"Help us, Auntie Gin," said Phyro. He put on his cutest smile and added a bit of whine. "Pleeeeease."

Gin had always liked Phyro the most of all of Kuni's children. This was only in part because Phyro was bright and always begged her for stories about the war. In truth, Gin had a better rapport with Consort Risana than Kuni's other wives. During the time of Kuni's rise, Jia was held by the Hegemon as a hostage while Risana rode by Kuni's side, and Gin had come to respect her as an adviser to the king. Secretly, she hoped that Kuni would designate Phyro the crown prince.

"It's true that I still have a few extra passes," said Gin. "But the rules say that they're meant for specific uses such as to replace the lost pass of another test taker from Géjira, not to get someone from Dasu into the Examination Hall."

"But this is an *extraordinary* circumstance," said Théra. "She lost her pass only because she was being brave; she was defending the innocent."

"She was defending Da's honor," added Phyro.

"Sometimes courage and honor have costs," said Gin. "She could always go home and wait another five years."

"But in five years, she'd have to compete against all the new and old *cashima* again for the few places allocated to Dasu."

"She's already passed the second-level examinations once. I'm sure she can distinguish herself one more time."

"Are you worried that she'll do better than the scholars of Géjira?"

Blood rushed into Gin's face and she stared at Théra for a moment, but then she laughed. "You're getting better at manipulation, Rata-*tika*, but I was deploying stratagems before you could even walk."

Théra's face turned red at having her trick seen through, but she refused to give up. "Would you have been happy if Prime Minister Cogo Yelu had not recommended you to my father back on Dasu but instead told you to wait patiently to distinguish yourself in time?"

Gin's face turned somber. "You're too bold, Princess."

"She deserves an opportunity, as did you. She's not some wealthy merchant's daughter, and she doesn't come from a family of scholars. In fact, she's so poor that she has to wear a painted sword because she can't afford to buy a real one. I thought of all people, you would have some compassion for her. Have you been a queen for so—"

"That's enough!"

Théra bit her bottom lip but said no more.

"Auntie Gin," Phyro piped up. "Are you scared of the empress?"

Gin frowned. "What are you talking about, Hudo-*tika*?"

"I heard the empress tell Prime Minister Yelu that she wanted him to administer this examination with extra fairness and adhere strictly to the rules. She told him, 'Too many nobles think they can get their friends' children a pass into the Examination Hall with effusive recommendation letters. You must ensure that the results are just.'"

"Did she?"

"Yes. She wrote an angry letter to Marquess Yemu because he gave one of his passes to his nephew, who didn't score as well as some of the other candidates, and the marquess had to apologize."

"What did the emperor say about this?"

Phyro scrunched up his brows. "Let me think . . . I don't think Da said anything."

"He didn't even offer Yemu a chance to explain himself?"

Phyro and Théra shook their heads.

Gin looked thoughtful for a while as she pondered this information, and then she locked gazes with Théra once more.

"Does the empress know about this friend of yours?" She spoke in the commanding tone of the Marshal of Dara, with none of the affectionate indulgence she habitually used with the Imperial children. "Don't lie."

Théra swallowed, but kept her gaze steady. "No. Mother wouldn't understand."

Gin waited a beat. "Just why are you so obsessed with getting this young scholar into the Grand Examination, Princess?"

"I told you. Because she's brave!"

Gin shook her head. "You know perfectly well how serious your parents are about the rules governing the examination; yet here you're almost begging for a scandal—"

"I am telling you the truth! Why would I—"

"I may not have Consort Risana's skill with reading what is in people's hearts, but I know there's more to this than being impressed by an act of bravery! What is it that you really want?"

"I want fairness!" cried Théra. "The rules are unfair!"

"What's unfair about the rules? Everyone needs a pass—"

"But I can't get a pass no matter how hard I try!" Théra shouted. Phyro, who had never seen his clever, imperturbable sister in such a state, stared at Théra, his mouth agape.

Gin waited.

Théra managed to get herself under control. "She's a girl just like me, but at least she has the option of taking the examinations to prove herself. Even if Father gave me an official position, the scholars would protest that it is unseemly for a princess to administer and everyone will whisper that it's only because I'm his daughter. No one will listen to a thing I say. I want to take the exam like the other *cashima* and prove that I belong. But since I can't, I'm going to make sure she gets her chance."

"You are much too young to sound so disappointed with the world. Haven't you studied Kon Fiji's precepts about the proper place for a noblewoman of great wisdom? There are other ways of exerting influence—"

"Kon Fiji is an ass."

Gin laughed. "You're indeed your father's daughter. He didn't have much use for the great sage either."

"Neither do you," said Théra defiantly. "Master Ruthi might not talk about you much, but I've heard the stories about you and him."

Gin nodded, and then sighed. "Sometimes I wonder if you're not unlucky to come of age in a time of peace. Many of the rules that the sages tell us are indispensable get suspended in a time of war."

Then she got up, looked through her traveling desk until she found a small stack of papers, and retrieved the top sheet.

"What is your friend's name?"

Phyro and Théra gave her the logograms for Zomi's name.

"'The Pearl of Fire'? That's pretty," said Gin as she dripped wax onto the blank form and then carved out the logograms with a few powerful strokes. "As the name is also derived from a plant, it is a good match for the House of Dandelion. Perhaps this is a good omen."

She retrieved the Seal of Géjira and pressed an impression into the wax skirt around the logograms. "Here." She handed the filled-out pass to Phyro.

"Thank you, Auntie Gin!" said Phyro.

"Thank you, Your Majesty," said Théra.

Gin waved dismissively. "Let's hope your friend is as worthy as you claim."

Long after the children had departed, Gin remained sitting at her desk.

At her back, a man emerged from behind a screen. He was lithe, long-limbed, and moved gracefully. Though the dark skin of his face was deeply lined and his hair graying, his green eyes shone brightly with an intense energy.

"It is a pretty name," the man said. "Perhaps as refined as her mind." He paused, as if deciding what more to say. Then he added, "She'll have more chances even if she doesn't get to attend this session of the Grand Examination, but you have just meddled in the administration of the examinations outside the bounds of your domain."

Gin did not turn around. "Don't lecture me again, Luan. I'm not in the mood."

The voice that replied was warm, though tinged with a hint of sorrow. "I've said all I had to say at the banquet in Zudi five years ago.

If you weren't going to listen to me then, you certainly won't listen to me now."

"I was once given a chance to rise; perhaps it is the will of Rufizo that I give this girl her chance."

"Are you trying to convince me or yourself?"

Gin turned around and chuckled. "I have missed that foolish earnestness that passes for your wit."

But Luan wasn't smiling. "I know why you wrote out that pass, Gin. You might be a great tactician, but you . . . don't know much about the game of politics. You suspect that my warning to you five years ago was right, and you're now trying to test whether Kuni's faith in you still holds as Jia is lining up the pieces for her son."

"You make me sound like an insecure and jealous wife. I know what I have done for the House of Dandelion."

"Puma Yemu's contributions were also great, Gin, but Kuni didn't even intervene to give him a chance to save face when Jia humiliated him. If you cannot sense the shifting winds—"

"I am not Puma Yemu."

"This is a clumsy move, Gin. It will not end well."

Gin flopped carelessly onto the bed. "We'll speak no more of this. Come and join me. Let's see if you've stayed in shape after five years of drifting about in a balloon."

Luan sighed, but he obediently came to bed.

CHAPTER FOUR

GRAND EXAMINATION

The Examination Hall was a breathtaking sight.

The hall was one of the only cylindrical buildings in the Harmonious City, with a diameter of about four hundred feet. Built atop the old site of Mapidéré's Imperial armory, right outside the walls of the new Imperial palace, it was about as tall as one of the watchtowers of the city, and concentric circles of gilt shingles on the roof gleamed in the sun, making the building appear as a gigantic blossom—some claimed they saw a chrysanthemum; others a dandelion.

The building also served as the centerpiece of the academic quarter of the city, which, in addition to the Examination Hall itself, consisted of the Imperial Academy, where the *firoa*—those who had passed the Grand Examination by scoring within the top one hundred of all candidates—could pursue in-depth study with specialists in various subjects; the Imperial Observatory, where astronomers surveyed the stars and divined the fate of Dara; the Imperial laboratories, where renowned scholars conducted research in various fields; and the neat rows of dormitories and individual houses for resident and visiting scholars.

After ascending to the throne, Emperor Ragin had made scholarship a centerpiece of his plan for rebuilding Dara, and Pan was now growing to rival Ginpen in Haan as a center of learning. Those who distinguished themselves in the examinations could serve the emperor through posts in civil administration or by exploring and extending the frontiers of knowledge.

The inside of the Examination Hall was airy and open, as the interior was simply one large, high-ceilinged, circular room. Multiple rows of windows honeycombing the top half of the cylindrical wall and a massive, eyelike skylight in the center bathed the interior in sunlight. The floor was divided into concentric rings of stalls by eight-foot-tall partitions for the test takers, with a capacity close to two thousand. At the center of the hall was a tall pillar that raised a platform into the air, just below the ceiling, like the crow's nest on a ship. The examination administrators sat on this platform, where they had a panoptic view of the proceedings to detect cheating. Halfway up the wall, above the test takers but below the administrators' platform, was an elevated walkway that went all the way around the hall for the patrolling proctors, adding further security.

As the sun rose over the walls of the palace, Duke Rin Coda, Imperial Farsight Secretary, looked over to Cogo Yelu, Prime Minister, who sat next to him on the central platform.

"Back when we were all in Zudi, did you ever think a day would come when the best and brightest of Dara would have to answer one of your questions and follow my directions if they wished to advance?" Rin asked.

Cogo smiled placidly. "I think it's best not to dwell on the past. This day is about the future."

Chagrined, Rin turned back to face the entrance of the Examination Hall and intoned, "Open the doors!"

 හ ෩ හ ෩

The *cashima* came from every corner of Dara: the fabled ancient academies of Ginpen, whose walls and porticos were draped with ivy and morning glory; the open-air schools of Müning, where lecturers and pupils roamed from hanging platforms to flat-bottomed boats floating over the sparkling waters of Lake Toyemotika; the fog-shrouded forums of Boama, where teachers and students debated ideas in the morning before heading to the sheep pastures for exercise and leisure; the hamlets scattered in the Ring-Woods surrounding Na Thion, where solitary scholars contemplated nature and art; the gleaming, grand, and richly furnished classrooms of Toaza, where cosmopolitan attitudes mixed with commercial purpose; the stone-walled learning halls of Kriphi, where ancient virtues were extolled to dull the pain of recent suffering; the private knowledge gymnasiums of Çaruza, where straw mats lined the floor so that students could study books as well as the martial arts of wrestling, boxing, and swordsmanship.

They were the best students in all of Dara. Emperor Ragin's system, devised by Prime Minister Cogo Yelu and Imperial Tutor Zato Ruthi, was a continuation and refinement of the ancient examination systems developed in the various Tiro states and under the Xana Empire. With standardized questions and uniform scoring systems, the goal of the Imperial examinations was to filter and sieve all the talent that Dara had to offer and bring forth the best to serve the emperor, regardless of the examinees' origins.

Every year, students from across Dara took part in the annual Town Examinations in the nearest large town. Answering questions on a variety of subjects from astronomy and literature to mathematics and aquatic and terrestrial zoology, those who passed earned the rank of *toko dawiji*. Out of a hundred students who took the exams, perhaps no more than ten or twenty accomplished this feat.

Then, every two years, the *toko dawiji* took part in the Provincial Examinations, in which the scholars had to compose essays on various topics. The essays were judged on criteria such as erudition, insight, creativity, use of evidence, and beauty of calligraphy. Out of a hundred *toko dawiji*, perhaps no more than two or three would pass and obtain the rank of *cashima*.

Finally, every five years—and this would be the first time since the founding of the Dandelion Dynasty—the *cashima* of each province and fief gathered at the regional capital and were selected to participate in the Grand Examination. Since each fief or province was allocated only a limited number of passes, the governor or king or duke or marquess would have to pick the attendees based on their test scores, character, recommendations, presentation, and a host of other factors. The selected *cashima*, the cream of the crop, gathered in Pan.

All of them had been preparing for this moment for years, some for the entirety of their lives. Some had passed the Provincial Examinations on their first try; others had tried multiple times during the days of the Tiro kings and under the Xana Empire without success, and then, as the rebellion and the Chrysanthemum-Dandelion War interrupted all examinations, did not get another chance until their hair had turned white. Their journeys here had been long and arduous, far more than just a ride in a bumpy carriage or a voyage across the sea, consisting also, as they did, of long hours spent poring over the scrolls of the Ano Classics and volumes of commentary codices, and the deprivation of the joys of youth, the lazy summers as well as the idle winters.

The dreams of entire families hung on them: Nobles who had won their titles by the sword and horse hoped their descendants would add honor to those titles with the writing knife and brush; merchants who had amassed vast fortunes sought the cloak of respectability made possible only by a learned offspring in Imperial service; fathers who had failed in their own pursuit of glory desired to see those dreams redeemed by their sons; clans who hoped to leap out of obscurity pooled their resources to support a single, brilliant child. Many had paid expensive tutors who claimed to know the secret of writing the perfect essay, and even more had paid charlatans who sold crib sheets and cram notes that were as expensive as they were useless.

The *cashima* streamed into the Examination Hall, each presenting a pass to the guards for careful inspection. Each test taker was also patted down to be sure that the voluminous folds of the robes and the long sleeves of the wrap dresses did not conceal sheaves of paper filled with dense notes written in zyndari letters as tiny as the heads of flies or precomposed essays by some hired ghostwriter. No one was even allowed to bring in a favored brush or writing knife, or a good luck charm obtained at the Temple of Lutho or the Temple of Fithowéo—the Grand Examination Hall, after all, *was* a battlefield for scholars! The stakes of the Grand Examination were so high that the temptation to cheat was great, and Duke Coda was determined to run a flawless test.

Rin Coda read from the instructions as the examinees found their assigned stalls and settled in:

"For the next three days, your stall will be your home. You will eat in it, sleep in it, and use the chamber pot you find inside. If you must leave for any reason, you forfeit your place in this year's exam, because we cannot permit the possibility of any outside contact.

"You will find in your assigned stall a scroll of fresh silk as well as scratch paper, brushes, ink, wax, and a writing knife. Your final composition must fit inside the wooden box in the upper right-hand corner of the desk with the cover closed, so plan your logograms carefully. Food will be brought to you three times a day, and two candles are provided for illumination at night.

"Do not try to communicate with any other examinee, whether by tapping on stall walls or passing notes or some other 'creative' method. Any such attempt will lead to immediate disqualification, and the proctors will escort you out of the Examination Hall.

"You have until sundown on the third day to complete your answer. I will issue a warning an hour before the end, but when I call time, you must already have the final composition inside the box, ready to be handed in. Do not try to beg for an extension."

Rin paused and looked around: Close to a thousand pairs of eyes stared up at him, hanging on his every word. Paper was laid out before them; brushes were inked and poised; clumps of wax lay in dispensers. Rin smiled and basked in the significance of this moment.

He cleared his throat and continued, "This year's essay topic has been chosen by the emperor himself.

"'If you were the prime adviser to the Emperor of Dara, what is the one policy you would immediately advocate to improve the lives of the people of the Islands? Consider history as well as the future. Thoughts from the Hundred Schools of philosophy are welcome, but do not be afraid to offer your own views.'

"You may begin."

For most of the examinees, the next three days would be recalled as among the most arduous in their lives. The Grand Examination was not merely a test of knowledge and skill of analysis, but also a trial of endurance and steadfastness of will and purpose. Three days was in fact much too long for one essay, and an examinee's worst enemy was self-doubt.

Some went through all their scratch paper in drafts on the first day and had to make do with writing palimpsests; some began transcribing to silk too quickly and ended up cursing as they changed their minds about an inopportunely placed wax logogram that could not be shifted or dislodged without marring the silk; some stared at the wall for hours, trying to remember that one perfect reference from the epigrams of Ra Oji that was just on the edge of recall, slipping out of grasp like some silvery fish darting into the dark sea; some bit their nails to the quick as they tried to divine the emperor's own thoughts on the question so as to craft an answer to flatter.

Six hours after the start of the test, the first examinee broke down. A fast writer, he had already finished his essay and begun to copy it onto the silk before he realized a fatal hole in his reasoning. Scraping off so much wax and starting over would ruin his calligraphy, but leaving the logograms in place would result in a flawed argument.

Seeing years of effort wasted due to a bout of impatience was too much for him to bear, and he began to scream and cut himself with the writing knife.

The test administrators were prepared for this eventuality. Four proctors were at his stall in a moment and carried him out of the Examination Hall to be treated by a doctor and then sent back to his hostel to recover.

"Shall we wager on how many will make it through the full three days?" asked Cogo Yelu. "My guess is fewer than ninety out of a hundred."

Rin Coda shook his head. "I'm glad that Kuni and I never had the ambition for the examinations."

As the first day came to an end, the duke and the prime minister left their observation platform to retire for the night, but the proctors continued to patrol around the Examination Hall. Large oil lamps were lit in the cardinal directions, and the proctors manipulated the curved mirrors behind the torches to focus the light into bright beams that highlighted individual stalls at random in order to catch any attempts at cheating.

The examinees were now faced with a dilemma: Was it better to use up the two candles on the first night to finish up a good draft and leave the revisions and calligraphy to the next two days? Or was the more strategic choice to get a good night's sleep on the first night and save the candles for an all-nighter the second night? As the hours ticked by, about half the stalls remained lit while the other half went dark, but sleep was hard to come by as neighbors rustled paper and shifted on their sitting mats, bright spotlights roamed overhead, and the fear that time was being wasted gripped the heart.

Three dozen more examinees had to be carried out of the hall during the night after breaking down under the pressure.

The second day and the second night were worse: The smell of unwashed bodies and leftover food and filled chamber pots assaulted the noses of the examinees, and some resorted to desperate measures to eke out every advantage. Some calculated how much wax would be needed for the final version of their answers and added the rest to the burning candles to stretch out the period of illumination; some, having run out of paper, began to use the walls of the stalls as scratch space; some heated the metal spoons that came with their bowls of soup and rubbed them against the other side of the silk to gently soften misplaced logograms so that they might be pried off without damaging the surface; some used the coconut juice they were served to thin out the ink and make it last longer; a few even started to carve their final drafts in the dark, feeling and shaping lumps of wax by touch.

The proctors noted each such instance of rule bending and came to consult with Rin and Cogo.

"I don't think these count as cheating," mused a frowning Cogo. "At least I don't think the rules explicitly prohibit such acts."

"We should give them a break," said Rin magnanimously. "I'm pretty sure Kuni would be impressed by some of these tricks."

A few dozen more examinees had to be removed as they fainted from exhaustion or lost control over themselves due to the intensifying stress. Clusters of empty stalls now dotted the Grand Examination Hall like calm atolls in a sea of activity.

Finally, as the sun rose on the third day, the examinees entered the final stretch of their competition. Almost all of them were now copying the finished essays onto silk, carving the wax logograms with meticulous attention to detail and inking the zyndari letters that served as glosses with flowing curlicues. The box for the final essay was very shallow, and the logograms had to be strategically placed on the scroll to allow it to be folded sufficiently flat to fit—each mountain needed a matching valley, and each exclamation required a subdued lament. The examination was not merely an exercise in reasoning and persuasion, but also a practical problem in three-dimensional geometry.

Those who had chosen to pull the all-nighter on the second night now realized their error: Their hands, shaking with exhaustion, could not hold the knife steady and left uneven surfaces and jagged cuts in the wax. A few decided that the only remedy was to take a quick nap, though a couple of them would, to their horror, find themselves oversleeping the deadline.

As the sun dipped below the walls of Pan, Rin Coda stood up on the observation platform and issued the one-hour warning.

But few of the scholars stirred from the general torpor. Most had decided that one more hour wasn't going to make a difference. They folded their essays, placed them in the boxes, and lay down on their mats with their arms over their eyes. A few leapt into frenzied motion, realizing that they would never finish in time.

"Knives and brushes down!" shouted Coda, and for the examinees, the declaration was the sweetest sound they had heard in three days. It was the order that released them from hell.

"I have done the best I could, Teacher," whispered Zomi Kidosu as she closed the cover of the box and sat back in *mipa rari* on the mat lining the floor of her stall. "The rest is up to chance."

She wished her teacher were still around so that she could ask him about the decision she had made on the way to Pan, the secret that she hoped would not ruin all she had accomplished. But she was on her own now.

So she prayed to both Lutho, the god of calculation and careful planning, and Tazu, the god of pure randomness, as her teacher had taught her to do.

CHAPTER FIVE

MIMI

On a winter day in the twenty-second year of the Reign of One Bright Heaven, which was also a year of the orchid and the last year of Emperor Mapidéré's life, a little girl was born to Aki and Oga Kidosu, a poor fishing-farming family in a small village on the northern shore of Dasu.

Though the family had few possessions, the tiny hut was always warmed by the glow of joy. Aki tended to the vegetable garden and mended the fishing nets and made stews out of leftover fish and wild herbs and garden snails and pickled caterpillars that tasted as divine to her family as the delicacies served in the grand palaces of Kriphi and Müning. Oga spent the days plowing the sea with the other fishermen and nights patching holes in the wattle-and-daub walls, entertaining his wife and children with stories he made up on the fly. The older children took care of the younger and learned their parents' trades by helping them. They led a life that was common but not commonplace, meek but not mean, tiring but not tiresome.

The baby girl cried loudly as she was born, but her voice was soon drowned out by the howling wind.

On that same day, Emperor Mapidéré's fleet left Dasu to explore the route to the Land of the Immortals.

During the last years of his life, Mapidéré became increasingly obsessed with the pursuit of life extension. Self-styled magicians and alchemists swarmed the court, offering elixirs, potions, spells, rituals, exercises, and other measures to halt or even reverse the ravages of time on the body. The dazzling array of solutions all shared one feature, however: a requirement of massive expenditures by the Imperial court.

Year after year, no matter how much money the emperor paid to the men with glinting eyes and whispered promises, no matter what exotic exercises, diets, or prayers the emperor engaged in, he grew older and more sickly, and even killing the lying scoundrels seemed not to improve things one iota.

Finally, just as the emperor was about to give up, two men from Gan, Ronaza Métu and Hujin Krita, came to him with a story that reignited the emperor's ashen heart.

There was a land to the north, they said, below the horizon, beyond the northernmost islands of Dara, beyond the scattered isles that provided haven for the pirates, beyond the reefs and atolls where the drift-gulls nested, beyond the reach of the fiery fingers of Lady Kana, goddess of death, where men and women enjoyed the blessing of immortality.

"The inhabitants of that realm know the secret of eternal youth, *Rénga*, and we know the way. All you have to do is to bring a few of the immortals back and ask them for their knowledge."

"How do you know this?" asked the emperor in a hoarse whisper.

"The merchants of Gan are always in search of new lands and new trade routes," said Hujin Krita, the younger and more well-spoken of the two. "We have long been intrigued by the many tales of the wonders of that land."

"And we have combed through ancient tomes for passing references and examined strange wreckages hoarded by storm-cursed fishermen for clues," said Ronaza Métu, who had a steadier, more calculating presence. "The web of deduction points to an inevitable conclusion: The Land of the Immortals is real."

Mapidéré looked with envy upon the men's strong limbs and handsome, arrogant faces, and the emperor seemed to hear the sound of jangling coins in the merchants' voices. "Stories may be just the insubstantial mirages of Lady Rapa's dream herbs, hardly worthy of belief."

"Yet what is history but a record of stories told and retold?" asked Krita.

"And wasn't a united Dara nothing more than a dream, *Rénga*, until you made it real?" asked Métu.

"The world is grand and the seas endless," said Krita. "All stories must be true in some corner of it."

The emperor was pleased by their speech. There was little logic to the men's reasoning, but sometimes logic was not as important as belief.

"Tell me the way then," said Mapidéré.

The men looked at each other and then turned back to the emperor. "Some secrets cannot be shared before their fulfillment, not even with the Emperor of Xana."

"Of course." The emperor smiled bitterly on the inside. He had learned a few things about men like these over the years, and he was sorry to detect the familiar signs of another swindle. But he could not resist the seductive song of hope. "What do you propose?"

"Well . . ." The men hesitated. "The Land of the Immortals is very far away, so we'll need a fleet of powerful ships, almost floating cities, to survive the long journey."

"What about airships?" the emperor asked.

"Oh, no! It will be a journey of months, perhaps even years—much too far for the meager supplies that airships can carry. You must build a special fleet for the arduous journey based on our designs."

Is skimming from the construction funds how they plan on profiting from this scheme? the emperor wondered. No matter, he had ways of dealing with such eventualities. "One of you will be in charge of the construction of the ships, while the other can gather the crews and supplies. I will give you whatever you need."

The two men looked pleased.

"When the expedition is ready," the emperor continued, "one of you will command it and the other will stay here to wait for the good news"—he watched the faces of the men carefully—"with me."

The men looked at each other. "You should go, old friend," said Krita. "You're the better sailor."

"No," Métu said. "You should have the honor of going because you're better at persuasion. I will stay and care for both our families. I know you will not disappoint us or the emperor."

There is no honor among thieves, mused the emperor. *If they're truly frauds, neither of them should want to stay and face my wrath when the other doesn't return. Yet they each have volunteered to stay and they're willing to leave their families behind, so perhaps they really do know of a way to the Land of the Immortals.*

Night and day, Mapidéré's shipwrights labored to construct great city-ships based on the merchants' designs: each as tall as the watch-towers of Pan and with a deck wide and long enough to allow a horse to gallop. They had deep holds for supplies that would last years and luxurious staterooms reserved for the immortal guests on the return journey. In total, a crew of twelve thousand skilled sailors, dancers, cooks, dressmakers, carpenters, blacksmiths, soldiers—some to impress the immortals with the height of Dara's culture and others to persuade the immortals of the wisdom of obeying the emperor's orders through more forceful means, should that turn out to be necessary—were conscripted for this expedition into the unknown waters of the north. A prince, born of one of the emperor's less favored wives, would come along on the expedition as a gesture of the emperor's esteem for the immortals.

Crown Prince Pulo personally came to send off the fleet from Dasu, the northernmost of the Islands of Dara. He led the crew in a prayer to Kiji, Lord of the Sky and Winds, and Tazu, Master of Sea Currents and Whirlpools. Then he gave the order to fill in the eyes painted on the bows of the ships so that they could peer through the mist and waves to find their way.

The day was cold, but the sky was clear and the sea calm. It was a good day to be off on an expedition.

The storm began as soon as the mast of the last ship had dipped below the horizon. The wind howled across land and ocean, tearing roofs off huts and bending trees until they snapped. Sheets of rain poured from the sky, making it impossible to see beyond one's outstretched hand. The dignitaries and officials who had come to see the fleet off ducked into basements, shivering with terror as thunder roared overhead and lightning flickered across the sky.

Three days later, the storm stopped as abruptly as it had begun, leaving a bright rainbow arcing over the sea.

Prince Pulo ordered airships to scout the seas for signs of the fleet. They returned after three days, having found nothing.

While the navy was being summoned, all the fishing boats of Dasu were immediately dispatched into the ocean. By this time, most suspected that the fleet had been lost, and the fishermen were told to look for survivors. In reality, the only one they cared about was the prince. Though it was doubtful if the emperor even remembered his name—why else would he have been chosen for such a fool's errand?—he was still a son of the emperor, and the governor and the magistrates of Dasu were terrified of the consequences if they didn't demonstrate sufficient zeal in this effort.

So the fishermen were not allowed rest. As soon as they returned, they were told to go out again, and to sail farther. No matter how tired or sleep-deprived they looked, they were not allowed to go home unless and until the prince was found.

Many never returned.

Prince Pulo waited by the coast. He had given up hope of seeing his little brother again, and he was just waiting for wreckage to be washed ashore. But none of the flotsam that showed up on the beach seemed to be from the fleet.

On the tenth day after the end of the storm, a large naval fleet finally arrived from Müning in Arulugi Island, but Prince Pulo said, "Call off the search. This is the season for storms and we don't need to put more lives at risk. I will inform my father."

Ronaza Métu, who had stayed behind to assure the emperor of the explorers' faith in their mission, swore that the fleet must have sailed beyond the reach of the airships and the fishing boats sent to look for it. The storm was nothing but Lord Kiji's unique way of speeding the ships along.

But Emperor Mapidéré had a different interpretation of the omen. Kiji and Tazu had broken up the fleet and devoured the pieces until there were no signs of the ships ever having existed. This was surely the gods' way of informing him that he had been duped again.

Métu was put to death, along with all the males of his and his companion's families within three degrees of relatedness. The emperor didn't particularly care if the blood would appease the gods, but at least he was satisfied. He hoped he had shown enough zeal for his dead son not to haunt him in this life and for himself to not feel embarrassed if they met again in the afterlife.

Storms like the one that had wiped out the fleet were not exactly unheard of in Dara. In the lore of Dasu and Rui, such storms were described as the result of tempestuous Kiji being angry with his sibling gods, and children born during such storms were sometimes said to be extraordinarily lucky. But the priests of Kiji and the clan headmen of Dasu didn't record this particular storm in their divination books or family shrines, for had the emperor not already spoken? The hour was cursed.

Yet Aki Kidosu wasn't willing to defer to their judgment. Her husband had spent only a few nights with their new baby daughter before the magistrate drafted him into the flotilla plying the winter sea to look for the unlucky prince on the expedition to the Land of the Immortals.

"Please, Your Grace, my wife and young daughter need me," Oga had said. "This baby is a surprise, coming as my wife thought that her childbearing days were long behind, and the nuns of Tututika warned us that she needed extra care—"

"Childbirth is a natural part of the life of women," the magistrate said. "Men of talent should be honored to serve the emperor. I am told that you're the best sailor and swimmer hereabouts. You must go."

"But my sons are already helping with the search, and surely we can take turns—"

"I have also been told that you're a teller of stories," said the magistrate, his voice turning severe, "a crafty fisherman with a tongue as slippery as an eel. Do not try to wiggle out of your duty."

"I'd like to return the next day—"

"No, you will go farther than anyone else because you win the spring boat race every year. If you return before any of the others, I will name you a traitor."

One by one, the other fisherfolk returned, weary and empty-handed. Crown Prince Pulo's departure had finally assured the magistrates that they had discharged their duty, and the wearied men and women were allowed to go home and rest.

But Oga was not among them.

"Please," Aki begged the magistrate. "The other fishing families of the village are too exhausted to go out to the sea again. Can you not ask the navy or the airships to search for him?"

"Impudent woman!" the magistrate chided. "Do you think the Imperial navy and air force should be redirected to look for a mere fisherman?"

"But he was out looking for the prince! He was serving the emperor!"

"Then he should be pleased to have given his life."

After the men and women of the village had recovered enough strength, they did go out on their own to look for Oga. They insisted that Oga's sons stay home with their mother—one potential tragedy was more than enough for a family. One after another, they returned with empty boats and mumbled apologies to Aki.

But she was not going to accept that he was gone until she had seen his body. The destitute and the humble were as powerless before hope as the emperor had been.

"Pa will be back when the sorghum is ready for the harvest," she whispered to the new baby after feedings. Aki called the baby Mimi because the way the baby smacked her lips and rooted for milk reminded her of a kitten. "I know he'll have so many great stories to tell you."

"My Mimi-*tika*, don't you worry. Papa'll be home soon, b'fore the next flurry," Aki sang in lullabies. "He'll give you piggyback rides and pretend to be your ship in a raging sea."

"I think he'll be home before the end of the summer. A year is a long time away at sea," Aki said, her voice singsongy with false cheer. "Maybe he was rescued by some pirates, and he's been regaling them with tales of adventure, like he used to do with the other fishermen on winter nights."

"You're already two! Papa is going to be so impressed when he sees you." Then Aki sighed when she thought no one could hear her.

She combed the beaches for wreckage every morning, and she continued to ask the crews of the fishing boats returning home if they'd seen anything while out at sea. She prayed to Lord Kiji and Lord Tazu every evening.

Once a year, when she went to the markets of Daye after the fall harvest to raise the rent for her landlord, she inquired at the governor's mansion for news of captured pirates and whether any of them matched the description of her husband. The officials shooed her away like a buzzing fly. They had more important things to worry about: A new emperor, Erishi, was on the throne, and there were rumors of distant rebellions. There was no time to deal with a crazy woman who refused to accept the fact of her husband's death when so many had already died in much less mysterious ways.

After leaving the governor's mansion, Aki also made sure to stop by the shrine for Lord Kiji to make an offering and seek advice. The monks and nuns told her to be patient and to trust in the gods, but they often abandoned her, sometimes midsentence, to attend to the well-dressed masters and mistresses who came into the shrine bearing chests filled with gifts for Lord Kiji and his attendants.

Like most children of the poor, Mimi was in the fields and on the beach helping her mother as soon as she could walk.

In spring, while her mother and brothers, who were almost a dozen years older, pulled the plow, she toddled after, pushing the sorghum and millet seeds into the soil step after step. In summer, she pulled fat caterpillars off the leaves in her mother's vegetable garden, crushed the heads and dropped the still-wriggling bodies into a lotus-leaf pouch so that they could be roasted later as a snack—this was how the poor who could not afford meat satisfied their craving for something savory. During fishing season, even before she was old enough to go out as an apprentice to the other fishermen, she patched nets and helped prepare the fish for drying and paste making, wincing as the sharp scales sliced her palms and the salt stung her fingers—until calluses covered her hands so that they looked like taros dug out of the ground.

"Your hands look just like mine," said her mother. It was neither praise nor lament, but a statement of fact. Mimi agreed that her mother's assessment was correct, though her hands were much smaller.

She wore the clothes that her two brothers had long outgrown, which were now barely more than rags. She made her own shoes out of bits of driftwood tied to her feet with spare fishing lines. She never knew the texture of silk, though she saw the sons and daughters of the wealthy pass by their field on horses sometimes, the hems of the iridescent robes and dresses fluttering like pieces of clouds torn from a sunset.

Mimi's life was no different from the lives of the innumerable children of the peasantry all over Dara. It was the fate of the poor to toil and endure, wasn't it?

But in play, Mimi stood out. It wasn't that she was unfriendly, but she seemed to have trouble fitting into the subtle web of power and hierarchy that held sway among children at play. While the other children of the village chased each other through the fields and had mud fights and elected kings and queens and reenacted the drama of society, she preferred to wander by herself, staring up at clouds drifting across the sky or watching the surf gently pounding the beach.

"What are you looking at?" the other children sometimes asked.

"I'm listening to the wind and the sea," Mimi answered. "Can't you hear it? They're arguing again . . . and now they're making up jokes to tell each other."

That was the other thing about Mimi, she could talk. She was conversing with her mother in complete sentences long before her second birthday, and she listened to conversations between adults with understanding in her eyes. Everyone remarked on her cleverness.

Perhaps the child is destined to speak to the gods, Aki thought. There were many legends of great priests and priestesses and monks and nuns being able to discern the will of the gods from the signs they left in nature. But she put the thought out of her mind immediately. She couldn't even afford to send any of her children to the village schoolmaster, let alone make the contribution to the Temple of Kiji required of a novice.

Then came the rebellion against Emperor Erishi and the Xana Empire, and new kings sprouted all over Dara like bamboo shoots after spring rain. War raged throughout the islands, though Dasu was thankfully spared the worst of it. When the Marshal of Xana, Kindo Marana, gave the call, many young men from this small island in the Xana heartland joined the army to put down the rebellion on the Big Island. Some went in search of glory; some went for food and pay; still others were taken by the army regardless of their wishes—including Mimi's brothers.

None of the young men ever returned.

"My sons will come home with their father," Aki said. She prayed even harder. Sometimes Mimi prayed with her. All the men in their lives were gone, and what else could they do? Hope was the currency that never ran out, and it was the fate of the poor to toil and endure, wasn't it?

Mimi tried to listen for signs in the wind and the sea, to read the tides and the clouds. Did the gods hear their prayers? She wasn't sure. The rumbling of the gods seemed to tell her their mood, but their speech was maddeningly just beyond comprehension. What did it mean that the winds that carried the voice of Kiji, patron of Xana, seemed to be filled with anger and despair while the tides that spoke for Tazu, the god of confusion and disarray, grew in wild pleasure? What was the import of this particular utterance? Of this other turn of phrase?

She strained to make sense of the world, but the world was shrouded in a veil that could not be pierced.

When Mimi was five, she woke up one night, disoriented. Her mother was soundly asleep by her side, and she couldn't remember the dream that had awakened her. She felt a premonition of something important happening beyond the walls of the hut, and she got out of bed, tiptoed her way to the door, and slipped out.

The sky was completely dark, with no moon and no stars. A faint breeze came from the sea, carrying the familiar briny smell. But out on the northern horizon, where the sea met the sky, flashes of lightning flickered, and the distant rumbling of thunder came to her, delayed and muffled.

She squinted and peered at the horizon. Indistinct shapes seemed to reveal themselves in the murky blend of sky and sea as the lightning flashes continued. A giant turtle, as large as a floating island, was limned in the hazy sky-sea like some hovering airship and swam jerkily to the west as the lightning bolts strobed. Behind it was the outline of an even more massive shark that snapped its jaws as it darted through the sky-sea, leaping up in powerful arcs from time to time and revealing teeth made up of jagged trails of lightning. Though the turtle seemed to be paddling its flippers leisurely and the shark swinging its tail in a frenzy, the shark never caught up to the turtle.

She knew that the turtle was the *pawi* of Lutho, god of fishermen, while the shark was the *pawi* of Tazu, god of the destructive nature of the sea. She watched the drama avidly like a show put on by one of the traveling folk opera troupes.

Then the eerie light show in the sky-sea changed again, and now she saw a ship with a strange design being tossed in the waves. It was circular in shape, like half of a coconut shell or a lily pad bobbing up and down in the tempest. A single massive mast, pure white in color, poked up out of the center of the ship like the stalk of a lotus flower, though the sails had long been furled or else torn away by the wind. Tiny figures were trying to hang on to the rigging and gunwales of the ship, but a few seemed to be shaken loose with each rise and fall and tumbled noiselessly into the waves. The unsteady illumination of the lightning seemed to emphasize the terrible fate that the ghostly ship found itself subject to.

The giant turtle swam up to the ship, dove down, and rose again with the ship lodged securely in the deep grooves etched into the back of its shell, as though the ship was a mere barnacle. Leisurely, the island-turtle continued to swim west, while the shark pursued close behind, tail whipping and jaws snapping. Slowly and inexorably, however, the turtle was pulling away.

Before the sea, all men are brothers.

Mimi felt the instinctive sympathy and terror of all the islanders for those who braved the whale's way. Before the vast brutality that was the sea, all humans were equally powerless. She cheered and cheered for the turtle and the ship it carried, though she was certain that whoever the refugees in the ship were—ghosts, spirits, gods, or mortals—they were too far away to hear her.

Once more, the great shark leapt into the air, higher than ever before, and, as it reached the apex of its arc of flight, shot out a long, twisting bolt of lightning. Like the tongue of a great python, it reached across the space between the shark and the turtle and struck the ship nestled on the back of the turtle.

Everything froze in the harsh, cold glow of the lightning for a moment, and then darkness hid the scene of destruction.

Mimi screamed.

Once again, the horizon lit up with flickers of storm-glow. The great shark on the horizon seemed to have heard her. Whipping its powerful tail, the shark turned toward the island, and its giant eyes, like the beacons of lighthouses, focused on her. The lightning-jaws snapped open, and after a few seconds, a massive peal of thunder boomed around her, and rain poured out of the sky in a sudden flood, drenching her so completely that she thought she was drowning.

Is this what it's like to defy the gods? she thought. *Is this how I will die?*

The shark swam toward the beach, its colossal figure now a looming island of roiling lights. It opened its jaws once more, and a long zigzagging lightning bolt shot out, reaching for Mimi like a long tentacle. Air crackled around the lightning bolt, energized by it and glowing with the heat.

Time seemed to slow down; Mimi closed her eyes, certain that her brief life on earth was about to come to an end.

Some hulking presence swooped over her head, so low that the skin over her skull tightened and tingled. She snapped her eyes open and looked up.

A gargantuan, shimmering raptor dove toward the ocean, toward that flickering tongue of lightning. The falcon's wings were so wide that they blotted out the sky over her head like a bridge made of liquid silver; the flight feathers at the trailing edges of the wings flashed like shooting stars. It was the most beautiful sight she had ever seen.

The falcon lowered its right wing like a shield to block the advancing lightning bolt shooting from the shark's jaws. The shark's eyes widened in surprise and then narrowed, and the hissing tongue of light connected with the raptor's wing. There was a brilliant, massive explosion of sparks like the eruption of a volcano. Bolts of lightning zigzagged in every direction.

One of the smaller bolts shot out at Mimi and struck her in the face.

She felt a searing tongue of liquid heat tunnel right through her. It was as if she had been turned into a funnel for molten rock that was being poured into the top of her skull; the sizzling lava flowed right through her torso to melt all her organs, and then left through her left leg to sink into the ground.

Mimi screamed. And screamed.

She couldn't believe how long she remained alert as the heat fried every cell in her body, and the last image she remembered before sinking into the bliss of unconsciousness was the giant falcon of light diving toward the shark while the shark leapt out of the ocean, as though the sky and sea were about to consume each other in a titanic battle.

The lightning strike left Mimi's face scarred and her left leg paralyzed. For days she lay in bed in a coma, waking from time to time screaming and babbling incoherently about what she had seen on that night.

"She was a pretty child," said the village herbalist, Tora. Then she sighed. In that sigh were a thousand things assumed but unsaid: the loss of a worthy husband perhaps; the denial of a secure future for Aki, who was without a son; a lament for the inconstant ways of the world.

"She is a hard worker," said Aki peacefully. "Scars do not take away from that. What can you do for her?"

"I can offer some iceweed for the fever and Rapa's Lace to allow her to sleep better," said the herbalist. "Keeping her comfortable is about all we *can* do. . . . You might also want to . . . ask the neighbors to help prepare a grave, just in case."

"The gods did not give her in my old age only to take her away before she can ask them her purpose," said Aki stubbornly.

Tora shook her head and mumbled something about the cursed hour of the child's birth, and then went away.

Aki refused to give up. She curled herself around Mimi in bed and kept her warm with her own body heat. Neighbors brought her the rare seawife's purse—the dyran egg sacks sometimes found attached to the tips of kelp ribbons in undersea forests—which Aki made into soup and fed to Mimi with a fish-bone spoon to add to the soup's strength.

Slowly, Mimi recovered. She woke up one morning and looked at her mother with a calm, steady gaze, and told her of what she had seen on the night she was struck by lightning.

"Many are the fantastic figures we see in our feverish dreams," said Aki.

Mimi did not think that her memories were dreams, but she couldn't be sure. She decided not to press the point.

Tora was summoned again to see if anything could be done about Mimi's left leg, which was numb and refused to obey her. It was as if the leg was no longer a part of her, but something alien attached to her body that she had to drag around. Her hip, where the leg connected with her torso, tingled with the pain of a thousand needles stabbing into her.

"I can give you a poultice made of shrimp paste and seaweed for the pain," said the herbalist. "But this leg . . . will never walk again."

Aki smiled and said nothing. It was the fate of the poor to toil and endure, wasn't it? Surely the gods would not deprive Mimi of the ability to do so.

"It hurts so bad that I can't sleep, Mama," said Mimi. "Tell me a story."

CHAPTER SIX

THE HUNDRED FLOWERS

DASU: A LONG TIME AGO.

Growing up, Aki had told Mimi many stories that she would recall in later days. But memory was a lump of wax that was reshaped by the knife of consciousness with each recollection, and as Mimi grew up and changed, the way she remembered the stories also changed.

Flowery metaphors replaced homely similes; sophisticated kennings replaced unadorned phrasings; echoes of the Ano Classics replaced the patterns of the sea in her mother's murmurs. It was as impossible to recall the words of her mother accurately as it was to hold on to the sand slipping between the fingers of a squeezing fist.

But the hearts of the tales remained, and the scent of home lingered in those memories: They were the landscape of her childhood dreams, the shores of her first narratives.

Now, my Mimi-tika, before your father and I had children, we used to entertain ourselves by telling each other stories on long winter nights, after we had coupled and before we could fall asleep. Sometimes the stories were told to us by our parents, and by their parents before them. Sometimes we added to the stories, the way daughters mend and alter the dresses inherited from their mothers, the ways sons adapt and reshape the tools inherited from their fathers. Sometimes we swapped the same story back and forth, changing it in each retelling, the way love is shaped and crafted and polished and built up by two pairs of hands in a space of their own.

This is one of those stories.

You know that the years come in cycles of twelve, and each is named after an animal or a plant. The cycle starts with the Year of the Plum, which is followed by the Cruben, the Orchid, the Whale, the Bamboo, the Carp, the Chrysanthemum, the Deer, the Pine, the Toad, the Coconut, and finally, the Wolf, before starting with the Plum again. The fate of each child is bound up with the plant or animal governing the year in which she was born.

But how did these animals and plants become selected for the calendar? That is a story worthy of telling and retelling.

Long ago, when gods and heroes still walked the earth together and fought and embraced each other as brothers, the years were without character. Each year was as likely to be gentle as a carp drifting in mountain streams, bringing with it bountiful harvest on both land and at sea, as it was to be fierce as an aged pine waving its gnarled branches, bringing with it strife and lean winters.

"My brothers and sisters," said Lord Rufizo, the compassionate god of healers, one day, "we have let time pass by as an undammed river for too long. But our mother, the Source-of-All-Waters, bid us to care for the people of Dara. We must discharge our duties better by bringing order to time."

The other gods and goddesses assented to this most excellent of suggestions, and the decision was made to divide time into cycles of twelve, much like the way the mighty Miru River is now tamed by dams and water mills every dozen miles or so along its course. Twelve was a good number, as it accounted for the four worlds of Air, Earth, Water, and Fire, multiplied by the three aspects of time: future, present, and past. And each of the years in the cycle would be named after an animal or plant of Dara so as to give it a guiding disposition. That way, the farmers, hunters, fishermen, and shepherds *would know what to expect and thus how to prepare for the long term.*

"Civilization is a matter of endowing nameless things with names," said Lord Lutho, who was always interested in giving everything a bookish sheen.

"I nominate a pair of ravens for the first year . . ." said Lady Kana.

". . . because everyone knows that ravens are the wisest of birds," finished Lady Rapa.

"No, no, no," said Lord Tazu, who loved contradicting his siblings. "What is the fun in all of us nominating our pawi? First, there wouldn't be enough of them to go around; and second, we've just fought a war over who among us is supposed to be the first among equals. Do we really want to start that again?"

"What do you propose then, Tazu?" asked Tututika, who also disliked the idea of further argument among the gods.

"Let's make it a game!"

The other gods and goddesses perked up at this, for the gods, like children, loved games most of all.

"We will let every flower, tree, vine, bird, fish, and beast know that the gods of Dara are selecting champions to guide time. On the announced day, we'll hide in a corner of Dara, and the first twelve living things to find us will be given the honor of governing the years."

All the gods and goddesses thought this was a brilliant idea, and the game was on.

"Mama! I want to look for the gods!"

"Whatever for? Don't you know that nothing good ever comes from bothering the gods when they don't wish to be bothered?"

"I want to know why! Why is Papa gone? Why have Féro and Phasu been taken away? Why was I struck by lightning? Why do we work so hard and have so little to eat—"

"Hush, child. There aren't always answers, only stories."

On the designated day, all the plants and animals raced to search every corner of Dara so that they might be among the lucky few to claim a year as their own.

Some subjects of the vegetable and animal kingdoms sought to accomplish their mission on their own: Sleek whales, largest among fish, raced around the islands to explore every hidden cove and visit every pristine beach before the others; golden chrysanthemums bloomed everywhere and saturated the air with their fragrance, hoping to entice a beauty-loving god or goddess out of concealment; clever ravens swooped over the cities of mankind, their eyes alert for anything that seemed divine rather than mortal; coconuts dropped into the ocean one after another, splashing out novel and pleasing tunes that they hoped might move a listening god to yield an exclamation of delight; golden and red carp danced through the ponds and rivers in scintillating formations, brandishing their diaphanous fins and waving their whiskers to mesmerize and delight the immortals; the lotus turned its thousand-eyed seedpods to every direction in the air and bared the hundreds of openings in its roots to listen for minute tremors underwater, a miniature all-seeing-all-hearing spy tower in operation; rabbits and deer raced across meadows on Écofi and Crescent Islands, each intent upon finding the unusual hump in the sea of grass that might be a god in disguise—unaware that the grasses were also plotting to weave false hiding places to divert the silly herbivores while they themselves sought the gods underground with their sensitive roots.

Others decided to form strange alliances to exploit the unique skills of each creature of Dara. The mighty cruben, sovereign of the seas, allied itself with the glowing sea cucumber—half animal, half plant—so that the illumination from the latter might reveal any gods hiding in the dark recesses of deep undersea trenches and enable the former to catch them; the winter plum, the bamboo, and the pine, the three hardiest plants of winter, allied with the heat-loving desert toad so that while the bamboo groves, pine forests, and winter plum copses whispered to each other across snow-capped peaks, the toads could scour the volcanic calderas; the wolf, fiercest predator on land, made a pact with the clinging vine so that as the wolf packs searched the deep woods and howled, the gods running and dodging might be ensnared by soft vine-webs.

From morning till noon, and from noon till evening, the gods were found one by one.

First, the pine forests, bamboo groves, and winter plum copses, surveying *every spot touched by ice in the islands, discovered Lady Rapa in the Wisoti Mountains as a delicate face carved into the glasslike surface of a frozen waterfall. Shortly after this discovery, the toads found Lady Kana as a jagged crack in a vitreous screen of obsidian.*

The alliance of fire and ice had paid off.

But not all alliances had such happy endings. The arrogant cruben dove straight for the heart of a swirling patch of turbulence in one of the deepest trenches of the sea, whose inky gloom was illuminated by hundreds of glowing sea cucumbers attached to the head of the cruben like jewels encrusting the tip of a ceremonial staff of power. But at the last minute, right before the cruben closed its jaws gently about the laughing form of shape-shifting Tazu, the sovereign of the seas shook its head and discarded the sea cucumbers from its adamantine scales like a water buffalo shaking loose the gnats clinging to its head. While the cruben shot for the surface in a triumphant surge, the poor, soft, glowing tubes drifted helplessly into the bottomless void like falling stars cast out of heaven.

Such was the risk of serving at the pleasure of the mighty and powerful.

"Mama, why are those with the most power always so bad?"

"Mimi-*tika*, is the fisherman evil who harvests the fruits of the sea? Is the farmer evil who cuts off ears of sorghum? Is the weaver evil who boils the cocoon of the silkworm and unravels its debut dress— now a shroud?"

"I don't understand."

"Great lords—whether mortal or immortal—do what they do because their concerns are not ours. We suffer because we are the grass upon which giants tread."

In a secluded cove on the northwestern coast of the Big Island, the whales plying the shores of the Islands of Dara discovered an ancient sea turtle whose shell was as cracked as the coral reefs peeking out of the sea.

The whales surrounded the turtle and splashed it playfully with sprays from their blowholes, painting a fine rainbow with the mist.

"Lord Lutho," said the leader of the whales, a massive dome-headed cow

*whose gray eyes had seen hundreds of springs, "you are hiding exactly the
way we predicted you would."*

*The ancient turtle laughed and transformed into the dark-skinned divine
seer, the fisherman of dreams and omens. "How do you know that you have
not found me exactly the way I predicted you would?"*

The whales were confused by this.

*"If you had foreseen that we would look for you here," asked the whale,
"why did you not hide somewhere else?"*

*Lutho smiled and pointed at the rainbow, now fading as the whale-mist
gradually dissipated.*

*"Was it because though you could foresee the future, you could not change
it?" The whale asked a different question.*

Lutho smiled and pointed to the rainbow.

*"Was it because you had foreseen the future but decided that the vision
was what you wanted after all?" The whale tried yet a third time.*

Lutho smiled and pointed to the rainbow, now barely a hint in the air.

*"Was it because—" But this time, the whale couldn't complete the question.
Lutho had disappeared along with the rainbow.*

"Mama, why did Lord Lutho point to the rainbow instead of answering?"

"Nobody knows, my baby. The whales didn't, and neither did your
father, our parents, grandparents, or their grandparents before them.
That's why it's called a mystery. I suppose sometimes the gods have
lessons for us we can't understand through words alone."

"I think Lord Lutho is not a very good teacher."

"Good teachers are as rare as the cruben among whales, or the
dyran among fish."

*It was no surprise that Lady Tututika, last born of the gods and the one
who took the most pleasure in beauty, was ensnared by the symphony of
coconuts rhythmically pounding the sea and the golden veil dance of the
carp—she manifested herself at the mouth of the Sonaru River, and it is
said that one can still get a glimpse of that heavenly dance in the motions of*

the veil dancers of Faça as musicians tap out beats on their coconut drums.

Neither was it a surprise when Lord Rufizo manifested himself when a yearling fawn tripped and injured himself in the rocky highlands near fog-shrouded Boama. How could the god of healing stand idly by when living creatures injured themselves in pursuit of the gods?

"At least Dara will enjoy a year mild as the deer every cycle of twelve years," said the green-caped divine healer, and the deer leapt around him in joy at being elevated among the Calendrical Dozen.

And finally, as the sun set in the west, Lord Kiji, the patron of ambitious flight and soaring fancy and wide-open skies, surveyed the Islands of Dara in the form of a Mingén falcon gliding over Dara. The bird, dizzied by a pungent pillar of floral aroma emanating from a garden of blooming chrysanthemums near the meeting place of the Damu and Shinané Mountains, fell out of the sky in a spiraling descent, and as he landed, a pack of wolves pounced on him, holding him down.

"I am caught by the king of flowers and the king of beasts!" said the god of all those who yearned to be above others. "I would call this not a bad way to end the day."

And there was much celebration in Dara, for the gods sometimes behaved as their natures dictated.

The wolf, however, was not quite as joyous as the others among the Calendrical Dozen; this was because the wolf was the pawi of Lord Fithowéo, and Fithowéo was missing.

"The god of warfare and strife?"

"Yes, baby, those are the domains of Lord Fithowéo."

"It would have been better if he had never been found. Without him, there would be no wars and all the suffering that comes from them."

"Ah my Mimi-tika, things are rarely that simple when it comes to the gods."

As you have probably already figured out, this contest came after the Diaspora Wars, when the divine siblings had fought along with vast armies, and brother had turned on brother, sister on sister.

In one of those battles, in order to protect the hero Iluthan, Fithowéo had fought Kiji for ten days and ten nights. In the end, Kiji's lightning bolts had taken away Fithowéo's eyes, blinding him. And so it was that the blind god had not participated in the discussion concerning the calendar but hid himself in an obscure cave deep under the Wisoti Mountains, nursing his wounds and avoiding all living creatures.

Water dripped from the stalactites high overhead, and other than clumps of mushroom glowing here and there like faint stars in the night sky, there was no illumination in the cave. The blind god sat by himself, unmoving and mute.

A scent tickled his nose, so faint that he wasn't sure whether he was just imagining it. But it was a sweet smell, simple and humble, like a trace of mint in a glass of water after a thundershower, like the lingering fragrance of soap bean on freshly laundered robes left in the sun, like the flavor of cooking fire that caresses a weary traveler's nose after a long night of hard hiking.

And so, without even realizing that he was doing it, Fithowéo got up and walked toward the scent, following his nostrils.

The smell grew stronger—a night-blooming orchid, he decided, and in his mind arose the image of a white flower with a large labellum like a rolled-up tongue that hid the stiff column in the middle, and four translucent petals that stood above the labellum like the translucent wings of a moth. He moved yet closer to the source of the smell, and as the diaphanous wings brushed his nose, he stuck out his tongue and traced the shapes of the petals. Yes, it was indeed the night-blooming orchid, whose shape was a faint echo of the moth that was said to be its sole pollinator, which emerged only in darkness and under starlight. It was a simple flower that was little valued by the ladies and gardeners, who preferred something more showy and ornate.

The tip of his tongue tasted the sweetness of nectar.

"I can taste sorrow on your tongue," came a whispered voice.

The god drew back, surprised.

"What could make a god sad?" asked the voice. Fithowéo realized that it was coming from the center of the flower he had kissed.

"What is the good of a god of war who cannot see?" a morose Fithowéo said.

"Can you not see?" asked the orchid.

The god pointed to his empty eye sockets, and when no reply came from the orchid, he realized that of course, in this dark cave, the orchid couldn't see either.

"I cannot," he said. "My brother blinded me with lightning bolts."

"But who told you that you were blind?"

"Of course I'm blind!"

"Have you tried to see?"

Fithowéo shook his head. The orchid was not a creature that could be reasoned with.

"I can see," said the orchid, "even though I don't have eyes."

"That's ridiculous," said Fithowéo.

"I saw you," said the orchid, utterly confident.

"What do you mean?"

"I reached out with my fragrance until the tendrils drew you to me," said the orchid. "It took a while, but I saw."

"That is not seeing," declared Fithowéo.

"I can tell you that there are a dozen bats hanging on the ceiling above us," said the orchid. "I can tell you that there is a swarm of moths who visits me every evening, though none of them is my match. I can tell you that there are furry moles who sniff around this cave when winters are rough. I know these things that you do not, and yet you tell me that I cannot see."

"That . . ." Fithowéo was without words for a moment. "All right, I suppose that is a kind of seeing."

"There are many kinds of seeing," said the orchid. "Didn't the Ano sages tell us that sight is simply light emanating from the eyes being reflected back by the world?"

"Actually—" Fithowéo started to say.

But the orchid didn't let him finish. "I see by shooting out lines of fragrance into the world and drawing back what they touch. If you don't have eyes, you must find other ways of seeing."

Fithowéo sniffed the air around him. He could detect the musk of the mushrooms to the left and a stronger, second floral scent—sharper, brighter than the fragrance of the orchid. "Is that a cave rose to the right?"

"Yes," said the orchid.

"And there's something else," said Fithowéo, sniffing the air again. "It smells like mud and the bog."

"Very good, there's a pool on the other side of me, filled with wormweed and tiny white fish who have lost their eyes because it's so dark here."

Fithowéo took a deep breath and separated the faint smell of the fish from the rest.

"You see," said the orchid, "you're already constructing a map of smells."

Fithowéo realized that it was true. As he turned his face from side to side, he could almost see the glowing mushrooms and the cave roses blooming next to the wall of the cave, as well as the pool of ice-cold water beyond the orchid. Their shapes were indistinct, like a blurry vision after he had had too many flagons of mead.

But after a moment of joy, he was plunged into depression again.

"I can't just stand around like you," said Fithowéo. "Smells may be sufficient for a flower rooted to the earth. But they're not enough for a god of rage and motion."

The orchid said nothing.

"When fate has taken away your weapons," said Fithowéo, "sometimes you must yield."

The orchid said nothing.

"When you have no more hope after a battle fairly fought," said Fithowéo, "the more honorable course is to give in to despair."

The orchid said nothing.

Fithowéo strained his ears in the darkness, and he heard something that sounded like the rustling of silk.

"Are you laughing?" Fithowéo roared. "You dare to laugh at my misfortune?"

He stood up and lifted his foot. The smell of the orchid was enough for him to fix her position. A step forward and he would be able to grind the orchid under his foot, flattening her against the jagged floor of the cave.

"I am laughing at a coward who claims to be a god," said the orchid. "I am laughing at an immortal who does not even understand his own duty."

"What are you talking about? I am the god of wars and battles! I must see the light glancing off a swinging blade and meet it with my battered shield. I must see the speeding arrow to bat it aside with my gauntleted arm. I must see the foe escaping on foot to pierce him with my enduring spear. What good is a map of smells?"

"Listen," said the orchid.

Fithowéo listened. In the silence of the cave, other than the irregular dripping of water, there seemed to be no other sound.

"Open your ears," said the orchid. "You have come to a place of darkness, where eyes that see only with light are useless. Do you think creatures who make this place home stumble through their lives?"

And Fithowéo listened harder: He seemed to hear shrill squeaks, so high-pitched that they were barely audible, crisscrossing the air overhead.

"The bats see by shooting out rays of sound from their throat and catching the echoes with their ears as they bounce back."

Fithowéo listened, and now he realized that the air was filled with another sound: wings beating rapidly against air. The bats were swooping gracefully in wide arcs near the ceiling of the cave.

"Dip your hands into the water," said the orchid.

And Fithowéo dipped his hands into the cold water, and he felt a tingling all over his hands, even after he got used to the numbing cold.

"The tiny white fish who live in the water flex their muscles and nerves to generate invisible lines of force that suffuse the water," said the orchid. "Like the mysterious force that fills the air before a thunderstorm, the invisible lines flex and twist around living beings, and so the blind fish see with their bodies."

Fithowéo concentrated and he could indeed feel invisible lines of force lapping at his arm, and he imagined the ripples of force echoing back to the tiny fish.

"You call yourself a god of war, but war is not merely the music of steel sword against wooden shield, or the chorus of speeding arrows thunking into leather armor. War is also the domain of struggling against overwhelming odds that neither Tazu nor Lutho would touch, the realm of snatching life from the jaws of fiery Kana without Rufizo as your ally, the province of depriving a superior enemy force of the comfort of restful Rapa using only your wits, the territory of finding an unexpected path to humble proud

Kiji despite the lack of all advantages, and the sphere of constructing out of ugliness beauty that would shock extravagant Tututika.

"You have become used to victory achieved at little expense against mere mortals, even if they are deemed heroes. But war consists of not only victories; it is also about fighting and losing, and losing only to fight again.

"A god of war is also the god of those who are caught in the wheel of eternal struggle, who fight on despite knowledge of certain defeat, who stand with their companions against spear and catapult and gleaming metal, armed with only their pride, who strive and assay and press and toil, all the while knowing that they cannot win.

"You are not only the god of the strong, but also the god of the weak. Courage is better displayed when it seems all is lost, when despair appears the only rational course.

"True courage is to insist on seeing when all around you is darkness."

And Fithowéo stood up and ululated. As his voice filled the cave walls and bounced back to his ears, he seemed to see the stalactites hanging overhead like bejeweled curtains, the stalagmites growing out of the ground like bamboo shoots, the bats careening through the air like battle kites, the night-blooming orchids and cave roses blooming like living treasure—the cave was filled with light.

The god of war laughed and bowed down to the orchid and kissed her. "Thank you for showing me how to see."

"I am but the lowest of the Hundred Flowers," said the orchid. "But the tapestry of Dara is woven not only from the proud chrysanthemum or the arrogant winter plum, the bamboo who holds up great houses or the coconut who provides sweet nectar and pleasing music. Chicory, dandelion, butter-and-eggs, ten thousand species of orchids, and countless other flowers—we have no claim to the crests of the great noble families, and we are not cultivated in gardens and not gently caressed by the fingers of great ladies and eager courtiers. But we also fight our war against hail and storm, against drought and deprivation, against the sharp blade of the weeding hoe and the poisonous emanations of the herbicide-sprayer. We also have a claim on time, and we deserve a god who understands that every day in the life of the common flower is a day of battle."

And Fithowéo continued to ululate, letting his throat and ears be his eyes, until he strode out of the cave, emerged into the sunlight, and picked up two pieces of darkest obsidian and placed them in his eye sockets so that he had eyes again. Though they were blind to light, they sowed fear into all who gazed into them.

And that was how the humble orchid joined the Calendrical Dozen.

CHAPTER SEVEN

TEACHER AND STUDENT

And so Aki helped Mimi get off the bed and gave her a crutch she made out of driftwood. She did not tell Mimi how unlikely it was that she would ever gain command of her leg. She simply expected her to figure out a way to do so.

Mother and daughter combed the beach and worked in the fields and helped the fishermen with their catch. Aki strode purposefully ahead, not looking back to see if the hobbling Mimi could keep up. For the common men and women of Dara, every day was a day of battle.

And Mimi learned to brush off the numbness in her leg; she learned to ignore the prickling pain in her hip; she learned to lean and shift weight and strengthen herself until she could walk with a crutch under her left arm.

One morning, as the pair combed the beach, they found pieces of some unusual wreckage. The remnants of spars and bulkheads were not made of wood, but some material closer to bone or ivory, carved with intricate designs of an unknown beast: a long tail, two clawed feet, a pair of great wings, and a slender, snakelike neck topped with an oversized, deerlike, antlered head. Aki brought the wreckage to the clan headman, but the elder could not recall ever seeing anything like it.

"It's not from the emperor's expedition," said Aki, and she made no more mention of it. The world was full of mysteries. The strange wreckage seemed to Mimi to be holes in the veil that hid the truth of the world, but she could not understand what she was seeing.

They brought the wreckage to market and sold it for a few pieces of copper to those who liked collecting curiosities.

But Mimi dreamt of the strange beast long after. In her dreams, the beast fought the storm turtle and the gale shark and the squall falcon, while lightning froze their poses momentarily, creating staccato, chiaroscuro scenes as spare and beautiful as they were terrifying.

She hoped that the turtle did manage to save that dream ship, just as she hoped that the gods had spared her father and brothers.

News arrived that the Xana Empire was no more. A great lord called the Hegemon had toppled the throne of Emperor Erishi in the Immaculate City and restored the Tiro kings of old. Few in the village mourned the empire's passing—patriotism, like white rice, was a luxury of the well-to-do.

It was said that the Hegemon had butchered the sons of Xana at Wolf's Paw, including all the young men from the village who had gone to fight for Marshal Marana. For days, people waited outside the door of the magistrate's home, hoping for news of their sons and husbands and fathers and brothers, but the doors remained shut as the magistrate convened with his advisers and clerks on how to properly conduct himself to curry favor with the Hegemon so as to keep wearing the official's dark silk hat. The lives of the dead soldiers were not even an afterthought.

Aki did not put up mourning tablets for her sons either. "I did not bury them with my hands," she said, "and I certainly will not bury them in my heart."

Sometimes, when Mimi woke up in the middle of the night, she saw her mother sitting on the floor next to the bed, her shoulders heaving, her face turned away. Mimi would put a hand out and touch her mother's back. The two would stay connected like that in the silence, until Mimi fell asleep again.

Eventually the people left the magistrate's courtyard and went back to their endless toil, which turned sweat into food and pain into drink. Private shrines to the dead and presumed dead were erected in their houses, but none made passionate speeches about the honor of Xana or spoke of vengeance against the Hegemon. The people were too numbed by sorrow to feel hatred—wars were personal to the great lords, but who could say for sure that the Hegemon bore more responsibility for these deaths than the marshal or Emperor Erishi?

While her brothers and father did not come home, a new king did arrive in Dasu.

King Kuni was a strange lord. He lowered the taxes, did not demand corvée service to build a new palace but paid the laborers to repair roads and bridges, and abolished the old, harsh laws of Xana that had meted out punishment for even sneezing too loudly. He let it be known that men and women of the other islands who had been displaced by the wars were free to come to his island, and he would even help them get settled with free seeds and tools. The elders and widows of Dasu rejoiced: The wars had drained the island of men, and husbands and fathers were in short supply. Though some women agreed to marry into existing households, especially if the families were wealthy, not all wanted such an arrangement.

It was also customary for women in love or in need of each other to be joined in Rapa marriages—the goddess was said to have once fallen in love with an ice maiden. As the folk opera troupes sang:

Their love was one that would play out over eons,
Through minute gestures measured in inches and centuries,
Through whispers that would echo down dusty shelves of
*   history,*

Through a single glance penetrating the scale of creation and a
Single dance that
Would outlast the eruptions of volcanoes and the sinking of the
Islands of Dara
Into the sea.

With the war, the number of Rapa marriages had grown so that women could support each other—it was easier to till the fields and to raise children together. Still, there were many women who preferred men and did not want to share, and strangers were indeed welcome.

Aki, who was asked but never agreed to bind herself in a Rapa marriage, paid no attention to any of the new men who came to settle in their village, though several seemed interested in her. She struggled to till their small plot of land with only Mimi's help and supplemented their income by helping the fishing crews.

"My husband is away," she said to anyone who asked. "He'll be back soon. And my sons, too."

"Do we have any talent?" Mimi asked her mother one day.

"Why are you asking that?"

Seven-year-old Mimi had returned home earlier to prepare dinner while her mother was finishing up in the field. She had to stand on a stool to reach the boiling pot on the stove—dangerous, but the children of the poor had to learn to do things earlier. A crier had come through the village bearing an announcement from the palace in Daye: King Kuni was looking for people with talent and was willing to reward them, no matter their present station in life.

Mimi repeated the message to her mother, word for word. It ended with this: *An oyster clasped in the branches of the most exquisite head of coral is as likely to hold a pearl as one mired in mud.*

She had always had an excellent memory: She could repeat stories from Aki after one telling, and she could perform entire folk operas in the long winters to entertain her mother.

"The magistrate's son is said to be going to the palace in Daye to show the king his skill with the brush and writing knife," said Mimi. "And the village schoolmaster is holding a contest for his students to select two who can recite the most Classical Ano poems to be presented to the king. I heard Uncle So on the other side of the village is going to show the king his new way of tying knots in fishing nets, and Auntie Tora is thinking she wants to present her collection of herbal remedies. Do we have any talent? Maybe we can also go to the king and live like the magistrate's son."

Aki looked at her daughter. *She is an extraordinary child. What if the king took an interest in her?*

Then she remembered what had happened to her husband. *Men of talent should be honored to serve the emperor.*

"Talent is like a pretty feather in the tail of a peacock, daughter. It brings joy to the powerful but only sorrow to the bird."

Mimi pondered this. The veil over the world seemed to grow even thicker.

King Kuni rebelled against the Hegemon. Once again, the men (and women also, this time) of Dasu left the fields and fishing boats to die in distant lands. Aki wasn't surprised. The dreams of the great lords of the world were built upon the blood and bones of the common people. The blossoming of the golden chrysanthemum required the fertilizer made from the ashes of the Hundred Flowers. That was an eternal truth.

Peace did not come again until Mimi had turned thirteen, when King Kuni became Emperor Ragin, initiating the Reign of Four Placid Seas.

∾ ∾

DASU: THE FIRST YEAR IN THE REIGN OF FOUR
PLACID SEAS (FIVE YEARS BEFORE THE FIRST
GRAND EXAMINATION).

One day, Mimi was in the markets at Daye. She was old enough for Aki to trust her to take care of selling the harvested grain and paying the landlord their rent all by herself. She was a better negotiator than Aki, in any event.

The sons and daughters of the wealthy rode through the streets on horseback, whips singing through the air, and Mimi and the other peasants dodged out of their way. Her hobbling gait and the heavy load of the grain sample bag meant that sometimes she was too slow, and several times the horses came close to trampling her. But Mimi only gritted her teeth and did not complain. Just as there were many ways of seeing, there were many ways of walking.

The scholars and bureaucrats of the emperor rode more sedately through the streets on comfortable carts pulled by teams of horses or men, and they kept their gazes averted from the dirty, numb, mal-nourished faces of the poor next to the sewer ditches hugging the road.

Mimi tamped down her anger. That was the way of the world, wasn't it? Emperor Ragin was supposed to care about the lives of the common people, but there were gradations among the commoners as well. As far as she could tell, it was only the people who were already well off who sang the praises of the new reign.

It was as useless to think about how she and her mother could also lead a life of ease and luxury, to be dressed in silk instead of rough hemp, to eat soft white rice instead of sandy millet that scratched their teeth, as it was for a dandelion to think that it could be honored like the chrysanthemum.

A crowd was gathered at the center of the market. Curious and hoping for some exciting performance of magic or acrobatics, she pushed her way through the thronging spectators, wielding her walk-ing stick like an oar through thick mud and water. She was disappointed to see only two men sitting face-to-face on a woven mat at the center, their hair styled in the double scroll-bun indicative of their rank as *toko dawiji*, scholars who had passed the first level of the Imperial examinations.

". . . knows that the closer something is, the bigger it appears, and the farther it is, the smaller," said the first scholar.

"It is your contention then that the sun is closer at dawn and dusk, but farther away at noon, thus explaining why it looks bigger at sunrise and sunset?" asked the second scholar.

"Plainly," said the first scholar.

"But everyone also knows that the closer a source of heat is, the hotter it feels. How do you explain the fact that the sun feels hottest at noon but cooler at dawn and dusk, if the sun is in fact farther away at noon?" asked the second scholar.

"Er . . ." The first scholar furrowed his brows, stumped by this puzzle.

"Simple. Your explanation is wrong!" said the second scholar.

"It is *not* wrong," said the first scholar, his face turning red. "The great sage Kon Fiji explained that nature, like human society, follows a discernible structure of hierarchy. The sun is as far above the earth as the emperor is above the common people. It only follows that the gods must have intended the sun to be at its greatest distance from the earth when it is at its apex, symbolizing the grace and nobility of the Imperial throne."

"But what about the noonday heat, my learned friend?" asked the second scholar.

"That is easily explained." The first scholar took a drink from his cup of tea and furtively glanced at the crowd around them. Now that so many people were watching, he had to win this debate to save face. He put the cup down and raised his voice, injecting into it an arrogant confidence—sometimes it was enough to sound like one knew what one was talking about.

"Your argument *assumes* that the sun is at a constant temperature. But that is not so. Employing pure reason, we discover that if the sun feels hottest at its farthest point from the earth at noon, it must also gradually increase in heat as it rises and cool down as it sets. The point at which the sun is hottest is also when it is highest, which is indeed the most perfect design."

Does the world follow a design that can be perceived? Mimi wondered. *Is nature a model for society so that what is natural is also what is just?*

She had never heard of such arguments before, and she was

mesmerized. The learned men seemed to think that the world itself was a kind of speech that could be decoded. She remembered her attempts to understand the conversation of the gods as a child. She yearned for such knowledge, knowledge that would allow her to interpret the signs of the gods, to see through the veil of the world and get a glimpse of Truth.

"You Moralists always assume the conclusion before the argument," said the second scholar contemptuously. "It is just as Ra Oji said: A disciple of Kon Fiji is the world's most powerful lens, for he bends all rays of evidence to focus on his desired opinion. Even if he is idle and has an empty belly, he would argue that it is the fault of the food for not recognizing his moral superiority and actively seeking his belly."

The crowd roared with laughter.

"In the end, a Moralist convinces no one but himself," continued the second scholar, pleased that he had the backing of the crowd.

"You Fluxists are good at poking fun at seekers of truth while offering up nothing of use yourselves except witticisms," said the first scholar, his voice trembling with rage. "What is *your* explanation for the sun's changing size then?"

"Who knows? It might indeed be the case that the sun moves farther away as it rises, as you contend, or it might be the case that the sun shrinks as it ascends, like a jellyfish contracting its cap to propel itself upward in the ocean. But your very approach is wrong: We need not force nature into models drawn by our desires. As the Ano sages told us, *Gipén co fidéra ünthiru nafé ki shraçaa tefi né othu.* We need only *conform* our life to the rhythms set by nature. I wake up in the crisp morning breeze and enjoy a breakfast of raw strips of whitefish, bought fresh off the wharf and spiced with ginger; I hide in the shade of a great parasol tree to take a nap at noon, dreaming that I am a cuttlefish with a fluttering fin skirt and that the cuttlefish is also dreaming of me; and I wake up at dusk to take a brisk walk along the cooling beach, admiring the looming blush of the setting sun. I much prefer my life to yours."

"Going with the flow is not the path to approach the reality of the universe. I'm no Incentivist, but Gi Anji was at least headed in the right direction when he pointed out that learned men must understand the world and improve it, for we're not dumb beasts or dandelions scattered by the roadside, but endowed with the godly impulse to transform the earthly realm to bring it closer to heaven."

"The reality of the universe must be *experienced*, not *constructed*...."

What's it like to ponder such questions all day? Mimi thought. *To not limit one's thoughts to the weather and the harvest and the fishing haul, to not have to struggle to plan for the next meal and the meal after that, but to be able to imagine and debate the substance of the sun and to believe that it is possible to read the larger patterns of life?*

The scholars went on debating in that vein, and the crowd cheered and offered their own observations from time to time. Eventually, the scholars tired of the argument and parted ways, having exhausted their store of classical quotations and learned citations. The crowd dispersed and only Mimi was left, still thinking and replaying the debate in her mind.

"The market is about to close, miss." A kind voice interrupted her reverie.

"Oh no!" Mimi looked around and saw that it was true. The grain buyers were packing up and driving their carts back to the warehouses. She would have to come back the next day. She was mad at herself—how could she have been so irresponsible?

She saw that the speaker was tall, gaunt, like the trunk of a seasoned pine. He was in his late forties, with graying hair that he tied up carelessly in a loose bun, and his skin was as dark as the shells of the great sea turtles. Though scars on his face marred his otherwise handsome features, his green eyes were friendly and warm in the light of the setting sun.

"You seemed fascinated by that debate," the man said, an interested expression on his face. "What were you thinking just now?"

Still a bit unsettled, Mimi said the first thing that came to her mind, "Why do so many sages have family names that end in 'ji'?"

The man looked stunned for a second, and then laughed.

Mimi's face flushed. She lifted the bag of sample grain over her shoulder and turned to leave, her humiliation making her stumble.

"I'm sorry!" the man said from behind her. "It's refreshing to hear an original observation. I meant no offense at all."

Mimi could hear the sincerity in his voice. He spoke with an accent from somewhere on the Big Island, and his enunciation was courtly and graceful, like the folk opera singers who played the nobles onstage.

"It was thoughtless of me," the man said. "I offer you my apologies again."

Mimi turned and set down her bag. "What was so funny about what I said?"

The man kept his expression very serious, and asked, "Do you know the work of any of the sages they quoted?"

Mimi shook her head. "I've never been to school." Then she added, "Well, I know the name of Kon Fiji, the One True Sage, because they have him in the folk operas sometimes."

The man nodded. "Your question makes perfect sense; I just never paid attention to the pattern you noticed. Sometimes we stop questioning things we take for granted. In fact, 'ji' is not a part of the family names of the sages. It is a Classical Ano suffix to indicate respect, roughly meaning 'teacher.'"

Mimi heard no condescension in his tone, which made her feel better. "You know Classical Ano?"

"Yes. I've been studying it since I was a little boy."

"You're still studying?"

"You never stop studying," the man said, smiling. "Not just Classical Ano, but also many other subjects, math, mechanics, divination."

"You understand the gods?" Mimi's heart quickened.

"I wouldn't go that far." The man hesitated, as though trying to figure out how to explain a complicated idea. "I've conversed with the gods, but I'm not sure they even understand themselves. It is possible that the more we know, the less we need to rely on the gods. And the gods are also learning, the same as us."

This was such a strange idea that Mimi was at a loss for words. She decided to change the subject. "Was it difficult to learn Classical Ano?"

"At first. But since all the important books and poems are written in it, my tutor made me work at it. Eventually it became as easy to read the logograms of Classical Ano as it was to read the zyndari letters."

"I don't know how to read at all."

The man nodded, a trace of sorrow in his eyes. "I come from old Haan, where every child had the chance to learn to read. Now that the world is at peace, perhaps that will be true not only in Haan, but all of Dara."

The vision seemed absurd to Mimi, but the voice of the man was so fervent and hopeful that she didn't want to make him sad. "What did you think of the debate?"

"I think they were both very learned," said the man, smiling again. "But that is not the same as wise. What did you think?"

"I think they need to weigh the fish."

The man was taken aback. "Oh? What . . . does that mean?"

"It's something my mother taught me. She used to ask me whether I knew why whitefish became heavier over time after you've hauled them out of the sea."

The man closed his eyes, pondering this. "That is indeed puzzling. I would have thought that as the water left the flesh, the fish would become lighter over time, not heavier. Is it something unusual about the structure of the whitefish? Maybe the flesh absorbs moisture from the air? Or perhaps the whitefish, when alive, contains some kind of gas that lightens it, like the Mingén falcon? Or—"

Now it was Mimi's turn to laugh. "You're acting just like I did, assuming what someone is telling you is true. Instead, you should be weighing the fish."

"And what would you find out if you did?"

"Whitefish doesn't get any heavier over time. It was a story made up by unscrupulous merchants who blew air into the bellies of their fish to make them seem bigger. And when their fish turned out to weigh less than other fish of the same size, they argued that their catch was fresher, which was why they weighed less."

"How would you apply this story to the debate?"

Mimi looked at the setting sun. "I have to go home before it gets dark, but if you come and meet me by the wharf north of the city tomorrow morning, I'll show you."

"I'll certainly do that. By the way, what is your name?"

"Mimi, of the Kidosu clan. And yours?"

The man hesitated for just a second, and then said, "I'm Toru Noki, a wanderer."

The next morning, Toru showed up at the wharf at the crack of dawn.

"You're prompt," said Mimi, pleased. "I wasn't sure if you would take me seriously, seeing as how you have the air of a learned man."

"I've had some experience with early morning appointments by fishing wharves," said Toru. "They usually end up teaching me much about the world." But he didn't elaborate.

Mimi stood without leaning against her walking stick, which was planted into the sand of the beach. Attached to the top of the bamboo pole was a horizontal crossbeam, at one end of which was mounted an old, small bronze mirror whose center was brightly polished. At the other end was a circular frame made from a thin stalk of bamboo with a banana leaf stretched taut across it.

She adjusted the mirror until an image of the rising sun was reflected onto the banana leaf. She carefully traced its outline with a piece of charcoal.

"You designed this yourself?" Toru asked.

"Yes," Mimi said. "I've always liked to look at things in nature: the sea, the sky, the stars, and the clouds. The sun is too bright to look at directly, so I figured out this way of looking at a reflection."

"It is very well conceived," said Toru admiringly.

"We'll have to do this again at noon. You can come back later or wait nearby. I have to go into the city to sell the grain. It's our only livelihood, and that can't wait."

"Your family doesn't fish?"

"My father used to," Mimi said, her voice dipping lower. "But my mother doesn't want me to learn. He . . . disappeared in the sea."

"I'll come with you," said Toru.

They went into the city, and though Toru offered to help carry the bag of sample grain, Mimi wouldn't let him ("I'm probably stronger than you"). The man did not insist, which Mimi appreciated. She never liked people to assume that because of her leg, she was less capable than others, and sometimes people had trouble understanding that.

Mimi wanted to try the open market, but Toru suggested that they try the royal palace first.

"The royal palace? But the government usually offers the worst prices."

"I have a feeling you'll be surprised."

Emperor Ragin had given his older brother, Kado, the island of Dasu as a fief and named him King of Dasu. But everyone knew that it was just a symbolic gesture, and King Kado stayed in reconstructed Pan, the Harmonious City, most of the time, leaving his kingdom to be run by the emperor's bureaucrats like the other provinces administered directly by the emperor. The royal palace used to be King Kuni's palace, and before that it was the governor's mansion under the Xana Empire. It wasn't much bigger than the other houses in Daye, as the city was never a great metropolis like the big cities on the Big Island or even Kriphi, the old Xana capital on nearby Rui Island. Ostentation had never been the emperor's style, even back when he was just King Kuni.

An acquisitions clerk sat in the yard of the palace, bored out of his mind. Emperor Ragin had a reputation for being frugal, and King Kado's regent—really the acting governor of Dasu—had given orders to keep the prices offered for grains low. Only peasants with the lowest quality grains, ones that they couldn't sell to the private merchants, came to try their luck with the government. The acquisitions clerk had had only one vendor approach him all day yesterday, and he expected today to be the same.

Oh, potential vendors! The clerk widened his eyes and took notice. *I wonder how bad their harvest has been that they're willing to come here.*

As the clerk examined the two people—the man with his long limbs and open stride, and the limping girl with a walking stick and the heavy bag of sample grain over her shoulder—approaching his desk, he sat up straight and rubbed his eyes.

What is he doing here? He had been in Pan with the regent during the coronation, and he remembered seeing the striking figure of this man standing next to Prime Minister Cogo Yelu and Queen Gin.

He jumped up as though springs had been installed under his bottom. "Er, Grand Sec—er—Imperial Sch—er—" *The man is supposed to have refused all titles. How am I supposed to address him?*

"The name is Toru Noki," the man said, smiling. "I have no titles."

The clerk nodded and bowed repeatedly like a shadow puppet whose tangled strings were being jerked by the puppeteer in an attempt at freeing them. *He must have very good reasons for disguising his identity. I'd better not blow his cover.*

The girl set the bag on her shoulder down on the ground. "Toru, would you help me loosen the string on the sack? My fingers are a bit numb from holding on to it."

The clerk watched in disbelief as one of the closest advisers of the Emperor of Dara squatted down like a common peasant to untie the string on the grain sack.

This girl must be very, very important. The clerk turned the thought over in his head and knew what he had to do.

He barely glanced at the grain. "Excellent quality! We'll buy everything you have. How about twenty per bushel?"

"Twenty?" Mimi sounded amazed.

"Er . . . how about forty then?"

"Forty?" She sounded even more shocked.

The clerk looked at "Toru Noki" helplessly. *This is already four times the going rate in the market!* He gritted his teeth. If the regent complained later, he'd just have to explain the situation the best he could.

"Eighty then. But that's really as high as I can go. Really. Please?"

The girl seemed in a daze as she signed the contract by drawing a circle on the paper with the inked brush.

"We'll send over the shipping carts in two days," the clerk said.

"Thank you," said Mimi.

"Thank you," said Toru Noki, smiling.

"Good negotiation," said Toru.

"That wasn't a negotiation at all," said Mimi. "Just who are you? That clerk acted like a mouse who had seen a cat."

"I really am just a wanderer these days," said Toru. "I'm not lying when I tell you I don't have a title."

"That doesn't mean you aren't important."

"Sometimes knowledge can get in the way of a friendship," said Toru, his tone serious. "I like how we can converse now as equals. I don't want to lose that."

"All right." Mimi nodded reluctantly. Then she brightened. "It's noon! We should take our second measurement."

She planted her walking stick into the ground and took out the mirror and the banana leaf and set up the contraption as she had before. The two looked at the image of the noonday sun projected onto the banana leaf. It matched exactly the outline she had traced in the morning.

"As I suspected," declared Mimi triumphantly. "The sun is exactly the same size at sunrise and at noon. It only *looks* bigger when it's near the horizon but actually *isn't*."

"Well done," said Toru. "It is just as you said: Always weigh the fish. I've always believed that the universe is knowable, but your phrasing cuts to the heart of the matter."

But Mimi felt disappointed. "Their debate sounded so interesting, though. I almost wish the sun did change in size."

"You can't build an elaborate house on a bad foundation," said Toru.

"If the basis for their dispute turned out to be illusory, it doesn't matter how good their reasoning was. There is wisdom in the words of the sages, but one must keep in mind that they didn't know everything. Models can be helpful in understanding the world, but models must be refined by testing against observation. You have to both *experience* reality and *construct* it."

Mimi pondered Toru's words. Somehow the veil over the world seemed to have grown slightly more transparent.

Is the world but a model for the ideal in the minds of the gods? Or is the world something beyond the reach of all models, in the same way that what I feel when I gaze at nature cannot be expressed in words?

"That sounds smarter than what both of those *toko dawiji* said."

"I can't take credit for that. It's a quote from Na Moji, founder of the Patternist school of thinking. I suppose I'm more of a Patternist than anything else, but I think all the Hundred Schools have some wisdom to teach us. They are like different tools for shaping and understanding reality, and a talented craftsman can gain insight into the world and remake it with their aid. I think you have Patternist instincts too, and you have much raw talent. But you have to cultivate it."

Talent, Mimi thought. The words of her mother came unbidden to mind. *Talent is like a pretty feather in the tail of a peacock, daughter. It brings joy to the powerful but only sorrow to the bird.*

"What do talent and wisdom have to do with the daughter of a poor peasant?" she asked. "The poor have one path in this world, and the powerful another."

"Don't you know the story of Queen Gin? She began as a street urchin, child, and yet she became the greatest tactician in all of Dara by cultivating her talent."

"That was a time of war, of chaos. Now the world is at peace."

"There are talents useful in war, and talents useful in peace. I do not know all there is to know about the gods, but I do believe it is not their will that a great pearl lie in obscurity, unable to shine."

What's it like to have so many tools of the mind at your disposal that you could dissect reality and put it back together as skillfully as my mother can scale and gut a fish within minutes and turn it into a delicious dinner?

Mimi had never envied the children of the wealthy who went to school and learned to read and write, but now she felt a keen hunger whose intensity was painful. She had been given a taste of the wider world out there, a glimpse of the Truth beneath the surface, a hint of the meaning of the speech of the gods. She wanted more. So much more.

Could not such knowledge be turned into silk clothes and white rice? Into servants and carriages and clinking coins that would relieve my mother and me from toil? Into arrogant looks and proud gazes directed at the road ahead instead of at the thronging poor to the sides?

Abruptly, she turned and knelt before Toru and touched her forehead to the ground.

"Will you teach me, Toru-ji? Will you help me cultivate my talent?"

But Toru stepped to the side, avoiding accepting her prostration. Mimi's heart sank. She looked up, her eyes narrowed. "What happened to that talk about a pearl not lying in obscurity? Are you too timid to dive into the dark sea to retrieve it?"

Toru laughed lightly, but there was a hint of sorrow and bitterness in it. "You have a fiery spirit, and that is a good thing. But you're also impatient and cannot hold your tongue, which is not always a good thing."

Mimi's face flushed. "I thought you were interested in the truth."

"It is not enough to sharpen a brilliant mind," Toru said. His eyes seemed to be focusing on something far in the distance, in time or space. "The road you ask me to lead you on is winding and rugged, and it requires knowing when to delay the truth and how to craft it so that it is more pleasing to powerful ears. These are not skills I possess in abundance either. I can enlarge your vision and show you how to pick out the patterns hidden all around you, but there are patterns, patterns of power, that I cannot teach you to read."

"Is that why you're roaming the Islands instead of helping the emperor in the Harmonious City?"

For a moment, Mimi was afraid that she had gone too far, but then Toru's face relaxed, and he stepped back to stand before her still prostrate form and bowed back to her.

"Perhaps it is the will of the gods that we meet, and who am I to defy their wishes?"

Mimi touched her forehead to the ground three times, solemnly, the way she had seen players from the folk opera troupes do when they portrayed students being accepted by great masters. Toru stood in place, accepting the honor.

"You may call me teacher," said Toru, "but in truth, we will be teaching each other. As the relationship between a teacher and student is one of great trust, it is important for us to know each other's true names. 'Toru Noki' is a name given to me by some friends long ago in a distant land. My true name is Luan, of the Zya clan of Haan. What is your formal name, Mimi-*tika*?"

The prime strategist of Emperor Ragin. Mimi stared at the man in wonder. *And he has just addressed me as though I am his daughter.* She couldn't believe she wasn't dreaming. "I . . . don't have a formal name. I've always just been Mimi, a peasant girl."

Luan nodded. "Then I will give you a formal name."

Mimi looked at him expectantly.

Luan mused. "How about 'Zomi'?"

Mimi nodded. "It sounds pleasant. What does it mean?"

"The Classical Ano logogram for the name means 'pearl of fire,' which was a plant in the Ano homeland across the sea. It was said that the zomi was the first plant to grow from the ashes of forest fires and to bring color to a world deprived of it by destruction. May your fiery nature be as auspicious."

CHAPTER EIGHT

A DRINKING PARTY

PAN: THE THIRD MONTH IN THE SIXTH YEAR OF
THE REIGN OF FOUR PLACID SEAS.

The celebration of the hundredth day after the birth—or in this case, the adoption—of the son of Mün Çakri, First General of the Infantry, was a wild and unorthodox affair. Not only had General Çakri invited everyone from within three blocks of his mansion—there were over three hundred banquet tables, which spilled out of his courtyard and filled most of the street in front of his residence—but the general had personally wrestled five pigs in a mud pen for the entertainment of all the guests.

So much wine and beer was consumed and so many pigs slaughtered for the feast that the butchers and tavern keepers and sauce vendors in that quarter of Pan would reminisce for years about the day they made "*real* profit."

But now that it was getting dark, and most of the guests had finally departed after offering their well wishes and taking home the lucky taros dyed in red, it was time for a more intimate after-party, where General Çakri would finally get to talk to his close friends.

Naro Hun, Mün Çakri's spouse, finally prevailed upon the redoubt-able general to bathe himself before coming out to greet his friends in the family dining room.

"You don't look much better than the pigs you wrestled," said a frowning Naro, who had always kept his desk spotless when he was a mere gate-clerk in Zudi. "I am *not* touching you until you wash."

"They've seen worse," muttered Mün. "I used to compete with Than to see who could go longer without bathing when we were at war." But he obediently went into the bathroom and quickly dumped buckets of hot and cold water over himself and came out with a towel wrapped around his waist.

"You can't possibly think that's appropriate—" But Mün pulled him into a kiss, and Naro relented. After all, people who had gone to war with you would hardly object to seeing your chest hair.

And so Mün Çakri, semi-naked and cradling the swaddled baby like a precious package, who was napping after his time with the wet nurse, and Naro Hun, handsomely dressed in a new father's water-silk robe embroidered with stags and swordfish, emerged into the warm dining room, where some of Dara's most powerful gener-als, nobles, and ministers were having tea and cakes around a large round table.

"Let me see the baby!" shouted Than Carucono, First General of the Cavalry and First Admiral of the Navy.

"Use both hands!" admonished Mün. "And cradle the head. The head! That's a baby, not a block of wood, you oaf! Be gentle!"

"He has handled babies before, you know," said a smiling Lady Péingo, Than Carucono's wife. "I've made a few with him. And the baby will be fine: He's almost six months old!"

"I cannot believe that I am being told to be gentle by a man who wrestles pigs," said Than. "I don't know how Naro puts up with you—you must break a bowl or cup every day. Aha, look at how your baby smiles at me! I'm certain that your beard frightens him."

"Let me have a turn," said Puma Yemu, Marquess of Porin. Than handed the baby to him, and Puma promptly tossed the little bundle high into the air.

"By the Twins!—" Mün cried, and Lady Péingo gasped, but Puma caught the baby and laughed.

"I'm going to kill you," promised Mün.

"I do this with my own kids all the time," said Puma. "They love it."

"I'm sure you only do it when Tafé and Jikri aren't around," said Lady Péingo, laughing. "You may act all tough among the men, but your wives definitely make the rules governing you."

Puma smiled and did not dispute this. Gurgling squeals emerged from the bundle in his arms. Naro and Mün rushed over to be sure the baby was all right.

"This is the first time I've seen him laugh!" exclaimed Naro.

"Of course," said Puma. "I told you he'd love it. Babies love to fly."

Mün pried the baby out of Puma's hands and glared at him.

"See," said Puma, "now the baby is going to cry. You look especially frightening with your beard like that."

"He likes playing with my beard!" Mün proudly stroked his bushy beard, which stuck out in every direction like the spines of a hedgehog. The baby continued to giggle in his arms.

"I certainly hope he turns out to resemble Naro more than you," said Than.

"That will definitely be the case," said Mün. "The boy was born to Naro's sister. She and her husband knew we were looking to adopt, and they were pleased to be able to help us. I will teach the boy everything I know, and nothing will please me more than for him to have Naro's looks and my skill at fighting."

Everyone understood that Naro's sister had likely offered the adoption as a way to gain an advantage for her own family, but there was no need to bring that up at a happy moment like this. It was possible to do something simultaneously out of love as well as self-interest.

"How did you decide on the name Cacaya?" asked Rin Coda. "It's very unusual."

Mün's face turned bright red. "I . . . like the sound of the name."

"Does it mean anything?"

"Why does it have to mean anything?" said Mün, getting more defensive. "This is just a nursing name. We won't have to pick an auspicious formal name for years."

But Rin, with his farseer instincts, sensed that there was more to this story. "Come on, spill it! It sounds Adüan to me."

Everyone turned to look at Luan Zya, who had lived among the people of Tan Adü for many years. Luan looked back at Mün with a smile.

"You can tell them," said Mün reluctantly. "I did ask you to help pick it, so I guess it's all right."

Luan coughed and slowly said, "The word is indeed Adüan. It refers to the thick and strong hair on the snout of the wild boar, a prized source of meat among the people of Tan Adü and a symbol of great strength."

Everyone digested this information, thinking of an appropriate comment of admiration.

"Wait, you named your son 'pig bristles'?" said an incredulous Rin. Then he whooped and laughed.

"I'm proud of my old profession!" said an irked Mün. "I want to be sure my son remembers his roots. Naro said it was okay, so I don't care what the rest of you think!" Naro patted him on his towel-covered buttocks for support.

A draft blew through the room and made the lamps and candles flicker. Mün shivered. Naro took off his robe and draped it around Mün like a cape. "I don't want you to catch a chill." Mün wrapped an arm around Naro's waist in response. His face relaxed.

"Look at you two," teased Puma Yemu. "Still acting like newlyweds!"

"Why don't you do stuff like that more often for me?" said Than Carucono, looking at Lady Péingo.

"I'd be happy to lend you one of my dresses if you're cold," said Lady Péingo. "Do you prefer the one with the pearl clasp or the one with the scarlet peonies? They both might be a bit tight on you, but I'm not judging. They could certainly emphasize the curves around that beer gut in a pleasing manner."

Than looked at Mün and Naro with a mock-wounded expression. "See, this is what I get at home. All day."

"Only when you behave," said Lady Péingo. Than and she looked at each other, grinning, their eyes glowing as softly as the moon outside.

"Naro and Mün certainly know the secret of long-lasting romance," said a smiling Cogo Yelu. "You would compare favorably to Idi and Moth of old. 'Weary wakeful weakness!' as the poets would say."

Everyone stopped drinking and there was an awkward silence. Cogo looked around. "What?"

"Why do you insult an old friend by calling him weak?" asked Théca Kimo, Duke of Arulugi, who had been quiet until now.

"I said nothing of the kind!" said a confused Cogo.

Luan broke in, "I believe Cogo was alluding to an old story. Centuries ago, King Idi of Amu was so enamored of his lover, a man by the name of Mothota, that when Mothota fell asleep in his arms and the king had to go to court, Idi ordered his courtiers to carry the bed with him and Mothota in it to the audience hall so as to avoid waking up his lover. The poets of Amu used the phrase 'wakeful weakness' as a kenning for romantic love."

"What's a kenning?" asked Mün.

"It's a poetic . . . Cogo just meant to pay a compliment to your affections for each other, that is all."

Mün looked pleased, and Théca, embarrassed, apologized to Cogo.

But Gin Mazoti, Marshal of Dara, now spoke up. "Have you spent so much time in the College of Advocates and the Grand Examination Hall that you've forgotten how to talk to your old comrades, Cogo?"

Luan was surprised at the harshness in Gin's tone, but she refused to meet his eyes.

"That's quite a question, Gin," said Cogo.

But the rather cold expressions of the generals made it clear that Gin was saying something they all thought.

"We know swords and horses," Gin said. "But even if you put Mün and Puma and Than and Théca and me all together, you wouldn't find more than half a book in our heads." Though Gin's tone was self-deprecating, there was definitely an edge to it. "So we'd appreciate it if you stick to drinking tea instead of spewing ink every chance you get."

"I sincerely apologize, Gin," said a humble Cogo. "I have, as you say, been spending too much time with the bookish and arrogant and not nearly enough time with old friends."

Gin nodded and said no more.

Luan tried to relieve the suddenly chill atmosphere in the room. "How about a game, everyone?"

"What do you want to play?" asked Mün.

"How about . . . Fool's Mirror?" This was a game in which participants took turns to compare themselves to specimens of a category—plants, animals, minerals, furniture, farm implements—and drank depending on whether the other participants judged the comparison apt.

Mün, Than, and Rin looked at each other and laughed.

"What's so funny?" asked Naro. Lady Péingo looked equally puzzled.

"Years ago, it was at a game of Fool's Mirror that the duke—er, the emperor—agreed to introduce me to you," said Mün to Naro.

"I've always wondered how you managed to get up the courage to get your boss to come to me! I see you had to get drunk first."

"I wasn't drunk! I was only . . . wakefully weak."

Naro laughed and gave Mün a peck on the cheek. The others in the dining hall chortled and guffawed.

"I think you need to stick to swords and horses," said Than. "You were not meant for poetry. Shall we use flowers and plants as the theme again and see how everyone has changed?"

Everyone assented.

"I'll start," said Mün. "I was once the prickly cactus, but now I think I'm a thorned pear." He looked lovingly at the baby in Naro's arms. "A child changes you, fills you with sweetness and light from the inside. It was a good thing the emperor recruited me before I was a father, or I would never have agreed to become a rebel."

The guests picked up their cups, ready to drink.

"No, no, no," said Than. "I cannot agree to this comparison unless you're an overripe pear—so sweet that it's sickening."

Mün glared at Than while others chuckled, but Naro came to his rescue. "I'll go next. I'm the morning glory whose vine has found the support of my one and true sturdy oak." He tightened his arm around Mün. "Sweet words are easy, but it isn't easy to find a love that lasts beyond the first blush of infatuation, and I know I'm lucky."

Mün turned to him and his face softened. "As am I."

Everyone drank without saying another word. Than Carucono drew Lady Péingo to him, and she sat blushing in his lap. Luan and Gin locked gazes for a moment, and Luan felt his face grow warm. But Gin's calm face was unreadable.

"It will be hard to follow up our loving hosts," said Puma Yemu. "But I'll try. I wasn't at that game years ago, but I've served the emperor for just about as long as the rest of you. I am the jumping bean of the Sonaru Desert. I may look no different from ordinary bushes in the wild, but when grazing animals come near, a thousand beans snap into action and make a noise that would frighten away an elephant!"

"I don't know about frightening away an elephant," teased Than Carucono. "But you certainly swear loudly enough when we play drinking games that the dogs in the city bark all night."

"That's because you cheat—" growled Puma Yemu.

"I think it's a lovely comparison," interrupted Lady Péingo. "I don't know much about war, but it paints such a vivid picture."

"It's very apt," said Gin. "Your surprise raiding tactics should be taught to every soldier of Dara."

There was no more commentary. Everyone drank.

Luan sipped his tea happily, but he was struck by the oddness of the moment. Given that Mün and Naro were the hosts, ordinarily they should have been the ones to give the definitive opinion of a participant's comparison. However, since Naro wasn't an official and Mün wasn't good at making speeches, it naturally fell to Cogo and Gin, the two highest-ranking officials present, to play the role of substitute opinion makers. Yet Gin had apparently assumed she would be the one in charge without even consulting Cogo.

"I'll go next," said Rin. He stood up and paced around the table. "I was once the night-blooming cereus, as I served the emperor in the dark, gathering underground intelli—er, nourishment. But now I think I'm rather more like the undergrowth in a forest of tall trees."

The silence that followed made it clear that others were rather befuddled by this comparison.

"Um . . . ," Mün tentatively said. "Are you also quoting from the Ano Classics or something? I know you went to school—"

Rin laughed and slapped him on the back. "I meant only that I get to enjoy the shade while the rest of you are exposed to the fiery sun and punishing rain! I've been lucky, I know that. I haven't had to risk my life or work as hard as the rest of you, and I'm thankful to be among your company."

"A gracious comparison," said Gin. "But not apt. You're a pillar of the House of Dandelion as much as the rest of us. You must drink."

Pleased, Rin drank.

Luan frowned. Rin might have made it seem like a joke, but there was a hint of insecure bitterness to his comparison. *He was looking for reassurance from Gin.*

"How about we hear from Luan next?" said Gin, interrupting his reverie.

"Hmmm." Luan stroked his chin thoughtfully. "I think I'm the pelagic anemone. I drift over the sea, riding on waves and drinking wind. All I need is a bit of sunlight, and I need not compete with the Hundred Flowers in color or fragrance."

"Sounds a little lonely," said Naro wistfully. Then he bowed to Luan quickly. "I meant no offense."

"Sounds like the ideal life for a man who has refused all titles at court," said a smiling Cogo. "I'll drink to that."

"You prefer to have no attachment?" asked Gin.

Luan looked at her. *What is she really asking?* "I prefer to live a life independent of the gardener's judgment."

Gin gazed at him steadily for a few moments, nodded, and drank. The other guests followed suit.

"I'll go next," said Théca Kimo. "I came to serve the emperor later than most of you, but I think I've done my share. I certainly have the scars to prove it." He got up on his knees and straightened his back to make himself look taller. "These days, I suppose I feel like that old apple tree in the courtyard that no longer bears fruit. My use, if any, is to be chopped down for firewood."

Like the hounds that are leashed after all the rabbits have been caught, and like the bows that are packed away after all the wild geese have been bagged. Luan recalled his conversation with Gin years ago. He looked over at the marshal, expecting a reprimand for these near-treasonous words.

The other generals looked at Gin as well, their cups a few inches from their lips. Luan noticed that most of them seemed to hold looks of sympathy rather than shock.

"I won't agree with that," said Gin.

And Luan let out a held breath.

But Gin went on, "That old apple tree was here before Mün built his house, and it will be here probably after the house is gone. Your loyalty is written in your scars, which are more lasting than any wax logogram carved by the busy bureaucrats. The emperor has not forgotten your service or the need for sword and armor to defend this precious peace. You will not be chopped down as long as I'm the Marshal of Dara."

Luan closed his eyes. *What are you doing, Gin?*

Théca bowed gratefully. "But Marshal, have you not heard rumors of the empress acting against the hereditary nobles, even those who founded the dynasty with the emperor himself? Several barons have already had their fiefs confiscated on pretextual charges of treason or disobedience. I fear—"

He wasn't able to finish his sentence, however. The steward of the house came into the dining room then and announced, "Her Highness, the Imperial Consort Risana, has arrived!"

∾ ∾ ∾ ∾

Risana swooped in with a retinue of porters and maids bearing gifts for the new baby and the happy couple: carved jade horses so that the young boy could play soldiers and rebels; bolts of high-quality silk for clothes and the nursery; delicacies shipped in from all corners of Dara by airship, including some that were ordinarily reserved for the Imperial household. . . .

She cooed over the baby held in Naro's arms and assured Mün that it was perfectly fine for him to be dressed only in a towel and a loosely draped robe.

"Don't forget I was in the camps with you during the wars!" she said, and to show that she meant it, took off her own formal robe so that she was dressed only in a simple underdress.

She moved around the room like a graceful spring swallow, nodding and smiling. "Théca! How's the fishing back on Arulugi? You must stay longer this time and go fishing on Lake Tututika with me. Puma! You haven't changed one bit. Phyro was just asking me the other day about visiting you for riding lessons. Both of you need to bring your families to the capital more often. Than! How are the children? Péingo! You need to come to visit me at the palace. . . ."

She stopped in front of Gin, who was already standing up. The two embraced warmly.

"Sometimes I miss the days we were at war," said Risana. "We got to see a lot more of each other."

"We did, Lady Risana. We did."

Finally, she came to Luan, and bowed to him deeply in *jiri*. Luan bowed back.

"You haven't changed one bit since the last time I saw you," said Risana, as she looked Luan up and down, a grin on her face. "I think you've discovered the secret of eternal youth!"

Luan chuckled. "Your Highness is far too kind." He did not pay her a compliment, though her beauty had only changed, but not diminished, over the years. Instinctively, he wanted to keep his distance.

"Actually, there is something. . . . I think you've found a new puzzle to solve."

Luan was only slightly surprised. Risana's talent was to intuit what people really desired, though it didn't work on everyone. "I have indeed found something that occupies my mind."

He took out a small piece of irregularly shaped white material. "What do you think this is?"

Risana examined the piece carefully. It seemed to be bone or ivory, and the design of a strange long-necked beast with two feet and a pair of wings was carved into it. "I remember seeing something like this a long time ago, when we were in Dasu. It washed onshore, didn't it?"

Luan nodded. "I've been collecting pieces like it—I bought this one in the markets of Pan. Though I can't be sure of their origin, every confirmed sighting seems to suggest that they are found on the northern shores of the Islands. I think there's a mystery up north worth investigating. It's part of the reason I've come to the capital, to speak to the emperor."

"You never want to stop learning, do you?"

As Luan and Risana conversed further, Luan realized how much he was enjoying the conversation. That was Risana's talent as well: She had a way of paying attention to people that made them feel as though they were the only one in the room. People liked her before they even knew it.

While Risana was catching up with everyone, her retinue set out incense burners and portable silk screens. Then Risana clapped her hands. "To celebrate Mün and Naro's new baby, I've brought some entertainment!"

The incense burners were lit, and lights erected behind the screens. Risana began to dance and sing to the accompaniment of the coconut lute and the nine-stringed zither:

The Four Placid Seas are as wide as the years are long.
A wild goose flies over a pond, leaving behind a voice in the
*   wind.*
A man passes through this world, leaving behind a name.

Will heroes be forgotten? Will faith be rewarded?
Though stars tremble in the storm, our hearts do not waver.
Our hair may turn white, but our blood remains crimson.

She leapt; she twirled; she bent and flexed and her long, loose hair spun gracefully through the air like the tip of a writing brush being wielded by a master calligrapher. As Risana's shadow flickered over the silk screens, her sleeves stirred the smoke from the incense burners into semisolid shapes: ships emerging from roiling waves and thick clouds; clashing armies on a dark plain; dueling heroes slashing at each other in the air; fleets of massive machines at war in air and under the sea.

The assembled guests were mesmerized by the show, and when Luan stole glances around at the others, he saw more than a few faces wet from this tribute to the martial splendor of Dara.

Even the longest celebration must come to an end. The guests said their good-byes to the hosts as the early morning stars rose in the east.

"Are things really as bad as I fear, old friend?" asked Luan. He had deliberately waited to leave with Cogo.

Ever cautious, Cogo waited until they were in the carriage. "It depends on what you mean." He relaxed into the seat and sighed contentedly.

"For example, I noticed that you've kept your family away from the Harmonious City."

"Not everyone is interested in politics," said Cogo. "Or good at it."

"I sense fear and uncertainty among Kuni's old generals."

"Thinking that the empress is intent on taking your fief and command away from you can certainly lead to some paranoia."

"*Is* it paranoia? I never spent much time with the empress."

Cogo gazed at Luan. "It is said that Consort Risana fears the empress because she cannot tell what the empress wants. It is the same with the rest of us. She has done much to promote the careers of scholars and bureaucrats, but whether that's just part of the emperor's need to shift from a time of war to a time of peace or a plot of her own design, no one knows."

"And what's going on with Gin? That was a strange lecture she gave you. She might not have attended a private academy, but she studied the Ano Classics on her own. We all know she's no unlettered soldier."

"Gin leads all of the emperor's old generals. I don't blame her for playing to her crowd."

"Does she resent the empress?"

"Gin keeps her own counsel, as you well know. But I do know that during the first year of the Reign of Four Placid Seas, the empress made an effort to befriend Gin. I believe that effort was rebuffed because Gin wanted to be loyal to Consort Risana, who she thought of—and still does—as a comrade."

Luan closed his eyes and sighed. *Gin, you're always so rash. I told you to keep yourself out of palace intrigue.*

"I notice that it was Consort Risana, but not the empress or the emperor, who came tonight."

"You are not the only one."

Does the emperor's absence indicate his support for the empress?

As if he had guessed Luan's unvoiced question, Cogo said, "The emperor is said to lean on Consort Risana's counsel more of late. He visits her often to discuss affairs of state, and it is said that he relies on Risana's judgment of character, as she can evaluate the sincerity of those who advocate passionately for a position. Yet the empress is not disfavored; she simply exercises her influence a different way.

"While Consort Risana is friendly with the wives of Kuni's old generals, several of Empress Jia's ladies-in-waiting have married high-ranking ministers and scholars or have become trusted house-keepers in their households."

"Weren't some of Jia's ladies-in-waiting young girls she had rescued from the streets of Çaruza during the time she was the Hegemon's hostage?" asked Luan.

"Indeed," said Cogo. "Jia has been like a mother to them. They're very resilient, resourceful, and—" He hesitated, searching for the right word.

"—extraordinarily loyal to Jia," said Luan. "Perhaps with more zeal than would make others comfortable."

Cogo chuckled. "The Imperial household is both harmonious and . . . not so."

Luan nodded. *It is very like Kuni to be comfortable with dissonant voices.*

"You never got the chance to compare yourself to a flower tonight," he said.

Cogo laughed. "The last time we played this game, I called myself a patient snapping flytrap, but the emperor insisted on comparing me to a stout bamboo for holding up his civil service. I'd rather not deviate from the emperor's metaphor. I suppose I feel more like a strained bamboo these days, bent so far that I fear I might snap."

"The empress must favor you, given her estrangement from the military commanders."

"It's hardly an easy thing to be 'favored' by the powerful," said Cogo. "You, who refused all titles to be a floating anemone, ought to know that."

"I'm sorry," said Luan. He wanted to have nothing more to do with courtly factions and warring Imperial consorts, but he could not help caring about the fate of his friends and lover. "Who do you really serve, old friend?"

"I have always served the people of Dara," said Cogo in a placid tone.

And the two rode on through the dark streets of Pan, each thinking his own thoughts.

By the time Consort Risana's retinue had packed up everything and left Mün Çakri's house, everyone was too tired to realize that two members were missing.

In the inner courtyard of the house, Naro kept a garden and a cottage that he sometimes used as a study. Two individuals dressed in the attire of Risana's dancers stood here now, admiring the carp swimming in the fish tank kept here for the winter. The fish—coral red, sunbeam gold, pearly white, jade green—surfaced from time to time from the dark water to display their shiny scales in the faint flickering light of an oil lamp, like thoughts glimpsed in a dream.

"So your student wants to go away again," said the woman, who was golden-haired and azure-eyed. Even the lovely carp seemed to dive deeper after they'd glimpsed her, embarrassed that they could not rival her in beauty.

"That does appear to be the case," said the man, whose wrinkled dark skin and stocky figure brought to mind a fisherman rather than a dancer.

"Don't you want to encourage him to help Kuni? There's a storm brewing; our brothers and sisters are eager to be involved. Tazu is already at it."

"Tazu will always be involved, and he makes life interesting for us all. But Little Sister, the more Luan learns, the less he needs my guidance. That is as it should be. A teacher can only lead the student down a path he already has chosen."

"That is rather . . . Fluxist of you, Lutho. I'm a little surprised."

The old man chuckled. "I don't think we need to disdain the philosophies of the mortals when they have something to teach us. It is the Flow of the world that children and students must grow up, and parents and teachers must let go. The gods have been retreating from the sphere of mortals over the eons as the mortals' knowledge has grown. They used to pray to Kiji for rain until they learned to divert rivers and streams for irrigation; they used to pray to Rufizo for every cure until they learned to use herbs and make medicine; they used to pray to me for knowledge of the future until they grew confident that they could make their future."

"But they still pray."

"Some do; but the temples are no longer as powerful as they were during the Diaspora Wars, and I suspect even those who pray know that the gods are more distant than before."

"You don't sound sad about it at all."

"When we made the pact that we would only intervene in the lives of the mortals though guidance and teaching, we all knew this was the inevitable result: They will grow up."

Tututika sighed. "And yet I cannot stop caring. I want them to do well."

"Of course we can't stop caring. It is the curse of parents and teachers everywhere, mortal or immortal."

And the two gods watched the ghostly carp in the tank, as though seeking the future in the murky, dark sea.

CHAPTER NINE

PALACE EXAMINATION

The carriage bringing King Kado and Lady Tete to the Imperial palace was late.

"What's the matter?" Tete stuck her head out and asked the driver.

"There's a crowd of angry *cashima* blocking the road, Mistress."

Indeed, about a hundred *cashima* milled about in the road, and passing carriages had to carefully thread their way between them. One of the *cashima* was standing on an upturned box for packing fruits and shouting at the crowd.

"Out of a hundred *firoa*, more than fifty come from Haan and only a single one comes from the old lands of Xana. How can that possibly be fair?"

"But the emperor himself began his rise in Dasu," said one of the *cashima* in the crowd. "And King Kado is the emperor's brother. Surely the judges would have taken that into account in scoring."

"He might have become a king in Dasu, but the emperor listens to his advisers. You all know how much sway Luan Zya, a nobleman of Haan, has at the court."

"Luan Zya hasn't even been in court since the funeral for the emperor's father!"

"All the better to whisper things into the emperor's ear in secrecy. We should march to the palace and demand an investigation! Release all the essays and let all of us judge together if those deemed well-matched to the fate of Dara are deserving and if the emperor's test administrators are worthy of his trust!"

The other *cashima* in the crowd shouted their approval.

Since the impassioned scholars were no longer talking about her husband, Tete ducked back into the carriage. "I think they're complaining about the results of the Grand Examination."

"Of course they are," said Kado. "If you didn't score high enough to place among the *firoa* so as to be guaranteed a plum position in the Imperial bureaucracy, complaining about the scoring is about all you *can* do."

"Do you know if the judges were really fair?" asked Tete. "Did any examinees from Dasu place?"

"What do I know of what the emperor and his advisers do in private council?" Kado smiled bitterly. "You know as well as I do that Kuni gave me this title only because our father begged him to do something for me before his death. I'm hardly a Tiro king of old."

Tete was embarrassed by this outburst—she knew what her husband said was true, but it was still hard to hear. Kuni still resented her and Kado for the way they'd treated him when he was a young man. Who could have guessed how things would turn out for Kado's idle little brother, who'd strutted through the streets of Zudi like a common gangster?

"Is Kuni satisfied these days?" Tete cautiously asked.

She meant whether Kuni was happy with Kado, but Kado took it to be a question broader in scope. "I don't know the details of what goes on at court, but it is said that Kuni's delay in naming a crown prince has caused factions to rise. The generals and nobles prefer

Phyro, while the ministers and the College of Advocates prefer Timu—and of course the empress and Consort Risana are involved. Both sides have done some ugly things."

"Inheritance disputes plague everyone, from the smallest shopkeepers to the Emperor of Dara. Are you going to offer to mediate?"

Kado shook his head vigorously. "The smart thing for us to do is to take the allowance Kuni pays us and stay out of his sight. We'll have our pleasures; let him run things the way he wants to. Ra Olu, my 'regent' in Dasu, is the real governor of the island, and he reports directly to Kuni. I know nothing, and I prefer it that way."

"Then why are we even going to the palace?"

"Some occasions require my presence as a decorative sign," said Kado, waving the sheaf of blank extra passes the regent of Dasu had sent him. "The people of the Harmonious City want to see the Imperial household enact harmony, and so we must play our bit parts. Let's just turn these in and nod and smile at whatever Kuni decides during the Palace Examination."

Although the top one hundred scoring examinees were given the rank of *firoa* and all could theoretically participate in the Palace Examination, only the top ten, honored with the designation of *pana méji*, were actually given the chance to do so. The rest would be assigned to a civil service pool where they would be matched with ministers and generals in need of junior staff, and these assignments would hopefully launch them into a glorious career in government service.

The *pana méji* now sat in two rows before the raised dais for the Imperial family at one end of the Grand Audience Hall; the emperor was about to question them directly.

On top of the eight-foot-tall dais, Emperor Ragin sat in his full court regalia: bright red Imperial robes adorned with hundreds of golden crubens playing with dandelions and exquisite embroidery depicting rearing waves and various lesser creatures of the sea; the flat-top crown with a curtain of seven strands of cowrie shells dangling from the front, obscuring his facial expressions from the viewer; and another curtain of seven strands of corals hanging in the back for balance. He knelt up in the formal position of *mipa rari* on the throne, a gilt ironwood sitting board overlaid with cushions stuffed with lavender, mint, and other mind-clearing spices formulated by the empress, the most well-known herbalist of the empire.

Speaking of whom—Empress Jia sat to the left of Kuni Garu, and Consort Risana sat to his right, both also dressed in formal court robes and crowns. Their robes were made of thick red silk because red was the color of Dasu, the island from which Kuni Garu had begun his journey to the Throne of Dara, though the robes of Jia and Risana were a shade lighter than the emperor's. Jia's robe was decorated with dandelion-mouthing dyrans, the rainbow-tailed flying fish that symbolized femininity, while Risana's robe was decorated with carp-derived motifs in honor of her home island of Arulugi. At the foot of Risana's cushioned seat was a small bronze censer topped by the figure of a leaping carp, and faint smoke issued from its open mouth. It was said that Consort Risana's health required her to partake of the fumes of certain herbs, and such censers often accompanied her.

Below the dais and flanking the two rows of *pana méji* scholars, the most powerful lords of the empire arranged themselves in a pattern that was meant to echo their relative influences in decisions of the state. Since Emperor Ragin's coronation years ago, it was rare for governors of the far-flung provinces and the enfeoffed nobles in their disparate fiefs to gather in the capital. This was a very special occasion, and the highest levels of courtly etiquette were on display.

Thus, to the Emperor's left, on the west side of the audience hall, the civil ministers and provincial governors who were in the capital knelt in a long column arranged by rank facing the center in *mipa rari*. Their gray-blue ceremonial formal robes, made of heavy damask water silk, were decorated with figures either symbolic of the province the governor was from: shoals of icefish for Rui in the north, towering oaks for ring-wooded Rima, cloud-fleeced flocks for northern Faça, sheaves of ripening sorghum and clusters of chrysanthemum-swords for central Cocru, and so on—or the sphere of responsibility of each minister—thousands of stylized eyes for Farsight Secretary Rin Coda, scrolls and codices for the Imperial Archivist, a scale for the Chief Tax Collector, trumpets for the First Herald, writing knives for the head of the Imperial Scribes, and so forth.

By rank, Prime Minister Cogo Yelu was the foremost among all the ministers and governors, and that meant that he usually sat closest to the throne. But today, the man closest to the throne was Luan Zya, who was dressed in a water-silk robe decorated with tiny remoras. Although he had no duties at the court and held no official position—in fact, he rarely visited Pan—Cogo had insisted that his old friend be given the position of honor as Emperor Ragin's most trusted adviser.

To the emperor's right, on the east side of the audience hall, the column of generals and enfeoffed nobles knelt, also in formal *mipa rari*. In contrast to the ministers and governors, these individuals, who obtained their positions mainly through wartime service, were dressed in ceremonial armor made of lacquered wood and wore decorative swords on their belts made of coral, perfumed paper, or fine porcelain. After all, other than the palace guards, no one was allowed to bring a functioning weapon into the palace, much less the Grand Audience Hall.

Queen Gin of Géjira, Marshal of Dara, leader of all the emperor's armed forces, sat conspicuously at the head of the column of generals and nobles. Next to her was Kado Garu, the emperor's brother, who looked ill at ease in the ceremonial armor that seemed too tight on his bloated body. Beyond him were the other men who had fought with the emperor during the rebellion and the Chrysanthemum-Dandelion War: Duke Théca Kimo of Arulugi; Marquess Puma Yemu of Porin; Mün Çakri, First General of the Infantry; Than Carucono, First General of the Cavalry and First Admiral of the Navy . . .

The two hierarchies were harmoniously woven together into a balanced whole. And above them, spouses and assistants of the Lords of Dara sat on balconies, where they would be able to observe the Palace Examination but have no right to speak.

Gin Mazoti looked across the audience hall at Luan Zya and smiled.

She did not notice the slight frown on Empress Jia's face as she glanced over at the nobles, her gaze lingering for a moment on Gin's steel sword, prominently worn on her waist, the only chilly reminder of death in the otherwise harmonious hall.

The formality and order of the Imperial court was a far cry from the relaxed atmosphere that had prevailed at Kuni's camp during the war years or the wild celebrations that had marked the empire's early days, when Kuni's followers had behaved more like friends than subordinates. As most of Kuni's retinue had humble backgrounds, their uncouth manners often shocked the old nobles of the Seven States and those who had followed the Hegemon.

At Kuni's coronation, for example, many of his old companions drank from bowls instead of the ritually correct flagons; grabbed food with their hands instead of using the correct eating sticks—one stick for dumplings and pot stickers; two for noodles and rice; three for fish and fruit and meat so that one could use two of them in one hand to hold the food while dividing it into smaller pieces with the last—and after they became inebriated, got up and danced with eating sticks and serving spoons as though they were swords, banging them loudly against the columns of the new palace.

Contemptuous whispers and titters among the old nobles and learned scholars grew in the capital, and so Cogo Yelu recommended that the emperor appoint a new Master of Rituals, explaining to Kuni that codes of courtly behavior, though tedious, were necessary now that the Islands were at peace.

"As Kon Fiji said, 'Proper rituals channel proper thoughts,'" said Cogo.

"So we're going to listen to Kon Fiji again?" asked Kuni. "I never liked him, even as a boy."

"Different philosophers are appropriate for different times," said a conciliatory Cogo. "The manners of a camp on the battlefield are not always the right etiquette for a court at peace. As the Ano sages said, *Adi co cacru co pihua ki tuthiüri lothu cruben ma dicaro co cacru ki yegagilu acrutacaféthéta cathacaü crudogithédagén.* The cruben who breaches freely in open sea may need to float gently in a harbor filled with many fishing boats."

"You could have just quoted the old village saying: 'Howl when you see a wolf, scratch your head when you see a monkey.' That's much more vivid than your flowery Classical Ano quotation—and you don't have to translate for me. I did pay *some* attention in Master Loing's class, you know."

Rin Coda, who had known Kuni longer than anyone, and Jia, who was used to Kuni's preference for the speech of the ordinary people, burst out in laughter. Cogo chuckled, his cheeks turning a shade of maroon.

Who should fill the new position of Master of Rituals? After more discussion, Cogo suggested Zato Ruthi.

"The deposed King of Rima?" asked the incredulous Kuni. "Gin did not like him at all."

"He is also the most renowned contemporary Moralist philosopher," said Cogo. "Rather than leaving him in his forest cabin, where he's penning angry tracts denouncing you, it might be better to make use of his reputation and knowledge."

"This will also send a signal to the scholars that you're ready to start a new era, when the book will be valued more than the sword," agreed Jia. "I know you like spearing two fish with one thrust."

Kuni was not sure about this, but he always listened to counsel.

"A fusty old book might not be fun to read, but it's good for propping a door open," mused Kuni. The order was given to summon Zato Ruthi into Imperial service.

Zato Ruthi was pleased with his elevation: Coming up with the protocols for the new Imperial court, to him, seemed a task far more important than mere minutiae like running an army or devising tax policies, the sort of tasks better relegated to people like Gin Mazoti— whom he grudgingly accepted as a colleague—and Cogo Yelu. After all, the Imperial courtly protocols would be the model of proper behavior for lesser courts and the learned, who would be exemplars for the masses. In this way, he had a chance to sculpt the soul of the people of Dara in accordance with Moralist ideals.

He threw himself into his task with gusto. He consulted ancient histories and the etiquette manuals of every old Tiro state; he collected all the Classical Ano lyrical fragments describing the golden age before it became corrupted; he drafted voluminous notes and drew detailed plans.

When he finally presented his ideas to the emperor, Kuni thought he was back in Master Loing's classroom again. Ruthi's protocol manual was a scroll whose length stretched halfway down the Grand Audience Hall.

"Master Ruthi," Kuni said, trying to keep the impatience out of his voice, "you have to create something that my generals can learn. This is so complicated that I can't even keep all the ritual phrases and ceremonial walks and seating arrangements and numbers of bows straight."

"You haven't even tried, *Rénga*!"

"I thank you greatly for your diligence. But why don't I take a stab at simplifying this?"

When Kuni presented his simplified plan—now a scroll only as long as he was tall—to Zato Ruthi, the latter almost fainted from the shock.

"This—this—this is barely a protocol at all! Where are the Classical Ano titles? Where are the model walks designed to cultivate the soul? Where are the quotations from the sages to guide debates? It's like something taken out of a folk opera to please an audience snacking on sunflower seeds and candied monkeyberries!"

Kuni patiently explained that Master Ruthi had misunderstood. He had simply refined Master Ruthi's ideas in a way that preserved their essence while remaining capable of being carried out by mere mortals. He did not explain that he had indeed taken much inspiration from the staging of folk operas, consulting Risana to gain her expertise. Thinking of the whole thing as a big play was the only way he could stomach working on it.

Back and forth the emperor and the Master of Rituals debated, trying to compromise on something that had enough formality to satisfy the desire for propriety by the old nobles and scholars and also contained enough fun to be accepted by the emperor and his wartime companions.

"Why am I the only one sitting?" asked Kuni, pointing at the latest illustration of formal court seating.

Ruthi explained that this was based on the protocols of the Xana Imperial court, which had been designed by the Imperial Scholar Lügo Crupo, a strict Incentivist. Emperor Mapidéré had preferred to sit in the extremely informal position of *thakrido*, with his legs stretched out in front of him, while all his ministers and generals stood at attention.

"Crupo believed that men were more efficient if they stood for meetings," said Ruthi. "Though he was wrong about many things, I do think his reasoning is sound in this regard. Efficient administration is important, *Rénga*."

"But I would look like some bandit king in council with his underlings! The ordinary people will view it as a play about despotism."

"I'm not asking you to sit in *thakrido*!" said Ruthi, a bit outraged. "I am not a barbarian. You should sit in *géüpa*, which would be appropriate by reference to the poem written—"

"The point is for everyone to sit," said the emperor.

"But *Rénga*, if you sit like everyone else in attendance, it will obscure the difference in your positions. Your person is a symbol of the state."

"So are the ministers and generals who serve me—if I am the head of the state, they're the arms and legs. It makes no sense to pamper the head and torment the body; formal court should model harmony among all the people of Dara. In this audience hall, we debate and decide the fate of the people as a whole, not just my personal preferences and dislikes."

Ruthi was pleased by this speech, which held a hint of the Moralist ideal for the relationship between the ruler and the ruled. He was forming a new opinion of Kuni Garu, the emperor who had turned Dara upside down, brought women into the army, and swept away the Tiro states in his rise to power. Perhaps there was—he thought hopefully—a Moralist soul deep within that beer belly. He would try to be more flexible and serve this interesting lord.

And so Kuni and Ruthi worked together for weeks, designing courtly regalia (or as Kuni thought of them, "costumes and props"), formal speeches ("scripts"), and etiquette protocols ("blocking")—they debated long into the night and used up reams of paper with rough sketches, frequently calling for midnight snacks and herbal drinks prepared by the empress that kept the mind alert—until the final result reflected Kuni's vision without offending Moralist traditions *too* much.

Kuni was willing to suffer for his art. The formal robe and crown took time to put on—even with servants—and the regalia forced him to kneel stiffly in uncomfortable *mipa rari*. But the example set by the emperor ended any complaints from the unruly generals—everyone put on the stiff robes, ceremonial armor, and heavy official headgear and knelt up in *mipa rari*.

Viewed from the ceiling of the Grand Audience Hall, Kuni's court resembled a cruben cruising at sea: The two columns of advisers along the walls outlined the scaled whale's powerful body, resplendent and sumptuous; the dais at the end was the head of the cruben, with Empress Jia and Consort Risana as the two bright eyes; and Emperor Ragin, of course, was the proud horn at the center of the forehead, charging through a turbulent sea and mapping an interesting path.

The First Herald consulted the sundial mounted on the southern wall, behind the Imperial dais, and stood up.

All the murmurs and whispers in the hall ceased. Everyone, from the emperor to the palace guard standing by the grand entrance, straightened their backs.

"Mogi ça lodüapu ki gisgo giré, adi ça méüpha ki kédalo phia ki. Pindin ça racogilu üfiré, crudaügada ça phithoingnné gidalo phia ki. Ingluia ça philu jisén dothaéré, naüpin rari ça philu shanoa gathédalo phia ki."

The herald chanted the words solemnly, sticking to the rhythm of the old meters of Diaspora-Era heroic sagas, as was deemed proper in Moralist treatises on the proper rituals for government. The Classical Ano words meant: *May the sky-lights careen smoothly and the whale's way sleep in tranquility. May the people be joyous and the gods pleased. May the king be well-counseled and the ministers well-led.*

The First Herald sat down while echoes of his voice continued to reverberate around the hall.

Emperor Ragin cleared his throat and intoned the ceremonial words that began formal court, "Honored lords, loyal governors, able advisers, brave generals, we gather today to praise the gods and to comfort the people. What matters do you wish to bring to my attention?"

After a pause, Zato Ruthi, Imperial Tutor, stood up. "*Rénga*, on this auspicious day, I wish to present to you the *pana méji* of this session of the Grand Examination."

Kuni Garu nodded, the cowrie strands hanging in front of his face clinking crisply. "I thank you and the other judges for your service. Having to carefully evaluate more than a thousand essays in such a brief period of time is no mean accomplishment. The examinees are fortunate to have their words weighed by minds as learned as yours."

To the side, King Kado shifted imperceptibly on his knees and gazed at the Imperial Tutor. He was thinking of the complaining *cashima* he had run into on the way here. *This old man may soon find out how much trouble he's in.*

Zato Ruthi bowed. "It was a pleasure to commune with so many supple and fresh minds." He pointed to the left-most scholar in the first row, a dark-skinned young man with delicate and handsome features, and the examinee stood up. "This is Kita Thu, of Haan. His essay was composed in an exquisite hand—the calligraphy calls to mind the best works of the late King Cosugi. Though his passion is the study of mathematics, his essay proposed a reform of the schools of Dara to emphasize the works of Kon Fiji."

Silence. Not a single murmur of admiration could be heard in the hall.

Kado frowned. *That sounds like the most boring proposal for reform I can imagine. Either this young examinee knows how to weave a dazzling pattern out of plain threads like a skilled lace maker of Gan, or else Zato Ruthi just revealed even more evidence of bias by giving high marks to a kid who knows only how to recite musty books by the Moralists' favorite sage.*

But the emperor only gazed steadily at the young man, and the dangling cowrie strands obscured his face so that no one in the Grand Audience Hall could discern his feelings. As he spoke, his tone was perfectly tranquil, expressing neither pleasure nor displeasure. "Are you related to King Cosugi?"

Kado sat up straighter, as did the others in the hall. *Interesting!*

The young man bowed deeply. "*Rénga*, you speak the honored name of my grand-uncle."

"He was a calm man in troubled times."

Kita nodded noncommittally. The emperor's words could be taken as either a compliment or criticism. Cosugi had generally been thought of as among the least effective of the Tiro kings during the rebellion against the Xana Empire, and his restored Haan had been the first state on the Big Island to fall to the armies of Emperor Ragin. It was best not to dwell on that history.

"I thought I recognized a regal soul in the gentle flowing outlines of the logograms!" said a pleased Ruthi. "You are truly skilled with the writing knife for someone so young." Then he seemed to realize how he sounded and coughed to disguise his embarrassment. "Of course, we knew nothing of your background as we reviewed all the essays anonymously."

Kado shook his head. *If word of what Ruthi just said gets out, those cashima will have even more ammunition in their accusations of bias and favoritism.*

"You observed in your essay that the current administration of Dara is impossible to sustain over the long term," said Kuni. "Can you review the argument for me?"

Excited whispers passed up and down the two columns of officials. Kado watched as Zato Ruthi surveyed the hall full of astonished officials, a satisfied smile on the Imperial Tutor's face. *Sly old fox! Of course he would state the argument of the essay in the most generic way possible, disguising its real bite. This way, he distances himself from Kita Thu in the event that the emperor is displeased with the argument, and that lavish praise of Thu's handwriting just lays the groundwork for more deniability if necessary—he could always claim to have been overwhelmed by the form rather than the substance of what was written.*

Once again Kado was glad that he stayed away from Kuni's court as much as possible. The Grand Audience Hall was a deep pool whose tranquil surface hid powerful currents and countercurrents beneath, and a careless swimmer could be easily pulled in and never able to get out. He knelt up even straighter, keeping his shoulders hunched and his eyes focused on the tip of his nose.

Kita Thu gazed back at the emperor, his face a perfect mask of awe and respect. "Of course, *Rénga*. I eagerly await your criticisms of my foolish ideas."

A heavy tapestry with a map of Dara hung behind the throne, and behind the tapestry was a small door leading to the emperor's private changing room, where he and his wives got ready for court. Now that formal court was in session, the room should be empty.

The other door to the changing room, the one opening to the corridor that led to the Imperial family's private quarters, opened slowly.

"Hurry! Get in there before someone sees us."

Timu, Théra, and Phyro slipped into the room and shut the door quietly behind them. This latest bit of mischief had been Théra's idea. Phyro wasn't sure spying on an examination would be any fun ("I don't even like taking my own exams!"), and Timu was worried about the wrath of their father and Master Ruthi if they were caught.

But Théra had painted a picture of thrills for Phyro ("Don't you want to see Father intimidate one of these bookworms?") and convinced Timu that he was going to get in trouble even if he didn't participate ("Isn't it the eldest brother's duty to prevent younger siblings from ill-advised adventures? And isn't he equally at fault with them should he fail in his duty?"). In the end, both boys—one eager, one reluctant—agreed to come with her.

The lamps in the changing room were still lit, and the children almost screamed with fright when they realized that it wasn't empty. Lady Soto, the empress's confidante and the caretaker for Timu and Théra when they were younger, glared at them from next to the door leading to the Grand Audience Hall.

"Don't just stand there," she hissed. "If you're going to eavesdrop, come closer!"

CHAPTER TEN

A BALLOON RIDE

SOMEWHERE OVER THE SEA NORTH OF
CRESCENT ISLAND: THE FIRST YEAR IN
THE REIGN OF FOUR PLACID SEAS (FIVE YEARS
BEFORE THE FIRST GRAND EXAMINATION).

Curious Turtle drifted leisurely over the endless sea.

"Look! Look!" Zomi shouted, pointing to the southeast.

The gentle swells broke, and a massive, sleek, dark body leapt out of the water. Even at this distance, it was clearly many times the size of the hot-air balloon they were riding in. The colossal fish hung suspended for a moment in air, thousands of black scales scintillating in the sunlight like jewels, before falling ponderously back into the water. A moment later, the muffled splash reached their ears like distant thunder.

"That is a cruben," said Luan Zya, "sovereign of the seas. They are often seen in the sea between Rui and Crescent Island. I think they like to dive down to the underwater volcanoes and linger in the heated water, much as the people of Faça enjoy hot spring baths near Rufizo Falls."

"I never thought I'd see one! It is"—Zomi hesitated—"beautiful. No, that's not right. It's beautinificent, brilli-splen-sublimeful, magnidazzlelicious. I'm sorry, I don't have the words. These are all the pretty phrases I know."

"The world is grand and full of wonders."

Luan smiled at the chattering girl, remembering the indescribable joy he had felt the first time he had seen a breaching cruben from the deck of a Haan trawler. He had been only ten, and his father, the chief augur of Haan, had stood by him to watch the leaping crubens, recounting the lore of the scaled whales while resting a hand gently on the boy's shoulder.

How do you know so much about the world, Father?

By following curiosity, the quality that Lutho prizes above all.

Will I ever know as much as you?

You will know much more than I do, Lu-tika. It is the natural flow of the universe that sons should exceed their fathers, and students shall surpass their teachers.

"Can we get a closer look?" asked Zomi eagerly.

"Maybe," Luan said. And he swallowed the lump in his throat and turned away to hide the fact that his eyes were wet. "Let's see if luck is with us today."

He leaned over the side of the gondola, uncapped his drinking gourd, and tipped it over carefully to let out a thin stream of red wine. The liquid line plunged straight down, but as it neared the sea, the stream twisted and pointed to the southeast, turning into a string of crimson pearls that scattered and fell into the waves.

"Good," Luan said. "The wind is coming from the northwest near the surface. We can ride it."

Reaching above his head, Luan twisted a dial about a foot across in diameter with both hands. The dial was connected through a system of gears and belts to the stove above them, filled with freeze-distilled liquor—meant for cleaning and stripping paint rather than drinking—and caused the thick flax wick to retract into the stove. The flame that roared overhead quieted and grew smaller, and the balloon began to descend.

"So we're entirely at the mercy of the winds?" asked Zomi. The balloon continued to fall until the northwesterly breeze caught it. "What if you can't find a wind headed in the direction you want to go?"

Luan reached up and twisted the dial the other way. The wick extended, the flame roared back to life, and the balloon stopped falling and drifted to the northeast.

"Then we'll have to go somewhere else," said Luan. "Ballooning is not for those too set on their destinations. *Curious Turtle* may not always find a way to get to where you want to go, but it will always take you somewhere interesting."

They reached the spot in the sea where the cruben had breached earlier, and Luan turned up the flames again to raise the balloon out of the breeze so that they hovered above the swell. The water parted again, and Zomi leaned eagerly over the side of the gondola, hoping to see another acrobatic breach up close. But this time, the cruben only poked its head above the water, its gigantic horn like the mast of a ship, and exhaled through the blowhole, shooting a fountain of mist high into the air near the balloon. Zomi cried out in joy and turned to face Luan.

"He was laughing at me!" Her face was bright with a smile and wet with the spray from the cruben.

Luan felt at once very old and also very young as he laughed along with Zomi.

As she slept, Zomi dreamed of home.

"I don't know how long I will be away," said Mimi.

Aki nodded. She was packing a stack of sorghum meal cakes soaked in honey and a small jar of salted caterpillars in a cloth. She spoke without turning to look at Mimi. "If you miss home, have a cake to remind you of the sweetness of our summers. If you are sad, eat a caterpillar to remind you of my cooking."

"Mistress Kidosu," said Luan, "I promise to take good care of your daughter. She is extraordinarily talented, but she cannot learn what I want to teach her without seeing the world."

"Thank you," said Aki. "I've always wanted Mimi to stay by my side

and live a life like mine, but that's a selfish desire, driven by the fact that the gods have already taken so many I love from me. Yet I've always known that she's special, and it surprises me not one whit that you've found her."

"I will learn the secrets of the world and come back to give us all a better life," said Mimi. She had so much she wanted to say, but she wasn't sure her voice would not crack, and so she simply said, "You'll eat white rice every day."

"Study hard, Mimi-tika," said Aki. "And do not think about me too much. You're my daughter, but you do not belong to me. The only duty any child owes to her parent is to live a life that is true to her nature."

Zomi woke up.

Overhead, the flame roared softly as *Curious Turtle* continued to ride the wind. All around her, she could see the stars, bright pinpricks of light like the glowing sea jellies that she was familiar with from swimming in the bay during the brief summers when the water was warm enough. She liked swimming: The water freed her from the bondage of her disobedient left leg, and she felt graceful, complete, not *lame* or *crippled*.

She liked flying in the balloon at night. It was like drifting through an empyrean sea.

Yee-ee-squeak, yee-ee-squeak . . .

The strange sound caught her attention. She turned and saw Luan sitting at the other side of the gondola with his legs stretched out in front of him. He had some contraption made of sticks and bundles of ox sinew wrapped around his right calf, and as he flexed his leg, the contraption made the rhythmic noise she had heard.

"What's that, Teacher?"

Startled, Luan stopped flexing his leg and looked over at Zomi. "Oh, nothing," he said. "Go back to sleep. I'll wake you up to steer the balloon in a few hours."

Zomi was going to ask more, but Luan draped a blanket over his leg and opened the thick book that he always carried with him, which Zomi had learned was called *Gitré Üthu*, which meant "know thyself" in Classical Ano. It was a companion that her teacher seemed to love more than anything else, or anyone—he never spoke of a woman, or a child, or parents. What would make an adviser who had helped a king build an empire prefer the company of unlettered children and wild seas? There were so many things about him that she didn't know.

As the stars spun overhead and the gondola rocked her, Zomi fell back asleep.

While Luan steered the balloon, Zomi practiced her zyndari letters on a slate with a piece of chalk. The breeze was steady and strong, scented with the clean smell of the open sea.

"How much longer until we reach Crescent Island?" asked Zomi. She stopped writing and yawned.

"If the wind holds steady, probably another two days, but the wind never is steady," said Luan. He looked at Zomi affectionately. "Already tired? You've only been writing for a quarter of an hour."

"I'm bored! I memorized all the letters and their sounds two days ago, and you're just making me write the same thing over and over again. When will you teach me the Ano logograms? Will it take more than five days?"

Luan laughed. "You'll have to learn Classical Ano along with the logograms, and it would take you many years to master them."

"Years! Then we'd better start right away."

"Don't be so impatient. I can't teach you how to carve wax in the gondola—the knife can be dangerous with the balloon swinging around like this."

"Come to think of it, I don't even know if I want to waste my time learning the Ano logograms. Isn't it enough to learn one way of writing?"

Luan had never encountered any student who thought it might be all right not to learn the Ano logograms, but then again, Zomi was not like the students who could afford private tutors or academics. "We'll talk about the logograms another time. For now, you still need more practice writing the Hundred Names with zyndari letters. Your handwriting is terrible."

"It's hard to fit the letters inside the small squares you've drawn! And why do I have to put them in the squares anyway?"

"The zyndari letters were invented long after the Ano logograms. We arrange them into word squares in imitation of the shapes of the logograms so that if they're used together, as sometimes happens when you need to gloss an obscure or new logogram, their shapes harmonize. It is not enough that one can write, one must also write with beauty."

"Why does beauty matter?" asked Zomi, an edge in her voice. "Isn't it enough that my meaning comes through?"

Luan looked at the scar on her face and the walking stick on the floor of the gondola next to her legs and realized that he had struck a sore point. "There are many kinds of beauty in the world, some of which are the province of gods, and some of which are the province of mankind. Beauty of expression when writing is within the control of the writer, and elegant calligraphy prepares the mind to be persuaded."

"Sounds like you're saying that the well-dressed will be listened to more," muttered Zomi.

Luan sighed. "That's not what I meant, but I can see why you feel that way. Since you've asked me to be your teacher, you must do as I say on this. Practice forming the letters within the squares in pleasing proportions; no matter how much you hate it, it's a vital skill."

Reluctantly, Zomi went back to writing. But after a few moments of silence, she piped up again. "This reminds me of carving the lucky cakes for the High-Autumn Festival. Mama always said I was too impatient to make the pretty patterns in the pastry before baking, but at least there you get something delicious at the end."

"Are you suggesting that I get you some sticky rice flour so that you can make edible word squares?" Luan asked sarcastically.

Zomi looked up. "Oh, that would be great! Teacher, can we? Can we? If we get some honey, I'll make a cone out of paper and cut off the tip so that I can write the zyndari letters using the dripping honey. And we can get some lotus seeds and coconut shavings—"

"If you put as much energy into practicing your letters as you do into dreaming up new foods, you'd have mastered proper handwriting by now!"

Zomi glared at him for a moment, lowered her eyes, and went back to writing. Her hand moved across the slate very, very slowly.

Luan sighed again. *Not every mind learns the same way. A knife needs to be sharpened against stone, but a pearl needs to be polished with soft cloth. I found infinite joy and comfort in the solitude of repetitious drilling and practice, but perhaps a different method is needed for this one.*

"Do you want to learn to fly the balloon instead?"

Zomi dropped the slate and climbed up to stand next to him in an instant.

"First, you have to find out where the winds are," said Luan. "Remember, a balloon has no way of propelling itself. It must ride the winds."

"Why do you ride around in a balloon instead of an airship?"

Luan laughed. "Airships require the special lift gas from Mount Kiji. They're reserved for the Imperial air force and government business."

"Maybe there are other gases that will do just as well."

"Maybe. But I don't know of any such gases. Besides, I like balloons. Airships are about getting from one place to another, and one worries constantly about propulsion. Flying in a balloon, on the other hand, is . . . more relaxing."

Zomi picked up Luan's drinking gourd, uncapped it, and turned it upside down over the side of the gondola. Luan leapt to grab the calabash.

"Easy! Easy! You just need a little bit to test the wind! Don't waste all the wine. This is all I have until we get to Ingça on Crescent Island."

"You drink too much anyway." But this time Zomi took care to tip the gourd over gently and watched as the thin stream went straight down into the sea. "No wind below us."

"No wind in a direction different from the one we're heading in," corrected Luan.

"How do you find out where the winds are above us?" asked Zomi. She squinted at the sky above them. A few wispy clouds dotted the empty blueness. "We can't pour wine upward—oh, how I wish I were a cruben, and then I could spray water up through my blowhole and see the winds!"

Luan rummaged in the footlocker at the bottom of the gondola and retrieved something that looked like a stack of paper. He pulled on a ring at the top and the stack of paper sprang up into a cube-shaped lantern with pleated paper sides and an internal bamboo skeleton that had been folded into a compressed shape. The bottom was open with a wire crosspiece that held a candle inside the paper lantern.

"That's really neat!" said Zomi.

"It's my invention," said Luan, pride in his voice. "These floating lanterns were known since time immemorial, but I came up with the collapsible bamboo skeleton that would allow them to be easily transported."

Luan attached a thin silk string to the bottom of the lantern, handed the string to Zomi, and lit the candle. As the air inside the lantern grew heated, the balloon began to float.

"Lean out the side of the gondola," Luan instructed. "Let the string out. This is a kite-balloon, and you can use it to sense the direction of the winds above us."

As Zomi guided the kite-balloon's flight and told Luan her observations of the direction of the winds at various heights, Luan noted them down on the slate. When Luan decided that they had taken enough readings, he asked Zomi to pull the kite-balloon back and extinguish the candle.

"Now, tell me: If I want to go in that direction"—Luan pointed to the southwest—"how would I do it?"

Zomi looked at the slate, upon which Luan had drawn a neat table of heights and wind directions based on her readings. "There's a strong northeastern wind if we go up . . . three hundred feet?"

Luan nodded. "You have just made Na Moji proud."

"Remind me who he was again?"

"Na Moji was the founder of the Patternist school of philosophy. He lived centuries ago, when Xana was a land far more primitive than the other Tiro states. He tied silk ribbons to wild geese and proved that the birds migrated south for winter and returned north for the spring. He was also the first to devise a kite with two strings so that they could be guided to trace out dizzying patterns in the sky.

"Na Moji believed that nature was a book whose language was mathematics. By careful observation and testing, we can plumb its depths and map out its patterns. Even the gods are subject to the patterns of nature, though they are able to read more of it than we can.

"You have created a map of winds with the kite-balloon, and now you're ready to fly wherever you wish. A balloon, of course, is at home in air, the natural element of Patternism."

Zomi looked around at the sky and the sea, but now instead of emptiness she seemed to see gusts of wind as broad, three-dimensional avenues and streets in an invisible city. A big smile broke out on her face. "I *like* Patternism! More! Teach me more!"

Luan chuckled. "Well, the next task you have to accomplish is to actually raise *Curious Turtle* into the wind, and that requires a different school of philosophy."

With Luan's help, Zomi grasped the dial overhead and twisted it. The flame shot roaring up out of the liquor stove, and with a jerk, the balloon began to rise.

"Gentle! You're trying to guide the flame, not wrestle it!"

Zomi twisted the dial back slowly and the flame quieted down a bit, slowing the ascent.

Luan continued, "The flame heats the air inside the balloon, which expands. The excess air escapes the balloon, causing the hot air inside to be less dense than the cold air outside. And in this way, the balloon gains altitude like the Imperial airships. Heated air acts a bit like the lift gas from Lake Dako on Mount Kiji."

The breeze picked up, and the balloon began to drift southwest. Zomi continued to twist the dial slowly, lowering and raising the flame by turns until the balloon leveled off.

"What you have just practiced is an illustration of the Incentivist school of philosophy," said Luan. "As the name indicates, its natural element is fire."

"I don't understand," said Zomi. "The Incentivists believe in burning things? Oh! Like the way Emperor Mapidéré burned books!"

"What in the world gave you—never mind. No, the Incentivist school was founded by Gi Anji, the youngest of the great sages. He's a modern, not an ancient Ano. Gi Anji believed that people are by nature lazy and resist change, and it is the duty of the wise ruler to incentivize them with proper rewards and punishments."

"My ma used to have a much simpler way of saying that: 'Get out of bed or I'll throw a burning lump of coal in the blankets.' So these Incentivists *do* like burning things."

Luan chortled. "I suppose that is one way of looking at it. What Gi Anji meant was that the stress the Moralists placed on cultivating virtue was misplaced. Most people are irredeemably selfish, and it is sufficient for the ruler to adjust the laws to encourage the right behavior. For example, if you increase taxes on farms but lower them for pastures—"

"What do you have against farmers?"

"Nothing! I was using an illustrative example."

"Can't you use another example? I don't like taxes. The tax collectors are always so mean to my mother and me."

"All right." Luan thought of his old friend Cogo Yelu, who could talk about taxes for hours, and smiled. "Suppose you want to encourage the arts and letters. Rather than exhorting the people to be more studious, it's better to make learning a requirement for positions of power."

"That doesn't sound very fair. You have to have money to go to school—"

"The point is: It's possible to think of the laws as a complicated machine, and by adjusting the right levers and dials, you can make people do anything, just as dialing up the heat on the stove drives air out, causing the balloon to rise, and dialing down the flame creates a vacuum for the cold air to fill, causing the balloon to fall."

"This philosophy sounds very . . . harsh."

"It *can* be. The greatest Incentivist was actually Lügo Crupo, Emperor Mapidéré's Imperial Scholar and later Emperor Erishi's regent. He carried Gi Anji's ideas to extremes and enacted harsh laws that finally led to the rebellion of the Scroll in the Fish."

"Like a pot boiling over if you set the heat too high."

"Exactly. But Incentivism is not, by itself, evil. It's just a tool to understand the world. There's a quote from Lügo Crupo, *Mirotiro ma thiéfi ro üradi gicru ki giséfi ga gé caü féno, gothé ma péü né ma calu, goco philutoa rari ma ri wi rénroa ki cruéthu philutoa co crusé né othu*, which means 'Men are only motivated by profit and pain, but that is no sin, for all such desires are the shadow of the desire to transform earth into heaven.'"

While Luan Zya lectured on, Zomi noticed a seagull, who had been flying right in front of the balloon, suddenly drop off before catching itself by flapping its wings vigorously. A tiny smile crept onto her face as she braced herself against the wall of the gondola.

". . . in fact, another of Gi Anji's students, Tan Féüji, managed to extend Incentivism with Moralist—"

The balloon lurched as the crosswind that had blown the seagull off course struck, and Luan Zya stumbled and grabbed onto the side of the gondola, his lecture cut off.

"You should have seen your face!" Zomi's laughter was as wild as the wind. "I saw a pattern, and I used it."

Luan Zya shook his head, but Zomi's joy was infectious. "You've been introduced to two schools of philosophy. Bored yet?"

"Are you kidding? This is fun! Teach me more philosophy about how to fly the balloon!"

"You see, you enjoyed my lectures on the Incentivists and the Patternists because I dressed them up as lessons on how to fly a balloon. A good idea is more easily absorbed if it is given the right expression, and that is why even when you have the right answers, you'll convince more people when you present them with good handwriting and proper sentence construction."

Zomi sighed. "Does this mean I need to practice more handwriting?"

"If you finish writing the Hundred Names fifty more times—to my satisfaction—we will look for more crubens."

Zomi sat back down, picked up her slate, and eagerly began to write. "Wait—" She stopped, looked up at the smirking Luan Zya, and stuck out her tongue. "I do *not* like it when you practice Incentivism!"

The banter between teacher and student was interrupted by laughter from time to time as the balloon continued to head for Crescent Island, the sun dappling the gentle waves below them.

CHAPTER ELEVEN

THE CRUBEN-WOLF

Instead of launching into an impassioned speech, Kita Thu turned around and clapped his hands together. "Quick! Go, go!"

And a group of servants who had been sitting behind the two rows of *pana méji* got up and started to unpack the trunks they had taken into the Grand Audience Hall. Swarming into the empty space between Kita Thu and the throne dais, they put on costumes, set out props, assembled elaborate paper-and-bamboo sculptures, put together intricate machines . . .

They were trying to put on a play for the emperor.

The Lords of Dara watched the proceeding with great interest while Kita Thu strode around, giving orders like a stage manager.

Since many of Kuni's most trusted generals had been men of little learning, many of the *pana méji* had figured—correctly—that a flowery speech that recited the points made in their essays would be of little interest. Given that the emperor himself was said to have little patience for scholastic rhetoric, it was crucial that the Palace

Examination presentations by the candidates take a more dynamic format.

And they had only had less than a month to prepare the presentations.

Once his servants had completed the preparations, Kita nodded and gave them the signal to begin.

The Lords of Dara and Emperor Ragin were then treated to a spectacle both amusing and horrifying.

Two servants stretched out a piece of shimmery blue water silk to represent the sea. As the waves parted, a monster rose out of the depths—portrayed by two players wearing a costume. The front half of the monster was a cruben, while the back half was a wolf. The monster lurched and struggled, as its legs could hardly propel the beast forward in the water. From time to time, the player in the front lifted the cruben-head out of the silk sea and sprayed fragrant rosewater into the air to simulate the gasping of the monster. The pleasing aroma gradually suffused the hall.

Titters could be heard around the hall and in the balconies. Even the empress and Consort Risana were charmed by the display.

Two more players came forward and placed a low platform laden with model mountains and valleys next to the silk sea to represent land. The cruben-wolf launched itself onto the platform, where the wolf legs finally found purchase. But now the heavy front half of the monster, no longer buoyed by the water, became a burden, and the monster still could not move effectively, as its fins flapped uselessly against the land and the wolf legs pushed the monster forward slowly, like an inch-worm.

Kita whistled to indicate that a new scene should start. And the players rushed around to change costumes and props. The Lords of Dara were treated successively to the spectacle of a falcon-carp, a stag-worm, a turtle-elephant—the trunk and legs could not retract into the tiny shell—and most amusing of all, a mushroom-shark that floundered in the sea, unable to eat.

"Emperor Mapidéré had divided all the Islands of Dara into provinces and ruled them directly through a bureaucracy loyal only to himself. Before his conquest, the Tiro kings had relied on enfeoffed hereditary nobles to handle the duties of administration. You took a path different from both of those systems. Half of your lands have been given to the nobles, who maintain some measure of independence, and the other half you administer directly through your governors. In this way, you have gained the disadvantages of both, and the advantages of neither."

As his servants cleaned up and packed everything back into trunks, Kita strode back and forth before the emperor, gesticulating passionately as he made his speech.

"If an Imperial edict announces a new tax, a governor must implement it while a neighboring duke or king might choose to ignore it. This leads to nonuniformity of laws and rewards the cleverly unscrupulous, who take advantage of such disparities to profit.

"You have created a monster that is neither fish nor fowl, and at home nowhere."

"A most impressive—and, I might add, entertaining—presentation. I don't fully agree, but do you have a solution?" asked Kuni. "Let the assembled Lords of Dara hear it."

Kita Thu took a deep breath and spoke deliberately, making sure that his voice carried throughout the hall. "*Rénga*, I propose that you restore the Tiro system in full."

The children had been mesmerized by the show put on by Kita Thu. The door to the changing room was to the side of the throne dais, and the seam in the door lined up with a few holes in the tapestry. By putting their eyes against the peepholes, the children could observe what was happening in the Grand Audience Hall without being seen.

"I want to try to play the cruben-wolf," whispered Phyro. "Will you do it with me, Rata-*tika*?"

"Only if I get to be the cruben part," said Théra.

"You always get the best part—"

"This Kita brought up the most complicated problem right away," interrupted Soto with a whisper. "That's a mathematician's mind-set all right."

"What do you mean?" asked Phyro.

"The nobles and the governors have been complaining about each other for years," said Soto. "The latest gossip is all about how several barons have had their fiefs taken away from them due to slight acts of insubordination that the scholars blew out of proportion. Have you been so busy playing that you haven't paid any attention?"

Théra came to the rescue of the embarrassed Phyro. "I've overheard Mother complaining about Imperial edicts not being obeyed. She thinks Father was too generous in awarding so much land to those who followed him and in giving them too much authority."

Soto nodded. "Your father was in a difficult position. Men and women who risked their lives for him needed to be rewarded, but having so many semiautonomous nobles makes it difficult to push uniform policies."

"But there's also possibly an advantage," offered Théra. "If an order from the Harmonious City is wrong, at least the lords of the fiefs could adapt it for the conditions of their realm or refuse to carry it out. Dara is large and varied, and maybe it's better to leave some room for the nobles to experiment in their own domains."

"I had not thought of such a justification. . . ." Soto looked at Théra with admiration. "But it is possible your father meant the parallel system to serve the purpose of counteracting against *too much* centralization, as you suggest."

"But surely he wouldn't approve of restoring the Tiro kings of old!" said Phyro.

Soto chuckled. "No, that he would not. But the fallen House of Haan has only one tune. I knew Kita's grand-uncle, Cosugi, and he was the same way. All he ever wanted was to be back on the throne in Ginpen. It seems that his dream lives on in a new generation."

∾ ∾ ∾ ∾

"The Tiro states should be revived, and men from noble lineages installed as kings," Kita continued. "However, the Tiro kings should acknowledge you as the sovereign and honor you as is your due, though they will administer each kingdom fully autonomously."

"How does this benefit Dara?" asked the emperor, his expression hidden by the dangling cowrie veil.

"In a thousand ways, big and small. While the bureaucrats, as men who serve at your pleasure, are inevitably motivated by thoughts of personal gain and will deceive you by exaggerating their accomplishments and hiding their errors, the Tiro kings will be men of noble character motivated by superior moral considerations. As they will not depend on your pleasure to maintain their hereditary positions, they will be motivated solely by honor and the good opinions of their fellows."

"Am I supposed to be content as a mere figurehead?"

"Not at all. Freed from the minutiae of administration, *Rénga*, you will roam from Tiro state to Tiro state and act as the conscience of the realm. With more time to devote to the contemplation of virtue, you will elevate the level of ethical thinking across the Islands. The Tiro kings will seek to emulate you, and their nobles will seek to emulate them, and so on down the line to the meanest peasant, who will wish to imitate the behavior demonstrated by his lord. With time, we may yet return to the golden age spoken of by the Ano sages in the sunken land in the western oceans, when people slept at night without locking their doors and those who lost goods in the streets might still expect to find them there untouched in the morning.

"The greatest rulers should be philosophers, not mere bureaucrats."

"This is an exceedingly pleasing vision," said Kuni, his tone still serene.

Practically everyone was now staring at Gin Mazoti to see her reaction to this proposal. Gin was no friend of the old nobles of the Seven States, but she was also known for pushing the boundaries of her own authority the furthest of all of Kuni's new nobles. But Gin sat still, her face betraying no hint of her emotions.

"You have explicated the essence of Moralism," said Zato Ruthi with a sigh. "Even Kon Fiji could not have envisioned a better future."

"No, he could not have," said Kuni, and those closest to him could hear a hint of a smile in the voice. "But I do have a question for you, Kita. Who is in charge of the army in your proposal?"

"Each Tiro king will be in charge of the defense of his state, of course. And should rebellion against your person arise, all the Tiro kings will come to your aid."

"I will have no army of my own?"

"A moral ruler should not resort to arms."

The emperor turned to his right to look at Consort Risana, who was staring at Kita intently. Carelessly, she waved her hands, as though to dissipate the faint haze of the smoke from the censer at her foot. Then she raised her right hand to gently touch the tiny red coral carp dangling from her earlobe.

Kuni turned back to Kita, his posture relaxing slightly, and nodded. "Thank you. The sincerity of your belief is commendable."

"I have come to this conclusion after much reading and thinking," said Kita, who straightened his back proudly.

"I have just the right post for you, I think. Your moral rectitude, mathematical aptitude, and affinity for coordination and management—that was a thrilling show you put on!—will make you an excellent fit for the administration of the Imperial laboratories in Ginpen."

Kita looked at the emperor, stunned. The post was of high rank, but far from the center of Imperial power.

The dream of every *firoa* was to be appointed to the College of Advocates, a new creation of the emperor. Composed of junior scholars who did not have specific areas of responsibility—and thus vested interests—the College of Advocates was charged with evaluating new policy proposals by the emperor's ministers and criticize them—all of them—by offering an opposite opinion.

The emperor had described it as a way to prevent ossification of ideas and practices in the bureaucracy by encouraging debate. Though the ministers had opposed the idea at first—having young people with no experience criticizing the policy suggestions of their elders seemed fundamentally wrong—the empress had persuaded Zato Ruthi and the other scholars that the College of Advocates was actually a way to implement the concept of the philosopher-king, and now a position in the College was deemed the best assignment.

But Kita's conversation with the emperor had not earned him the honor he craved. Time passed as he stood rooted in place, trying to process this assignment.

Zato Ruthi stepped forward and broke the uncomfortable silence. "Thank the emperor!"

Embarrassed, Kita bowed. *At least I will be close to family back in Ginpen.* But he wasn't sure whether they would view this outcome as a success. He gritted his teeth and tried one last time before stepping back to sit among the ranks of the *pana méji*. "*Rénga*, I hope you will give my proposal due consideration."

"I will discuss it with my daughter Fara when I put her to bed tonight."

Scattered laughter from the assembled ministers and generals echoed around the hall.

"This Kita is an exceedingly silly man," whispered Théra.

"What makes you think he has failed?" asked Soto.

"It's such a ridiculous suggestion! Father just compared it to a fairy tale!" Théra said.

Phyro agreed. "This is his chance to impress the emperor, and he completely botched it. Everyone knows how much attention my father pays to the army—"

"And now he's ruined this *one* precious opportunity that he got after years of study, something that others who have worked equally hard will never get!" finished Théra.

"I thought what he said was reasonable," said Timu hesitantly. "Master Ruthi's glosses on Kon Fiji's *Morality* said—"

"You do remember that Father used to call the One True Sage the One True Sap, don't you?" said Théra. Phyro started to laugh and had to cover his mouth with his hands until his face turned red from the effort to be quiet.

"A dutiful child does not repeat the opinions of a parent given after an evening of drink and revelry," said Timu, his tone rather cold. "The emperor also said—"

But Soto cut in. "Do you think any of the *pana méji* are the children of simple peasants?"

Timu, Théra, and Phyro peeked through the seam in the door at the ten figures sitting at the center of the Grand Audience Hall. All of them were young, good-looking, and dressed in fine silks—except for the young woman kneeling at the end of the last row, who was dressed in a plain hempen robe dotted with patches like a map of Dara.

"Hey, that's Zomi!" Phyro whispered.

"Yes! I knew we were right to help her!" said Théra, her face flushed with joy.

"Except for her," Soto said, "all the rest of them come from big, important clans, families with power and money and the best tutors, families that could count on many future *pana méji* among their ranks. They're playing the long game. When these examinees speak, you can't interpret what they're saying as the words of an individual."

"Why don't they just deliver a petition to the governor or noble in their region if they have something to say to Da?" asked Phyro.

"Because . . . they already know how Father will react to the message," said Théra. "Don't they? It's more about the forum."

Soto nodded approvingly. "How often does anyone get a chance to voice an opinion directly to the emperor as well as all the Lords of Dara? The Palace Examination is a rare opportunity for these families. You've just heard what some of the deposed old nobles of the Tiro states think of your father's reign."

Théra nodded. It was as if a veil had been lifted from her eyes. "So that fairy tale from Kita was really a threat. A threat of treason."

Timu looked at her, shocked. "Théra! If that were true, the emperor would have had the guards seize him instead of making a joke. How can you say such outrageous things?"

Soto sighed inwardly. Not all of Kuni's children had the same natural instinct for politics as their father. Patiently, she explained, "The emperor's joke was not directed at Kita. It was certainly not the spoiled princeling's reaction that your father cared about."

"What do you mean?" Timu asked, his expression still one of bafflement.

Soto tried again. "When your father sits down to share a meal with one of his advisers, do you think they're really interested in the food? When your mother invites Consort Risana to attend an opera, do you think they are really interested in the performance? Sometimes the show that is on the stage is only an excuse for a conversation among the audience that would be too awkward without the distraction."

Théra peeked through the seam in the door again. While most of the ministers and governors on the west side of the Grand Audience Hall chuckled, only a few of the generals and nobles on the east side were laughing. Some of the nobles even looked . . . tense.

"Do you think many of the newly enfeoffed nobles are growing restless? Would they ally with the old nobles of the Seven States against my father?" asked Théra. The idea seemed so far-fetched. *Queen Gin and Duke Kimo and Marquess Yemu . . . they are all friends with Father, aren't they?*

"Or perhaps your father *thinks* they are growing restless, which is and isn't the same thing," said Soto. "It's no secret that the empress sides with the governors and the bureaucracy and suspects the nobles and generals. Your father respects her opinion. The joke was the real test."

"I don't understand—" began Timu.

"Or"—Théra bit her bottom lip, deep in thought—"perhaps some of the nobles think that my father suspects them of ambition, and *they* are testing my father by laughing or not laughing."

"Argh!" Phyro wrapped his arms around his head dramatically. "You're making my head hurt. Why do you have to make everything so complicated, Rata-*tika*? If anybody really dared to rebel, Da would just ride out with his army and fix it, the same way he fought the

Hegemon. Auntie Gin will teach them a lesson they won't forget!"

Soto smiled. "It's possible to be *too* clever. In any case, nobody knows the truth in the hearts of these nobles, but that is what everyone is trying to find out. The message delivered by Kita Thu is a stone tossed into a pond, and now everyone in the Grand Audience Hall is trying to read the ripples."

"I don't think we should be discussing such things," said Timu. He looked distinctly uncomfortable.

Soto looked at him pityingly. "What if the emperor makes you crown prince? Then it would be your job to think about such things."

CHAPTER TWELVE

CRESCENT ISLAND

CRESCENT ISLAND: THE FIRST YEAR IN
THE REIGN OF FOUR PLACID SEAS (FIVE YEARS
BEFORE THE FIRST GRAND EXAMINATION).

Except for a few coastal towns and trading ports, Crescent Island was largely unsettled.

The landscape was a patchwork of shield volcanoes with miles and miles of frozen, ropy lava flow on which barely anything grew—as though the gods had carved ruts into a muddy road with massive carriages—and dense forests divided by rugged mountains, where the fauna and flora between neighboring valleys were as different as two islands divided by the open ocean.

In the days of the Tiro kings, the southern part of the island was administered by Amu, and the kings of Amu used it as a royal hunting preserve, though foreign kings and nobles from all over Dara were sometimes given license to hunt there as a reward or gesture of friendship. Mountain deer, lava fowl, white-cap monkeys, and parrots with bright plumage were all favored quarry, though the most prized game of all was the boar, which seemed to develop tusks of different shapes and sizes and coloration in each of the hundreds of valleys on Crescent Island. Some of the kings of old Amu became obsessed with collecting them all and spent more time hunting than administering in Müning, and the Amu poet Nakipo, who was also renowned as a lady of fashion at the Müning court, once wrote:

Crescents by your snout.
Crescent in the sea.
You've seized the king's heart.
My beautiful, wild glee.

The policy of keeping Crescent Island largely wild was maintained under Emperor Mapidéré, and then later, under Emperor Ragin. Initially, Kuni had tried to settle some of the veterans from his wars on new land claimed from the wilderness, but the soil turned out to be mostly poor, and few wanted to be so far away from the rest of civilization. The scattering of coastal settlements were populated with families who found employment as guides and porters for the trophy-hunting parties of the nobles, supplementing their income by fishing in other seasons.

Small garrisons were maintained to keep the island from becoming a haven for pirates, though there were also small villages scattered in the interior of the island populated by descendants of the princes and princesses who had founded tiny principalities on the island during the Diaspora Wars. They paid no taxes to the Imperial Treasury and did not heed the Imperial edicts, and traveling storytellers and court poets attributed to them wild customs and improbable beliefs.

"There!" Zomi shouted, pointing to the southwest. At the foot of a towering cliff was a small clearing with about a dozen tiny thatched-roof houses huddled in a circle.

"That's right, we'll have lunch there and then hike up into the mountains. You can land in the clearing in the middle of the hamlet. The people here recognize my balloon."

Zomi moved away from the dial overhead. "Teacher, I think you should land this."

"Nonsense. *Curious Turtle* is in your hands," said Luan. "Everyone has trouble with their first landing, but the real test is whether you view that as a failure or just a lesson."

Zomi's face flushed, remembering how her first attempt to land the balloon in the coastal settlement of Ingça had resulted in a hard bump against the earth, causing the gondola to tip over, spilling both her and Luan Zya onto the ground like two flopping fish.

She reached up and twisted the dial deliberately, reminding herself to go slow. The breeze was gentle and the balloon was drifting slowly, and as the flame overhead quieted, it lost altitude slowly.

"Keep your eye on the landing spot," instructed Luan. "Envision the line of descent and follow it. Think of yourself as sliding down a slope."

Zomi tried to imagine herself as part of the balloon, reacting to the nudges and bumps of the air currents with minute adjustments to the dial. She was not going to fail and disappoint her teacher.

As the balloon skimmed low over the ground, about fifty feet up, Zomi struggled to lift the anchor—a heavy metal claw attached to a length of silk rope—over the side of the gondola. Her bad leg made it hard for her to get leverage, but Luan did not come forward to help her, knowing that she preferred to do everything on her own.

The anchor dropped, and *Curious Turtle* jerked up suddenly with the loss of weight. But Zomi was prepared and held on to the side of the gondola. The claw of the anchor smashed into the grassy ground with a muffled thump and skipped over the grass a few yards, throwing up clumps of earth until it caught, and the anchor line stretched taut for a moment before drooping gently like a kite line. The balloon was held fast.

"Well done!" said Luan.

As Zomi worked the winch to bring the balloon down to the ground, a few villagers came out of the houses and gazed up at the billowing balloon coming out of the sky like a jellyfish. Zomi noticed their curious clothing: rough hempen robes cut in strange styles, with belts and waist-purses made from animal hide.

"They look like folk opera players dressed in costumes from the Diaspora Wars," whispered Zomi.

"Their ancestors came from Arulugi a long time ago," said Luan. "After generations of living away from the ever-changing fashion on the other islands, they're like a still pool by the side of a rushing river, a world unto themselves."

"You sound like you almost envy them."

"Hmm?"

"Do you want to live like that? Away from everyone else?"

Luan pondered this. "When I've been away from the bustle of the great cities of Dara, I miss their noise and color. When I've spent too much time in them, I miss the clarity and solitude of nature."

"Sounds like you're never satisfied."

Luan smiled. "I suppose that is true. It's complicated."

Finally, the gondola settled on the ground. Zomi extinguished the flame overhead, and the balloon began to lose air and billow in the breeze. Zomi climbed out of the gondola, connected several bamboo segments into a long pole, and pushed against the sagging balloon so that it would fall neatly along the ground and not become tangled.

An old man with a flowing white beard came forward to greet the visitors. Luan climbed out of the gondola as well.

"Weal be hale, all'vry-choon," said the elder.

"Goad 'orrow, Comi," replied Luan. *"Hale thu weal."*

They bowed to each other deeply, and Elder Comi swept his sleeves across the ground between them three times—just like hosts in folk operas about ancient heroes did to greet their guests—and both sat down in *géüpa*.

"What dialect are you speaking?" whispered Zomi as she scampered to sit next to Luan.

"It's the vernacular of Amu."

"It doesn't sound like how the Amu merchants I've met in the markets talk—wait, is this how they talked thirty generations ago?"

"Not exactly. The way we speak changes quickly—have you not noticed how even elders in your village do not speak the exact same way you do? I'm sure the speech of Elder Comi's people has changed over time as well. But because they are isolated, they've managed to retain some pronunciations and vocabulary from the past that others on Amu have lost. I know how to say a few phrases and can understand a few more, but I have not spent enough time to really learn the language."

"So how will you talk?" Zomi asked.

"Watch."

A boy and a girl, both younger than Zomi, came to them from one of the houses. The boy was holding a tray filled with some gray, mud-like substance, and the girl was holding a tray with a crude ceramic teakettle, four cups, and a few dishes of snacks. The children set the trays down between Elder Comi and Luan Zya, bowed, and left.

Elder Comi poured tea for everyone—including a fourth cup for the gods—and gestured for them to taste. Zomi sipped the tea: The infusion was cold, with a floral flavor that was pleasant but unfamiliar.

The elder rolled up his sleeves and picked up a knife on the side of the tray. The edge of the knife was so dull that it resembled a small spatula. He used the knife to carve a grid of squares into the gray substance as though he was slicing a cake. Then he put down the knife and began to sculpt the gray, gooey material in each square with his hands.

"It's clay," said Luan.

Zomi watched, fascinated. The elder sculpted the clay squares into little mounds and pyramids, and then began to carve with the knife.

"Is he *writing*?" whispered Zomi. "These are Ano logograms, aren't they?"

Luan nodded. "Since the zyndari letters simply represent the sounds of speech, I can no more read his writing than understand his speech if he wrote with letters. The Ano logograms, on the other hand, are not tied to the everyday speech of the people, but are frozen along with the departed language of the Ano, which we both know."

"So he's writing the exact same way the first Ano did?" Zomi felt awed at the prospect of seeing someone writing in the same manner as ghosts of people dead for millennia. It seemed like a kind of magic.

"Not exactly. Though Classical Ano is no longer used for daily speech, it is the language of poetry and scholarship, and so it has changed over time to accommodate new words and new ideas invented since the coming of the Ano to these islands. But because Classical Ano is seldom spoken now—and then only by the learned—it is tied to the logograms, which evolve much more slowly than fickle common speech. Even at the time of Mapidéré's Unification, the logograms used by the Seven States were sufficiently similar to each other that it was easy to master another state's logograms if you were properly educated and good at seeing patterns. His logograms are slightly different from the ones I learned, but it is not difficult for me to figure them out. We can converse via clay and knife."

Zomi watched as Elder Comi and Luan Zya took turns shaping the clay and carving them into speech. Elder Comi's sight was failing, and so he read Luan's replies by caressing the logograms gently, using his fingers as eyes.

"What does that first logogram you wrote say?" whispered Zomi.

"What does it look like?" asked Luan, taking a sip from his teacup. "Oh, this plum-morning-orchid infusion is wonderful. I've missed it."

The logogram was simple: a squat cone with three peaks poking up at the top. "A small mountain?" said Zomi, her voice betraying some trepidation.

"That's right; that's the logogram for mountain, which is read as *yeda* in Ano. What about the next one?"

Encouraged by the success, Zomi looked at the next square in the tray with more confidence. This logogram was more complicated: It appeared to depict a little person on the side of a slope.

"Person-on-the-side-of-a-mountain?"

"Which way is the person facing?"

Zomi crouched down to get a closer look. The head of the person was triangular, and the tip pointed to the top of the slope.

"The little guy is heading up the slope, I think." Zomi pondered this. "Climb?"

"Good! Very good! It's read as *cotothu* in Ano." Luan took a bite from a piece of pastry he held with a pair of eating sticks. "You should try this, Mimi-*tika*."

Zomi struggled with the eating sticks for a while, gave up, and picked up a piece of pastry with her hand despite the glare from Luan. It was really good!—sticky rice cake with coconut shavings, and the inside was filled with something that tasted like papaya and yet wasn't papaya.

Still chewing, she managed to say between bites, "So you're talking to the elder about climbing the mountain behind the village?"

Luan Zya smiled. "Good guessing. These are among the first logograms I learned as a child."

"Are all the logograms just sculptures of what they say? These are easy to figure out! Why would you need years of schooling to learn them?"

Elder Comi had finished reading Luan's question. He began to sculpt a response in the remaining squares in the writing tray.

"If you think it's that easy, why don't you tell me what Elder Comi is saying?"

Zomi examined the logograms as Elder Comi's hands and carving knife shaped the clay, one square after another.

"That looks like a . . . scallop shell? But it's in the same square as these two other things . . . Is that a really fat winter melon? And is that a banana leaf?"

Luan coughed and almost dropped his teacup. As he shielded his mouth with his sleeve, his face turned red as he laughed with his eyes until tears came out.

Zomi gave him a wounded look. "Kon Fiji said that it is not proper to laugh at those seeking knowledge."

"Oh, so you *can* remember quotes from the One True Sage when you think they might be useful against your teacher."

"Come on! Explain!"

"All right, all right. Ano logograms are much more than just sculptures of objects. How would you distinguish a hill from a mountain? How would you refer to anything complicated like a new type of waterwheel if you had to give an exact portrait of the thing you're talking about? How would you say anything abstract like 'honor' or 'courage'?"

Elder Comi put down the writing knife and made a *please* gesture at Luan.

Luan flattened the first logograms he had made and began to carve a response while continuing his explanation for Zomi.

"The 'fat winter melon' is actually a closed fist, and the 'banana leaf' is an open palm. A lot of Ano logograms incorporate stylized representations that are easy to carve but aren't very close to the original anymore."

"What does Elder Comi mean when he put a scallop shell next to a closed fist and an open palm?"

"The secret of the Ano logograms is the art of combinations . . . let me think—you like building things, so I'll try to explain this to you the way an engineer would. Tell me, what is a machine?"

Having never given this question much thought—*isn't it obvious what a machine is?*—Zomi struggled to formulate a response. "A machine is a . . . thing with gears and levers and other stuff." *It's really hard to put into words what should be obvious.* "Oh, they make work easier, like the ox-drawn plow is better and faster than a hoe."

"Not bad! The great engineer Na Moji defined a machine in *The Mechanical Art* this way: A machine is an assembly of components put together to accomplish a purpose. But what are components?"

Zomi scrunched up her face in confusion. "I don't understand."

"Think back to the sun-measuring scope you built. You put together two poles, a banana leaf stretched across a bamboo hoop, and a handheld mirror. What are each of those? Do they each have a purpose?"

Zomi thought about this. The two poles formed a cross for support; the bamboo hoop and the banana leaf, modeled on an embroidery hoop and cloth, provided a surface for recording; the mirror, made of a wooden handle attached to a bronze plate, was for reflecting light and casting a clear image. "They are each also . . . machines, made from their own components."

"Exactly! A machine is made from sub-machines, each with its own purpose, and the machine orchestrates all these purposes together to accomplish a new purpose. And you can imagine that your sun-scope can be made into a component of an even larger machine—say, a device for tracing the reflection of an original image onto a new piece of paper: a copying machine."

Luan put down the knife and gestured for Elder Comi to respond.

Zomi's head was reeling. She pictured her crude sun-scope refined and enlarged, attached to a sitting board and an artist's easel and systems of mirrors and lights and supporting struts so that a painting could be copied with exactitude. "That's . . . amaze-licious and wonder-utiful."

"When you constructed your sun-scope, you borrowed a mirror's ability to reflect light, the bamboo poles' resilience and flexibility, and the banana leaf's smooth surface and combined them to do something that had never been done before. Engineering is the art of solving problems by combining existing machines into new machines, and harnessing the effects of the sub-machines to accomplish a novel effect. This is true whether you're a fisherman weaving nets out of ropes and weights, a blacksmith hammering and shaping a plow on an anvil, or a cooper making a barrel from staves and hoops."

Zomi sat there, slack-jawed. She had never heard of the idea of making things described this way. It sounded like art, like the poems sung by the traveling folk opera troupes, like . . . glimpsing the truth of the gods.

"It is possible, Na Moji said, to think of engineering as a kind of poetry. A poet assembles words into phrases, phrases into lines, lines into stanzas, and stanzas into poems. The engineer assembles raw components like nails and planks and ropes and gears into stock components, stock components into contraptions, contraptions into machines, and machines into systems. A poet marshals the words and phrases and stanzas for the purpose of moving the listener's heart; an engineer marshals components and devices and effects for the purpose of changing the world."

Zomi's heart sang.

"The ancient sagas tell us that Man is the word-hungry animal, but I rather like to think of us as the idea-hungry animal. The Ano logograms are the most sophisticated machines ever devised for working with ideas."

Elder Comi set the writing knife down one more time and straightened his back, a smile on his face. *"Well'en. Gramersie."*

"Gramersie," said Luan Zya.

He turned to Zomi, who was still staring at the clay logograms and turning over Luan's words in her head. "Mimi-*tika*, Elder Comi and I have reached an agreement. We will lunch here first, and then he will send a few villagers to act as our guides as we climb the mountain to survey the flora and fauna. Can you help me get the trading goods from the gondola?"

Still a bit dazed, Zomi followed Luan to carry back baskets of goods. Some of them had been brought from Dasu, and others had been bought at the port of Ingça: cast-iron cooking pots, large knives for cleaving meat and chopping vegetables, bolts of hemp cloth, packets of spices, sugar, and salt. She handed them to the boy and the girl, who had come to gather the tea service and used dishes.

Elder Comi stood up and grinned, revealing his surprisingly healthy and strong teeth. *"Hale repast."* He bent to pick up the writing tray.

"Wait!" Zomi shouted.

Luan and Elder Comi both turned to look at her.

"Please leave the writing tray." Zomi gestured at Elder Comi to make herself understood. She turned to Luan. "Can you teach me the logograms?"

Luan chuckled. "I thought you weren't interested in them."

"You didn't tell me earlier they were for engineering ideas!"

ഗ ~ ഗ ~

Being rather far inland, the hamlet didn't offer the fresh fish that Zomi was used to consuming for main meals; instead, lunch consisted of dried fish, small nodules of steamed bread, and rice noodles in a soup of wild greens and melons.

"You never explained how to interpret the logogram with the scallop shell and the two hands," said Zomi, as she sipped the soup.

"Remember to use two eating sticks for the noodles instead of your hands," said Luan. "Kon Fiji said that—"

"Yes, yes," interrupted Zomi. "One eating stick for dumplings and pot stickers; two for noodles and rice; three for fish and fruit and meat so that you can use two of them in one hand to hold the food while dividing it into smaller pieces with the last. And as a woman, I have to take care to always leave my eating sticks on the table so that they lay chastely next to each other when not in use. You've been telling me these rules at every meal! I *have* been listening."

"I know you think these rules are silly, but proper manners, like good handwriting, will soothe the minds of others so that they are more receptive to your ideas."

Zomi picked up two eating sticks and halfheartedly stuffed some noodles into her mouth. Since she couldn't talk with her mouth full—more lessons on manners—she pointed at the logogram impatiently.

Luan laughed, shaking his head. "You truly are hungry for knowledge. All right, think of each Ano logogram as a small machine, made up from components with distinct effects. The scallop shell is a semantic root, which designates the overall semantic domain of the logogram. Since the ancient Ano used shells as their first currency, the scallop shell references all things having to do with trade, finance, and wealth. There are hundreds of these semantic roots that you must learn to master the logograms."

Zomi swallowed the noodles in her mouth. "What about the hands?"

"Chew the food, child! Chew! The hands are more complicated. They are motive modifiers, which means that they narrow and refine the semantic root to point to a more specific meaning. The combination of the open hand and the closed fist is a standard way to represent change or transformation. Putting them all together tells you that this logogram means 'trade,' or *ingcrun* in Classical Ano."

"And that's what you and Elder Comi were discussing!" Zomi said. "You were talking about climbing the mountain, and he proposed a trade."

"That's right. But take a look at this pair of logograms down here." Luan used his eating sticks to point to two other logograms in the writing tray.

Zomi stared at them and muttered to herself. "Hmm . . . both of these seem to have smaller versions of the logogram for 'trade' in them . . . And they both have a flat slablike thing on top . . . are these supposed to be fish fillets?"—Luan almost choked on a mouthful of pastry as she said this—"They look the same, Teacher."

"Do they really?"

Zomi crouched down again, examining the logograms from every angle. "Oh, I see what you mean. The flat fish fillet thing has different symbols carved into them: This one has a semicircle with a line in the middle that ends in a swirl; that one has a semicircle with a line poking between a pair of triangles."

"That's right. The 'fish fillet'—why do you always have food on your mind? Haven't you eaten enough? The 'fish fillet' is called a phonetic adapter. The first logogram is the Ano word *crua*, which means 'to buy,' and the second logogram is the Ano word *athu*, which means 'to sell.' The phonetic adapter is marked with symbols that give you a hint of how the logograms are supposed to be pronounced—in this case, whether the tongue is rolled or positioned between the teeth. Phonetic adapters allow words that are semantically closely related to be distinguished. Indeed, the phonetic adapters inspired our ancestors to invent the zyndari letters. But you still haven't discovered all the details. Examine the 'trade' component some more."

Zomi reached out to explore the logograms with her hands, trying to detect details that were hard to see given the uniform gray of the logograms. "I can see there are other marks and patterns carved into the side of the shell—the semantic root. Do these mean anything?"

"Those are called inflection glyphs, and they mark the conjugation of verbs and declension of nouns, adjectives, and pronouns. In formal writing, they're usually colored to make them easier to see—and also for aesthetics—but in calligraphy, they're often omitted for a more elegant outline. Also, by changing the height or angle of the logograms, a writer can indicate tone, emphasis, and—but we're now probably getting too advanced. You'll pick these up in time."

"So you make complicated logograms out of simpler ones, just like you build a new machine out of machines you already have."

"Exactly!" Luan was finished with his meal and pushed the rest of the dish of pastries at Zomi. "Let's start with a simple example: Take the logogram for 'mountain' and combine it with the logogram for 'fire'"—he quickly sculpted the merged logogram with a few well-placed motions of the knife—"what do you get?"

"A . . . volcano?"

"Yes! All right, let's try something a little more complicated. If you take the logogram for 'volcano' and add the motive modifier for 'blossom,' what do you have?"

Zomi pondered this. "A volcanic flower?"

"You're thinking too literally. Remember how the mirror can be used not just for seeing yourself, but also for projecting an image onto another surface? Think metaphorically."

Zomi imagined a flower blooming . . . and she sped it up in her mind. "A volcanic eruption."

Luan's face exploded into a wide grin. "Yet one more example. What do you get if you use the logogram for a volcanic eruption as a motive modifier, and place it next to the semantic root of air-over-heart, which means 'mind' because the ancient Ano believed that thoughts originated in the heart, not the brain?"

Zomi stared at the new logogram Luan sculpted. The sub-logogram of air-over-heart was formed from a small pear-shaped nodule decorated with three wavy ridges, which rather reminded her of a chicken's brain. "Explosion . . . mind . . . fury?"

Luan laughed out loud. "You're indeed quick! That is why the

Amu poet Nakipo's famous poem 'Fury' is written like this."

He sculpted the poem in the tray: the elaborate logogram for "fury" at the top, and then two lines of four logograms each below it.

Zomi parsed the logograms one by one:

Air-Heart-Fire-Mountain-Blossom
Air-Heart. Fire. Mountain. Blossom.
Fire-Blossom. Mountain. Air. Heart.

"I don't understand. What sort of silly poem is this?"

"You don't recognize all the inflection glyphs or phonetic adapters yet, so let me read it and then translate for you."

Séfino.
Ingingtho ma doéthu. Roaféru phiçan co maca.
Oféré, pharagi co ügidiraü ca géüthéü! Ingingtho co aé ki gophicrupé.

Fury
A mind on fire. A flower of frozen lava.
Open, my stony soul! A breeze over the heart.

"Lovely, isn't it? Nakipo wrote it after an argument with one of her closest friends, and this is deemed one of the finest examples of the imagistic school of poetry popular in old Amu. Each of the poem's two lines is written with variations of the five sub-logograms found in the single logogram in the poem's title, combined in various ways to give rise to new meaning. The poem is a finely crafted machine, as carefully designed as an Imperial airship or a jeweled water clock."

Two young women came toward them from the hamlet. They wore large wicker baskets strapped to their backs and nodded at Luan and Zomi.

"Our guides are here," said Luan.

Zomi seemed to not hear him; she continued to caress the logograms in the writing tray, the unfinished pastry forgotten to the side.

CHAPTER THIRTEEN

MERCHANTS AND FARMERS

One by one, the other *pana méji* were introduced, and they presented their ideas with various degrees of panache. Some put on skits like Kita Thu; some unveiled models or illustrations. One had his servants run around the Grand Audience Hall trying to fly some kites that were supposed to illustrate the elevated tone of his arguments—the lines got tangled and the kites crashed into the balconies, leading to much embarrassment and jokes about the "tangled skein" of his logic. Another chose to engage the Lords of Dara by making them participants in a mini-opera where they'd sing the chorus—that experiment fared about as well as one might expect.

Emperor Ragin quizzed each, jumping from their essays onto new subjects that seemed to interest him more. Now clued in to the true nature of the event, Théra was more appreciative of the stiff, odd answers given by the examinees as well as the subtle flow of power in the Grand Audience Room. It was as if the emperor, the *pana méji*, and all the attendees at court were playing some elaborate game in which a conversation happened beneath the conversation.

The next examinee, Naroca Huza, was from Géjira, Queen Gin's realm. He spoke with the crisp, bright vowels of Gan, and the jade hairpins he wore in his triple scroll-bun gleamed in the slanting rays of sunlight.

"*Rénga*, I will open my presentation with a marvel to honor your wisdom and the diligence of Prime Minister Cogo Yelu."

Naroca's servants unpacked their trunks and began to assemble a massive machine in the middle of the Grand Audience Hall. It consisted of two large vertical spokes on either side, and a massive scroll of paper was installed on the right and spooled onto the spoke on the left. The audience could see that the scroll was divided into large rectangles, within each of which was painted a picture.

In front of the spokes was erected a rectangular frame whose size matched the size of the pictures on the scroll. The top and bottom of the frame were each an axle that turned freely. A pair of flat boards was attached to each axle, like a water mill wheel with only two vanes. These flaps were designed so that the vanes in the top and bottom wheels met just in the middle of the frame. As the wheels spun in synchrony, they acted as two rotating doors alternately blocking the view of the scroll behind them—when the flaps met in the middle—and revealing the scroll—when the flaps were parallel to the ground.

An intricate series of gears and belts connected the spools and vaned wheels to a set of foot pedals connected to cranked wheels to the side. The servants sat down on seats located above the pedals and readied themselves.

Everyone in the hall held their breath, waiting to see what sort of magical feat this strange contraption would perform.

Naroca looked around the hall, satisfied that all attention was directed at him. "You may begin!" He waved his hand forcefully.

The servants began to pedal at a steady pace. The gears and belts transferred their motion to the vaned wheels so that they began to flap open and closed, letting light through in rapid succession. At the same time, the massive scroll of paper began to rotate, spooling the paper from the right to the left.

Everyone in the hall gasped.

The images on the scroll seemed to come to life. A ship appeared to be sailing through a tumultuous sea, laden with bags of grain, bolts of silk, and boxes of other goods. Bravely, the ship made it through rain and lightning to arrive at a dock, where a cheering crowd welcomed the sailors.

Then came a map of the Islands of Dara, and the goods of each region appeared on the map one after another as though drawn there by an unseen hand: the prized fish and crabs of Zathin Gulf; the heavy red sorghum and glistening white rice of Cocru; corals and pearls from the coast of Wolf's Paw; taro and animal pelts from Tan Adü; thick stacks of lumber from Rima; fruits and wines and wool from Faça; incense and silk made in Géjira . . .

And tiny ships appeared on the map, sailing from one region of Dara to another, leaving trails behind like strands of spider silk. Gradually, the Islands of Dara were woven into a whole, connected by the shining trails of the ships that plied its seas. The ships flickered and grew brighter, as though they were meteors leaving brilliant trails in a dark sky.

Abruptly, the animated images stopped. The entire massive scroll of paper had been unspooled from the right to the left, and the loose end of the paper flapped rhythmically against the machine. The servants slowed down and then stopped pedaling.

The Lords of Dara were unwilling to believe that the marvel had come to an end. It was simply too magical.

Luan smiled knowingly. Though the demonstration was impressive, he understood its principle right away. The animated image had been produced in a similar fashion as the rotating lanterns made by folk artists at the Lantern Festival or schoolboy drawings done in the corners of thick codices. Each successive image differed only slightly from the previous one, and when they were moved with sufficient speed behind a flickering shutter, persistence of vision produced the illusion of motion.

". . . if merchants were given the recognition they deserve and the protections they require, then Dara's prosperity would surely follow."

"You're protesting the Imperial edict raising port imposts?" asked Kuni.

"Among other policies," said Naroca.

"I find the suggestion intriguing," said Kuni Garu. "Old Gan, of course, was renowned for its trade ships, but it was the view of Kon Fiji that while farmers, weavers, craftsmen, smiths, and similar tradesmen *made* things, traders simply moved things around and profited from the needs, deprivations, and hungers of others. Your presentation, while marvelous, was sparse on justification. Can you elaborate?"

"That is the best demonstration *ever*," said Phyro. "I wish we could make moving pictures like that."

"I don't think you'd have the patience," said Théra. "Hundreds of artists must have worked nonstop since the Grand Examination to make that. Naroca's family is very wealthy, and this isn't a very subtle display. Father isn't going to like that."

"I thought Da liked traders," whispered Phyro. "He's always going on about how much he did to protect them back when he was the Duke of Zudi."

"Remember that sometimes the emperor must ask questions that aren't his," said Soto, "and sometimes the answers he elicits are meant for other ears."

"The Moralists have much to teach us, *Rénga*," said Naroca, "but the One True Sage lived during a different time, when villages were small and inhabitants never traveled more than ten miles from home. Different times require different wisdom."

"Some truths are eternal verities," said Empress Jia. Her voice was not loud, but it carried crisply across the hall.

Although no one said anything or made a sudden move, Théra

could feel the mood in the Grand Audience Hall shift as everyone perked up their ears.

It was rare for the empress to appear at court, and even rarer for her to speak. The courtly protocols originally designed by Zato Ruthi had adhered to the customs of the Seven States by excluding the participation of the emperor's family from formal court. But Kuni had insisted on including seats for his wives next to his throne, to the protests and consternation of Moralist scholars. It was Empress Jia who proposed the compromise of voluntarily limiting her and Risana's appearance to special occasions, at which she and Risana mostly remained silent.

Naroca bowed to the empress in acknowledgment. "That is true, Your Imperial Majesty. Yet the Moralists do not have a monopoly on truth. The great-spirited Ra Oji once said that the ebb and flow of the sea were at the heart of every search for happiness."

"What does that Fluxist adage have to do with the jangling of coins and bargaining for advantage?" asked Jia.

"The essence of the tides is movement and change. It is the constant flow that prevents stagnation and refreshes life. To say that merchants produce nothing is a misunderstanding. We bring goods from places of abundance to where they're wanted, so that excess may make up for shortage. The tide of commerce fulfills desires and spreads new ideas."

"That is a pretty speech," said Jia. "But coming from the son of Géjira's wealthiest merchant, who is no doubt unhappy with the Imperial edict to raise port duties so as to lower farmers' taxes, one rather suspects its sincerity."

For a moment, it seemed as if Naroca was cowed. But he soon rallied. "All men and women are driven by self-interest. Merchants are simply more honest about this fact. Without profit and trade, fields will lie fallow and mines abandoned—"

"I think the farmers and miners who labor for their food will be very surprised to hear that you claim to be the purpose of their life." The empress did not relent. "Emperor Ragin had settled veterans from the rebellion and the Chrysanthemum-Dandelion War on small plots of land in the hope that they would become self-sufficient farmers leading stable lives. But unscrupulous merchants bought up these plots with promises of quick pay—which many of the veterans quickly frittered away in gambling parlors—and now the former landowners have to scrape for a living as tenant farmers or laborers. Raising the taxes on trade was a way to stop this trend."

"But small family farms are not as efficient as large farms—"

"Oh, do not lecture to me about efficiency! I know well the tricks you employ. Once you've bought up enough plots of land, you turn them into sugarcane fields or silk plantations to make more profit, instead of growing rice and sorghum and vegetables. There are entire regions of Géjira where food has to be imported, a truly bizarre situation for some of the best land in Dara. Staking the lives of entire provinces on the fate of a single crop makes Dara more unstable, and when the crop fails, the unemployed laborers have to resort to banditry. We should heed the lessons taught by the ancient Tiro states of Diyo and Keos well, for Keos fell due to being dependent on Diyo grain shipments."

"Regional self-sufficiency is not desirable, Your Imperial Majesty. You speak of ancient Diyo and Keos, but the patterns of more recent history support my view. Rima declined because it strove for self-sufficiency and achieved only stagnation. Emperor Ragin's Dasu, on the other hand, rose in part because of the pursuit of commerce."

At this, Emperor Ragin chuckled. "Cogo, do you still remember those 'Authentic Dasu Cooks' you trained?"

Prime Minister Cogo Yelu smiled and inclined his head.

Empress Jia ignored this side exchange. "Your arguments dance from Fluxism to Incentivism, and then to Patternism. Yet at its heart, trade is exploitation. When the harvest is good in Géfica, you lower the prices you offer so that the farmers barely make more than they do in other years; when locusts strike Tunoa, you raise the prices you demand so that families must choose between going into debt or starvation. The very word 'trade' is a misnomer—you prey upon misery!

Why is it that the farmers of Cocru who till the fields still go hungry while the merchants of Gan dress in silk and eat meat at every meal?"

"That is but the natural consequence—"

"Silence! Who recommended you for the Grand Examination?"

The arrogant grin on Naroca's face froze.

"Why is Mother so outraged?" whispered Timu. "This isn't like her at all."

"Watch," said Soto. "Sometimes you kick the dog because you're aiming for the master."

"I did," Queen Gin of Géjira intoned coolly—the old Tiro state of Gan had covered both Géjira and Wolf's Paw, though now Wolf's Paw was an Imperial province while Géjira was Gin's charge. "He might be a bit arrogant, but I thought he showed signs of brilliance in his Provincial Examination answers."

"He argues like a paid litigator, with no integrity or steadfastness of principle."

"Lady Jia," Queen Gin of Géjira said, "I apologize for the rash way this young man from my fief spoke." Her tone, on the other hand, suggested no regret at all. "However, is it not the custom at Palace Examinations dating back to the time of the Seven States for the examinee to speak frankly without fear of offense?"

Luan Zya frowned while the other ministers and generals kept their eyes focused on the ends of their noses, not even daring to take a deep breath.

"*Lady* Jia?" the empress repeated, dumbfounded.

"Forgive me, Your Imperial Majesty," said Queen Gin, pronouncing the honorific stiffly. "Sometimes it's hard to change old habits. My mind still acts as it did in the days of old, when the emperor was just Lord Garu and I his marshal." Still seated, she bowed to the empress, though not very deeply, as her stiff ceremonial armor allowed her only a soldier's greeting.

The sheathed sword on her waist clanged against the stone floor, and the sound reverberated in the Grand Audience Hall.

~ ~ ~ ~

Soto shook her head and muttered, "Foolish."

Timu and Phyro looked at her, uncomprehending.

But Théra was thinking, *Is she talking about Mother or Queen Gin?*

"Gin, Jia, *please*," said Kuni.

Jia turned her eyes away from Gin and looked straight ahead.

Gin straightened her back, her sword gently scraping against the floor.

"I hear that you canceled the plan to renovate the palace in Nokida this year, Gin," said the empress, her voice as calm as the stone pool in the garden for the birds to bathe in. "Is the treasury of Géjira in need of assistance?"

"I thank Your Imperial Majesty for being so solicitous of me," replied Gin. "But Géjira is doing just fine. I follow the example of the emperor: A fine palace for me is not as important as the welfare of the people."

"Then you're to be commended for upping your contribution to the Imperial Treasury this year without increasing the burden on the people," said the empress, now a trace of mockery creeping into her voice.

"I know my duty," said Gin evenly.

Though it was impossible to see the expression on Emperor Ragin's face, the way the crown's dangling cowrie strands suddenly clinked against each other was audible to those closest to him. Ever sensitive to her husband's moods, Risana turned to Kuni and almost reached out to hold his hand, but then she remembered where she was and stopped herself at the last moment.

Luan Zya looked at Gin, the grimace on his face growing more pronounced.

"What was that exchange about?" asked Phyro.

"If the emperor has issued an edict to increase port duties, wouldn't you expect the taxes collected in Géjira, filled with wealthy merchants, to go up?" Soto asked.

The children nodded.

"And the portion of the taxes turned over to the Imperial Treasury from Géjira would also go up," said Soto.

"Prime Minister Cogo Yelu is wise to have designed a taxation scheme that harmonizes the needs of the emperor with the needs of the provinces and fiefs," said Timu. "This is just as it should be."

Soto looked at him. "And you've heard nothing in that exchange that you find odd?"

Timu looked back at her, his face confused. "I do not like riddles, Lady Soto."

Soto sighed inwardly again. *Jia has a difficult task in front of her with this child.*

Théra jumped in. "Why would Queen Gin have to put off plans to renovate her palace if the tax revenues were up?"

Soto turned to her and smiled. "A very good question."

Timu struggled to make sense of this. "Are . . . you accusing Queen Gin of refusing to implement the Imperial edict and paying the expected increase in the portion that is due to the Imperial Treasury out of her own pocket?"

"Your mother did say 'without increasing the burden on the people,' remember?"

"But why would she do that?"

I can only explain so much, thought Soto. *I can't hold your hand every step of the way.*

But Théra came to her brother's rescue. "Because she feels the Imperial edict is wrong or because she wants her people to like her— even more than they like Father. Either way, Mother . . . doesn't like it."

"Perhaps we should speak to the next scholar." Consort Risana broke the silence.

Kindly, she gestured for Naroca Huza—who had been forgotten by everyone—to return to his seat. The young merchant's son, relieved that his ordeal was over, rushed back to his place among the other *pana méji* and sat down.

Kuni looked at Risana, who raised her right hand casually and touched the red coral carp earring. The emperor nodded and turned back.

"You may join the College of Advocates," intoned Kuni. "I suspect your perspective will be of great use to everyone at court."

This was certainly not the result Naroca had expected. He stood up and bowed deeply to the emperor and sat back down.

Empress Jia resolutely refused to look at him.

Zato Ruthi, stunned by the heated exchange between the empress and Queen Gin, recovered. "Uh . . . yes. Of course. Next is Zomi Kidosu, of Dasu. Her essay was written in a rough and indelicate hand, yet there was something powerful in the carved logograms that reminded me of the finest stone calligraphers of Xana from centuries ago, who worked with a difficult material in an uncultivated land. I was surprised to find that . . . that . . ."

Gin Mazoti looked at him, amused. Back when Zato Ruthi had been the King of Rima, he had repeatedly declared his disapproval of Kuni Garu's choice of a woman as the Marshal of Dasu, citing Moralist adages about the proper relation between the sexes. However, after the emperor made it clear that he intended to open up the examinations to women and that as Imperial Tutor, he was to teach all the princes and princesses the same curriculum, he had managed to discover new support in Kon Fiji's writings that suggested at least highborn women were *sometimes* suitable for scholarship. Ancient texts were apparently as malleable in the hands of a master scholar as lumps of warm wax, able to bear any construction.

Still, old habits died hard. He must have been pretty surprised to find out that one of the ten *pana méji* selected by him and the other judges was a woman.

"Ahem." Ruthi cleared his throat and went on. "Her essay was bold and original, harmonizing the Fluxists with the Moralists in a way I have never seen before. I think her proposal for reviving the simpler rituals of the Ano sages of old is well worth listening to."

Zomi stood up from the back row of seated scholars.

Whispers and murmurs passed among the assembled ministers and generals. Consort Risana looked puzzled while the empress frowned.

The most surprised of all, however, were Luan Zya and Kado Garu. *She made it!* Luan suppressed the urge to jump up and shout in joy. *Who is she?* Kado thought over the list of names he had been sent. . . .

When she had been kneeling, the sad state of Zomi's attire had been hidden, but now that she was standing and the center of attention, the shabbiness of her clothing was on full display. The hem of her plain hempen robe was frayed, and her leggings showed through a rip. Bits of a harness around her left leg also peeked out, which explained her limping gait.

Luan Zya looked over at her and offered an encouraging smile. She smiled back.

"Why are you dressed so poorly?" asked Emperor Ragin.

"Because I *am* poor," said Zomi.

Zato Ruthi glared at the officials behind the kneeling scholars, who were supposed to be in charge of teaching the *pana méji* court protocol for today.

"We offered to buy her a formal dress for today," said one of them in a trembling voice, "but she refused."

"A piece of jade wrapped in a dust rag remains a piece of jade," said Zomi. "But dog turds wrapped in silk will still stink up the room."

After a stunned moment of silence, Consort Risana's laughter rang out in the Grand Audience Hall. The other *pana méji*, finally realizing that they had been insulted, turned to stare at Zomi angrily.

Smiling behind the curtain of cowrie strands, Kuni leaned forward and said, "Why don't you share with all of us your proposal for reforming Dara?"

The door leading to the corridor banged open. The four eavesdroppers in the changing room turned around and saw little Fara, four years old, standing wide-eyed in the door.

"Are you playing hide-and-seek?" she asked. Then her face broke into a big smile as she jumped and shouted. "Hide-and-seek! Hide-and-seek!"

Her shouting was so loud that it was certain that the people in the Grand Audience Hall heard.

The children looked at each other.

"I told you this was a bad idea," said Timu. "The emperor and the empress are going to be furious!" Then his face looked even sadder as he muttered, "Master Ruthi is going to assign a dozen essays for this, and probably double that amount for me, for not stopping you."

A maid stood in the doorway leading into the corridor, her body quaking with fright. "Lady Soto! I'm sorry! Princess Fara ran away when I went to prepare her snack, and she was too fast for me to catch up."

Soto waved her away. She was just about to tell the children to run off and she would face the emperor's wrath by herself when Théra pulled Fara to her and said, calmly, "That's right. We're playing hide-and-seek, and we just found you."

"But *I* found *you*!"

"It's opposites day. Play along with me." She gestured for Phyro and Timu to leave.

Then Théra pulled the door leading into the Grand Audience Room open, took a deep breath, and shouted. "There you are, Ada-*tika*! What a nice hiding spot you've found! I'm sure I wouldn't have found you if you hadn't cried out. Now, where does this door lead to?"

CHAPTER FOURTEEN

THE HIKE UP THE MOUNTAIN

CRESCENT ISLAND: THE FIRST YEAR IN THE
REIGN OF FOUR PLACID SEAS (FIVE YEARS
BEFORE THE FIRST GRAND EXAMINATION).

What had appeared from the distance as a sheer cliff turned out to have a winding path carved into its face. By pulling on vines and protruding stones, the sure-footed guides, Képulu and Séji, made their way up the mountain.

The two women were sisters, and they kept up a constant stream of chatter as they climbed up the mountain. Though Luan and Zomi couldn't understand what they said, occasional glimpses of their expressive faces and comically exaggerated gestures as they paused from time to time made the teacher and student chuckle. The sisters were excited to go up the mountain for the first time after a long winter: Springtime was good for collecting herbs, wild greens and shoots, and useful insects with medicinal properties.

The path was simply too steep for Zomi's leg, and so Luan strapped her to his back as he followed closely behind the guides, copying their steps and holding on to the same handholds. All four were connected to each other by rope for safety. The necessity for her teacher to carry her dampened Zomi's joy, and bored, she made the mistake of looking down the side of the path once, which made her wrap her arms around Luan's neck and hang on for dear life.

"If you wanted to go up the mountain, why didn't we just fly up there in the balloon?"

"The forest up top is too dense for the balloon to land," said Luan. He tugged on the rope gently to signal to the guides that they needed to stop until Zomi felt calmer. "And it's impossible to get a close look at the things we came to see if we only survey it from air."

After a while, Zomi's breathing returned to normal, and she nodded for the party to keep on climbing.

From time to time, Képulu and Séji paused to collect leaves, berries, lichen, insects, and mushrooms found by the side of the path and store them in the baskets they carried on their backs. Luan would occasionally ask the women to stop and hand him a specimen, which he carefully pressed between the leaves of *Gitré Üthu*—though if the object in question was too thick, he would try to sketch it in the book with a piece of charcoal.

"Why are you so interested in getting up there?" asked Zomi. She was beginning to enjoy the climb. They were high enough that the mist obscured the long drop down, and riding on Luan's back made her feel as though she was floating among clouds.

"Treasure."

"Treasure?" Zomi's heart sped up. *Now this is exciting.* "From pirates?"

"Er . . . not exactly. Though I've been here twice before, this year is different. Over the winter there was a volcanic eruption atop the mountain, and I've never had a chance to observe how nature repairs itself after such a disturbance. Did you notice how dry things were down in the village? I expect that's related to the eruption too." He patted the book in his hand affectionately. "This book may be big, but it is but a pale copy of the book of nature, the greatest treasure of them all."

"You gave up a life in the palace just to travel all over Dara collecting plants and sketching animals?"

"Some like to hunt trophies; I like to gather knowledge."

Zomi thought of her own long walks along the beach and the days she spent wandering through the fields and woods of home, noting the patterns of racing clouds and blooming flowers and murmuring winds, hoping to understand the voices of the gods—yes, odd as her teacher was, Luan was a kindred spirit.

She sensed from Luan's breathing that he was getting tired, and as they were at a relatively flat section of the trail that widened into a small ledge, she pointed to a small bush growing at the side of the path. "What's that?"

"Hmm . . . I'm not sure." Luan pulled on the rope again to ask the guides to stop. "Let me examine it more closely."

"Put me down first so you can climb up to it," said Zomi. Luan gently let her down and made sure she lodged her good foot securely between two rocks and grabbed onto secure handholds.

While Luan studied the plant, Képulu and Séji untied themselves from the safety rope—having made sure to secure it first to the cliff for Luan's protection—and climbed up the dangling vines to reach otherwise inaccessible spots on the cliff face, where they gathered bird eggs, dug out tubers, and sniffed at the succulent leaves of various plants before stuffing handfuls into their baskets. Zomi admired the way they moved about the cliff face as securely as spiders traversing a web. For a moment she was jealous of their perfect, balanced limbs, their powerful muscles and limber sinews—then she pushed the thoughts away. That way lay madness. The choices of the gods could not be questioned.

"This is fascinating," muttered Luan Zya. He took out a knife and started cutting branches from the small bush.

Zomi couldn't see what was so fascinating about it at all. It looked just like the common clinging birch that grew on steep slopes back home in Dasu. She had asked the question only in the hope of eliciting some botanical lecture about a plant she was already familiar with so that Luan would get a longer break from having to carry her, but her teacher treated it like some exotic species that had never been seen.

"What is so special about it?"

"Look at how strong and flexible these are."

Luan now had in his hands a bundle of cut branches, each of which was about a foot long and about the thickness of a finger. He flexed them to gauge their resilience and test for weak spots. Satisfied, he shortened the safety rope and tied it to a rocky outcrop, braced his feet in two depressions in the cliff face, took out some lengths of rope and ox sinew from the sack attached to his waist, and tied the branches together into a framework.

"What are you building?" asked Zomi, curious.

"I've come up with an idea that will help you, but you have to trust me. Can you sit over here, hold on to the vines, and give me your leg?"

Zomi looked at him suspiciously. She did not like it when people paid attention to her weak leg, much less when another person touch it.

"Are you scared?" Luan said, a teasing smile at the corners of his mouth as he held up the strange contraption he had built.

That settled it. Zomi crawled near him, wrapped the vines around her own arms, and held out her left leg with some effort so that it rested in Luan's lap. "I'm afraid of nothing."

"Of course not," said Luan, and he wrapped the framework around Zomi's leg. Once the branches were braced around her calf, he tightened the ox sinew so that the branches dug into Zomi's skin.

"Ouch!" Zomi cried out. But then she immediately bit her lip to stifle the cries.

Luan slowed down so that his movements were more deliberate and gentler. Zomi closed her eyes and gritted her teeth as he flexed and bent her leg in ways that caused her skin and nerves to tingle as though a thousand ants were crawling up her leg.

"While your body is getting used to this, I might as well teach you about the third and fourth schools of philosophy, Fluxism and Moralism."

"You can't even let a single idle moment slide by?" Though her tone was petulant, Zomi was grateful for the distraction.

"Life is short, but knowledge grows ever more abundant. The founding sage of the Fluxists is Ra Oji, the ancient Ano epigrammatist. '*Dothathiloro ma dinca ça noco phia ki inganoa lothu ingroa wi igiéré néfithu miro né othu, pigin wi copofidalo,*' he once said, or 'A Moralist is someone who can tell you how everyone ought to behave except himself.'"

Zomi laughed. "I like him."

Luan took off Zomi's left shoe, placed another set of branches right under Zomi's foot, going from the ball to the heel, and wrapped lengths of sinew around her ankle and foot to hold them in place. He tightened the sinew by twisting another short branch and locked it into the framework wrapped around Zomi's calf.

"Yes, Ra Oji was quite a character. We don't know much about his life except that he was about a generation younger than Kon Fiji. He must have come from a very learned family, as his knowledge of ancient Ano traditions from before their coming to the Islands of Dara was extensive. Many Ano books lost during the Diaspora Wars are known to us now only as fragments that have survived in his poems and parables, and he wrote a lively, moving biography of Aruano, the great lawgiver who created the Tiro states.

"But those accomplishments came later. As a young man, Ra Oji made his name by debating Kon Fiji."

"He debated the One True Sage? I've never heard of such a thing."

"Oh, I think the Moralists don't like to be reminded of how their great teacher could also be challenged."

Luan bent the branches in the brace this way and that, notching some of them with a knife. Then he started to carve two thicker branches, peeling off the bark to reveal the smooth wood below.

"What was the debate about?"

"Kon Fiji came to the court of the King of Cocru to advocate a return to the funeral rites of the ancient past, as practiced on the sunken continent in the west that was the ancestral homeland for the Ano. The rites were rigidly defined for different classes, and involved lengthy mourning periods for the deceased. For instance, a king's death mandated mourning by all subjects in the realm for three years; a duke, one year; a count or marquess, six months; an earl, three months; a viscount, a month; and a baron, fifteen days. The commoners had a different set of rules based on their professions—merchants were at the bottom, and farmers were at the top because Kon Fiji viewed merchants as exploiters who produced nothing. There were also rules about the sizes of the mausoleums, the types of clothing to be worn at the funerals, the number of pallbearers, and so on and so forth."

"These sound about as useful as his rules for how many eating sticks should be used to eat noodles."

"I can tell you'll get along fabulously with the Moralists at the emperor's court."

"Let me guess, Kon Fiji probably also had different rules for men and women."

"Ah, you're thinking like a Patternist—and you'd be right."

"It figures."

Luan fitted the two longer, thicker sticks into the notches in the branches sticking out beyond Zomi's heel, and then connected the other ends to the brace around her calf with strong hoops of sinew.

"The King of Cocru was as skeptical as you. Kon Fiji argued that the rites were important because they enacted and embodied the respect due to each rank. Ranks are made real—the technical term in Moralism is *reified*—through practice. Abstract principles are given life through performance. Just as applying the same rules to friends and foes alike gives meaning to *honor*, giving away possessions supplies content to *charity*, and reducing punishments and taxes provides significance to *mercy*, the adherence to seemingly arbitrary codes of behavior can reify a structure for society that leads to stability."

Zomi pondered this. "But there is no soul to such performances. All that everyone would be doing is acting out roles dictated by Kon Fiji. It wouldn't be real honor or mercy or charity if all the king is doing is following rules."

"The One True Sage would say that just as intent drives action, action can also drive intent. By *acting* morally, one *becomes* moral."

"This all sounds terribly stiff and inflexible."

"That is why the element of the Moralists is the earth, the stable foundation for statecraft."

"What did Ra Oji say?"

"Well, he began his debate by saying nothing."

"What?"

"You have to realize that Ra Oji was a very striking young man, and it was said that when he came into the court of the King of Cocru on that day, all the men and women just gawked."

"Because he was very handsome?" asked Zomi, slightly disappointed. She had been thinking of this Ra Oji, who debated the stuffy old Kon Fiji, as a hero of sorts. That he was handsome seemed to . . . detract from the vision. "Wait, there were women at the court too?"

"Ah, this was in the early days of the Tiro states, when noblewomen were often in formal court to give their opinions. It wasn't until later that the scholars convinced most of the kings that women shouldn't meddle in politics. But to answer your first question: No, it was because he came in riding on the back of a water buffalo."

"A . . . buffalo?"

"That's right, a water buffalo that you'd find wallowing in the rice paddies of a Cocru peasant next to the Liru. In fact, its legs were still caked with mud. Ra Oji sat on its back in *géüpa*, happy as you please."

Zomi laughed out loud at this, wholly forgetting the Moralist prescription to cover her mouth. Luan smiled and did not correct her. He continued to make adjustments to the harness around her leg, and Zomi was growing so used to it that she no longer paid much attention to it.

"The King of Cocru asked in consternation, 'How can you come into the palace on the back of a muddy water buffalo, Ra Oji? Have you no respect for your king?'

"'I am not in control of the buffalo, Your Majesty,' said Ra Oji. 'When our ancestors came to these islands, they let the flow of the ocean's currents carry them wherever the ocean pleased, and likewise, I let the buffalo wander wherever he will. Life is much more enjoyable when I ride the Flow instead of worrying about how many times to brush the ground with my sleeves or how deeply to bow.'

"At this, the King of Cocru realized that Ra Oji was challenging Kon Fiji. So he stroked his beard and asked, 'Then how do you answer Master Kon Fiji's advocacy for a return to ancient rites to achieve a more moral society where each knows his duty?'

"'Simple: Our ancestors came from a continent where the earth dominated everything, and stability of life in small villages was paramount. But we now live in these islands, where the shifting currents of the ocean determine all. Our people must contend with migrating shoals of fish, unpredictable typhoons and tsunamis, and volcanoes that erupt and release rivers of fire—and even the ground trembles at these moments. We've had to invent new logograms to describe new sights, and the only certainty of life is that it's uncertain. With new circumstances come new philosophies, and it is flexibility and resilience, not rigid adherence to tradition, that will serve us well.'

"'How can you say such things?!' demanded Kon Fiji. 'Our lives may have changed, but death has not. Respect for the elderly and honor given for a life well lived connect us to the accumulated wisdom of the past. When you die, do you wish to be buried as a common peasant instead of as a great scholar worthy of admiration?'

"'In a hundred years, Master Kon Fiji, you and I will both be dust, and even the worms and birds who feast on our flesh will also have traveled through multiple revolutions of the wheel of life. Our lives are finite, but the universe is infinite. We are but flashes of lightning bugs on a summer night against the eternal stars. When I die, I wish to be laid out in the open so that the Big Island will act as my coffin, and the River of Heavenly Pearls my shroud; the cicadas will play my funeral procession, and the blooming flowers will be my incense burners; my flesh will feed ten thousand lives, and my bones will enrich the soil. I will return to the great Flow of the universe. Such honor can never be matched by mortal rites enacted by those obeying dead words copied out of a book.'"

Zomi cheered and stood up, shaking a fist.

Luan looked at her, his face breaking into a smile.

Zomi looked down and realized that her left leg was supporting her weight. Incredulous, she gingerly shifted her weight and tested her leg by flexing it. The complicated framework of supple branches and tough sinew flexed as well, lending her strength and support as though magnifying the movement of her atrophied muscles.

"How did you do this?" Zomi asked, awe and wonder in her voice.

"When I used to work with Marshal Gin Mazoti in the emperor's army, we had many veterans who had lost limbs in battle or from working on Emperor Mapidéré's projects. The marshal and I devised artificial limbs to help these soldiers recover some of their lost abilities. I was inspired to adapt one of them for your condition." Luan leaned down and showed Zomi how the sinews and supple branches cleverly stored and magnified the energy from her muscles. "It's acting a bit like a skeleton, but on the outside of your legs instead of inside, giving you both support and mobility."

"You're a magician!" Zomi was getting the hang of it, and she moved around in delight. She felt as though she was swimming in air; she had not been able to move about so effortlessly since the night she was struck by lightning. Though she would still need some help to make her way up the mountain, she should be able to move around on flat ground as though her leg were almost perfect.

She looked back at the kind face of Luan and remembered the secret contraption he had been working on in the balloon. This was clearly not something invented at a moment's notice. How long had he been thinking and working on a prototype in secret? He knew how sensitive she was about her leg, and he hadn't wanted to embarrass her by drawing attention to it until he had figured out a solution.

Spontaneously, she ran up to Luan and gave him a great big hug.

Luan hugged her back.

The guides, who had been quietly observing the construction and testing of the brace, cheered and clapped.

Zomi didn't dare to speak because something seemed to be stuck in her throat and she didn't want to croak like a frog.

∾ ∾ ∾ ∾

Finally, the four of them climbed through the sea of mist and emerged at the top of the cliff. A great, dense forest spread around them, though most of the trees crawled along the ground and were no more than the height of a person due to strong winds at the top of the peak.

They picked their way through this forest. As the guides stopped from time to time to add to the collections in their baskets, Luan hurried over to ask them for explanations of the uses of the plants and fungi, the three conversing by carving logograms in the soil and humus.

Zomi took advantage of her new freedom by wandering around on her own. She particularly loved the birds flitting about on the branches, half-hidden behind the leaves and singing a hundred different songs.

"What's that bird called?" asked Zomi, pointing at a mottled green-blue bird.

"The fluted thrush."

"And that one?"

"Scarlet siskin."

"And that one there with the bright yellow tail?"

"Sun-through-clouds."

As he told her each name, he sketched for her the logograms.

"Some of these birds seemed similar to the birds the Ano knew in their homeland, and so they gave them the same names; others were new, and new words and logograms had to be invented. But see, all the names of the birds have the *bird* semantic root, and so even if you didn't know what the logogram meant, you could guess that it was the name of a bird. This is one of the ways that the Ano logograms can give you hints about knowledge of the world. They are machines that transform the book of nature into models in our minds."

Zomi thought about this, and then asked for the names of various flowers and mushrooms. Luan patiently told her the names and sketched out the logograms on the ground. He loved how curious she was. It made him feel young again.

"Why is the flower semantic root in the logogram for this mushroom?" asked Zomi.

"A matter of history. Back when the earliest logograms were devised, the ancient Ano thought of mushrooms as a kind of plant. It was only much later that scholars and herbalists decided that the fungi were distinct from the vegetable kingdom."

"Yet the error in classification persists in the logograms."

"Knowledge is a vehicle that progresses through errors and blind alleys. It is the nature of history that the ruts left by earlier events persist down the centuries. The wide paved roads in Kriphi follow the course of earlier dirt paths when it was but an Ano fortress, and those roads, in turn, followed the trails of the wandering sheep flocks when it was but a hamlet. The Ano logograms are a record of our climb up the mountain of knowledge."

"But why study the record of errors? Why force generations of students to make the same mistakes?"

Luan was taken aback. "What do you mean?"

"When the Ano came to these islands, they saw new animals and new plants, and yet they persisted in naming and classifying them using outdated machinery, with a system of logograms that was full of accumulated mistakes. They learned that the seat of thought is in the head, yet 'mind' is still written as air-over-heart. Why not start something entirely new?"

"You ask a very good question, Mimi-*tika*. But I would caution that the desire for perfection, for a fresh start, is very close to a philosophical tyranny that disregards the wisdom of the past.

"In the debate between Kon Fiji and Ra Oji, it is not clear-cut that Kon Fiji had the worse argument. True, things are different in the Islands from the Ano homeland, but the hearts of people—with all their ideals, passions, greedy covetousness displayed side by side with high honor, selfish interest driving noble sacrifice—are not. Kon Fiji was not wrong to say that respect for the wisdom of the past, for paths carved out by generations of lived experience, should not be disregarded overnight."

"Hmmm."

"I've never seen you at a loss for words before," said a grinning Luan. "You're actually making Kon Fiji sound like . . . a true sage."

Luan laughed. "I haven't always given you the fairest presentation of the Moralists, I suppose, and that is my fault. But just as the four major schools of philosophy and the Hundred Schools of minor branches of learning all have something to teach us, it is a balance between the new and the old that we must strive for."

"I thought we're striving for Truth."

"We're not gods; we can't always tell truth from error, and so it's better to be cautious."

Zomi looked at the logograms Luan had carved on the ground, unconvinced.

Hidden by the misty woods, Képulu and Séji shouted excitedly from some distance ahead. Luan and Zomi hurried to follow the voices, and the air around them was filled with the acrid smell of smoke and fire.

Growing worried, Luan wanted to stop and assess the situation, and he called out for Zomi to slow down. Still a bit uncoordinated, she stumbled ahead on her brace but refused to heed Luan's admonitions. Luan had no choice but to rush to follow behind.

They emerged into a narrow clearing like a scar in the forest.

And a scar it was. The volcanic eruption had carved a burnt tongue into the green flesh of the mountain. The thick, ropy solidified lava, like the mythical River-on-Which-Nothing-Floats, should have been devoid of life and vegetation. It would take years before life would recover in this inhospitable landscape.

But instead of a black surface filled with folds and twists like the shell of a giant walnut, the lava flow was bright red, as though it was still fresh from the depth of the earth. The smell of smoke and burning was overwhelming.

Startled, Luan reached out to pull Zomi back from danger before noticing that Képulu and Séji were dancing in the middle of the burning lava.

"Those are flowers!" said Zomi, and she pulled free of Luan and danced onto the bright red lava flow.

Luan looked again and realized that indeed, the entire surface of the lava flow was filled with a carpet of bright red plants. Each plant was about a foot high, and shaped like spikes of hyacinth. The leaves, stems, and flowers were all fiery crimson, with bunches of scarlet berries dangling from spikes where the flowers had wilted.

Luan plucked some of the berries and found them to have a hard finish, almost like lacquered beads. The flowers exuded a strong fragrance that was spicy and smoky, as though the plants were burning. The smell from the berries was fainter, but still strong. The entire plant was like a miniature flame.

"Careful of the fumes," said Luan. "Don't breathe in too deeply. I'm no expert herbalist, but such strong and unusual smells generally indicate poison or mind-altering capabilities."

Képulu and Séji carefully gathered some of the plants for their collection. Luan looked at the specimens they showed him and saw that the roots, also a faint red, spread out like strands of spider silk and clung to the inhospitable rocky surface. Only with a faint pop did the roots detach from the rocky surface. This was a tenacious plant that made its home where no other flower dared to tread, a floral pioneer.

"What are these called?" asked Zomi.

"The eruption occurred sometime last fall, and our guides say that they have never seen this plant before. It is a brand-new discovery!"

Képulu and Séji chattered excitedly at Luan, and then made a *please* gesture. Seeing the confusion on his face, they quickly sculpted some logograms on the ground. Luan grinned.

"They've asked me to give this plant a name. That's a high honor."

"What will you name it then?" Zomi asked.

Luan pondered the plant and smiled. "Since this fiery plant is so impatient to explore lands where others fear to tread, why don't we name it zomi, for Pearl of Fire?"

Zomi laughed, delighted, and gathered more of the berries to stuff into her pocket. "I will make a necklace of these to wear."

Luan stood up, thinking that he would ask the guides to gather more of the plants for study back at the hamlet, but the faces of the women, frozen in shock, made him pause. He turned to look in the direction of their gazes and saw thick columns of smoke rising in the direction they had come from.

CHAPTER FIFTEEN

A REBELLION OF SCHOLARS

Kuni turned around on the throne and called out, "Théra? Is Timu with you too?"

A moment later, a quivering male voice replied, "*Rénga*, your faithful servant is here. I am terribly sor—ARGH—*mmf*—"

The muffled gurgles—as though a hand had been clamped over his mouth—played a bass line to the whispering voices of other children engaged in urgent debate, with occasional phrases loud enough to be heard by the assembled Lords of Dara.

"... shut up ... the plan ..."

"... I'm not leaving ..."

"... obey! ... Big Sister ... *trust me* ..."

"... better together ... *no essays* ... my fingers will fall off ..."

And a four-year-old's girlish giggles punctuated it all.

The atmosphere in the Grand Audience Hall now resembled that of a children's playroom. Jia and Risana looked mortified; the ministers and generals and nobles struggled to maintain serious miens, their bodies shaking with suppressed laughter.

Zato Ruthi trembled with rage as he stood up and headed for the changing room behind the throne dais with long strides, his hands fumbling through the folds of his robe for the ferule that he usually kept with him—though regretfully he had left it in his room today because it interfered with the clean outline of his formal court attire.

But Kuni gestured for him to sit back down.

"You might as well all come in," the emperor called out. The urgent whispering of the children ceased. "This is a formal occasion where the presence of children is usually unwelcome, but I think Timu, at least, is old enough now to be exposed to more affairs of state."

The heavy curtains behind the throne parted, and the children streamed out with Lady Soto at the end.

"Children go where they will," said Soto, as though that explained everything.

Kuni nodded. "They do have quick feet. Perhaps the gods led them here today for a reason." After a pause, he added, a hint of a smile in his voice, "A child who takes no risks is not going to lead an interesting life."

"I'm *so* sorry, Father," said Théra. "Fara is too young to know better, and I was too caught up in the game to realize she was hiding in a room she wasn't supposed to be in."

Fara took in the large number of people in the hall and then buried her cute, innocent face in the skirt of the dress of her big sister, who put her arms around her in comfort.

"So many people here, Da," said Phyro. "We had no idea!" He also looked around, hamming it up by opening his eyes as wide as saucers.

Kuni pushed the strands of cowries dangling in front of his face aside and smiled at Phyro. "The Lords of Dara are here to celebrate scholarship. You should be inspired by their example and be more diligent!"

"*Rénga*," said Timu, bowing deeply. He was very nervous—as he always was—in front of his father, and though his lips kept on moving, no more sound would emerge.

"You're here," said Kuni. It was hard to tell by his tone if it was a simple observation, an encouragement, or a lament. After a moment, he let the cowrie veil fall back in place. "All of you, sit at the base of the dais and observe."

Jia frowned. Of course the silly performance by the children did not for a minute fool her into thinking they hadn't been deliberately eavesdropping—Timu was always terrible at lying, a personality trait that had both benefits as well as drawbacks. But at least Théra's explanation offered everyone a way to avoid losing face. She resolved to speak later to Soto and Dafiro Miro, Captain of the Palace Guards, about better security procedures within the palace.

Kuni turned back and was just about to pick up the conversation with Zomi when a loud clang came from somewhere far away. It sounded like hundreds of gongs were being struck. The Grand Audience Hall quieted, and now the assembled lords could hear the faint sounds of a crowd shouting in the distance.

"What's happening?" asked Risana. Color drained from her face.

Kuni glanced at Dafiro Miro, who was standing to the side. The Captain of the Palace Guards nodded and beckoned to one of the guards, who left the Grand Audience Hall in a jog.

"Let's continue with the examination," said Kuni, whose voice revealed no anxiety. He turned back to the almost-forgotten *pana méji* standing before him. "Zomi Kidosu, you have the floor."

Everyone's attention was drawn back. Given the poor state of Zomi's dress, no one expected a spectacular presentation. A few of the generals stifled yawns as they prepared themselves for a long speech.

"I have already begun my presentation," said Zomi.

"You have?"

"The best of the best in Dara are rioting in the streets. *That* is my presentation."

The Lords of Dara perked up their ears. Now *this* was getting interesting.

"The *cashima* who failed to place in the ranks of the *firoa* are assembling in Cruben Square in front of the palace to protest," Zomi said. "Judging by the noise, they have drawn many onlookers, some of whom may take advantage of the situation to engage in a bit of looting under the theory that the law cannot punish a mob."

"You *started* this riot?" asked Kuni, his tone severe.

"I may have been the spark that began the fire," said Zomi. "But trust me, I was not responsible for the dangerous accumulation of fuel."

Kuni glanced again at Dafiro Miro, who started to head for the exit to the Grand Audience Hall.

"Captain," said the empress, "you may need to summon the city garrison. A riot in the streets must be swiftly put down."

"No!" Kuni said.

Dafiro Miro halted and turned back to look at Kuni and Jia.

"They are just students," said Kuni. "Whatever happens, do not harm them."

Jia narrowed her eyes, but she said nothing.

Dafiro nodded, turned around, and left.

Kuni turned back to Zomi Kidosu. "Since you call yourself a spark, what, exactly, is their grievance?"

"They think the Grand Examination has not been fairly administered."

"What?" Zato Ruthi sputtered.

"I'm simply repeating the whispered complaints among the examinees," said Zomi. She looked at the other *pana méji* in the hall. "My colleagues can confirm."

Ruthi looked to the seated examinees; they nodded reluctantly.

Still kneeling, Ruthi shuffled around to face the emperor and bowed so deeply that his forehead touched the ground. "*Rénga*, I and the other judges are willing to have all our records re-examined. I assure you there has been no favoritism."

"Sit up," said Kuni. "I'm not going to doubt your work because of a few hotheaded students who can't bear the thought that they're not as intelligent as they think."

"But this is a serious charge, *Rénga*! I cannot have my good name sullied in this manner. I demand that you order a full audit of the process we used and a rejudging of the Grand Examination essays. You will find that we followed the most exacting procedures to ensure fairness—"

"There's no need for that," said Kuni.

But a red-faced Zato Ruthi went on, spittle flying from the corners of his mouth as his sentences piled into each other. "Prime Minister Cogo Yelu and I came up with the most scrupulous, careful process. We ordered the clerks who collected the essays to examine each one to be sure that the students followed the rules and left no identifying marks—any violators were immediately disqualified. Only the anonymous essays were brought to the judging panel.

"Each essay was assigned a random number in the judging queue so that the order in which the essays were read would bear no relationship to the stall assignments of the examinees, further preventing judges who were present at the examination hall from being able to guess the author. The seven judges on the panel and I read all the essays and independently assigned each one a score between one and ten. The final score was determined by tossing out the highest and the lowest scores for each essay and summing up the rest. I am utterly confident that there is no basis to sustain a charge of bias."

"I *know* that," said an impatient Kuni. "Master Ruthi, you're fair to a fault. Even back when you faced Queen Gin on the battlefield, you would not attack her until she had rested her troops and arranged them into formation. Of course I give no credence to the charges of these sore losers."

"That is fairness only in the method, not substance," said Zomi.

Everyone stared at the young woman, stunned, but she gazed fearlessly at the emperor.

"You—you—" Ruthi was shaking so much that he had trouble getting the words out. "Wh-what are you saying? This has nothing to do with your essay!"

"My essay was merely a pastiche of your old ideas—the best way to please a judge is to regurgitate his own ideas back at him in new clothing—of course I won't present *that* to the emperor."

Ruthi's eyes bulged, as did the eyes of practically everyone else in the hall. This young woman was either beyond bold or insane.

But she went on as though she hadn't said anything surprising. "Master Ruthi, can you tell us how many of the *cashima* examinees who entered the Grand Examination were from Haan?"

Ruthi shouted at the palace guards, who scrambled to follow his orders. A few minutes later, a young palace guard brought Ruthi a thick ledger. The elderly scholar flipped through the pages until he found the list of examinees by region of origin and counted. "Seventy-three."

"And how many were from Wolf's Paw?"

"A hundred and sixty-one."

"From Rui?"

"Ninety-six."

Zomi nodded. "That's about what you'd expect based on their respective populations. But out of the hundred *cashima* who achieved the rank of *firoa*, how many are from Haan?"

Ruthi flipped to another page in his ledger. "Fifty-one."

"From Wolf's Paw?"

"Ten."

"From Rui?"

"There were no *cashima* from Rui who achieved the rank of *firoa* this year."

Zomi nodded again. Then she looked at the nine other *pana méji* seated near her. "Can you tell me where you're from?"

"Haan."

"Géjira."

"Haan."

"Wolf's Paw."

"Haan."

"Haan."

"Arulugi."

"Faça."

"East Cocru."

Zomi looked around the Grand Audience Hall, her eyes flashing. "I am, of course, a daughter of Dasu. Master Ruthi, you're from Rima, and the Prime Minister is from Cocru, but where are the other six judges on your panel from?"

"One is a learned scholar from Arulugi, and the others are all famous teachers in Haan."

Zomi gazed at the emperor. "I think the numbers speak for themselves."

"What do you think you've proven by this recital?" sputtered the fuming Zato Ruthi. "I'm a man of Rima. If I were as unscrupulous as you intimate, wouldn't I have elevated at least one scholar from Rima into your exalted rank?"

While Ruthi's voice grew louder like a raging storm, Zomi kept her voice as calm as a glacial pool. "Master Ruthi, I do not impeach your integrity. But an honest man may still administer an unfair examination."

"What does it matter where the judges are from when we *couldn't tell who wrote each essay*?"

"Can you not see how the results appear in the eyes of the people of Dara? When the distribution of honors is so lopsided, one must presume a flaw in the process. It is substance that matters, not procedure."

Ruthi was so angry that he started to laugh. "You speak like that fool in Kon Fiji's fable who lamented that copper was not valued as much as gold. Far from indicating bias, the numbers you point to actually prove that the panel did their job!

"It is well known that the people of Haan are dedicated to learning and scholarship, and the Ano Classics are taught to children as young as two. Rui, on the other hand, has few academies of renown, and the rulers of old Xana were never as devoted to the pursuit of wisdom. This was why Mapidéré had to recruit Lügo Crupo from Cocru and why even Emperor Ragin, when he was King of Dasu, had to scour the rest of Dara for talent.

"The *cashima* represent the best minds of each province, but when they are gathered in one place, it is natural that the *cashima* of Haan would excel the *cashima* of Rui or Dasu. Do you complain that the apples in the orchards of Faça are bigger than those from Cocru? Or that the crabs caught in the Zathin Gulf are tastier than those caught off the shore of Ogé?

"I'd think something had gone horribly wrong if *not* as many Haan scholars had achieved the top rank."

"Is Haan all of Dara? Are the people of the other provinces of Dara of less worth?"

Ruthi slammed his ledger onto the floor and gesticulated wildly with his arms. He was beyond caring about decorum and appearances. "The emperor's charge to me is to seek men—and women—of talent. I have faithfully carried out my duty. Your presence here is proof that the method is sound. Though you're from a humble land of illiterate peasants, yet today the emperor and all the Lords of Dara have lent you their ears!"

"'Talent' is a loaded word," said Zomi. "Is it truly talent that the examination measures or mere habits of mind?"

Ruthi laughed. "I'm familiar with that criticism of the examinations. Indeed, as a young man, I disdained the civil service examinations of Rima for the same reasons. Rima's exams required students to regurgitate obscure epigrams from Ra Oji or fill in less-known dialogues by Kon Fiji. The only skill that truly mattered was memorization, and the narrowness of focus disgusted me.

"That is why I have redesigned the Imperial examinations to reward creativity, insight, boldness of thought, and refinement in expression. Do you think it's possible to do well on the exams without a mind as sharp as the writing knife or as supple as heated wax? To know how to craft an argument, to support it with clever allusions from the Classics and well-drawn examples from life, to consider and anticipate opposing points of view—all while planning for the practicalities of fitting the logograms into a constrained space and making the most of limited resources under great pressure—this *is* a test of true talent."

Zomi shook her head. "You see but the sun-dappled surface of the sea instead of the Hundred Fishes beneath. The examination prizes beauty of expression and fine calligraphy as well as sharpness of argument, but do you not see that these are judgments shaped by habit?

"For years, you and the other judges have studied together and read each other's essays until you have formed a consensus of what is persuasive and what is pleasing. You have then taught these to your students, who in turn taught theirs, propagating a certain ideal. This ideal is most concentrated in the academies of Haan but thin elsewhere. What you call beauty and grace and suppleness in writing are nothing but the consensus of men who have grown used to hearing each other. When you judge an essay good, it is only because the words seem to you to echo your own thoughts. Even if you cannot see the faces behind the logograms, you pick men who are just like you! I am here because I learned to write as the image in the mirror you so love!"

Ruthi stared at Zomi, eyes bulging and breath labored. "You arrogant, disrespectful child—"

Before he could finish, Dafiro Miro entered the hall. "*Rénga!* I have urgent news."

CHAPTER SIXTEEN

FIGHTING FIRE

CRESCENT ISLAND: THE FIRST YEAR IN
THE REIGN OF FOUR PLACID SEAS (FIVE YEARS
BEFORE THE FIRST GRAND EXAMINATION).

By the time the four of them made their way down the tortuous cliff path back to the hamlet, the place was in chaos.

About a mile distant, a semicircle of gigantic, roaring tongues of flame licked the sky, and roiling columns of smoke drifted over the clearing, obscuring the houses and making it hard to breathe. Even at this distance, the heat was palpable.

A nobleman stood next to *Curious Turtle* with a retinue of about a dozen men dressed for the hunt. A few carried the tusked heads of boars, whose dead eyes stared at the world in a permanent grimace of rage.

"Get this balloon ready!" shouted the nobleman, who was coughing and gasping for breath. His men scrambled to obey, and it was evident that all of them had just run hard through the woods to get here.

A few yards from them, Elder Comi stood with the rest of the villagers, looking on mutely.

"Don't just stand there!" shouted the nobleman. "Why don't you organize the peasants to go fight the fire?"

The villagers looked at him, uncomprehending.

Fighting a forest fire like this is utterly preposterous, thought Zomi.

"Get shovels and buckets and whatever else you can find!" declared the nobleman. "If you concentrate your efforts, you may be able to delay the fire long enough for the balloon to take off."

The villagers looked at each other, but no one moved.

"Oh, by Tututika's blood! These savages don't understand human speech." He jumped up and down and mimed shoveling dirt onto fire and pouring buckets of water. He raised his voice, as though this would help the villagers understand him. "Go on! Go! I'm the Earl of Méricüso. Are you afraid to die? It's an honor to die for the life of a great lord!"

Elder Comi turned away from him. He spoke to the villagers in a low but firm voice, and pointed at the cliffs. A few of the young women and men shouted at him and shook their heads. The elder smiled, pointed at his legs, and sat down with some difficulty on the ground in *mipa rari*. He bowed his head, pointed to the cliffs again, and spoke resolutely.

As Luan and the others ran to join the commotion, Zomi had the eerie feeling that she was watching a folk opera being performed. When she had first been exposed to the operas, she had found the lyrics, with their flowery language and complicated vocal decorations, hard to understand, and she had filled in what was happening by using the expressions of the players and their body language as clues. She could seize the strands of emotion in the air and color in the blanks.

Children, the village is doomed. Houses may be rebuilt and gardens replanted, but people cannot be replaced. Go and escape by the cliff route.

But Grandfather, you won't be able to make it with your legs.

Do not trouble yourselves about me. Go on. Go!

Zomi felt her eyes grow warm and her throat constrict. She was thinking of her mother, and how she would behave if a fire approached and Zomi couldn't get away because of her leg.

"You'll never get the balloon up if you tangle it like that," Luan calmly told the soldiers, who, being inexperienced with the workings of a hot-air balloon, were making a mess of things.

Glad to find someone whose speech he could actually understand, the nobleman immediately ran over and grabbed Luan by the lapels. "Is this your balloon? Excellent! Excellent! Quick, get it ready to fly."

"What happened?"

"I came to this benighted valley because I heard that there were boars here with tusks in a pattern no one had captured. Since some of the boars were hiding deep in the woods, one of my followers had the clever idea to start fires to drive them out."

"Don't you know how dangerous that is with such a dry spring?"

"The idea worked! I got six excellent trophies. It's not my fault that the wind shifts so quickly around here. We had to leave behind everything at our camp and barely managed to escape with our lives. Thank Tututika that you're here!"

Luan shook his head. He and Zomi ran to straighten out the tangled balloon and to start the liquor-fueled stove. As the flame roared to life and the balloon began to fill, the nobleman and the soldiers cheered.

"It is best to start loading the gondola," said Luan to the Earl of Méricüso.

"But this gondola is so small!"

"Toss out anything that is not necessary for flight. Get rid of the beds, the blankets, the food and water, and anything else you can free," said Luan, exasperated.

"Right. Right. Good thinking!" said the earl.

As the soldiers scrambled to obey the earl and tore out everything that wasn't bolted down in the gondola, Luan and Zomi continued to use the bamboo poles to straighten out the balloon so that it could be filled evenly with hot air.

"Mimi-*tika*," whispered Luan. "Our first priority is to save Elder Comi's life. He can't climb the cliff to escape, so this balloon is his only chance. Later, no matter what I tell you to do, you have to obey, do you understand?"

"What are you thinking?" Zomi's guard was up. Luan's tone was too strange.

"Don't argue! You're the student. You must obey."

"I won't obey an order that is wrong!"

Luan laughed. "Now you sound like a Moralist. It was Kon Fiji himself who said that the duty to the Just and True supersedes all others, even a command from a teacher. I thought you didn't like Kon Fiji."

"Even an idiot can be right sometimes."

"Ha! I dare say Kon Fiji never thought he'd be defended in these terms."

The earl and his soldiers had finally succeeded in stripping the gondola of everything. They scrambled to pile in. Four of the soldiers sat on the bottom and crossed their arms to form a comfortable seat for the earl. The rest of the soldiers either climbed in and stepped on top of their comrades or hung on to the side of the gondola.

"Careful! Careful! Don't damage the tusks!" shouted the earl as the boar's heads were loaded in and carefully held up by the men around the earl. Luan shook his head at the ridiculous scene.

"Who told you that you get to fill the balloon with only your people?"

"The villagers can climb the cliff. That's what they want to do anyway."

"Why can't you climb the cliff instead? You are fit and strong."

The earl looked at Luan as if he were crazy. "Who knows how long I'll be stranded on top of that mountain? These trophies won't be properly preserved if I don't get them to a taxidermist in time."

Luan put a hand on Zomi's shoulder to restrain her. "You have to make room for Elder Comi at least," he said. The balloon was almost filled, and it strained against the tethering stake on the ground. "And Zomi and I have to be in there to pilot the balloon, unless one of you knows how to fly it. I warn you, fire can do strange things to air currents, and you need an experienced pilot."

The earl looked at Luan and Zomi suspiciously. "This girl knows how to fly the balloon? I don't want someone useless in here."

Luan looked at the cringing flunkies holding up the earl's muscular thighs and bit back a sarcastic remark. Instead, he simply said, "She's young, but she's an excellent pilot."

The earl's lips parted in a cold grin. "Then I won't need you both, will I? Seize her!"

Several of the men hanging on to the side of the gondola hopped down to the ground, grabbed Zomi, and dragged her back to the gondola. Zomi screamed and kicked, but she was not strong enough to overcome the men. Luan rushed over to help, and one of the men unsheathed his hunting knife and slashed at Luan, who stumbled and fell to the ground.

The villagers rushed over. Without saying a word, Séji ripped open Luan's leggings to reveal the sickening wound in his thigh. While she ripped strips from Luan's robe to fashion a tourniquet to stop the bleeding, Képulu rummaged through her basket for leaves that she chewed into a poultice, applied it to the wound, and bandaged the leg.

Meanwhile, the earl's men maneuvered the screaming Zomi into the gondola. The four "cushions" shifted to make space so that she was directly under the dials and levers for controlling the balloon's stove, and then they squeezed in and held her legs so that she was trapped next to the earl and his pile of boar trophies.

"Let me go!" Zomi shouted. "I won't fly the balloon for you."

The angry villagers shouted and approached the balloon. The earl's men unsheathed their hunting knives and brandished them threateningly.

"Stop!" Luan shouted to make himself heard above the commotion. There was such a natural authority in his tone that both sides halted. In a calmer tone, he continued, "Mimi-*tika*, listen, you have to fly the balloon without me."

"Absolutely not! I'm not leaving here without you."

"We must save Elder Comi! We can dangle a harness under the gondola to carry him to safety. The rest of us can make our way up the cliffs."

"You can't climb the cliffs with your leg like that!"

"Sure I can!" Luan got up. Séji reached out to support him, but he pushed her away, and stood as straight as a crane. "You managed to climb the cliff before with a brace, and I can do the same. Do not underestimate the medical arts of the villagers."

Zomi still looked skeptical, but she was calming down. Maybe this was a solution after all.

"Hurry, hurry!" shouted the earl. "If you want that old peasant saved, do it now!"

As Luan explained what he wanted with gestures and roughly carved logograms on the ground, the villagers quickly fashioned a harness out of sticks and pelts to support Elder Comi and to tie it to the walls of the gondola.

The balloon was almost completely filled, and the earl's men pulled in the anchor. The gondola wobbled on the ground, held only by a tethering line.

"Mimi-*tika*," said Luan, "we don't have much time. I have one more lesson for you."

Zomi stared at Luan in disbelief. She couldn't understand why her teacher was choosing this moment to engage in another philosophy discussion. *And why is he just standing there?*

"No matter what else you think of the Moralists, their core belief is right: Sometimes you must do the right thing even if it hurts you. Actions reify ideals. We must never stop striving to do good, to protect the weak and the powerless. This is the charge to all men of learning."

Zomi nodded, but she continued to stare at the stiff figure of Luan. Having dealt with a weak leg all her life, she was sensitive to the way people distributed their weight on their legs.

"You're a brilliant young woman, Mimi-*tika*. You have the curiosity to seek out the terra incognita beyond the bounds of dogma, and you have the quickness of mind to cut through a thicket of confusing questions. But you're like a raw ball of wax, undisciplined, unshaped, unpurposed. You must apply yourself to the tedium of study, which is like the carving knife, to shape your mind into an intricate logogram for processing ideas. Do you understand?"

Zomi nodded, not really listening. *Teacher really is standing like a crane, with all of his weight on one leg.*

"Go, go, go!" shouted the earl.

The villagers had finished tying Elder Comi's harness to the gondola. They backed away from the wobbling balloon, which was being buffeted by strong winds. The smoke had grown thicker and the fires closer. One of the earl's men cut the tethering rope.

"Get your passengers to safety, and when the fire is burnt out, you can come and retrieve me on the other side of the mountain. Watch the wind currents carefully, and fly as high as you can!"

Zomi put her hands up to the dial and turned the stove output to maximum. As the fire roared overhead, the balloon struggled to lift off.

"Go, go!" Luan gestured at the villagers. When the villagers refused to move, he grabbed a carrying pole from one of them and began to write on the ground.

He's not even bending down, thought Zomi.

The balloon's ascent jerked to a stop. Elder Comi's harness dragged along the ground, failing to lift off.

"There's too much weight!" shouted the panicking earl. "Cut off the harness."

"No!" Zomi said. "We have to save the elder. Why don't you ask one of your men to jump off? They're much heavier and they can climb the cliffs."

"How dare"—but realizing that Zomi was necessary for them to get out of the maelstrom of scalding winds buffeting the balloon, the earl swallowed his curse—"you can't possibly think a wild peasant's life is worth more than one of my servants."

"Then toss your boar's heads out! The six of these must weigh more than the elder."

"Absolutely not! They are the whole reason we came here." The earl gave the men around him a meaningful look, and one of them swung his hunting knife quickly and severed the lines tying the harness to the gondola while the rest held on to Zomi to prevent her from doing anything.

"Damn you! I will ki—" One of the men slapped her hard to choke off any more outraged words. Zomi was momentarily stunned.

The gondola tumbled crazily as the balloon finally lifted off.

Zomi recovered and looked below through the tangle of arms and boar's heads and the earl's hateful face. Elder Comi struggled out of the remnants of the harness while some of the villagers ran over to help him. And Luan, still standing in the same place, continued to write on the ground with his pole as the rest of the villagers watched. The carrying pole's awkward length meant that he had to carve the logogram in broad strokes, and even from the height of twenty feet, Zomi could see what he was writing.

It was a single logogram composed of three components:

A river flowing. A volcano. A stylized outline of a flame.

The Flow. The red volcano, the symbol of Lady Kana, goddess of fire, ash, cremation, and death. But skin-of-fire? What's that?

"I have to pilot the balloon," Zomi said to the earl, and then coughed uncontrollably. She sounded frightened. The smoke had grown so thick by now that it was hard to see the sky. The roiling columns twisted about in complicated patterns, marking the chaotic air currents that made the gondola swing about wildly so that all of the earl's men had to hold on for dear life.

Thinking that the girl had finally come to her senses, the earl nodded for his men to let her go. Zomi adjusted the dial so that the flame was lower, slowing the ascent of the balloon.

"What are you doing?" the earl asked, alarmed.

"Wrestling a pig, of course." Zomi grabbed one of the heads and slammed it into the earl's face, aiming one of the tusks at his eyes. As the earl screamed and the men in the gondola scrambled to protect him, Zomi turned the dial all the way up, causing the gondola to jerk suddenly, tossing the men in the gondola into a jumbled heap. She scrambled over them and climbed over the side of the gondola and let go.

"Mimi!" Luan cried out.

Though she tried to roll as she made contact with the ground, she heard the bones in her left leg snap and felt the sharp stab of pain a moment later. She couldn't move. She couldn't even breathe.

Luan dropped his pole and tried to get to Zomi, but his leg collapsed, and he fell to the ground. Séji and Képulu rushed over, ripped the now useless harness from around her leg, and worked quickly to set the broken bones and stabilize the break with splints.

Zomi finally managed to recover enough from the fall to suck in a lungful of air. She screamed with the pain.

Overhead, the balloon continued to ascend as the men hanging on the outside of the gondola screamed, digging their fingers into the wicker with every ounce of strength. The earl's curses came to them in a hailstorm that grew fainter as the balloon continued to rise, twisting about in the hot winds.

Luan crawled over to Zomi on his hands and one knee, dragging the useless leg behind him.

"How could you do such a stupid thing as to jump from the balloon? Why don't you ever listen to me?"

"Because you lied!" Zomi screamed back. "You couldn't even walk, but you told me to get in that balloon to fly that pig to safety. And he dropped Elder Comi anyway!" As Luan sat up and tried to cradle her, she slammed her fists against his chest, on his shoulders, at his arms.

"It is the duty of the learned—"

"You lied! You were going to send me away and die here! My father abandoned me for duty, but I will *never* abandon someone I love for duty, no matter what the Moralists say. I won't."

Luan made no effort to defend himself as her barrage continued. After a while, she wrapped her arms around his neck and wept.

"Mimi-*tika*, my stubborn child." Luan stroked her back and sighed. "Remember what I taught you about the Fluxists. The Flow is the inexorable current of the universe. To live life gracefully is to accept it, and find joy within each passing moment. Every journey must have a final stop, and every life must come to an end. We're like dyrans in the vast sea, silver streaks passing each other in the watery depths, and we should cherish the time we have been given."

"I refuse to live life with such passivity!"

"Accepting the Flow is *not* passive. It's to understand that there is a balance in the universe, an ultimate accounting." Zomi looked up and saw that Luan's face was somber. "There's a time for Kana's fiery call to arms, and a time for Rapa's gentle call to slumber. I am meant to die here today, but you're not."

"Why? Why do you think you are meant to die?"

"I once advised a king to commit an act of betrayal that I thought was the right thing to do, and I've never been able to forget the lives lost because of me. . . . I've been trying to atone for it since. The signs tell me today is my day."

"If you're such a believer in the Fluxists, maybe we're meant to end our journeys together."

"But you're so young! This cannot be right."

"How can you claim to know the ways of the Flow?"

Luan chuckled. "I have never claimed to be a very good Fluxist, and I see that I cannot match you in debate." He hugged Zomi tighter, and the child hugged him back.

By now the roaring of the fire was so loud that it seemed as if they were in the middle of a typhoon. The thickening smoke and searing heat made everything around them appear shimmery and hazy, like a dream.

But Zomi did not share Luan's serenity; she refused to believe that the Flow, whatever that was, meant that they had to die. Certainly her teacher could think of *something* to do. "The act of betrayal by the earl may be a sign that we are not meant to die at all."

"Oh?" For a moment Luan's eyes, reflecting the approaching fire, lit up. "But what *can* we do?"

"You are supposed to know that!"

"Since neither of us can climb up the cliffs, we must urge the villagers to leave as soon as possible."

But the villagers refused to abandon either Elder Comi or Luan and Zomi, and it appeared that everyone was going to die together in the oncoming conflagration. The flames were so close now that only a thin band of forest lay between them and the clearing for the hamlet.

The villagers and Elder Comi all sat down in *mipa rari* in a semicircle around Luan and Zomi. "*Tiro, tiro,*" said the elder, a peaceful smile on his face. "*Tiro, tiro,*" the other villagers repeated, and reached out to link their arms into a wall of flesh.

Since Luan and Zomi were guests, the villagers were carrying out the ancient duty of hosts to shield them, even if their sacrifice would only slow down the flames for but a second.

Luan and Zomi bowed their heads. "All men are fellows before the bleak, endless sea and the fiery, explosive volcanoes," Luan said, reciting an old Moralist adage.

Once more, Zomi looked for and found *Curious Turtle* in the sky. Because it was so overladen, the rate of ascent was extremely slow even though the stove was working at full power. It was barely fifty feet up in the air, and it was accelerating toward the flames.

"I guess even Lord Kiji, bringer of winds, is not very pleased with the cruel earl and his lackeys," said Zomi. "He's pushing them toward the fire. They'll never get high enough in time to escape being roasted."

Luan squinted and shook his head. "It's possible that Lord Kiji is angry at him, but I've learned over the years to attribute as little as possible to the gods. I've come to rely on the precept laid down by Na Moji: Since the will of the gods cannot be ascertained, it's always simpler— and more likely correct—to explain things by verifiable patterns."

"Aren't you the son of an augur? That . . . almost sounds like the words of an atheist!"

"The best way to honor the gods is to blame them for less. They may guide and teach, when it suits them, but I prefer to think of the universe as knowable. The balloon's drift is easily explained. As the fire heats the air above, it grows active and light, rising to leave behind a vacuum, and the cold and heavy air outside the fire is drawn toward it."

"Like the hot-air balloon when we inflate it? When the cold air rushes in to make the flame stand straight up?"

Luan nodded and smiled. "Exactly." He cupped his hands around his mouth and shouted at the receding balloon, "Drop your anchor! You'll never get high enough in time. You can still escape by the cliff route!"

But the men in the balloon did not respond.

"Maybe they're too far," mused Luan. "Can you shout at them? Your voice is higher pitched, and may be easier to hear over the roar of the flames."

Zomi shook her head. "I will not do anything to save them."

"That's not the moral—"

"I don't care! I only care about people close to me."

Luan sighed and pulled her close again as powerful gusts of hot wind whipped around them. He hugged her and said nothing more as they watched the balloon disappear in the thick smoke over the roaring fire.

Perhaps there were screams, but the balloon was too far for them to be sure.

Suddenly, Zomi struggled and pulled away. "Teacher! I think there is a way!"

While Luan and Zomi remained where they were, the villagers ran into their houses and emerged with jars of cooking oil, medicinal liquor, rags, sheets, small tables, cradle beds.

Instead of sacrificing themselves for their guests, it looked like they were ready to escape with whatever possessions they could carry. Elder Comi stood in the middle of the hamlet, gesticulating and calling out orders.

But instead of heading for the cliffs, the villagers smashed the wooden furniture apart and wrapped oil-soaked rags around the ends of the pieces of lumber. Then they divided themselves into two groups. One group lit the makeshift torches and carried on their backs bundles of firewood and more jars of oil; another grabbed shovels and hoes. Both groups then headed for the raging flames advancing on the hamlet.

The heat was like an invisible wall. A few stumbled, fell, got up again, and pushed on. Rags soaked with an infusion made from herbs intended to reduce fever were wrapped around their noses and mouths so that they could breathe in the suffocating smoke. A few daring ones had chewed herbs that could fool the mind into believing anything. *There is no fire. There is no danger,* they muttered to themselves, and pressed on.

The running villagers in their ragged clothes flapping in the wind resembled a swarm of moths headed for the flame.

By the time the rising heat made it impossible to move forward another inch, the villagers had reached the shrubs and saplings at the edge of the woods. The forest fire, like a caged monster, was about to smash through this flimsy screen and emerge into the clearing for the final carnage.

Séji shouted the order, and the villagers went to work. Those with shovels and hoes started to dig a shallow ditch, ripping away the grass, fallen leaves, and surface soil. They worked quickly and efficiently, and carved out a shallow defensive moat at the edge of the forest— but what could such a small ditch do against the rampaging flames that they faced? The fire would easily be able to leap across it and devour the hamlet.

The other group, meanwhile, had spread apart and dropped bundles of firewood in an arc on the farther side of the shallow moat. They emptied bottles of oil and liquor over the firewood, and then they set the bundles alight.

In the face of fire, they added more fire.

An observer might well wonder if the desperation of their situation had driven them into the belief that it was better to die in flames started by their own hands.

The villagers continued their work, extending both the ditch and the arc of flames at either end. They seemed intent on surrounding the village with it.

The new fires grew stronger, brighter, louder. Soon, they were as high as a man, and then two men, three men. The crimson tongues extended to lick at the trees at the edge of the forest.

Strangely, instead of leaning over to jump over the shallow, apparently useless ditch, the new wall of flames leaned toward the greater fire in the forest, like a child yearning for a hug from its mother. The wind grew even stronger, whipping the new flames into a frenzy.

The trees at the edge of the forest caught, and the flaming arc roared in joy as it rushed for the embrace of the much greater fire on the other side, consuming anything that stood in its way: undergrowth, fallen logs, living trees, thick layers of half-rotten leaves. Branches snapped, green leaves curled and burst into bright sparks, columns of smoke merged and thickened.

The villagers, their hair singed and throats parched, stumbled back into the clearing. The wall of flames they had nursed had carved out a much wider swath of land on which nothing combustible remained.

Fire, driven by the hungry winds generated by the forest fire, had deprived itself of fuel.

"A bold move," said Luan, his voice full of admiration.

"All thanks to your teaching, of course," said Zomi, inflecting her voice as though she were an old man. "Combining the preference for fire from Incentivism and the understanding of wind from Patternism, it required but the confidence and grace of secure Fluxism to implement a Moralist plan."

Luan stared at her, mouth agape. "I'm not sure that this interpretation, um . . ."

Zomi's face twitched, and she broke down into peals of laughter.

Luan shook his head and sighed. "You are clever, Mimi-*tika*, but I'm afraid you are a ball of wax too slippery for me to carve."

Zomi grabbed him by the arm and tried to get her giggles under control. "You have to admit, that was a pretty good impression of you."

"Not a good impression at all! Have I been playing the zither to a stubborn calf?"

"All right, all right. I apologize for mocking you," said Zomi. "But to tell the truth, you did give me the inspiration."

"Oh?"

Zomi pointed to the logogram Luan had carved on the ground with the carrying pole.

A river flowing. A volcano. Skin-of-fire.

"This is a single-logogram epigram from Ra Oji," said Luan. "It speaks of serenity in the face of all-consuming death, of letting go into the Flow."

Zomi shook her head. "That is not how I read it." She pointed at the components one by one, and intoned, "A flowing current. A mountain-like wall. Fire-on-the-outside."

"But that is not how—"

Zomi wouldn't let him finish. "I don't care how it's *supposed* to be read. I reorchestrated the components of your logogram into a new idea-machine to accomplish a new purpose: Instead of giving up in the face of death and feeding myself reasons, I sought to preserve life through an agent of destruction."

"You are truly a Pearl of Fire," said Luan. He rummaged through the baskets that Séji and Képulu had left by their side and retrieved the bright-red zomi berries. "It was fate that led us to these berries today, and may your mind ever stay as sharp as their scent and your will as strong as their shell."

As the teacher and the student sat stringing the berry-beads on a string to make a necklace, the villagers approached with bowls of refreshing, cool well water. In the distance, the forest fire was already weakening and burning itself out, powerless to intrude upon this peaceful haven.

For years, the teacher and the student wandered the Islands of Dara.

Sometimes they traveled by balloon, sometimes on horseback. They spent summer evenings drifting over the Zathin Gulf in a small fishing boat, counting and classifying the fish and seaweed they hauled out of the water. They spent winter mornings gliding through the snowbound forests of Rima on sleds pulled by teams of dogs and hiking up the mirror-hard glaciers of Mount Fithowéo. Once, they soared through the skies over the hidden valleys in the

Wisoti Mountains on two stringless kites, though the huntsmen who happened to be glancing up thought they were watching two eagles circling overhead.

While they studied the wonders of the book of nature in their travels, Luan also took care to give Zomi a classical education whose breadth and depth even the famed academies of Haan could not match. Luan taught her the surviving fragments of the dialogues of Aruano the law giver; the epic tales of the heroes Iluthan and Séraca during the Diaspora Wars; the treatises of Kon Fiji and the commentaries by other Moralist masters; the witty epigrams and fables of Ra Oji and his Fluxist disciples; the principles and best practices of engineering as laid out by Na Moji and the accumulated elaborations thereon by Patternist thinkers; the political and legal essays of Gi Anji and the differing Incentivist developments under Tan Féüji and Lügo Crupo; the lyrical poetry of the great Classical Ano poets like Nakipo and Lurusén; and even selected excerpts from the Hundred Schools like Pé Gonji's military strategies, Huzo Tuan's biting criticism, and Mitahu Piati's memoirs of life in Rima during the early years of the Tiro period.

Gradually, the movements of Zomi's carving knife and writing brush became more confident, more expressive. "The art of calligraphy is for the mind like the art of dance is for the body," as Luan reminded her again and again.

She learned to carve logograms with sharp, simple surfaces in monochromatic wax, like the ancient Ano who had first come to the Islands and left their tales in stone steles scattered in ruins; she learned to write in the florid style of the Amu poets, where every edge or arris was chamfered, every corner rounded and polished, and liberal use of color for shades of meaning and emphasis was an art in itself; she learned to compose in the abstract, lyrical style of the Cocru scribes, full of abbreviations and simplified logograms whose clean lines and rough surfaces evoked the sword dance of Cocru soldiers; she learned to draft in the unique plain brushstrokes of Xana engineers, who combined zyndari letters with barely sketched flat projections of Ano logograms to create a script that eschewed the emotive qualities of language in favor of the precision and elegance of numbers. She learned the one thousand and one semantic roots, the fifty-one groups of motive modifiers, and all the phonetic adapters, inflection glyphs, and tone elevation techniques that allowed a scholar to wield the knife and the brush to marshal the Ano logograms into complicated idea-machines for purposes of persuasion, explication, exploration, and artistic pleasure.

From time to time, the two visited towns and villages to obtain supplies and to rest. They never stayed long, as Luan preferred the solitude of the wilderness to the bustle and complications of modern life. But one evening, as they walked along the beach outside a small town in Haan after a long trip down the Miru River in a flat-bottomed boat to study the construction of water mills, Luan and Zomi stopped to admire an astonishing sight.

Thousands of baby turtles were emerging from their nests. The hatchlings struggled out of the sand, and after some time spent stumbling about and observing their surroundings, they awkwardly headed for the white surf, where the rhythmic pounding of the waves promised them a watery, vast world where their flippers would give them the freedom to move through it with grace and ease, instead of the difficult, halting steps they were forced to take on land.

Luan glanced at the pier in the distance and realized where he was. He remembered the crisp morning, so many years ago, when he had dived from that pier into the ice-cold sea to retrieve an old fisherman's shoes like a baby turtle's first tumble into the sea.

Perhaps this is a sign.

Luan turned to look at Zomi thoughtfully. She was now as tall as he was, no longer a child.

"This is where my teacher met me and also said good-bye," he said.

"Was it a long time ago?" asked Zomi.

"It was," said Luan, and for a moment he looked wistful. "There comes a time when every hatchling is ready for the sea, and every student is ready to say good-bye to her teacher."

Zomi looked confused. "But I still have so much to learn!"

"As do I. Do you not feel the call of the world, though, Mimi-*tika*? There will always be more books to read, but I think you're ready to perform your own deeds that will be written about one day."

"What about you? If I leave you, who will make your tea in the evenings? Who will argue with you at lunch? Who will ask you—"

"I will be all right, child." Luan laughed. "Besides, I have been thinking of starting another adventure. There are intriguing pieces of wreckage we have seen in our travels that suggest new worlds beyond the sea."

"Like the pieces you showed me with the strange winged and antlered beasts carved into them? I told you my mother and I found them when I was younger, too."

Luan nodded. "I'd like to ask the emperor for help to find those new worlds. There has always been a restlessness in my soul that cannot be denied."

"Then let me come with you!"

"I am content to drift through the world in a balloon or on a barge, letting the Flow take me where it will. But I'm an old leatherback; you, on the other hand, are not yet ready to embrace life as a Fluxist. As the waves pound the sand, so does the empire call for men and women of talent. The Grand Examination will be next year, and you're ready to make your mark. You must enlarge your spirit and take up your duty."

He reached out and caressed the necklace around Zomi's neck. The berries had long since dried out, and over time, contact with skin and clothes had polished the surfaces to a smooth, shiny sheen, though the bright red hue had not faded one whit. "We will set out for Dasu in the morning so that you can attend the Town Examination, the first step in a long journey to the sea of power."

"Teacher, I must ask you for a favor."

"Anything."

"Is it all right if I never mention that I am your student until after the examination?"

Luan was surprised. "Why?"

"If I succeed, I want it to be because of my talent, not because of your name—the way that clerk in Dasu once offered me such a good price for my grain. And if I fail, I do not want to sully your reputation and have people think that you were not a good teacher when the truth was that I was too stubborn to study well."

"Ah, Mimi." Luan was moved by her combination of pride and solicitousness. "Do as you will. But I know that I will never have another student as good as you. I eagerly wait for the day you soar to heights I can only aspire to."

Zomi did not trust herself to speak, for suddenly her vision had grown blurry and her throat constricted. So instead of more words, Zomi bent down and started to sculpt logograms in the sand.

Air-over-heart. A man. A child.

Heart-in-man. Heart-in-child. Open-hand-closed-fist.

Water-over-heart.

The Ano word for "teacher" literally meant "father-of-the-mind," and what was love but an exchange of hearts?

Luan hugged her, and both stood there until the wind had dried the heart-water on their faces and the silent music of the stars had soothed their souls.

Aki Kidosu made all of Mimi's favorite dishes: scrambled eggs with dried caterpillars, fresh mushroom stew flavored with spring herbs and bitter melons, sticky rice cake filled with sweet green-bean-and-lotus paste. There was no money to afford pork, but the caterpillars were well seasoned and especially tasty.

Mimi ate heartily. "I have so missed this!" It was wonderful to be home after all these years. "The caterpillars have such a sweet fragrance. It reminds me of a poem:

White drops between white beads;
Red sticks between red lips.
Girls crunching lotus seeds;
Smoothly gliding lean ships."

"Is that from a folk opera?" her mother asked. "I don't think I've seen it."

"It's . . . a poem by Princess Kikomi of Amu," Mimi said, embarrassed. "It's nothing."

She and Luan Zya had liked to quote bits of poetry at each other. To make old lines say something new was a way to practice the mentality of an engineer who often needed to make old parts accomplish new purposes. But here, in this simple hovel where she had grown up, where the walls were cracked and the floor was bare dirt without a mat, it seemed wrong to quote the words of the dead princess of the Tiro state most dedicated to the ideal of elegance and refinement.

"Try the bitter melon! It's from the garden."

"Mmm, mmm!"

Between bites, Mimi noticed that the hair at her mother's temples had grown white, that her spine had grown more curved, and Mimi's heart ached to think of her struggling all by herself to maintain the farm and keep up the rent.

Then Mimi saw that her mother, who had been chewing contentedly on a piece of sticky rice cake held in her hands, had stopped and was staring at her.

Mimi stopped as well, the single eating stick held daintily in her hand with a piece of rice cake on the end suspended awkwardly a few inches from her mouth.

"You eat like the daughter of the magistrate," said Aki. It was hard to tell whether her tone was admiring or regretful.

"It's just a habit," Mimi hurried to explain. "The teacher and I—we sometimes liked to discuss the intricacies of a particularly obscure logogram during meals, and it was easier if we kept our fingers free from grease . . . and Kon Fiji said that—"

She stopped, embarrassed by herself: She was reciting Amu poetry and quoting Kon Fiji at her mother. Resolutely, she pulled the rice cake off the end of the eating stick, careless of how it stuck to her fingers, and took a big bite from it. When she put down the eating stick, she deliberately set it down so that it crossed obscenely with its companions on the table.

Her mother nodded and went back to eating, but her motions were now awkward, uncertain, as though she was sitting with the daughters of Master Sécru Ikigégé, their landlord, at the symbolic New Year's meal where the landlord was supposed to express thanks for the tenants, and the girls always sneered at the uncouth manners of the tenant farmers.

As she counted the new wrinkles on her mother's face and the new patches on her dress, Mimi's heart twitched.

How can I go to the Town Examination and think of leaving her here by herself? I will stay with Mama always.

She tried to continue the conversation. But after Aki politely dealt with her praise for the food ("Oh I'm sure you've had much better out there in the world") and her inquiry after her mother's health ("Still many more years left in this sack of bones!"), Mimi ran out of things to say. After years of chattering away at Luan Zya at meals about philosophy and engineering and politics and poetry and math, she had forgotten how to converse with her mother.

Mimi was utterly ashamed.

"Why don't you take a nap after the meal?" her mother said, breaking the awkward silence. "I'll flip over the sheets on the bed so that they're clean." The tone she used seemed to suggest that Mimi was a guest, the daughter of a magistrate or scholar.

"I don't need to nap," said Mimi. "I can help you around the farm or the house. What do you need?"

Her mother smiled. "Oh, this would bore you. I need to go over to Master Ikigégé's house and help his oldest daughter cut paper butterflies for her wedding."

"Isn't she supposed to do that herself?"

"Well, she's got fat fingers—though she's trying to lose weight before the big day."

Aki and Mimi giggled. For a moment it felt like the old days, but then Aki added, "I'm already late. If I don't go over quickly, he'll add another five coppers to my rent."

Mimi's face froze. "How can Ikigégé do that? The rent is fixed by the lease."

Aki put the dishes into the sink and started to wash, her cracked fingers flitting through the water like scaly fish. "Master Ikigégé says that the regent has raised the taxes at Emperor Ragin's orders. Since taxes are not discussed separately in the lease, all of his tenants have to bear a share of it."

This made no sense to Mimi. Why was the emperor, who supposedly cared about the lives of the people, raising taxes on the poorest of the poor?

Wiping the dishes, Aki continued, "But Master Ikigégé is generous, and offered to reduce the share I have to pay if I do chores at his house. I work as a maid over there so that he doesn't have to hire one, and at least this way I can afford the rent."

The idea of her mother slaving away at her landlord's beck and call sickened Mimi. "Ma, don't go. I'm home now, and I'll go in your place. I'm sorry I was away for so long, but you won't have to suffer anymore."

This is the right thing to do, isn't it? I'm sure Kon Fiji would approve.

But Aki stacked the dishes and shook her head. "You have a new name now, Zomi Kidosu. You are no longer a simple farmer's daughter."

"What are you saying, Mama?"

Aki turned around and folded her hands against her lap. "Remember the story about how if a golden carp leaps over the Rufizo Falls, it turns into a rainbow-tailed dyran? You've leapt over the falls, Mimi-*tika*. You have a future, but it isn't here. It isn't with me."

Mimi closed her eyes and remembered the time she and Luan had flown in stringless kites: After seeing the world from such a height, could she spend the rest of her life in this small one-room dwelling, within the bounds of a few acres of land and a thin sliver of beach? Could she bend and scrape for a few coppers from their landlord after having critiqued the philosophies of the Hundred Schools? Could she endure the tedium of this way of life after having been exposed to so much more?

"There's a restlessness in your soul," said Aki. "It's always been there, but now it's grown."

Mama is right, Mimi thought. *This is no longer home. I have to make a new home.*

"I will make you proud, Mama. I will register for the Town Examination; I will bring you honor and wealth; I will make sure that you eat white rice every day and dress in silk and sleep on feather-filled mattresses at night."

Aki came over and held Mimi, and she had to reach up to caress her daughter's face. "All I care about, my child, is that you're happy. You are setting out into the wide sea, my baby, and I'm sorry that Mama does not have the knowledge or skills to help you."

What do I care about the duty of the learned? Mimi thought. *Why should I try to make the lives of the Earl of Méricüso or Master Ikigégé better? All I care about are the people I love.*

Mimi hugged her mother back. "I will give you a better life. I swear it."

CHAPTER SEVENTEEN

THROUGH THE VEIL

PAN: THE THIRD MONTH IN THE SIXTH YEAR OF
THE REIGN OF FOUR PLACID SEAS.

"Zomi Kidosu was right," Dafiro said. "The *cashima* who were not ranked among the *firoa* had formed a mob outside the palace gates. They were banging on gongs and singing songs, demanding that the Grand Examination essays be reviewed by a new panel of judges. Their antics attracted a large number of idlers and curious passersby."

Kuni waved for everyone to be quiet. He listened. There were no sounds of banging gongs or singing students or shouting mobs, muffled or otherwise.

"I said *were*." The captain's tone was humble, but there was a hint of smugness to it. He waited as the silence lengthened, like a story-teller playing his audience.

Kuni parted the cowrie strands dangling from his crown impatiently so that Dafiro could see his face and what the emperor thought of the captain's attempt at drama.

Dafiro bowed and hurried to explain. "I told the rioting *cashima* that you, *Rénga*, were interested in understanding their complaint, but as there were many voices among the students, you preferred to receive a single petition signed by the most insightful scholar among them. 'Emperor Ragin will personally review the petition, bypassing Imperial Tutor Ruthi,' I said—and I may have winked. 'You *may* even get a private audience with the emperor himself.'"

Kuni let the cowrie strands fall back in place to hide his smile. "Clever, Daf."

Dafiro's eyes twinkled. "I have an excellent teacher, *Rénga*."

Even the empress and Consort Risana couldn't quite keep their faces straight at this, and a few of the generals and ministers who had followed Kuni the longest chuckled. Kuni's reputation for shameless tricks as a young man was well known.

Dafiro bowed to Zato Ruthi. "I beg your pardon, Master Ruthi. I figured you would not want to meet with these spoiled children." Ruthi waved his hands dismissively, indicating that he was not offended by Dafiro's fib.

"Wait, wait!" Phyro jumped up from his place at the foot of the dais. "Da, how did what Captain Miro said stop the riot? I don't understand."

Kuni looked at him affectionately—though the boy couldn't see his face—and then glanced at Timu, whose face was equally confused. Only Théra stood there grinning knowingly like the ministers and generals in the hall. The emperor sighed quietly to himself. "Daf, why don't you explain for the benefit of the young prince?"

Dafiro nodded. "Prince Phyro, what do you think happened among the scholars after I told them about the petition and the private audience?"

Phyro spread his hands helplessly. "I have no idea."

"Think, Phyro," Kuni said, a hint of impatience in his voice. "You're being lazy."

Risana cut in gently. "Just imagine yourself in the scholars' place. Remember what it was like when you and your friends played war? Who got to be the marshal?"

"I did," Phyro said, looking even more confused.

Kuni shook his head almost imperceptibly. Phyro did often play with the children of ministers and nobles who were in Pan, but of course Phyro always got to pick the game and always got the best roles because he was the emperor's son. He had too little experience of the dynamics of a group, of politics. *This has to be remedied.*

Dafiro smoothly came to the prince's rescue. "Your Highness, the rioting *cashima* are ambitious scholars. Most of them are used to being the cleverest boy—or girl, in a few cases—out of everyone they know. When I mentioned that the emperor would accept a petition only from the best among them, it was natural that all of them would want to claim that title—and I added fuel to the fire by implying that one of them might get a private audience with the emperor, which is almost as good as being a *pana méji.*"

Phyro's eyes glinted with the light of understanding. "So . . . they started fighting over who was 'most insightful'?" He rubbed his hands together in glee, sorry to have missed an exciting fight.

Dafiro nodded. "But they're scholars, Your Highness, so their fighting is . . . how should I put this . . . of a different quality than wrestling matches among the soldiers."

"I bet they competed to see who could quote the most obscure passages from Kon Fiji," said Phyro, chuckling. Timu gave him a reprimanding look and subtly pointed at Zato Ruthi, who pretended not to see any of this.

"There was some of that, yes," said Dafiro. "And then they started pointing out each other's grammar mistakes, and then the mistakes in the corrections, and then the mistakes in the corrections to the corrections. One started to sarcastically remark on the accents with which Ano epigrams were recited; another pointed to the anachronistic style of the declaimed speeches. I let them go on in this vein for a bit until they'd gotten red in the face and properly thirsty with all that oration, and I showed them how to get to the best pubs in Pan. They'll be there arguing and debating for the rest of the day. The *cashima* took their gongs with them, and the rest of the crowd either followed to enjoy more free theater or dispersed."

"This is why Ra Oji once said, *Dogido çalusma co jhuakin ma dümon wi cruluféü lothéta, noaü lothu ro ma gankén do crucruthidalo*," added Kuni. "If ten scholars were to start a rebellion, it would take them three years of argument just to agree on a name for their faction."

Phyro laughed so hard that he started to cough. "It sounds like—*ahem*—you'd fit right in with them, Toto-*tika*."

Timu stood awkwardly, his face flushed a furious shade of red, unable to come up with a retort.

Théra noticed the embarrassed expressions on the faces of the other *pana méji* at this bout of jeering at their fellow examinees. She stopped grinning and turned to Dafiro. "Thank you for your quick thinking, Captain Miro. I'm sure Father is grateful that you diverted the momentary rage of the learned scholars, the backbone of the Imperial bureaucracy, without any harm. They're the true treasure of Dara."

The princess bowed to Dafiro in *jiri*, and Dafiro bowed back deeply, his face now also serious. Timu and the *pana méji* relaxed.

Kuni looked on, pleased. "I will speak with the students once they pick a representative. The stakes of the exams are high, and it's understandable they would react this way to disappointment, but I am satisfied that the integrity of the exams is unassailable, and I will persuade them to see reason."

Zomi Kidosu, silent through the entire exchange between Miro and the children, now cut in. "You may have pacified the disappointed *cashima* today with a distraction, but the fundamental problem, the unfairness of the exams, remains."

Everyone in the Grand Audience Hall was reminded that they were still in the middle of a Palace Examination. Dafiro retreated to the side of the hall, the children quieted and sat down, and Kuni sat up straight and once again gave Zomi his full attention.

"You spoke of the way prized essays tended to reflect the tastes of the academies of Ginpen in Haan," said Kuni. "It is a fair criticism, perhaps. But it will take time for other regions of Dara to become as devoted to learning as Haan."

Zomi shook her head. "*Rénga*, that is not all. Even if all the other provinces of Dara had academies as respected as those in Ginpen, the examinations are still not selecting for talent. Look at the *cashima* who were so easily manipulated by the captain's tricks: They are narrow-minded fools who have memorized ten thousand Ano logograms and think they know all there is to know. Such poverty of spirit cannot lead to true beauty or grace or suppleness of thought."

Kuni was momentarily stunned by her vehemence, but Risana broke in. "Zomi Kidosu, do you have a different view of what is worthy of being called beautiful and graceful and supple in thought?"

Zomi nodded. "Master Ruthi speaks of the power of examples drawn from life to persuade, but the lives of his students are different from the lives of most of the emperor's subjects, as distinct as the life of the pampered rose in a hothouse is from the lives of the dandelion in the fields.

"This man paints a picture of a world in which his family again holds absolute sway over a kingdom. That man over there wishes for an ideal world in which all laws and taxes have been redesigned to allow his family to accumulate wealth. They dress up these visions with citations to dead philosophers, but all I see is ugliness and hypocrisy. Look at these men"—Zomi pointed at the other *pana méji*—"Not a single one of them has ever had to work for his next meal or had to beg a corvée administrator for a reprieve."

Kuni Garu's face, hidden behind the dangling cowrie veil, flinched.

"I doubt any of them can tell an ear of sorghum apart from an ear of wheat, or knows the weight of the fish in the boat after a day of trawling in Gaing Gulf. They have never sweated after an honest day's labor or bled from blisters made by swinging the sickle or hauling in the net.

"Has anyone in the College of Advocates ever told you that your policy of increasing the taxes on the merchants would end up harming the small farmers you aimed to help?"

Kuni shook his head.

"When the taxes go up on the merchants, who, as the empress has noted, also tend to be large landowners, they pass on the tax to their tenants and increase their burden."

"That is not supposed to—"

"I know that isn't supposed to happen. But it does—it happened to my mother. You may have your edicts and policies, but in the villages, the wealthy do what they will and the poor must obey. The voices of the poor are not heard in these halls, and so you do not understand their plight."

"I was not always the Emperor of Dara," said Kuni Garu quietly. "I was once a boy who stood by the side of the road to watch Mapidéré's procession and wandered the markets of Zudi, tempted but not able to afford anything. There were days when I did not know where my next meal would come from."

"All the more reason that you should weigh the fish instead of trusting self-serving reports, imaginary models, or hopeful visions!"

Kuni was about to defend himself, but Zomi would not be interrupted.

"And look at them." She swept her arm at the *pana méji*. "They are all men! You may have opened the civil service to women, but only a few dozen of the *cashima* who came to Pan for the Grand Examination are women, and out of those barely a handful made it into the ranks of the *firoa*.

"What do those in your College of Advocates know of the beauty prized by women that isn't for the delectation of men? Or the plight of women who must raise children without any of the advantages given to men? Or the reasons some sell themselves to the indigo houses? Or the causes that make the choice of a marriage akin to bondage seem reasonable to so many?"

Risana could not help but nod vigorously as Zomi spoke. She remembered the life she had led with her mother, before she met Kuni Garu. She berated herself inside for having been so absorbed by the worries of life in the palace that she had not done more for all those others who lived just like she had. This young woman was an inspiration.

"Can your *firoa* react with anything but condescension toward a fisherman's song composed from rough and simple words of his dialect?" Zomi went on. "Can they see the creativity and love imbued in a leaping carp a farmer's daughter folds out of wrapping paper saved from parcels of roasted nuts? What appreciation can they—and you—have for examples drawn from *the people's* lives? You've forgotten—"

"We cannot give up on heading out to the sea just because we know we cannot catch all the fish!" The emperor stopped himself, and, after a moment, continued in a calmer tone. "Before Mapidéré's time, some states administered everything through hereditary nobles while others restricted civil service testing to families who owned land. Mapidéré was the one who opened up the examinations to all men, though in practice his judges could be bribed. I have expanded the examinations to all candidates without regard to sex or status and enforced fairness with standardized questions and grading criteria across the realm. Imperfect as my examinations are, are they still not better than anything that came before?"

"*Rénga*, I mean no disrespect, but you sound like a fisherman with a hold full of rotting fish laughing at another with a bigger hold of rotting fish."

"Perfection cannot be achieved in a brief span of time! The ladder of Imperial testing will not elevate all men and women of talent, yet it offers a beam of hope for the studious and the poor. You come from a sharecropping family without power, yet today you stand among the most honored of Dara's scholars. You are the fulfillment of my trust and hope for the system."

"I am hardly a good example," said Zomi. "I have been blessed with instruction from . . . a teacher few could aspire to, and when it seemed I was about to be denied the chance to take the examinations, strangers came to my aid. Luck is not much of a promise."

Despite the surging pride Luan Zya felt in his student, he had to keep his emotions hidden. Zomi was determined to make it through the examinations on her own merit, and he could not reveal his relationship to her no matter what. *You are a fledgling eagle heading for the skies; you're the hatchling turtle diving into the sea.*

"Then it is the will of gods that you should be elevated above others," said Kuni. "I ascended to the Throne of Dara by equal measures of skill and luck, and random chance governs our fates more than we'd like to admit."

"That is the counsel of despair, *Rénga*. If you seek true talent, then your system of examinations resembles the man who seeks pearls only by diving from the wharf because it is safe and convenient, all the while arguing that the random motion of the tides will move pearls of great value into his reach."

For a long while after, the Grand Audience Hall was silent.

Unexpectedly, Prince Phyro spoke up. "It sounds like you are just jealous that they're rich while you're not. But their families have worked as hard as yours to accumulate their wealth, and why should their children not gain the advantage of having been born to a wealthier family?"

Both Risana and Kuni looked at the young boy. Risana was about to reprimand the boy for speaking in this solemn hall, but Kuni waved for her to be quiet.

"I suppose that is one way to look at it," said Zomi. "But let me try to explain it another way." She walked to the side and stood in front of Zato Ruthi and bowed.

"May I borrow these?" she asked, pointing to the stack of thin wooden boxes for holding the examination essays. "I haven't prepared a presentation, as you now know. So I must improvise."

Surprised, Ruthi nodded.

Zomi picked up four of the boxes, walked back, and laid them out in a row on the floor. She knelt down and hid the boxes from view with the hem of her robe, appearing to place some objects into the boxes. Then she stood up and unveiled the boxes, walking to stand behind them.

"I have placed some humble gifts for you in these boxes," Zomi said, looking at each of Timu, Théra, Phyro, and little Fara. "One of them contains a piece of thousand-layer cake, steeped in sweet honey and filled with lotus seed. The other three boxes are empty. The princes and princesses may each pick a box, and whatever you find in the box, that is your dessert for tonight. If you find yourself in possession of the thousand-layer cake, you have no obligation to share with your siblings. And if you find yourself holding an empty box, you must not complain. Do you like this arrangement?"

"Um . . . ," said Phyro.

"That's unfair," said Fara, her voice crisp and childish. "We should share!"

"Why is it unfair?"

"I didn't do anything wrong," said Phyro. "Why should I get an empty box?"

Zomi looked at Phyro. "Before birth, all of us are mere potentials. We have no control over the moment of incarnation, when we might end up as the son of an emperor or the daughter of a peasant. The veil is lifted as we come into the world, and we find ourselves holding a box that determines our fates without regard to our merit. Yet all the great philosophers have always said that our souls are equal in weight in the eyes of the World Father, Thasoluo. It would be most strange if our own sense of justice, after being cultivated by the wisdom of the sages, cannot match that of a child of four."

Phyro's face turned red, but he had no response.

Unexpectedly, Prince Timu came to his rescue. "That is mere sophistry, Zomi Kidosu."

Zomi Kidosu regarded him coolly.

"You misunderstand the Classical philosophers. That our souls are equal in the eyes of the World Father does not mean that we're meant to achieve material equality. The sages teach us that men and women are born into different ranks, but all of us have our roles to play in the harmonious play of life. You speak as though it is bad to be a peasant, but there is also the nobility of being virtuous in poverty; you speak as though it is good to be a king, but a king's cares are as great as his fortune. Neither one is inherently better than the other: Each should strive to excel in his assigned position. Not everyone prefers thousand-layer cake. *That* is true wisdom."

"I see," said Zomi. "Prince Timu, you will surely not object then if I eat the thousand-layer cake and give you the wrapping paper to lick? In fact, why don't we switch places so that I can experience the suffering of your many cares in the palace, and you get to experience the nobility of poverty in my muddy hut?"

It was now Prince Timu's turn to be at a loss for words. "You—you—"

Empress Jia looked at Zomi, her face frosty. "Timu, speak no more."

"So which box holds the thousand-layer cake?" asked Fara, still staring at the boxes. "Can I see?"

Zomi nodded.

Fara opened the first box; it was empty.

"Can I try again?" she looked at Zomi, who nodded.

Fara opened the second box, then the third, and finally the last. All were empty.

"Where's the cake?"

"There never was any cake."

Fara squinted at her. "But you said there was!"

"For most people of talent in Dara, that is the kind of promise made by the Imperial examinations."

"You clearly have a proposal that you did not write down in your essay," Kuni said. "Perhaps it's time to present it."

Luan Zya had been staring at Zomi, his face tense. But Zomi refused to meet his eyes, instead gazing calmly at the emperor.

"I propose that we abolish the use of Ano logograms and Classical Ano in the Imperial examination altogether." Her voice was steady and sure. "Testing should be done using only zyndari letters writing in the vernacular."

Kuni froze, as did all the assembled ministers and generals and nobles. The Grand Audience Hall was so silent that the noise of the distant crowd was the only sound.

Murmurs of incredulity began to grow among the assembled ministers, and a few began to chuckle.

Théra hung on every word of the young scholar. She had never heard anyone so bold, so original. Zomi was like a lightning bolt that had lit up a dark sky; she had never believed that it was possible to turn the world upside down like this, to reimagine it as though nothing that had come before mattered.

"Surely you—" Kuni started to say.

"Preposterous!" Ruthi seemed to not realize or care that he was interrupting the emperor. "Without knowledge of the Classical Ano logograms, you might as well abolish literacy!"

"That isn't true. It takes only about a month for a child to learn the zyndari letters and to start composing in the vernacular. Yet we deem writing with only zyndari letters to be unacceptable and require years of schooling to learn the intricacies of the dead words of Ano philosophers and twist our thoughts to fit their mold. Schools constructed around the logograms can only be attended by those who do not have to live off the fruits of their own labor.

"The kind of arguments prized under such a system are sclerotic, lifeless, oriented toward the past. If we abolish the need for the Ano logograms and write the wisdom of the new age in the vernacular using only zyndari letters, there will be such a flourishing of learning across Dara that you will have a much better chance of finding the talent you desire. Instead of seeking pearls in the shallow reefs near the wharfs of Haan, you will be casting the net far and wide across the entire ocean.

"I do not advocate that we discard the logograms altogether. I well know their advantages in beauty, in literary expressiveness, in maintaining a connection with the past, in allowing people who speak differently to communicate, in crafting and shaping a worldview that offers joy and comfort. But the cost they impose on the examinations is too high. I love the logograms as much as any of you, perhaps even more, yet just because we love something doesn't mean we must hold on to it when circumstances have changed. It's time to abandon old machines and remake the minds of Dara."

The Grand Audience Hall exploded with voices of outrage and argument.

Now, she thought, *if only my secret can stay hidden.*

CHAPTER EIGHTEEN

HEIR TO THE EMPIRE

PAN: THE THIRD MONTH IN THE SIXTH YEAR OF
THE REIGN OF FOUR PLACID SEAS.

In the back of the palace, behind the wall that divided the public halls from the private quarters of the Imperial family, there was a garden.

About equal in area to a medium-sized farm, it wasn't large by the standards of the old Tiro kings, who often had private hunting grounds and seaside resorts that took up thousands of acres of land, but it was intricately laid out and reflected the tastes of the Imperial family.

The western end of the garden belonged to Empress Jia, who had filled it with decorative flowers and useful herbs. Varieties of chrysanthemums and roses in every hue bloomed in coral-and-obsidian lined planters arranged in concentric rings that echoed the whorls of individual flowers (the planters made it easier to move the plants into hothouses during the cold months). Herbs collected from all corners of Dara were grown here in grids, each square clearly labeled with the herb's name, place of origin, and a warning if the plant was toxic. A work shed constructed in the style of a medicine shop of Cocru sat in the middle of the herb plots as though it had been plucked from the streets of Zudi.

The eastern part of the garden belonged to Consort Risana, who had chosen to build a maze made up of thick, trained hedges; deep-lake rocks full of wrinkles and perforations that resembled massive sponges; coral formations taken from the sea; and small ponds that held schools of colorful carp and tranquilly reflected the sun like tidal pools. Herbs known for their mind-altering qualities were grown here and there, and Consort Risana sometimes entertained the children by practicing her smokecraft, turning the maze into a fantasyland filled with friendly immortals who provided sage advice, as well as mythical monsters who delighted the children with fits of terrified laughter.

But the few visitors who had the privilege of being allowed into the garden all agreed that it was the central part of the garden, the emperor's own preserve, that was the most distinctive.

The children, who had lingered in the Grand Audience Hall after the conclusion of the Palace Examination to observe the rare sight of all the Lords of Dara leaving the hall by rank and seniority as though performing some choreographed dance—in truth, they were also motivated more than a little by the thought of avoiding having to deal with Empress Jia and Master Ruthi's inevitable scolding for their interruption of the proceedings—finally left the hall to return to the family quarters at the back of the palace.

They went through the guarded door at the Wall of Tranquillity, crossed the small arched bridge that traversed the thin stream that flowed from west to east and marked the division between the public and private sections of the palace, and entered the garden.

On their left was a flooded field that would become a rice paddy later in the spring. On their right was a taro patch and a vegetable garden filled with trellises for climbing vines. Had one not known that this was the Imperial garden, one might have thought the princes and princesses had just stepped into a Cocru farm.

And there was even a man dressed in the traditional garb of the Cocru farmer: white leggings made from long strips of hemp cloth, a large-brimmed hat woven from reeds to keep the sun off his face and neck, and a thin robe with the hem tucked into the belt to allow freedom of movement. He was hauling two buckets of water dangling from the ends of a carrying pole from the stream over to the vegetable garden.

"*Rénga,*" Timu called out. "Your obedient children give you their respects."

The man in the reed hat stopped, slowly turned around to keep the water in the buckets from spilling, and smiled at the children. It was indeed Kuni Garu, Emperor Ragin of the Islands of Dara.

Though Féso and Naré Garu had been farmers by trade, they owned their land and were not sharecroppers. By the time Kuni was a young boy, the Garus had settled inside the city of Zudi and rented out their farm to support their other business interests. Kuni had but the vaguest recollections of life on a farm. But after he became emperor, and especially after the death of his father, Kuni had taken up farming as a sort of hobby that he pursued with dedication in the Imperial garden. Perhaps it was a way for him to honor the roots of his own family and indeed the economic foundation that supported all of Dara.

"Come and help me," said Kuni. "I can show you the budding taros and string beans."

"Most Revered and Honored Father," said Timu, "this is a most delightful invitation that humbles me. Your solicitude of the well-being of the lowliest subjects of Dara is unprecedented! To debase yourself to perform the task of coaxing sustenance from the earth is akin to a cruben deigning to act the part of a mere shrimp. By experiencing the life of the common people, the virtuous sovereign may feel himself closely attached to the people. Indeed, Kon Fiji, the One True Sage, once said—"

"It's all right, Timu," Kuni interrupted him. He was still smiling, but a hint of impatience was in his eyes. "All you have to say is: 'I'm busy. Thanks but no thanks.'"

"Er . . . Master Ruthi indicated earlier that there are some important lessons he wishes to impart to his foolish student. I am caught in the difficult position of having to choose to obey my father, Sovereign of the Empire and mold of my body, and my teacher, Sovereign of the Realm of Knowledge and author of my mind—"

"Go, go!" Kuni said, one hand waving as though chasing a pesky fly. The motion disturbed the pole balanced over his shoulder, and some of the water spilled from the buckets.

"I am most grateful for your indulgence, *Rénga*." Timu bowed and hurried away.

Kuni chuckled, but he sighed inside. *I know well that you think it's beneath you to dig in dirt and perform physical labor, because you think Kon Fiji meant it literally when he said that menial tasks made the mind mean. Sometimes I wonder if reading so many books is a good thing. Why are you so unlike me?*

He turned to Phyro. "Hudo-*tika*, what about you?"

"Da, I'm busy. Thanks but no thanks."

Kuni laughed out loud, and more water spilled from the buckets. "I see. And what are you busy with?"

"Captain Miro promised to see me and tell me more about how he got those scholars to start drinking instead of rioting, and I want to ask Auntie Gin and Uncle Théca for tales about the Hegemon."

Kuni nodded and waved him away also. *Phyro is a lot like me when I was younger, but he's too attached to the romance of daring and war. He's had a life of ease, and I do not know when or how he will learn the patience necessary. . . .*

Finally, he turned to the girls. "What about you, Rata-*tika* and Ada-*tika*? Are you busy as well?"

"I love playing in the dirt!" Fara yelled, and ran over to hug Kuni. She was so fast that Kuni had no time to set the carrying pole down, and more water spilled as Fara wrapped her arms around her father's legs. Then she let go and happily ran into the empty rice paddy and splashed around, careless of how the mud and water soaked her opulent dress.

"Father." Théra came up to Kuni and gave a low bow in *jiri*. She glanced at the buckets. "I think we might as well go back to the stream and refill these."

"You're right," said Kuni. "Your brothers and sister managed to make me spill most of the water."

He set the carrying pole down and released the two buckets, handing one to Théra. Father and daughter walked back to the stream and refilled them. Théra struggled with the heavy weight as she followed Kuni, and as the water in the bucket matched the rhythm of her steps, it sloshed over the edge.

"Here, let me help you," said Kuni. He bent down and picked up a small wooden plank and set it to float in the middle of Théra's bucket. "Now try."

This time, though Théra continued to struggle with the weight, the plank dampened the waves in the bucket and water didn't spill out.

"Being a ruler is a lot like carrying a bucket of water," Kuni said. "There are always competing forces that threaten to make waves, and it is the ruler's job to find a way to balance the various forces from spilling out of control so that the land may be irrigated and the people fed."

"Why not just set the bucket down so that it wouldn't be agitated?" asked Théra, her breathing becoming labored.

"Then we'd be left with a bucket filled with dead water, and nothing would grow. Forward motion is essential, Rata-*tika*. Change is the only constant."

Théra couldn't help but feel that this speech had perhaps been rehearsed and intended for her brothers. But she was glad to have this moment with her father. She had always enjoyed listening to him talk about politics and economics, and he had always stopped whatever he was doing when the children wanted to spend time with him, though she tried not to bother him often.

"Are there a lot of people pushing on you, Father?"

"Too many to count. The nobles want more independence; the civil ministers want more uniformity; those in the College of Advocates want more say in policy; the generals want more money to pay their soldiers; the veterans want more land to settle on; the merchants want more spent on fighting the pirates and competent magistrates—I've even had to revive the profession of paid litigators; the farmers want more aid for irrigation and reclamation; everybody wants somebody else to be taxed more. I am a kite buffeted by the winds from every direction, and it's all I can do to stay aloft."

Théra imagined her father flying through the air like the legends of the Hegemon, and she felt a wave of tenderness for him. Not pity, exactly, but it was strangely moving to hear that her father, who had always seemed so sure of himself, didn't know everything.

"It's good that you have so many wise ministers and generals to advise you."

"Ah, but they all see but a slice of the whole, and they depend on me to keep them in balance. That is why, Rata-*tika*, I designed my crown to shield my face so that they cannot see my expressions as I struggle to figure out what to do. Half of my work is hiding what I think so that I won't be manipulated too much."

They made it to the vegetable garden, and with Kuni's guidance, Théra used a ladle made from a calabash cut in half to gently water the baby shoots and sprouts just poking out of the soil.

"Rata-*tika*, do you know why we don't plant the vegetables with the rice, or mix the climbing vines with the taro patch?"

If this question had been addressed to Timu, he would have replied that it was a matter of keeping each plant with its own kind to ensure respect for their natural places in the chain of being. If this question had been addressed to Phyro, he would have replied that it was a matter of preventing the plants from fighting each other. But Théra somehow understood that it was a test.

She looked at the way the emperor's garden was laid out, which seemed rather careless: The rice paddy was irregularly shaped; the taro patch was much too tiny to yield more than a few meals; the vegetable garden had a mix of beans and melons and leafy vegetables in apparent disarray; and beyond the vegetable garden was a weedy area where wildflowers like dandelions bloomed in abandon.

No real farmers would do things this way, right?

She walked around the garden, looking at it from every angle. Though she had walked by it countless times and even examined it up close a few times, she had never realized that . . . *wait, that's it!* The shapes of the different crop patches reminded her of the Islands of Dara.

Cautiously, she said, "Because different plants require different nutrients and different amounts of water. A rice paddy needs to be inundated, while the vines do best with plenty of air and little water. And even the weeds are a part of your domain, and they have their own needs."

Kuni nodded, apparently satisfied. "Different policies are needed for different regions."

Théra's heart thrilled. *I was right! The independence given to the nobles is meant as an experiment.* "And perhaps when planting a new crop, it's best to try to plant it in different plots subject to different regimens and see which one works best."

Kuni laughed. "My daughter has a talent for farming . . . and perhaps much more."

"I could come out and farm with you more often."

"I would like that," Kuni said. Then, after a pause, he added, "It was clever of you to remember to help the *pana méji* and Master Ruthi save face after what Captain Miro did at the Palace Examination. If only your brothers had your sense."

Théra's face flushed, pleased at the compliment. "What did you think of Zomi Kidosu's proposal?" she asked, eager to hear her father's views concerning her protégée.

Kuni glanced at her, curious. "Do you know her?"

"Um . . . no. But she was so striking."

Kuni continued to look at her but did not press the question. "Some seeds would thrive only when the soil is prepared properly." He did not elaborate.

Théra pondered this answer as she continued to water the garden with her father.

Plunk, the gourd scraped the bottom of the bucket and came up empty. Théra stood up and wiped her forehead with a sleeve. "Shall we go back and get more water?"

Kuni looked at her sweat-drenched face, and his face softened. "It's all right. You've already helped me a great deal. Girls shouldn't get all sweaty and sunburnt. You can take Ada-*tika* to play in the shade of your mother's part of the garden."

Théra regarded Kuni, biting her bottom lip. Then, steeling herself and standing up very straight, she said, "Father, did you tell Queen Gin during the war that she shouldn't have gotten all sweaty and sunburnt?"

For a moment, Kuni's expression was suspended between surprise and embarrassment; then his features relaxed into a smile as he bowed to his daughter. "My apologies, Princess Théra. Strength may wear a robe or a dress. I had not intended an insult, but you're right, my words were ill considered. You have your mother's temper and spine, and that is a good thing."

Théra bowed back deeply in *jiri*. "My father is a lord of capacious mind."

Just as they were preparing to return to the stream with their empty buckets, a friendly voice cried out from some distance away, "Luan! What are you doing here?"

Kuni and Théra turned and saw that Rin Coda, Imperial Farsight Secretary, was coming over the arched bridge. He was speaking to Luan Zya, who was standing under the bridge, as though trying to meld into the abutment.

Luan stepped out from the shadow of the bridge and bowed. "My apologies, *Rénga*. I did not want to intrude upon your private moment with the children."

"Intrude!" said Rin. "You're practically family! Though you have been absent for much too long! We must have at least six cups of wine later; I dare say I have a much better liquor collection now, and I'm sorry we haven't been able to spend much time together for your visit. While you've been away, my people have had a very difficult time keeping an eye on you—for protection!—for you're like an elusive turtle in the ocean, popping up in some town for a few days and then disappearing for months!"

Luan chuckled. "Thank you for your concern for my safety, but perhaps it's best for our chief spy not to admit in front of the emperor that your employees have been having trouble keeping a simple itinerant scholar under surveillance."

Rin waved dismissively. "Kuni knows that I keep a close watch on the real troublemakers. I just wanted to be able to get you back here in case some crisis happened and we needed your advice." As the emperor's childhood friend, Rin Coda had always gotten away with being very informal with him.

"I'm certain the emperor is surrounded by men and women of far greater wisdom than a simple engineer."

"Oh, stop that! That sort of excessive humility comes across as bragging!"

Kuni listened to their banter happily. It reminded him of a simpler time.

"Father, I will retire with Ada-*tika* so that you can discuss matters of state," said Théra. She knew that when Rin came to speak with her father, it was usually about something secret. She bowed to Luan and Rin in *jiri*, called for Fara to follow her, and left the Imperial garden for the private quarters of the Imperial family.

Kuni turned to Rin.

"The *cashima* are still drinking and arguing," said Rin. "No more trouble from them, for now." Then he looked contrite as he added, "I'm sorry I had not anticipated the riots."

Kuni waved dismissively. "It's all right. I will have to deal with their petition eventually. I'll talk to Cogo and Zato about how to address the imbalance between the regions. Perhaps a system whereby scholars from regions outside of Haan and Gan are given some bonus points is necessary. It will require some relaxation of the anonymity requirements."

"Good luck convincing stiff-spined Ruthi of the wisdom of that plan," said Rin. "He'll tell you that any candidate who gets in because of extra points will always feel inferior to the candidates from Haan, and thus your cure is worse than the disease."

"He wouldn't be entirely wrong," said Kuni. "That is why this is a difficult problem. But compromise is the lubricant that keeps the machinery of the state running." Kuni grinned as Luan lifted his eyebrows at this engineering metaphor. "I've been saving that for your return."

Luan laughed. "The emperor is a most interesting lord."

"You're already spending so much money in stipends to lure good teachers to move from Haan to the other provinces," said Rin. "These bookworms don't seem to realize how much you've been doing behind the scenes to address their complaints."

"It takes as much time to watch a sapling grow into a towering oak as it does to cultivate scholarship in regions without a tradition of learning," said Kuni. "But young men do not have such patience, and interim measures are needed. Besides, I'm also trying to encourage more children of the poor to attend schools to add to the talent pool, which I'm sure these children of the wealthy will object to as they'll perceive it as increasing competition. Well, we'll cross that bridge when we come to it. What else do you have to report?"

"Not much. A few deposed nobles are making trouble—two of them actually met recently in Pan. But I don't think they'll amount to much. More worrisome is the cult of the Hegemon, which is growing in the Tunoa Islands, and there are signs it's spreading to other regions. So far, I've limited myself to surveillance. Should I do more?"

Kuni's face darkened, but after a moment he relaxed. "It's easy for Mata to grow kinder in the people's memories now that he's only a ghost haunting Dara and not an insatiable lord who rides from one end of the Islands to the other, demanding tribute in blood."

"These ingrates—"

"No! As long as they are peaceful, let the worship of my brother grow unimpeded."

"But Kuni—"

"No. A forceful response would only encourage those who wish me ill. I betrayed Mata on the shores of the Liru because I thought it in service of a greater honor, and if some believe that the House of Dandelion is founded on a sin, I will not confirm their opinion with a vain attempt to dam up the mouths of the people. Mata truly was an extraordinary individual, and veneration of honor and faith is no threat to me."

To the side, Luan nodded.

"What about the Golden Carp?" asked Kuni.

"It's been difficult. The parents of the young women sometimes require the most persuasion, especially when they're wealthy."

"Then focus on the poor," said Kuni. "Those enjoying fewer advantages from the way things are may be more ready to be persuaded."

Rin nodded. "Let me keep at it." He turned to Luan. "Remember the drinks later—I'll invite Cogo and Gin along. But first, let me . . . um . . . check on something from the empress's garden."

He hurriedly bid his farewell and left for Jia's part of the garden.

Kuni laughed. "Jia is always complaining to me that someone has been taking her happy herbs without permission. I've always suspected Rin was the culprit." He turned around and saw that Luan had a strange look on his face. "What is it?"

"As one without a position at court, I do not think it is my place to comment—"

"Come on," said Kuni. "Why do we have to play this game? I've already indulged your desire to not be entwined in the politics of the court, but can't I have my old friend speak honestly to me?"

Luan nodded, comforted that his lord still thought of him that way. "Then permit me to speak plainly. It is not good to indulge our appetites unchecked. Though it ought to be celebrated that you're still so vigorous that you seek out new . . . beauties, yet I'm reminded of a tale from Pan, after you conquered the palace of Emperor Erishi, when you entered the women's quarters—"

"What in the world are you talking about?" interrupted Kuni, whose eyes had been growing wider and wider as Luan prattled on.

"Er . . . this Golden Carp program . . . is it not a reference to the idea that a golden carp leaping over the Rufizo Falls will turn into a dyran? And Rin mentioned young women . . . so . . . I'm glad that I amuse you, *Rénga*."

Kuni was now laughing so hard that he was bent over at the waist. "Oh Luan, Luan! You *have* been away for too long. I should be wounded that you think so little of me as to believe that I'm holding some sort of beauty pageant to choose for myself new wives from among the commoners of Dara. The very idea!"

"Then what is it that you're asking Rin to do?"

Kuni struggled to get his laughter under control. "Ahem . . . Zomi Kidosu is right that the Imperial examinations, as fair as I've tried to make them, are not a good way to attract the talents of *all* of Dara. Though I've opened the examinations and the civil service to women, few have applied to take the examinations and even fewer have risen through the ranks. I have been asking Rin to find girls of promising talent and to secretly offer their parents a stipend to encourage them to attend school and take the tests—*that* is what I meant by the Golden Carp. But so far the results have been poor, even in Haan. Most parents do not want their daughters to leave home and seek a career in the service of the Imperial bureaucracy."

"Custom is a hard thing to change," said Luan. He was very relieved to see that his guess had been wrong. Perhaps he had been too cynical about Kuni Garu. After all, he was a lord who had been willing to take the most interesting path, to gamble for success.

"It takes time," agreed Kuni. "I've had to keep the project a secret because the Moralists are so ascendant and loud. If this became public knowledge, I'm certain that the College of Carping"—Luan smiled at Kuni's alternative name for the College of Advocates— "will bury me under a mountain of petitions denouncing me for ignoring tradition and straying from virtue. My life is all about compromises."

"Why don't I help you carry water, Lord Garu?" asked Luan. For a moment, he was concerned that slipping into the old familiar form of address would upset the emperor, but Kuni's relaxed face assured him. Not all customs were bad.

"You should be at court and help me carry the burden of administration."

"I am an old buffalo, Lord Garu, suitable for wandering the wilderness but no longer capable of taking up the plow."

"Ha! There you go again. Excessive humility disguising a boast. It's all right, I know you love your freedom. If I were in your position, I wouldn't want to come back to court either."

"I do have a request for you."

"Oh?"

"Will you fund an expedition to the north? The records of Emperor Mapidéré's voyage to the Land of the Immortals bother me. We know so little of the sea. The ancient books speak of walls made of storms and living islands that devour all travelers, but the truth is hard to come by."

Luan retrieved the strange pieces of wreckage—filled with carvings of winged and antlered beasts—from his sleeves and explained his plan.

"You really have made up your mind not to stay at the court, haven't you?" asked Kuni, disappointment evident in his voice. But he shook it off. "All right. I can't force you to stay. But I won't be able to afford an expedition on the scale of Mapidéré's folly."

"A few small but capable ships—equipped to my specifications—are all I require."

"I will do my best."

As the two men carried water to the vegetable patch and continued to converse about family and work, Luan realized that there was a dark cloud under Kuni's easy manners.

"Though you're steering the ship of state through treacherous waters," Luan said, "the hand on the wheel seems confident enough. But perhaps there is something deeper that concerns you?"

Kuni glanced at him. "There is. Maybe it's a good thing that you've decided not to come back to court." The emperor looked around to be sure that none of the servants were nearby in the garden, but he nonetheless lowered his voice further. "Without a place here, you might be able to give me more objective advice. Like the ship of Métashi, the House of Dandelion faces a coming storm."

Luan paused to consider the reference. Métashi was the name of an ancient Tiro state. Though the balance of power between the Seven States prior to the Unification Wars of Emperor Mapidéré had persisted in some form for more than a thousand years, they were not the only Tiro states of history. After the Diaspora Wars, the Islands of Dara had been divided into many more, smaller Tiro states that fought each other, and the Seven States were the ones that had managed to survive the early period of chaotic warfare.

Métashi, one of the smaller states established on the northern shore of the Big Island, had attempted to unify the Big Island more than a thousand years ago. King Gota of Métashi managed to secure all the territories north of the Damu and Shinané Mountains, and established a capital at the site of present-day Boama. However, after Gota's death, his three most powerful generals, Haan, Faça, and Rima, each supported a separate heir and tore the nascent empire apart. The partition of Métashi into three separate states was memorialized by the Boama court poet Para with the following lines:

The first storm of merciless spring;
The fall of the walls of Boama.
A summer of fame for a king;
The sundered ship feels winter's sting.

"You're still young, *Rénga*," said Luan.

Kuni gave him a bitter smile. "We're all young in the eyes of the gods and old in the eyes of our children. A young dynasty must pass through a wall of storms before the first succession—no less treacherous than the mythical walls in your ancient tomes. If we succeed, this empire might last as long as the Seven States; if we fail, my fate will be no different from that of Mapidéré. Jia and Risana both have been pushing, in their own ways, for me to name the crown prince. Who would you choose?"

Startled, Luan lowered his head diffidently. "I do not know the princes well."

"I know you had been standing under that bridge before the children's arrival," said Kuni evenly. "A single move is sometimes enough for an observer to judge the strength of a *cüpa* player."

Realizing that he had no choice but to voice an opinion, Luan proceeded carefully. He thought over what he had observed of the children's performance at the Palace Examination and their interactions with their father. "Prince Timu is learned in the ways of the Ano sages; he will no doubt gain the support of the civil ministers and the College of Advocates. He's prudent and respectful, and he'll be an able administrator."

Kuni said nothing, but nodded for Luan to go on.

"Prince Phyro yearns for honor and glory, and he has a natural charm that appeals to the generals and nobles. I can see echoes of you in his easy manners, and I believe he'll be a good leader in a time of war."

Kuni looked at Luan. "Did I ask you to tell me which of my children should head the College of Advocates or suit up in armor and ride by Gin's side? You know well that it takes more, much more, to steer the ship that is Dara."

Luan sighed and remained mute.

"Your silence is more telling than what you did say." Kuni said. "So now you see my dilemma."

"Either of the princes would succeed at the task, if properly advised."

"If. *If!* But that is precisely the problem—the advisers want to run the show. They're already lining up and waiting for me to die."

"Surely things are not as bad as that!"

"No, perhaps not. But . . . so far you've been speaking of talents. What of a father's heart?"

Luan took a deep breath. "There is a natural affection between you and Prince Phyro, which is lamentably absent between you and Prince Timu."

Kuni winced but did not look away. "The gods keep an accounting of our errors and mistakes, and sooner or later we are asked to pay. I was absent from Timu's life for much of his childhood, and things have always been awkward between us. But is it right to deprive the firstborn of his natural inheritance for choices he did not make?"

"Guilt is not the best way to pick an heir."

"I know that!" Kuni took a deep breath to calm himself down. "But I am not a scale made of insensate ironwood; I cannot ignore my own feelings. Risana stayed by my side throughout the war years, and Phyro grew up in my lap. Yet without Jia's sacrifices as a hostage of the Hegemon, the House of Dandelion would not be on the throne today. I owe her too much."

"Then the empress was wise to have chosen to step off the airship in Zudi that day."

"Who knows how much of her choice was made from love, and how much from calculation for a day just like this?" Kuni said, and heaved another sigh. "I do not want to see brothers take up arms against each other, or my wives locked in a deadly war of succession. They each have the support of a faction of the court, and it is all I can do to keep my choice hidden."

The way Kuni said *brothers* gave Luan pause. Once more, he reviewed what he had seen and heard, and suddenly he understood what Kuni was really saying.

"*Rénga*, you're indeed a lord of capacious mind!" said Luan.

Kuni looked at him, an eager expression on his face. "What do you think of the solution?"

"It will take time," said Luan cautiously. His mind was still reeling from the revelation of Kuni's true plans. *A crown princess, not a crown prince.*

"A *very* long time. That is the true aim of the Golden Carp: As long as Gin is an exception, my choice of heir will never be accepted by the College of Advocates or the nobles and ministers. Only when those qualified to enter the Grand Audience Hall are as likely to wear a dress as a robe will it be possible for Théra to ascend to the Throne of Dara."

Though Luan had already figured out Kuni's plan, it was still a shock to hear the name of Kuni's true chosen heir spoken aloud. Luan imagined the angry protests from the College of Advocates and the denunciations from the Moralist scholars. It had no doubt taken a great deal of effort for Kuni to convince the court to tolerate attendance by the empress and Consort Risana due to their long service as his advisers. But to persuade them to accept a woman as the empress regnant would require a revolution—or a change in the composition of the court.

"I was especially pleased to see your student at the examination today," said Kuni. "It's as if you've found a golden carp for me without even being asked."

"How . . . did you know she was my student?"

Kuni quirked a brow at him. "You and I have had many debates over the years, and I saw echoes of your style in her rhetoric, though she is entirely original. She is bold and brash like a newborn calf who knows no fear of a pack of wolves; her ideas are so radical that they cannot be implemented—at least not yet."

Luan was reminded once again how people had always underestimated Kuni—including even sometimes himself.

"She will learn humility in time," said Luan. "Raw iron must be refined by the crucible of experience to become steel."

"If the young do not have radical ideas, the world will never change," said Kuni—and Luan was reminded of the legend of a young Kuni Garu who had gazed upon the face of Mapidéré and saw his eventual downfall. "Each fresh wave coming to land from the sea is brash, bold, radical, and wild like a newborn idea; the wave is worn down by the unyielding reality of the hard land and eventually dissipates, exhausted, to be replaced by the next wave in an apparently futile endeavor. Yet the cumulative efforts of such successive surges, over generations and eons, carved the coastline of Dara. Like me, she will learn the art of the possible; I'm patient."

"Sometimes I think you're a kite rider in time," said Luan. "Your visions are so far beyond the horizon of the present."

"It is the only way, Luan," continued Kuni. "Of all my children, Théra is the only one who has the judgment, the instinct for politics and theater, to grasp the helm of the empire. She gets along well with both her brothers, and with her ascent, she'll be able to find ways to moderate their rivalry and find ways for both of them to help her, something that neither of the boys can do on their own.

"Yet in order for her to be accepted, I must play the long game, and subtly pave the way for her ascent while keeping everyone in the dark. What's more, I must ensure that she has no obvious base for power until the moment is ripe. Phyro and Risana have the generals while Timu and Jia have the scholars, but if I encourage Théra to build up a power base of her own, it will only lead to even more intense factional fighting at the court. Only by keeping her apparently powerless could I ultimately help her take over the reins."

"Why haven't you confided in the empress?" asked Luan. "Surely she would be as supportive of a bid by her daughter as her son?"

Kuni shook his head. "She will not tolerate the risks involved in such a radical change; besides, she's proud, and will not give up her own chosen path."

"Has the court become so divided that you and she can no longer see with one mind?"

"We never have been of one mind," said Kuni. "Oh, do not mistake me. The love between us has not faded, but to love someone does not mean giving up your own will. You underestimate Jia. She believes that stability is more important than anything else, and my plan requires a revolution that—if not carefully managed—may plunge the empire into civil war. Besides, she has thrown her lot in with the scholars and promoted their interests for years, and she is too proud and certain to gamble away all she has built on my impossible dream."

"A most interesting dream," said Luan, and the two shared a smile, thinking of deeds of daring in the past.

"Interesting enough to tempt you back?" asked Kuni.

Luan shook his head. "Your goal is admirable, Lord Garu, but I would rather brave the wild seas than the politics of the court."

"Do you really think my palace is more deadly than the realm of capricious Tazu?"

"I know my talents as well as their limits."

Kuni sighed. "I had to try."

"I wish you success with every fiber of my being."

"I have to be in control long enough to see the seeds I plant germinate and blossom—in some ways, the older I grow, the more I become sympathetic to Mapidéré, who also begged the gods for more time. So I keep myself in good health with Jia's herbs that regulate the humors, and vigorous exercise." Kuni picked up the buckets for another trip back to the stream. "As long as I can keep things from spilling over, I think I have a chance of preparing Dara to weather the wall of storms."

And so the emperor and his adviser continued to labor in the farm in the middle of the Imperial palace, nourishing an old friendship and new sprouts.

"Rin!" the empress called out from the work shed.

"Ah!" A surprised Rin jumped up from the patch of Rufizo's fingers—an herb whose leaves could be smoked to relieve pain as well as to induce a sense of euphoria. "How did you know—er, yes, I'm here!" Quickly, he stuffed the leaves he had collected into his sleeves, brushed the dirt and grass off his robe, adjusted his hat, and walked into the shed confidently, prepared to deny everything.

The shed was suffused with the smell of a thousand herbs that made Rin dizzy. He rarely came here, as the place seemed to him full of things that could harm him: Plant specimens—possibly toxic—and strange animal parts dangled from crisscrossing lines, drying in the sun; cabinets along the walls were filled with tiny drawers labeled in Jia's neat hand; sea horses, jellyfish, centipedes, spiders, tiny snakes, and other exotic creatures floated in jars of distilled liquor; notebooks overflowing with Jia's recipes and experiments lined the bookshelves.

Jia herself was working at the counter. She was pounding on some mixture in a mortar, the muscles in her forearms bulging with the effort. The sound of the pestle scraping against the bowl and crushing the ingredients made Rin fear the worst.

To his relief, the empress made no mention of the missing herbs. She stopped what she was doing and greeted Rin with a casual bow as though they were meeting in one of the taverns in Zudi.

"We've all been so busy that we haven't had a chance to chat like in the old days. Here, I've created a few new pills that I think you'll like." She opened one of the tiny drawers in the cabinet and retrieved a few paper packets and handed them to Rin. "The first one is good for cold nights—it keeps the chill out of your bones and can give you a quick energy boost. I know the emperor works you hard and sometimes you have to stay up late. The second one is a sleep aid, but it also gives you peaceful, vivid dreams; I know you like happy herbs." Rin blushed at this, but Jia went on, "And as for that last teal packet . . . well, let's just say that the next time you are with a woman, try it. I'm sure she and you would both appreciate it." She grinned at him and went back to her mortar and pestle.

Rin's face was now bright red. He managed to mumble a few words of thanks and put the packets away. He had never married and started his own family, instead devoting all his efforts to serving the Imperial family. He knew that he wasn't the most talented of Kuni's advisers, and he had obtained his position in large measure because he had grown up with Kuni—well, also because he was able to bend the rules and do things that Kuni needed done without having to know about them. He had always been a bit insecure about his own place in Kuni's life, and Jia's solicitousness warmed his heart.

"Are things going well with the farseers?" Jia asked casually.

"It's all right," said Rin. "Things are peaceful. There are always some dissatisfied old nobles and veterans who had served the Hegemon complaining about their bad luck, but nothing that you or Kuni need to worry about."

"If that is so, I suppose your requisitions from the Imperial Treasury haven't been very extensive? And you haven't had to hire many people?"

"That's right," said Rin, pride in his voice. "I've actually asked for a reduction in my budget." He wanted to make sure Jia knew that while he might still be tapped into the world of organized crime and making a small profit—mostly by keeping his spies away from certain gangs who offered information as well as bribes—he wasn't skimming from Kuni.

Jia chuckled. "Rin, you are honest to a fault sometimes. Don't you know the basic rules of bureaucratic maneuvering?"

Rin was confused. "I'm . . . not sure I understand."

"Zato Ruthi complains to the emperor constantly about the amount of work involved in administering the Imperial examinations fairly, and so year after year, he gets a bigger budget and hires more of his friends and students. Cogo Yelu comes up with one new scheme for the emperor after another, and he thereby enlarges his staff and occupies more offices. Those in the College of Advocates are always discovering new ways they can be helpful to the emperor and write more detailed critiques, and so they are allowed to review more types of petitions and pay for more research. Even the generals and enfeoffed nobles know to describe the pirates and bandits in their territories in meticulous—perhaps even exaggerated—detail so as to justify the bloated sizes of their armies and fleets. If you don't find things for yourself to do, how do you expect to keep a seat at the table? What need is there for a Farsight Secretary if there are no plots and rebellions against the emperor?"

Rin was even more moved. Jia was like a big sister who was watching out for his interests, knowing that he didn't have the native talent to keep up with clever people like Gin and Cogo. "So . . . should I be telling Kuni that . . . that there are more malcontents plotting rebellion, like those scholars and Hegemon cults, and ask for a bigger budget?"

Jia didn't turn around but continued to pound away at the mortar, punctuating her speech with the rhythmic noise. "Well, *exaggerating* will only get you so far. The rule of bureaucratic life is that all the departments are competing for a limited pool of funds, and everyone is trying to enlarge his empire. To really secure your position, you have to show Kuni results."

"But . . . how? Dara is at peace. There are always complainers, but few are serious about starting a rebellion."

Jia stopped and looked at Rin, amused. "If there are no rebels, can't you . . . create some?"

"What?" Rin wasn't sure he was hearing right.

"There are many who dislike this time of peace," Jia said, and there was no longer a smile on her face. "But they don't act because they lack funds, weapons, and men. Suppose, however, that you find a way to get them weapons and money and light the fire of ambition in their hearts, don't you think that, in time, you'll be able to reveal to the emperor a massive plot and demonstrate the need for your department?"

"But why would I encourage a plot against Kuni?"

"Not *encourage*," said Jia, "not exactly." She reached up and pulled down a leaf drying on one of the lines stretched across the shed. "Do you know what this is?"

Rin looked at the leaf. It was thin and wrinkly, and resembled nothing so much as an octopus. He shook his head.

"This is a plant called drainwright grass, often found in Géjira. Because Géjira is so industrious, many landowners build workshops to supplement their income, and the dyes and acids and bleach they use make the soil toxic. Later, if they wish to restore the land to farming, the inhabitants plant drainwright, which delights in pulling the salt and pollutants out of the soil and incorporating them into itself as a way to deter herbivore animals. The farmers then cut down the drainwright grass, burn the leaves, and cart the ashes away. A few cycles of this would cleanse the soil and make it suitable for planting again.

"Do you understand what I'm saying, Rin?"

Rin struggled to make sense of Jia's obscure hints. "You are saying . . . that if I make money and weapons available to those who I suspect of disloyalty, it is a way to get them to come to the surface, a way to extract the poison hidden in the empire's soil."

Jia nodded. "And when you expose such plots, you'll earn Kuni's eternal gratitude and gain yourself a bigger budget."

Rin thought through the plan and grinned. It reminded him of the way low-level bosses in rival gangs sometimes colluded to secure their positions in the eyes of their respective bosses through manufactured conflict. He bowed deeply. "I can't thank you enough, Jia. A single conversation with you is worth ten years spent in a schoolroom."

Jia chuckled. "Flattery does not suit you, Rin. If you carry the plan out, Kuni and I will both have much to thank you for. But of course, this will only work if you keep it a secret, otherwise Kuni will not be so impressed with the plots you foment and uncover."

Rin nodded like a chicken pecking at rice. "Of course. Of course!"

Jia watched as he left, the smile on her face gradually fading like a ghost.

CHAPTER NINETEEN

PARTINGS

PAN: THE FOURTH MONTH IN THE SIXTH YEAR OF
THE REIGN OF FOUR PLACID SEAS.

Though it was good to catch up with old friends and to indulge
in the fruits of civilization, there were only so many banquets one
could attend and only so many teahouses one could visit before the
appetite waned. It was time for Luan to leave the Harmonious City.

Gin came to the city gates to see him off.

"Will you come to Nokida to spend a few days with me?"

Luan shook his head.

"I had hoped you would come so that you could meet . . ." Gin's
eyes dimmed for a moment before turning resolute again. "You have
your journey, and I have mine. I take it you'll head north to prepare
for your search for the Immortals?"

"Yes," said Luan. "But first, I have some ideas for outfitting the
expedition on the cheap that will take a bit of time to work out."

He wanted to embrace her but stopped himself. Ever since the
night of the celebration held for Mün Çakri's son, Gin had been acting
cool toward him. Perhaps it was a way for her to dull the sorrow of

parting by not getting too entangled in the first place. And who was to say he wasn't doing the same thing himself?

Still, it was not easy to leave a lover without saying what was on his mind.

"Be careful, Gin. You're too proud. Don't make enemies with those who will always have the favor of the cruben."

Gin looked at him, her eyes narrowed. "Have you ever known me to shy away from a fight?"

Before Luan could reply, a crisp voice called out from the side. "Teacher!"

Luan turned and saw Zomi Kidosu striding toward him from the city, holding a satchel over her shoulder.

"I thought we already said our good-byes, Mimi-*tika*."

"Did not Lurusén say that it was the duty of a student to accompany her teacher for ten miles at the start of every journey?"

To the side, Gin shifted and cleared her throat.

Zomi turned to her as though realizing that the queen was there for the first time. "Your Majesty, I meant to come by and thank you earlier. I was very fortunate that Princess Théra was able to secure your help on my behalf."

Gin nodded imperiously. "Don't mention it."

"I'm curious, Your Majesty. How did she—"

Gin interrupted her. "I said *not* to mention it. Don't you understand?"

Zomi's face flushed, and she nodded.

Luan observed the exchange quietly, suppressing his irritation at Gin. She was clearly annoyed that Zomi had not acknowledged her, a queen, before acknowledging her untitled teacher—Gin's pride verged on arrogance. He was a bit puzzled that Gin and Zomi would know each other, but he decided not to pry as it was clearly not a topic Gin wanted discussed.

Gin glanced back at Luan, seemed about to speak, stopped, tried again, stopped again. Finally, she said, "A pelagic anemone cannot be cultivated in an aquarium. I wish you well."

She turned to leave.

"You never looked at yourself in the Fool's Mirror!" Luan called out.

Gin stopped. Without turning around, she said, "You say I am proud; so why should I not compare myself to the winter plum?"

Then she left.

"You look sad, Teacher," said Zomi.

"Oh, it's nothing," said Luan. "Just thinking that we all have to be true to our natures."

The winter plum was a poetic companion to the chrysanthemum. Just as the chrysanthemum was the last flower to bloom before the onset of winter, defiant against death, the winter plum was the first flower to bloom before the coming of spring, refusing to shield its powerful fragrance from frost and snow.

Have you ever known me to shy away from a fight?

"The emperor finally decided on a position for me!" said Zomi.

"Oh, what is it?" asked an excited Luan. At the end of the Palace Examination, there had been so much consternation and outrage at Zomi's performance that the emperor said that he needed some time to think about a suitable assignment.

"He has appointed me to the College of Advocates!" said Zomi. "I'm starting at second rank, above all the other new appointees."

"Deservedly so!" Luan was pleased. Zomi's voice would be exactly what the emperor needed to carry out his plan.

And the two walked ten miles together, stopping every mile or so to drink from the bottle gourds Zomi carried in her satchel. Zomi told him her plans for reshaping Imperial policy and for bringing her mother to Pan, and Luan nodded and laughed, seeing hints of the shape of the future.

"Teacher." For the first time, doubt and hesitation crept into Zomi's voice. This was the end of ten miles, the last chance for her to ask her question. "What if I were to tell you that I've done something terrible, something that would change the way everyone sees me?"

Luan looked at her. "I once counseled a king to break a peace treaty so that thousands would be slaughtered in order to save hundreds of thousands of future lives. The emperor once betrayed his best friend to give Dara a better future, elevating the grace of kings above personal honor. Let the past be the past, Mimi-*tika*, and endeavor to make the future that resulted from your choice be a better one."

Zomi carefully considered this advice, and then she nodded and bowed.

"Teacher, may you continue to find treasure everywhere you go."

Luan drained his cup, turned it so that Zomi could see it was empty, and then bowed back and left without another word.

Let old heroes fade into story and song; the world will be remade by new heroes.

"Brother, I'm glad we have a chance to chat before you leave," said Jia, raising a cup of plum wine. She sat in relaxed *géüpa*, her legs folded easily under her. "It is so rare for the Imperial family to be together."

Across from her, a nervous Kado Garu raised his cup in response. He remained in stiff *mipa rari*. "Sister, I'm honored by your invitation."

Kado and Jia had never been close. He was certain that the empress had summoned him for some purpose.

"You've done an excellent job with Dasu," said Jia. "You know how special the island is to Kuni—it is his second home, in some ways. He gave the island to you because he couldn't trust anyone else to run it."

Kado turned Jia's words over in his mind. *What does she mean? She knows very well that I'm doing nothing in Dasu. I haven't even visited the place more than half a dozen times since I was made the "king," letting Kuni's governor-regent do whatever he wants in my name.*

"I've been blessed by an able assistant picked by Kuni," said Kado. He hoped that the answer was what Jia wanted to hear.

"You don't need to be so modest," said Jia. "To have a scholar recommended by you take the first place in the Palace Examination! No one expected that of poor little Dasu."

Ah, so that's it, thought Kado. He had seen how Jia seethed as Zomi Kidosu embarrassed Prince Timu during the Palace Examination. Rumor had it that the empress was extremely protective of her son since Kuni seemed to favor Phyro over Timu. A cold sweat broke out on Kado's back. *If Jia thinks that somehow this Zomi Kidosu is my way of further strengthening Risana's push for Phyro to be designated the crown prince . . .*

"I have a confession to make, Sister," he said. "I didn't recommend Zomi Kidosu."

"Oh?" Jia lifted her eyebrows.

"I was not being modest when I said Ra Olu, my regent, really runs everything on my behalf. For the Grand Examination this year, I signed the blank passes ahead of time, and he filled in the names of the top *cashima*, sending the list to me later for ratification. I really had nothing to do with the candidates."

"Still, you could have revoked her pass. You're the one who sent her on her path to fame and glory."

"That's just it, Sister." Kado put down the cup and leaned forward conspiratorially. "Zomi Kidosu's name wasn't among those sent to me for ratification."

Jia froze. "What?"

"When I saw her at the Palace Examination, I was surprised." Kado smiled. "But I didn't say anything because . . . uh . . ."

"Because you figured if she did well, you could take credit for recommending her. Why mess with success?" Jia said, smirking.

"Ahem." Kado cleared his throat awkwardly. "I can't hide anything from you. Yes, I'm sorry, but such a thought did cross my mind. I should have been more circumspect, of course."

"So if you didn't recommend her, how did she come to be in possession of a pass to the Examination Hall? Was it a forgery?"

"I did do some discreet investigating afterward. She got in with a proper examination pass, but it wasn't one signed by me."

"Who did sign it?"

"Queen Gin of Géjira."

Jia looked thoughtful. Then she smiled and raised the cup again. "Thank you, brother. Thank you."

A breeze passed through the courtyard outside, caressing the nodding blossoms of the dandelion.

GUSTS AND GALES

CHAPTER TWENTY

THE MAGIC MIRROR

TUNOA: THE SIXTH MONTH IN THE EIGHTH YEAR
OF THE REIGN OF FOUR PLACID SEAS.

The veneration of the Hegemon had begun with his death on the shore of the Big Island, across the channel from Farun.

Eight years earlier, Mata Zyndu, the greatest warrior who had ever walked the Islands of Dara, had committed suicide along with his faithful consort, Lady Mira, after being betrayed by his erstwhile friend, Kuni Garu. When news arrived that the Hegemon had refused to cross the channel because he could not bear the shame of facing the people of his homeland, many had vowed to fight Kuni Garu to the bitter end to avenge their lord.

However, instead of sending an invasion force, Kuni had pardoned all of the Hegemon's followers and planned a lavish burial outside Çaruza to show his great affection and admiration for the man. The gods of Dara had also cooperated by intervening at the last minute to take the body of Mata Zyndu into the realm of myth and legend.

In the rest of Dara, people whispered of the generosity of Kuni Garu, now known as Emperor Ragin. Scholars competed with each other to write biographies and compose odes to the emperor, celebrating his friendship with the Hegemon and the tragic flaws of Mata Zyndu that had made the breach in their friendship inevitable.

But in Tunoa, commanders of the last army units loyal to the Hegemon reminded the common people that those who were victorious by sword and horse never lacked willing accomplices who wielded the carving knife and the brush. After all, the greatest flaw of Mata Zyndu was trusting that wily Kuni Garu, the bandit-of-a-thousand-lies, too much.

Then the emperor announced that the Tunoa Isles would not be enfeoffed to a noble, but would remain directly under Imperial administration. To honor the man the emperor had once called brother, the people of Tunoa would not have to pay taxes for five years. The palace would buy all the dried fish it needed exclusively from Tunoa at guaranteed prices as well as offer positions in the palace for the women of Tunoa to work as Imperial embroiderers. Finally, Zyndu Castle would be renovated and turned into a mausoleum for the Hegemon, and the Imperial Treasury hinted at a large roster of local masons, carpenters, blacksmiths, and general laborers who would be employed.

It was a transparent ploy, as was the wont for vulgar Kuni Garu. Still, people needed to eat and drink, and children needed to be fed and clothed. The Hegemon's remaining captains and lieutenants found fewer and fewer people who echoed their calls for vengeance, and eventually, they stopped. Quietly, their soldiers deserted the garrison forts, sold off their uniforms to collectors, and faded into the fishing villages.

By the time the emperor's emissaries arrived at Farun harbor, bearing the headless body of Réfiroa, Mata Zyndu's famous black steed, and his weapons, the magnificent bronze-iron sword Na-aroénna and the fearsome toothed war club Goremaw, the people of Tunoa stood onshore silently to welcome the relics of their lord. Without having to fire a single arrow or spill a drop of blood, the emperor's emissaries accepted the surrender of the Hegemon's last commanders.

Réfiroa was buried in the family cemetery for the Zyndu clan, and, after months of work to renovate and enlarge the ancient structure, the sword and the cudgel were installed in the highest room in Zyndu Castle, a place of honor they shared with the weapons left behind by past generations of Zyndus. Priests and priestesses of Rapa and Kana, paid a stipend by the emperor himself, maintained an everlasting flame in the ancestral hall, and pilgrims came from everywhere in Dara to hear about the deeds of the great man and to view the weapons that had transformed Dara.

The emperor had carried out his promise, and the people of Tunoa smiled as copper pieces jangled in their pockets. There was no more talk of vengeance or honor.

That was the way of the world, wasn't it?

But keeping alive the memory of a spirit had its costs: It was hard to keep such a spirit confined.

Mota Kiphi had grown up hearing stories of the brave deeds of his father, one of the Hegemon's original Eight Hundred warriors.

He had been born after his father had already left Tunoa with the Hegemon for the Big Island seventeen years ago to join the rebellion against the Xana Empire. It was said that Mota's father had killed twenty Xana soldiers at the siege of Zudi and that he had fought by the Hegemon's side during the charge at Wolf's Paw, killing three Xana hundred-chiefs and earning the rank of hundred-chief for himself.

His father had never returned, which only made the stories truer.

What boy didn't wish to emulate his father?

But the two men in front of him now didn't look like deposed Tiro kings. In fact, with their ragged clothes and scraggly beards, they looked like desperate robbers who had turned to begging. The Tunoa seaside cave in which they "held court" was small and dank, and the stuffy, hot air was infused with the stench of briny sea and rotting garbage.

"I was the first to discover Kuni Garu's treachery at Thoco Pass," said one of them, who called himself Doru Solofi, King of South

Géfica. He seemed insulted that Mota did not know who he was.

"Did you really know the Hegemon?" Mota asked, skeptical.

Solofi chuckled. "What a time we live in that a king could be interrogated by a child."

"Any fraud could claim to have known the Hegemon," said Mota. "I used to play at being the Hegemon myself when I was little."

"Here, I'll show you proof," said the other man, wiry and dark-skinned, who called himself Noda Mi. From somewhere deep in the cave, he retrieved a long bar of jade carved with intricate patterns. "This is the Seal of Central Géfica, the Tiro state created by the Hegemon for me."

Mota examined the jade bar carefully. Though he couldn't read any of the Ano logograms, he could tell it was very valuable and the workmanship was exquisite. He decided there was a chance that these men could have been nobles—or at least they were pirates or robbers who had stolen this artifact from nobles.

"If you were Tiro kings, how did you end up here in this cave, not even able to afford to pay me for the food I brought you?"

"We didn't ask you here to talk about food and money!" snapped Doru Solofi. "I saw you showing interest at that dancing troupe's performance honoring the deeds of the Hegemon, and I thought you might be willing to serve the Hegemon again."

"What do you mean? My family already venerates the Hegemon. Not only do we go to the mausoleum in Farun once a year, but we have a private shrine set up behind the house—"

"That isn't serving," an impatient Solofi interrupted him. "Are you willing to fight for him?"

Mota backed up a few steps. "That is talk of treason! I won't join some plot against the emperor, who's been respectful of the Hegemon's memory."

"What if the Hegemon himself told you that it's your duty to avenge him?" asked Noda Mi, a cold glint in his eyes.

"Wh-what do you mean?" Despite the heat, Mota felt a chill going down his spine.

Noda walked to the back of the cave, where a crack in the ceiling let in a single beam of bright sunlight that fell against a natural ledge. He knelt at the bottom of the ledge as though at a shrine, retrieved a silk bundle, and reverently unwrapped it.

"Come," he said, beckoning to Mota. "Gaze into this."

Gingerly, Mota walked closer and picked up the mirror. It was made of bronze and very heavy. The back of the mirror was carved in relief, and by the illumination of the beam of sunlight, he could see that it was the figure of the back of the Hegemon, standing tall with Na-aroénna in his right hand and Goremaw in his left, both pointing at the ground. He flipped the mirror around and looked into the smooth, brightly polished surface. A reflection of himself stared back. Nothing out of the ordinary.

"I've seen mirrors like this all over the place," said Mota. "This is better made than the one my mother has—"

"Be quiet!" said Noda Mi. "Now, watch."

He placed the mirror under the beam of sunlight and tilted it until the reflection, a much larger circle of light, fell against the opposite wall of the cave.

Mota stared at the image, his eyes wide open and his jaw hanging. Then he fell to his knees, and he touched his forehead to the ground. "I am yours to command, Hegemon!"

Noda Mi and Doru Solofi looked at each other and smiled.

On the wall of the cave was the clear projection of an image of the Hegemon, this time from the front, a grim, determined look on his face. Both weapons were raised in the air as he prepared for another immortal charge. A line of zyndari letters curved around him like a halo: *Kuni Garu must die.*

As word of the magic mirror spread, more bold young men and a few bold young women came to the mysterious cave to gaze upon this apparition. They examined the mirror carefully and could find no flaw in its perfectly smooth surface. Yet when placed under a beam of sunlight, the ghostly image of the Hegemon in battle invariably appeared.

The only explanation, however improbable, had to be true: The Hegemon was speaking to them from beyond the grave.

Noda Mi gathered them into groups to practice what he called "spiritual dancing" at night, where the young worshippers had to follow certain choreographed steps that were a blend of traditional sword dancing and parade-ground marching. After they worked up a sweat, Noda handed out bowls of hot soup that smelled strongly of medicinal herbs, and as they drank, the ghost of the Hegemon watched over them from a projection against the mountainside, cast there by a bright full moon or the light of a flickering torch.

And as the medicine took effect, the image of the Hegemon would start to move before their eyes, leaping, dodging, charging, rushing. The worshippers would start to chant, falling into a hypnotic trance:

> My strength is great enough to pluck up mountains.
> My spirit is wide enough to cover the sea.
> In life I was the King of Kings.
> In death I am the Emperor of Ghosts.
> Na-aroénna will once again drink blood.
> Goremaw will once again sup on marrow.
> Let us redeem honor from a dishonorable land.
> Kuni Garu must die!

"Excellent take tonight," said a satisfied Noda. He loved the sound of coins jangling in his purse, the collected donation from the evening's congregation.

"Don't we already have plenty of money?" asked Doru. "I'm sick of dressing like beggars all the time. When can we change into clean clothes and go visit the indigo house again?"

"Patience, my brother," said Noda. "We don't want to draw the attention of the Imperial governor or Kuni Garu's spies. We've been lucky, but let's not push our luck too far. The funds we're gathering must be turned into weapons."

They had indeed been extraordinarily lucky. After several failed rebellions and months of running and hiding from Duke Coda's spies, they'd decided to make their way to Tunoa, where they hoped the strength of the cult of the Hegemon would provide them with fearless warriors.

The farseers pursued them into the isles, where they suddenly seemed to lose interest in the two deposed Tiro kings. Not only did they fail to capture Noda and Doru, but, perhaps overconfident with their past successes, Duke Coda's agents began to make mistakes.

In teahouses where Noda and Doru thought they were trapped, the hunters spoke of their plans in voices loud enough to be overheard by their prey and departed without making an arrest. Careless and lazy, they left behind in hostel rooms maps and orders signed by Duke Coda himself, from which Noda and Doru gathered important information about the movement of Duke Coda's funds.

At first, the two kings could not believe the intelligence revealed by these documents. According to what they read, a few of the convoys shipping precious jewels for the duke were practically unguarded, relying for protection on the fact that they were disguised as garbage haulers. Noda and Doru tried their luck by raiding one of these and were rewarded with a large haul of treasure without any loss of life—Duke Coda's drivers practically ran away the moment they realized they were under attack. The two kings had a good laugh over the cowardice of the emperor's spies.

The money allowed them to extend their reach, to hire spies who infiltrated noble courts and Imperial magistracies across Dara. It was delicious to use money intended for spying to spy on the spymasters.

Their luck had taken an even better turn as they visited an indigo house, where a pretty girl with dark hair chatted incessantly of her skill and boasted of the gossip she had heard from her important clients. But her face flushed red after just a single cup of plum wine, and she was asleep before the flask was even empty. Noda had then searched her room and found her trunk unlocked, confirming his suspicions that her foolish clients had made her quite wealthy.

Noda grabbed the money purse and left in a hurry, and only later did he and Doru realize that the satchel contained more than jewels. There was an herbal recipe for inducing a hypnotic trance—no doubt one of the girl's tricks—as well as a discarded draft in beautiful calligraphy critiquing the emperor's policy of decreasing funding for the armies of the independent fiefs—perhaps a memento left by one of the girl's customers.

Noda had immediately concocted the plan to approach the nobles for surplus weapons. With the reduction in Imperial funding, the nobles had no choice but to reduce the sizes of their armies, increase taxes, or begin selling weapons on the black market, and he was sure more than a few would choose the last.

But the luckiest find of all had been a mirror, which was packed at the bottom of the girl's money purse, wrapped in a sheet of paper. At first, they had thought it another piece of jewelry, as it was made with a gilded handle and back. But one day, while idly admiring himself in the mirror, Doru Solofi discovered that the mirror cast an image of a naked woman onto the wall despite its perfectly smooth surface. The wrapping paper around the mirror had given the name and address of the mirror maker, an obscure shop in Haan.

Noda had immediately dispatched trusted messengers to the place, and, as he suspected, found out that the shop had a secret technique for mirror making that they had developed only recently. Though the shop owners were reluctant to produce words of treason, a combination of money and threats against the family had persuaded them to collaborate and make the mirrors that would play a key part in the shows that Noda and Doru put on for their followers.

"Do you remember how we thought the gods might be in favor of our plan when we pledged to be brothers in Pan two years ago?" asked Noda.

Doru nodded.

"I'm beginning to believe it."

CHAPTER TWENTY-ONE

MOTHER AND DAUGHTER

PAN: THE FOURTH MONTH IN THE NINTH YEAR OF
THE REIGN OF FOUR PLACID SEAS.

"The emperor agrees with me that adding more biography to our curriculum is a good idea," said Zato Ruthi.

A spring breeze wafted through the instruction hall, bringing with it the fragrance of early-blooming flowers.

"As the sons and daughters of the emperor, it is my hope that the great deeds of important historical figures will inspire you to greater virtue and that the patterns of the past will warn you of pitfalls for the future. I want each of you to spend the next month focusing on a figure of your choice from the recent past. You will study that person's life in detail and explain his rise and fall, connecting that experience with the broader patterns of history.

"Fara, why don't we begin with you? Who do you want to study?"

"I want to hear stories about Lady Mira," said seven-year-old Fara. Three years had passed since the first Grand Examination of the Reign of Four Placid Seas. Though she had lost the baby fat that had once charmed the Lords of Dara, her eyes remained full of mischief and insuppressible delight.

"The Hegemon's consort?" Ruthi pondered this request and then nodded approvingly. "Lady Mira tried to mitigate the Hegemon's more volatile tendencies, and in the end she died to demonstrate her faith to her beloved husband. She was a paragon of virtuous womanhood, and a fit choice for a young lady to study. Now, Prince Timu, who is your favorite?"

Timu, now sixteen years of age, knelt up very properly, placed his hands together one behind the other, and slid them up the opposite forearms so that the flowing sleeves covered both—this was a formal gesture he had learned from reading old books, as it showed respect for the teacher by not sullying the teacher's eyes with leftover wax and stray ink on the student's fingers. He bowed his handsome face. "Master, I would like to study the deeds of King Jizu."

Phyro rolled his eyes. Fara giggled and covered her mouth.

"Ah." Ruthi's eyes glowed with pleasure. "That is an admirable choice. Of all the Tiro kings during the rebellion, Jizu was certainly one of the most virtuous. He loved the people more than life itself, and his sacrifice is rightfully celebrated by poets and wandering story-tellers alike. Designating him as a model for emulation speaks well of your character. What about you, Prince Phyro?"

"I want to hear all about the Hegemon and Queen Gin," said the stocky twelve-year-old, who had grown much taller and more mus-cular in the last three years.

Ruthi hesitated. "The Hegemon did have nobility of character—a fact that the emperor recognized in his eulogy; I can understand the appeal. But why Queen Gin?"

"The Hegemon was the greatest warrior of Dara, yet Queen Gin defeated him—what tales of daring must lie behind that fact! Uncle Yemu and Duke Kimo often reminisce about the time they fought with her, but I'm sure there are stories they won't tell me. Please, Master Ruthi, you have to satisfy my thirst for knowledge!"

Ruthi sighed. "I shall do my best, but you have to do the reading!

I may begin by assigning you my essay on her conquest of Rima. . . . Remember, not all the rumors you've heard are true."

Théra and Phyro exchanged knowing smiles.

Ruthi turned to the last student. "Princess Théra, what about you?"

The fourteen-year-old princess, whose face combined the beauty of her mother with a hint of her father's impish looks in youth, hesitated only for a moment before replying, "I want to study Princess Kikomi."

Ruthi frowned. "Théra, Kikomi chose to betray the rebellion out of her foolish devotion to Kindo Marana, Marshal of Xana. She played upon the affections of the Hegemon and the Hegemon's uncle, seducing both with her wiles. She was fickle of character and unwise in her actions—a most unsuitable choice."

Théra's eyes flashed. She took a deep breath. "I respectfully disagree, Master. I believe Kikomi was misunderstood, and I intend to rehabilitate her name."

"Oh? How do you mean?"

"The charge that she was motivated by love for Kindo Marana is based only upon the words she uttered before her death. There is no hint in any of the records of Kindo Marana that such a romance existed between the two."

"We know that she took him to bed after the fall of Arulugi—this was attested in the trusted memoirs of palace officials in Amu."

Théra shook her head. "She was his captive by then. Her actions might have been an attempt to seduce him to save Amu. Müning fell but wasn't sacked, which suggests she accomplished the same feat as Jizu: a deal with the conqueror to save the city."

"Then what of her manipulation of the Hegemon and Phin Zyndu?"

"Could the ploy not have been the price exacted from her by Marana in exchange for sparing Amu? Marana was known to press every advantage to divide and conquer his enemies."

"But she proclaimed her love for Marana even unto death!"

"She had to! If her plot were revealed, the Hegemon would have sought vengeance upon Amu. Her dying words could be an attempt to divert the Hegemon's rage toward Marana."

"This is a bold theory . . . but . . ."

"It's no bolder than the ploy of Tututika, who during the Diaspora Wars played a similar game of seduction to save Amu from the wrath of Iluthan's armies."

"But you're talking about a goddess—"

"Who is also the patron of Amu. She would have served as a natural inspiration for the princess."

"You have no evidence—"

"I have read everything I could find concerning Kikomi *not* written by scholars and historians: memoirs by her adoptive family as well as by mere acquaintances; everything she wrote and was said to have written; gossip, legend, and lore. Practically all these sources agree that she was devoted to her people and ambitious, and I found her essays to be full of insights on the nature of power and the path of history. Her character simply does not match that of the foolish caricature drawn by court historians."

"Yet history is full of examples of women who have done worse for love—"

Théra shook her head. "That's just it, Master. If Kikomi were a man, would you have been so convinced that she betrayed her people for a misguided romance?"

"Men can certainly fall prey to the same disease. Indeed, Phin Zyndu was entrapped by Kikomi's feminine wiles."

"But you also speak of Phin Zyndu's bravery and long-suffering preparation for vengeance, and the Hegemon's courtship of Kikomi is but a single episode in the storytellers' expansive repertoire based on his life. On the other hand, the women of history are defined by the men they loved. We never hear anything about Lady Mira except that she killed herself out of love for the Hegemon—Fara, did you know that Lady Mira's art was once desired by all the nobles of Çaruza?— and we never talk about Kikomi except as a seductress blinded by love, though she was one of the most important leaders of the rebellion. Talent can wear a dress as well as a robe. Why the discrepancy?"

"Hmmm . . ." Zato Ruthi was at a loss for words.

"You see the patterns you expect to see, Master, and I believe Kikomi took advantage of that tendency—not just in you, but in the soldiers who rushed into Phin Zyndu's bedroom. To accomplish her goals, she chose to sacrifice her own good name."

"That is an act of great courage and wisdom to attribute to a woman. . . ."

"Master, you once misjudged a woman's ability to fight a war, and you lost your throne. I say this not as an insult, but as a reminder that the lessons of history are not always easy to see. I can never prove to the satisfaction of all that my theory is right, but I choose to believe my version because it's more interesting."

She sat back in *mipa rari*, fully expecting to be berated by her teacher for bringing up a painful episode in his life.

After a long silence, Ruthi bowed down to Théra.

Surprised, Théra bowed back.

"The proudest moment in a teacher's life," said Ruthi, "is when he learns something new from his student."

Quietly, the empress stood outside the instruction hall, listening to the proceedings within.

To accomplish her goals, she chose to sacrifice her own good name.

She smiled bitterly. History was full of tales of rival queens plotting palace intrigue for the benefit of their children, and that was how they would tell her story.

But they would be wrong, so very wrong.

She loved the people of Dara, and they would hate her. That was the price to be paid for truly grand and interesting ideas.

As the children continued to converse with their tutor, Jia silently walked away.

Chatelain Otho Krin came into the work shed.

"The messengers have returned, Lady Jia." That was what he always called her in private.

Jia came up to him and gave him a quick kiss.

"The donations were delivered successfully," Otho said. "But though I am in charge of the palace budget, I don't think I can find any more money without raising suspicion."

"I will find you more funds," declared Jia. "You're certain that neither the leaders of the Hegemon cult nor the farseers know the source of the money?"

Otho nodded. "I was very careful never to reveal my identity to the messengers."

"Rin watches Tunoa closely. It couldn't have been easy to sneak the money in."

"It would have been difficult without Lady Ragi's idea of using a traveling folk opera troupe as messengers."

A smile flitted across Jia's face. Ragi was one of her former ladies-in-waiting, who had married Gori Ruthi, Zato Ruthi's nephew and Under Minister of Transport and Carriage. "Ragi always did like the traveling shows. Do you remember how when she was a girl in Çaruza, she begged you and me to take her to the shows even when the Hegemon placed me under house arrest?"

The memory of those more dangerous but also more carefree days made Otho's heart throb with pain. He shook off the reminiscences and continued, "Rin Coda's spies keep a close eye on shipping through the ports by merchants and large landowners as well as the bigger smuggling gangs, but they rarely pay attention to itinerant entertainers, especially the women. The actresses recommended by Lady Ragi were able to hide the funds and other goods in prop trunks and bring them into Tunoa without Duke Coda's spies ever suspecting that anything was amiss—it also helped that the troupe had a letter of introduction from Lady Ragi's husband."

"So many men think of women as mere props and entertainers," said Jia. "It's easy to hide in their blind spots."

Otho flinched. He didn't like it when Jia spoke like this, so cold and calculating. But he was in love with her, and love made it necessary to ignore certain feelings.

"How did they get them into the hands of the cult leaders?"

"This was slightly trickier, but the opera troupe was able to sell one of their actresses to an indigo house, again hiding the goods in her trunk. When one of the cult leaders came to visit, she was able to give everything to him without making it appear that she was doing so. Once the deed was done, the troupe redeemed her freedom and they went on their way."

Jia nodded. "Clever. I'm sure he's as blind as Rin's spies." But her elation soon faded as she clenched her fists in frustration. "Now if only those fools would make use of all the resources I've given them! I can't do everything for them."

"What do you want me to do with the opera troupe?"

"Give them the promised pay," said Jia. "And also this." She handed him a few paper packets. "Tell them it's a formula for experiencing communion with the gods—it will be true if they try it, at least for a while."

Otho nodded and did not ask for more information. He had decided long ago that not knowing all the details of what Jia planned was best for his peace of mind. One time he had seen one of the messengers running naked through the street, screaming that he was burning up from the inside before throwing himself under the hooves of a team of spooked horses. Another time he had heard rumors of men who had died in the throes of passion in an indigo house. Jia was creative with her formulations.

"Just to be sure," she added, "leak the fact that the troupe is flush with money to a few gangs of thieves."

Sometimes he felt that he didn't understand her at all, but she needed him, and he would always be there for her.

"Don't be troubled in your conscience, Otho." Jia graced him with a regal smile. "I have tried to explain what I'm doing to you, but politics is not your natural realm. Trust that I act to protect the dream of Dara, the fragile peace that Kuni and I have built."

And seeing that Otho was unconvinced, she affectionately wrapped her arms around him. "Then try this: Know that I act out of love for Kuni, even if he would not understand. Love makes us do strange things."

Otho nodded. He *could* understand that sentiment.

∽ ᗆ ∽ ᗆ

As Théra and Kuni worked in the garden-farm, Consort Risana strolled by and stopped.

"I was just looking for you, Kuni!" she called out.

"Auntie Risana," Théra said. "Sorry I can't greet you properly. I'm a bit muddy at the moment."

Risana waved to indicate that it was all right. "It's so nice to see you two enjoying the spring sun together. I wish Hudo-*tika* would join you."

"Hunting is good exercise, too," said Kuni.

He wiped his sweaty face with a towel and left the field to join his wife.

"You look like you have some good news to share," he said, smiling.

"I do indeed. Cogo has looked at my draft proposal for model leases between landlords and tenant farmers and thought it a good idea."

"Of course he would," said Kuni. "Standard lease terms will help curb the sort of abuses that Zomi Kidosu spoke of, and place the tax burden where it belongs. Getting the nobles to promulgate these models in their domains will be trickier, however. They'll view it as more Imperial interference in their affairs."

To the side, Théra continued to plant sweet lantern seedlings. Her ears perked up and her hands slowed down at the mention of Zomi's name.

"I have a solution for that," said Risana. "When you issue the edict, you can couch it as a request for comments. That way, each of the nobles will be able to offer suggestions and adapt the model for conditions unique in each fief."

"Good," said Kuni. "That way, they'll feel consulted rather than imposed on."

"And I will write privately to the wives of the most recalcitrant lords. I know what most of them are really afraid of, and by assuring the wives that this policy has nothing to do with the empress, they'll pass the sentiment on to their husbands."

Théra knew that both Consort Risana and her mother exercised much of their influence through informal means, and her father depended on them to maintain a web of social ties and unofficial communications to help smooth the running of the empire.

"Thank you," said Kuni. "You are always so circumspect."

"It's enough that you know what I've done," said Risana, and she and Kuni shared a kiss and continued to talk in lowered voices.

It's too bad that she can't take credit for her ideas, Théra thought.

"What do you think of Roné, Than Carucono's nephew?" the empress asked.

Théra and Jia were arranging flowers in the courtyard outside the empress's private suite. They'd always enjoyed doing this together, ever since Théra was a little girl and brought dandelion puffs to her mother so they could blow on them together.

"He seemed really full of himself," said Théra. The Carucono family had come into the palace for a visit earlier, and Théra served them tea as they chatted with Jia.

"He's a *firoa* who barely missed the cutoff for the Palace Examination," said Jia. "And Than treats Roné as though he were his own son. He has reasons to be proud."

Théra scoffed. "I'd be more impressed if he had bolder ideas." The memory of Zomi Kidosu's performance at the Palace Examination three years ago came unbidden to her mind. She smiled to herself.

Jia stopped trimming the flower stems to look at her. "Then what do you think of Kita Thu? He certainly set the tone for boldness of presentation."

It took Théra a few moments to remember who her mother was referring to. "The one who advocated for a return to the Tiro system? He was a joke!"

"There are more than a few in the Islands who support his ideas," said Jia. "What may seem like a joke to your father doesn't always appear that way to others."

"I thought he was without vision," said Théra stubbornly.

"What of Naroca Huza? The prime minister speaks well of him."

It finally dawned on Théra that her mother's tone was not at all casual. *Why is she asking about my opinion of these men?*

"I am perhaps too young to judge the character of men," said Théra, now very cautious.

Jia went back to trimming the flowers. "Are you really? Half of the noblewomen your age have already been contracted in marriage."

"But I don't even like any of these people!"

"Our choices are limited, and you need to think about the most advantageous way to position yourself for the future. You're a clever girl, but a suitable alliance is the best way to ensure that your cleverness is not wasted. Do not define your life by romantic notions."

Théra's heart pounded. She dared not speak lest she scream. *Are these alliances for my sake or for the sake of my brother?*

CHAPTER TWENTY-TWO

THE EMPEROR'S SHADOWS

PAN: THE FOURTH MONTH IN THE NINTH YEAR OF
THE REIGN OF FOUR PLACID SEAS.

The small airship drifted over Lake Tututika, which glistened in the sun like an endless mirror. From this height, the small fishing boats appeared as water striders, and even the eagles hunting for fish circled below the ship like small gnats. A dozen palace guards manned the feathered oars, pulling to the beat of a light drum. Inside the gondola, the emperor, the empress, and Consort Risana sat around a small table, snacking on sugared lotus seeds and drinking hot green tea. It was rare for the Imperial family to find the leisure to enjoy a spring day together, away from the concerns and intrigue of the palace.

"Phyro is begging to visit Gin again," said Risana.

Jia said nothing as she methodically wiped the porcelain teacups with a white cloth.

"That boy has always liked the company of generals more than books," said Kuni. He chuckled. "I can understand that."

"In a time of peace, books are more important than swords," said

Jia, as she carefully deposited powdered tea into the cups with a bamboo scoop.

"Phyro grows restless," said Risana. "He complains that Master Ruthi's lessons, while valuable, are not teaching him what he needs to know."

Kuni closed his eyes for a moment to breathe in the fragrance of the powdered tea. "There is only so much you can learn from books. No book could have prepared me for being emperor, and I doubt my children would be any different."

This was as close as Kuni ever got to acknowledging the awkwardness of his lack of a plan of succession. Risana glanced over at Jia, but Jia seemed to be concentrating only on the brazier over the hot coals.

Risana bit her lip and decided that she had to risk it. "It's best for both princes to learn the art of administration." She kept her eyes on Jia as she continued, "Phyro can help Timu as an adviser when the day comes for Timu to take over." She hoped that she had done enough to assure Jia, whose moods she had always found hard to read.

Jia waited until the water was just boiling in the brazier, the bubbles covering the surface like the foam blown out by fish over a quiet corner of the pond. Then she lifted the kettle off the brazier and poured the scalding water into the three teacups, flexing her wrist so that the stream of hot water shot out like a concentrated beam of light, dipping into the cups in quick succession.

"The princes do need practice to understand how to drive the carriage of state," said Jia. "Please, have a taste. Lady Fina's parents sent this from Faça."

Risana sipped the tea. "It is excellent. Honored Big Sister, your skill at bringing out the best qualities of each variety of tea is unparalleled."

Jia smiled in acknowledgment. "Kuni, you're not the eldest in your family, and yet it is you, not your brother, who has become Emperor of Dara. We should not be tied to the idea of primogeniture. The prince who is most suited to rule should ascend the throne."

Risana almost felt pity for Jia. It must have taken Jia every ounce of strength to acknowledge her weakness. Kuni had come to power with the aid of men (and women) who were more at home in a saddle than in a court, and almost all of them found Risana the more sympathetic queen and Phyro the better future heir. And although Kuni had never explicitly broached the idea of designating Phyro as the crown prince, anyone who had eyes could see how Kuni favored the younger boy.

With her last statement, Jia was practically conceding the struggle at this point.

"You are truly an extraordinary woman," said Risana, determined to be gracious in victory. "I am humbled by your grandness of spirit."

Jia sighed inwardly. The awkwardness between Kuni and Timu was a complicated matter that many thought was rooted in the prolonged separation between father and son during the Timu's earliest years, when Jia and the children had been the Hegemon's hostages. By the time father and son were reunited, Timu had become more attached to Jia's lover, Otho Krin, than his father. Timu's formal demeanor and timid nature in the following years had not helped things.

But she knew that it would be a disaster if Phyro were to become the emperor. It was up to her to see that future never come to pass, not just for the sake of Timu and herself, but all of Dara.

"I have an idea," Jia said. "The best way to tell who is most suited to rule is to observe them in practice—a friendly competition, if you will."

Kuni chuckled. "It is good that we have only two princes to worry about."

Years ago—after the death of Consort Fina—Kuni, Jia, and Risana had all agreed that Jia should prepare herbs for both wives that would prevent further pregnancies. Even with the skill of someone like Jia at hand, childbirth was an extraordinarily dangerous event for women, and Kuni didn't want to see anyone else close to him die in that manner. There were enough children, he had declared, and though he didn't voice it aloud, he was perhaps also worried about more children intensifying future rivalries over succession.

"A kingdom is not as large as the empire, but it has similar problems on a smaller scale. It would be good for the princes to get some experience at ruling." Jia sipped her tea. "Just like a shadow puppet play can portray the world in miniature, the princes can play at being the Emperor's shadows."

"The Emperor's Shadows," mused Kuni. "I like it. Where do you suggest the princes be given their realms?"

"Kado is not doing much in Dasu," said Jia. "In fact, I get the feeling that he would be perfectly content to retire from the throne in favor of one of his nephews. You might as well leave Kado and his family with a hereditary title with no fief—they'll be taken care of, but they won't have to bother with the responsibility."

Kuni nodded. He wasn't particularly close to Kado, and this seemed like a good solution. "Timu or Phyro?"

"Dasu is in need of a ruler with more care for the spiritual and intellectual development of its population," said Jia. "Advocate Kidosu had said as much. I think Timu would be more suited for the fief, and Imperial Tutor Zato Ruthi can assist him."

The suggestion made sense to Kuni. "What about Phyro?"

Risana tensed and disguised her anxiety by sipping from her cup. She regretted not seizing the opening earlier to suggest that Phyro be an apprentice of sorts for Gin Mazoti—that would have given Phyro the experience he needed as well as bringing him even closer to the most powerful general in the realm. But Jia now had the initiative, and she could do nothing but wait.

Jia looked thoughtful. "This is the Year of the Wolf, potentially a time of strife and danger. Since forces loyal to the Hegemon are plotting mischief in Tunoa, why not send Phyro to the new fief and give him the power to fully pacify the land? Rin Coda could be his adviser. After all, you cannot fight all your sons' battles for them."

Risana turned over Jia's suggestion in her mind. She could find no fault with it. Both Dasu and Tunoa were similar in size and population (indeed, Tunoa was slightly bigger). Jia's idea matched the skills of both princes with local needs, and it really did seem that she was trying to do the best for both boys. "I'm grateful for your thoughtful care for our children," said Risana.

"I'm only doing my duty," said Jia. "You're the sister I never had."

And the three continued to drink tea and admire the lovely lake laid out beneath them. Between the sky and the water, the airship was a single pearl that connected everything to everything else in a web of light.

The announcement of the Emperor's Shadows set all of Pan abuzz.

Many wondered whether this meant that the emperor was thinking of a bigger role for the princes to play—and a smaller one for himself; some praised the decision to send Prince Timu to focus on the cultural development of Dasu; others worried that the appointment of Prince Phyro indicated a rise in the dissatisfaction of old nobles with Emperor Ragin's rule; still others thought of the whole thing as an episode in some exciting shadow puppet show, wherein rival princes built independent bases of power at the ends of Dara.

Lady Soto was reading to Fara in the western end of the garden when Jia came down the path, a small basket in hand.

"Aunt Empress," said Fara. She stood up and bowed in deep *jiri*.

"Go on and play by yourself in the orchard," said Soto. "I'll come and find you later, and we can finish the story." Fara scooted away, and Soto laid the book down next to her.

Jia glanced at the title on the book. She frowned. "Isn't Fara a bit too young for the story of the Queen of Écofi and the Seven Princes?"

"Children can deal with bloody tales a lot better than we give them credit for," said Soto. "It's real bloodshed that we should save them from."

Jia inclined her head and considered Soto. The corners of her lips lifted. "Soto, I think we're far past the time when we need to be playing games. If you have something to say to me, say it."

Soto took a deep breath. "I've been trying to figure out what you're doing, but I confess I'm stumped."

Breezily, Jia said, "I'm on my way to the hothouse to pick some oranges for the children."

"I think I've earned the right to be spoken to without jest. I've gone through the palace accounts—Chatelain Krin may be careful, but it's impossible to not leave marks when so much money is involved."

The smile faded from the empress's face. "You're wondering if I'm still trying to ensure that Timu will be the crown prince. The answer is yes."

"I know that. But I can't figure out how the Emperor's Shadows will accomplish that, or what it has to do with your secret diversion of funds from the Imperial Treasury. You once worried that Phyro was going to gain the loyalty of Kuni's generals with his easy manners and admiration for the martial arts, and I can only imagine you'd try to remedy that by either reducing the power of the generals or by gaining Timu some respect with them. But your plan doesn't seem to do either of those things."

"When you try something repeatedly and it doesn't work, continuing along the same path would be madness."

Soto took a deep breath. "I'll always be loyal to you, Jia. But I have affection for all the children. I don't like to see any of them hurt."

Jia looked back, her eyes level. "Why is it that a mother's actions are always assumed to be selfish? I've watched all the children grow up together, and I have affection for them all, even if I didn't give birth to every one. But I've also seen blood flow when men grow ambitious and wish to seize by force that which is not theirs. I must do what I can to prevent that future. I am the Empress of Dara, and my first duty is to the people."

"Do you see such a future with Phyro on the throne?"

Jia looked away for a moment and seemed to come to some decision. "Soto, you chose to serve my husband because you believed that he would give Dara a better future than the Hegemon. Do you still believe that's true?"

Soto nodded.

"Your belief is the greatest danger of them all."

"I don't understand."

"Like the Hegemon, Kuni places too much faith in personal trust. During the Chrysanthemum-Dandelion War, he allowed Gin Mazoti to declare herself queen, gambling that the gesture of trust would buy her loyalty. He allows each of his nobles to keep an army large enough to bring ruin upon the land, though the Islands are at peace. Like the man he once called brother, Kuni has decided to build his empire upon bonds of trust between him and those who serve him."

"And why is that wrong?"

"Because trust is fickle and will not bear a heavy load. Kuni has made the empire dependent on him because he thinks only he can see a path forward. That is a fragile state. Phyro, though he is young, shows the same tendencies."

"But in a time of great tumult, is it not best to be sure the reins are held by a man strong enough to guide the carriage? Timu does not have such strength."

"Perhaps not. But instead of a Dara kept tranquil by vows of loyalty and friendship, I want a Dara founded upon systems, institutions, codified behaviors that, through repetition, become *reified*. The only way to build lasting peace is to strip power away from individuals and invest it in structures. Kuni thinks that when men are moral, they will do the right thing. But I think it is only when men are doing the right thing—regardless of reasons—that they can be said to be moral."

"You might speak the language of the Moralists, Jia, but at heart I think you're an Incentivist. The only way to achieve what you wish is to reduce governance to a system of punishments and rewards."

Jia smiled wistfully. "It could be said that all good kings are Incentivists dressed in Moralist clothing, perhaps assisted by able Patternist ministers."

"What of the Fluxists?"

"They live in a realm beyond mere mortals. In the sublunary sphere, we must always think the worst."

Soto sighed. "Risana is playing sparrow tiles while you're playing *cüpa*."

Jia laughed. "You make me sound so calculating and . . . cold."

"Aren't you?"

"I have said all I can. Even a trusted friend . . . well, I have been frank on what I think of trust."

Soto searched Jia's face. Eventually, she sighed. "You have grown ever more subtle. I cannot tell what is in your mind."

"Remain my friend, and think not so lowly of me. When you think well of someone, all their actions appear to you in a kinder light. What if the plot you think you see is but an echo of your own fears projected onto an innocent act?"

"Advocate Kidosu!"

Zomi stopped just beyond the bridge over the stream that led to the private part of the palace. She turned and saw that it was Princess Théra, who was walking toward her from the middle of the emperor's vegetable garden. Though she was dressed in a plain robe meant for the field and her hands were muddied, her graceful movements and confident demeanor proclaimed her status as though she were dressed in silk and wore gossamer gloves.

Zomi suppressed her impatience and nodded. "Your Highness." Every time she came to the palace—which wasn't often, since a junior advocate like Zomi might be summoned to court only a handful of times a year—Théra seemed to find some excuse to talk to her. But the princess never had anything interesting to say.

"Are you busy?" the princess asked. "I haven't seen you in a while."

"How can I be of assistance?" Zomi asked, failing to keep the stiffness out of her voice.

She berated herself for her rudeness. She could not explain to herself why she felt such annoyance with Théra every time she saw her. In truth, she ought to be grateful to her. Théra was the one who'd managed to secure her a pass into the Grand Examination and gave her a chance.

But she didn't *feel* grateful. In fact, the intervention of Théra and her brothers had, in some way, taken away from the purity of her victory—yes, that was it: They were from different classes, as different as a chrysanthemum was from a dandelion, and yet Théra insisted on acting as though they were equals, without acknowledging her privileged life, without the delicacy to be embarrassed by the gulf between their circumstances. What was a mere game for her and her brothers—getting that pass to the examination—had meant the difference between achieving a dream and having it dashed to pieces.

She disliked the way Théra *played* at being other than who she was: the way she'd disguised herself as a commoner at the Three-Legged Jug, the way she dressed up to play at being farmer here in the Imperial garden, the way she asked after Zomi as though they were friends when, in fact, their lives had nothing in common.

"Oh, nothing," said the princess. "I didn't mean . . . I just wanted to . . ." Her face turned red.

Zomi waited.

"I've been thinking about your proposal for abolishing the use of Ano logograms," said the princess, her words tumbling over one another in a jumble. "I found a reference in a poem Kikomi once wrote that reminded me of it I wasn't sure if you had read it I could copy it out for you if you want or you could get it at the library of course you could—"

"Your Highness, I can't be late to see the empress, who has summoned me."

"Oh," said the princess, disappointed. "I'm sorry." Then she seemed to screw up her courage and blurted out, "I admire you, Advocate Kidosu. In fact, I envy your life. You're free to live by your merit, while my only worth is bound up with my birth, a tool to further the ambitions of others."

It took every ounce of Zomi's strength not to lash out at her. Instead, after a few deep breaths, she simply said, "Your Highness, do not use the word 'envy' so casually when you do not know the paths others have trod on. Few women—no, few *people*—have the advantages you possess. If you lament that you cannot live as you like, perhaps it is because you have not tried to live as yourself at all."

"I am honored beyond words, Your Imperial Majesty," said Zomi Kidosu, sitting in formal *mipa rari*. She felt extremely apprehensive. The empress had never summoned her, and she still felt flustered from her encounter with Princess Théra.

"Not at all," said Jia. "Relax." She shifted into *géüpa* and gestured for Zomi to do the same.

They were in the empress's small audience hall, a part of her private suite. The straw sitting mats were smooth under them, and the fire in the wood-burning stove kept the room comfortable against the early spring chill. A flask of warm plum wine rested on the table between them, along with two cups.

"I hear often of your petitions to the emperor. He is very impressed with your work."

With some effort, Zomi suppressed her surprise. Since her appointment to the College of Advocates three years ago, she had worked on dozens of detailed petitions critiquing policy proposals put forward by the various ministers, including some by Prime Minister Yelu and even some that originated from the emperor himself. She had always received the same comment back from the emperor: *I have read it.* None of her bolder ideas had ever been implemented.

She had despaired of ever making a difference.

"Please, try the wine," said the empress.

She poured from the flask and filled both cups. The fragrance of winter plums filled the air. Zomi took a sip to be polite. The wine was strong, and she felt her face grow warm.

"I understand that your mother has not agreed to come to Pan."

Zomi tensed. She never spoke of her private affairs at court.

"Thank you for your solicitousness, Your Imperial Majesty. My mother is used to her way of life, and she thinks she will be unhappy in the bustle of the capital."

The empress nodded. "My parents are the same. They do not want to come and live in the palace, no matter how often I've invited them. They far prefer their home in Faça, where they get to do as they like, instead of having to watch everything they say and do here at court."

Oddly, Zomi was touched. The woman who sat across from her was nothing like she had expected.

"Of course, my situation is much simpler," said the empress. "I may not be able to discharge the duties of a daughter by serving at their side, but I can send them whatever I like: treasure, a musician who I think they'll find pleasing, or an airship to bring them a team of Imperial cooks to make authentic Dasu meals for their birthdays."

She grinned at Zomi, who laughed as she imagined the sight of an airship being dispatched to shuttle a surprise birthday celebration to aged parents. Then she looked wistful.

The empress turned somber as she continued, "But I imagine it is much more difficult to provide a better life for your mother on the small salary of a member of the College of Advocates. The emperor wants to run the college as a lean organization, but your colleagues either come from much better off families or have other ways to supplement their income."

The empress's sympathetic tone broke down Zomi's last shred of guardedness. The stipend paid to the College of Advocates was meager, and life in Pan was expensive. Though she scrimped and saved every copper piece, she had not been able to send much money back home to her mother.

Moreover, she refused to play the games that her colleagues engaged in. Other advocates in the college often visited the expensive restaurants and opera houses of Pan in the company of ministers whose policy proposals they were supposed to critique; sometimes they left carrying discreetly wrapped packages under their arms, a satisfied smile on their faces. This was how one became friends with the powerful and received favorable promotions. Zomi understood that as she watched her colleagues being promoted away from the college into policy positions, one after another, but she could not bring herself to join them. She was too disgusted.

"The emperor believes in rewarding those of talent, and so do I. I think I may have a solution to your problem."

"I fear that this foolish advocate may not be up to the task Your Imperial Majesty has in mind," Zomi said.

"Queen Gin wrote to the emperor asking for a prime adviser. I recommended you."

Zomi looked at the empress, utterly amazed. Becoming prime adviser to an important noble like Queen Gin was akin to becoming prime minister to a Tiro king of old. Such officials had great powers, and she was sure to be able to get some of her ideas implemented—a far preferable change to writing ineffective critiques of other people's ideas. And out of all the nobles, she admired Queen Gin the most. Furthermore, since the queen had recommended her to the examination, it seemed that her secret would be safest if she served Gin.

It also didn't hurt that such a promotion would come with a massive increase in her salary. Finally, she might be able to carry out her promise to her mother.

But it was strange for the empress to take such an interest in a noble's affairs. By all accounts, the empress was dedicated to reducing the powers of the nobles. In fact, last year, Zomi Kidosu had critiqued the empress's proposal—ultimately carried out—of reducing Imperial funding for the nobles' armies in order to divert more funds into civil infrastructure projects. She had actually been in favor of the proposal, but it was the job of the advocates to poke holes in every policy suggestion regardless of personal feelings.

While Zomi was still reeling from the revelation, the empress continued, "Despite the rumors, I value highly the vital role played by the independent fiefs as places of policy experiment. Queen Gin is an able warrior, but . . . she lacks finesse in civil administration. Your help would be much appreciated. Besides, she is likely to trust you implicitly because you're Luan Zya's student."

It didn't surprise Zomi that the empress knew who her teacher was—the emperor had guessed, after all. She nodded at Jia's discreet reference to the relationship between her teacher and the queen.

Though what Jia said made sense, Zomi couldn't help but feel that the empress had something else in mind. She might not be skilled in politics, but she knew that such a favor usually came with a price.

"Do you have any special instructions for me?" she probed. The discord between the queen and the empress was an open secret. If Jia wanted her to betray Queen Gin in some way, she had to find a way to turn down the post.

"Only one: that you do what is right for Dara, no matter the consequences," said Jia.

Zomi looked at her questioningly.

"Prince Phyro is clever but inexperienced," said Jia. "Duke Coda is skilled at his work but is likely to be overzealous. I'm afraid that while pacifying Tunoa, the two might harm the innocent in a way that the emperor might come to regret. Not all criticism of the emperor is treason, and if the prince and the duke press men and women of talent who hold a different opinion too severely, they'll need a refuge in Dara."

Zomi thought over the empress's words. They also made sense. Her performance at the Palace Examination and her strident critiques at the College of Advocates had already established her reputation for being brash. An argument from her to protect dissenters would seem natural—indeed, she smiled as she remembered the Three-Legged Jug.

"You do not intend to eliminate the fiefs?" she ventured. "I confess that I thought—"

"You can't trust everything you hear," said Jia. "I have always wanted only what is best for Dara. An open mind is open to persuasion, and your advocacy of more independence for the fiefs is very persuasive."

Zomi blushed, pleased that her petitions had been read by the empress and found compelling. *Maybe I haven't been wasting my time after all.*

She knelt up in *mipa rari* and bowed deeply to touch her forehead to the ground. "Empress, you are truly in possession of a capacious mind."

Jia gestured for her to rise. "One more thing: Never reveal this conversation to anyone else."

Zomi looked up, a question in her eyes.

"The scholars grumble when the wives of the emperor interfere in the affairs of state," Jia said, a light, bitter smile on her face. "We must minimize the extent to which my role is visible. Such is the plight of women who have not risen through the ranks by merit, as you have."

Zomi nodded and bowed again. "I swear that I will never reveal the confidences you have entrusted to me."

They finished the flask of wine, and Zomi left, a spring in her steps.

"Ah, vanity," whispered the empress, long after Zomi was too far away to hear her.

For hours Théra locked herself in her room, tears of humiliation flowing down her face.

She had admired Zomi Kidosu from afar for years, living vicariously through her, imagining adventures that Zomi got to have that she couldn't. To have the woman talk to her the way she had shattered into a million pieces the illusion she had built up inside her head of a kind, wise, caring friend.

Something Zomi said echoed in Théra's mind and refused to fade: *Perhaps it is because you have not tried to live as yourself at all.*

The young princes and princesses decided to go for a ride in the spring air. Fara rode in a carriage while Timu, Théra, and Phyro took horses. Two dozen palace guards surrounded them, and carriages and pedestrians respectfully moved to the sides of the road as they approached.

"Have you thought about what you'll do in Dasu?" Théra asked Timu.

"I'll probably start by visiting the places that were important to the start of the emperor's rise: the entrance to the Grand Tunnels, the false shipyard that fooled Kindo Marana, the beach where he used to sing with Aunt Risana, and so on. Then I'll try to devise a way to fund schools to help young people like Zomi, and consult with Master Ruthi as needed."

"Is he morose that he has to leave Pan and go so far away?"

"Not at all. He's very excited. He wants to be able to do more research in the archives there to fill in some gaps in the history of the

Chrysanthemum-Dandelion War, especially about Queen Gin's role early on."

Théra saw that Timu was sitting straighter on the back of his horse, and he was talking more animatedly than usual. The prospect of being on his own, away from a father he couldn't ever seem to please, seemed to invigorate him.

"What about you, Hudo-*tika*?"

"Uncle Rin and I have already planned out several traps for the traitors!" Phyro rubbed his hands in glee.

Théra grinned. "Tunoa is a rough land. Are you sure you're going to be okay with no thousand-layer cake for dessert every night?"

"Do you still think I'm Fara's age?" Phyro looked wounded. "I'm going to catch fish for myself just like the Hegemon once did! Tunoa is full of history; it's the birthplace of generations of the marshals of Cocru. I'll be strolling through the ruins of ancient castles and communing with the ghosts of grand heroes. What can be sweeter than sleeping upon a bed of grass on the slope of a storied hill after a day of hard marching, a canopy of stars over my head?"

"You kind of butchered that quote from Ra Oji," said Théra, laughing. "Ra Oji was talking about death being a natural consequence of the flow of life, and he didn't want an elaborate funeral—"

"I get to interpret Ra Oji's words however I want," declared Phyro. "The words are dead, but *I* am alive."

Théra smiled and said no more. Phyro really was a lot like their father in many ways. She just hoped that he would learn to govern his impulses better as he grew up.

Looking at her happy brothers, Théra felt the pangs of another bout of envy. They were going to go into the wide world and experience life. Still mere boys, they would make decisions that changed the lives of the people—albeit with some supervision and advice from Zato Ruthi and Rin Coda. They were starting down the path to a life of accomplishment, of judgment and rule. She, on the other hand, was going to be cooped up in the palace, preparing for the only future that she could see: a marriage to some mysterious man.

But she was assuaged by the thought that she had taken a small step to change that future.

"Father, what of your other shadows? Do they not deserve a chance as well?"

"What would you like, Rata-tika?"

Dust motes had danced in the slanted sunbeams in her father's private study, as chaotic as her thoughts.

"Do not contract either Ada-tika or me in marriage without our assent. Will you promise that?"

"Of course! I wouldn't think of it."

"Not even if Mother tells you to?"

He had looked at her as though assessing a student at the Palace Examination. "No, not even if your mother says so."

She had sighed with relief. Then she added, "Don't assign a new tutor for us after Master Ruthi leaves. I will teach Ada-tika myself, and I want to study what I like."

It was only a small step, but it was the start of finding out who she was besides the dutiful daughter, the loving sister, the polite princess, or the conscientious student.

"Look, a wild goose!" shouted Fara. She stood up in the carriage to point with her hand. Théra moved closer to the carriage in case she fell.

But Timu and Phyro had already ridden ahead. While Timu shaded his eyes to gaze up at the flight of the wild goose and muttered something about the weather patterns, Phyro took the bow off his shoulder and notched an arrow.

"Don't!" Théra cried out, but it was too late.

Though he was strong for his age, Phyro still lacked the strength to draw the bow fully. The arrow fell harmlessly short of the wild goose. But the palace guards, to please the prince, had all stopped and shot their arrows in a barrage, and the wild goose, with a pitiful cry, fell from the sky.

"This is almost the same as if I had shot it myself," said Phyro.

The palace guards cheered in assent.

"Poor goose," said Fara.

"Yes, poor goose," said Théra.

CHAPTER TWENTY-THREE

LETTERS FROM CHILDREN

NOKIDA: THE SIXTH MONTH IN THE ELEVENTH
YEAR OF THE REIGN OF FOUR PLACID SEAS.

Dearest Mama,

*I was surprised to hear from your last letter that you
were thinking of leaving Dasu for an extended period of
time to visit relatives in Rui. Is the house I built for you not
satisfactory? Are the maids not doing good work? Reading
between the lines, I suspect that the neighbors are jealous of
your daughter's success and have made you uncomfortable.
Do not let them spoil your enjoyment! The queen pays me
well, and I wish to make your life better, as I promised.*

*Sorry I haven't written in so long. It's not much of an
excuse, but I've been busy because work is going very well.
I'm given a lot of responsibility, and the queen, I think,
trusts me more with each passing day. Right now I'm
working on a pet project whereby I try to teach the daughters
of the farming families of Géjira the zyndari letters and
have them read the Ano Classics in vernacular translation,*

without forcing them to learn the Ano logograms. They love it! There is so much beauty in Classical Ano literature, but so few get to enjoy it because they cannot read the logograms. Already the girls are writing beautiful stories full of Classical Ano allusions—and other than the fact that they're in vernacular translation, I think they're better than the stories written by the boys their age in the private academies.

Oh, this will amuse you. I've taken to peppering my reports to the queen and the other ministers with fake Classical Ano allusions translated from folk sayings you used to lecture me with. Here are a couple of examples:

Crudigada ma joda gathéralucaü rofi, crudigada wi joda giratha, üü ingro ça fidagén.

That's "Nothing good ever comes from bothering the gods when they don't wish to be bothered."

Méüdin co daükiri ma géngoa co üri kiri né othu.

That's "Every day in the lives of the common man is a day of battle."

I know you can't get the full effect because I'm only sketching the logograms with shorthand instead of sculpting them with wax, but trust me, they're lovely to look at.

The best part is that not a single minister has recognized them for what they are! They all act as if they know exactly which Moralist treatise or religious scroll I'm quoting from, even though these are not real Classical Ano quotes at all. They're so afraid of being seen as not learned that they'd rather nod their heads and sigh and tell me what a great allusion I've made.

The queen, though, looks at me funny when she runs into one of them. I think she sees through my little jokes (and enjoys them, hopefully).

Do take care of yourself, and please let me know if there is anything I can do for you.

Your Mimi

∾ ᔈ

DASU: THE SIXTH MONTH IN THE ELEVENTH YEAR
OF THE REIGN OF FOUR PLACID SEAS.

Most Honored Rénga,

*Permit your unworthy son to wish you a thousand
happy days in the space of a hundred, which is to say: May
each of your days be ten times as happy as each regular day,
which is not to say that there is a such a thing as a regular
day for the overburdened and wise Emperor of the Islands
of Dara, since each of your days must be ten times as
worrisome as a day in the life of someone like me, therefore
making the wish of a day ten times as happy, on balance,
merely appropriate and deserving. . . . Ah, words trip over
one another when this unworthy son tries to express his
genuine affection and awe for his most august sovereign
and father.*

*Your query in the last letter quite shocked and surprised
me, and I have devoted all of my time to finding an answer.
I believe I can now offer you a not-unsatisfactory response,
which, to wit, is as follows.*

*Your query: Confirm that the candidates sent by Dasu
to the Grand Examination this year are indeed from
Dasu.*

*Answer: To fully answer this query required much
research and precise definition of terms, as concepts such
as "Dasu" and "from" and "sent by" are all contested and
require some careful parsing. . . .*

[About thirty pages of dense Ano logograms later]

*I remain, ever lovingly and obediently,
your most devoted servant and child,
Timu, Prince of Dara, Regent of Dasu*

Jia jabbed Kuni in the ribs.

"Aw! Ahem! Excellent reading, excellent!" Somewhat disoriented, Kuni shouted at the mostly empty private audience hall.

"*I* was doing the reading," said Jia, "not some scribe. Did you really fall asleep?"

"Asleep? No! I was merely resting my eyes."

"How could you!"

"Jia, you can't possibly blame me for this! Timu's letters have gotten more and more tedious over time. He has always tended to pleonasm, but I'm afraid his prose has grown as out of control as the weeds at the edge of my garden."

"Prince Timu's style is . . . ornate," said Risana.

"He takes ten sentences to say what could be said in one, which is to say, what others may—oh, look, he's even gotten me to do it!"

"He's just nervous when he has to write to you," said Jia.

"Let's focus on the answer he gave you," prompted Risana.

"Can one of you summarize for me? I confess that I . . . didn't quite get his answer."

"He explained that yes, your suspicion was right. Of all the candidates sent to the Grand Examination from Dasu, almost half were from families who had moved to Dasu from the core islands within the last five years," Jia said.

"I knew it!" Kuni called out triumphantly. "These rich families are all the same, always looking for a way to game the system."

"It wasn't a bad idea to reach a compromise with the protesting *cashima* from five years ago," said Jia. "We all agreed that adding points to the scores of examinees from provinces outside of traditional areas of scholarly excellence like Haan and Géjira would achieve more regional balance among the *firoa*."

Kuni sighed. "As soon as I agreed to the change, I suspected enterprising families from the core islands would move to places like Dasu and Tunoa in hopes of securing an advantage in the Imperial examinations for their offspring."

"This is hardly in the spirit of your policy," said a frowning Risana.

"No," said Jia. "Though I suppose if the policy entices some Haan families to move to Dasu, it will, in a way, also help elevate the spirit of scholarship there."

"I shall write to Timu to ask him to adjust the Provincial Examination system to reward those families who have been in Dasu longer—"

"Or you could just inform him of what you think is the problem and let him figure out the solution," said Jia. "He's supposed to solve problems for you, not the other way around, you know?"

Kuni agreed this was very wise.

∾   ∽

TUNOA: THE SIXTH MONTH IN THE ELEVENTH
YEAR OF THE REIGN OF FOUR PLACID SEAS.

My Dearest Father,

Between the time of my last letter to you and now, there has been a sudden spate of assassinations of officials and posters denouncing the House of Dandelion tacked to magistracy gates. Garrison soldiers have grown fearful and would not leave camp unless in twos or threes.

This was most surprising, as I thought the threat from the secret cults was on the verge of being eliminated.

An accounting of my reports to you will reveal that since our arrival in Tunoa two springs ago, Duke Coda and I have uncovered more than two hundred secret cults centered around the worship of the Hegemon. The cults varied in membership between a dozen to a few hundred, and most were harmless, composed of simple peasants venerating the memory of Tunoa's favorite son. However, a small number of the cults used reverence for the Hegemon as a cover to foment rebellion, progressing as far as assassinating low-level Imperial officials and amassing weapons.

Pursuant to my decision early on to outlaw all private worship of Mata Zyndu and to direct all who wished to honor the Hegemon to the mausoleum in Farun, Duke Coda has been leading the effort to crack down on the troublemakers. You and I both have commended the speed with which he uncovered these nests of poisonous snakes and captured their leaders—sometimes it seemed as if he had a preternatural sense for where they would be found, as befitting the reputation of the Imperial Farsight Secretary.

Most of these cults were started by dissatisfied nobles of the old Tiro states, though a few were funded by Géjira merchants unhappy with your new policy of supporting the farmers at the expense of merchants by setting a price floor. We have been coordinating with Queen Gin to reveal the identities of all the merchants involved.

Meanwhile, we've also been mindful of your admonition to pair the whip with sweet apples. While we have executed the cult leaders publicly, ignorant men and women who supported the leaders out of a misguided devotion to the Hegemon were treated with leniency. Youthful scholars who possessed much passion but little wisdom and who published tracts against you were handed back to their parents so that they might stay home and reflect upon the errors of their ways. We've also increased the funding at the Hegemon's mausoleum: The more worshippers who can be drawn there, the less fertile Tunoa becomes for would-be cultists.

Nonetheless, the recent upsurge in acts of defiance against the Dandelion Throne suggested that our policy required adjustment.

In the past, the secret cults tended to build their bases deep in the woods and hills, far away from the villages. This

actually made them easy to spot by airship, as the cooking
smoke from the camps would be visible from far away.
However, no such signs were seen on recent air patrols.
Duke Coda suspected that the cultists have adapted by
hiding themselves better. He came up with a plan, which I
heartily approved.

I restricted the shipment of wax and whale oil into Tunoa
until most towns and villages had used up their supplies.
Then I lifted the restrictions, but with an announcement
that there might be further supply shortages down the road.
Meanwhile, Duke Coda's spies monitored the sale of wax
and whale oil across Tunoa, noting where unusual amounts
were being purchased. Duke Coda reasoned that the cultists
must be sleeping during the day and operating at night.
They would need candles and oil lamps for illumination,
and the recent supply constraint and my announcement
would induce them into purchasing large amounts for a
hoard.

We soon identified multiple towns where sales of candles
and lighting oil seemed far in excess of the people's ordinary
needs. More spies were sent to investigate in depth.

What they discovered was shocking: Noda Mi and Doru
Solofi, two of the Tiro kings created by Mata Zyndu, had
been building up a network of secret societies dedicated to
the cause of rebellion. They had been operating out of caves
and cellars at night, out of sight of our airships, where
followers gathered to worship the Hegemon and to plot
treason by the thousands.

Garrisons and priests from the mausoleum were
dispatched to raid these cells. In the past, arresting and
hanging cult leaders, followed by priests explaining that
the only way to properly worship the Hegemon was at the
mausoleum, was usually sufficient to end the cults. But this
time, the soldiers had to fight. Not only did the followers

of Mi and Solofi resist violently, they even slaughtered the priests, claiming that they were not the proper spokespersons for the Hegemon.

Rumors that Mi and Solofi could converse with the spirit of the Hegemon could be heard on every street corner, and we finally tracked down their source when we captured about a dozen mirrors endowed with strange magic. Although they seem plain enough, when placed in the sun, they project an image of the Hegemon in a supernatural manner. Duke Coda and I have studied these mirrors in depth, consulting expert mirror makers and scholars, even destroying a few of them in the process, but none could discover their secret. Noda Mi and Doru Solofi are now in open rebellion, and more foolish men and women rally to their cause daily, inspired by the belief that they have the aid of the dauntless spirit of Mata Zyndu.

I have sent a few of these mirrors with this letter in the hopes that you can help discover their secret. Though the rebels' ranks are swelling, though they seem to be finding weapons out of nowhere, and though we have suffered some setbacks, yet we'll fight them without fear, without relent, trusting in your guidance.

Very lovingly,
Your Phyro

∽ ∽

PAN: THE SIXTH MONTH IN THE ELEVENTH YEAR
OF THE REIGN OF FOUR PLACID SEAS.

"Phyro has really grown up," said Risana. "He sounds more confident with every letter, leaving behind childish sentiments. Listen to that final line—such courage." She glanced at Jia and quickly added, "Still, he has to do more to match his brother. Dasu has done amazingly well at the Grand Examination this year, managing to produce three *firoa* and sending one candidate to the Palace Examination. Despite the problems we've uncovered in Dasu, no doubt much of the credit should also be given to Timu's hard work in that remote outpost."

"Or perhaps Master Ruthi just unconsciously taught the scholars of Dasu how to please the judges at the examinations," said Jia, a faint trace of a smile on her face. "Phyro is doing the difficult work of keeping this hard-earned peace."

"I detect the hand of Rin in this one," said Kuni. "He used to be a letter writer, you know? He's trying to make the best of a bad situation by emphasizing their efforts. Phyro might have written the report, but Rin can't help adding in his special touch."

Jia nodded to herself. *Rin probably regrets taking my advice now. But this is only the start.*

"Are you saying things are worse than the letter says?" an anxious Risana asked. "Shouldn't you send aid?"

"Fathers cannot always fight all the battles for their sons," said Jia.

Kuni pondered this. "Jia's right. That last line is not quite a call for reinforcements. If I send aid now at the first sign of difficulty, I would undermine his authority by expressing a lack of confidence. Phyro was too quick and harsh in his dealings with the cults, but I have to let him work this out by himself."

"How did things deteriorate so fast? I thought Rin and Hudo-*tika* had it all under control," said Risana.

"It's not how strong the rebels are *now* that worries me. It's how much stronger they could become," Kuni said. "This is one of those times when I really wish for the counsel of Luan Zya, who was always so good with strange contraptions."

He tossed the letter aside and picked up one of the bronze mirrors from the platter. Walking near one of the windows in the private audience hall, he let the bright sunlight fall against the mirror and contemplated the projection on the ceiling.

The face of the Hegemon stared back at him. The carving was very skilled, with powerful lines that captured his angular features and unorthodox cross-hatching that gave the face depth. Mata Zyndu's famous double-pupiled eyes stared down at Kuni in a confident scowl. As the mirror's reflection shimmered in the heat from the sun, the image seemed to come to life.

"Hello, brother," whispered Kuni. He shivered despite the heat.

"This is just a trick," said Jia. "Even Fara wouldn't be fooled."

"But tricks like this can be far more convincing to the common people than the intricate arguments of learned scholars," said Risana. "I've performed enough in my youth to know how effective spectacle can be."

"Risana is right," said Kuni. "Huno Krima and Zopa Shigin began their rebellion with a silk scroll stuffed into a fish, and they were able to bring down the Xana Empire. As long as the people believe this 'magic,' it has power."

"We could dispatch all the airships to search for Luan," said Jia.

"That requires knowing where he is," said Kuni. "The sea is vast, and we . . . haven't heard from him since his departure. I hope he's at least safe."

For a moment the emperor seemed at a loss as he imagined the fate of his old friend.

"But if anyone can survive the wrath of Tazu, it's a disciple of Lutho, the aged and wise turtle, and a man who once rode on the back of a cruben. The gods help those who help themselves. I will get Cogo's counsel. What really matters aren't these mirrors. We must find out how the rebels are getting their weapons."

He strode resolutely out of the private audience hall.

CHAPTER TWENTY-FOUR

AN OUTING

LAKE TUTUTIKA: THE SIXTH MONTH IN
THE ELEVENTH YEAR OF THE REIGN
OF FOUR PLACID SEAS.

Théra and Fara sat on the wharf, dangling their feet into the cold water. Dressed in plain robes of rough hemp cloth, they looked like two peasant girls taking a break from the heat. In front of them, lotus leaves covered the surface of Lake Tututika as far as the eye could see, while giant pink-and-white flowers bloomed over them like dancers swaying with the wind. Small boats wove between the leaves, and young women sang as they harvested the lotus seeds.

The lotus blooms, my darling,
Do you see how it blushes at the sight of you?
My heart beats, my darling,
Do you not know how brief the summer is?

"This is fun," said Fara. "We should have adventures like this more often."

Seventeen-year-old Théra put an arm around her nine-year-old little sister and pulled her affectionately against her side.

Since taking over the education of herself and her sister, Théra had stopped reading the Moralist tomes. Instead, she let their enthusiasms be their guide as they sampled the vast collection of the Imperial library: One day they might gorge themselves on Faça folklore, the next day they might admire the drawings in military engineering treatises, and the day after that might be spent on lyrical poems of the Diaspora Wars, whose obscure logograms they puzzled out with the aid of volumes of dictionaries. They spent more time reading than they ever did under the tutelage of Zato Ruthi.

But as much as they enjoyed reading, sometimes the girls just wanted to be away from the palace, away from the guards and courtiers and servants and maids, away from the roles of Imperial princesses.

They had snuck out of the palace by hiding inside the carriage of the farmers who delivered fresh produce to the palace kitchen; then they had hitched rides with merchants and farmers until they got to the shore of the lake.

"If we did this more often," Théra said, "I'm afraid my mother would tear all her hair out. When we get back, she'll probably make you write the hundred-stroke logograms a hundred times."

"It's worth it."

"It is indeed worth it," said a new voice.

The girls turned around. The speaker was a lady of extraordinary beauty. Golden-haired and blue-eyed, her brown skin was as smooth as polished amber. A blue silk dress floated around her like a veil of water. Her voice was gentle and cool, like a breeze passing through the leaves of a weeping willow.

Théra stood up and bowed to her in *jiri*, thinking she was the mistress of the nearby large estate that probably owned this private wharf as well as all the farmland in the area. "We apologize for trespassing; we'll leave immediately."

The lady smiled and shook her head. "Why leave? There are four great pleasures in life, and this is one of them."

"What are the four great pleasures?" asked Fara, instantly curious.

"That would be sitting by a cozy fire in winter while snow falls outside the window; climbing onto a high place after a spring rain to admire a revitalized world; eating crabs with freshly brewed tea next to the fall tides; and dipping your feet into a cool lotus-covered lake in the middle of summer."

"Oh," said Fara, a bit disappointed. "I thought you were going to say something more . . ."

"More impressive?" asked the lady.

Fara nodded.

The lady chuckled. "When you've lived for as long as I have, you realize that the greatest pleasures in life are not very impressive at all. It's better to have one true friend who can understand the voice in your heart when you pluck out a hesitant tune on the zither than to have the unthinking adoration of millions."

Théra looked closer at the woman's placid face and realized that she couldn't tell how old she was: For a moment she seemed as young as Théra herself, but as the sparkling lake changed the light reflected onto her face, she suddenly seemed as old as the grandmothers who tilled the nearby fields.

Théra turned the lady's words over in her mind. She wasn't sure she agreed with them, but at least the lady was interesting. "I take it you're a Fluxist, Mistress?"

"I don't care much about labels, but I do think Ra Oji was closer to the truth than the other Ano philosophers. Emperor, beggar, princess, maid—for all our toils and struggles, in the end the Flow governs us all."

"But what you said can't be right," Fara suddenly piped up. "I mean . . . about the great pleasures."

"Why not?"

"You didn't mention the love of a handsome man!" said Fara. "That's the most important thing."

"Whatever makes you think that?"

"It's all the stories the ladies—er, the older girls tell her," said Théra. "And all the plays put on by the traveling puppet opera troupes: Lady

Mira killing herself for love; Princess Kikomi killing for love; Lady Zy jumping into the Liru for love."

The lady sat down on the wharf, careless of the delicate fabric of her dress. She took off her wooden clogs and dipped her feet into the water. Théra saw that her feet were calloused and rough, and instantly she liked her more.

"Come and sit," said the lady. Then she quirked her brows at Théra. "By your tone, I take it you don't approve of love much."

"Songs about men are about friendship, war, sights of faraway lands, and sounds of the eternal sea," Théra said. "But songs about women—just listen."

They quieted and listened to the women in the little boats collecting lotus pods.

I am ripe for harvesting, my sweet dear.
If you don't pick me, another hand will.
I am heavy with need; my face bends near,
Ready for the night of veil and trill.

"I know what the song is about!" said Fara excitedly. "They serve lotus seeds at weddings because it's good luck: The bride will be pregnant soon and bear many children, like the lotus seedpods."

"See?" Théra said.

"You sound like another young woman I once knew," said the lady. "She was not much older than you when we met, and she also had much to say about the fate of women and the price of beauty. But I think you might be judging this song too harshly. Listen."

The young women in the boats continued to sing, their voices as cool and refreshing as the water at their feet.

But perhaps no hand will ever pick me,
And that is not so terrible a fate.
I'll kiss the water and release my seeds
To see them wander the watery ways.

How far will they go? What will they behold?
What distant shores will they touch and visit
Before they sink and sprout and grow and bloom—
To sway over sun-dappled waves anew!

"That is lovely," said Théra.

"Very lovely," said Fara.

"There's much wisdom in flowers," said the lady, "though they're often dismissed as frivolous."

"My mother tried to teach me about flowers," said Théra, "but I suppose that's why I wasn't very interested in them. A lotus is a bit like the dandelion. While dandelion seeds ride the wind, lotus seeds ride the water. Both have adventures." Her eyes dimmed as she spoke. "Even flowers get to do more than some people."

The lady waved at one of the small boats, and the young woman oared it over, her powerful arms flexing in the sunlight like the firm roots of the lotus. The lady bought a few lotus pods from her, paying with an ingot of silver.

"I don't have enough money to give you change for that," said the young woman, laughing. "Mistress, everything in my home added together isn't even worth that much."

"Keep it," said the lady. "Think of it as a gift from Tututika, like the lotus pods themselves."

The young peasant woman looked at the wealthy lady and nodded solemnly. She crossed her arms before her chest and bowed in *jiri*. "Thank you. May Tututika always walk amongst us."

Théra knew that in Géfica, especially in the countryside, the people were pious in their worship of Tututika, the goddess of fresh water and agriculture. It was the custom to be generous to strangers, for the goddess was said to take on human form from time to time to test the beauty of people's character. Random acts of kindness were not unheard of.

The peasant woman oared away, leaving a wake over the smooth surface of the lake. The lady took out a small bone knife and cut open one of the spongy pods to retrieve the seeds. Then she peeled off the rubbery shell to reveal the white kernels inside.

Fara stared, mesmerized. She had eaten plenty of sugared lotus seeds and loved lotus paste in desserts, but she had never had fresh lotus seeds before. "I'd like one."

"Fara!" Théra scolded. "That is very rude."

"I bought them to share," said the lady, laughing. "But you have to wait. If I give this to you now, you'll not like it at all."

As the girls watched, the lady put away the knife, took a hairpin out of her bun, and poked it through the center of the seeds, one by one. "There is a green core in each seed, the germ, which is among the bitterest things you'll ever taste."

She handed the cored seeds to Fara and Théra, who thanked her and put them in their mouths. The taste was exquisite: cool, refreshing, sweet but not too sweet.

Fara laughed and splashed her feet in the water. "I think having fresh lotus seeds you didn't pay for should be added to your list of greatest pleasures."

Théra sighed.

The lady looked at her, amused. "What's the matter now?"

"My heart grows bitter . . . at the thought of a future I can't master."

"No one can master the future," said the lady, "not even the gods. But let me tell you a story. On Arulugi, the teahouses prepare a delicacy by filling the cored lotus seeds with various foods using a toothpick: mango paste, thin bits of bacon, crab roe, apple-flavored shaved ice, sea salt, and so forth. The mixed seeds are then served in a large dish to a group of guests, and everyone enjoys the surprise of whichever flavor they happen to pick up."

"What if someone left an uncored seed in as a joke?" said Fara while making a face.

"I see that I can't have you help me out at dinner parties," said the lady, her laughter crisp and cool. "The Fluxists like to speak of a heart of emptiness as an ideal state. With a heart of emptiness, there is also infinite potential for the future: joy, anger, sorrow, happiness.

How we fill our hearts has much to do with our fates, far more than our native talents, the circumstances of our birth, the vicissitude of fortune, or even the intervention of the gods. If you do not like the stories you've been told, fill your heart with new stories. If you do not like the script you've been given, design for yourself new roles."

I am named Dissolver of Sorrows, thought Théra. *When the bitterness in my heart has been dissolved, what is left is potential.*

She looked at the lady, imagining her own heart growing lighter, more hollowed out and spacious. She was pretty sure now she knew who the lady was. It was a moment of wonder, to be so close to the presence of the numinous. "I have found a new pleasure in life: hearing you speak for an hour."

The lady chuckled. "Each of the pleasures I mentioned is better with a friend. A real friend is a mirror that reflects the truth back to us."

"A mirror?" For a moment Théra's heart grew heavy again as she recalled how Zomi Kidosu had impatiently brushed her off. Who was her real friend? But then she remembered the strange mirrors that were troubling her father.

An impulse seized her to make the most of this encounter with a goddess—that was the most interesting choice, wasn't it? "What can you tell me about the nature of smooth mirrors that can conjure ghosts?"

"Ah, I see I'm dealing with a mind as subtle and willful as your mother's," said the lady. "I suppose it wouldn't be breaking the rules, not exactly, for me to tell you another metaphor."

The lady tossed one of the lotus seeds at the lake. Just as it was about to make contact with water, a golden carp hopped out of the water and captured it with its mouth. The carp then stayed near the surface to wait for more food, bobbing up and down in the water and creating an expanding series of concentric waves.

"What a pretty fish," Fara cried out.

"My favorite creature," said the lady. "But watch the ripples."

The ripples expanded until they struck the straight edge of the wharf, which reflected them back toward the center of the lake in a new series of concentric waves. The waves from the carp and the reflection intermingled, forming an interlocking pattern.

"That looks just like the scales on the fish," said Théra.

"When the crests of the two waves are added together, the result is a higher wave. When the troughs of the waves overlap, the result is a deeper trough. When the crest of the one meets the trough of the other, the two cancel out. And that is the cause of the pattern," said the lady.

"Is this a metaphor about friendship?" asked Théra. "That our strengths may strengthen each other and make up for our faults, but our faults added together may also lead to a worse result. It is thus best to have many friends."

"You are a good student," said the lady. "That is a lesson I had not even intended. I only meant that you should think about waves and reflection, for light, in its true nature, shares much with these waves."

Théra wasn't sure she understood, but she watched the waves and tried to memorize the pattern.

They ate lotus seeds until it was late and the girls had to go home.

CHAPTER TWENTY-FIVE

TESTS AND COUNTERTESTS

PAN, ARULUGI, AND THE KARO PENINSULA:
THE SEVENTH MONTH IN THE ELEVENTH YEAR OF
THE REIGN OF FOUR PLACID SEAS.

"Is it taken care of?" asked Jia.

Chatelain Otho Krin nodded. "The mirror makers have been silenced."

"And the workshop burnt so that no trace of their secret remains?"

A wave of nausea struck Otho Krin. Even when he was a bandit, he had not liked the sight of blood. He had hoped Jia would comfort him, but that was not to be. It seemed to him she was changing more and more from the woman he had known, but he pushed the thought aside. Lady Jia—*the empress*, he silently corrected himself—had always known the right thing to do, and he was going to help her, no matter how he felt about the details.

Love demanded sacrifices.

"And the other thing?" Jia asked.

"An anonymous note was passed to Duke Coda's spies. The ship from Arulugi will be searched on arrival at Tunoa."

Jia let out a held breath. "Once Rin's men begin to focus on Théca

Kimo, be sure to let Kimo know. I will do what I can to help things along." She put a hand against Otho Krin's cheek. "You've done much for the future of Dara. The people may not know or understand, but know that you have my gratitude."

And Otho was again reminded of the very first time he had met Jia, and how she had made his heart feel grand and full of courage.

You're loyal, Jia had said. *That's not nothing.*

Otho Krin bowed. "All I care about is your good opinion."

Kuni paced in the private audience chamber. He stopped from time to time to scrutinize the new letter from Tunoa held in his trembling hands, though he had already read it so many times that he could recite it from memory.

"Perhaps Phyro is wrong," offered Jia.

"Phyro might be young," said Risana protectively. "But Duke Coda is very careful. He would not support Phyro in making such an accusation without ironclad proof."

"Still," said Jia, "a charge like this against one of the emperor's most loyal followers is extraordinary."

"I have always trusted Théca," mumbled Kuni.

"You have indeed, and your trust has served you well. But trust is a fragile string; sometimes kites do break loose and set out on their own," said Jia.

"Perhaps you should summon Gin Mazoti?" asked Risana.

"That might be awkward," said Jia. "If the charge turns out to be false, a preemptive strike would chill the hearts of all the nobles loyal to the emperor."

"What do you propose then?" asked Kuni.

"If Théca Kimo were really supplying the rebels in Tunoa with weapons, he must be observing your movements with care. You could announce a tour of the Islands, starting with a visit to the Karo Peninsula, across from Arulugi. Ask Than Carucono to accompany you with a sizable detachment of Imperial forces. If Kimo is innocent, he will do nothing. But if he really is planning to rebel . . ."

"Big Sister," said Risana in admiration, "you're as wily as Luan Zya. This is like one of my old smokecraft tricks. Kimo will see a mirage, and how he reacts will tell us what is truly in his heart."

Reluctantly, Kuni nodded.

"You're still undecided?" asked Cano Tho, commander of the Arulugi palace guards.

He and his lord, Duke Théca Kimo, sat in a small flat-bottomed boat in the middle of Lake Toyemotika, the only boat this far out from shore. There was a slight drizzle, and the mist made the stalk-like buildings and vine-suspended platforms of the city of Müning in the distance indistinct like a watercolor sketch.

Duke Théca Kimo said nothing but drained his cup. One might have expected it to be filled with one of the thousand varieties of orchid-bamboo-shoot tea that Arulugi was known for, or some expensive wine from one of Faça's ancient vineyards, as befitting one of Kimo's station, but instead, it was filled with the cheap, burning sorghum liquor favored by the poor of Dara.

"The emperor's intent could not be any clearer," said Cano.

"Do we have any more roasted pork?" asked Théca.

Silently, Cano opened the basket at his feet and refilled the dish on the low table between them. Both of them were sitting in *thakrido*, like a pair of gangsters instead of the cultured elite of an island known for its grace.

In truth, Kimo had never felt at home in Arulugi, the Beautiful Island. He had earned the fief by conquering it during the wars between Emperor Ragin and the Hegemon, at the direction of Marshal Gin Mazoti. But though he was its master, he had always felt like an unwelcome peasant in a wealthy man's house. The hereditary nobles of Müning might bow to him and speak to him reverently, but he could feel them whispering behind him, laughing quietly at his uncouth ways and the tattoos on his face that revealed his past as a convicted felon—*how dare they! He could have slaughtered them all instead of allowing them to keep their estates.* He found himself grasping for topics of conversation with his wives, highborn ladies of the old Amu nobility, and all three seemed to prefer one another's company to his. He found orchid-bamboo-shoot tea and the elaborate ceremonies around it fussy, and the singing and dancing of the girls in the teahouses and the ducal palace—formal, stately, and full of obscure allusions to Amu's illustrious past—usually put him to sleep.

"The airships make passes over the shores of Arulugi and the Amu Strait daily, and a naval fleet is gathering in the strait," said Cano. "Than Carucono has amassed his troops on the Karo Peninsula. Do you not understand what this means?"

"The emperor wants to tour the Islands. Some security measures are perfectly reasonable," said Kimo. "The emperor is trusting and honorable, and since I've cut off the supplies for Noda Mi and Doru Solofi, he'll not act against me."

Though he was the most powerful man on the island, and his word was law, he did not find the administration of a realm to his liking. He liked shiny treasure, greasy food, the company of loose women and brawling men—not the minutiae of tax policy and implementing Imperial decrees via detailed regulations. Yet now that the world was at peace, the only outlet for his energy was hunting for elephants on Écofi or wild boars on Crescent Island. But his ministers, steeped in the Moralism of Kon Fiji or the Incentivism of Gi Anji, lectured him incessantly on how a proper ruler should be more dedicated to the welfare of his subjects and not waste all his time in the slaughter of defenseless animals—*defenseless! Have they ever faced a charging bull elephant?*

Thank the blessed and luscious Tututika that he still had Cano Tho, the only man who was willing to accept him as he was instead of judging him. That was why he had always listened to his counsel.

He regretted that decision now. He had never thought Noda Mi and Doru Solofi would succeed in their mad scheme, and he had flat-out refused their invitation for him to rebel against Kuni. He had even thought he would capture the two and send them to Pan, with their arms bound behind them to show his loyalty.

But Cano had convinced him to let them go, arguing that the men were harmless and revealing a plot against the emperor in his realm would only invite more scrutiny against Arulugi. Instead, Cano had suggested that he sell surplus weapons to the two.

"The Imperial Treasury has cut off funding for the armies of the independent fiefs," said Cano. "You'll have no choice but to reduce the size of the army."

Kimo had not liked that prospect. The army, after all, was the foundation of his throne.

"If you don't think Noda and Doru would ever amount to much, what's the harm in selling them weapons to help maintain your army? But should Noda and Doru become more than a nuisance, the emperor will surely call upon you to suppress their rebellion, thereby confirming your value to the Imperial throne."

Kimo liked scenarios where he always came out ahead, no matter what happened.

Unfortunately, the rebels *were* successful, but it was Prince Phyro, not he, who was called upon to suppress them. And though he had cut off all further dealings with the rebels, Duke Coda's spies were now swarming the island, looking for evidence that he had been part of the plot. He dared not speak of it with any of his ministers in the ducal palace, afraid that some of them were already working for the Farsight Secretary, just waiting for him to slip up.

Once more, he drained his cup, savoring the burning sensation of the liquor going down his gullet. He yearned for sleep and for dreams in which he could revisit the times of glory, when he had slept in the open with a saddle as his pillow, and the shedding of blood was not seen as some kind of sin but the true measure of a man. He had once killed a king! Yet now he was cowering on a boat in the middle of a lake to complain about his fate in secret.

A pious man once took a trip to Wolf's Paw,
Thinking he would like to dive for pearls.
"Do not go," said the merchants of Toaza.
"Sharks are especially fierce this year."

Another small boat emerged from the mist and drizzle and sailed closer. A man in a raincoat woven from banana and lotus leaves stood at the stern, holding on to the long single oar. Around his neck he wore a necklace of shark's teeth—rather incongruous on this tranquil, freshwater lake. At his feet were a basket and several fishing rods. Not recognizing the duke and the captain, the man waved at them in a friendly gesture, and continued to sing in his loud, hoarse voice.

"I am pious and respect the gods," said the man.
"Tazu will surely protect me."
He bought an oyster knife and tied stones to his feet,
And headed for the harbor for a boat.

"Do not go," said the fishermen at the shore.
"Sharks have turned the sea into a realm of death."
"I'm pious and respect the gods," said the man.
"Tazu will surely protect me."

He rowed into the sea, as fast as he was able.
He rowed and rowed until the shore had disappeared.
He stood up and got ready to dive, and the seagulls
Dove at him and squawked, "Do not go. Do not go."

"I'm pious and respect the gods," said the man.
"Tazu will surely protect me."
He plunged into the sea, searching for pearls,
But a great shark snapped its jaws about his leg.

"Lord Tazu, why?" the man gasped at the surface.
Blood stained the foamy sea and pain racked his mind.
"If you were truly pious," replied Lord Tazu,
"You would have heeded my three warnings."

No more prayers were heard
As the man sank beneath the waves.

The fisherman disappeared into the mist, though the sound of his singing lingered.

"Lord Kimo, let me be plain," said Cano Tho. "You must heed the warning signs. Kuni Garu is a man who will smile at you one moment, and stab you the next. If you don't act soon, you will join the Hegemon in the afterlife."

Théca Kimo looked at his friend, astounded. "You speak of treason. But why?"

A succession of expressions flitted across Cano's face before he came to a decision. "For the Jewel of Amu."

"Kikomi? That inconstant woman?"

"Do not speak of her that way!"

Kimo set down his cup, his face darkening. "You forget yourself, Captain Tho."

With an effort, Cano Tho lowered his voice. "I apologize for that outburst, Lord Kimo." He sat up in formal *mipa rari*. "I rescued Princess Kikomi from the prison ship of Kindo Marana, and she was a woman of incomparable courage and wisdom. I will never believe the lies told about her after her death."

"Her betrayal is known to every child—"

"How can the man whose very victories were founded on betrayal speak of honor? After the rebellion, Kuni Garu honored all the great nobles who died during the rebellion against Xana. Jizu is venerated in Na Thion and Mocri is worshipped in Wolf's Paw; even the Hegemon himself has shrines erected in Tunoa with the emperor's approval. Yet Kikomi is an exception. We have never been allowed to erect a temple to her memory in Arulugi, and the craven scholars, careful to please the emperor, continue to smear her reputation in the history books."

"It's understandable for the emperor to feel this way about her.

She killed Phin Zyndu, a mentor to the Hegemon as well as the emperor—"

Cano laughed. "Kuni Garu may disguise his dark past with pious words of honor, but truth lives on in the hearts of men. He is terrified of Princess Kikomi because the lies about her speak the truth about himself. He is a lord of inconstant affections, skilled at manipulation but undeserving of loyalty. He will turn on you."

Théca Kimo pondered Cano's words. When Kuni was at war, he had needed men like Théca Kimo, and after his victory at Rana Kida, it would have been impossible not to reward those who had risked their lives in his ascent to the throne. But now that the world was at peace, how much longer would the emperor need him? As memories of Théca's contributions faded, why wouldn't Kuni Garu treat him as he had treated the Hegemon?

"Queen Gin has promised that she will never let anything happen to us," said Kimo.

"Where is the marshal now? Why isn't she at the Karo Peninsula pleading for you?"

Kimo said nothing. The signs were ambiguous, like the fog of war.

"Arulugi is skilled at war over the sea," said Cano. "If you steel your heart and strike first, you may still seize the initiative from Kuni Garu. A victory will secure the independence of Arulugi and make you the master of your own fate. Do you wish your children to inherit the life you've fought for? Then heed the warning of the gods, Lord Kimo."

Kimo might not understand court intrigue and subtle plots, but Cano's words made perfect sense if he applied his experience as a criminal in the streets. The leaders of the great street gangs respected men who showed that they were willing to fight to protect their turf, and a powerful gangster survived only by demonstrating that he still had teeth.

The burning liquor brought tears to his eyes as he drained his cup. "I suppose it doesn't hurt to be prepared."

෧ ෨ ෧ ෨

"He's mirroring my moves," muttered Kuni. "What is Théca Kimo thinking? Why has he moved his army onto the shore and his navy into the strait?"

"Perhaps his ships are gathering to help secure the seas for your crossing," suggested Jia.

"When I haven't even indicated I was going to cross?" huffed Kuni.

"We've been here for weeks," fretted Risana. "Yet he has not come to pay his respects. This bodes ill for his intentions."

"The Ano sages tell us that trust is hard to earn, but easy to lose in a moment of doubt," said Jia.

"What does that even mean?" snapped Kuni. "Trusting the untrustworthy is no sign of wisdom."

"Théca had proven himself during the war," said Jia evenly.

"That was more than a decade ago!" said an irritated Kuni. "I have to think not just about myself, but also about the children. If I pass away tomorrow, will Timu or Phyro . . . be able to handle him?"

The emperor walked away, agitated; Risana followed close behind, trying to soothe him. Jia stood in place and watched them leave.

"Lord Kimo, you can't go," said Cano Tho.

The duke's grand audience hall should have been filled with his ministers and generals, like a miniature version of the audience hall in Pan, but now only the generals, all veterans who had served under Théca for more than a decade, and a few nobles trusted by Cano, sat along the two walls. The nobles belonged to the oldest and most illustrious lineages of Arulugi, a faction that had long wished for Amu to regain its independence and could be counted on not to be tainted by the emperor's spies. Though they had never liked Théca Kimo much, they desired to regain their diminished power even more.

"To disobey a direct order from the emperor would be open treason," said Théca Kimo.

"The emperor already has enough evidence to manufacture the crime of treason," said Cano. "Consider your state, Lord Kimo. Weapons from your armory have been found in Tunoa in the hands of the rebels shouting the name of the Hegemon; you've amassed ships in the Amu Strait, warily watching the emperor's fleet; your soldiers are gathered around Müning, ready to do your bidding; you've distanced yourself from ministers and advisers recommended by the emperor, suggesting a secret plot."

"But I thought these were just precautionary measures—a reminder that I still have teeth! The emperor should know that I have no intent to rebel."

"Actions do not have meaning by themselves," said Cano. "All that matters is the perspective in which they are seen. If the mirror is distorted, a fat man will appear thin, and a loyal man will appear as a traitor."

"All the more reason that I should answer the emperor's summons to explain myself."

"Lord Kimo, have you forgotten the banquet held by the Hegemon after he entered Pan? He invited Kuni Garu to the banquet because he intended to kill the man for his betrayal after separating him from his men."

"But Kuni Garu escaped unharmed!"

"Kuni Garu had a tongue as clever and quick as that of a paid litigator. Do you? And do you imagine Kuni intends to repeat the mistake of the Hegemon? If you go, you'll not return."

"This must be a bad dream," Kimo muttered. "What have I done?"

"You've done nothing but what is logical. The emperor has forced your hand. When the hunter comes to you with his axe sharpened, do you continue to play the loyal dog waiting for slaughter, or will you turn into a fierce wolf and fight for your survival? Lord Kimo, you may not wish to rebel, but the emperor has taken the choice away from you."

Théca Kimo sat and pondered. Slowly, his body began to tremble as his muscles tensed, and the tattoos on his face stood out as the vessels in his face filled with blood. With a loud *crack*, the bamboo cup in his hand shattered.

"How did things get this way, Kuni Garu?" asked Théca Kimo. He howled with rage. "How?"

"He's *ill*?" Kuni repeated, disbelief and rage infusing his voice. "He's *ill*?"

"It is a most puzzling letter," said Cogo, who had been summoned from Pan, where he was acting as Kuni's temporary regent. "Théca claims that he cannot travel too far due to bad health, and thinks he can only go to the middle of the Amu Strait before having to turn back."

"I don't think *puzzling* quite captures it," said Risana. "The word you're looking for is *preposterous*. Not only has he declined to come to Karo to pay his respects to the emperor, but he's now suggesting that the emperor meet him in the middle of the Amu Strait, each with a single ship. Who does he think he is?"

"He thinks we're two Tiro kings negotiating," said Kuni. "Or, knowing him, two street gang bosses sitting down to have some tea and discuss the division of protection money from indigo houses and bars and gambling parlors. He has rebelled. Oh, he has already rebelled."

Everyone could hear the pain in his voice.

"I'm sorry that I had been so trusting of him before," said Jia.

"Don't be," said Kuni. "It was your suggestion of a tour to the Karo Peninsula that finally allowed us to see the darkness in his heart."

"Do you want to summon Gin Mazoti to prepare for an attack?" asked Risana.

"Kimo and Mazoti fought together for years against the Hegemon," said Jia. "She might object to an invasion of Arulugi when you still don't have ironclad proof. Besides, open warfare with Théca Kimo will confuse the other nobles and embolden the rebels in Tunoa—if you're not careful, you might find even more old nobles raising the flag of rebellion, thinking to take advantage of the chaos. The more quietly we can resolve this, the better."

"The empress is right," said Cogo. "It might be best to agree to Kimo's demands and meet him in the Amu Strait."

"Why?" asked Risana. But then she saw the sly grin on Cogo's face. "Ah, a plot."

"Kimo helpfully 'suggests' that we each ride to the midpoint of the Amu Strait without escort ships to avoid 'giving the appearance of disharmony to the other Lords of Dara,'" said Kuni. "I have no confidence that a single ship of mine can overcome his in a sea battle—"

"It's also far too dangerous," interrupted Jia.

"—and I can't have airships to help, as they would alarm him. Cogo, just what are you planning?"

"He will *see* you arrive at the appointed spot on a single ship," said Cogo. "However—"

"What you *see* is not always what you get, in smokecraft as well as in war," said Risana.

Risana and Cogo smiled at each other.

Kuni looked from one to the other, and realization dawned on his face. He chuckled. "We might not have Luan Zya here with us, but this is a trick worthy of Dara's prime strategist."

"The emperor has agreed to my conditions?" Théca Kimo read over the letter a few more times to be sure he hadn't missed something. "Cano, it looks like our plot has worked. Kuni Garu must have decided that he isn't willing to go to war after all and will negotiate with me."

"Kuni Garu is wily and full of tricks," said Cano. "I suspect that things are not as simple as they appear."

"It will be easy to verify if he's adhering to the conditions I named in my letter," said Théca confidently. "What can he do in the middle of the open sea? I'd be able to see any ambush coming from miles away. You worry too much."

"It's best to prepare for the unexpected," Cano insisted.

The emperor and the duke, each riding on an ordinary merchant ship, approached to about a boat length of each other and dropped anchor. Both emerged from their respective cabins and sat down upon platforms erected on the deck for this purpose. Each had a small table in front of him, on which were placed food and drink. They would share a meal this way across the waves—though a far wider gap now separated their hearts.

Something about the scene triggered a memory in Kuni Garu's mind—fifteen years ago, he and the Hegemon had sat across from each other on two flat-bottomed boats over the Liru to discuss ending a bloody conflict, and now he was sitting down with another fighting man across the water to discuss preventing one. History had a strange sense of humor.

"I'm glad to see Duke Kimo appears well," Kuni called out across the water. "Your letter made it sound like you were on the verge of death."

Kimo did look in the prime of health. Though he was dressed in thick, voluminous robes that would be more suitable for winter, there was no doubt that he wasn't "ill" as he had claimed.

Kimo had the good grace to blush. "*Rénga*, hearing news that you were willing to be reasonable sped my recovery."

"Oh? How have I not been reasonable?"

Kimo took a deep breath and started in on the speech Cano Tho had written for him. "Lord Garu and I were once coequal lords of Dara, dedicated to the ideal of overthrowing the despotism of Xana."

Kuni's face didn't change at Théca's addressing him as "Lord Garu." That was to be expected.

Kimo continued. "Yet after the success of the rebellion, instead of returning the world to its familiar tracks, Lord Garu embarked on a path to replicate the abuses of Mapidéré. Instead of dividing the land into Tiro states all equal to each other, as the Hegemon had tried to do, Lord Garu assumed the title of emperor and kept most of Dara for himself. Only a few scraps were thrown to me and the other Lords of Dara."

"A few *scraps*," muttered Kuni. "I see, having three major islands and a territory greater than several of the old Tiro states counts as mere scraps."

Kimo went on. "Yet even so, Lord Garu appears dissatisfied. Over time, your decrees have evinced the intent to weaken the enfeoffed nobles and strip them of their arms and land. It does not seem that Lord Garu would stop until all of Dara is under a single fist. For the sake of my heirs and those who have followed me, I demand justice from Lord Garu."

"You demand justice?" asked Kuni. "You have supplied the rebels in Tunoa and amassed your troops and ships against me; I summoned you to explain, and you refused to come; feigning illness, you dictated terms to your lord, showing a heart intent on treason. I have been tolerant beyond reason because I do not wish more blood to spill, and yet *you* dare demand justice?"

"If you have already made up your mind that I will betray you, then nothing I say matters. Lord Garu, I ask you to grant me the title of king, and declare Arulugi, including Crescent Island and Écofi, to be an independent Tiro kingdom that owes you no submission. Then we shall stand together, you in the east and I in the west, as brothers in eternal friendship."

Kuni laughed. Though Kimo had memorized a passingly well-composed speech, he still sounded like a street gangster demanding his cut. He shook his head. "And if I do not agree?"

Kimo gritted his teeth. "The navy and army of Arulugi stand ready to enforce my claim. We have prepared firework rockets in advance against your airships. Though my realm lacks the strength to invade the Big Island, yet I do not think you will find conquering Arulugi an easy task. And if you do declare war against me, the other enfeoffed Lords of Dara will see their future in mine, and rally to my aid. Think carefully, Lord Garu, before you make a rash decision you may come to regret."

"It's a good thing that I won't give you the chance to put your dark plot into operation," said Kuni. He slammed his fist down on the table, and ten guards below the raised platform lifted speaking tubes toward the sea and shouted as one: "Ram the ship!"

As the stunned soldiers on Kimo's ship scrambled to lift anchor and get the ship underway, thinking that Kuni intended to ram their ship with his, the sea beneath the ships began to churn.

"A whale?" asked one of the soldiers.

"A cruben?" asked another.

Than Carucono peered out of one of the thick pieces of crystal that acted as the mechanical cruben's eyes. The great underwater boat was hovering about fifty feet below the surface, and faint sunlight made the water appear a dark green. From time to time, fish swam past the porthole.

Behind him, soldiers inside the dank interior of the mechanical cruben stood at the ready to open the valves of the steam engine powered by heated rocks picked up from underwater volcanoes. Cogo Yelu had followed the secret maps drawn by Luan Zya more than a decade ago and designated a meeting spot for Emperor Ragin and Duke Kimo near one of these underwater volcanoes.

Carucono's ear was held against the opening of the breathing tube that extended to the buoy disguised as a clump of seaweed bobbing at the surface.

He heard the order he had been waiting for.

"Go, go, go!"

The crew leapt into action, some throwing levers and twisting dials, others running toward the tail of the mechanical cruben in disciplined motion to shift its internal balance and tilt up the bow. The underwater boat was about to surface.

The sea exploded.

The ironwood horn slammed into Kimo's ship from below, lifting it almost out of the water and breaking it in half instantly. The sound of masts breaking and spars snapping deafened ears as the smell of the hot sulfuric steam that powered the mechanical cruben overwhelmed noses.

Sailors and marines were tossed from the deck, screaming for mercy and praying to Tazu and Tututika. As broken pieces of the hull and masts tangled in rigging fell back down and slammed into the water, it was clear that Kimo and his men had no choice but to wait to be rescued and then shackled by the emperor.

But Kuni Garu stared up at the sky, his jaw hanging open. There, tracing out a graceful arc of flight, was the figure of Théca Kimo. He tumbled in the air a few times, and then the voluminous robes he wore spread open like the wings of a giant bird. Spring-loaded bamboo rods snapped into place, stretching the robes into a massive kite. Like the Hegemon in his surprise attack on Zudi fifteen years earlier, Théca Kimo slowly glided toward Arulugi, suspended beneath a stringless kite.

The craftsmen of Arulugi had always been skilled with the construction of flexible structures, lacing bamboo and vine into the graceful hanging platforms of the city of Müning, the diadem that floated over Lake Toyemotika. Cano Tho had designed the platform on which Kimo sat to act as the end of a catapult. The arm, made of strong bamboo, was winched down and held in place with rope. However, as soon as something went wrong, Kimo could trigger the catapult and cause himself to be ejected into the air, out of harm's way, and then glide back to Arulugi on a kite combining the design elements of Luan Zya and Torulu Pering. The kite, with its complicated folding frame so that it could be worn in disguise, was fragile and prone to accidents and certainly not reliable enough for regular use. Cano had insisted that Kimo wear it only as a last measure of desperation, but as it turned out, it would save Kimo's life today.

Archers scrambled onto the deck, but the kite was already too far. As Kuni watched Kimo glide out of reach, he sighed, knowing that the peace that had ruled the Islands of Dara for ten years had come to an end.

CHAPTER TWENTY-SIX

LIGHT AND REASON

PAN: THE SEVENTH MONTH IN THE ELEVENTH
YEAR OF THE REIGN OF FOUR PLACID SEAS.

- *Grant me this boon, brother,* said the musical voice of Tututika.

- *Why have you chosen to aid Kuni's daughter, instead of your own island?* asked Fithowéo the Warlike.

- *I act out of respect for the memory of Kikomi.*

- *But Théca has promised Cano Tho to erect a shrine in her honor if his rebellion succeeds.*

- *The best memorial for Kikomi isn't a shrine of stones or wood, but a princess free to fulfill her potential.*

- *Why not continue the lessons yourself?*

- *The crafting of mirrors is your art.*

- *And so you've come to the sightless god to help her see.*

- *As a sightless orchid once helped you.*

- *I'm the god of warfare. Tutoring young girls isn't really . . . something I've done much.*

- *You're the god of all those who find joy in dauntless struggle. Not all wars are fought with swords and spears, and not all foes are found on the battlefield. The times are changing, brother, and we must change along with them.*

Théra leaned against the balustrade overlooking the carp pond in a secluded corner of the palace. The ornamental fish—vermillion, gold, black, white, sapphire, jade—swam below her, creating endless ripples that interfered with each other in complicated patterns.

What did the lady mean? Light is a wave? How does that help with the mystery of the magic mirrors?

A pretty tune came to her from somewhere deeper in the palace. She didn't recognize the instrument on which it was being played. The high tones were clear as wind chimes, the low tones as solemn as the song of the cruben. Each note lingered in the air, blending with the next and the next one after that.

She went in search of the source of the sound, and after many winding corridors and long porticos, she came into the music hall, where the emperor and Consort Risana sometimes retired to play the coconut lute, sing, and dance.

Fara skipped over to her. "Rata-*tika*! Isn't this pretty?"

Surprised, Théra hugged her. "It is, Ada-*tika*."

A wooden frame about the height of a man had been installed in the middle of the hall. The frame had two horizontal beams, one at the height of the head, the other at the height of the waist. From each beam hung eight smooth bronze slabs of various thicknesses, each about the size of a very large book.

A lean, middle-aged man knelt at the foot of the frame in *mipa rari*, and he was playing the music by striking the slabs with a pair of long-handled mallets. He wore a short-sleeved tunic, and his arms bulged with muscle, and the skin was marked with scars both old and new. Théra found it a bit odd to see these arms, which seemed to belong to a blacksmith or soldier rather than a musician.

The sisters stood listening to the music. It took almost the time of burning a full stick of incense before the man finished. He sat back and gently set the mallets down, and waited until the last note slowly dissipated.

He turned around and bowed. "I hope the rough music was pleasing to the princesses."

Fara clapped. "It was wonderful! Auntie Risana will love to hear this when she's back."

Théra bowed back. Now that she could see the man's face, she was startled by his eyes: They were so dark that she couldn't see the pupils at all, as if they were made of solid obsidian. These eyes were so distinctive that she certainly would have remembered him if she had seen him in the palace before today. His muscular build and the scars on his arms made her uneasy. It was nearly inconceivable for an assassin to make it through the security of Captain Dafiro Miro, but given the fact that the emperor was away and the rebels were raging in Tunoa . . .

Smoothly, she stepped before Fara. "I don't believe I've had the pleasure of knowing the master's honored name."

The man laughed, a deep, belly-rumbling sound. "Princess Théra's reputation of intelligence is known far and wide, but I had not known that she is a lady of courage as well as refined manners. Your greeting is courteous, and yet you have shielded your younger sister in case I mean you harm. You're solicitous of my feelings while preparing for the worst. Even Kon Fiji would admire the solution."

Théra blushed at having her intent seen through so clearly. But the man continued amiably, "My name isn't very important. I'm just an old smith who happens to have an interest in music. Do not blame the guards—I come and go as I please, and I play music for an audience in whom I have great hopes. We're all in search of the one true friend who can understand the voice in your heart when you play a hesitant tune on the *moaphya*."

The familiarity of the man's last sentence made Théra relax. Whoever this man was, she felt that she could trust him. "If master will not share his name, I won't press. You call this a *moaphya*? I've never seen one before."

"It's an old Ano instrument, rarely seen after the Diaspora Wars," said the man. "The name means 'square sound.' You can spot mentions

of it in the old heroic sagas. The hero Iluthan was a skilled player."
He beckoned at Fara. "Would you like to try it?"

While Fara enthusiastically banged on the slabs without much
skill, Théra asked, "Can you tell me more about it?"

"The Ano divided musical instruments into eight families: silk—
that would be stringed instruments like the lute and the zither;
bamboo—flutes and reed pipes; wood—xylophones and rhythm
sticks; stone—tablets and echo bowls; clay—ocarinas and porcelain tubes; gourd and vine—maracas; hide and leather—drums and
singing bellows; and finally, metal—bells and chimes, of which the
moaphya is a member. Each of the gods of Dara has a favorite family,
and each family of instruments expresses a unique quality that cannot be replicated by the others."

Théra sighed. "Now I really wish I knew more about music. I enjoy
the dancing lessons with Consort Risana, but I've never had the
patience to learn an instrument. My brother Timu is better at that sort
of task."

"The *moaphya* is my favorite. It's a hard instrument to play, but even
harder to make. Each slab must be cast to exact measurements to produce the right tune. Any flaw would mar the sound."

"How do you ensure that the slabs are properly made?"

"Watch."

The man took out a thin, translucent silk cloth marked with a grid
of dark lines and beckoned Théra closer to examine one of the slabs.
Théra saw that the bronze slab was also marked with a grid of lines,
an exact echo of the lines on the silk cloth. The man wrapped the silk
cloth around one of the slabs, ensuring that the grids matched up
exactly.

Then he picked up a mallet and struck the silk-wrapped slab. As
the slab clanged, the grid on the silk seemed to come alive, vibrating everywhere with an even tremor. But in one corner, something
seemed to be wrong: The grid appeared slightly out of alignment, and
the tremors looked out of sync with the rest.

"Have you ever tried to line up two identical pieces of silk and watched the patterns they make as the grids are overlaid and rotated?"

Théra nodded. She had delighted in watching such patterns as a young girl. Indeed, one of her favorite pastimes had been to overlay one of the embroidered portraits of the Hegemon made by Lady Mira with another piece of silk and observe as the shifting layers of silk made Lady Mira's abstract art come to life.

"The principle is the same here. While the naked eye cannot see the imperfections in a cast slab, by using a reference grid such as this, it is possible to detect minute flaws during the casting process." He looked regretful. "This one will have to be recast. Even the gods aren't free from errors."

Théra stared at the grid on the vibrating silk. The patterns made by the two overlaid grids reminded her of the interfering waves over the surface of Lake Tututika. *Two waves . . . a mirror . . . flaws and imperfections . . .* She seemed on the verge of understanding something, but she couldn't quite say what it was.

In her mind, the image of the Hegemon cast by the magic mirror became overlaid with the embroidered portrait by Lady Mira, and the two visions, one detailed and lifelike, the other formed from abstract geometric shapes, interfered with each other as though in battle. Light and shadows, honor and cruelty, the colossus who strode across Dara and the ghost who haunted the Islands. *Which is closer to a true portrait of the man?*

"Rata-*tika*, where did he go?" Fara asked.

Startled, Théra looked up. The man was gone.

You must weigh the fish. Théra remembered the colorful phrase from Zomi Kidosu's Palace Examination performance. *The Prophecy of the Fish had been a trick; why should the "magic mirrors" be any different?*

Théra threw herself into her task with abandon. Never before had she been given such a complex, intricate puzzle to solve, and she found joy in facing off against such a foe. *Perhaps,* she thought, *this is something like the battle lust that the Hegemon always spoke of and Hudo-*tika *always yearned for. There is a pleasure in dedicating yourself to overcoming* *overwhelming odds, in bringing all your strength to bear against the unknown.*

She found every Ano and modern treatise on the nature of light and read the scrolls from end to end; she asked Captain Dafiro to summon master mirror makers and asked them questions until they had run out of answers; she took over a workshop in the Imperial Academy and worked with scholars and metalsmiths and lens makers to construct experimental prototypes.

And then, news arrived from Tunoa.

CHAPTER TWENTY-SEVEN

REBELS OF DARA

TUNOA: THE NINTH MONTH IN THE ELEVENTH
YEAR OF THE REIGN OF FOUR PLACID SEAS.

To the accompaniment of war drums, five thousand rebels of Tunoa
chanted as one:

> *The ninth day in the ninth month of the year:*
> *By the time I bloom, all others have died.*
> *Cold winds rise in Pan's streets, wide and austere:*
> *A tempest of gold, an aureal tide.*
> *My glorious fragrance punctures the sky.*
> *Bright yellow armor surrounds every eye.*
> *With disdainful pride, ten thousand swords spin*
> *To secure the grace of kings, to cleanse sin.*
> *A noble brotherhood, loyal and true.*
> *Who would fear winter when wearing this hue?*

Noda Mi and Doru Solofi, now dressed as Tiro kings, stood on a
dais constructed out of packed earth. Behind them, a large piece of

canvas stretched between two tall trees, forming a backdrop. The tall, swaying trees around the dais left the backdrop in shadow.

Slowly and reverently, Doru Solofi held up a mirror and tilted it in the sun. A colossal image of the Hegemon on his trusty steed, Réfiroa, appeared against the canvas backdrop. The rearing horse foamed at the mouth while the rider brandished Na-aroénna and Goremaw, his double-pupiled eyes staring into the face of every rebel, sending shivers down their spines.

"Companions of Tunoa," intoned Noda Mi solemnly. "More than nineteen years ago, the Hegemon composed this poem to express his determination to rid Dara of tyranny. Tragically, his illustrious career was cut short by the despicable Kuni Garu, a lowly bandit who betrayed the Hegemon, a man he once called brother, in order to steal the throne of Dara."

He paused and surveyed the rebels: Within a few short months, they had coalesced into a formidable force. Suspecting his once-loyal nobles of ambition, Kuni Garu had finally showed his hand and forced Théca Kimo to rebel. Inspired by the examples of Théca Kimo, Noda Mi, and Doru Solofi, others who were unhappy with Imperial rule had pledged support of various kinds. Hereditary nobles in Haan offered treasure, idle and landless veterans offered their experience, and even men of learning who had failed to place in the Imperial examinations came with advice.

Now that they were awash in funds, Mi and Solofi equipped all the rebels with gilded armor and even better weapons from Arulugi— Théca was now quite eager to restore trade, given the Imperial embargo of his realm—as well as formal regalia for themselves as befitting their station as Tiro kings ("There's a time to appear as men of the people to gain their faith," said Noda Mi, "as well as a time to appear to be above them to inspire awe").

It was really too bad that they had to make do with their existing supply of magic mirrors to inspire the rebels in their cause. Noda often regretted not kidnapping the family of mirror makers when they were still alive.

Of course, with the new money, the ranks of the rebels also swelled with the inevitable inrush of faithless bandits and desperadoes interested only in making a fortune, who posed a threat to discipline. On the whole, however, the Tunoa rebels appeared to be a formidable force.

"But the Hegemon had made a prophecy," Noda Mi shouted. "He said that the double nine would be a special day. Two years ago, during the ninth month of the ninth year of the Reign of Four Placid Seas, the Year of the Wolf, the goddesses Kana and Rapa handed us these spiritual mirrors . . ."

Doru Solofi had to keep himself from laughing as he listened to Noda's bombast. He and Noda had hardly thought to endow the date of their discovery of the mirrors with such significance until much later, of course, but he supposed that if he squinted really hard, what Noda Mi was saying wasn't exactly a lie. The prostitute from whom Noda had stolen the money purse with the first magic mirror was indeed dark-haired, and the girl he had been with that night had been a blonde. They certainly had been billed by the indigo house as of "goddess" quality. Anyway, as Noda Mi always said, "The grace of kings lies in graceful lies," which he claimed to be a palindrome when written out in Ano logograms.

". . . This is the Year of the Cruben, a time when greatness rises and ambition is rewarded. We shall make the prophecy come true and march into Pan to avenge the Hegemon!"

The rebels clanged their golden spears against their golden shields, and shouted as one. The noise drove the birds and beasts out of the woods for miles all around.

"How did things get this way? How?" Phyro, who had always been close to "Uncle Rin," now screamed at the spymaster.

Rin winced. How he wished he had never listened to the empress. At first, he had been pleased with the growth of the rebellion, thinking of the extra funds he'd be able to request to fight such a sizable insurgency. But the news from Arulugi made him realize that he was no longer in control, as he had thought.

The rebels of Tunoa had surrounded Zyndu Castle. Phyro and Rin weren't in immediate danger, as the castle, even after it had been turned into a shrine, still retained its ancient, thick walls. Even the rebels seemed to have been surprised by their own success and had not come prepared with heavy siege machinery, only flimsy ladders. Well provisioned, the five hundred defenders under Prince Phyro's command should be able to hold out for a while. Still, gazing down upon the golden-armored host, Phyro felt his stomach tighten.

"I didn't realize how much they had turned the population against us," protested Rin. "In the past, Imperial administrators were able to gather a lot of useful information from the villagers. . . ."

Phyro's glare made Rin think better of bringing up how the policy of outlawing all private veneration of the Hegemon had likely played a role in souring the population against them.

"But these mirrors . . . they've changed things. Now, practically every person in Tunoa, from a child barely able to walk to old women with all their teeth fallen out, really believes that the Hegemon has returned and is manifesting through these mirrors. Even those who aren't fighting with the rebels secretly give them shelter and aid—we lost the patrol airships because the cooks at the airfield set fire to them! Our garrisons have lost every encounter against the rebels during the last two months."

"But you were telling me everything was going according to plan!"

"It was . . . sort of."

"Have you sent for aid?"

"Three waves of pigeons have already been dispatched."

Phyro said nothing, but he now deeply regretted not asking for aid earlier. He had wanted to show his father that he was no longer a child and able to take care of a few superstitious bandits in these far-flung isles. With the rebellion of Duke Kimo raging on Arulugi, the last thing the emperor needed was this further distraction.

He hoped that once aid arrived from the Big Island, he would be able to redeem himself.

ᔕ ᔕ ᔕ ᔕ

The rebels camped beneath the walls of Zyndu Castle for three days and three nights as their numbers continued to swell. By now, almost eight thousand men laid siege to the keep. But the rebels didn't go into the forest to cut down trees and construct catapults or arrow towers. They mostly sat and listened to speeches, chanted, and prayed.

Phyro and Rin watched them, puzzled but also slightly relieved.

Then, on the morning of the fourth day, the rebels attacked.

It was a most disorganized assault. The rebels simply rushed up, pushed the rickety ladders against the walls, and started to climb, holding up only flimsy wicker shields. Mi and Solofi and a few of their personal guards held up magical mirrors and projected images of the Hegemon onto the castle walls to inspire the rebels.

Phyro watched the brazen but chaotic scene in astonishment. The attackers were completely unprotected, and the defenders on the ramparts, ready with boiling pots of oil and night soil–infused water, as well as rocks, heavy beams of wood, and thousands of arrows, ought to make short work of them. This was a mistake even the rawest of military commanders would not make.

"This is why Noda Mi and Doru Solofi crumbled before Marshal Mazoti during the Chrysanthemum-Dandelion War," Phyro muttered. "You can dress a sheep in wolf's clothing, but it's still a sheep." He gave the order for the defenders to begin the slaughter.

But few of his soldiers moved.

"What are they waiting for?" Phyro shouted, panic creeping into his voice.

Rin Coda rushed away and returned a few moments later, his face ashen.

"Some of our men, especially the locals, believe that the rebels have the Hegemon's protection. They think that arrows cannot pierce the rebels' armor, and spears and swords cannot harm the rebels' limbs. They believe that the rebels have been endowed with the spirit of the berserkers of Mata Zyndu and anyone who stands against them will be cursed."

Phyro stamped his feet in frustration. "Madness. The world has gone mad!"

"I'm going to gather the soldiers from the Big Island and hope that some of them haven't fallen under the sway of this debilitating witch-craft."

"Wait," Phyro said. "I have an idea. Do what you can to hold them off, and I'll be right back."

Rin Coda did what he could to rally the few men who still believed in the Imperial cause, and by threatening, beating, and whipping the rest, managed to organize some semblance of resistance. As rocks and wooden beams fell from the ramparts and pots of boiling liquid tipped over, the rebels on the ladders screamed and tumbled to their deaths.

"They do not have sufficient faith in the protection of the Hegemon!" Noda Mi shouted. "The Hegemon only defends those who are without doubt. The Doubt-Ender has been unsheathed! Sing with me, sing! *The ninth day in the ninth month of the year . . .*"

As thousands of rebels took up the chant, they made an impressive din. Noda and Doru's men regained their courage, and scores again climbed up the ladders. Despite the falling stones and wooden beams crushing the rebels into meat pies, more of them lined up to test their faith against doubt. Faced with this fearless horde whose eyes glinted with the zeal of madness, the defenders began to lose their heart.

Rebel archers finally lined up below the ladders and arced their arrows high overhead to strike at the defenders over the ramparts. Screams of dying and injured men filled the air.

It seemed only a matter of time before the walls would be breached.

"Who dares to make another move?" shouted Prince Phyro, who emerged at the top of the walls, breathing hard.

He was holding up a portrait of Mata Zyndu, which was usually hung in the main hall for the pilgrims who came to pray for the Hegemon's blessing. But Phyro now held it up like a giant shield and advanced on the attackers, who were just about to overwhelm the ramparts.

"You dare to desecrate the image of the Hegemon?" asked Phyro. He leaned the portrait over the edge of the wall. "This was one of Lady Mira's famous embroideries and captured the very essence of the Hegemon's spirit. Are you so impious that you wish to swing a sword against the soul of the Hegemon himself?"

The barrage of arrows from the attackers ceased. None of the archers dared harm the portrait of their lord. The attackers on the ladders hesitated and then stopped, afraid that if they pushed forward they might inadvertently stain the sacred painting.

"Despicable!" shouted Noda Mi. His face turned red with fury.

"A contemptible trick!" shouted Doru Solofi, spit foaming at the corners of his mouth.

"Am I so despicable?" asked a grinning Phyro. "Then why doesn't the Hegemon's portrait slip from my hands? I've always liked the Hegemon, you know? I might even be a bigger fan than you! Anyway, I'm going to hold the picture and stand right here. *I* will not be the one to defile the Hegemon's memory."

Rin Coda gestured at some of the most trusted defending soldiers, who seemed to wake from a trance. They also ran into the castle and returned a few minutes later: some of them carrying large figures of the Hegemon from wishing shrines and others crates of embroidered souvenir portraits for pilgrims. Soon, the ramparts were topped with a row of Mata Zyndu pictures and statues.

"You're indeed a son of that loathsome Kuni Garu," said Noda Mi. "This is a shameless trick worthy of the great betrayer himself." He and Solofi hurled a stream of curses and invectives at Phyro, but Phyro only smiled at them. The rebels halfway up the ladders stopped in place, unsure what to do.

In reality, Noda Mi and Doru Solofi had half a mind to order the archers to shoot fire arrows and burn the portraits so as to put an end to this farce, but they knew that reverence for the Hegemon was the foundation for this rebellion, and they were sure that if they ordered the destruction of the portraits, not only would they be disobeyed, but their men might even turn on them.

While the two sides were stuck in this stalemate, men both above and below the ramparts suddenly pointed up at the sky and shouted:

"An airship!"

"We're saved!"

"But why is there only one?"

Indeed, a slender airship was drifting over Zyndu Castle, its wing oars beating gracefully and rhythmically. Had the emperor's aid finally arrived?

The expression on Phyro's face, at first ecstatic, gradually turned to consternation. "That's *Time's Arrow*, the Imperial messenger ship," he whispered to Rin Coda. "It holds a crew of no more than a couple dozen. Where are the rest?"

Noda Mi, recognizing that the new ship was no great threat, was about to order another round of assaults on the far side of the castle—surely Phyro and his soldiers couldn't surround the entire castle with images of the Hegemon, could they?—when someone leapt out of the airship.

As soldiers from both sides gawked, the person tumbled a few times in the air before diving straight down. But just as everyone was about to close their eyes, not willing to see the tragic impact with the earth, the diver let out a giant silk balloon on their back. The balloon puffed up and filled with air, and slowed the descent of the rider.

"That was how the Hegemon took Zudi, years ago!"

"A spirit? A messenger of the Hegemon?"

Everyone could now see that the rider was a woman, and she was dressed in elegant, formal court robes with long sleeves and trains that drifted in the air like the tails of a kite.

Like a dandelion seed, the woman slowly spiraled down and landed on top of the walls of Zyndu Castle.

"Théra!" said an amazed Phyro. "What are you doing here?"

"Saving your butt, apparently. Three waves of pigeons! I was sure you were on the verge of death—since it would take too long to inform Father over by the Amu Strait, I commandeered *Time's Arrow* and came myself."

Phyro watched his big sister in undisguised admiration. He had always worshipped her, but now she seemed to have grown even more marvelous.

Théra disconnected the silk balloon from her robes and stepped up to the edge of the battlement. "Followers of the Hegemon, you have been misled!"

The rebels looked up at her. Princess Théra was regal and dazzling in her bright red court robe, embellished with silver-embroidered dandelion seeds and pearl-mosaic fish designs. "I've been sent here to show you the truth of the Hegemon's will."

She retrieved from the folds of her robes a large bronze mirror.

She held it up so that everyone below could see how smooth the highly polished surface was, like a pool of clear water. Everything around was reflected in it perfectly: the still-boiling pots of oil; the bloody figures of the defenders, some with arrows still sticking out of their torsos; the golden-armored rebel host.

She raised an arm and pointed into the sky behind the rebels. Everyone turned and saw that the airship had stopped just behind the rebels. Long bamboo poles extended from both ends of the gondola, from which a gigantic silk cloth was draped like an immense sail or curtain.

Princess Théra tilted the mirror so that the bright sun struck it and threw a projection onto the screen.

The defenders of Zyndu Castle and the rebels of Tunoa alike were stunned into silence.

There, on the screen, a gigantic figure of the Hegemon stood next to an equally gigantic figure of Emperor Ragin. The two stood with arms around each other's shoulders, their faces placid and gentle. Below the projected image were a few lines of text in zyndari letters:

A noble brotherhood, loyal and true;
Let not arms again cause Dara to rue.

Someone dropped his sword, and then another, and soon, the clanging of swords against ground filled the air.

"How? What?" Phyro was full of questions.

Théra pointed in the direction of Noda Mi and Doru Solofi, and imperiously ordered, "Seize them!"

But the two men had already cast off their bright royal regalia and faded into the dark woods like cuttlefish escaping into the deep sea, leaving behind only clouds of ink.

"Don't move it too fast," said Théra. "And don't press down. Pretend that you're the gentle breeze driving a boat evenly over the pond."

Carefully, Phyro moved the semispherical glass lens over the mirror. The light passed through the lens, struck the smooth bronze surface underneath, and was reflected back. Rainbow-sheened rings appeared in the lens, like concentric ripples, like the whirls of a fingerprint.

"What are these?"

"I call them Tututika's Rings," said Théra.

"Very pretty," said Phyro.

"They're more than pretty. They tell you if the surface beneath them is smooth. The light reflected from the mirror interferes with the light reflected by the lens itself, and if the surface is perfectly smooth, you'll see the rings as perfect circles. But if the surface is not perfectly smooth, you'll see the rings as deformed, revealing dips and protrusions undetectable by the naked eye."

As Phyro moved the lens around, he found that he could indeed trace valleys and ridges in the mirror by the deformation of Tututika's Rings in the lens.

He removed the lens and felt the surface again: nothing, no bumps or depressions at all. He gazed into the mirror: The reflection appeared completely faithful.

He sighed in admiration. "These patterns in the surface must be minuscule. But they cause the image to appear in the projection?"

"Precisely," said Théra. "I was certain that there was some trick to these mirrors. With the aid of Tututika's Rings, I finally figured out their secret."

"Including how to make them?"

"I don't know exactly what Noda and Doru did, but it turns out that the relief carving on the back is the key. To make my mirror, I had the image I wanted projected cast in relief in the back and then scraped and ground the surface vigorously. The embossed back meant that some parts of the mirror were thicker than others, and as a result, the tension and stress of the polishing caused tiny wrinkles in the surface that reproduce the design on the back without being visible to the eye."

"But how do you get a design of the back view of Father and the Hegemon on the back of the mirror but a picture of their fronts to be projected from the front?"

"Easy. The mirror was cast in two parts. First, we embossed the image we wanted into the mirror, polished it, and then added a new backing."

Phyro held up the lens. "And how did you discover Tututika's Rings?"

"I had excellent teachers," said Théra, somewhat mysteriously. "One showed me that light was like waves, and the other showed me that deviation from an expected pattern of interference could be used to detect minute variations in thickness. The rest was just a lot of experimentation."

Phyro held up the mirror in the sun and admired the projection of the emperor and the Hegemon on the wall. "Knowing how this was done, I can now admire the craft. Before, even I felt a bit awed by them."

Théra nodded. "Absolutely. Noda Mi and Doru Solofi relied on 'magic' to fool their followers. But once we figured out the secret, the magic belonged to everyone."

CHAPTER TWENTY-EIGHT

REFUGE

NOKIDA: THE NINTH MONTH IN THE ELEVENTH
YEAR OF THE REIGN OF FOUR PLACID SEAS.

Gin Mazoti surveyed the two men kneeling before her, experiencing a sense of déjà vu. Years earlier, the very same two men had also knelt before her, when she had captured the city of Dimu as the Marshal of Dasu.

Noda Mi and Doru Solofi had disguised themselves as Tunoa fishermen and arrived in Nokida earlier after braving the unpredictable currents of the Kishi Channel. They had come straight to the palace and begged to see the queen.

They now spread out their hands, bowed, and touched their foreheads to the stone floor, which was pockmarked and in need of repairs. "Your Majesty, Honored Queen of Géjira, Marshal of Dara, we are at your mercy!" They continued to strike their foreheads against the floor tiles until the dull thudding had stained the stones crimson with blood.

"That's enough."

Noda and Doru stopped moving, still prostrate.

"You've committed treason against the emperor. What good is pleading for mercy from me?"

Noda parsed Gin's words carefully. The very fact that Gin was asking questions instead of throwing them into a prisoner wagon bound for Pan was a good sign. The fact that she spoke of the emperor and herself in two separate sentences was another.

"Most Sagacious and Honored Queen, Paragon of Virtue!" he said, still not lifting his face from the floor. "We have been foolish in thinking that it was possible for mere grass to resist the might of the Imperial scythe, or for lowly praying mantises to dare stand against the march of the Imperial carriage. We can only blame our own greed and ambition for our sorry state and know that death is our just desert. Emperor Ragin is truly peerless in the arts of war and a commander of men without equal."

Gin listened, a slight frown creasing her brows. Noda stole a quick glance at the brightly polished surface of the sword lying at Gin's feet and saw the reflection of the queen's face. He almost smiled but quickly lowered his head again. *Ah, vanity.*

"You were arrogant," said Gin, standing up. "*That* was why you lost to a mere child on the battlefield. Trusting in the prowess of men lost in a feverish dream is a tactic that Mata Zyndu relied on to great success, but you two are no Mata Zyndu. Had I been—" She checked herself. "This is all beside the point. There is nothing I can do for you. I will give you a comfortable bed and a good meal tonight, and send you on your way to Pan in the morning."

Noda and Doru crawled forward and each grabbed one of Gin's feet. "Mercy! Mercy! Oh, Merciful Queen, Lord Rufizo Reborn, if you send us to Pan, we'll be faced with a fate worse than death! The emperor will make us into examples. He will slaughter our families and followers, and all the members of their families within three degrees of relatedness."

"What is that to me?"

"Once before, when we fought on the side of the Hegemon against the emperor, you showed mercy and let us go. We pray that you again repeat that act of great courage so that your immortal name may live on in song and story. In war, it has always been the rule that the nobles are treated differently from common men at arms."

"Is that so?" said Gin. "I suppose that's true—you certainly deserve a fate far worse than the fools who followed you. I doubt you'll find a single Lord of Dara who would disagree on this point."

"Yet surely it is not true that *all* the Lords of Dara are equal! Everyone knows that of all the emperor's advisers, the only one who can bring her sword into the palace and whose counsel the emperor heeds is you!" Once again, Noda went back to knocking his forehead against the floor, and Doru copied him.

Gin frowned again. Though their effort at appealing to her pride was rather transparent, she had to admit that it was working—after all, who had done more to build Kuni's empire than she? If he was going to listen to anyone, he should listen to her.

But she wasn't so foolish as to want to risk her reputation for the likes of Noda Mi and Doru Solofi. She was far more curious about the fact that the two of them had gotten as far as they had—and managed to drag Théca Kimo into their plot as well. Considering how much effort Rin Coda had put into the Imperial security apparatus, something didn't smell right.

"If you want me to help you," said Gin, "tell me everything that's happened to you since the time you decided to rebel. Leave no details out."

As Noda and Doru recounted their run of good luck, Gin's face gradually darkened, and then brightened.

Finally, she extricated herself gently but firmly from their groveling. "Gentlemen, do not debase yourselves further. You are my guests for tonight, and I will decide what to do on the morrow."

Zomi Kidosu frowned as she surveyed the open plaza before the queen's grand audience hall. Dozens of men and a few women were camped out on bedrolls, making the place appear as a beggar's lane.

"Who *are* these people?" asked ten-year-old Princess Aya Mazoti, who walked next to her. She had the wiry frame of her mother and the same sharp features, though her skin was darker. The queen had never said who her father was, and none of Mazoti's generals and ministers had dared to probe. The kings of Dara had never felt the need to explain to their followers who they pleased to bed, and Mazoti had always acted as though the same rules applied to her. She had taken many men to bed, but none dared to think that deed made them special.

"These are the followers of Noda Mi and Doru Solofi," said Zomi. "They escaped Tunoa and are seeking asylum with your mother."

"Is she going to protect them?"

"I'm not sure," Zomi said. It had been a few days since Mi and Solofi had arrived with their retinue, and Gin seemed unable to make up her mind. As soon as Zomi saw Doru Solofi's shifting mien, arrogant and groveling by turns, she had recognized him as the brute who had attempted to extort her and the other patrons of the Three-Legged Jug years ago. Unsettled by emotions and memories she had long pushed out of her mind, Zomi had avoided going to the queen, as she did not trust herself to offer objective counsel. But the queen had summoned her, and Zomi was glad to run into Princess Aya on the way to the audience hall—it would delay the unpleasant discussion a little further.

"If they're traitors, then Mother should kill them on the spot," said Aya.

Gin Mazoti had never shied away from letting her daughter know how she came by her throne, and Zomi was used to the way the princess spoke easily of killing and warfare. In truth, since her arrival in Géjira, she had been working to moderate some of Gin's more militaristic instincts to administer the realm with a gentler hand. For instance, she had encouraged Gin to freeze the military budget and divert more funds into building village schools for the poor modeled on the learning huts of old Haan. She was using them to experiment with a new curriculum that emphasized writing in the vernacular and practical skills like mental arithmetic and geometry that eschewed proofs. Gin had been far more amenable to her suggestions than the Imperial bureaucracy, and Zomi felt that she was finally finding a perch from which she could shine. Gin's generous stipend also allowed her to send a lot more money home to Dasu. Everything in her life seemed to be moving in the right direction.

"That looks like fun!" Aya said.

Zomi followed her gaze and saw one of the fugitives, a young man about eighteen or nineteen years of age, exercising with one of the hitching stones at the edge of the plaza. With both hands, he grabbed the protruding ring to which the horse's lead was supposed to be tied and, with a grunt, tossed the stone into the air. Although the stone must have weighed close to two hundred pounds, he managed to toss it up about ten feet or so. Then he caught it with both arms and gently set it down. He repeated this several more times. The other fugitives, having grown inured to the sight of this feat of strength, ignored him.

Aya ran up to him. "You must be a great warrior," she said, her voice full of admiration. Ever since she was a toddler, Gin had been teaching her wrestling and knife fighting, and she was a tomboy through and through.

Mota Kiphi put the stone down and wiped his face. "Thank you, young mistress."

"You should call me Your Highness," said Aya.

"Your Highness," said Mota dutifully.

Zomi called to the princess. "Come, Your Highness. The queen doesn't like to be kept waiting."

"I want to talk to this man," said Aya stubbornly. Zomi had no choice but to walk over. She had been avoiding the fugitives in order to maintain objectivity and advise the queen properly, but now that she was here, it seemed impolite to say nothing.

"Have you always been this strong?" As soon as Zomi asked the question, she felt foolish, but she had never been good at small talk.

Mota shook his head and smiled shyly. "I was a lot like my father, rather sickly and weak as a child."

"So what happened?"

"My father left to fight with the Hegemon against Mapidéré before I was born, and he never returned. I've always wanted to be like him. I remembered the tales about how Marshal Dazu Zyndu had also been weak as a child but carried a calf around until he became strong as an ox. So I plowed the fields for my neighbors and hauled their fish until things changed."

Though he told his tale in a matter-of-fact manner, Zomi could hear behind it years of sweat and dedication, years of yearning for a dream.

Zomi thought of her father, who had died to look for a prince. She thought of her brothers, who had died because a noble called for them to fight. She thought of the way Princess Théra had managed to get her into the Grand Examination with a single word.

We suffer because we are the grass upon which giants stride.

She also thought of the complicated meaning of the word "talent." She thought of her own years of hard work and toil. She thought about the ways in which she did not feel at home among the nobles at the Imperial court and the refined scholars who were her colleagues in the College of Advocates. She thought about the ways in which she did not feel at home when she was actually home in Dasu.

If a carp has leapt over the Rufizo Falls, does the carp-turned-dyran not owe a duty to do what she can for the other carp?

This was why she had not wanted to know these men at all. Knowing someone's stories made you vulnerable.

"You *are* strong," she said, not knowing what else to say.

"Yes, I am," Mota said. He wasn't bragging, just acknowledging a truth. "But I wish I had listened to my mother, who didn't want me to come fight at all. She said that the great lords like King Noda and King Doru like to gamble, but it's always the people who have to scrabble for a living who pay the price."

Zomi said nothing.

"My mother will make whoever hurt you pay," said Aya. "She's a greater lord than them all."

Zomi went around to talk to the other fugitives. Some were scholars who had failed to place in the Imperial examinations and hoped to find an outlet for their talent; some were desperadoes who thought of the rebellion as an opportunity to accumulate wealth; but most were simple young peasants like Mota Kiphi, who fought because they were told it was the right thing to do, and they trusted the nobles to know better.

Zomi left for the audience hall.

"You cannot do this," said Zomi.

"I *cannot*?" asked Gin Mazoti, amused. "Why not?"

"Because it would be wrong to offer up Noda and Doru's followers to the emperor's executioners when those two are responsible! That they would even suggest such a thing is beyond the pale."

"I can't offer up Noda and Doru," said Gin, her voice hard. "They came to me, thinking that I could save their lives. I would have no shred of honor left if I don't even try."

"You're talking about saving face—"

"Honor is everything!"

Zomi took a deep breath. "But then why offer up their followers?"

"Because things are no longer as they were in Pan," said Gin. "The emperor has not asked me to lead the war against Théca Kimo, though I am still nominally the Marshal of Dara. Neither did he come to me for aid with the situation in Tunoa. I suspect that . . . Never mind, there are things you're not meant to understand. I have to give him something."

"You think the winds have changed in Pan?" asked Zomi. "Do you . . . think the emperor suspects you of ambition?"

"I don't know *what* to think," said Gin. "The signs from Pan are conflicting, and I think this rebellion in Tunoa is more complicated than it might appear. Someone powerful in Pan is plotting against those who have done the most to bring about the rise of the House of Dandelion."

"If you think the empress . . . I must say that you are wrong."

"How do you know this?"

I can't betray the empress's trust, thought Zomi. *I can't let the queen know how the empress has been misunderstood.* "I just know. But if you really must reassure yourself, surely you can go to Consort—"

Gin silenced her adviser with a cold and proud glare. "If you're going to suggest that I go to Consort Risana for protection, hold your tongue. I made my name upon the tip of my sword. I will not go groveling to the wives of my lord."

"You speak of honor in shielding Noda and Doru, yet you would give up their followers to assure the emperor. I do not think the two can be reconciled."

Gin laughed bitterly. "Consistency has always been a trap into which only small minds wish to leap."

"Are you certain that you're not simply offering protection to Noda and Doru to see if you still have the emperor's trust, to see that you are still the Marshal of Dara in his heart?"

Gin looked away, saying nothing.

If the prince and the duke press men and women of talent who hold a different opinion too severely, they'll need a refuge in Dara.

This must be the moment the empress had meant, thought Zomi. *Oh, Queen Gin, if only you knew that the empress and you are on the same side!*

"If you intend to preserve your honor and influence," said Zomi, "you must protect not only Noda and Doru, but also all their men."

Gin quirked a brow at her.

"I have spoken to the men who followed them here. They have been misled or have become dissatisfied with the emperor, but many of them are men of talent.

"Prince Phyro is young and rash while Duke Coda is embarrassed at having almost lost against the rebels. It's natural that they'd portray these men as unredeemable traitors. Presently, the emperor is enraged by Théca Kimo's betrayal, and if you hand these men over, he will no doubt execute them, only to regret the decision later.

"Blood begets more blood, Your Majesty, and Dara cannot afford more blood. The wise course of action is to shield all these men until the emperor has had a chance to calm down, and then he will thank you for your steady hand and cool counsel. This is the best way to secure your honor in his heart and to prove your loyalty."

Gin gazed severely at her. "Are you certain that you're not trying to protect these men because they remind you of you? Of your rise from base birth to greatness?"

Zomi shot back, "You were once just like them!"

"This is dangerous counsel."

Do what is right for Dara, no matter the consequences.

Zomi had never been more certain in her life that she was doing the right thing.

"Yet you have made your name upon the tip of your sword."

As Gin continued to look at Zomi, her face gradually relaxed.

"Tell Noda and Doru's men to move into the guest quarters with their lords. Tonight, we feast and welcome them all to Géjira."

CHAPTER TWENTY-NINE

EMPRESS AND MARSHAL

"*Rénga*, I must advise against this course of action," said Prime Minister Cogo Yelu. "Puma Yemu may have suffered some defeats, but risking yourself is not going to be the answer."

"Puma Yemu has always been so effective," said Jia. "One wonders why this war is going so poorly."

Cogo looked at the empress and was about to speak, but then he thought better of it and kept his mouth shut.

"I don't know what Puma is thinking," said an irritated Kuni. "I don't seem to know my generals at all anymore. But I have no choice but to go to war. Shall I stand by while the people whisper that I have lost my will to fight?"

"You could summon Queen Gin," said Jia.

"I did not summon her earlier because I thought it would be awkward for her to fight against one of her old friends," said Kuni. "And now that things are going poorly, you want me to crawl to her for help? Will you make me into the laughingstock of Dara?"

"She *did* win Dara for you," said Jia quietly.

A long, awkward silence. Kuni's face darkened.

"I think what the empress meant to say," Risana broke in timidly, "is that Gin Mazoti has a certain skill—"

"You do not need to explain what she meant," said Kuni. He swept his sleeve through the air angrily. "If even my wife thinks that I must rely on the sword of Gin Mazoti to keep my empire, then so must half of Dara. Is my throne so insecure that I must beg her to intervene whenever one of the nobles grows ambitious? Is she the emperor or am I?"

"I spoke rashly, Kuni," said Jia. "I'm sorry."

Kuni ignored her. "Risana, prepare your luggage. We leave with the army in the morning. I'm going to Arulugi personally to oversee this war, and I will not come back until either Théca Kimo is dead or I join the Hegemon."

Kuni stormed away.

"Do not hold this against him," said Risana to Jia. "He's just used to having me with him on campaigns. He is . . . under a great deal of stress."

Jia inclined her head and smiled. "Thank you, sister. I had not thought my husband and I were such strangers that I needed marital advice."

Risana blushed, bowed, and hurried away, leaving Cogo Yelu and the empress alone.

"What is your counsel, Prime Minister?" asked the empress.

"I am certain that the emperor will do what is right for Dara," said Cogo, bowing and keeping his eyes calmly focused on the tip of his nose. "As will the empress and Consort Risana."

Jia laughed. "How many years have we known each other now, Cogo? You need not act like Consort Risana in one of her dances: waving her long sleeves in every direction, pleasing admirers from every vantage point. If you think I've made a mistake, you have but to speak plainly to me."

"It did seem ill-advised to bring up the topic of Queen Gin when the emperor had already decided to go to war himself."

"Because he would be insulted?"

"The emperor is still a man," said Cogo. "None of us is free from vanity."

"Oh, I was counting on it," said Jia.

Cogo's eyes snapped to focus on her, but the look of surprise lasted only a fleeting moment before being replaced by his habitual serene expression.

"The emperor may have at one time or another reprimanded all of his generals and advisers except you and Luan," said Jia. "Luan stays away from the court, while you are smooth as a polished piece of jade, the master politician." She paused and looked at him.

"I am but a loyal servant of the emperor," said Cogo, his face impassive.

"And of the next emperor as well, I hope?" asked Jia.

Cogo hesitated only a beat. "Of course."

"Remember that."

Jia turned and left.

Cogo stood rooted in place, and only long after the empress was gone did he raise his sleeve to wipe the cold sweat from the back of his neck.

While Emperor Ragin and Consort Risana were away in Arulugi to oversee the war against Théca Kimo, while Prince Timu remained in Dasu to maintain vigilance against the pirates, while Prince Phyro—and Princess Théra, who refused to obey her mother's commands to return to the capital—remained in Tunoa to sweep up the remnants of the Hegemon's cult, Empress Jia became Imperial regent in Pan.

Since this was the first time the empress had ever been the regent, the ministers and generals were not quite sure what to expect. Her reputation for possessing a fiery temper filled everyone with trepidation.

But she soon reassured everyone. She visited the city garrison, thanking the soldiers for defending the capital against acts of sabotage by Théca Kimo's spies or the remnants of the insurgency in Tunoa; she went to oversee the shipment of grains and feed for the emperor's expedition in Arulugi; she gathered the scholars and spoke to them about the importance of stability.

Everyone at court whispered that Empress Jia was indeed an extraordinary woman surpassing others of her sex like the dyran surpassed all other fish, a much-needed careful and stabilizing influence.

On the ninth day after the emperor left, Jia summoned all of Kuni's ministers and generals who were in the capital to formal court.

She sat in her customary seat next to the throne, though now next to her sat the Seal of Dara on a small sandalwood table. The ministers and generals lined the Grand Audience Hall, all sitting in formal *mipa rari*.

"Honored Lords of Dara," said the empress, "we gather today to speak of examinations."

The ministers and the generals looked at each other, puzzled. The Grand Examination wouldn't happen for another five years, so what was the empress talking about?

The empress turned to the side and called for Princess Fara. The young princess timidly entered the Grand Audience Hall and knelt before the empress.

"You don't need to be afraid," said the empress kindly. "I'd just like to ask you a few questions and see if perhaps the emperor's advisers could learn something from a child."

The gathered ministers and generals felt their stomachs tighten. *What game is the empress playing?*

"Ada-*tika*, suppose a man of Haan must go to Faça on a trip of a few months, and he leaves a sum of money to his good friend, asking him to take care of his children. However, when he returns, he finds his children starving and in ragged clothes, while his friend enjoys rich meals and dresses in silk. What shall he do with such a friend?"

Fara smiled. "This is a story from Kon Fiji's *Treatise on Moral Relations*. The answer is: The man should break off all contact with this friend because he cannot be trusted to be faithful."

The empress nodded. "Very good. Now, suppose a minister is

unable to govern his clerks well, and they disobey his directives and shirk their duties while he imposes no discipline, what should the king do with the minister?"

Fara giggled. "This is from the same story. The answer is: The king should dismiss the minister because he cannot be trusted to be competent."

The empress again nodded. "A third question then. Now, suppose an enfeoffed noble ignores threats to his lord's well-being, offers comfort and succor to his lord's enemies, instigates discord and harmony in the family of his lord, forms factions and parties among his lord's followers, what shall the lord do with him?"

Fara was stunned. "That's—that's—but that's not how the story went . . . I don't know."

Jia smiled. "It's not your fault." She gestured for her to leave, and the young princess bowed and ran away quickly.

The Grand Audience Hall was completely quiet. Though all the ministers and generals were full of questions, none dared even to breathe too loud.

"Would anyone care to answer?"

No one stirred.

Kado Garu, who sat to the side, at the head of the column of nobles and generals, silently congratulated himself on having yielded his fief to Timu. *Jia really is going to go after the nobles.*

Jia looked around and settled her eyes on Cogo Yelu. "Prime Minister, would you care to answer the query that Princess Fara could not?"

Cogo Yelu bowed and said, "The empress is citing one of Kon Fiji's famous tales. If I recall correctly, the One True Sage was speaking to the King of Faça."

"Indeed. What was his original third question to the King of Faça?"

"Kon Fiji asked, 'Suppose then that the state is ill administered, that the laws are unreasonable, that the people complain about corruption and misrule, what should be done with the king?'"

"What did the King of Faça say?"

Cogo Yelu reluctantly went on. "The King of Faça was silent for a while. Then he looked to the left, looked to the right, and then began to speak of the weather."

"How are you different from the King of Faça, Prime Minister, if you will not answer my query?"

Cogo touched his forehead to the ground and said nothing.

Jia looked away from him and swept her eyes over the court.

"When Théca Kimo rebelled, Gin Mazoti never came to Pan to offer her aid, despite her position as the Marshal of Dara; when Noda Mi and Doru Solofi escaped Tunoa, their little plot in shambles, Gin Mazoti offered them refuge; when Gin Mazoti attended court five years ago, she spoke rudely to me while conspicuously flaunting her friendship with Consort Risana; when a *cashima* lost her pass to attend the Grand Examination, Gin Mazoti offered her aid in secret, thereby hoarding for herself the loyalty of a talented person—have you nothing to say to any of these charges?"

Cogo remained kneeling with his forehead to the ground. But when it was clear that the empress would not go on until he gave an answer, he spoke reluctantly, pausing between words, "There must be ironclad proof, lest the people speak ill of Your Imperial Majesty."

Jia waved her hand, and Chatelain Otho Krin came forward. "Spies have returned with a new report from Géjira. Queen Mazoti feasts every night with Noda Mi and Doru Solofi, as well as many of their followers."

Jia waited.

Cogo looked up. "I serve the emperor," he said. Then he bowed again and touched his forehead to the ground. "And the empress."

The other ministers, generals, and nobles bowed and said together, "I serve the emperor and the empress."

Jia looked impassively at them and nodded, once.

As *Cruben's Horn* descended toward Pan, Gin and Zomi looked down at the carriages and pedestrians streaming through the wide avenues of the city like blood through the vessels of some giant.

Zomi pointed at the golden, circular roof of the Grand Examination Hall. "Five years ago, that place had seemed the center of the universe, a hub around which everything revolved. I could not conceive of a more important place anywhere else in Dara. Yet today it appears as just an ordinary building, and my heart is no longer filled with awe at the sight of it."

"That is because the Examination Hall was necessary to your success back then, and of little use now," said Gin.

Zomi was startled for a moment, and then she nodded. "I had not thought of it that way before, but I suppose it is true. I am thankful, in any event, that the hall where so many scholars' dreams died ultimately brought me to you."

"Such is the fate of all things and people," said Gin. "One day we're street urchins and peasant girls from distant provinces, and the next day we could be queens and high officials deciding the fates of hundreds of thousands because our talents are necessary to those who need them. But who knows what will happen the day after that?"

Zomi wasn't used to such morose sentiments coming from the queen. She wondered whether it was because Gin still felt some trepidation at being summoned by the empress out of the blue. The messenger had explained that the empress wished to discuss the rebellion in Arulugi, and that as time was of the essence, Gin had to leave right away in the Imperial messenger airship. The ship's small capacity allowed Gin only a single attendant, and she chose Zomi Kidosu. She had none of her guards and trusted generals with her.

"Zomi, do you know who Aya's father is?" asked Gin.

The question surprised Zomi. She had always assumed that this was a topic that Gin did not wish to broach.

"You know him," said Gin. "You are the daughter of his mind as Aya is the daughter of his flesh."

Zomi was stunned by the revelation.

"Aya does not know the truth. I've always hidden it from her because . . . I suppose I wanted her to be prouder of me than of her father. Vanity is a sin none of us can be free from. I've never told him either because . . . I wanted him to stay because of me, not because of duty.

"If something should happen . . . would you . . ." The queen's voice trailed off, as if she could not bear this moment of weakness.

For a moment, Zomi wondered if Gin's suspicion of the empress's intentions was right. But the empress had been her bene-factress, and thinking that way felt like a betrayal.

The empress bears you no ill will at all, Zomi wanted to shout at the queen, but she had sworn an oath of secrecy. *You will find out the truth soon enough,* she thought.

"I swear to protect Princess Aya," said Zomi, "with every fiber of my being."

Gin said nothing, as though she didn't even hear her.

The grand plaza in front of the Imperial palace loomed as the ship began the final approach to the landing site.

Gin arrived in Pan in the afternoon, but the empress did not see her right away despite the rush to get her into the capital. She was apparently absorbed with the affairs of state and could only attend to Gin on the morrow. Gin was not invited to stay inside the palace because, as the empress's secretary explained, the empress found the sight of swords at the present time an ill omen.

Shaking her head at Jia's pettiness—the empress had never liked the fact that Gin could enter the palace with her sword—Gin went to the quarters assigned to her in the guest complex right outside the walls of the palace. This was where visiting nobles and import-ant officials from the provinces stayed when they came to the capi-tal on business. Gin settled in with a pot of tea and conversed with Zomi Kidosu, certain that soon generals and ministers who wished to curry favor with her would come to visit.

But no one came for most of the afternoon.

Though Gin continued to joke and laugh and speak of inconsequential things, Zomi saw that the queen's hand involuntarily trembled as she poured tea. Whether it was from rage or fear she could not tell.

Zomi grew uneasy as well. She had never been very sensitive to the winds of politics, but even she could see this was unusual. *What is going on in Pan?*

Finally, Mün Çakri, First General of the Infantry and one of Gin's most trusted friends, arrived in the evening.

"What interesting gossip is being passed around the court?" asked Gin, after they had finished greeting each other.

"I didn't realize you were interested in gossip, Marshal," said Mün. "In any event, I wouldn't know. I've been away in Rui, helping to prepare the island against an assault by Théca Kimo should he become desperate enough to try such a thing. I returned only this morning and I have to leave again tomorrow to escort the grain shipment to the emperor in Arulugi."

"Ah, so you've been away as well," said Gin, disappointed. "Have you heard any news of Luan Zya?"

"That old turtle? No, nothing. But I wouldn't worry about him. He's dived from the sky and ridden on the back of a cruben—I doubt sailing through unknown waters could harm him."

"How's Naro and Cacaya-*tika*?" Gin asked.

"I've been so busy these last few months that I haven't seen much of them. But I've already started to teach the boy to wrestle piglets."

Gin laughed. "I wouldn't expect anything less."

"I started my life as a butcher, and I don't want my son to forget it. Where we start is important, you know?"

Gin turned somber. "Have you ever wished you could have stayed a butcher instead of . . . this life?"

Mün shook his head. "Never. Why would a kite wish to stay on the ground instead of shooting for the sky?"

"Even if a storm is coming?"

Mün glanced out the window. "It does look like it will rain soon. I better get back before Naro starts to worry."

Gin refilled both cups and drained hers in one gulp. "To old friends and flying kites in storms."

Mün drained his cup. He smacked his lips, praising the fragrance of the wine.

He didn't catch the fleeting trace of sorrow in Gin's eyes.

CHAPTER THIRTY

ZOMI'S SECRET

"I will not!" declared Zomi.

She was once again sitting opposite the empress in her private audience hall, a pot of freshly brewed tea between them.

While Mün and Gin were conversing, Chatelain Otho Krin had come to the guest quarters and summoned Zomi for an urgent meeting with the empress. The "report" she had been asked to sign shocked her to the core of her being.

"The proof for Gin Mazoti's intent to rebel is ironclad," said the empress, calmly pouring tea for both of them. "You'll simply be confirming what we already know."

"The queen never intended to rebel."

"Then why has she been harboring Noda Mi and Doru Solofi as well as dozens of their followers? At this moment, generals loyal to the Throne have already seized control of the army of Géjira and occupied the queen's palace. The fugitives have been arrested."

"But you told me—" Zomi stopped. A complex series of expressions transformed her face: disbelief, anger, fear, and eventually bitter acceptance. "Only now do I understand the true purpose of my assignment—I was but a stone in your *cüpa* game. You have lied to me, Your Imperial Majesty."

"Speaking of lies, I have something to show you." Jia got up and walked over to her desk. She rummaged in a drawer and returned with a stack of paper. She set the stack down on the desk between them and pushed it over to Zomi.

Zomi looked at the stack closely. It was actually a single sheet of paper that had been folded over multiple times. She reached out and touched it: Golden threads were embedded in the material, and it was clear that the sheet had once been cut into small squares and then painstakingly pasted back together with strips of paper and glue. Many of the squares had names written on them, along with the seals of the various governors and enfeoffed nobles.

She didn't need to unfold the paper to know that there would be a square missing.

Her mind drifted to that momentous night years ago.

Regent Ra Olu, King Kado's representative on Dasu, was holding a party for all the cashima *of Dasu. He was supposed to meet with each of them individually and then determine which ones would be recommended for the Grand Examination based on a combination of their scores in the Provincial Examination and their character and reputation.*

Zomi had been sure that she would be selected. She had the highest score of all the toko dawiji *who had achieved the rank of* cashima *in years, and out of the ten or so recommendations that Regent Ra Olu would hand out, one would have to have her name on it, wouldn't it? After all, that was the point of the examinations, to pick out men and women of talent to serve the emperor.*

Many of the cashima *had gone to school together or knew each other by the prominence of their families, and they now conversed in small cliques. Zomi didn't know anyone and wandered around by herself: There was much wine and fish, served raw and dipped in the spicy sauces that Dasu was famous for.*

Her stomach was unused to the wine—no doubt expensive—and the rich fish roe—a delicacy. Soon, Zomi had to go to the toilet. When she was done, she was confused. She couldn't find the customary box of soft, dry tissue grass next to the toilet. How was she supposed to clean herself?

She waited until another cashima, a man, came in. She whispered through the thin privacy partition.

"Do you have anything to wipe with?"

"Have they run out?" the man asked. "The regent will be very unhappy with the toilet attendants. Let me help you out."

He went to the next stall, came back, and reached under the privacy partition. Zomi gratefully took what he was holding in his hand.

She was stunned: It was a stack of silk handkerchiefs, just like the ones in the box in her stall. She had thought they had been left behind by a lady of the house by mistake. The silk was smooth and soft; she had never owned anything that expensive.

So this was how the wealthy lived.

She seethed as she wiped herself. She thought about the muddy hut she had grown up in; she thought about her mother going to Master Ikigégé's house to wash the floor and clean the toilets; she thought about her own childhood spent hauling fish and working the fields until the skin of her hands had grown as rough as the soil itself. Meanwhile, the regent of Dasu was cleaning his ass with silk.

She returned to the party, now feeling even more of a stranger, someone who didn't belong.

"I saw that the beggar girl was hungry, and so I ordered a servant to give her some leftover porridge," a well-dressed lady said. Zomi did not recognize her, but she was surrounded by a crowd of cashima, who seemed to hang on her every word.

"She squatted down right there in the kitchen and started to slurp the porridge. Embarrassed, I told her, 'A girl does not squat, dear. You should sit in mipa rari when you're in the presence of a superior lady. And you should take small sips, not slurp like an animal.' She looked at me and said, 'Ma and Da squat too. And if I don't slurp, how would you know I like the food?' And then she asked me if I had any preserved caterpillars to go with the porridge. Caterpillars! Can you believe it?"

The lady giggled.

The cashima *around her laughed as though she had truly told an amusing story.*

"I wish Lady Lon had not been exposed to such a primitive side of Dasu," said one of the cashima. "In truth, even we are embarrassed by the uncouth manners and disgusting eating habits of the peasantry, a legacy from the days when Xana was little better than a land of barbarians. I have yearned to see the superior, refined society of the Big Island, and it is so good that you're with us, Lady Lon, to provide us all a worthy example to emulate."

"Oh, don't be so modest," said Lady Lon. "I know you are different. You are the educated cream of Dasu and would not appear too out of place at one of the parties I used to hold in Pan. Though, if I may be so bold, it will serve all of you well to seek a teacher of elocution and polish your speech slightly. I'm afraid that the tones of Dasu may sound a bit coarse to the ears of the inhabitants of the Big Island."

The gathered cashima *thanked Lady Lon for her generous instruction.*

"Lady Lon, you judged the young girl wrongly." Zomi couldn't hold her tongue any longer.

The other cashima *fell silent. Lady Lon turned to her, amazed.*

"The young girl's family was in the habit of squatting because they were too poor to afford sitting mats. When she saw the clean tile floor of your kitchen, she didn't want to sit because she was afraid that her muddy clothes might dirty your floor. She slurped your porridge to show that she appreciated your act of charity, for that is how the poor of Dasu express enjoyment of our food. Kon Fiji said that having good manners means acting out of a sincere desire to be considerate of the feelings of others. I see nothing uncouth or unrefined about the young girl's manners, but much that needs improvement in yours."

Lady Lon's face flushed bright red. "Who are you? How dare you lecture me?"

Zomi strolled over to one of the tables, filled her plate with pieces of raw fish dipped in sweet and spicy sauce, and then squatted down next to the table, her spread legs facing Lady Lon.

"You—you—" *Lady Lon, enraged and embarrassed, could not continue.*

"It is said that even the emperor, when he was King of Dasu, once sat down with the elders of my village to share a meal, and he squatted like everyone else and drank from the same cups and ate from the same plates. Should we not emulate the emperor?" She opened her mouth and chewed a piece of fish loudly and vigorously, not bothering to ensure that her lips remained closed.

She relished the way Lady Lon turned away from her in embarrassment. She delighted in the way the other cashima looked at her in disbelief. In a way, she also pitied them—they were so afraid of power that they behaved like boneless sponges when the Imperial examinations were meant to bring the powerless into the ranks of the powerful. She knew she had done better on the examination than them all.

Only later in the evening did she find out that Lady Lon was the favored wife of Regent Ra Olu. She waited with the other cashima for the elect to be announced, and she heard the regent call out nine names and then stop, instead of giving the expected tenth. As the cashima left the party, she went up to the regent.

"I have the highest score in all of Dasu, perhaps all of old Xana." She was certain there had been a mistake.

"Scores aren't everything," said the regent, and turned away as though she was nothing but an inconsequential fly.

And Zomi understood what she should have always understood: Talent was not enough. There were webs of privilege and power that were just as important, if not more important, than talent. The ideal of the Imperial examinations was a lie.

So she turned away, and quietly let down her hair from the triple scroll-bun of a cashima. In her plain clothes, she looked indistinguishable from the servants clearing away the dishes and cups scattered around the room. She grabbed a stack of plates and stopped by the table on the raised dais where the passes for the Grand Examination were held, and slipped the last signed, but blank, pass into her sleeve.

It had been an impulsive decision.

She had not thought it wrong to steal the pass that should have belonged to her. Later, she had rationalized that if she did well on the Grand Examination, her theft would remain a secret because the regent would say nothing—he would be rewarded for having recommended a successful candidate to the emperor, so why would he argue with success? She had been counting on his self-interest.

She had hoped that success would make her feel like she *belonged*, but deep down, she had always known that her honor was stolen. There was a stain at the origin of her success that could never be erased.

"King Kado never saw your name on the list of recommended candidates," said the empress, "which means that you had forged your name in the hand of the king's regent."

Zomi said nothing.

"It was really a stroke of luck that you then lost your pass, and Gin Mazoti signed a replacement pass for you—otherwise you would have been caught when Rin Coda assembled the passes back together and noticed that the handwriting on one of the passes from Dasu was different from all the others."

Zomi closed her eyes. The empress was right. That brute at the Three-Legged Jug had actually been her savior. So much in life depended on these coincidences, wild, unpredictable turns that were the province of Tazu. Were they just another name for fate?

"But maybe instead of luck, we could say that Gin Mazoti was involved in a plot to cheat at the Grand Examination to enlarge her influence."

"The queen knew nothing about any of this!"

"Who would believe the words of a disgraced cheater?" asked the empress placidly. "Let's imagine what will happen after I announce your treachery: You will be tossed in prison; your mother will lose everything and perhaps be whipped for breeding a daughter of such poor character; Gin Mazoti will still be a traitor."

Zomi thought about her mother.

"I will give you a better life. I swear it."

Zomi thought about her teacher.

"That's not the moral—"

"I don't care! I only care about people close to me."

Zomi thought about Queen Gin.

"Aya does not know the truth. . . . If something should happen . . . would you . . ."

What was the right thing to do?

If Zomi were disgraced, she would have no power to protect any of the people she cared about at all. But if she remained in the empress's good graces, then her mother would continue to be cared for, and there would be a chance, however slim, that she could rescue the young princess from the usual fate of traitor to the Throne.

Zomi swallowed, hard. To carry out her promise to the queen, she must first betray her.

"I shall be guided by you, Empress," said Zomi.

CHAPTER THIRTY-ONE

A VISIT TO THE LAKE

PAN: THE TENTH MONTH IN THE ELEVENTH YEAR
OF THE REIGN OF FOUR PLACID SEAS.

At the crack of dawn, the empress and the prime minister came to see the queen.

Gin stood in bare feet at the door awkwardly, not having had a chance to put on her socks or shoes to greet the empress because she had been given no notice. She was certain that Jia was doing everything on purpose—delaying seeing her when she arrived in Pan, forcing her to stay outside the palace, keeping visitors away, and then showing up so early unannounced—to keep her off balance, unsure of herself. But just because she understood what Jia was doing didn't mean that the tricks weren't effective.

"I heard that years ago, back on Dasu, Lord Garu himself once dashed out the door of his house without shoes to welcome you back," said a wistful Gin. She emphasized *Lord Garu* deliberately, but the empress did not react to her breach of decorum. "He thought you had run away."

Cogo laughed, though the mirth sounded a bit forced. "I left to chase you."

"I owe all my successes to you," said Gin with feeling. "Old friends are hard to come by."

"And the prime minister may bring you yet more success," said the empress, also smiling. "I apologize for not being able to meet you yesterday, but unexpected troubles come up when you are the regent. I hope we can take a ride together."

"A ride?" Gin found the empress's request odd. But since Cogo was with her, she felt reassured. "I am yours to command, Your Imperial Majesty."

The three of them rode together, side by side, while the palace guards escorted them through the streets of Pan. They rode for much of the morning, always heading west, while the empress kept the conversation light, touching upon various bits of gossip in Pan, the latest popular stories being told in bars and teahouses, and the outrageous critiques of Imperial policy put forth by the learned minds in the College of Advocates. She made no mention of the rebellion, and Gin felt even more jumpy and uneasy.

Finally, they arrived at an Imperial dock on the shore of Lake Tututika. A small boat was tied up, and a kite was attached to its bow, flying high in the sky.

"This is one of the new inventions from the Imperial Academy based on a design by Luan Zya," said the empress. Gin's heart leapt at the mention of her former lover.

The empress continued, "This is a small model, of course, but I'm told that with a large kite to catch the powerful winds high above the clouds, it is possible to achieve speeds greater than with sail or oar. I wanted to get your opinion on it since you were once so helpful on the design of the mechanical cruben, another novel boat."

Gin wasn't sure how such a boat, even if effective, could be relevant to the current war in Arulugi, which was no longer a naval war. The empress seemed to speak only in enigmas.

"Why don't you try it?" the empress pressed.

Cogo went to the boat and made a gesture. *Please.*

Gin approached. The palace guards lined up along the wharf, apparently cutting off her retreat.

I'm being paranoid, thought Gin. *I must not show fear.*

"You should leave your sword," said Cogo. "This is a very small model, and we calculated the ballast for your weight only."

Gin hesitated. She looked into Cogo's face, but he avoided her gaze, looking only at the boat.

She sighed and took off her sword and laid it on the ground. She stepped into the boat and sat down, feeling as though she was following a script that was very old.

"I'll have to fasten this about you," said Cogo. He indicated the ropes attached to the gunwale. "The boat moves very fast when the wind catches the kite, and it's safest to tie you down."

Gin nodded. Every instinct in her told her to refuse, to jump up and pick up her sword and demand from the empress the truth of what was going on. But she knew that there would be no retreat from such a gesture, from open treason.

She held still.

Cogo wrapped the ropes around her waist and tied the knot behind her. She could see that his hands were trembling. She wanted to laugh. Her success on the battlefield had never been based on her swordsmanship, and yet here the empress was treating her like a cornered wolf, a thrashing shark, another Mata Zyndu. She let herself be bound.

Kuni will never turn against me, she thought. *It doesn't matter what the empress thinks. If she acts against me, it will only prove what I've surmised from Noda Mi and Doru Solofi.*

"Gin," Cogo whispered. "How could you?" He stepped back.

"Gin Mazoti," said the empress. "Do you confess your sins?"

Gin heard the sharp clang of dozens of swords being unsheathed at once. She couldn't get up because she was tied in place, and she no longer had her sword with her. She felt the tips of a few swords pressing against her back.

She laughed mirthlessly. She realized that she wasn't even surprised.

"Cogo, my old friend," she said, "you are the cause of my rise. It is only proper that you are also the cause of my downfall."

CHAPTER THIRTY-TWO

BATTLE OF ARULUGI

ARULUGI: THE TENTH MONTH IN THE ELEVENTH
YEAR OF THE REIGN OF FOUR PLACID SEAS.

Théca Kimo, though no naval expert, deduced that the mechanical crubens would make short work of Arulugi's navy. As soon as he returned safely to Müning, he ordered the ships scuttled in the port of Müningtozu to seal off that route of access to the capital.

Puma Yemu, who had been designated commander of the Imperial forces, had no choice but to land his troops on beaches on the eastern shore of Arulugi. But dense jungles around Müning meant that the only practical way his troops could approach Müning was over the broad expanse of Lake Toyemotika.

Kimo, of course, was prepared with a fresh-water navy that patrolled the lakes, while Yemu was faced with the prospect of having to construct a new fleet from scratch.

The two sides thus settled down to a kind of stalemate. Without surface support, Imperial airships could do little to seriously damage Müning, the City in the Lake, as firebombs and burning oil fizzled uselessly in the canals and channels between the isles that formed the city's foundation. Meanwhile, Kimo's ships dominated the lake and harassed Yemu's workers and soldiers onshore. Yemu could make little progress to overcome this advantage as the dense, mist-drenched jungles of Arulugi lacked the dry timber necessary to construct seaworthy ships.

But Kuni's arrival on Arulugi revived the Imperial army with a fresh boost of morale. Eager to demonstrate their valor—and motivated in no small measure by the emperor's promise of additional titles and fiefs for exceptional performance—Puma Yemu's troops banged their spears against their shields and pledged to break through the defenses of Müning even at the cost of many lives. The din of their shouting and clanging drifted across the calm waters of Lake Toyemotika and caused Théca Kimo's heart to palpitate.

Ever resourceful, Yemu decided to apply the "noble raider" tactics that had served him so well on the Porin Plains to water. He directed the Imperial airships to work in concert and airlift some small assault boats from the sea to a secluded cove of Lake Toyemotika under cover of darkness—he rejected the thought of airlifting any mechanical crubens, as they would be essentially powerless without underwater volcanoes in the lake.

Then, during the darkest hours of each night right before dawn, he ordered the airships to harass Kimo's navy. However, instead of dropping firebombs and burning oil, for which Kimo's sailors were well prepared, the airships doused the ships with water. Surprised at this tactic, Kimo's men watched helplessly as torches and lamps on deck were extinguished, essentially blinding those aboard. The unexpected water assault also ruined the firework powder rockets the Arulugi ships carried as anti-airship weapons.

A dense fog settled over the fleet. Starlight and moonlight became hazy, and it was impossible to see even from one end of a ship to the other. As frightened Arulugi sailors peered into the inky mist, they detected the smell of smoke—but where was the smell coming from? What was burning? Was Marquess Yemu preparing yet another aerial assault, this time with fire? Had the emperor somehow acquired seaworthy ships on the lake, which were oaring toward them at this moment?

Indistinct shapes seemed to loom in every direction. As lookouts shouted, pointing excitedly, volleys of arrows were let loose at these ghost ships, and the archers ran from one side of the ship to the other, responding to new threats that arose each minute.

While the sailors and marines of Arulugi shouted and shot at these insubstantial foes, small Imperial assault boats advanced on the large Arulugi ships through the inky night like tiny remoras silently approaching much larger sharks and whales. The soldiers aboard drilled holes through the hulls of the warships and filled them with bombs made of firework powder. After lighting the fuses, the assault boats pulled away.

Kimo's men were able to get the torches relit just as the bombs exploded, ripping out huge chunks from the ships' hulls.

"Consort Risana's smokecraft is as wondrous as the legends," said an admiring Yemu from one of the assault boats, now safely out of the way.

"It's but a small stage trick," said a smiling Risana. "Making men see what they most fear to see is the easiest arrow in a smokecrafter's quiver."

The Arulugi ships turned into floating pyres, and Risana and Yemu stood and watched as tiny figures, like moths around lit lamps, dove off the sides of the burning hulks. The terrified screams of sailors drifted over the water as the ships slowly sank.

"We should head back before the emperor finds out I'm gone," said Risana. "He's grown overprotective, but I miss the days of doing interesting things."

Two Arulugi warships sank that first night, which was not, in the grand scheme of things, a big loss. But damage to matériel was never Puma Yemu's goal. Thereafter, Kimo's sailors lived in constant terror of another "noble raid" by Marquess Yemu. Everyone onboard stayed up all night with their hearts in their throats, peering through the darkness for signs of Imperial airships and assault boats. Despite the exhortations of Cano Tho and even King Théca himself, morale sank among the rebels.

Nothing happened for two or three nights, but then, just as the alertness of Kimo's men slackened, Yemu ordered another aerial water assault, once again dousing the torches and lamps on Arulugi ships.

This time, the Arulugi fleet did not wait around for the next stage. Most of the captains made the decision to immediately set sail, eager to get out of the way so that Yemu's phantom assault boats would sink their fangs only into the sides of any member of the herd that got left behind. In the impenetrable darkness, the fleet lost its carefully designed formation; oars became tangled; ships rammed into each other; and curses and screams and angry, futile shouts to restore the chain of command filled the air.

This time, four ships were lost due to being rammed by other ships of the fleet, and Puma Yemu didn't even bother sending out the assault boats.

Marquess Yemu varied his tricks in the following nights: Sometimes Imperial airships dropped firebombs when the Arulugi fleet had prepared for another water attack by erecting lotus-leaf shelters over torches and lamps; sometimes the airships only teased the Arulugi fleet by buzzing low overhead at night without doing anything else; sometimes the airships even dumped foul-smelling water that rumors said came from the latrines of the Imperial army and the air force—here, Yemu was taking advantage of superstitions common among sailors, who believed that the urine of women was particularly unclean and brought bad fortune to those who plied the whale's way, and who knew that the Imperial air force, as a part of the legacy of Marshal Gin Mazoti, was mainly staffed by women.

Théca Kimo denounced these tactics as utterly shameless and challenged Puma Yemu to personal combat, perhaps with battle kites over the surface of Lake Toyemotika.

"Your lord must be truly delusional if he thinks I will agree to such an outdated ritual," said a grinning Yemu to Kimo's messenger. "As for his 'unclean' complaint, I have fought by the side of women since the Siege of Zudi—in fact, both he and I served under Marshal Mazoti, so I hardly understand his outrage. But if Kimo's men feel it's better to be peed on by a man than a woman, all they have to do is to surrender and crawl to my camp, and I'll happily oblige them."

Just as Kimo's men grew used to the nightly harassment by airships and no longer panicked, Yemu resumed the attacks with his ghost assault boats. Three more Arulugi warships were sunk this time by exploding firework powder.

Morale completely collapsed. The sailors, after night after night of living in terror, threatened to mutiny. Cano Tho ordered the fleet to retreat into the city of Müning itself and promised the sailors a night of revelry and drink to restore their spirits. Since the Imperials still had no large ships to transport troops across water—the airships and tiny assault boats were limited both in number and capacity— King Kimo thought one night of leaving Lake Toyemotika unpatrolled was a risk worth taking.

As the sailors of Arulugi, drunk and exhausted from an evening of dancing, teetered over Müning's hanging walkways, shouts erupted from around the City in the Lake.

"The city has fallen!"

"The emperor promises leniency for any officer or soldier who surrenders and fights for the empire!"

"Whoever captures the traitor Théca Kimo will be given a fief of his own!"

Cano Tho and Théca Kimo rushed onto the suspended platforms around the Palace, situated on one of the largest isles that made up Müning, and they found a city burning around them. The suspended platforms were collapsing in thick columns of acrid smoke, turning the city into a fiery web. Soldiers rushed around, aimless, while officers shouted ineffectually. Groups of men dressed in Imperial uniform swung from spire to spire, setting more fires and slaughtering the confused, drunken Arulugi soldiers stumbling around.

"We were fooled by Kuni's tricks!" said Cano Tho in despair. There was no choice for Théca Kimo except to escape the city immediately.

If the king and his adviser had spent their night seated by Lake Toyemotika, they would have seen how Marquess Yemu's troops had, under cover of darkness, crossed the lake on large rafts made by lashing together gourds, coconuts, and sheep's bladders with the vines of Arulugi's jungles—an old trick taught to Yemu by Gin Mazoti herself.

While Yemu's raiders had harassed the Arulugi navy, the Imperial army had been secretly collecting vines from the jungle onshore. The distracted Arulugi forces had not detected any massive construction effort in the jungle and assumed that the Imperials were not building ships. In fact, they had completely missed the primitive and rickety rafts, which could only be of use across an unguarded, serene lake.

"Not letting them see what they fear to see is an even harder task," said a smiling Risana.

"War is a subspecies of smokecraft," said Puma Yemu, rather proud of himself.

During the fall of Müning, many of Théca Kimo's generals had surrendered when they realized that Kimo's rebellion was hopeless. Now bereft of support save for about two thousand hardened rebels under the command of Cano Tho, Théca Kimo was making a last stand at the western tip of Arulugi. With his back to the endless sea and the dense ranks of the Imperial troops before him like so many impenetrable walls, Théca Kimo's days were numbered.

He came to Kuni's camp alone, his arms bound behind his back; he knelt, demanding to see the emperor.

Kuni's soldiers seized him and brought him to the execution grounds.

"Kuni Garu!" Théca Kimo shouted in the direction of the large commander's tent. "I was wrong to rebel and I beg you now for mercy. Remember that I abandoned the Hegemon to serve you at a time when it was not clear who between the two of you would emerge victorious, and I delivered three islands to you! You owe me at least an audience."

Kuni's soldiers held him down against the execution block.

"Kuni Garu! Your son called me uncle and I taught him how to swing his toy sword! I lost two toes from the bitter cold at the siege at Rana Kida, and I have hundreds of scars over my body from fighting your wars. I should never have listened to Noda Mi and Doru Solofi, and I should never have let my fears feed my ambition. I ask only that you leave me my life, and I will exile myself to the distant isles of the north as a beggar."

Kuni's soldiers untied his hair and stripped off his shirt so that his neck could be stretched out across the execution block, with four soldiers holding down his torso and another pulling on his head by his hair on the other side.

"Kuni Garu! Why won't you come and see me? I know if you see me you won't give the order. You've always been a merciful lord! Have I not earned my life with all that I've done for you? Look into my eyes and tell me I deserve to die!"

The executioner lifted the axe.

"Where are you, Puma Yemu? Do you not know that you're next? Where are you, Than Carucono? Do you believe your friendship with the emperor shields you? Where are you, Marshal Mazoti? Did you not promise me that I will not be chopped down as long—"

Even with his head separated from his body, Théca Kimo's eyes glared at the commander's tent in the distance.

Kuni Garu never emerged.

For three days, the emperor refused to see anyone. Only Consort Risana was allowed inside the tent. The guards at the door could only hear faint snatches: crying, singing, angry and drunken shouting.

The empress's messenger arrived in Kuni's camp on the evening of the third day, and Than Carucono pushed Kuni's tent guards aside to deliver the letter himself.

Long after he had read the letter, Kuni sat still like a man in the second month of mourning. He did not shout or curse or rend his clothes or smash the furniture; he did not ask for drink or herbs to soften the pain in his heart; he did not demand to be taken to Pan immediately to confront the woman to whom he had given his own sword, made a queen, elevated above all other men and women of ambition.

The marshal, one of the three truest companions of Kuni Garu, an equal of Luan Zya and Cogo Yelu, had rebelled.

I came to power from an act of betrayal; perhaps it is justice that I may fall from just such another betrayal.

After a man had been drenched by one wave of grief, sometimes he was numb to far greater waves.

"There must be some mistake," said Than Carucono, who had long admired Gin Mazoti. "The marshal would never betray you."

"Can you see into the hearts of men and women?" asked Kuni.

"But the empress has never liked—"

"Jia tells me that Gin has been found to be harboring Noda Mi and Doru Solofi—do you think the empress could conjure them out of thin air? Even Gin's closest adviser has confirmed Gin's guilt, and I remember Zomi Kidosu: She showed no fear during the Palace Examination and denounced me to my face. She would never join in a lie because she has no instinct for politics."

Than Carucono held his tongue. The emperor's logic was unassailable.

Still, Kuni neither affirmed nor objected to the order of execution drafted by the empress.

What is the truth? Kuni thought. *Why is it that logic tells me one thing, but my heart another?*

Eventually, he got up and summoned a messenger.

"Go to Pan in secret and give this to Captain Dafiro Miro; watch him read it and destroy it before returning."

CHAPTER THIRTY-THREE

MATTERS OF HONOR

PAN: THE TENTH MONTH IN THE ELEVENTH YEAR
OF THE REIGN OF FOUR PLACID SEAS.

Gin Mazoti sat in the windowless cell, facing the iron bars that made up one of the walls. Hers was but one of many arranged in a circle around a central hall, though the other cells were all empty. This prison was reserved for nobles and high-ranking ministers who had been accused of treason, and the empress had refused to grant Doru Solofi and Noda Mi, mere deposed nobles with visions of grandeur, the honor of being housed here after they were retrieved from Nokida.

In the center of the ceiling was a square opening for the light-well—a vertical tunnel that led up to the roof, from where mirrors reflected the sun down into the hall, providing it with its only source of illumination.

Deprived of her armor and sword and dressed in a plain tunic, Gin Mazoti appeared as a novice nun in one of the temples, perhaps an order dedicated to Rufizo. She contemplated the dust motes floating through the square shaft of light, saying nothing.

The table reserved for the guards at the center of the hall was empty, as was the rest of the hall save for the man who had come to talk to her in secret.

"I will not," said Gin in a hoarse whisper.

Her interlocutor was Dafiro Miro, Captain of the Palace Guards and one of Emperor Ragin's most trusted men.

"We don't have much time," said Miro. "The guards served under me during the Chrysanthemum-Dandelion War, and that is why they've been willing to risk their lives to give you this chance. The drugs I gave them will keep them in slumber for three more hours, but if you're not away from Pan by then, there will never be an opportunity like this again."

"Is this what my service to the House of Dandelion has earned me? To live out the rest of my life as a fugitive?"

"The evidence gathered by the empress against you is ironclad. Even your closest adviser, Zomi Kidosu, has denounced you."

"A lie, no matter how often repeated, does not become the truth. Let Kuni come to me, and I will show him how flimsy this evidence is. Indeed, I will show him where lies the true threat to his throne."

"He can't do that."

"Why not?"

"The empress has the support of all the civil ministers, from Prime Minister Yelu down. Even the emperor cannot ignore such overwhelming opposition."

"But he knows in his heart I am inno—"

"That is why he has sent me in secret to aid your esc—"

"If I do as you ask, I will never be able to clear my name of the taint of treason. A wild goose flying over the pond leaves a shadow, and a person leaves behind a name. My name is everything to me."

"If you leave today, who knows what will happen in ten, twenty years? In time, the empress's mind may change and she will no longer see you as a threat. But if you are . . . executed, all will be lost."

"I will not give Kuni the satisfaction of having it both ways. He wants to assuage his conscience while his wife does the dirty work of clearing his doubt. He wants the love and trust of his old retainers while they're disarmed, disgraced, and distanced from the levers of power. He thinks he can have the love of the people as well as the praise of the lords, the loyalty of his old friends as well as the bought affection of old enemies. He thinks he can balance all the forces around him and resolve everything by secret compromise, but in matters of honor, there is only wrong or right.

"Let him choose and live with his choice."

She turned away from Dafiro to face the wall, indicating that the conversation was over.

CHAPTER THIRTY-FOUR

UNEXPECTED NEWS

ARULUGI: THE TENTH MONTH IN THE ELEVENTH
YEAR OF THE REIGN OF FOUR PLACID SEAS.

"You don't really believe that Gin has rebelled," said Risana. "Harboring fugitives is not the same as open treason."

Kuni remained hunched over his table. He was reading over the rest of Jia's report, dense with columns of figures and long explanations concerning the various policies she was implementing to stabilize the empire in a time of rebellion.

"Speak to me, Kuni," said Risana.

Kuni sighed and put down the report. After a moment, he turned around.

"It may not be possible to see into the hearts of men and women," said Risana. "But you know I can tell the desires and fears of many, including you and Gin."

"But not Jia," said Kuni.

"No," admitted Risana. "That has ever divided us. But I do not think you fear Gin, and I do not think Gin's loyalty to you has ever wavered."

Kuni lowered his head. "I cannot lie to you."

"Then why? Why let the empress do this? She has worked steadily to weaken the power of the nobles, including those who fought for you and paved the way for your rise. She has chilled the hearts of those who are most loyal to you. How can you stand by and let Gin die?"

Kuni flinched. "Gin is not blameless in this affair. Her flaw has always been pride. In Faça, she killed Shilué and claimed the Throne of Faça and Rima as a test of my trust. Despite Jia's obvious enmity for the enfeoffed nobles, Gin never made an effort to placate her, preferring to again and again flaunt her status and past contributions. I have already done all I can for her—Dafiro—" He shook his head, unwilling to go on.

"But Jia has gone too far! She mistrusts Gin and Kimo and Yemu because she thinks they are closer to me—"

"Kimo *did* rebel! What makes you think my trust in Gin is not equally misplaced?"

"Even if Gin has committed indiscretions, more than Théca Kimo, she deserves your mercy!"

"If I step in today, I will only make things worse. Even if I stay Gin's execution, the empress has made out a strong enough case that I will have no choice but to strip Gin of her title and command. She won't be able to live with such a humiliation, and resentment and rage, over time, will turn even the most loyal heart onto the path of rebellion. She is such a skilled commander that a rebellion led by her will be unstoppable. Can Timu stand against her? Can Phyro? Can—it's the duty of fathers to fight so that their children may live in peace. I cannot leave my children to fight wars that they cannot win."

"Then you are conceding everything to Jia's will, including the matter of succession, and though I am blind to Jia's desires, I fear now that she will not stop until my son and I are both dead."

"It will not come to that," Kuni muttered. "It will not."

"Are you saying that . . ." Risana hesitated. Then she bit her lip as she made up her mind. "Don't be angry with me, husband, but do you think your judgment has been blinded by affection for the empress and guilt at what she suffered on your behalf during the war with the Hegemon?"

Kuni's face shifted through a series of expressions like a roiling sea before finally settling down to an impassive mask. "You think that because I feel sorry that I left her, alone, at the mercy of the Hegemon for years, I'm now putting the throne and the future of Dara at risk to assuage my conscience?"

"It's sometimes hard for those at the center of a storm to see their own position clearly. The best creations of smokecrafters are drawn from the hearts of the deceived because we tell the most convincing lies to ourselves."

Before Kuni could reply, the flap of the tent swept open, bringing with it the chilly evening breeze of autumn. Risana and Kuni turned together. It was Than Carucono, with a somber expression and a tense pose.

"*Rénga*, urgent news from the north, Prince Timu—"

Kuni dashed over and grabbed the scroll from Than. He read over the message quickly and then stood frozen in place.

Risana walked over and pried the scroll from his hands. She turned still as well as soon as she read it.

"*Rénga!*" cried Than Carucono. "*Rénga!*"

Eventually, as though slowly awakening from a dream, Kuni willed his limbs to move. Step by step, he made his way to a corner of the tent and retrieved his coconut lute. He began to play a mournful old Cocru folk tune.

The wind blows, and clouds race across the sky.
My power sways within Four Placid Seas.
Ebb and flow: ambition, pride, talent, will.
Where are the brave who will guard my borders?

Risana and Than listened to the song quietly, each thinking their own thoughts.

Kuni put away the lute. He had recovered his habitual serenity, and the shock of the news was fading.

"Summon two messengers," said Kuni. "One will go to Théca Kimo's remaining troops and offer them amnesty; the other will go to Pan and bring the empress a copy of this letter."

"Any orders to the empress from you?" asked Than.

Kuni shook his head. "Jia will know what she must do."

TEMPEST
FROM THE
NORTH

CHAPTER THIRTY-FIVE

THE COMING
OF THE CITY-SHIPS

DASU: THE TENTH MONTH IN THE ELEVENTH
YEAR OF THE REIGN OF FOUR PLACID SEAS.

On the northernmost beach in all of Dara, a few children played in the lingering, tired heat of an autumn afternoon. They picked out pretty shells and looked for interesting bits of wreckage that washed up onshore from time to time, not neglecting to pocket the stray clam or oyster, for food was always on the minds of the children of the poor.

"Pirates!" one of the boys called.

His companions stopped to gaze at the sea. A flotilla of ships, all different sizes, appeared on the horizon: slender fishing boats following the designs of old Xana; broad, shallow-drafting cargo vessels taken from the merchants of Wolf's Paw; sleek wave-riders seized from Arulugi; even a few aged warships captured by the pirates from the Tiro kings in years past. Oars protruded from every deck, and the ragtag sails flapped in the wind. Dipping and rising over the waves, the ragtag fleet appeared as leaves strewn over a pond.

"So many," a girl muttered. "I've never seen so many."

"It's a raid!"

A few of the adults in the terrace fields on the hill stopped their work, staring at the approaching flotilla in horror. How many ships were there? Dozens? No, hundreds. It was as if all the pirates of the northern isles were heading for Dara. This would be the largest pirate raid anyone could remember, or even remember hearing tales of.

As the news spread, everyone headed for the hills. People emerged from huts and houses, dropped their farm implements and fishing gear, and ran as fast as their legs could carry them—old, young, male, female, rich, poor . . . none of that mattered as far as the pirates were concerned. A few villagers had the presence of mind to run to the garrison commanders to report the raid. Hopefully the report could be passed on to Prince Timu in time to organize some semblance of a rescue operation after the pirates had satiated their appetite for destruction and left Dasu.

By the time the pirate ships landed, the beach and the nearby fields were deserted. Pirates spilled out of the vessels onto the sand and headed inland like a swarm of termites over a new house. They leapt over the fences of vegetable gardens and trampled through fields of taro, their legs and arms pumping in a frenzy—woe to any who stood in their way.

Prince Timu might not know much about military affairs, but he knew when to defer to those with better judgment. The Imperial garrisons on Dasu were well trained and knew how to take advantage of terrain and choke points.

A detachment of Imperial soldiers appeared at the top of the ridge. Arrayed in neat formation, the archers pointed their arrows at the approaching tide of pirates. The commanding officer raised his arm, ready to give the order to fire.

The pirates were shouting something.

"... mercy ..."

"Run for your lives! ..."

"... my eyes ... horror ..."

The officer hesitated. Something was wrong. But the pirates

weren't slowing down at all, despite the arrows pointed at them.

"Fire at will!"

Volleys of arrows shot toward the pirates, and dozens fell.

Normally, pirate raids retreated in the face of such disciplined resistance—they were bandits of the sea, more interested in plunder and captives than concepts like honor and victory. But not this time. Pirates scrambled over the bodies of their fallen comrades and kept on charging. They were running faster and harder than any assault force the officer had ever seen; it was almost as if they were berserkers—

The commanding officer stared, unable to believe his eyes. The oncoming human tide resolved into individual men and women, some holding babies and children. Most of them wore no armor, and their hands bore no weapons. Instead of a pirate crew seized by battle lust, this was a mob of desperate refugees fleeing from unspeakable terror.

"Mercy! Mercy! Mercy!" the refugees shouted.

Even the most hardened veteran soldier, faced with such a sight of thousands of men and women crying for mercy, could not remain unmoved. The archers' arms slackened, and most stopped shooting as they looked to the commanding officer for direction.

But he was no longer looking at the pirates. Beyond the crowd of refugees, beyond their abandoned ships, a wooden wall topped with immense sails, clean and white like the surf, loomed over the horizon.

Twenty massive ships, each as tall as the watchtowers of Pan and as big as a small town, bobbed over the waves.

Prince Timu gathered his advisers in Daye to discuss the strangers that had landed on the northern coast of Dasu and set up camp. For now, they seemed content with their tent city on the beach.

"The pirates raid the coasts of Dasu and Rui every year," said Ra Olu, King Kado's former regent in Daye and now Prince Timu's prime civil minister. He wore his sleek hair in a neat triple-scroll bun, and his expensive yellow silk robe complemented his dark complexion perfectly. "They're desperate, ruthless men, but they do not lack courage. Yet now, these strangers have so frightened them and broken their will to resist that they're willing to throw themselves at the mercy of the emperor. What manner of monsters must they be? We should attack immediately."

"On the contrary," said Zato Ruthi, the prince's old teacher and his adviser. "The pirates cannot be said to possess true courage as they are without morals. The tales they tell of these strangers are confusing, contradictory, and must not be given credence. Fire-breathing serpents? Death raining from the skies? These sound like the feverish ravings of madmen.

"Even if they did attack the pirates, it may be that the pirates provoked the strangers first, and all civilized men who ply the seas bear a natural antipathy toward piracy. These ships match the description of the city-ships in the legendary fleet of Emperor Mapidéré. Might they be envoys of the immortals from beyond the seas? We should not act as the aggressor."

"If they are, in fact, immortal guests retrieved by Mapidéré's fleet," said Ra Olu, "don't you think we would have seen an old courtier from Mapidéré's time emerge from the tents by now?"

"It is possible that Mapidéré's men and the immortals are waiting for us to act as proper hosts and apologize for the rude sight of those pirates, who were hardly fitting greeters at Dara's door."

"If you won't believe the words of pirates—who are, after all, men of Dara—why would you assume that the intention of the strangers is friendly?" countered an exasperated Ra Olu.

"Because the pirates have proven themselves to be lawless criminals motivated only by greed, but we know nothing of these strangers. As Kon Fiji said, 'Embrace the stranger who comes over the sea, and the stranger will embrace you.'"

"Kon Fiji was hardly thinking of strangers who could make ruthless pirates tremble like leaves in autumn. We should immediately ask for aid from Rui and the emperor himself."

"The emperor is busy with putting down a rebellion and should not be distracted without more proof of danger," Ruthi said. "If Prince Timu runs to his father for aid now, he'll appear as a child who still hasn't grown up."

This last argument convinced Timu. "It's best to find out more about them before overreacting. Master Ruthi, will you act as our envoy to the strangers?" Seeing that Ra Olu was about to object, Timu quickly added, "But it *is* good to take reasonable precautions. I'll ask for a fleet of airships from the Imperial air base on Rui to act as an escort. If the strangers are friendly, the ships will be seen as a sign of our esteem of their visit. And if they're hostile, we'll be prepared."

Twenty great airships hovered above the hill overseeing the beach in a straight line. They were each about 180 feet in length, with hulls shaped like sleek dolphins. These were not the largest ships of the fleet, which, following designs dating back to the time of Emperor Mapidéré, tended to approach three hundred feet in length, but they were newer and faster, and were far more kind on the Imperial Treasury.

Below them, a two-thousand-strong honor guard arrayed itself on the slope of the hill. The finest examples of Dara arms, the soldiers stood completely still and silent, their armor glinting in the sun and their polished spears raised like a forest of bamboo. The only sound that could be heard was from the crimson war capes of the officers on horseback flapping in the breeze.

Behind the phalanxes, hundreds of expensive carriages were parked helter-skelter on top of the hill. Temporary shelters and viewing platforms constructed from bamboo and silk stood in the blank spaces between the carriages. Many of the noble and wealthy families of Daye had come out to witness this historic sight: Prince Timu's representative was about to make contact with immortals from beyond the sea.

"Do you think the immortals will be looking for wives?"

"Ha! Are you thinking of engaging a matchmaker for yourself?"

"Oh, I'm quite happy with my own prospects, thank you very

much. But since no boy on Dasu seems good enough for you, maybe only an immortal from overseas can satisfy you, both out of and in the bedroom—aw! Stop pinching!"

"Maybe I don't want to marry one . . . but it would be fun to bed an immortal, once. And maybe I can learn their secret and become an immortal! Wouldn't that be something?"

"Do you think immortals have bad breath in the morning?"

The pampered men and women treated the whole spectacle as a holiday. Excitement swept the crowd as they sat on the comfortable cushions under diaphanous silk roofs, munching on snacks and sipping tea, observing and commenting on the conical white tents that filled the beach like a mat of conch shells, which were dwarfed by the massive ships behind them.

An occasional glimpse of one of the strangers walking between the tents brought exclamations and giggles. Minor nobles imagined the prospects of befriending the immortals and using them to elevate their own status. Wealthy landlords whispered about plans for selling small plots to the immortals at inflated prices and getting them to abandon their tents for luxurious houses. Merchants watched the distant great ships rising and falling on the swell, speculated on the cargo they held, and made bets as to what sort of goods the immortals would be most interested in.

This was the Year of the Cruben after all, a time when the sea was supposed to be especially bounteous in treasure and opportunity.

Behind them, the poor villagers who had been displaced from their homes by the arrival of the strangers watched the scene in a more somber and anxious mood. The only thing they were interested in was when they'd be allowed to return to the fields and resume their lives. They dared not sketch any hopeful visions of the future dependent on the arrival of the immortals—if that was who they were. Whenever things changed in Dara, it seemed that the wealthy and powerful reaped the benefits and left the rest behind.

Calmly, Zato Ruthi set out for the foreign camp on top of a pure white horse. He was escorted by a dozen soldiers also on horseback, bearing gifts from Prince Timu. A giant flag of Dasu, showing a red field charged with the blue figure of a breaching cruben, flapped at the head of the small procession.

Ruthi and his guards merged into the distant camp. Everyone's gaze followed the flag, now flickering like a tiny flame in a snowfield. What sights and wonders was Ruthi witnessing?

CHAPTER THIRTY-SIX

STRANGERS

DASU: THE TENTH MONTH IN THE ELEVENTH
YEAR OF THE REIGN OF FOUR PLACID SEAS.

The tents, squat cylinders about the height of a man topped with flat, conical tips, were made of hide, Zato Ruthi realized as he approached the encampment. The strangers' camp was surrounded by a low fence built of animal bones lashed together with sinew, each post capped with a sharp-jawed skull, and from the tips of sharp white poles—were they the ribs of some beast?—planted in front of the tents the tails of various animals flapped, much like banners and flags. Behind the tents, the mountainous city-ships undulated with the waves, like whales at rest against the beach.

The immortals certainly have an odd sense of architecture, thought Ruthi. He had always imagined the immortals as ethereal beings who built with gossamer web and silky clouds, with flower petals and dewy leaves. He had imagined them as sophisticated poets and philosophers who communed with the gods and transcended all material needs. The reliance on bones and skin here, on the deaths of animals, seemed rather jarring.

There was an opening in the fence, a gate of sorts, formed from the giant jaws of a shark. The entire scene exuded a sense of stark strength and discipline, a spare simplicity of functional elegance.

As he approached the gap, men emerged from the tents. Some fifty or so came outside the opening and blocked his way. He stopped his horse to observe them closely.

They were generally light-skinned—though heavily tanned by the sun—and the colors of their hair and beards ranged from pure white to a light brown. Dressed in skins and hides, they held war clubs made of bone or driftwood, tipped with shells and stones. Some had their hair entirely shaven off while others wore neat braids that hung against their backs; a few wore helmets made from the skulls of animals. He saw few signs of metal weapons or armor, and no silk or hemp cloth. Many of them looked emaciated and short in stature, and the hides on their bodies were ragged and torn, as though they had been on a long journey with no opportunity to replenish supplies.

The sad state of their clothing made Ruthi realize with a start that some of the "men" were in fact women. He blushed. *What sort of immortals would force the women to wield clubs and fight? And so immodestly!*

They look like characters who have stepped out of old Ano sagas, Ruthi thought. *This must have been how the barbarian natives of these isles looked to our ancestors when they first arrived on the shores of Dara as refugees from the destruction of their homeland in the west.*

Though disappointed that the strangers were not immortals after all, Ruthi maintained a respectful expression as he got off his horse. His guards followed suit.

"I come in peace," he declared to the strangers. "The Emperor of Dara welcomes you to these shores. If you need assistance, my lord, Prince Timu, stands ready to provide whatever you may need."

One of the barbarians, a tall man who appeared to be in his forties or fifties, stepped forward. He said something to Ruthi, but the latter could make no sense of the string of strange syllables.

Undaunted, Ruthi gestured for his guards to bring the gifts they had prepared to a point about halfway between the two sides and leave them on the ground: a platter of roast pig, a trencher of raw fish cut into designs resembling the Ano logograms for "peace," a bolt of silk, a scroll upon which Prince Timu had written in calligraphic logograms the words *Within the Four Seas, all men are brothers*—a quote from Kon Fiji. Ruthi had carefully chosen these gifts to demonstrate Dara's generosity to strangers while preserving the dignity of the emperor as well as Prince Timu, the emperor's representative on Dasu.

After leaving the gifts on the ground, Ruthi's guards stepped back. The tall barbarian, while keeping his eyes on Ruthi, gestured for a few of his retinue to approach the pile of gifts. They poked at the pork and fish, tried some, and then excitedly shouted for more of their companions to join them. They ate ravenously, pushing and shoving each other to get at the food, and soon the pork and fish were gone. The silk was carried back into the camp by two greasy-fingered men. The scroll, on the other hand, was examined and then carelessly dropped.

The impassive expression on the tall barbarian's face never changed.

Ruthi frowned. *This isn't an auspicious start.*

The tall stranger smiled and pointed at himself. *"Pékyutenryo,"* he enunciated slowly. Then he swept his arm around to indicate the encampment. *"Lyucu."*

Now we're getting somewhere, thought Ruthi. He tried to repeat the unfamiliar syllables as well as he could.

Pékyutenryo—whom Ruthi decided must be some kind of barbarian chief—nodded, apparently satisfied.

Ruthi pointed at himself, and slowly said, "Zato Ruthi." Then he imitated Pékyutenryo and swept his arm to indicate the distant Dara army and airships. "Dara."

Pékyutenryo grinned, baring two rows of uneven teeth. Somehow the expression seemed feral and threatening, rather than friendly. But afraid of offending the barbarians, Ruthi imitated the grin.

These people who call themselves the Lyucu may not be immortals, but they don't seem impossible to deal with.

Pékyutenryo now pointed to Ruthi's guards and mimed a series of motions that reminded Ruthi of undressing. Ruthi blushed, as did the rest of the men of Dara. *Were these barbarians without shame?*

Seeing Ruthi and his guards hesitate made the chief frown.

A few of the barbarians came to the aid of their king. They laid their weapons on the ground next to their feet and took off the ragged pieces of hide and fur on their bodies—both men and women!—until they were dressed only in rough loincloths woven from some kind of grass fiber.

Ruthi blushed even more furiously and was about to order the rest of his retinue to avert their eyes to preserve the modesty of these brazen barbarians when the undressed barbarians stopped, pointed to the weapons, and then pointed at themselves again, slapping their hands up and down their bodies.

"Oh, he means for us to disarm! It's a security precaution." Ruthi nodded vigorously to show that he finally understood. He turned to his guards. "Go ahead, do as they ask."

"Master Ruthi, is this wise?" asked Jima, the captain of the guards, who was also responsible for bearing the standard of Dara. "Not knowing their intentions, we should not enter their camp defenseless."

"This is the problem with spending your life fighting instead of studying the books of the sages," admonished Zato Ruthi. "Where's your capacity for empathy? You have to try to think about this from their perspective. Look at how primitive their equipment and dwellings are! Not a single metal weapon to be seen anywhere. Look at how quickly they devoured the food we presented! Imagine yourself in a strange country far from home, hungry, terrified, surrounded by a powerful army with weapons and armor far more advanced than yours. If a group of them wished to enter your camp, wouldn't you also demand some gesture of good faith?"

"I've been a soldier all my life, Master Ruthi. Trust me, though we may have better weapons, I can tell you these people are not afraid of us."

"Dara is the land of civilization," said Ruthi severely. "Our ancestors came to this land and pacified the savages, and I expect the gods have spread our fame far and wide beyond these shores.

"These barbarians have braved the unpredictable whale's way to come to us, drawn by the shining beacon of our way of life. We must demonstrate to them our superior grace. A just man has no cause to fear treachery, and even if they have some plot against us, our righteousness and good faith will surely shame them into realizing the error of their ways. Disarm now lest we stain the honor of our lords, the Emperor of Dara and his faithful firstborn."

Reluctantly, Captain Jima and the other guards disarmed, leaving their weapons and armor in a pile next to the empty platters that had borne the other gifts.

Pékyutenryo grinned even wider, and he waved his hands in a decisive gesture. His retinue parted to the sides of the shark's-jaw gate, leaving the way into the encampment open.

Up on the hill, the spectators of Dara cheered.

"They're going in!"

"You have sharp eyes, Dümo. Can you see what's happening?"

"They're too far away. But I think the strangers just bowed. Maybe Master Ruthi really impressed them with his learning? And they bowed again!"

"But they were doing it after Master Ruthi and his men already went in. Why would they bow when he couldn't see them?"

"Well . . . this is where your lack of schooling holds you back. I remember reading once about the customs of the natives of Crescent Island at the time of the arrival of the Ano. Bowing after someone has left is a sign of even greater respect than bowing to their face—"

"I had no idea you were such an expert on the heroic sagas, Yehun! Was this in the Saga of He-Whose-Name-Is-a-Mouthful? I read it too!"

"Um . . . yes, that's the one! Very obscure—I'm surprised you know it. Now, as I was saying, this was an ancient custom that existed in the Islands long before the settlement of the Ano, but it makes perfect sense if you remember—wait, why are the three of you laughing like hyenas behind my back?"

"Oh, Yehun, you poor, arrogant ass, there is no such thing as the

Saga of He-Whose-Name-Is-a-Mouthful! Just because you're the only *toko dawiji* among us doesn't mean you have to have all the answers all the time."

"A superior mind need not be troubled by the petty—"

"Do you want us to continue to pay you the only kind of 'respect' you deserve, bowed over in laughter?"

Zato Ruthi knelt down in formal *mipa rari* in the middle of the great tent, which was about the height of three men stacked foot-to-shoulder and about twenty yards wide. The floor was carpeted in the soft fur of some unknown animal. Ruthi stared at the walls of the tent with some interest: The hide was translucent, reminding him of the thin, furry membranes of bat wings. Though he was well-read and knowledgeable, he couldn't tell what beasts the hide was taken from.

The barbarian chief strolled to the front of the tent and sat down in cross-legged *géüpa*. Other barbarians—nobles and chieftains, to judge by their massive war clubs and the elaborate bone and shell jewelry they wore—sat down around the perimeter of the tent in a chaotic jumble, some in *géüpa*, and some even in *thakrido*, with their legs spread and stretched out, including the women.

Captain Jima, who knelt behind Ruthi, frowned. Ruthi was the representative of the emperor himself, and for Pékyutenryo and his chieftains to treat Ruthi with such disrespect was unacceptable. But before he could say anything, Zato Ruthi restrained him with a hand.

"They may not share the same understanding of our sitting positions," whispered Ruthi. "The mark of a civilized people is to be tolerant and not take offense at ignorance. We shall honor this Pékyutenryo as the king of his people."

The captain gritted his teeth and said nothing. Something about the way the barbarian nobles and chieftains laughed and whispered at each other bothered him. This did not seem like a king receiving an ambassador from another land, or even a gathering to welcome friendly strangers. He couldn't put his finger on it, but . . . why did Pékyutenryo look so satisfied?

A few young barbarians brought in the weapons and armor left by Ruthi's guards at the entrance to the camp and deposited the pile in front of the king. Pékyutenryo said something to the young people, who nodded and left.

"You see," said Ruthi to Jima, "there's nothing to worry about. They even brought your weapons in. I'm sure soon, after we've established trust, they'll give the weapons back to you."

Pékyutenryo looked at Zato Ruthi and his men, sitting awkwardly in the center of the tent, and grinned some more. Ruthi nodded and returned the same ridiculous grin. The Lyucu nobles began to pass around a large, crude ceramic bowl and took sips from it in turn, and the noise of conversation gradually filled the space.

After taking a drink from the bowl himself, Pékyutenryo gestured for one of his men to bring the bowl to Ruthi. Ruthi accepted the bowl reverently and examined the contents: something that smelled of alcohol and milk, with frothy foam around the bowl's rim.

"*Kyoffir!*" Pékyutenryo said, pointing at the bowl. Then he mimed quaffing heartily.

Ruthi brought the bowl up to his mouth. It didn't smell like cow's milk or goat's milk or even mare's milk; rather, the fragrance was . . . herbal. Tentatively, he took a sip. The taste was pungent, faintly medicinal, and the liquid burned his throat as he swallowed. The consistency of the drink was thick, not unlike an alcoholic yogurt. It also had a very strong kick, and Ruthi, not much of a drinker normally, coughed and sputtered as tears welled into his eyes.

The Lyucu nobles roared with laughter, and even Pékyutenryo himself chuckled. Ruthi wiped his eyes and set the bowl down, once again grinning foolishly.

Thankfully, the barbarian guards who had been sent away earlier returned, carrying with them more weapons and armor. They left these in a separate pile by the equipment taken from Ruthi's men, and Pékyutenryo got up, walked over, picked up a helmet from each pile, and compared them, paying no attention to Ruthi.

"The weapons from that other pile also have the look of being from Dara," said Captain Jima. He didn't bother to whisper, as the barbarians clearly could make no more sense of the conversation between him and Ruthi than the two of them could make sense of Lyucu speech. "Where did they get them? The pirates?"

"That sword"—Ruthi squinted—"appears to be of Xana design. If I'm not mistaken, it is a helmet from the time of Mapidéré, more than two decades ago."

"Emperor Mapidéré's expedition?"

Ruthi nodded. "Has to be."

Pékyutenryo continued to pick out objects from one pile—a sword, a gauntlet, a helmet, a shield, a bow—and find counterparts from the other pile, scrutinizing and comparing them. From time to time he called for a few of his nobles to approach, and the small group would confer and examine the weapon or armor, arguing or agreeing with each other loudly.

Ruthi and Jima stared at the mysterious exercise, utterly baffled.

"Perhaps they're comparing the artistic styles in the pieces to authenticate that we're indeed the origin of the wondrous artifacts they received from Emperor Mapidéré," said a hopeful Ruthi.

Eventually, Pékyutenryo seemed satisfied with whatever he was doing and ordered his guards to take all the weapons and armor away. Then the guards brought out a large, shallow, circular tray that seemed to be made from a thin layer of hide stretched across a frame of curved bones and set it down before Ruthi. It was filled with beach sand.

Pékyutenryo sat down opposite Ruthi—in *thakrido*, naturally—with the tray of sand between them. Then he picked up a stick and drew on the sand.

Ruthi watched as Pékyutenryo drew a line across the sand, and then a small circle in the upper portion. The barbarian king then looked at Ruthi and pointed up at the ceiling of the tent.

He's telling me that circle is the sun, and this line is the land, Ruthi thought.

Pékyutenryo drew a few ovals in the sky, with long wings sticking out of them. The drawing might be crude, but it was clear that these were meant to represent the Imperial airships. He continued by drawing some mushroom-like objects on the land at the other end: apparently, the barbarian encampment.

Then Pékyutenryo mimed ducking in fear as he looked up at the ceiling of the tent. Grinning again, he handed the stick to Ruthi, who was not at all clear as to what was wanted.

Pékyutenryo took the stick back and drew some arrows shooting out of the airships at the camp, and handed the stick back to Ruthi. He gave Ruthi a questioning look and mimed terror again.

Ruthi laughed. "No, no! The ships are just here as part of the welcoming ceremony; not an attack force."

Pékyutenryo looked at him, a look of incomprehension on his face.

Ruthi tried again. He erased the arrows from the sand and tried to draw some flowers dropping from the airships to fall on the camp—but the flowers came out looking like snowflakes. "Peace," he shouted, as if speaking louder would make the barbarian understand. "Not war!" Then he mimed smiling and hugging and drinking from the large bowl, smacking his lips.

Pékyutenryo looked even more confused. Then he appeared to have thought of a new tack. He drew some stick-figure men on horses below the airships—the Imperial phalanxes—and then drew the barbarians rushing out of their encampment, war clubs raised high overhead as they charged at the Dara army.

Grinning, he handed the stick back to Ruthi.

Ruthi looked at him with a tense expression, spreading his hands in supplication and question.

Pékyutenryo mimed laughing, holding his belly as though some joke was killing him. He pointed at the sand tray again.

"Ah, he's talking about a hypothetical," said the relaxed Ruthi. "A joke, as it were."

"I don't think so," said Jima. "This is not a matter of jokes; he's probing our defenses. Master Ruthi, we should leave immediately."

"Nonsense," said Ruthi. "This is about two minds coming together to communicate. Exercise your atrophied empathy, Captain Jima! Since he's curious about how we'd respond, wouldn't it be better to show him the might of Dara's arms in a sandbox than to have him find out through actual warfare? The emperor has always wanted to minimize the loss of lives."

So Ruthi started to draw on the sand. As the former King of Rima, he was quite knowledgeable about classic military tactics. Using a series of diagrams, he showed Pékyutenryo how the Imperial pha-lanxes would shift in formation, falling back in the center while flanking the barbarian charge with both wings until the attackers were surrounded. Then he illustrated how the barbarians, outclassed in weapons and armor, would be slaughtered or captured.

The expression of both admiration and terror on Pékyutenryo's face appeared genuine.

"Now, you don't need to worry!" Ruthi hurried to reassure his host. "This is just a hypothetical. Hy-po-the-ti-cal! Pretend!" He mimed holding his belly and laughing.

Pékyutenryo nodded vigorously and grinned ingratiatingly at the Imperial envoy.

Zato Ruthi felt elated. He might once have met a humiliating defeat at the hands of Gin Mazoti in the woods of Rima, but here, today, he had managed to intimidate and impress a barbarian king into will-ing submission to the Emperor of Dara just by drawing pictures in sand!

Pékyutenryo wiped the sand tray clean and drew the Lyucu encamp-ment and the Imperial airships overhead again. He pretended to cower in fear while looking up at the sky again; then he mimed hold-ing his belly and laughing.

Hypothetically, how would the Emperor of Dara attack me from the air?

All the other barbarian chieftains gathered around the sand tray. Pékyutenryo handed the stick to Ruthi and gestured for him to con-tinue.

"Master Ruthi," pleaded Captain Jima. "This does *not* feel right.

You should not reveal to them our capabilities or explain airship-to-ground tactics. We know almost nothing about how they fight!"

"Shush! You are acting like some paranoid, silly peasant, instead of a confident officer of the Imperial Army. What's wrong with showing them what our airships can do? Our might will fill them with awe and inspire them to give us due respect. This is how a great civilization impresses lesser ones."

And so Ruthi continued to draw in the sand, showing the barbarians how Dara's airships attacked with firebombs.

Pékyutenryo held out five fingers, paused, balled his hand into a fist, paused, and then held out five fingers again. He pointed to the airships and then spread out his hands, giving Ruthi a questioning look.

Ruthi pondered for a bit, and then understood what Pékyutenryo was getting at. He drew an airship and filled it with little circles, showing a few of the circles dropping from the airship at the camp—a volley of firebombs. He held out all ten fingers to Pékyutenryo, balled them into fists, and then held them out again . . . he repeated the process five times to show that each airship carried around fifty firebombs, more than enough to do massive damage to the Lyucu encampment. Then he erased the little circles inside the airship to make it appear empty.

Pékyutenryo grinned and said something to his nobles, who all laughed. Then Pékyutenryo picked up the bowl of alcoholic yogurt—the "kyoffir"—and handed it to Ruthi. Ruthi drank from it happily. The strong drink was having a positive effect on his mood.

"Thank you for your information," said Pékyutenryo. His accent was heavy, but the words were clearly understandable.

Ruthi looked over the rim of the kyoffir bowl, stunned. Behind him, Jima and the rest of Ruthi's men leapt up in alarm. But they were too late. Pékyutenryo's war club had already crushed Ruthi's skull, and the other Lyucu nobles made short work of the rest of the delegation from Dara.

∽ ∾ ∽ ∾

"Something's happening! They are coming out of the big tent!"

"But where's Master Ruthi?"

"Why is the Imperial standard on the ground?"

"Are they lining up to surrender?"

The chatter among the crowd died down as they watched the barbarians stream out of the encampment, form into long lines, and then march toward the Imperial phalanxes, war clubs waving. The sea breeze carried their shouts to the crowd—unmistakable war cries.

Although the Lyucu host, about a mile off, outnumbered the Imperial troops, Ra Olu wasn't worried. He ordered the phalanxes to move forward to meet the oncoming barbarian charge. Flag signals were given for the airships to approach the barbarian horde and begin bombing.

"These clowns dare to challenge the might of Prince Timu!"

"They're going to die before they even know what hit them!"

"Drive them back into the sea!"

The barbarians got closer. Those with sharp eyes among the crowd noticed the wretched state of their weapons and clothing; even the pirates had been better equipped. The audience from Dasu, instead of being fearful, grew excited at the prospect of witnessing a one-sided slaughter.

"This is going to be a day that will live on in song and story."

"Can they not see how overmatched they are?"

"I can't believe how foolish these savages are!"

"Are some of those barbarians women? How cruel must their husbands and fathers be!"

The Lyucu charge stopped just outside the range of the archers under Ra Olu's command.

Have they suddenly realized the futility of their attack? Ra Olu thought. He gave the order for the airships to dive and begin bombing.

Like well-choreographed dancers, gasmen inside the airships tightened the straps around the gasbags to reduce lift, and the oarsmen pulled hard against the feathered oars. Like giant Mingén falcons spiraling down to seize prey, the bamboo-and-silk airships dove.

Soldiers inside the gondolas prepared the buckets of burning tar and opened the bomb bay doors as the ships streaked over the barbarian formation.

The Lyucu commanders whistled, and the horde broke up into small groups of fifty or so each. Most of the individuals in each group ducked in place while those at the edges of the formations raised their war clubs and planted them at their feet like spears. The squatting barbarian warriors helped unfurl and stretch sheets of some hide-like material—clearly the same material that made up their tents—over their heads, to be held up by the war clubs erected at the edge. The effect was as if small tents suddenly sprouted over the heads of groups of barbarian warriors.

This seemed a desperate measure—the hide-like material looked so thin and light that it was nearly translucent; surely the firebombs would make short work of it.

The tar bombs struck the shelters and exploded. A few of the bombs hit the ground near the tents and splashed burning tar onto the exposed legs and bodies of the Lyucu warriors at the edges of the formations. They screamed, howled, dropped their war clubs, and rolled around on the ground, but their nearest companions immediately took over the duty of holding up their war clubs to keep the tents from collapsing.

As the sizzling tar burned into their skin and flesh, their pitiable shrieks first grew louder, and then weaker as their flapping limbs and gyrating bodies slowed down, and then stilled.

Dara soldiers and onlookers cheered. This slaughter was even more exciting than they had imagined.

But soon, the cheers turned into cries of astonishment.

The exploded tar bombs had turned the temporary shelters over the heads of the barbarians into pools of flaming lava, but somehow, the thin material managed to hold. The sizzling, smoking tar burned brightly atop the tents but seemed unable to set the material itself ablaze.

The Lyucu warriors who were ducked down at the center of the fire shelters poked up their war clubs in a rhythmic pattern, and the cover of each tent began to undulate like the surface of the sea. Most of the burning tar, carried by the waves, soon sloughed off the tents and fell harmlessly to the ground.

The airships swooped around and began a second bombing run. Realizing that the tents themselves were more fire-resistant than anticipated, the airship captains now changed tactics and ordered the bomb crews to shift their aim so that the bombs would explode on the ground near the tents rather than on the tents. The hope was that this would injure enough of the tent-pole holders by splash damage that the tents would collapse.

But the Lyucu warriors were prepared for this. As the airships dove toward the fire shelters, the warriors in each formation began to move as one: Hundreds of legs pumped in sync and the tents headed toward the diving airships to ensure that the bombs again exploded harmlessly against the protective umbrellas overhead.

A few formations, unable to adjust their speed properly, did end up running into the pools of burning tar on the ground, and the injured warriors had to roll around on the ground in an attempt to put out the fires while the rest of the individuals in the formation scrambled to get out of the way of further damage. Most of the moving shelters, however, escaped the second bombing run also unscathed.

Ra Olu realized that he had underestimated the barbarians, who appeared to be surprisingly well prepared for airship assaults. But he had been an experienced low-level field commander during the Chrysanthemum-Dandelion War and knew how to quickly adjust to changing circumstances. Immediately, he gave additional orders for the flag corps to issue to the airships.

The airships turned around once more and headed for the barbarian encampment. As they passed the line of many-legged, temporary field tents—wriggling like jellyfish over a placid sea—they dropped another volley of firebombs. The ships flew low and synchronized their motion so that all the bombs landed approximately in a line between the barbarian attackers and their camp. As the bombs exploded, the burning tar coalesced into a flaming barrier that separated the barbarian horde from their home base. The huddled barbarians could only watch as their route of retreat was cut off.

Ra Olu grinned and gave the order for the Imperial phalanxes to advance. As soon as they were in range, Ra Olu was going to give the order for the archers to fire: The barbarians would be trapped between the wall of fire behind them and the wall of arrows ahead of them. Meanwhile, the airships would go on to bomb the barbarian ships. The entire Lyucu invasion force was going to die here on the shore of Dasu today.

The airships approached the encampment like the great Mingén falcons approaching a fresh fishing ground. The city-ships were fat, juicy fish trapped in the shallows, ripe for picking.

Ra Olu's phalanxes advanced steadily. With each step, the invaders were closer to their deaths.

"Fire!" ordered Ra Olu.

Thousands of arrows shot out, traversing the distance between the Imperial phalanxes and the barbarian line in seconds.

However, the Lyucu warriors had shifted their defensive postures so that the sheets of strange hide-like material, stained with remnants of the burning tar, were now stretched like wide screens across the front of the line. The warriors near the front stepped on the bottom edge of the hides and leaned forward, bracing their war clubs in front of them, while those behind them pulled back on the top edge of the hides so that everyone was shielded behind the protruding "pouch."

Arrows thudded against the hides and fell harmlessly to the ground, though some of the warriors who were bracing against the front of the shelters grunted with pain as the force of the arrow strikes bruised their bodies, even cracking a few ribs and arm bones.

What is that extraordinary material? marveled Ra Olu. *I have never heard of such a tough hide. What kind of beast does it come from?*

But he didn't have the opportunity to ponder this mystery for too long. Cries of alarm and shock rose from his soldiers and the civilian onlookers. Ra Olu looked up, and the signal trumpet in his hands dropped to the ground.

In the distance, gigantic, nightmarish beasts emerged from the great city-ships and climbed into the air.

The creatures were unlike anything Ra Olu had ever seen, an impossible amalgamation of features from different species: a barrel-shaped body about the size of three or four elephants—using the airships hovering nearby for scale; a serpentlike tail that trailed in the air; two clawed feet, like those on falcons, extended below the belly; a pair of great leathery wings that spanned 120 feet or more; and a long, slender neck topped with a deerlike, antlered head.

Ten, twenty, thirty, more of them kept on rising into the air. With their massive wingspans and long necks, each appeared about two-thirds the length of an Imperial airship, though the torsos were much smaller. The beasts swooped, and, with a speed that seemed unimaginable for their bulk, flew at the airships.

Stunned, the first airship captain didn't even have the chance to order a response before two of the beasts tore into the hull. They slashed with their claws and snapped with their jaws, whipping their necks about violently. The silk surface and the bamboo frames snapped beneath claws and teeth like toothpicks, and the gasbags inside were punctured within seconds. The crew screamed and leapt from the gondolas, plunging hundreds of feet to their deaths.

The other airship captains recovered from their initial stupor and ordered flame arrows to be shot while the oarsmen pushed with all their might to guide the airships in retreat. But the arrows bounced harmlessly off the wings and bodies of the beasts like mosquitoes trying to sting elephants, and some instead struck other airships and started fires.

Ra Olu finally understood what material the tents and barriers of the barbarians were made from.

The beasts descended on the fleet of Imperial airships, which had once seemed so graceful and nimble, but now appeared clumsy and lumbering next to the speedy flight of these deadly creatures. None of the airships lasted more than a minute under the assault by two or three of the creatures.

Flaming wreckage fell from the sky, drifting in the wind like clouds at sunset. Dying crewmen dove from the fiery hulks, screaming as they plunged to their deaths. Many in the crowd of Dasu observers averted their eyes from this horror. A few began to pack up their carts in preparation to flee.

Soon, the sky was cleared of airships, and the dreadful beasts gathered into a loose formation and headed for the Imperial phalanxes.

Only now did Ra Olu understand that the initial Lyucu charge had been but a ruse. It was designed to test the strength of the Imperial forces, to lure them into attacking and demonstrating their tactics while the barbarians held them in place until the aerial beasts could be summoned.

Ra Olu knew that he had to be decisive; he had only one chance.

"Charge!" he gave the order.

The stunned Imperial forces were still sufficiently disciplined to obey. Archers stepped forward, let loose another volley of arrows, and then dropped their bows and switched to their defensive short swords. They fell back as the spearmen marched forward and the ordered ranks of spear tips, aimed at the barbarian horde, rushed forward.

The barbarians dropped their hide-barrier, let out a deafening war cry, and rushed to meet the Imperial charge with their war clubs.

Like a surging tide crashing into a rocky beach, the two sides clashed. Bone struck shield, and spear and sword tore into flesh. Men and women howled and hollered, bled and died.

Overhead, the beasts flew right over the maelstrom of opposing forces and headed for the audience behind the Imperial soldiers.

The Dasu civilians who had come to witness the drama of first contact with the strangers screamed and scattered. Carriages crashed into each other; horses trampled over people; and the wealthy shrieked for the help of their servants—but all the servants sensible enough to be of any use had already fled. All was chaos.

The beasts dove down, pulling up only when they were thirty or forty feet from the ground. Their wings beat furiously as they hovered near the earth, the rush of air from their great wings making those below them cower.

A few daring men and women looked up and their hearts were chilled by what they saw: The torso of each beast was covered by a fine web of netting made of some tough fiber mixed with sinew, and a dozen or so barbarian warriors strapped themselves into the webbing on either side of each beast like sailors clinging to the rigging of a tall ship, holding bone spears and wishbone slingshots. A single barbarian pilot wearing a helmet made of an animal skull sat at the base of each beast's neck, securely strapped into a saddle.

The eyes of the men and women riding the beasts were as dark and implacable as the reptilian eyes of their mounts.

The beasts reared back, opened and closed their massive jaws rapidly a few times to reveal long, sharp upper canines like curved swords, and then snapped their necks forward, letting loose jets of fire from their mouths.

It was as if Mount Kiji had finally erupted. Dozens of fiery tongues made of flames, each almost a hundred feet long, lashed across the crowd and turned the ground into boiling lava. Some were instantly incinerated while others ran screaming from the scene, their bodies on fire. The smell of charred flesh filled the air and acrid smoke obscured everything. It was truly a scene from hell.

The Imperial soldiers in their phalanxes glanced back and were utterly stunned. The barbarian warriors, seeing the devastation wrought by their aerial support, roared with approval and shouted as one, *"Garinafin, garinafin! Pêkyutenryo! Pêkyutenryo!"*

The will to fight left the army of Dara and the Imperial lines collapsed as soldiers stumbled and ran. The barbarians rushed forward and bashed their skulls open with their war clubs while overhead the beasts swooped and chased after survivors, who were dispatched by the riders with precise strikes from their slingshots. . . .

In the distance, Ra Olu whipped his horse to run even faster. He had started to run as soon as he had given the order for the charge.

His heart ached for the young men he had sent to their deaths, but this was the only way to buy himself some time to escape and bring the news to Daye.

All the stories told by the pirates were true. The invaders were powerful beyond measure, and Dasu was doomed.

CHAPTER THIRTY-SEVEN

THE PRINCE'S STAND

DASU: THE TENTH MONTH IN THE ELEVENTH
YEAR OF THE REIGN OF FOUR PLACID SEAS.

In Daye, a fast Imperial messenger ship was readied to bring news of the invasion to the emperor.

To make the vehicle fly as fast as possible, the ship would have no crew except the oarsmen—most of them women picked for a balance of light weight, strength, and endurance. Instead of relying on the drumming of a coxswain, the rowers would try to keep in sync by singing popular folk songs with strong beats. Every bit of weight that could be dispensed with was eliminated: Interior bulkheads within the gondola were taken out; weapons and armor were abandoned—it wasn't as if arrows or pikes or grappling hooks for boarding would do much good against the barbarians' flying beasts, which apparently were called "*garinafin*"; and the ship would carry no provisions or water, the crew relying on the water condensed against and collected from the fog-catching silken hull as the ship passed through the clouds to slake their thirst.

Despite Ra Olu's strenuous urging, Prince Timu refused to board the ship to escape.

"It would be useless to include me among the crew," said Prince Timu. "I would be winded after no more than a quarter of an hour manning one of the oars. Now I wish I had listened to Théra and Phyro and paid more attention to athletics."

Ra Olu stamped his foot in frustration. "No one is asking you to row the ship! Your safety is the primary concern right now."

"Nonsense. Master Ruthi had always taught me that without faith and loyalty, men are little better than beasts. The emperor sent me here to make the lives of the people of Dasu better. Now that they're under threat, it would be a betrayal of their trust and the trust of the emperor to abandon them."

Thinking of his own escape from the battlefield, Ra Olu blushed.

Mistaking Olu's silence for sorrow, Timu tried to comfort him. "Don't be too sad at the loss of Master Ruthi. He had always wanted to live his life in accordance with the precepts of the Moralist sages. And I'm certain that he died with no regrets."

For an hour, Timu sobbed inconsolably for the death of Zato Ruthi, his teacher and the shaper of his mind. There would never be another scholar as gentle and forgiving in all of Dara.

Then he wiped away his tears. He did not forget his duty.

Based on Ra Olu's description, Timu was prepared for garinafin riders to appear in the sky at any moment, ahead of barbarian foot sol-diers marching across the land. However, the sky in the east remained clear.

By questioning some of the refugees who were streaming into the city from the Dasu countryside, Ra Olu learned that the garinafins were not scouting ahead of the advancing barbarian army; instead, they were resting on the beach where they had slaughtered the two-thousand-strong army of Dasu.

"Do they seek to desecrate the bodies of the martyred soldiers?" asked Prince Timu, his voice quivering.

Ra Olu shook his head. "The barbarian king, this Pékyutenryo, is crafty. He spoke with Master Ruthi for a long while before attacking, and one may surmise that he was trying to pump the master for useful information. The attack that he launched was carefully planned and seemed intended to cause us the greatest injury possible. I don't think he would give up the chance to launch a lightning attack and take over all of Dasu if these garinafins were capable of it."

"What do you mean?"

Ra Olu explained patiently. "After bursts of exertion, most animals need some time to recover. Consider the long-legged leopard of Écofi, which is said to be the fastest animal on land: It dashes through the grass fast as a bolt of lightning to chase down quarry, but then it must rest for half a day before it can even get up and move again. Considering that display of fiery strength I witnessed from the garinafins, it would not surprise me that they would need time to recoup."

"Time to recoup . . . ," muttered Timu. "Then . . . they're not invincible after all. Even though they breathe fire and seem to have hides of steel."

"No. I'm certain that they're mortal, the same as you and I. They cannot fly across all of Dara without pause, raining down fiery death upon everyone."

Prince Timu called for his brush and inkwell, and hastened to compose an addendum to the report he had drafted for Emperor Ragin on the invasion.

The messenger airship left without Prince Timu aboard.

By the time the barbarian horde finally reached the city of Daye later that day, they found a city with its gates wide open. The garinafins, about thirty in number, waddled amongst barbarian warriors like awkward, oversized whales-with-chicken-feet struggling to make their way on land, their wings folded neatly around their bodies.

Prince Timu, who stood with Ra Olu in front of the city gates, was reminded of the fantastic creations of Kita Thu years ago at the Imperial examination, when he had tried to analogize Emperor Ragin's empire to a cruben-wolf that was at home neither on land nor in water.

"I heard the men of Dara prize honor," declared Pékyutenryo, who was riding at the base of the neck of a pure white garinafin that appeared even bigger and taller than the other beasts. "But are they so cowardly that they will not even fight me before begging for their lives?" Despite his accent, the arrogance in his voice was easy to perceive.

Timu looked up into the face of the barbarian king and answered, "King Pékyutenryo, you misunderstand. I'm not here to beg you for my life at all; you may take it if you wish."

Pékyutenryo looked down at the young prince, amused. "My name is Tenryo Roatan. 'Pékyu' is a title, much like your 'emperor.' Who are you?"

"I am Timu, Prince of Dara and Lord of Dasu."

Tenryo looked at Timu with even more interest. "You don't know how to fight, do you? Look at your smooth skin, your thin arms, your frail frame. With a prince like you, your father's empire is but a child's play tent."

Timu refused to take the bait. "You have already killed thousands— but they were soldiers, and it was their duty to die in defense of the people, a duty that I am bound by as well. To carry out that duty, I've given orders for the people of the city of Daye, and indeed of the entire island of Dasu, to cease all resistance. There is no honor in fighting a hopeless war. Lives are more important."

Tenryo now looked at Timu with something approaching respect. "If you're not interested in saving yourself, then what are you doing blocking my way into the city?"

"I come here to warn you that if you dare to harm the unarmed people of Dasu, then even as a ghost, I will lead the people in a war against you until you are driven back into the sea!"

Though Timu was but a young teenaged boy who appeared more comfortable with the writing brush than the sword, he made this speech with a steady voice and a serene demeanor.

Ra Olu felt a thrilling joy as he watched Timu. *Prince Timu may not have the frame or build of a warrior, but Fithowéo is also the god of those who are armed with only their pride, who strive and assay and press and toil, all the while knowing that they cannot win.*

King Jizu must have looked just like this when he stopped the destruction of Na Thion by Tanno Namen.

After a pause, Tenryo laughed. "Prince Timu, you are very much mistaken if you think I'm afraid of ghosts. I care not for the petty musings of your philosophers, and I have slain more people than you can imagine.

"I have been betrayed countless times in my life, and I, in turn, have betrayed those who thought me subjugated by a promise. Experience has taught me that even the bond between parent and child is no guarantee of faith. Obedience can be enforced only through terror and death, not grand gestures invoking the names of the gods or invisible spirits. A scene of carnage will pacify an unruly population more than all the pretty speeches in the world."

Timu stared at Tenryo, and for the first time, the reality of what he was facing seemed to be sinking in. "That . . . is a philosophy of evil."

"Good and evil are mere labels we place on deeds that benefit or harm us, and I have wagered the lives of my thanes and warriors upon a mere hope for refuge in the shoreless sea. To them I owe every duty, but to you and yours: nothing. A better life for my people is the only good for which I strive.

"I intend to conquer all of Dara, and I'll not stop until all the men of these islands lay prostrate at my feet, living or dead, and the lamentation of their women has overwhelmed the tides."

Timu's face twisted in a mixture of terror and defiance. Tenryo gazed down at him, and the pékyu's voice was almost compassionate as he spoke again.

"Do not be afraid for your own life—you're more useful alive. But you will watch as we make an example of Daye: It is perhaps the most valuable lesson of all."

The slaughter of Daye lasted three days.

CHAPTER THIRTY-EIGHT

THE EMPRESS'S REQUEST

PAN: THE TENTH MONTH IN THE ELEVENTH YEAR
OF THE REIGN OF FOUR PLACID SEAS.

Footsteps echoed through the circular hall. Still the only prisoner in these lonely cells, Gin Mazoti looked up.

Two figures emerged from the shadows and stopped on the other side of the bars. One was a guard holding a large ring of keys. Behind him was Empress Jia, holding a wooden tray on which sat a porcelain flask and a single cup, both of which glowed with a pale white light. The guard opened the door to the cell.

Empress Jia nodded at the guard. "You may leave."

The guard looked at Gin, who remained seated, and then looked back at the empress.

"Leave," said the empress, less patiently this time.

The guard bowed and left, the jangling of his keys gradually fading until they disappeared into the silent shadows.

Jia came in, set down the tray in front of Gin, and sat opposite her in *géüpa*, as though she and Gin were simply friends sitting down for an afternoon chat. Slowly, she poured for Gin, her movements steady and methodical. When the cup was filled, she pushed the cup toward Gin.

The fragrance of osmanthus, sweet and mind-cleansing, filled the air and relieved the cell of some of its dankness.

Just one cup, thought Gin. *She doesn't even bother to pretend anymore.*

"This is from the basement of an old Amu noble family in Dimushi whose property escheated to the state when they were found to be plotting treason. The vintage is among the best for osmanthus wine, I'm told, though I'm no expert. Since you were from Dimushi, I thought you would appreciate it more than I."

"I suppose that Amu noble's acts of treason were more substantial than mine."

"You don't consider harboring the leaders of a rebellion under the banner of the Hegemon treason?"

"I consider it a duty to protect witnesses to a plot brewing at the side of the emperor as he lies asleep."

The way Jia froze told Gin that her guesses had been right. It was cold comfort, but it was some comfort.

"Noda Mi and Doru Solofi were fools," said Gin. "They never understood that they were mere stones in someone else's *cüpa* game. And Rin . . . ah, Rin . . . he was always too insecure."

"I always knew that you would be the one to figure it out," muttered Jia. "You were always the better tactician."

"Not as good as you," said Gin.

"You waited too long," said Jia in agreement. "I never thought you'd be so bold as to harbor those two. At most I hoped that Zomi Kidosu might convince you to save some of their followers. But when you saved Mi and Solofi, I knew that I had to move right away."

"I thought the emperor would listen to me."

"You relied on his trust; that was always your blind spot."

Gin picked up the cup, and still saying nothing, drained it in one gulp. The wine was excellent, pure and dry, probably the best Gin had ever had.

She waited for the burning to start in her stomach. She hoped that the poison would act quickly. Considering all her service to the House of Dandelion, she should at least be owed that.

But there was no scalding sensation in her stomach, no pain. She didn't feel drowsy, either.

She looked up at Jia, surprised.

"It isn't poisoned," said Jia. "I harbor no personal ill will toward you, Gin. I know you don't believe that, but it's true."

"A test then," said Gin. "Did I pass?"

"You passed it long ago," said Jia. "You could have seized me the moment I came down here, defenseless save for a single guard. You could have demanded whatever you liked: an airship to take you away to the far corners of Dara; trusted units to escort you back to Nokida; an audience with Kuni. But you didn't."

"It would have been pointless," said Gin. "That you came down to see me like this means that you were prepared for such contingencies. If I did seize you as a hostage, I would only be confirming my charges as a traitor."

"A tactician to the last," said Jia, and the admiration in her voice was genuine. "I doubt I would ever be your match if you weren't . . . so proud."

Gin refilled the cup from the flask, and she drained it again. "It is indeed very good wine, though not the kind of thing I had when I lived in Dimushi. I was an urchin on the streets of the city, and sometimes I was so hungry that I ate the leftovers the wealthy families dumped into feeding troughs for the dogs and pigs. I know that we have never been close, Jia, but the emperor was the only one who gave me a chance and gave me the life I had, and I would never have betrayed him. So tell me why . . . why this elaborate ruse?"

"We do not know our own hearts as we think we do," said Jia. "You're a warrior, Gin, but I thought Dara no longer needed warriors. Kuni's power may have come from swords, but to rule, he must rely on writing brushes. When a sharp sword is lying around the house with young children around, someone is bound to be hurt."

"I might not think Prince Timu the best choice for the throne, but

I would have acquiesced in the emperor's decision, no matter what it was."

"It is precisely because you speak of 'acquiesce' that I had to do what I did. In a time of peace, it should never be the place of those who lead armies to say who should or shouldn't ascend to the throne. That way lie wars, division, madness."

"I would fight for Timu. My ambition is to serve the House of Dandelion."

"You might," said Jia. "But would Phyro? Would Théca Kimo or Puma Yemu? If Phyro raised the banner of rebellion, how many nobles and generals would side with him? And should that day come to pass, would you not rationalize to yourself that you were being loyal to Kuni by taking up the cause of the child who most resembled him in spirit?"

Gin laughed. "So, because your son is weak, you believe it gives you the right to deprive the House of Dandelion of those who fought for it and might fight for it again. That is a deeper betrayal than any plot you think you've uncovered."

Jia didn't even flinch at this. "I care not for labels like 'betrayal,' because my only duty is to the people of Dara. It isn't for Timu that I do this, though I know you and others will think so. I would have held to the same course even if Phyro were the heir. Especially so, then."

Gin stared at Jia. "I don't understand."

Jia sighed. "When a cruben breaches, he leaves behind trails of mangled fish and seaweed; when a ship traverses a wall of storms, she leaves with broken masts and tattered sails; when an empire rises, it finds itself atop a hill of skulls and bones. Violence has a cost, Gin, and sooner or later, that debt must be repaid. I wanted to ensure that the cost isn't so high as to cause the cruben to fall back into the sea, for the storm to catch up to the ship, and for the ghosts and vengeful souls to topple the House of Dandelion."

Gin pondered this. "You distrust all those who wield arms. As long as the House of Dandelion does not monopolize the use of force, you believe the emperor's heirs cannot sleep soundly at night."

"Not just Kuni's heirs, but all the people of Dara," said Jia. "Kuni has kept all the nobles and generals in check because of their personal loyalty, and perhaps Phyro can keep it for a generation longer. But what of his heirs, and the heirs who inherit the domains held by you, Kimo, Yemu, Carucono, Çakri and others? At some point, the tales of friendship between their parents and grandparents will fade into mere legends, the fire of ambition will grow inflamed, men with command of armies will become restless, and Dara will once again plunge into the old ways of death and blood, when the strong prey upon the weak. The people of Dara deserve better."

"You think like Mapidéré," said Gin, "who tried to preserve his empire by taking away weapons from the common people. That plan did not work out so well."

"That is because he had no system to replace the competition of warfare," said Jia. "I don't put my trust in the fragile bonds of personal loyalty forged on the battlefield celebrated in old poems. I want to replace it with obedience to a system of rules and codes, of energy and ambition channeled into a web of roles and duties recorded in books and reified by repetition until they become invisible chains as real as the roads and trade routes that crisscross the seas and bind together the Islands of Dara. It would not matter then that an heir is weak or strong. The people of Dara need a system that will serve them no matter who is emperor."

"And so you elevate the Moralists and their visions of a society governed by repetitious ritual and well-worn models from the past. You think that if you eliminate all independent military commands and put scholars in charge, at worst they'll hew to the adage that if ten scholars were to start a rebellion, it would take them three years of argument just to agree on a name for their faction."

"Events have proven me right. Noda Mi, Doru Solofi, and Théca Kimo did rebel."

"None of them would have done anything to challenge the throne had you not continuously advised the emperor to reduce their powers, to chip away at their sense of security, and, in some cases, to outright incite rebellion. You forced them into doing what you wanted to see happen."

"I did nothing more than encourage their natural tendencies, which, given time, would have come to full bloom. No matter how much I may have paved their way, the choice to rebel was ultimately theirs. A wolf can never be an obedient dog, nor a shark a tame porpoise."

Gin laughed. "A pretty speech to justify entrapment."

"You think I poisoned the ground; I think I merely drew poison out of it. You think I tipped a bucket; I think I merely made it fill faster. I expect we'll never agree, as we each only see what we expect to see. I do not regret what I did because I know that somewhere deep down, you and Kuni both know I am right. Kuni is too softhearted to go as far as I did, but he knows it's better to cauterize a wound now than to let it fester into a disease that his children cannot heal. You know that you've been tempted before, and that having resisted such temptation before is no guarantee for the future."

"You make me regret not listening to a beggar in a white cape a long time ago, who advised me to aid neither the emperor nor the Hegemon, when I still had the chance to carve out my own fate," Gin said.

Jia looked up sharply at this.

Gin sighed and looked away. "And I'm angry at myself now for remembering that day with regret, which seems to only confirm your way of looking at the world, an ugly, brutal world that I do not want to live in."

"It is the only world we have," said Jia. "For the stability of the empire and the security of the people, I'm willing to do anything and let history be my ultimate judge."

"You win," said Gin. "I may be a good tactician and fearless of death, but Luan was right. I don't have the heart for this kind of politics." She poured from the flask again and drank.

"Have I really won?" Jia asked. Gin waited for more, but Jia seemed lost in thought.

Only after a long while did the empress speak again. "If my husband were to go to war personally, how many men do you think he could command effectively?"

Gin was surprised by the question. After giving it some thought, she said, "Lord Garu would be a good hundred-chief." Almost unconsciously, she fell back into the familiar forms of address and speech patterns of the old days, when she, Kuni, Cogo, Luan, and Risana had debated strategy by a bonfire on the beaches of Dasu. "If pressed, he might do all right leading a detachment of a thousand if given clear plans and goals. But beyond that, I think he would be more of a liability than an asset. He is not a tactician by nature, and he is far too impulsive and unwilling to make the right kinds of sacrifices to be a good general."

"What about you? How many men can you lead?"

Gin looked at her contemptuously. "I was the Marshal of Dasu and then the Marshal of Dara. I have sent tens of thousands to their deaths, and I have also killed hundreds of thousands. No matter how large the army, I could wield it as well as I dance with my sword."

"Then why do you serve him? How can you claim that you will never rebel or do harm to the House of Dandelion when you admit that you think you surpass your lord in skill?"

Gin gazed at Jia calmly. "I never said that. The skill of leading soldiers is different from the skill of governance and rule. I served Lord Garu because he could do what I could not: make Dara a better place for all the boys and girls in the streets of Dimushi I could not save. I have never wavered from that belief."

Jia sighed. "I sincerely wish we could have been friends. My desire is the same as yours, and yet I know that for Dara to have lasting peace, men and women like you must fade away like the night mist at dawn."

The two sat for a while more in contemplative silence, and then Gin said, "I'm tired of waiting. Either give me a length of rope or a flask of poisoned wine. I ask only that my daughter—"

"She will not be harmed," said Jia.

"She may also have an aptitude . . ." Gin's face, which for a moment had appeared vulnerable, hardened again. "She will make her own way in life, the same as me. I am ready to fade away as you desire."

But Jia shook her head. "Having you fade away is only desirable if Dara were at peace. The gods often delight in thwarting our carefully laid plans."

"The rebellions have not grown out of control," said Gin. "Even the emperor's children will be able to handle them, given time."

"No, there is something else." From the folds of her sleeves, Jia retrieved the report from Prince Timu and handed it to Gin.

Gin spread it open and read it slowly. When she looked up, her expression was unreadable.

"I ask you to save my son, Gin Mazoti. I ask you to save Dara."

"Then proclaim me innocent, and confess your plot to the people of Dara," said Gin. "I will not fight unless my name is cleared."

For a long time, Jia said nothing. Gin waited.

"I can't," Jia said.

"Ah, vanity," said Gin.

"No," said Jia. "If I do as you ask, all that I've worked for will come to naught. No one will dare to speak against the enfeoffed nobles and their personal armies for generations, and all of Dara will be plagued with war far into the future."

"I have already named my price," said Gin. "You must choose."

News and rumors of the Lyucu invasion quickly spread throughout Dara as refugees fleeing Dasu and Rui struggled onto the shore of the Big Island.

"The barbarians ride on flying elephants that could spit fire!"

"They're called garinafins and they do more than spit fire. Just looking into their eyes turns you into stone, and then they smash you into smithereens with their eagle-claws and wolf-teeth."

"Rui fell within five days! Pékyu Tenryo sent the garinafin riders over the Gaing Gulf on city-ships, and just like that, more than fifty airships went *poof!* Can you believe it? They say five thousand people died, including the governor and his whole family, and not a single barbarian was even injured."

"I saw a woman who lost all her children in a single fiery blast. Oh gods! The fire just missed her, but she was holding on to the hand of her little girl and that hand is all she has left. She won't let the charred stump out of her hands. We got her into the boat, but now we have to watch her every hour lest she hang herself. . . ."

"I saw a man whose eyes turned red as fire after the Lyucu killed his parents, wife, and three children in front of him. He went after the Lyucu with the only weapon he had—a shovel—and they struck him so many times with their clubs that there was nothing but a paste of meat and pulverized bone left in the ground after they were done. . . ."

"I saw such horrors as the Lyucu entered my village while I hid inside the overturned fishing boat. They killed everyone they thought was too old or sickly or crippled to make good workers, and then made all the mothers strangle their babies so that they would be free to become concubines for the Lyucu warriors. . . ."

"I was the only one to escape from my hometown because the Lyucu wanted to make an example of it. They competed to see who could toss babies the highest and let them smash against the ground; they made the children pick which of their parents they wanted to keep alive before killing them both anyway; they forced all the rest of us to run into the woods so they could hunt us for sport. . . ."

"Can't the flying elephants carry the barbarians across the sea to the other islands?"

"Of course they can! And now that the emperor has lost the air base at Mount Kiji, we won't even be able to replenish the gas in our airships—not that the airships have done much good so far."

"Can't Marshal Mazoti do something? They say that the empress has asked her to return to her old position and to defend Dara to redeem her treason."

"But what can the marshal do? She's just a mortal, the same as us, but the barbarians fight like evil immortals."

"May the gods save us."

"I wonder where they've been?"

CHAPTER THIRTY-NINE

THE FARSEER'S DEPARTURE

PAN: THE ELEVENTH MONTH IN THE ELEVENTH
YEAR OF THE REIGN OF FOUR PLACID SEAS.

Having wiped up the remnants of the Mi-Solofi rebellion in Tunoa, Prince Phyro, Princess Théra, and Duke Rin Coda returned to a capital in disarray.

After a brief family reunion made somber by the absence of Timu, Kuni left with Rin to discuss the situation in Dara. Jia went to the Temple of Tututika to pray for Timu. And Phyro and Théra each had someone they wanted to visit.

Risana objected as soon as she heard what her son wanted to do.

"Why can't I go see Auntie Gin?" asked Phyro. "She's the only one who can rescue Timu!"

"You have to learn to control your emotions," said Risana. "Think! Gin is now a traitor who has refused to fight for the emperor. If you go see her, it will be seen by everyone as a gesture of doubt and shake the foundation of Imperial authority. That is the last thing we need right now."

"I hate this."

"Image is everything in the arts of war and politics," said Risana. "You ought to know this by now."

Théra, on the other hand, tracked down Zomi Kidosu, who was staying at the guest complex outside the palace with Princess Aya. The empress had not wanted her to leave Pan while the case against Gin was pending.

The princess had never seen Zomi look so lost. She arranged and rearranged the papers on her desk, trying to appear busy but accomplishing nothing.

"What are you doing?"

Zomi looked up, as if startled to find the princess still there. "I'm taking care of the civil affairs of Géjira remotely while it's . . . under Imperial occupation. I've created some programs for the queen that the emperor's generals won't understand—"

"That's not what I meant," said Théra. "Is what you wrote about the queen true?"

Zomi looked away. "Your Highness, I . . . I don't . . . please."

Théra sighed. Seeing Zomi like this felt wrong, as though she had caught her naked. *Is this why Kon Fiji warned his disciples against hero worship? "To admire anyone excessively is to set yourself up for disappointment."*

She had wanted to tell Zomi about her exploits in Tunoa, thinking that the woman would be interested in the magic mirrors. She had wanted to show Zomi that she had changed, had grown. This was not how she wanted them to meet: under clouds of doubt and betrayal.

"Do *you* have the life you want?" Théra asked. And before Zomi could answer, she left.

> To My Dearest Friend:
>   I've often thought about the time you saved me from arrows raining down from the sky when we were both boys skipping school to watch Emperor Mapidéré's procession . . .

Rin Coda hesitated, uncertain what logogram to carve next. He had always been good with words, but now, nothing seemed capable of expressing the sorrow he felt.

> *My best friend's child has been seized by cruel invaders*
> *from across the sea, and the woman who could save him has*
> *been accused of treason and thrown into jail.*
> *How could it have all gone so wrong?*

The soft block of wax in his hand continued to drip, and eventually, an ungainly, amorphous blob formed on the silk after the line of carefully carved logograms, as chaotic and conflicted as the maelstrom in his own mind.

He sighed and blew out the fire and set the wax block aside.

Théca Kimo has been executed, and Gin Mazoti's reputation is ruined. Many men and women have lost their lives in meaningless wars. All these things happened because I felt insecure and wanted to enlarge my influence, to feed and create a rebellion that I could then reveal and suppress.

He carried a small table under the central beam in the room, got up on it, and looped a silk scarf around the beam, tying the ends together.

I can't blame it on Jia. She might have given me the idea, but it was I who did the deed. I provided Noda Mi and Doru Solofi with the funds for their rebellion; I allowed Théca Kimo's weapons to get into Tunoa, miring him in a plot from which he could not extricate himself; I let Noda Mi and Doru Solofi escape to Géjira, thinking that they could still be useful in the future. While I created phantom threats and congratulated myself for overcoming them, I neglected my duty and let a real threat into the empire.

He put his chin through the silk loop, wrapped the silk once more around his neck so that his head could not be extracted, and tested the loop for strength. It would hold.

I owe everything I have to Kuni, and yet I betrayed him worse than anyone. I cannot face Théca Kimo. I cannot face Gin Mazoti. I certainly cannot face my friend.

He kicked the table away; his body fell a few inches and stopped as the silk loop took his weight; his legs kicked, jerked, and then slowed; the smell of urine and feces filled the room; the sound of muffled struggling stopped.

Jia and Kuni sat in *mipa rari*, facing each other across a small table. Rin Coda's unfinished letter lay between them.

"This is your doing," Kuni said.

Jia said nothing. She was thinking about Otho Krin.

Rin's suicide ten days ago had led to a massive investigation by Cogo Yelu. He was particularly zealous—no doubt an attempt to clear his own role in the downfall of Gin Mazoti—and he revealed many instances of corruption and complicity, as well as outright fomenting of rebellions by the farseers. Many scapegoats had been found and executed.

"How could we have drifted so far apart?" muttered Kuni. "And yet, you have forced me into keeping your secret for you. If I reveal the truth about Rin's suicide and your role in all that has happened, the empire will fall apart at the moment when we can least afford it. Rulers, like gods, cannot be seen as making mistakes, and so you have yoked me to this lie that I cannot repudiate."

Jia bowed her head.

Eventually, Cogo had come to suspect the involvement of Otho Krin, the chatelain. But despite the application of threats and torture, Otho had refused to divulge the empress's role.

He had died in prison. They said it was suicide. Maybe it was true; maybe not.

Love made one do strange things.

His silence had been valuable. Though Kuni suspected what she had done, Cogo could not gather any proof. Even though Kuni knew the truth, as long he couldn't prove it, her position was secure.

And eventually, she hoped, he would understand why she had done what she did.

Love made one do strange things.

They sat in silence for a long time. Jia's shoulders heaved, and tears dropped onto the table.

"I will give him a lavish burial," muttered Kuni. "Oh Rin, foolish Rin." He looked at his wife, sorrow infusing every wrinkle in his face. "You can't even apologize."

He got up and left.

Jia never lifted her face.

Soto came into the room and draped a blanket around the sitting figure of Jia. She hadn't moved from her position for hours, not even after the emperor left.

"I know you think I'm a monster," said Jia.

"I don't know what to think," said Soto. "But I am still your friend."

"Thank you," Jia whispered. And the two women held hands for a moment in the flickering light of candles.

"I had a dream once," said Jia. "In it, Lady Rapa spoke to me of the importance of lasting structures and systems, as slow to change as rivers of ice. She spoke to me also of the impermanence of bonds of loyalty and faith, as unstable as flickering tongues of fire."

"It's a lazy mind that blames our errors on the gods."

"Oh, I'm not placing blame. Dreams often just reflect our thoughts in metaphor."

"Your dream-vision has the allure of simplicity," said Soto. "But like the models of the philosophers, the real world has a way of being more complicated."

Jia looked away. "Without dreams and the striving to achieve them, how are we better than the kelp and seaweed that merely drift with the current?"

"Do you regret what you've done?"

Jia shook her head. "Everything I did was for the benefit of the people of Dara. It just didn't work out. Had the Lyucu not arrived, I would have brought peace to the land for generations. I can't apologize when I don't think I did anything wrong."

"But your methods . . . Jia, I wish you could have chosen a

different way. To spill blood should be a last resort, not the first."

"I have not the charisma of Kuni, who could have perhaps found a way to disarm the enfeoffed nobles over a drinking game; I have not the power of Mata, who could have enforced peace by the sword and cudgel; I have not the craft of Luan Zya, who could have lured the ambitious into traps of more cunning design. But they have not my vision, so I had to use the methods available to me as a woman of the palace: intrigue, plot, provoked rebellions."

Soto sighed. "I both agree and disagree with you. The lives lost . . . I do not think you can be free of that debt."

"I am willing to be judged for my choices. The same as Kuni, as anyone who would wield power."

Soto nodded. "Then why are you sitting here?"

Jia looked at her. "I am in disgrace; there's nothing to do."

"Yet you're still the Empress of Dara, and the lives of the people you care about are threatened by invaders from the north."

"I think the days of my meddling in politics have come to an end."

After a moment of silence, Soto said, "Do you remember going to the shadow puppet shows as a young girl?"

Surprised, Jia nodded.

"The shows would start in the evenings, before the sun had set. And usually the first act would end on some tragedy: The lovers would be divided by jealousy and suspicion; the evil minister would have forced out the loyal general; the faithful maid would have been dismissed by her mistress over a misunderstanding."

Jia chuckled softly. "And by the time of intermission, night would have arrived. The stars would be out twinkling in the sky, and I thought they had come at the worst moment to catch the show."

"But there is always a second act," said Soto. "Always."

The two women looked at each other. Finally, Jia nodded and squeezed Soto's hand.

CHAPTER FORTY

THE CORRUPTION
OF RA OLU

RUI: THE ELEVENTH MONTH IN THE ELEVENTH
YEAR OF THE REIGN OF FOUR PLACID SEAS.

A chill wind blew across the roiling waves of Gaing Gulf. A giant Mingén falcon hovered overhead along with two ravens, one black, one white, and a dove. Meanwhile, a monstrous shark circled through the flickering shadows under the waves. The clouds were limned in a golden light like the scales of a carp, and if one listened closely, the pounding spray seemed to coalesce into the howling of wolves.

The shark, *pawi* of Tazu, Master of Unpredictable Waters, leapt out of the sea, its toothy grin glinting in the sunlight.

The Mingén falcon, *pawi* of Kiji, Lord of the Winds, swooped down to let out a challenging cry at the dagger-fanged fish.

- *What are you laughing about, Tazu?*

- *The God of Birds has been driven out of his home by winged barbarians. I think most would find it funny.*

- *Have you lost all compassion? You laugh now, but they will come for your home on Wolf's Paw, too.*

- I laugh at everything, brother. You laugh at nothing. That is the root of your problem.

The scale-clouds roiled as Tututika, the last born of the gods, interrupted in her clear, musical voice:

- Stop bickering. All of Dara is under threat. All the Islands, all the people, all the gods. We must do something.

The wave-wolves howled as Fithowéo the Warlike joined the discussion:

- Are you suggesting that we go to war against the Lyucu? What of our pact to not directly interfere in the affairs of the mortals?

- The Lyucu aren't the people of Dara. The pact doesn't apply.

The great shark showed off its deadly grin again.

- Such sophistry! But what does "the people of Dara" mean? This is not the first time invaders have come to these shores. These islands were inhabited before the coming of the Ano, which was not even that long ago in the eyes of the eternal stars. We didn't do much to protect those people of Dara from the slaughter, did we?

Since the other *pawi* looked away, shamefaced, Tazu went on:

- During the Diaspora Wars, some of us fought against them, some of us fought with them, and some of us did both. And it seems all of us ended up preferring the incense and music and sacrificial meals and great temples offered up by the descendants of the Ano more than the rough-hewn woodland shrines of the people whose remnants now live on Tan Adü. Isn't this but another turn in the eternal wheel of change? Remember, we're not mortals; their concerns aren't the same as ours.

The other gods were silent for a while, but eventually the gentle dove of Rufizo spread its wings over the brooding sea.

- The coming of the Ano was a time of bloodshed and widespread death, and you're right that all of us did things we aren't proud of during the Diaspora Wars. But we were different then, younger, more like children who did not know the difference between good and evil. Just as the descendants of the original inhabitants of these islands have merged with the Ano to become the people of Dara, we have also changed. We've altered the way we dress, the way we speak, the way we fight and debate and love because of

the Ano. All of us have walked among them in mortal form and taken them as lovers—

The clouds turned crimson as several of the gods remembered old flames, and Tazu's shark chuckled, a most unpleasant sound.

—The Ano have changed us with their worship and philosophy and culture as much as we have changed them with our guidance and persuasion. I would hope we have grown in our sense of responsibility.

The shark's grin was now more like a sneer as he answered:

- You sound like a mortal Moralist, but how do you know that in a thousand years these strangers who call themselves the Lyucu will not also build great temples to us and praise our names and think of themselves as the people of Dara? The spears of the original inhabitants of these islands have rotted away and their bones lie deep in the soil, but the Islands are still here and so are we. I say let them fight as they will and we can go on playing our games with them as before. Doesn't Kuni Garu always speak of doing interesting things? I think it's most interesting to watch people kill each other, especially when the Lyucu have these wonderful beasts.

Now came the turn for the Twins of Cocru—stubborn and patient Rapa, the goddess of sleep and rest, and impulsive and volatile Kana, the goddess of death and fire:

- We have shaped the people of Dara—

- Just as the people of Dara have shaped us, my sister. And we're responsible in part for the crisis facing Dara today.

The black crow of Kana looked at the shark of Tazu, who carelessly flipped in the water, and the white crow of Rapa, who looked away and said nothing.

- We can't just stand by.

Once again, the Mingén falcon of Kiji swooped over the other *pawi*.

- The Lyucu worship their own deities. Tazu, you are the jealous sort. Aren't you worried that if they win, we will be forgotten and fade away?

But the shark was unfazed.

- Among the gods they worship is one they call the All-Father and another they call the Every-Mother; who knows if the All-Father isn't just another

name for our father, Thasoluo? He was called away by Moäno, the King of All Deities, and it might be that he went to other lands and begot other children. The sea is vast and other worlds lay beneath the horizon, as these Lyucu have proven. Would you break the spirit of the promise we made to our mother and go to war against our father's children from beyond the sea?

The white crow of Rapa screeched angrily at the shark.

- That is pure speculation! We haven't even met these other gods! You just want more people to die.

- What of it? I thought your twin sister would welcome the prospect. Who says I don't look out for my siblings?

The black crow cawed.

- Death is my domain. But that doesn't mean it's all I care for.

The shark flicked its tail as though wagging a finger.

- I still say we can't interfere directly, not until we know more about these people and the gods they've brought. I do enjoy games, though, and so I will play with these strangers on their magnificent mounts.

The waves howled again like wolves.

- I wish Lutho were with us. He always has the best ideas.

The shark nodded at this.

- Where is that old turtle? I haven't seen him since the appearance of the city-ships.

None of the gods could recall seeing their storm-braving brother, wisest of the gods.

In this vein, the gods went on debating listlessly; there was no consensus about what to do by the time the gathering broke apart.

"What do you have to say, barbarian of Dara?" asked Pékyu Tenryo. He and his chieftains were seated in the great hall in the Palace of Kriphi, the capital and biggest city on the island of Rui.

All the Lyucu were bedecked in strings of pearls and coral beads seized from the unfortunate inhabitants of the city. Jewelry, vessels made from precious metals, and gold and silver coins were piled all about them as they quaffed bowls of kyoffir and wine taken from the governor's stores. Young women and a few handsome young men, the sons and daughters and wives of the wealthy inhabitants of Daye, sat in the laps of the chieftains or next to them, giggling and laughing, flirtatiously pouring drink for the chieftains and kissing them as the captives wrapped their arms around their conquerors.

In the middle of the hall knelt Ra Olu, former regent of Dasu, who touched his forehead to the carpet. "This fool begs to know when the Great Pékyu wishes to bring the blessing of his glorious army to the rest of Dara."

Pékyu Tenryo let out a loud burp and pushed the woman in his lap away—she was Lady Lon, Ra Olu's wife. Tenryo took particular pleasure in humiliating the conquered nobles of Dasu and Rui with ostentatious displays of dominance of this kind. "Why do you want to know?"

"Planning an invasion of the core islands is a big undertaking, and . . . perhaps this humble servant can be of assistance."

"Oh?" Tenryo looked at Ra Olu suspiciously. "Timu tells me every time I see him that the spirit of the nobles and officials of Dara is indomitable and you will never yield to me. Are you telling me he's wrong?"

Timu and the other nobles and officials who refused to surrender and serve the Lyucu had been laboring with the rest of the commoners in the late autumn fields, gathering feed for the garinafins and herds of long-haired cattle brought by the city-ships, constructing weapons and defensive fortifications for the Lyucu army, and generally being treated as little better than animals by the conquerors. Timu, though frail and bookish, proved to be an inspiration for everyone around him. He bore the lashes from the Lyucu overseers without complaint and kept on reassuring the enslaved population that the emperor's army was going to arrive any day to drive out the invaders.

Until now, Ra Olu had stuck by his lord. This sudden change in tone was . . . intriguing.

"Prince Timu is a stubborn man," said Ra Olu. He gazed at the treasure piled around the Lyucu chieftains—who were also called thanes—and the dishes full of meat and fish in front of them, and the glow of greed in his eyes seemed to take on a life of its own. He swallowed. "But most of the people of Dara are more reasonable."

"I thought you men of Dara were contemptuous of us, calling us barbarians." Tenryo deliberately put his arm around Lady Lon and caressed her breasts. "Does it not bother you that your husband seems to show no anger that I have claimed you for my bed every night?"

"Everyone wants to do better," said Lady Lon, her face flushing crimson. Her gaze and Ra Olu's met briefly, and she immediately looked away. Curling an arm around Pékyu Tenryo's neck, she giggled and kissed him. "Who doesn't want to eat meat and drink wine instead of fighting with peasants for a share of rough sorghum biscuits out of a trough and lapping water from puddles?"

Pékyu Tenryo laughed. The regimen of humiliating these Dara nobles was finally having the intended effect. He had always known these people were soft.

"The Great Pékyu is invincible," said Ra Olu, touching his forehead to the ground again. "My wife has only shown her wisdom in choosing to serve you; all of us could learn a lesson by emulating her submission, which is the only course in the face of a superior force. But I have been an administrator for this population for far longer than you. Wise as you are, perhaps I can offer ideas that would help."

"What exactly do you have in mind?"

"Though the heavenly Lyucu army is all-powerful and all of Dara is surely to fall under your sway in no time, yet it is a fact that the people of Dara are many while the warriors of Lyucu are comparatively few. I have observed that many warriors are occupied with the unproductive task of keeping watch over the peasants and nobles, much like cowherds watching over unruly cattle lest they hurt themselves . . . and every day dozens, even hundreds, of the people of these islands have to be killed in unfortunate incidents of suspected sabotage.

"Would it not be best if you could bring most of your warriors to the battlefield with you instead of having to worry about a possible rebellion at home incited by a few evil-hearted, stubborn Dara nobles?"

"I'm listening."

"Most of the common people would be willing to serve the Lyucu, though some might be tempted by the lies of the emperor and his hollow promises of a counterinvasion. I propose that we organize the families of Rui and Dasu into units of ten, and each such unit shall elect a deci-chief. The deci-chief is responsible for maintaining a watch over the ten families in his charge, and if anyone within the ten families is found to be a traitor to the Lyucu, every member of the ten families shall be put to death. Since the peasants will now be given oversight by their own elders and nobles, instead of the invader, superior Lords of Lyucu, instances of misunderstanding will be reduced and fewer of the valuable slaves will have to be killed."

"Oh . . . ," Tenryo mused. "You're suggesting that the people of Dara watch each other instead of having us watch them." His eyes began to glow. "This is quite a trick."

"We can enhance it with other additions," added Lady Lon. "For example, you can reward those who reveal to you plots of rebellion or anyone who dares to whisper words of dissatisfaction about the Lyucu occup—er—the gentle and generous reign of the Lords of Lyucu by giving them certain privileges." She blushed again and fed Tenryo a mouthful of wine from her own lips.

"Ha-ha-ha!" Tenryo kissed Lady Lon. "I do not intend to invade the core islands until next spring. The garinafin are tired and skittish after the long journey across the ocean, and they'll need to recuperate over the winter. It will indeed help for the population here to be pacified before I renew my efforts next year."

"I will endeavor to help you in whatever way I can," said Ra Olu. "All I ask is some token of recognition—though all the people of Dara are barbaric beasts, some beasts are better than others, and some quicker to learn."

"It turns out that the moralistic people of Dara are shameless hypocrites," said Tenryo. The gathered Lyucu thanes laughed.

"But I confess that your suggestions are pleasing," Tenryo continued. "Well, if you and your husband implement this plan well, I will surely reward you richly. You may move into the governor's mansion from the fields tonight, Ra Olu; and Lon, I may even allow you to go back to your husband's bed one of these nights."

"The Great Pékyu is a most generous lord," said Lady Lon and Ra Olu together.

Their eyes met, and none of the thanes noticed the look they shared with each other.

Pékyu Tenryo gave the order that the temples of the gods of Dara and their priests and monks were not to be disturbed. After all, the Lyucu were not barbarians, despite the charges of outraged Dara scholars. They were a pious people also.

Curious Lyucu chieftains and warriors visited the shrines to see what kind of gods the people they'd conquered worshipped.

"Doesn't this Kiji remind you of Péa, son of the All-Father and Maiden-of-the-Wind, who gave us the gift of the garinafin?"

"That makes sense! Doesn't the Mingén falcon remind you of a garinafin, just a lot smaller?"

"Maybe the barbarians of Dara didn't understand the revelations of the All-Father and got their statues wrong?"

The Lyucu chieftains began to make offerings of meat and rendered fat at the altars to Kiji. As far as anyone could tell, the burnt offerings went up into the heavens just like any other offering, and presumably Lord Kiji consumed them.

For days, priests at the Temple of Kiji on the western shore of Lake Arisuso debated the question of whether they should accept such offerings, but in the end, the abbot voted in the affirmative when it was discovered that many chieftains were willing to donate gifts of jewels and gold to the temple.

"Lord Kiji is a compassionate god," said the abbot piously. "All who wish to be bathed in his light should be allowed to do so."

He made no mention of the fact that the Lyucu pilgrims prayed to the god as Péa-Kiji; neither did he bring up the fact that a few of the Lyucu thanes had asked that the likeness of a garinafin be added over the shoulder of Lord Kiji's statue, opposite the depiction of the Mingén falcon, Kiji's *pawi*.

Still, a small carving of a garinafin did appear over Lord Kiji's shoulder, and when the Lyucu came to the temple, the priests who chanted prayers with them called the god "Péa-Kiji."

- *I see that my winged brother has a new look!*

- *Tazu, I'm not in the mood for any more of your tiresome mockery.*

- *Who's mocking? I'm envious! You are back in your home, and you've gained so many more worshippers. Now if only the rest of us could get the same treatment.*

- *This is a complicated situation.*

- *Sure, sure. But I will note for the occasion that you're not so gung-ho about going to war against the Lyucu now.*

The God of Birds—and now also patron of garinafins, albeit reluctantly—made no reply.

CHAPTER FORTY-ONE

THE INTERPRETATION
OF A LETTER

PAN: THE TWELFTH MONTH IN THE ELEVENTH
YEAR OF THE REIGN OF FOUR PLACID SEAS.

There were no bars on the windows, and the floor was covered with soft sitting mats. Embroidered images of snow-covered winter plums hung from the stone walls, brightening the space. A stove kept the room warm as well as the pot of tea hot. The fragrance of incense cleared away any lingering traces of the chill of winter.

But Gin didn't think her new home was particularly different from the dank cell where she had been kept. She was still a prisoner; if she tried to leave the room, dozens of palace guards would bow to her, their hands on the pommels of their swords.

The emperor handed the sword to Gin.

She accepted it. This was the second time that he had given this sword to her. The first time had been many years ago on a high dais, when she had stood in front of a surprised and skeptical army and told them that they would, one day, defeat the Hegemon of Dara.

It seemed like a dream.

"You agree then?" asked Kuni.

Gin swung the sword through the air a few times, slowly. Kuni did not blink.

"My conditions have not changed," said Gin. "You will announce my innocence and reveal the plot of the empress against those who helped you to become emperor. You will apologize to all the nobles, including the spirit of Théca Kimo and all who died needlessly. Then you will imprison Jia for the rest of her days, and make Risana the new empress. Only then will I consider the request."

Hope faded from Kuni's face. He shook his head.

"I can't do any of that, Gin. What Jia did . . . was wrong, but she did prove that Théca was temptable."

"Who isn't? If we were all judged by—"

"If I do as you ask, there will be chaos. All faith in Imperial administration will be lost: Every noble will demand concessions for their domains, taking advantage of this error in my judgment; every potential rebel will be emboldened, thinking that the farseers are corruptible; every scholar and governor will lose faith in my authority, realizing that I'm fallible and can be deceived. Dara will never recover from this damage to Imperial authority, and we will have weakened this fragile peace more than any act of treason."

"You only have yourself to blame for that."

Kuni closed his eyes. "If we were truly at peace, I would be willing to risk it to right this wrong against you, counting on the passage of time to heal the wound gradually. But we're not at peace. A greater threat looms over Dara than any we've faced before. If Dara cannot stay united before the Lyucu, if the nobles do not fight with me with one heart, if the people doubt my judgment, if the governors and scholars mistrust my hand—then darkness will descend over all the Islands and many more will die, and all we've fought for will be lost."

"So you want me to live with a lie and go to battle for you as a traitor who has been forgiven and fights to redeem her stained name."

Kuni nodded. "I know it's unfair. But there is no other course. We are not always in control of our own fates, and sometimes we must live with mistakes—and even beg others to live with them. The roles we play dictate courses of action."

Kuni knelt down before Gin and touched his forehead to the ground.

For a moment Gin was seized by the desire to step forward and lift him up by the arms, to tell him that she understood, that she would do as he asked. After all that had happened, she still believed that it was sweet and proper for people to die for great lords who recognized their talent.

But then the bitterness of her own humiliation returned. She recalled the moment Cogo had secured her into the boat by the lake like an animal bound for the sacrificial altar, the way Jia had dismissed the bonds of loyalty as fragile and worthless, the way Dafiro Miro had come to try to sneak her away like some embarrassing fugitive.

"What pains me," said Gin, "is the fact that you cannot deny that at some level, you agree with Jia. That was why you had taken Faça and Rima away from me, years ago, and sent me to Géjira. You also believe that power is always corrupting, and because of that, you wanted to weaken my power base. Suspicion poisoned the bond between us long before today."

Kuni sighed. "How is it different from you? You declared yourself queen without waiting for me to give you the title, afraid that I might be jealous of your accomplishments. We're not perfect, and we strive to do the best we can despite our sins."

"You're right," said Gin. She strode over to one of the walls of the room, and, with a forceful thrust, plunged the sword into a crack between two of the stones. Then, with a powerful drive against the handle, broke the sword in half.

Leaving the tip embedded in the wall, she came back and handed the broken sword to Kuni.

"I'd rather break than bend to preserve a lie," she said. "I'm tired of letting power wield us, Lord Garu. I cannot be your marshal unless you clear my name; you must fight this war on your own."

Kuni got up, accepted the broken sword, and left silently.

ও ন ও ন

Princess Théra found Zomi Kidosu by the gates of Pan. She was hobbling along with a walking stick and begging for the caravan drivers to give her a ride.

"Advocate Kidosu!" Théra called out from her horse, and pulled to a stop by her.

"I haven't gone by that title for years, Your Highness," said Zomi. "I don't have any titles now."

"I heard what happened from Father," said Théra. "You've resigned all your posts and asked to be allowed to head back home. Do you really wish to live as a slave of the Lyucu?"

"Then you know I'm a worthless person," said Zomi. "Do not sully your eyes with my sight. I betrayed my queen in a moment of weakness to preserve my own secret and to give my mother what I hoped was a good life. Without my lies, Prime Minister Yelu would not have sided with the empress, and the marshal would be leading the army against the Lyucu. The marshal is right: Without a foundation of honor, everything else is a mirage. Since Princess Aya is safe, I have awakened from my nightmare and now must head home to be with my mother."

"What happened to your leg?"

"My harness needs to be replenished with fresh, supple branches from the greenhouses in winter. Since I've given up everything acquired with ill-begotten gains, I can no longer afford to buy them."

"You really are a fool," said Théra indignantly.

"I beg your pardon?" said Zomi, her face flushed with anger.

"You have a simple need and the resources to fulfill that need, and yet you prefer to feel sorry for yourself, believing that somehow makes you noble."

"What do you know of—"

"Oh, I don't know everything you've been through, but I recognize the symptoms of your malaise. You once scolded me for lamenting my fate when I had advantages others did not, and you told me that if I did not have the life I wanted, perhaps it was because I had not tried to live as myself at all. I throw these accusations in your face today."

"I am not in the mood—"

"You made mistakes. So what? Were you not the best student of the greatest strategist of Dara? Did you not impress all the Lords of Dara with your daring and insightful critique of the hollowness of my father's vision of a meritocracy? Have you not ably assisted a queen with the administration of her realm and accomplished more than countless others your age?

"Yet today you slink away like a wounded puppy instead of pledging all your talent and power to help your lord *and* yourself in a moment of need? Can you not do more to help those you love by staying at the court, bearing the shame of your disgrace?

"Next year is the Year of the Orchid, your birth year! Have you forgotten that it was the lowly representative of the Hundred Flowers who reminded Fithowéo of his duty to strive and fight against the eternal darkness that is self-doubt?"

Zomi looked up at the princess, and for the first time, she realized that the careful, self-pitying girl of her memory was gone. There was a quality to her that could only be described as *regal*.

She nodded and held out her hand as the princess helped her onto the horse behind her.

Zomi came to the suite of rooms where Gin was held. Though Zomi no longer had an official position at the court, after she showed the guards the letter written by Princess Théra and signed with her seal, they let her through.

Zomi knelt at the entrance to Gin's sitting room and waited. The sunlight cast her shadow against the silk screen of the sliding door. There was a pause in the chatter between Gin and Aya inside; then, after a moment, the talk went on.

No one came to the door.

The sun set, and the moon rose. The guards came to ask Zomi if she wished to eat and drink. She shook her head.

As the stars careened through the sky, she thought over her life. She thought of all those who had believed in her and how she had disappointed them all: her mother, Luan, Théra, Gin. She thought of her own boldness and how it was sometimes indistinguishable from arrogance and selfishness. She thought of all the words of the Moralists that she had mocked without understanding the truth they spoke. She cried with utter shame.

The sun rose again, and just as she was about to get up and leave the marshal's presence forever, the door slid open.

"Come in and have some tea," said Gin, her voice as mild as the morning breeze.

"Men and women should die for those who recognize their talent," said Zomi. "I'm sorry." She felt like that young woman who had first ridden the balloon with Luan Zya years ago: She did not have the words. "I'm sorry," she said again.

"I know," said Gin. "But the past is the past, and all we can do is learn from our mistakes. You betrayed me because you believed you had no other choice—but as you have learned, such are the moments when we see our own souls and strive to enlarge them."

Zomi began to cry. "I have disappointed you. I am more ashamed than there are words in the world."

"You have had too many successes at too young an age," said Gin. "But humiliation can be a good teacher as well. I once crawled between the legs of a man and thought I would never again be able to lift my head; yet he taught me the need to play the long game. You have talent, Zomi Kidosu, but you must learn to guide that talent with wisdom, which can only be taught by failures."

"Please punish me," said Zomi.

"You have been punished enough," said Gin. "That is why I left you here for the night by yourself. We are always our own harshest critics." She bent down to lift her up. "What you need now is forgiveness and the resolve to go into battle against doubt anew."

To the Emperor of Dara:
  Rénga's threats of an invasion have quite surprised
  us. Does the emperor seek to emulate the fools of

ancient legends told by Ra Oji, who sought to strike at stones with eggs and hope for success?

The emperor speaks of raising armies and navies and fleets of airships, but we have already defeated your army once, and why should you expect the outcome to be different in a repeat contest? You may hold an advantage in numbers, but what is the use of such advantage when each garinafin under the guidance of brave Lyucu warriors is capable of defeating a thousand men-at-arms of Dara? We have seen the capabilities of the best that the fighting men of Dara can offer, and we're not impressed.

Moreover, with the passage of time, our advantage grows while your strength diminishes. Without a source of lift gas, how will you keep your airships aloft over time? We will upgrade the equipment of our warriors with the seized weapons from the armories in Dasu and Rui. The people of Dara already tremble at the mention of the Great Pékyu's name, and the more time passes, the greater the fear grows. They will not fight for you with conviction. To seek to threaten the stronger when you're the weaker is not the act of a wise sovereign.

Prince Timu is a happy guest here and has no wish to return, and we have no doubt he will come to see the wisdom of submission to a superior lord. In time, perhaps, Timu will ascend the Throne of Dara and rule some parts of Dara as a loyal thane of the Lyucu.

While the wondrous garinafins enjoy the well-deserved respite of the fragrant hay after their soaring victories in Rui and Dasu, the Great Pékyu is looking forward to seeing you soon. I hope our first encounter will be akin to the ancient spearman prostrating himself to welcome the arrival of the sun, symbol of the

*Great Pékyu himself. Our winged beasts, riding on the
city-ships gifted by Mapidéré, shall determine just who
is the true master of Dara.*

*—Pékyu Tenryo, Protector of Dara,
speaking through your erstwhile servant, Ra Olu*

"Shameless! Shameless!" Emperor Ragin roared as he stomped through the Great Audience Hall. "We must attack immediately."

Mün Çakri and Than Carucono focused on reading the letter and made no reply.

"Kuni, you must consider this carefully," said Risana. "We don't know how to defeat the garinafin riders, and a rash attack will not benefit Timu but cause needless deaths."

"But as times goes on, more and more of our airships will have to be grounded without a new source of lift gas. Waiting will only make us weaker," countered Jia.

"I am most enraged by Ra Olu's betrayal," said Kuni. "How could a man who studied the books of Kon Fiji and worked alongside Zato Ruthi be so utterly without shame? I truly was blind when I made him regent of Dasu and then asked him to assist Timu."

"*Rénga*, I think it's more concerning that you may be blinded by concern for the safety of the prince," said Cogo Yelu.

"What are you talking about?"

"The prime minister is right," said Zomi Kidosu. "It's too late to worry about mistakes made in the past; best we focus on how to make the most of what we have."

Kuni glanced at Zomi suspiciously, not bothering to disguise his distaste for the woman. He had accepted Zomi's resignation without any regret, believing her character to be suspect after she confessed her stolen pass to the Grand Examination—which, in truth, didn't bother Kuni much—and recanted her accusation against Gin Mazoti, which did. The only reason she wasn't punished more was because digging for the truth behind her errors would have created a great scandal for the Imperial family.

"The path you're advocating is rather convenient for yourself, don't you think?" asked Kuni.

Zomi's face flushed, but she refused to back down.

"Even if a knife has injured you in the past, it's still a good knife if you wield it right."

Princess Théra had vouched for Zomi and asked for her to be made into one of her personal advisers. With Dara once again in all-out war, Kuni had decided that it was time to give Théra more responsibility, as scholarly objections to the participation of women in political and military affairs had to be temporarily checked in favor of finding talent wherever talent chose to reside. Théra's role in putting down the rebellion of Tunoa certainly proved that she had some skills in the mechanical arts, and having Zomi, the prized student of the great engineer Luan Zya, assist the princess could be a way to build up a new, untapped base of power for Théra. Thus, Kuni had named Théra a consulting liaison to the engineering academies of Ginpen and Pan, with the charge to research weaponry for Phyro and the generals and to coordinate intelligence analysis with Rin Coda's former department.

"Father," Théra whispered, and pulled on the emperor's sleeves. "Please!"

The emperor sighed and gestured for Zomi to continue.

"Even though Ra Olu has betrayed your trust by acting as an amanuensis for the barbarian king, his desire to please his new master with florid prose may provide us with useful intelligence. In my experience, Ra Olu and Lady Lon are a vain couple who feel the constant need to boast and strut and cannot suffer humiliation—this may explain the ease with which they betrayed you as well as give us an advantage."

"You speak like an Incentivist," said Kuni.

"Incentivism has its uses," said Zomi.

"What useful intelligence have you gathered from this letter then?" asked Risana.

"In an effort to cover the shame of his own betrayal, Olu speaks of Prince Timu as a 'happy guest.' But this tells us at least that Prince Timu is not in immediate danger, so you need not act rashly."

Jia's face, tense until this point, relaxed slightly.

"And his boast of a strategic imbalance between the two sides is confirmed by our own scouting, which tells us that the Lyucu are confident and their morale is high," said Cogo. "A frontal assault is not a good idea."

"But we can't just wait for them to invade! How will we defend against these aerial beasts, who seem invincible?"

"Perhaps Ra Olu's letter has unwittingly given us more clues in that regard as well," said Théra. "We just have to know how to read the letter."

The emperor paced some more and seemed deep in thought. Zomi and Théra shared an encouraging smile with each other.

"It is the next-to-last sentence that is most odd," said a thoughtful Cogo Yelu. "I'm not aware of any Classical Ano allusion to a spearman welcoming the sun."

"Maybe it's a reference to some barbarian legend," scoffed the emperor. "Why should he limit himself to Ano allusions now that he serves a different master?"

"No, that's not it," said Zomi Kidosu.

Everyone turned to gaze at her. Struggling to hold back her excitement and appear calm, Zomi said, "Ra Olu has always had a contempt for the natives of Dasu, but he fancies himself a good regent and makes an effort to study local phrases and references that he finds colorful and exotic. Sometimes he peppers his speech and writing with them in an effort to appear to be close to the people. The Spearman is the name of a summer constellation recognized by the peasants of Dasu, and the only time it can be seen in the east, right before dawn, is early spring."

"So Minister Olu may have inadvertently revealed to us the Lyucu's plan to invade in the spring," Théra said.

"That gives us some time to prepare," said the emperor. The way he looked at Zomi Kidosu was now friendlier, and the young woman nodded back in acknowledgment.

"I think there's even more," Zomi said. As she continued to speak, her demeanor grew more confident. This reminded her of the experience of deciphering obscure Ano logograms with Luan Zya on those carefree nights riding across Dara in the swaying gondola of *Curious Turtle*. "The mention of the city-ships tells us that the garinafins are incapable of long-distance flight. I think this means they're like the long-legged leopards of Écofi, and flight is a matter of enormous exertion that they're capable of only in short spurts. For transportation across the sea, they need ships."

"And the reference to hay is also interesting," said Jia, who was catching on to this method of reading. "It suggests that the garinafins live on grass, not meat." Her eyes suddenly lit up. "They must be cared for in a similar fashion as cattle. The journey across the sea has weakened the creatures significantly, which is why they need to rest over the winter and put on some weight." Since Jia's family had been ranchers in Faça, she knew the habits of ranching quite well.

"But that means the best time to attack is now!" said Kuni. "If we're making the right inferences from Ra Olu's careless disclosures, then the Lyucu will never be as weak as they are now, and we should take advantage of this opportunity to strike."

This seemed reasonable, and Kuni's advisers agreed.

"We need to come up with a plan to counter the garinafins as soon as possible," said Than Carucono.

"I'll prepare the army for an invasion," said Mün Çakri.

"We should be ready to attack in no more than two months, while it's still winter," said Kuni. "Puma Yemu can wrap up his affairs in Arulugi and lead the vanguard."

The fact that he didn't name a commander in chief was not missed by anyone. Everyone thought of the marshal, who refused to emerge from her house arrest.

Mün Çakri and Than Carucono looked at each other, and both were just about to volunteer when Jia spoke up.

"You are Timu's father. The soldiers will be more inspired if you take the lead and act as commander in chief yourself."

Risana, Phyro, and Théra were all about to object, but Kuni stopped them. "The empress is right. Sometimes we all have to fight our own battles. Maybe this is the only way to restore full faith in the throne after recent . . . irregularities."

The panic that had seized all of Dara gradually subsided, now that the Lyucu appeared to be content with only Rui and Dasu, at least for the moment.

The nobles of Dara sent secret detachments to the northern shore of the Big Island to await orders for further deployment, but even after two weeks, there was no announced date for when the emperor's vanguard would leave the Big Island.

Rumors went around the camps that the emperor's generals, at a loss without their marshal, were bickering incessantly and could not come to agreement on a suitable plan.

Four women came to visit Gin Mazoti in her suite.

This was a rare sight. The disgraced marshal seldom had visitors these days, as nobles and military commanders wished to avoid the complications of having to explain their association with a traitor who refused to repent.

Captain Dafiro's eyes widened when he realized who these visitors were, but he kept his silence and simply bowed and stepped aside.

"How may I assist Your Imperial Majesty?" asked Gin. Her tone was respectful, but the tension in the air was as cold as the wintry wind outside the door.

Empress Jia nodded and came into the room; behind her was Consort Risana, and then Princess Théra and Zomi Kidosu.

"The emperor intends to invade Rui," said Jia. "We come to ask for your help." She presented a copy of Ra Olu's letter with both hands. "There is some valuable information in this letter."

But Gin did not accept it. She turned away from the women. "I am no longer the Marshal of Dara. A broken sword has no business to be thinking of warfare. I've been doing nothing but composing poems and sampling the wines Your Imperial Majesty has so generously supplied me with."

"Mün Çakri and Than Carucono cannot come up with a plan to defeat the beasts," said Jia.

"And Phyro has been trying to help, but though he's clever, he is no tactician," said Risana.

"Planning an invasion of this scale is not like plotting the downfall of a recalcitrant and foolish noble," said Gin. "It takes time."

Jia's face flushed, but she kept her voice even. "Timu must be suffering daily as a prisoner. As a mother, surely you must understand how I feel."

Gin did not turn around, but her shoulders softened. "Aya has nothing to do with your political games. It is unfair of you to try to manipulate me that way."

"Is there anything I can say that will not be interpreted as manipulation by you?" asked Jia, heat finally coming into her voice.

Théra broke in, "Auntie Gin, the generals have always relied on your leadership, and it is not their fault that they've been put in this position. Please, I know you've always cared for the lives of those who follow you. Help us for their sake, if not the sake of my family."

Gin turned to look at her. The familiar form of address brought to mind happier times, when mistrust and doubt had not crept between her and Kuni's family. She sighed. "Give me that letter."

While Gin paced back and forth in the room, the other women sat in *géüpa*, watching her intently.

"... so these beasts rely on hay and feed ... and they require rest ..."

The other women looked at each other and smiled, glad to have their own interpretations confirmed by the great marshal.

Gin stopped. "I haven't been entirely idle—old habits die hard. I've been thinking about the beasts' methods of attack as reported in Timu's letter and considering countermeasures, but they are simply too massive, tough, and fast for most of our weapons."

The faces of the women fell.

"This letter does give me some new ideas," Gin added.

Hope flared on everyone's face again.

"The key, for me, is this passage near the beginning: 'each garinafin under the guidance of brave Lyucu warriors.' He seems to be saying that the garinafins require the riders to be effective."

"So they're not quite intelligent enough to attack on their own?" asked Théra. "Is it like the stories of the wars in ancient Écofi, when the Ano were able to defeat the elephant-towers of the natives by aiming for the riders instead of the armored beasts?"

Gin nodded approvingly. "That's one theory that's worth testing, in the absence of anything better."

"It's easier to strike at the pilots than the mount," said Risana. "Just as it's easier to catch the king than all his soldiers."

"In theory," said Gin. "But what is really needed, of course, is better intelligence and understanding of the beasts. Knowing the enemy is more than half the battle."

Everyone nodded. The discussion only highlighted the value of Ra Olu's letter.

"But the mirror situation is also true," said Gin. "Much of the initiative during that initial engagement on Dasu was lost due to the Lyucu's apparent familiarity with our airship tactics and capabilities. They were perfectly prepared for everything our ships could throw at them, so to speak. I do not like to speak poorly of the dead, but I suspect Master Zato Ruthi's belief in Kon Fiji as a guide in military affairs was at least partly responsible."

Théra and Zomi both found themselves nodding at this.

Gin continued, "Now that they think they know everything our airships can do, it also gives us an opportunity to surprise them."

"My mother has an idea along those lines that we wanted your opinion on," said Théra.

"Oh?"

"It is perhaps an idle thought," said Jia. "I have never been very knowledgeable about the ways of war. But Théra said I should at least bring it up and see if you could help make it better."

Gin nodded, gesturing for the empress to continue.

"I grew up as a rancher's daughter," said Jia. "And though my interest was in herbs and medicines, I played the same kind of games that children of ranchers everywhere did and perhaps still do." Her face turned red for some reason, as if what she was about to say was rather embarrassing.

"She had a lot more fun than I did," said Théra. "While I was cooped up in a palace most of my life, my mother ran around in the fields all day and got into plenty of trouble."

Gin looked at Jia, who looked regal even in a plain yellow robe instead of her courtly dress, and had a hard time picturing her as a young girl running wild after herds of cattle and sheep.

"Our laborers gathered the manure of cows, sheep, and pigs into pits and fermented it to produce fertilizer that could be sold to the farmers nearby," said Jia. "Such pits were quite dangerous, as the fermenting manure produced noxious fumes that could be fatal and were very volatile."

Gin nodded. "The use of dried cow and horse dung as a fuel is well known to every soldier."

"But you probably didn't play the same games we did. Some of the more adventurous children and I used to grind up dried dung and place the powder in a sealed jar with water, and let the fumes out through a bamboo tube that could be lit to produce a lamp of sorts. If we let the pressure build up enough, the flame could shoot out quite far, as though the jar were breathing fire. This was quite dangerous, and I knew a boy who was severely injured when one of the jars exploded in his face. The adults forbade us from playing in this manner, and I only brought it up because Théra often begs me to tell her stories about my youth."

"You can fight fire with fire," said Théra excitedly. "Just like I fought the mirror cult of the Hegemon with more mirrors."

Zomi was reminded of the incident from years ago, when she had used fire to chase away fire. Vague plans were forming in her head as images of mechanical components flitted through her mind: pumps, tubes, massive jars . . .

"You have my attention, Lady Jia." Gin went on to inquire into the details of the construction of such jars and asked Jia to draw up detailed plans.

They conversed until late into the evening, and Gin provided many ideas that Théra and Zomi recorded on sheets of paper with tiny letters and simplified diagrams.

"We should head back," said Jia. "Otherwise Kuni will wonder where I am."

"He never used to worry when I visited the marshal late at night in camp," said a smiling Risana. "In a time of war, the rules of peace are suspended."

Gin recalled the times when Risana had come to her to discuss matters of military strategy, long before the seeds of discord. She was reminded again that great ideas could come from anywhere, and hadn't the Hegemon erred also by ignoring her own ideas during the Chrysanthemum-Dandelion War?

"I have enjoyed your visit, Empress. I apologize if I seemed dismissive at first." She was going to say *Had we conversed like this in the past, perhaps we could have become friends*. But she held back. It was too late for that.

Jia bowed to her in *jiri*. Gin responded with a soldier's salute.

CHAPTER FORTY-TWO

INVASION OF RUI

RUI: THE SECOND MONTH IN THE TWELFTH YEAR
OF THE REIGN OF FOUR PLACID SEAS.

To the consternation of many Moralist ministers, the final Imperial edict that authorized the secret battle plans drawn up by Mün Çakri, Than Carucono, and Prince Phyro included a final sentence thanking the contributions of Empress Jia, Consort Risana, Princess Théra, and Special Assistant Zomi Kidosu.

While many in the College of Advocates began drafting petitions criticizing the emperor for permitting his household to participate so heavily in affairs of state, several of the women advocates, including the new *firoa* admitted during the last Grand Examination, celebrated by gathering at the Three-Legged Jug, the place where Zomi Kidosu had first made her name, where they shared drinks and discussed ways to make their own work also more visible.

Puma Yemu, commander of the Dara vanguard, divided the Imperial fleet into small flotillas and ordered them to approach Rui from the south and west in a wide, scattered arc.

"Why is he doing this?" asked Pékyu Tenryo of his gathered thanes in council.

The chieftains offered their opinions.

"Maybe the barbarians of Dara are trying to minimize losses. If they concentrate all their invasion force on one beachhead, a garina-fin strike will incinerate the entire army. This way, they hope to land in scattered pockets along the whole shoreline, and at least some detachments will survive."

"Maybe they are trying to sneak in ships to land spies for sabotage. With so many ships on the sea, it will be hard for us to catch them all."

"Maybe this is a blockade, which I understand is a common tactic among these maritime savages. But we're not dependent on trade like them, so this will bother us no more than dolphins dancing in the sea would bother the tusked tiger sleeping on the steppes."

"Whatever the reason, what can we do about them? Our city-ships are far too cumbersome to be sent after them: It would be like dispatching horrid wolves after gnats."

"We could wait for them to come closer and hit them with the gari-nafins."

"But watching such a long coast day and night with sky-riders will exhaust the mounts after a few days."

As the debate continued, there were many theories but no firm proposal for a response.

"Loyal Thanes of Lyucu," a new voice spoke up. "To know the intent of the prey, we must study its spoors."

The speaker was a young woman about twenty years of age: tall, limber, and powerfully built, with a pale complexion matched by hair so blond that it was practically white. Her name was Vadyu Roatan, though most of the warriors called her "Tanvanaki," which was short for *Tanvanaki-garinafin*, or Flash-of-the-Garinafin, due to her skill as a sky-rider and with the slingshot.

"Daughter, what is your counsel?" asked Pékyu Tenryo. Tanvanaki was his favorite daughter, and the only one of his children to come with him on this expedition.

"I have observed the flags flown from those ships with the aid of barbarian airships." Cries of consternation and outrage erupted from the other thanes. "Why should we not make use of these perverse machines we have captured as long as they are useful? We came here on their ships, did we not? The airships can stay up far longer than my trusty Korva, and those barbarian dirt-diggers can row very fast when sufficiently motivated with the lash. They make excellent scouts."

Pékyu Tenryo waved for the other thanes to quiet down. "Focus on your explanation, daughter."

"After gently persuading a few of the captured barbarian officers"— Tanvanaki smiled at this, and the other thanes chuckled in agreement: The barbarians of Dara could not come close to matching Lyucu warriors in their ability to endure torture—"I found out that the ships approaching our islands belong to one Puma Yemu, a crafty commander known for hit-and-run tactics."

"A coward then!" shouted one of the other thanes.

"It isn't cowardice to fight with guile," said Pékyu Tenryo. The face of the thane who had spoken turned red, and he shut up.

"I suspect that he intends to use the small flotillas to harass and raid our coast in an attempt to exhaust our garinafins and warriors and to grind down our morale in preparation for a full-scale counter-invasion."

Pékyu Tenryo nodded. "Do you have a response?"

"Of course," said Tanvanaki, her eyes flashing. "The best way to deal with a swarm of buzzing flies is to swat them!"

"Then you are in charge of the Lyucu fleet, Tanvanaki-garinafin," said Pékyu Tenryo.

Aboard *Time's Arrow*, Princess Théra and Zomi Kidosu stood around a tray of sand upon which tiny paper models indicated the positions of the Lyucu and Dara ships in the wine-dark sea between Rui and the Big Island.

While Phyro was on the Big Island helping the generals prepare for the rest of the plan, Théra had asked to be given the fast, sleek Imperial messenger ship for scouting purposes.

"I wish we could get even closer," said Théra, "close enough to see Timu. Phyro and I used to tease him a lot when we were younger, but he's a good man. I hope they aren't treating him too poorly."

"Kiji will surely protect him, Princess," Zomi said.

Zomi knew that at least part of the reason Théra had brought them here, so close to the front, was so that both of them could feel closer to their loved ones, trapped on Rui. She was grateful for that—just being physically nearer to her mother made the knives of anxiety twisting in her gut feel slightly better.

"Enough sentiment," said Théra, and she resolutely shook her head. "What do you think of the Lyucu response?"

Zomi pondered the battlefield map as though contemplating a scroll of Ano logograms or reading a complex engineering schematic. "We were counting on the limited range of the garinafins to leave gaps on the coast, give us more landing spots, but this strategy of using the city-ships as floating islands has multiplied their aerial advantage."

The Lyucu fleet, which now consisted of both massive city-ships that had brought the invaders as well as smaller vessels captured from Rui and Dasu, had been reorganized by Tanvanaki into independent flotillas of about a dozen ships each. Each flotilla was centered around a single city-ship that acted as a carrier for two or three garinafins, while the smaller Dara vessels served as escorts. Captured airships surveilled the sea and located Puma Yemu's ships, after which garinafins took off from the city-ships and struck the targets from the sky with deadly fire, and the escort ships then mopped up the wreckage by killing all survivors. Yemu had already lost multiple ships this way.

"I'd say it's more than just an advantage," said Théra. "These carrier battle groups have completely dominated the sea south of Rui. Taken separately, the city-ships and the garinafins are each limited and vulnerable, but they complement each other really well when put together this way. It's as if they've built a new kind of war machine."

Zomi nodded. "It's a clever use of their existing matériel to achieve a new purpose." She really enjoyed working for the princess, who thought in a way that matched her own patterns. They understood each other and made each other's ideas better in a way that reminded her of the carefree days she had spent with Luan Zya in *Curious Turtle*.

"They must also be doing some incredibly cruel things to make the airship crews and captured Imperial sailors serve them," mused Théra. "We have to advise Puma Yemu to pull back."

"But maybe we don't need to order a full retreat," said Zomi.

"What do you mean?"

"General Yemu is known for his skill at evasion," said Zomi. "If he's careful, he could turn this into an opportunity—"

"—to gather some intelligence," finished Théra, eyes flashing.

The two shared a knowing smile and clasped each other by the arms.

Puma Yemu's ships began to retreat from the encroaching carrier battle groups. Wind filled the sails; rowers flexed their muscles; and the sleek hulls cut through the water, scattering in every direction.

Puma Yemu sent out ostentatious kite signals to the Imperial fleet that the captain of any ship found to flee instead of engaging the enemy would be executed. This caused the Imperial ships to behave like jittery water striders: Timidly, they attempted to approach the Lyucu battle groups, but as soon as it appeared that a garinafin was about to launch, they turned around and sped away, sending up kite signals to declare that the enemy had an OVERWHELMING NUMERICAL ADVANTAGE, no doubt an attempt to save the necks of their captains from courts-martial.

Yet they dared not run too far away. When it was clear that the garinafins would not pursue, the ships slowed down, turned around, and began the process of inching back toward the carrier battle group like reluctant children being called home to dinner.

Tanvanaki laughed after the various kite signals used by Puma Yemu's ships had been deciphered for her by captured Imperial sailors.

She ordered the battle groups to give full pursuit, as it was clear that the spirit of the men of Dara had been broken.

As the battle groups moved farther and farther from Rui into open sea, Zomi and Théra tracked their positions carefully on their map. Sometimes Yemu's ships failed to escape in time, and a few more fell to the fiery breath of the garinafin; sometimes the garinafins had to turn back before running out of energy. With so many separate encounters between Puma Yemu's ships and the carrier battle groups, Zomi and Théra were finally able to calculate a precise value for the maximum effective strike range of the flying beasts.

Prince Phyro proposed a plan to use underwater boats to attack the garinafin-carriers. Since they were now so far away from shore, the garinafins would not have enough energy to fly to safety if they lost their floating platform.

"This is not a bad idea," said Théra. "But don't you realize that if you use the mechanical crubens now, you would be revealing their capabilities to the enemy? The art of war requires withholding information from the enemy as long as possible, and not every victory is worth the pursuit. This is similar to the principle of *cüpa*, where sometimes it's better not to capture the enemy's stones in order to secure a better position for yourself."

Phyro agreed with Théra's analysis, but the princess was troubled by the impatience of the young prince. That had always been Phyro's weakness, and it was apparent that even years of acting as the emperor's shadow had not cured him of it.

"Puma Yemu has done his part," declared Princess Théra. "Now it's up to the others to make use of this dearly bought knowledge."

Once again Than Carucono peered through the eyes of the great mechanical cruben at the murky underwater scene.

Schools of bright-colored fish flitted across his field of vision from time to time, and once in a while a shark swept past as well. Nine other mechanical crubens followed his, a pod of giant artificial scaled whales plying the trackless deep.

Puma Yemu's raids to the west were just one part of the plan. The purpose of their harassment was to keep the garinafins from paying attention to the sea to the east of Rui, where a serpentine line of underwater volcanoes dotted the seafloor.

Looking back at the cramped and dim interior of the boat and the sweaty, dirty faces of the skeleton crew, Carucono couldn't help but compare this trip to the last time he had sailed this route from the Big Island to Rui, more than a decade ago. Back then, he had been headed in the reverse direction as the forces of Dasu prepared for a secret invasion of the Big Island, and the underwater boats had been packed with soldiers buoyed by determination and hope. Today, he was also on a secret mission, but this time the boats were filled with many fewer men, and they were far less certain of the success of their mission.

Navigating the mechanical crubens across the sea in a multiday journey was an arduous process. The submarine boats depended on the underwater volcanoes to provide the heated rocks for the steam engines that powered the energetic tail fins. Even with detailed maps of the locations of the underwater volcanoes, the process was crude and full of danger. Minor deviations in route could lead to missing the next volcano, and the boats were simply too massive for the few men aboard to make much headway as rowers. If they missed the volcanoes, they would have no choice but to surface and launch signal kites and wait for rescuers, which would likely also reveal their location to the enemy and doom them.

And so, during the day, the mechanical crubens relied on the murky illumination from the surface to identify underwater landmarks, canyons, and coral formations. At night, the crew had to rely on dead reckoning, and their hearts were at their throats as they gazed through the portholes for the dim glow of distant volcanoes, like stars in the dark abyss. From time to time, they had to guide the boats close to the surface and poke up breathing tubes to refresh the air, made turbid and heavy by their breathing, before they became light-headed and drowsy.

∽ ∾ ∽ ∾

The night was moonless, the sea, calm.

The Lyucu city-ships, anchored amidst smaller vessels captured from the harbor of Kriphi like resting whales surrounded by skittish seals and dolphins.

The peasants of Dara, after another long day of backbreaking labor under the watchful eyes of their own deci-chiefs and Lyucu guards, were finally allowed to rest. The Lyucu thanes and warriors, in turn, had finally fallen into a drunken slumber after another evening of revelry. In their dreams, they imagined riding on well-rested garinafins who swooped over the grand cities of the heart of Dara, where endless treasure and a population terrified into docility awaited their plunder.

A few miles out to the sea, just beyond the maximum effective range of the garinafins calculated by Princess Théra and her assistant, the waves parted to reveal the horn of a breaching cruben. The head and front of the scaled whale erupted straight out of the water, hung suspended in midair for a moment, and crashed back down.

Behind it, nine other crubens followed suit.

By the time the thunderous noise reached the coast, it was barely audible. A few of the patrolling guards on the decks of the city-ships and in the crow's nests of the captured Dara vessels turned to gaze into the dark sea, but the faint starlight made it impossible to see anything. The guards blew into their cupped hands to keep their fingers warm against the chill and pulled the fur hats down lower over their brows as they resumed their watch. The noise didn't particularly worry them. Breaching whales and crubens weren't exactly rare this far north, away from the busy shipping lanes near the core islands.

Puma Yemu's navy was still fleeing like terrified mice before the haughty cats played by the garinafin-carrying city-ships, and patrols by airships of the sea near Kriphi harbor had revealed nothing unusual. Unless the people of Dara had invented ways to make their clumsy, slow airships invisible, this would be yet another uneventful night.

Finally assured that the surfacing crubens had not been detected by the patrolling guards onshore, Than Carucono let out a held breath that glowed white in the faint starlight. The air was biting cold and the water frigid enough to kill a person in minutes. However, in some ways, the most dangerous phase of the mission had only begun.

In the dark, the crews fought against the wind and the swells with short oars until they maneuvered the massive crubens into a large circular formation with their heads pointed toward the center. To provide more stability to the bulky vessels—which were not optimized for surface operations—Than ordered the mechanical crubens' long pectoral fins to be extended from the retracted position used during fast swimming. Then, the crews slowly winched the jaws of the crubens open. The ten boats now resembled a pod of crubens bobbing lazily with impossibly wide yawns.

Piece by piece, the crews brought up their secret cargo from deep within the holds to the jaw-decks. Pontoons made of sheep and cow bladders attached to bamboo poles were dropped into the water surrounded by the crubens and lashed together into a frame, and then thin planks were laid over the frame to form a large floating platform the size of a suspended walking park in airy Müning.

The cruben-men gingerly stepped onto the platform, found it stable, and raised their arms in a gesture of victory.

From the bellies of the crubens, teams of sailors carried up what appeared to be tightly tied bundles of bamboo, each as long as thirty feet and as thick as a tree trunk. After setting their heavy load down in the middle of the platform, the crew cut the ropes tying the bundles together and quickly jumped out of the way as the mass sprung and flexed, like a sleeping cat uncoiling and stretching upon awakening. The bamboo stalks unfolded, extended, stood up, connected to each other . . . it was like watching the unfurling of a piece of fancy paper craft from Amu, where skilled artists folded smooth sheets into flat packets that, upon release, turned into animals, houses, or the likenesses of famous people; or a sped-up version of the germination, growth, and blossoming of some plant as the stem uncurled from underneath the soil and reached into the heavens.

Soon, the bamboo frames of ten small airships stood on the bobbing platform.

Zomi Kidosu, inspired by the thought of the folding hot-air balloons that Luan Zya had shown her during their travels, had sketched out their original, rough design. After Phyro and Théra understood the implications, they had advocated vociferously for Zomi's idea to the generals and the emperor. The ingenious mathematicians and scholars of the academies and laboratories of Pan and Ginpen, both private and Imperial-supported, had worked nonstop to devise ways of compressing and folding the frames of the airships until they could be folded up and stored inside the cramped holds of the mechanical crubens.

Next, the crew retrieved bags of lift gas and attached them to the frames. These had been compressed as much as possible to reduce their volume, and they now resembled bamboo-leaf-wrapped rice dumplings where the strings were tied too tight prior to cooking, and the bags bulged everywhere between their lashings. After ensuring that the frames were securely attached to the floating platform, the ropes around the lift gasbags were loosened, and they strained against the bamboo frames, seeking to return to the sky, their natural element.

More cargo was carried out and loaded onto the airships and tied securely to the frames: massive ceramic jars, flexible hose made from animal intestines, heavy bags of a material that the sailors treated very carefully. The gondolas, also broken down into compact pieces that could be put together like a puzzle, were carried out and assembled.

The relatively small size of the crubens meant that there was no room to store the bolts of lacquer-painted silk that usually wrapped over the frame and made up the surface of the airships—this meant that the bamboo-framed, gasbag-equipped airships now resembled animals whose skin and muscle had been made magically transparent, revealing the skeleton and pulsing and pumping organs within. The absence of the silk skin made the airships slower due to drag and more vulnerable to missiles like arrows and bolts that aimed at the lift bags, but considering the Lyucu did not seem to rely on ranged weapons except slingshots firing stones, the loss wasn't fatal. Moreover, the open bamboo frame meant that the crew was no longer limited to the gondola as a place for staging offensive weaponry. Instead, the crew members could climb all over the bamboo struts like the rigging of a naval ship, and the airships were now capable of dealing with threats coming from every direction.

There was one more advantage provided by stripping the airships down to their skeletons, an advantage Than Carucono counted on for the success of tonight's mission.

The bamboo frames and the silk gasbags had all been painted black, and the specially trained crews, also dressed entirely in black, attached themselves to various perches on the exposed frame. The airships were ghosts made out of the substance of the night, stealthy and unseen.

Pon Naye, leader of this special airship squadron, saluted Than Carucono. "Admiral, the fire-birds are ready."

Pon had been among the first women recruited by Gin Mazoti into the air force. An able commander who had once faced down the legendary Hegemon when he soared over the Liru River on a battle kite, Captain Naye had volunteered to lead this expedition.

Naye took off a cloth sack attached to her waist and tossed it at Than, who caught it easily. "If we don't come back, please bring this back to Pan."

Than hefted the sack. It was very light. "What is it?"

"The last will and testament of every member of my squadron," said Naye.

Than Carucono squeezed the bundle tight against his chest. His eyes felt stung in the sea breeze as he said, "I'll make sure these get delivered to the families if . . . May Lord Kiji and all the gods of Dara protect you."

Naye laughed. "People say that airmen are a superstitious lot, but I've never been particularly pious. I've lived one step away from falling thousands of feet the entire time I've been in a uniform, and

I've never prayed. If the gods of Dara want to fight alongside me, I welcome them. But if they don't, I know I have what I need." She patted the slender barrel of the new weapon strapped to the frame next to her.

"Where do you live?" Than asked on an impulse. "I'll . . . deliver yours personally."

"I didn't leave one," said Naye. "I've never learned to read or write, and talking to the letter writers about what happens after I die just doesn't . . . feel right. Besides, there's no need. I've been an airman for more than fifteen years now, and every copper I've earned has either been pissed away, gambled away, or given away to lovers. I'm as light as my ship."

"Don't you have any family? I'm sure they'd want to know. . . ."

Naye's face grew somber. "My father died fighting for Emperor Mapidéré, and my mother died of starvation. I had a son once, but I don't know him because I didn't want to get married and settle down, so his father raised him somewhere on Dasu."

"On Dasu," Than Carucono repeated mechanically. Suddenly it made sense why Naye had volunteered for this mission.

"I haven't been much of a mother to him," said Naye. "But if the Lyucu have already killed him and his father, then I'm here to avenge them. And if he's still alive, I hope someday he'll hear a story about what happened here today and know that his mother was not an unbrave woman."

"A good name," Than Carucono said. "In the end, it's the only thing we leave behind that matters."

"Something like that, I guess," said Naye. "I'm not much good with words, Admiral."

She whistled to get the attention of the air crews.

"Last check for secure hold. . . . Loosen the bindings around the gasbags. . . . Taking off on my command in ten. . . . Brace! Brace! Brace! . . . three, two, one, liftoff!"

The crew members near the bottom of the frames, where the airships were tied to the floating platform, swung their short swords in synchrony, and the skeletal airships shot into the night, quickly fading against the darkness of the starry heavens. The platform, which had been raised slightly out of the water by the lift of the airships, dropped back into the water with a dull splash.

Gliding through the night like jetting squids, the skeletal airships approached the city-ships silently.

One of the on-watch Lyucu guards strained his eyes against the dark sky, trying to discern the ghostly figure that he thought he had seen.

Was it a flock of birds? A breeze? Didn't the stars appear to be obscured for a moment by some shadow?

Abruptly, a great tongue of flame erupted out of the dark sky.

Extending, unfurling, uncurling like the roiling clouds at sunset or the surf at dawn, by the time the tongue of flames reached the guard and caressed him, it was as thick as the massive columns that held up the roof of the palace in Kriphi and almost fifty feet long; the air crackled around it as the stars wavered in the heat.

The tongue retracted, as suddenly as it had flicked out; a charred corpse stood where the guard had been; and the crow's nest had turned into a flaming pyre.

"Sneak attack! Sneak attack!"

The other guards on the ship and the guards on the other ships cried in alarm, uncertain of the strength and number of enemies involved in the assault. They ran helter-skelter across the decks, searching in every direction. The angle of attack was such that the view of the guards on the other ships had been blocked by the massive sails. It appeared as if firebombs had been lobbed by catapults across the water, but how could a fleet from Dara have arrived without being noticed by the airships or the garinafin-carriers?

Torches were quickly lit and lookouts peered intently into the night. But no ships were visible over the dark sea, and the dock was deserted.

Another flaming tongue shot out, gently licked another ship, and left its main mast in flames.

This time, the lookouts realized that the attack had come from the air. But try as they might, they couldn't see the Imperial airship that must have launched it. With their bright, lacquered silk surfaces, they ought to have been easily visible by the glow from the burning ships, and even if they weren't illuminated by firelight, their massive size meant that they would block out chunks of the starry sky.

It was impossible to hide Imperial airships. Yet, somehow, the airships that attacked them now were nowhere to be seen, like ghosts.

Messengers were dispatched to the city of Kriphi to rouse the slumbering thanes and drunken warriors. They'd need to hurry over with Dara slaves to put out the fires if the ships were to be saved.

Another flaming tongue, another scream, another ship bursting into flames.

Four concerted tongues this time, and one of the city-ships was on fire at both bow and stern.

Finally, one of the lookouts was able to catch the source. As a tongue of flames illuminated the dark space around it, the lookout caught a glimpse of something impossible: A warrior of Dara was standing in the air, completely unsupported, and she was wielding the tongue of flames like a long spear.

The lookout, actually a fifty-chief in the Imperial army who had surrendered to the Lyucu and gained their trust by ruthlessly whipping and pushing the enslaved Rui civilians to work harder, was reminded by the hallucinatory vision of the sight of Fithowéo fighting with a spear of flames.

He shuddered. *Have the gods of Dara finally decided to intervene?*

More scrambling and shouting aboard the ships. Sailors lit bright signal lamps and used curved mirrors to reflect beams of light into the sky, searching, hunting for the phantom Imperial airship.

There it is! The ship was truly spectral. Its thin bamboo skeleton, painted so dark that it seemed to meld into the night, reflected little light. Even the feathered oars that propelled it were dyed black. Clusters of soldiers could be seen lashed to the frame at various stations, wielding the infernal machinery that spewed forth deadly flames.

These *flamethrowers*, as the irrepressible Prince Phyro dubbed them, had been invented by Zomi Kidosu based on the childish pranks of the empress's youth.

Drums full of manure had been left fermenting for weeks to build up the deadly, flammable gas; dried manure had been ground into a powder mixed with solid pellets and packed in jars to serve as ammunition. For deployment, a hose was attached to each drum of gas under pressure and then connected to a thin, straight tube that could be wielded like a spear. One end of the tube was then connected to a bellows and jars of pulverized manure. As soldiers pumped the bellows to drive the manure pellets and powder through the hollow tube, a valve was opened on the drum to release the pressurized manure-gas, and the gas-powder mixture was lit by a ring of pilot fire near the free opening of the tube. All this resulted in a powerful fiery jet that incinerated everything in its path.

Beams of light roamed about, probing the dark sky like the panicked antennae of some insect. Other ghost airships were revealed, hovering about the fleet in the harbor like giant moths that augured ill fortune, and spitting deadly flames at the Lyucu ships.

The few archers onshore—mostly surrendered Dara soldiers—shot arrows at the ghost ships. Most fell harmlessly wide, and the few that came close to the women aboard were deflected by skillfully wielded wicker shields.

The skyline of Kriphi lit up as torches came to life and the Lyucu warriors scrambled to respond. The deep rumbling of giant beating wings could be heard over the commotion on the docks: The garinafins and their riders had been roused.

Bright beams from rotating mirrors near the torches focused on the wraithlike airships to prevent them from disappearing into the night. Having lost the cover of stealth, the airships changed their tactics. The oarsmen set the oars aflame so that the Imperial airships now resembled fiery birds or glowing jellyfish whose natural element was the empyrean sea. The fire-limned oars, like poisoned tentacles, set sails aflame as the airships brushed past them and pushed back the men onshore trying to put out the fires.

A loud, piercing screech, a sound that was at once mournful and prideful, echoed through the night. Naye's heart shuddered as the alien noise probed at the part of her mind whence nightmares came. Her crew and the crews of the other airships stopped shooting flames, and the Lyucu onshore stopped waving their clubs and shooting arrows.

Everyone waited, holding their breath.

The Lyucu warriors onshore exploded into a thunderous cheer as the great shadow of a garinafin swooped up from behind the lights and dove at Naye's airship.

The beast was so much larger than the airship that it was as if one of the Mingén falcons were diving at a grazing calf. And the Imperial airship, whose burning wings had stopped flapping as though the crew had been frightened out of their wits, drifted helplessly like a hot-air balloon as the garinafin approached.

The pilot of the garinafin, a thin, wiry man about forty years of age, allowed a feral grin to spread across his face. He turned back and shouted for the rest of his crew to hang on tight. The garinafin was going to rip this airy bamboo cage into shreds.

Closer and closer the garinafin came; still, the doomed airship did not move.

The pilot of the garinafin whooped in delight.

The garinafin whipped its wings forward to hover in place as it reared back its neck, ready to incinerate the airship.

Naye's airship jerked through the air as though an invisible hand was moving it out of the way. The bellows on the airship weren't just for powering the flamethrowers; through a series of tubes and flared trumpets, they also stored compressed air in containers that could be released through rear-facing openings. Taking a page from the squids that darted through the oceans with jets of water, the engineers of the Imperial Academy had added air jets to the phantom airships as a surprise escape mechanism.

The fiery plume from the garinafin missed most of the airship. Only the very tail section of the airship was set on fire, and a lone, unlucky airman fell from her perch, screaming as she plunged to her death like a burning meteor.

The rest of Naye's crew scrambled to accomplish two goals. Some climbed over the frame to bring hoses connected to tanks of water to suppress the fire before it got out of control; others turned their flame-spears to aim at the garinafin, which was momentarily stunned after its fire-breath attack and defenseless.

Abruptly, the world lit up as though a volcano had just exploded; jets of fire shot out from multiple locations on the airship, all converging on the garinafin.

In regular combat against other garinafins, the riders would be protected under bulky shelters made out of tough garinafin leather, which would hang like saddlebags from the netting draped across the body of the garinafin. But given that the riders had to be roused in the middle of the night and had never encountered any Dara airships that could breathe fire, they had not bothered with the full suit of armor.

As the marshal had hinted at the women who had come to see her, such arrogance gave the people of Dara an advantage.

As the flaming plumes stroked the body of the garinafin, the sizzle of cooking and the stench of roasted flesh filled the air. Some of the terrified riders managed to scramble over the netting to the safety of the other side of the garinafin like spiders scuttling into the shadows as an explorer approached with a torch, but most could not get out of the way in time and fell, howling and burning, into the frigid sea far below.

The pilot had enough presence of mind to give new commands to his mount, and with strenuous beatings of the massive leathery wings, the garinafin backed up and retreated with the wounded riders hanging on to the netting for dear life.

The crew on Naye's ship and the other Imperial airships cheered. The fearsome Lyucu warriors were, after all, not invincible.

CHAPTER FORTY-THREE

A TASTE OF VICTORY

RUI: THE SECOND MONTH IN THE TWELFTH YEAR
OF THE REIGN OF FOUR PLACID SEAS.

As Pon Naye directed her phantom fleet to continue to spread fire
on the Lyucu ships anchored in the bay, a dozen more garinafins
approached the airships but kept their distance. The giant beasts and
their riders alike were confused by these new contraptions shooting
flames in every direction like burning hedgehogs, so different from
the defenseless, slow Imperial airships they had easily dominated in
the past.

Since the flamethrowers wielded by Naye's crews could shoot
fire farther and with more sustained force than the natural fire breath
of the garinafins, there was a decisive shift in the balance of power.
Although garinafin wings and skin were tough, the intense heat generated by the flamethrowers still felt unpleasant to them. As much
as the pilots urged them on, the garinafins hung back and warily
circled at a safe distance from the airships, unsure what to do.

Meanwhile, ships burned and sank below them. Sailors jumped
into the frigid water and attempted to swim to safety. The garinafin

riders watched the living hell that was the port of Kriphi helplessly.

But one of the pilots, a young woman with hair so blond that it was almost pure white, was undaunted. Vadyu Roatan, also known as Tanvanaki, daughter of the pékyu, was the leader of this group of garinafin riders, and her mount, a pure-white beast named Korva, was also the largest and wiliest in the herd.

As Tanvanaki surveyed the situation from her mount, she poked the narrow end of her speaking tube against the large bump situated right before her saddle, under which was one of Korva's vertebrae.

Since the necks of the garinafin were so long, the only practical ways for pilots to communicate with the beasts during flight were to kick at the tough skin at the base of the neck with sharp spurs or to speak through trumpet-shaped tubes made from the hollow ear bones of the garinafin, which allowed voices to be carried into the beasts' heads through vibrations in the spine.

"Girl," Tanvanaki said, "we have to try something new." She stroked the back of her mount's neck while she explained what she wanted into the speaking tube.

Korva nodded to show that she understood. Then she bellowed and moaned, a deep noise that was akin to the song of crubens and whales. After a moment, the other garinafins answered back in their deep, mournful voices, and their pilots crossed their arms overhead to indicate to Tanvanaki that they understood. The winged beasts began to circle around the airships, carefully keeping just out of the range of the flamethrowers. From time to time, one of them darted in and tried to find an opening to breathe fire at the skeletal airships.

"Watch out," shouted Captain Pon Naye through a trumpet made out of a bull's horn that was eerily similar in shape to the one held by the pékyu's daughter—though of course she was speaking through the narrow end to broadcast her voice to her crew and the other airships. "They're herding us!"

Indeed, the garinafins appeared to be working in coordinated fashion. Like a wolf pack circling around a herd of sheep, the garinafins' constant harassment forced the airships to fire repeatedly to defend themselves and to use the air jets to escape from the garinafins' fire breath. But even though they understood the situation, the airship crews had little choice but to drift gradually closer to each other as the garinafins tightened their encirclement.

Finally, the ten airships were backed into a cluster with their tails bumping into each other while the bows pointed out like the rays of a starburst. The oarsmen retracted their feathered wings and stowed them temporarily. In this formation, although the airships were no longer free to strike at the anchored Lyucu ships and the men onshore, the cluster was also perfectly protected against attacks from every direction. Each airship was also protected by the crossfire of flamethrowers on sister ships to either side, giving the garinafins no opening to take advantage of. The circling garinafins and the cluster of airships had reached a stable, if tense, stalemate.

But Naye couldn't help but feel that something was wrong. She reminded herself not to be complacent. The Lyucu had shown themselves again and again to be wily opponents. She surveyed the garinafins circling around at a steady pace, their distinct coloration—stripes, speckles, irregular mottled patches, even pure coats—like the patterns on the revolving lanterns of her childhood.

"Conserve your ammunition," she shouted into the trumpet again. "Don't fire unless you have to. They may be trying to exhaust our supplies." But that didn't make sense. Based on what they had learned about the garinafins in past encounters by Ra Olu and Puma Yemu, the garinafins had less endurance in their fire-breathing ability and would tire out before the airships used up their flamethrowers.

The pattern of garinafins circling around the airships began to repeat: speckled, stripes, pure coat, spotted . . . Idly, Naye counted them. *One, two . . . ten, eleven. Speckled again, now the stripes, the pure coat . . . wait! Eleven?*

She looked about frantically; then she looked below her: the dark ocean, flickering with the light of burning ships. Her heart sank with dread as she looked up, and her suspicion was confirmed.

She picked up her trumpet to shout out a warning, but it was too late.

While the other garinafins surrounded the airships and kept them occupied, Vadyu Roatan had urged Korva to fly away undetected and fade into the night. After achieving sufficient distance from the maelstrom of action, the Lyucu princess had urged her mount to fly straight up, high above the cluster of airships and encircling garinafins.

This was a direction that, she suspected, Imperial airship captains rarely took notice of due to their ingrained habits. As a result of the history of their evolution and the single source of lift gas in Lake Dako, airships were seldom possessed in large numbers by more than one power, and air-to-air combat was extremely rare. Imperial airships were mainly used to reconnoiter and bombard ground- and sea-based targets, and the few air battles that had occurred in history were slow, ponderous affairs that resembled naval engagements where the opposing sides approached each other in the same plane to exchange missiles and arrows and to attempt boarding. Although Dara strategists understood that the side achieving higher altitude would have a decisive advantage in an aerial battle, such theoretical understanding was never put into practice. Airmen never drilled firing their weapons upward because the airships with their hanging gondolas were designed to attack targets below them or at the same level, but not above them—a direction normally blocked by the opaque silk-draped hulls in any event.

Tanvanaki urged Korva into a fast dive, heading straight for the center of the cluster of airships. By the time Pon Naye realized her error and was about to alert the rest of her squadron to turn their attention above them, Korva and her crew were almost atop the airships.

Tanvanaki squeezed her knees against Korva's neck, and Korva reared up in the air, halting her dive with massive swipes from her wings; then she lunged forward with her neck and spewed out a plume of flames at the center of the cluster, where the airships were bumping into each other. At the same time, the riders hanging on to the webbing of the great beast let loose with a hail of stones from their slingshots to suppress the return fire from the flamethrowers. A few of the Dara airmen were struck in the head and slumped noiselessly against their harnesses.

But Korva's tongue of flames stopped just short of the ships' bamboo frames. Though the airmen cringed, terrified, at the roaring fire and the oppressive heat, the plume eventually fizzed out without setting any of the ships afire.

Pon Naye shouted with joy. The skeletal airships' unfamiliar shapes must have made it hard to judge distance accurately, and Tanvanaki had brought her mount to a stop just a moment too early. Now the garinafin would have to take a few moments to recharge, giving the Imperial airships the needed time to prepare a defense.

Airmen scrambled over the open lattice framework to bring their flamethrowers to bear on this new threat from above. Without opaque hulls, the airships should be able to hold foes from this direction at bay as well and create a protective barrier of flamethrowers in every direction.

Naye looked at the activity around her, and abruptly, a terrifying realization came to her. Vadyu had not misjudged the distance. The attack from the garinafin had done exactly what it was meant to do.

"No!—" she screamed, but it was too late.

The panicked airmen at the tails of the airships, their hair singed by the heat from the garinafin's fiery breath, had opened fire with their own flamethrowers without waiting for an order from Pon Naye. The hose man opened the valve to the pressurized manure gas while the bellows operators pumped as if their lives depended on it: From the tails of the ten airships, ten flaming tongues flicked out at the hovering beast like ten frogs aiming for the same fly. Since the flamethrowers had greater range than the garinafins, Korva—or at least her crew—was sure to be severely injured.

But that reaction was precisely what Vadyu had been counting on. The plumes of fire shot upward, but long before reaching their target, they began to curve down, like the arced flight of the dyran falling back into a sunlit sea. Ten flaming tongues struck at ten airships, following graceful parabolic arcs as though they had been aiming at each other.

The flamethrowers were designed to mix the pressurized manure gas with pulverized and pelletized manure, which provided the mass to carry the flames farther than using gas alone. But this also meant that the flames from the flamethrowers were really streams of burning missiles, and missiles were bound by gravity. If the airships attacked upward, the flaming tongues would eventually fall back down to their own level.

The closely packed airships had been tricked into firing upon each other.

Instantly, bamboo frameworks were set aflame, and the screams and howls of the crews, their bodies covered by fire, filled the air. The extent of the fire damage was beyond the ability of water hoses to control; gasbags burst and the ships began to lose altitude.

As panicked crew members untied themselves from their harnesses and tried to escape the burning tails of the airships toward the bows, the airships became unbalanced and began to list and tilt as they lost attitude. Soon, all would plunge into the dark ocean, already littered with the burning wreckage of Lyucu ships.

Naye stared at the hovering figure of the giant, pure-white garinafin and the tiny figure of the pilot on its neck, and her heart was filled with admiration. *This woman is a worthy foe,* she thought. Though the Lyucu princess had never encountered the flame-throwing ghost airships before, she had devised a plan to defeat them within minutes.

Am I to fail? Will my name be forgotten as whispers into the winter wind?

The burning frames started to crack and fall apart; the airships lost altitude more quickly. The other garinafins closed in and spewed more fire, and some attacked with their claws and teeth. More screams and shouts. The airmen at the flame-throwing stations had either abandoned their posts in a futile attempt to find safety or were standing still, their eyes closed and their arms held over their faces defensively. Some of the crew, realizing that all hope was lost, even untied themselves and jumped, plunging into the dark, frosty water below. If they didn't drown or freeze to death quickly, they would be captured by the Lyucu and perhaps meet a fate worse than death.

Naye untied herself from the frame, and picked up her speaking trumpet.

"Soldiers of Dara, we are already dead!

"We knew that before we took off this evening. There is no doubt.

"All that remains to be determined is whether the bards and story-tellers of these islands will recall our names as bywords for glory or cowardice. Will our parents, brothers, sisters, husbands, wives, and children live as free men and women of Dara or enslaved to the barbaric Lyucu?"

The panicking crew stopped, held on to supports, and listened to this speech, even as their ships disintegrated around them and the garinafins continued their assault.

"Follow my example, sisters!" Naye retied her safety harness around the manure-gas drum of a flamethrower, a massive ceramic jar that was taller than her and many times wider. She nodded to her bellows operators. "It's time. Do it."

This was the last surprise in the design of the phantom ships, an option of last resort.

"I cannot demand this of you," Naye had said to her crews and commanders, before they disappeared into the mechanical crubens for this mission across the sea. "And neither can the emperor, no matter what the ministers and priests say about the sweetness of dying for duty. I may not have studied the Ano Classics, but I know that life is sacred.

"I want to give you this choice because sometimes we who follow the ways of Fithowéo must decide between a terrible fate for one and a terrible fate for many others. A soldier does not always have many choices, but I wanted to give you the choice to live up to an image you want others to remember."

The bellows operators hesitated only one second before nodding back.

"It's my duty as captain to go down with the ship," said Naye. "But I'm afraid I won't be able to do it this time."

"We will go down with the ship," said one of the bellows operators, her voice solemn.

"We will see you soon on the other shore of the River-on-Which-Nothing-Floats," said another of the bellows operators.

"Perhaps the Hegemon will welcome us," said Naye, smiling. She waved her hand decisively.

One of the bellows operators unsheathed her short sword and cut the cords tying the drum to the frame of the airship.

A set of bamboo poles had been bent and held in place beneath the drum. Modeled on the design of the catapult that had launched Théca Kimo to safety at his meeting with the emperor, the straightening bamboo poles now launched the drum out of the burning hulk of the airship high into the air. At the top of its flight, just as it was about to begin its fall, a pair of kite wings snapped out of the sides of the drum and turned the fall into a glide. Tied to the drum, Naye manipulated the ropes attached to the wings to aim her flight at one of the garinafins.

The riders on the back of the garinafin, too excited by the sight of the burning, sinking airships, didn't see this new flying assailant. The garinafin did see, but for it, the tiny winged contraption was like a gnat or mosquito, and it paid the machine no mind. It was only after the flying drum had landed on the back of the garinafin, in the midst of the riders attached to the webbing in various harnesses, that shouts of surprise and alarm arose. A few of the Lyucu riders unstrapped themselves from their harnesses and climbed up the webbing with their bone clubs, ready to finish off this impudent escapee from the burning airships.

As soon as the drum landed, Naye took out a pair of grappling hooks and dug them into the webbing on the back of the garinafin, ensuring that the drum and herself would be securely attached to the back of the beast. As the Lyucu warriors approached gingerly on the heaving, unsteady back of the great beast, and the garinafin curled its serpentine neck so that its antlered head peered over its shoulder and loomed above the Dara captain, Naye laughed.

She ripped off the hose attached to the drum and the safety valve, and stabbed the straight fire spear with its burning pilot light at the end into the drum.

For a second, nothing happened, and then, it was as if a small sun had risen over the back of the garinafin. In an instant, the explosion incinerated Naye, the Lyucu warriors, the pilot, and much of the face of the garinafin.

The drums, besides being filled with manure for generating the flammable gas, had also been packed with sharp stones and iron scraps to increase their deadly potential. As powerful as the bombs were, they would do little against the thick hide of the garinafins unless they happened to explode against soft tissue like eyes and tongues, but the bombs were lethal to the riders and pilots, which was their chief aim.

The gigantic beast, blinded, deafened, and pilotless, howled with rage and pain; it then somersaulted in the air and dove for the other garinafins, breathing fire and brandishing its massive talons.

The rest of the garinafins, unprepared for this sudden turn of events, didn't get out of the way of their berserk companion in time. Talons slashed, men and women screamed, tongues of fire lashed out, and it was only when five garinafins coordinated their efforts that they were finally able to bash in the skull of the out-of-control beast. Those sky-shadowing wings flapped once more, stopped, and the body plunged hundreds of feet into the burning hulk of a city-ship below, throwing fiery spars and wreckage everywhere like a volcanic explosion.

On the other airships, other Dara captains had followed the lead of Naye, and more tiny aircraft launched into the night air and headed for the great garinafins. Not all of them landed on their targets. A few of the garinafins caught the drums with their jaws, but a moment later, their heads exploded in similarly bright halos. Others were caught by the garinafins' great claws, and their lower bodies then disappeared in spheres of heat and light. The thunderous explosions, accompanied by the screams of the dying men and women and the crazed howls and moans of injured garinafins, created a fresh hell in the sky.

The pain-crazed beasts, deprived of the guidance of their pilots, lashed out and swerved through the air unpredictably, attacking any-thing and everything that stood in their way, breathing fire in plume after fiery plume. Surviving garinafin riders were flung from their safety harnesses by the jerky maneuvers, and the blind, rampaging garinafins smashed into ships and incinerated sailors in vast numbers. They crashed into one another, heads snapping, jaws biting, talons slashing, tails whipping, mouths breathing fire, until one or the other finally fell from the sky, lifeless, like a fallen god.

In the end, after most of the garinafins had died, three surviving beasts wrestled for a long time in the air. Evenly matched in strength, none of them could gain a decisive advantage, and they clung to each other as their torn wings made it impossible for any one of them to stay aloft alone. The tangle of leather and flesh and wings and claws and jaws and fiery breath formed by the three beasts in midair resembled a dark cloud full of thunderous roars and flashes of fierce lightning.

Tanvanaki had piloted Korva away from the commotion as soon as she realized what was happening. Struggling to hold back tears of rage and terror, she looked over in the direction of Kriphi and saw a set of foxtails flapping at the top of the flagstaff in front of her father's Great Tent, lit by bright torches from below.

Pékyu Tenryo had issued the order to retreat.

She couldn't believe it. *Why? Even if we've lost most of the garinafins around the city, aren't all the airships gone?*

But then, as she looked over at the walls of the city, she understood. An army from Dara had somehow landed onshore, and they were systematically moving through the camp of the Lyucu like a slow wave rolling through detritus on a beach. From time to time, a tongue of flames shot out from their advancing ranks, setting tents aflame and causing Lyucu warriors and the surrendered soldiers of Dasu who had not gotten out in time to die in an inferno. The Imperial army must have been brought here by the same secret means they had used to bring the airships.

Now, with the complete panic caused by the airship assault, no credible ground or naval defense could be mounted. And with the garinafin force at Kriphi destroyed and the last of the garinafins, her own Korva, almost out of fire breath, there really was no choice but to retreat.

Tanvanaki sighed and put her trumpet against the backbone of Korva again. "Exercise mercy, and then let's go."

Korva moaned to show that she understood. She flew at the tangle of fighting garinafins and reared back, shooting the last of her fire breath at them. The beasts, injured and stunned, stopped fighting, and Korva reached out with her claws and gracefully snapped their necks in midair.

Then she turned to the west to follow the retreating ranks of the Lyucu army. Behind her, the hulks of the burning Imperial airships and the dead garinafins fell into the sea, where they joined the sizzling garinafin corpses and the embers of the wreckage of the Lyucu ships.

The first rays of dawn peered over the horizon and lit up this scene of quiet horror.

Than Carucono's landing at Kriphi shocked all the Lyucu thanes. Though the exact details were still unclear, torture of surrendered Dara soldiers suggested that perhaps two waves of underwater boats were involved, one to carry the phantom airships that acted as shock troops and another holding the main invasion force. Pékyu Tenryo was furious that the full capabilities of such weapons had not been revealed in the past, and he had a hundred surrendered Dara soldiers incinerated publicly by garinafin breath, vowing to treat anyone who dared to withhold valuable military information in the same manner.

Timid whispers by the soldiers that no one had imagined that the mechanical crubens would be used in this manner were ignored.

The garinafin-carrying city-ships and their escorts, which were engaging Puma Yemu's troops far out at sea, now became the only effective navy left to the Lyucu. Messenger airships from the Lyucu ordered them to return immediately to the western shore of Rui, which was also where the retreating Lyucu army was headed.

As Pékyu Tenryo marched with his army, the enslaved civilians of Rui were forced to move with him, leaving behind only empty villages and warehouses for the invading Imperial army. Children as young as eight and elders as old as eighty-eight were made to march for miles every day, and any who lingered behind were often executed on the spot with a forceful blow to the skull. Young babies were ripped out of their mothers' arms and tossed to the side of the road and the parents whipped to march on despite their piteous cries.

"Please, please! Mercy!"

But the guards, many of whom were not even Lyucu but surrendered soldiers of Rui and Dasu, were implacable. The former Imperials knew that their fates were now inextricably linked with those of the Lyucu. If the emperor's forces ultimately prevailed, their prospects as collaborators and spies weren't favorable. They had no choice but to display even more zeal in their service for their Lyucu masters.

Ra Olu and Lady Lon were especially notable examples. They worked hard at motivating the reluctant civilian population forced to move with the Lyucu army. As the columns of men and women slowed down with exhaustion and hunger in the cold winter air, Ra Olu spread a rumor that hot meals were being prepared up ahead. Excited by the promise of food, the people picked up their pace, only to find out that the turncoat minister had been lying to make them move faster.

"You will all have plenty to eat once we reach Dasu," Ra Olu said by way of apology, and the refugees only then understood that the plan was for the remaining city-ships to ferry the Lyucu army back across the Gaing Gulf to Dasu, where they'd presumably make a last stand. And the people of Rui would be shipped across as well, like mere cattle to serve their Lyucu masters.

The people cursed Ra Olu and Lady Lon's names. They gritted their teeth and said nothing in front of the guards, but if the chance ever presented itself, they resolved to tear these two into pieces with their bare hands.

෴   ෴   ෴   ෴

While Than Carucono and his troops searched through the liberated Kriphi for Lyucu spies to interrogate to gather intelligence about the enemy, Zomi Kidosu focused on recovering the carcasses of the dead garinafins.

Some of the bodies had landed on burning city-ships, where they were consumed by the fire and sank with the wreckage of the ships. But others had fallen into the sea, where the water extinguished the fires and preserved them. Although the creatures were massive, the bodies seemed surprisingly light and floated on the water.

Zomi picked out two especially well preserved carcasses and asked to requisition some of the mechanical crubens to haul the bodies back to the Big Island.

"Princess Théra directed me to recover garinafin specimens," explained Zomi. "Since we've not been able to capture any alive, especially not juveniles, these are the best we can do. These carcasses represent vital military intelligence and we must get them back to the Big Island as soon as possible."

Carucono assented. He had seen how the princess and Zomi had been able to concoct unusual weapons that allowed surprising battlefield tactics, and if the princess thought dead flying beasts were useful, he wasn't going to argue.

Four mechanical crubens dragged the garinafins back to the Big Island. Long cables were attached to the carcasses and then connected to the mechanical crubens, who dove down to reach the underwater volcanoes for the heated rocks that powered the engines, unwinding the cables behind them like kite strings because the carcasses stayed afloat on the surface. In this manner, the garinafin bodies were slowly "flown" back to the port of Ginpen, where the scholars of old Haan and their colleagues from Pan set about the task of exploring them at the princess's direction.

Than Carucono ordered messengers dispatched to bring the emperor to Kriphi immediately.

"The emperor must be anxious to see Prince Timu. Once he is here with the rest of the army, morale will be so high that we'll sweep the Lyucu into the sea with little effort, just as we did with that rebellion by Théca Kimo."

"I don't agree with this course of action," Zomi Kidosu said.

Everyone in the audience hall of the palace of Kriphi turned to look at her. The place still stank of stale milk and rotting food from the Lyucu occupation.

Zomi swallowed. "Something isn't right here. Though Admiral Carucono's invasion went according to plan and Captain Naye's sacrifice was effective, the Lyucu still have close to fifty garinafins. Even with our flamethrowers, the most we dared to hope for was to establish a dug-in position near Kriphi and hold it until more reinforcements arrived. But the Lyucu have continued to retreat to the west, and the garinafins are nowhere to be found."

"Perhaps the garinafins refuse to fight after witnessing what happened to their peers at the Battle of Kriphi Harbor," said Carucono. "Or perhaps morale among the Lyucu is so low that Pékyu Tenryo cannot rally his men to fight. That is why the Lyucu are planning to retreat to Dasu."

Zomi shook her head. "We only know that because a few escaped refugees tell us that Ra Olu suggested this was the plan, but I'm beginning to doubt the Lyucu trust him enough to reveal to him their true plans."

Carucono was about to reply when the meeting was interrupted by a commotion at the entrance to the audience hall. People were shouting, demanding to see Admiral Carucono.

"What is going on there?" demanded Carucono.

"They claim that two of the prisoners insist on seeing you," said one of the guards. "They say this cannot wait."

"Men of Lyucu?" asked Carucono, a bit surprised. So far, interrogating the Lyucu prisoners—most of them the wounded who had been left behind during Pékyu Tenryo's retreat—had been fruitless. The barbarian warriors either didn't know the speech of Dara or refused to say anything beyond demanding to die.

Carucono gestured for the guards to let the small group of soldiers and the prisoners in.

Soldiers entered carrying two stretchers. In one of them was a gaunt, bandaged figure who lay very still; in the other was an old man who struggled to sit up as they came in.

"We thought so at first," responded one of the soldiers escorting the prisoners. "We found the two of them in the sea, almost drowned. Both of them had been chained in the hold of one of the city-ships, but the destruction of the ship had freed them by breaking the bulkhead to which their chains were attached. Though they were dressed in Lyucu clothing, we realized they were in fact men of Dara."

Carucono approached the stretchers to examine the prisoners. Both of them had long white hair that was tangled and dirty, matched by bushy and tangled white beards. Their frail bodies were covered in the same kind of hides that the Lyucu wore, patchy and full of holes. Through the holes one should see the scars, lesions, and pus-oozing boils that indicated many hours spent shackled in bug-infested cells.

The old man who was struggling to sit up had a hunched back and the pale skin and gray eyes of a native of the Xana homeland, while his companion's face was the familiar dark shade of Lutho Beach.

As Carucono examined the dark-complexioned man's face, he gasped. The man's eyes were empty sockets covered by wrinkled flaps of skin, and though his lips quivered and moved, no sound emerged. But despite the hideous mutilation, Carucono knew the face well.

"Luan Zya!" he cried out.

"Teacher!" Zomi ran up and knelt down next to the stretcher, holding one of the man's gnarled hands in both of hers. The stick-thin fingers squeezed her hand back, hard.

Still, Luan Zya did not speak.

"Why won't you talk to me, Teacher?" Zomi asked, hot tears falling from her face.

"They burned his eyes and cut out his tongue," croaked the old man in the other stretcher.

Most of those present had never seen the legendary prime strategist of Dara. They now stared at this wasted figure on the verge of death, disbelief in their eyes.

Zomi noticed that Luan's other hand was gripping a sack made from a cow's bladder. She tried to free it from his hand, but Luan's fingers held on like talons. She looked questioningly at one of the soldiers carrying the stretcher.

"We found it drifting with him in the sea," said the soldier. "He wouldn't let go of it even after we pulled him into the boat."

"Teacher, you're safe now," said Zomi. And slowly, gently, she pried the fingers loose and opened the waterproof sack. She paused. The contents were very familiar to her, though she hadn't seen the book in years.

"That bag holds something more precious than life for Master Zya," the old man said, his voice wheezing. "A book of knowledge."

"And who are you?" asked Than Carucono.

"Oga Kidosu," said the old man, "a fisherman of Dasu."

Zomi whipped her head around to stare at him. Though the man's voice was barely above a hoarse whisper, it reverberated in her head like thunder.

Father.

CHAPTER FORTY-FOUR

THE VOYAGE OF LUAN ZYA

SOMEWHERE NORTH OF DASU:

THREE YEARS EARLIER.

The tiny flotilla made up of *Lutho's Luck*, *Proud Kunikin*, and *Stone Turtle* had been heading north for weeks, having left the last of the pirate isles behind them days earlier. Around them was the endless ocean sparkling in the noonday sun, and schools of dyrans leapt out of the water from time to time, gliding over the waves in graceful arcs.

Eight men aboard *Lutho's Luck*, stripped to the waist and covered in sweat, leaned against the horizontal spokes radiating from a central drum to take a break. At the moment, the drum was prevented from spinning by wedges driven into slots in the side. Attached to it was a cable made up of many twisted strands of silk whose other end shot into the sky and disappeared into the distance. Though the cable hung between the sky and the ship in a gentle curve familiar to all kite fliers, it was clearly under great tension.

A person knowledgeable about the sailing arts would have noticed something else odd about *Lutho's Luck*: Although there was a light wind coming from the north, instead of tacking against it with sails fully trimmed, the ship was headed directly into the wind with its sails fully extended perpendicular to the ship's hull. In other words, the sails were acting as air brakes and slowing the ship down as much as possible. As the ship heaved in the choppy sea, sailors scrambled over the deck and rigging, struggling to keep the sails trimmed for this unusual purpose.

In addition, the oarsmen were also hard at work, bracing themselves against the oars to slow the ship down even further. Even so, *Lutho's Luck* was plowing ahead through the ocean at a fast clip. Behind it, *Proud Kunikin* and *Stone Turtle* tacked zigzag courses and sailed as close to the wind as possible, struggling to keep up. As *Lutho's Luck* hesitated at the apex of each swell before dipping down into the trough, it almost seemed about to be lifted out of the sea by whatever was attached at the distant end of the cable.

Captain Thumo of *Lutho's Luck* paced the deck anxiously, glancing from time to time at the hourglass next to the large drum. The hourglass had been flipped over four times, indicating the passage of four full hours. He was getting concerned about the fate of the life at the other end of the line.

He stopped at the end of another full walk across the deck, turned abruptly, and was about to give the order to terminate the experiment when everyone stopped at a piercing, shrill noise coming out of the sky.

Fweeeeet!

A metal hoop descended from the sky along the cable, whistling loudly as the breeze passed through its specially shaped rim. Finally, with a sharp clink, it stopped against the drum.

The eight men at the giant winch at the center of the deck of *Lutho's Luck* jumped into action. As soon as they braced themselves against the spokes of the hub, another sailor brought out a large mallet and knocked free the wedges keeping the drum in place. For a few seconds, the feet of the eight men slid against the deck as the cable strained against the drum and spun it almost a quarter turn, but the men soon found their footing and stopped the drum dead in its tracks. As the muscles along their thighs and arms bulged and flexed, they pushed hard against the spokes, and, slowly but surely, began to spin the drum the other way and to winch the cable in.

As they worked, they chanted:

> Taki had two chests and no gold;
> He went into Tazu's wet hold.
> "Give me a large share of treasure,
> Lest I piss and wreck your pleasure."

> Heave-heave, push! Heave-heave, push!

> Tazu got ready to call for a storm,
> But Nogé gave him a slimy worm.
> The pirate and cook escap'd the wrath
> Of the god who follow'd no fixed path.

> Heave-heave, push! Heave-heave, push!

> The frothy whale's way has no end;
> Each stranger is also a friend.

A tiny black spot appeared at the far end of the cable. It grew as the men continued to sing their sea shanty and winched the tethered contraption down until it resolved into the figure of a kite, but one that was unlike any that had heretofore been constructed in Dara.

Diamond in shape, the kite measured eighty feet from corner to corner. The frame, constructed from the stoutest bamboo cut from the slopes of Mount Rapa and Mount Kana, supported three layers of wings made of lacquered silk. The rigging system was as complicated as any oceangoing ship's, and the main cable itself was a thick bundle of silk that cost the lives of millions of silkworms. The triple-decked wings provided enormous lift, allowing the kite to fly higher than any conventional battle kite or airship.

As the men continued to winch the kite down, it soon became

apparent that the kite was almost as big as the ship itself. A tiny gondola dangled beneath the enormous triple-wings like a silkworm moth cocoon; such an enormous craft was apparently capable of supporting only a single passenger.

Since the kite-sail was no longer above the cloud cover, where it caught the powerful winds that blew only at that altitude, *Lutho's Luck* slowed down, and the sailors and oarsmen finally got back the control of their vessel. *Stone Turtle* and *Proud Kunikin* tacked ahead to provide assistance as the kite lost more altitude, eventually splashing down gently in the sea.

A small pinnace was lowered into the water, and the recovery crew rowed over next to the bobbing hulk of the kite. With sharp knives, they cut the gondola free from the kite and heaved it into the boat. Made from hard jujube wood that was then sealed with layers of wax and silk, the cocoonlike gondola was airtight. The anxious crew on the pinnace peered into the glass porthole at one end of the cocoon.

Dimly, they glimpsed the face of Luan Zya, whose eyes were tightly shut, either in deep slumber or already dead.

"Master Zya," said Captain Thumo, "you should have given the signal to return much earlier!"

Luan Zya, recuperating in his hammock, smiled weakly. His hands and feet, frostbitten, were wrapped in bandages. The effects of the loss of consciousness induced by lack of air were still visible in his sluggish movements.

"Well, the view was so incredible that I kind of didn't want to return. The pristine ocean stretched endlessly beneath me like a blue mirror, only marred here and there by atolls like dust motes. Even the horizon itself appeared curved, providing further confirmation for Na Moji's theory that we live upon a vast globe. And the color of the empyrean! It was a hazy purple through which you could see the twinkling of the stars . . . I imagine that is what the gods and the immortals see."

Although the cocoon, designed by Luan Zya himself based on the knowledge gathered from several earlier attempts to conquer heights far above that reachable by airships and balloons, had been wrapped in layers of insulation against the frost at such altitudes and had also been equipped with an external balloon to hold extra air for breathing, he had pushed the craft beyond what it was designed to do by ascending higher than he—or any person in recorded history—had ever done.

"Had you waited even a minute longer, you might never have returned! You may wish to see what the immortals see, Master Zya, but you're still trapped in a mortal body!"

"We are explorers, Captain Thumo. It's no shame to die while experiencing heights and depths beyond the known limits of human endurance. Before leaving on this journey, I made my peace with the possibility that I would not return."

"You may be content to die, Master Zya, but not all of us can be so carefree. Sailing with that kite was like walking Fithowéo's *pawi* on a leash—it was unclear whether we were flying the kite or the kite was flying us, so powerful was its pull. Several times I almost made the decision to winch you down despite your strict orders to the contrary. Who knew that the winds above the clouds would be so powerful?"

"Indeed." Luan Zya nodded. "I was already thinking about that! It might be possible to construct ships that rely on kites as sails to move far faster than conventional ships—though there would have to be new ways to build hulls to survive the sustained force and overcome the drag of the water . . . maybe a way to skim above the waves so that the ships are almost skipping—"

"I will *not* sail on such a boat," said Captain Thumo firmly. "I like my ships solidly in the water, thank you kindly."

Luan Zya laughed. "It's just a thought. Well, as much as you disapprove of my lust for extremes, my flight did result in valuable information. I believe I have found the cause of failure by all other explorers to the far north."

"Oh?"

"Riding on a kite like this allows you to see quite far. During the early days of this expedition, remember how I spoke to you of the way the Islands appeared as mere indistinct tan patches set against a blue background from such heights? Mountains, valleys, waves, the spouts of whales and crubens—none of these details were visible. All that was left were large patterns, trends that could not be seen from up close.

"When I lived among the people of Tan Adü, I learned that the ocean was not a featureless expanse, but a tapestry woven with intricate patterns visible only to those whose hearts were still and whose minds had been primed for generations to appreciate its rhythms. The Adüans had detailed maps of the currents that flowed across the ocean, both on the surface and below it, like gilt strands in plain cloth. The currents reflected the forces of nature, of underwater valleys and volcanoes, of winds and rivers, of austral typhoons and boreal storms—their sacred shell-and-twine maps formed the foundation of the detailed maps of underwater volcano ranges that I eventually created.

"What I saw from my cocoon in the sky today reminded me of those maps. The ocean in the north was a pale blue canvas upon which were inscribed a masterpiece of complex patterns: long, flowing arcs like the tentacles of the octopus; intricate curlicues like the swirl of the nautilus; bold, thick strokes of starburst passion that demonstrated the brush painter's skill and soul. The canvas was tinctured in deep aquamarine and pastel periwinkle, purplish black and salt-pale white—it was a painting the likes of which I had never seen, an abstract seascape drawn by the gods.

"And far in the north, almost at the edge of my vision, was a wall of white. It was like seeing the spray and foam at the top of a line of waves headed for the shore, but at that scale, the spray must have been as high as mountains. Entranced, I stared at that distant wall, and it eventually resolved into individual whorls—dancing, circling, jostling against each other, it was a dance of typhoons, a parade of hurricanes, a celebration of cyclones. And, as the wall was at the limit of my vision, I could not see beyond it."

"What does that mean?" asked Captain Thumo. "A wall of storms?

Were you perhaps seeing the ramparts of the Palace of Tazu?"

Luan Zya shook his head and smiled weakly. "I do not know, Thumo, but I suspect that previous expeditions were . . . stopped by that wall."

The captain drew in a sharp intake of breath. "What you really meant to say is that without the benefit of your far sight, those expeditions would have come upon the looming wall of storms with little warning, and the ships would have been torn to shreds. We must stop sailing any farther. This is the edge of the world, beyond which we are not meant to go."

"No!" Luan Zya's eyes had taken on a fervent ardor that had been absent from them for years. It was the same look as when he had plotted for the fall of the Xana Empire, for the death of Mapidéré, a look of madness and passion that frightened and also compelled Captain Thumo. "We are to sail into and *through* it. I *must* find out what is beyond!"

"But that means certain death!"

"Do you not desire to push beyond your fears to see just how far you can go?" Luan Zya's voice was gentle but tinged with a trace of disappointment.

Captain Thumo shook his head. "I'll not demand the crew to undertake such a mission, not even for you, Master Zya. Sailors understand that death dealt by the unpredictable hand of the sea is a part of our profession, but now that we know the nature of danger, to court it deliberately is folly."

Luan Zya closed his eyes and nodded. "All right, but let's at least sail closer so we can confirm my guess. If you wish to return once we've glimpsed the wall of storms, I won't object."

The sails fluttered in the light breeze. Above them, a bright sun gleamed.

Every pair of eyes on the three ships was focused straight ahead; no one said a word.

From west to east, a towering wall of water and roiling clouds blocked the horizon. Made up of powerful cyclones and sinuous twisters dancing, jostling, battling each other like spinning sword dancers, the wall was the very image of primordial chaos devoid of light save for spider cracks of lightning flashing from time to time through the murk. The unceasing rumbling of thunder made the ocean quake, shaking the very deck on which they stood.

"We are gazing upon the very face of Kiji, bringer of lightning, and Tazu, master of typhoons," said Captain Thumo. He placed his hands piously on his chest and prayed.

"Only in the ancient sagas of the Ano did I read of such a thing," said Luan Zya, his voice full of awe. "And I had always dismissed the tale of the journey though the Wall of Storms as an allegorical myth. No matter how much we think we know or have seen, the world is still full of wonders undreamed of by mankind."

All stared at the incredible display of the raw power of nature in dread silence.

Eventually, Thumo broke the silence. "This is as far as I will go, Master Zya. You've seen what you came to see. This is a barrier placed by the gods, beyond which none may pass."

Luan Zya nodded. "Let me go up in my kite. It would be a shame to come so close to the faces of the gods without a kiss."

"You are mad!"

"I might be. But let me have this pleasure."

"The kite may pull *Lutho's Luck* into the storms."

"The wind here is still manageable. If you sail south some distance before launching the kite, you should have plenty of room to maneuver in safety. Should you feel you're unable to overcome the kite's pull, you may cut the cable before endangering the ship."

"But what about you?"

"Just as you cannot ask the crew to undertake a journey that you believe will mean certain death, I cannot return from this marvel without having tried to investigate it."

And so the kite was sent aloft with the dangling cocoon after the ships had sailed some miles south. Soon, the kite was so high in the sky that it disappeared from view. The cable extended up and to the north, bringing Luan Zya closer and closer to the wall of storms.

The force pulling on the cable grew stronger. *Lutho's Luck*'s southern progress slowed, and then gradually stopped. It began to drift back to the north. Once again, the wall of roiling water and clouds loomed before the flotilla.

The cable shuddered and the winch groaned; the kite had been caught in the storm. Sailors aboard all the ships watched the vibrating line with equal measures of fascination and terror.

There was still no ring that came whistling down the cable, indicating Luan Zya's wish to return.

Captain Thumo was a dutiful man. Though he gritted his teeth and glanced at the taut cable and the distant flashes of lightning with dread, he gave an order that was passed to *Stone Turtle* and *Proud Kunikin* with flag signals.

The other two ships sailed closer and grappling hooks were tossed across the decks. Soon, the three ships were lashed together in a column, and the oarsmen aboard all three ships leaned into their labor with all their strength.

Like three fish hooked on a single line, the vessels strained against the pull of the kite, trying to hold their position.

Fweeeeet!

The shrill whistle sounded like celestial music to Captain Thumo's ears. The ring swooped down the line from the slate-gray sky and struck the central drum of the winch with a loud clang. He was about to give the order to start winching the kite back down when the deck lurched beneath his feet and surprised shouting erupted on all three ships.

Captain Thumo looked up and saw that the cable, which had been taut until then, had slackened and was drifting down from the sky. The sudden disappearance of the force that the three ships had been straining against had caused the vessels to career forward, out of control, with prow bumping into stern, and oars becoming snarled. Thankfully, the damage was slight, and it didn't take long before the sailors disentangled the ships from each other. Thumo rushed over to the now-useless drum and picked up the signaling ring. There was a fluttering silk ribbon attached to it.

I can't come so far without taking a final step. Be safe.

Captain Thumo cursed. He stared at the wall of storms, where each gyrating column of water and air was as tall as a mountain and as thick as a city.

Nothing could survive that.

Thumo closed his eyes in mourning. Though he did not know his famous patron well, he had come to respect and love the gentle old man during this brief voyage. There was a quality of grace to his every word, his every motion, that marked him as a man who did not belong merely to the mortal plane, but was in communion with the divine. He dared to do what none other dared, and even the manner of his death brought him closer to the gods.

With a desolate heart, the captain shook his head and gave the order to trim the sails for the voyage home.

But there was no cheer of joy from the sailors; instead, moans of terror and incoherent screams greeted the captain's ears.

"What's the matter?" Thumo shouted. "Master Luan Zya has released us from his mission. We are headed home!"

The sailors pointed behind him, their eyes mirrors of fright and dismay.

Thumo turned to look in the direction they were pointing in and froze.

One of the cyclones in the wall of storms had separated from the rest like a dancer moving away from the pack. Dwarfing even the Tazu whirlpool if the maelstrom were lifted into the air, it headed straight for the ship, a sinuous, gyrating, predatory monster that intended to devour all in its path.

A wall of water as high as the tallest tower in the palace in Pan rose before the cyclone and rushed at the boat like baying hounds before a hunter, a great wave that made tsunamis appear as mere ripples in a pond.

Thumo shouted for his crew to man the sails and the oars, but he already knew that they were doomed.

Luan Zya braced himself against the walls of the cocoon. Cutting himself loose had not been an impulsive decision, but one that he had planned ever since Captain Thumo had stated that he was unwilling to risk the lives of his crew for the unknown. In a way, Luan had been relieved by the refusal—he didn't want to be responsible for the deaths of others in the pursuit of a goal whose attainment he desired with every fiber of his being but for which he could offer no rational explanation.

That is perhaps also why I have not wanted any post of authority under Kuni, he thought. *And why I sought to flee the capital when the emperor asked me to help him continue a revolution with his unexpected, secret choice of an heir.*

He had always played the role of adviser, someone whose legacy was tied to the decisions made by others. He would strategize and scheme, but when the moment came to order men to die for his visions, he lacked the necessary conviction of purpose and the willingness to accept the consequences of his decisions.

Better to soar through the sky on a kite, alone. That had always been the role he was more comfortable with. Whatever he decided, the only life he was responsible for was his own.

He peered through the thick glass portholes and gripped the handholds tightly. He was surrounded by magnificent, roiling clouds that formed the spinning walls of the typhoons, each the size of an island, one merging into the next. The howl of the winds and the roar of thunder filled the interior of the cocoon as though he were inside a set of drums being played by the gods.

Ropes connected to pulleys and rigging fed into the cocoon, and by pulling on them he could change the angle and tension in the wings of the kite and direct its flight to some degree. As streaks of water collected over the portholes and blurred his vision, he experienced the illusion that he wasn't in the sky, but undersea, and the cocoon was a one-man submersible diving through a strange, fantastic ocean.

As he glided into the clouds lit up by flashing lightning bolts, he felt an exhilaration that he had last experienced on that long-ago day when he had dived from the Er-Mé Mountains toward the procession of the tyrant Mapidéré, certain that he was going to die but also certain that he was going to spend the last moments of his life in incandescence.

He would be the first man to fly through a typhoon laced with lightning, the first man to try to pierce the Wall of Storms that blocked the path to the legendary land of the immortals to the north.

Laughing, ululating wildly as though he was again that young man driven by passion and purpose, he pulled hard on the wings of the kite and dove into the heart of the stormy wall.

Then the rumbling of thunder shook the entire cocoon and made his teeth clatter; there was a bright flash that seemed to blot out the entire world; his skin tingled as though it had a separate life; and the last thought he had was: *So being struck by lightning feels a bit like being lit on fire.*

He woke up. He did not know where he was: in the land of the living or on the farther shore of the River-on-Which-Nothing-Floats.

He could feel the bruises all over himself, but no bones seemed to have been broken. The pain was like a dull knife that poked at the cobwebs in his mind.

I'm not dead.

He felt himself being gently lifted up and then set down, as though the storm clouds had acquired mass and become thick and sluggish.

The thunderous rumbling continued outside. A dark blue light filled the interior of the cocoon.

Am I still flying?

A bright orange shape with black stripes glided across the porthole above him. He marveled at how slow this bird flew—as slow as his thoughts.

What a marvelous bird to fly through such a storm! Is this its native habitat?

He was feeling very light-headed.

The last time he had felt like this was when he had run out of air after the kite ascended to previously unattained heights. He had put the feeling down to fatigue, to simple exhaustion, but now he understood that it was a sign that the cocoon was running out of breathable air.

He hadn't equipped the cocoon with an air balloon this time because he wasn't flying for height. Why was he running out of air?

A yellow shape with blue stripes glided across the porthole.

Another bird?

No, the wings are too small.

It's swimming, not flying.

A fish.

Water. I'm under water.

The thoughts wriggled into his mind with great difficulty, struggling against the dizziness and confusion that filled his brain like the thick mud at the bottom of lotus ponds.

I must get out.

His frantic fingers finally found the latch to the cocoon's door, squeezed around the handle, and pulled.

The shock of the water flooding in caused him to gasp before he remembered to hold his breath. The cocoon, which was designed to float, had been pushed under the surface by the weight of the wreckage of the kite. He kicked away from it, struggling to find the surface. All around him, stiffened silk pressed down on him. He had to swim away from the cocoon and get around the wings to reach the surface, the air.

His lungs were on fire, and his arms and legs felt weak and heavy. He was too far away from the edge of the kite. He was never going to make it.

He stopped struggling. The heavy robe, worn for warmth, had taken on water and was dragging him down toward the bottom of the ocean.

It would have been nice to see new lands before I die, but every journey has an end.

We come from the Flow, and to the Flow we shall return.

He was about to close his eyes and open his mouth to gulp down the cold water that would end his life when something stirred next to his heart like a struggling animal. Curious, with the last glimmer of consciousness, he released the unknown object from the folds of his robe.

A book emerged. Its pages fluttering like the wings of a bird in slow motion, like the undulating skirt-fin of a cuttlefish, the book swam for the surface, leaving trails of dissolving ink behind it. In the murky underwater light, the pale pages seemed to glow with golden letters.

It was *Gitré Üthu*, the magic book that had been given him by Lutho, the god who had changed and saved his life more than once.

Luan Zya reached for the book and grabbed onto its spine with the last of his strength; he felt himself being dragged toward the surface.

With a loud splash, he broke through the water. He clung to the frame of the floating kite and gulped air hungrily, much as decades ago he had emerged onto the shores of Tan Adü from his wrecked raft. In the distance, he could see the Wall of Storms, whose constituent typhoons and cyclones still connected the sky with the sea.

But the part of the sea he was in was perfectly calm. The frame of the downed kite creaked as the gentle swells lifted it and set it back down, as though rocking a baby to sleep. He was bathed in bright sunlight, and a warm breeze caressed his face.

A rainbow appeared in the eastern sky, the right end disappearing into the gyrating storms. Realization slowly dawned on him that the Wall of Storms was to his south.

He had somehow traversed it in his kite.

Shivering with pangs of joy, relief, and terror, he heaved the soaked *Gitré Üthu* out of the water onto the rolling surface of the kite to dry. All the notes he had taken in it over the years had been washed away by the water, and the blank pages seemed both a cleansing of the past, with its intrigues and betrayals, and a promise of the future, terra incognita.

A golden line of text appeared on the still-wet page: *You are on your own.*

And a moment later, another line: *That's a good thing.*

"Thank you, Teacher," croaked Luan Zya. And then he laughed.

Luan Zya drifted over the endless ocean on his makeshift raft, fabricated out of salvaged parts from the giant kite. He lashed the bamboo poles in the frame together to provide a base and then built a tent over it with pieces of silk to shelter himself from the sun and the rain. He fashioned a crude sail and mast out of more bamboo and silk, but the strong current that gripped the raft meant that he had only very limited control over the path of his craft. The cocoon, still attached to the kite, drifted alongside the raft like a buoy.

Day after day, the current, like a mighty river, ran west toward the setting sun. To his left was the Wall of Storms, a constant companion on the horizon. To his right was the open ocean, and he wondered what lands lay beneath the horizon, lands that might be inhabited by immortals or other beings who created the exotic artifacts that he had seen. Schools of dyran, trailing their rainbow-sheened tails, glided just above the water, while crubens and whales breached and spouted in the distance from time to time. He whispered his prayers to the scaled sovereigns of the sea in the tongues of Dara and of Tan Adü, whose inhabitants seemed to have a special relationship with the creatures. When he was hungry, he fished with string torn from his robe and a hook made out of the bronze clip for his hair bun. When he was thirsty, he drank the rainwater collected on top of his tent—and it rained nearly every day.

He wondered if he might soon reach the location of the sunken continent that was the fabled homeland of the Ano. Would he see the tops of mountains peeking out of the waves, the last atolls of a once-great civilization? Would he pass, unknown, over the great cities of myth and legend like an airship whose view was obscured by thick clouds?

From time to time, the typhoons and cyclones that made up the Wall of Storms would part and reveal a narrow opening, like a channel between two landmasses. These calm valleys between storm-mountains sometimes lasted for hours or even days before the Wall closed up again.

Luan speculated that if one could discern the pattern in their movements, it might be possible to sail through the Wall safely. Once in a while, one of the cyclones left its place in the Wall and wandered erratically over the open sea, causing Luan's heart to leap into his throat with concern that it might be headed for his raft. Luckily, the gyrating twisters seemed to always steer clear of his course, but he wondered if other travelers who had come this way had been as fortunate. After all, he knew of no man who had seen the Wall and returned to Dara to tell of it save for a few cryptic references in ancient sagas. Perhaps the Wall had its own ideas about who it would let through and who it would allow to depart its vicinity unmolested.

Lacking other ways of occupying his time, Luan Zya began to write in his book. One of the fish he caught, a young marlin, had just eaten a meal of squid. After gutting the marlin, he took out the half-digested squids and squeezed out the dark liquid in sacs between the gills to use as ink. For a pen, he used the snout of the marlin. He recorded the new fishes he caught and sketched the movements of the components of the Wall; he composed poetry and spoke to *Gitré Üthu* of his thoughts like an intimate friend.

No more glowing letters appeared in *Gitré Üthu* after that first day. Luan was used to such unexplained long absences from his immortal benefactor, and he did not cry out for divine intervention—a teacher could not always watch over his students, after all.

But there was a deeper fear that he did not even want to admit to himself. What if the gods of Dara were limited to Dara and had no influence beyond the Wall of Storms?

He focused on mapping the Wall of Storms, doing his best to judge distance and direction by the shape of shadows and dead reckoning. Sometimes the pages he wrote on still held faint traces of his old notes, and he smiled as he remembered what a different man he had been when he had written those notes, when overthrowing Mapidéré had appeared as a task more important than any other in the world.

Killing the emperor was easy. Building a world that is more just and persuading those in power to exercise it wisely have been far harder.

After a few weeks, the Wall of Storms curved away to the south, but the current Luan Zya was riding on continued west. It appeared that the Wall formed a barrier all around the Islands, perhaps another consequence of Daraméa's tears, which had formed the Islands of Dara. Luan knelt down on the raft and bowed to the Wall. Though it was violent, unpredictable, a force of nature that could not be comprehended, it had come to symbolize for Luan a final connection to home. Unbidden tears flowed down his face.

The Wall of Storms disappeared behind the kite-raft. His umbilical cord cut, Luan Zya was now alone at sea, truly adrift and away from home.

After a few more weeks, the current shifted to the south.

The stars appearing at night began to change, turning into constellations more familiar to Luan Zya. He was to the west of the Islands of Dara now, and as he lay on his raft at night, gazing up at the stars, he wondered what his friends, Cogo, Gin, Kuni, Risana . . . were thinking and doing. He hoped that Gin would finally take his advice to heart and give up her pride and the yearning for ostentatious displays of honor and glory.

And then what? Would you have her come with you on this fool's errand, to brush by death only to drift over the endless sea, subsisting on rainwater and fish foolish enough to be caught?

He tried to imagine Gin by his side, living the life he was now living, and the sight brought forth mirthful chuckles. The very idea was preposterous.

She has her own path in life, and having her give up the title and power of being a queen—an accomplishment that she has striven for all her life—would depress her as much as giving up learning, studying, wandering, and exploring would depress me.

Gin was like fire, and he was like water. They each had their own natures and characters, and what was right for one wasn't right for the other.

As the weeks went by, the patterns in the sky continued to change. Now Luan Zya spent each night charting the new stars. He could feel the weather changing as well, the sun rising higher at noon, the temperature growing warmer, more like the climate of Tan Adü or even hotter. He made up new constellations and gave them names, some serious, some whimsical: the General, the Loving Mother, the Diving Cruben, the Blossoming Dandelion, a Dish of Spicy Dasu Raw Fish . . .

The fish he caught now were of different species, some unknown to him. Not all of them were fit to eat. Some had sand in their bellies that probably helped the fish grind up their food, but cleaning such fish was a tedious chore. Some had flesh so filled with tiny bones that it was impossible to eat them without fire to soften the spikes, and others left his stomach in painful knots and he had to vomit up what he had eaten. One even caused him to become light-headed and to lose feelings in his limbs. By the time he woke up, weak and dehydrated, he wasn't sure how many days had passed.

He vowed to be more careful, and meticulously painted pictures of the fishes, labeling their patterns with colors and noting their tastes and effects when consumed. He wasn't sure if these notes he wrote would ever be read, but he had to feel like he was doing something useful to keep sane.

Day after day, week after week, the sun grew brighter, hotter, and more merciless. The raw, salty water of the ocean made him itch all over, and his skin began to blister and ooze pus. Rain stopped, and he was forced to drink his own urine and to suck out the moisture from the organs and flesh of the fish to slake his thirst.

How many days had it been since it last rained? How many days had he been drifting? Was he still heading south or had the current turned east? In his sun-induced delirium, he was no longer sure of the answers to any of these questions. He lacked the energy to even crawl out of the stuffy shelter of the tent, to make the effort to catch fish and obtain sustenance. He knew he had to get up and fight for his life, but he just couldn't summon the strength.

Let me die, he thought. *Let me die.*

Funny. He had not given up when it had seemed that the entire Xana Empire had been hunting him; he had not given up when he had tried to conquer the Imperial Palace in Pan with just a few dozen men behind him and Duke Kuni Garu by his side; he had not given up when the Hegemon's might had seemed impossible to overcome, when his lord had possessed but a single isle and needed to challenge the strength of all the rest of Dara—yet here he was, asking for the peace of death, too tired and hungry and thirsty to continue the basic struggle to stay alive.

What courage it took for the starving and the poor to continue the mere act of existence, of survival, of endurance. Such quiet acts of heroism were not celebrated, and yet they made up the foundation of civilization, far more than all the honorable sentiments of the Ano sages and the pretty words of the nobles.

He drifted off to sleep, thinking that he would not wake up again.

But he did wake up. He had fallen asleep at the edge of the raft, with his head partly extended over the sea. Now something bobbing in the water was bumping against his face. He looked, trying to get his blurry vision to focus: coconuts.

He seized them with shaking hands and fetched as many as he could out of the water and piled them onto the raft, his thick, stone-dry tongue almost choking him as he imagined the delicious, refreshing liquid inside.

But then he realized that he had no tools with which to open them.

The small bone writing knife that he carried—really more a decorative piece of jewelry—was suitable for carving raw fish but was useless against the hard shell of the coconut. He looked around frantically for a nail, a hammer, a machete, or even a large rock, knowing that he didn't possess any of these things. In despair, he picked up a coconut and banged it against the bamboo frame of the raft, knowing the futility of the act. He was separated from the lifesaving water by only a shell thinner than the palm of his hand, and yet such a shell seemed at this moment to be even more impenetrable than the Wall of Storms.

He broke down then and called for the gods to help him. He had not been in the habit of praying to them in his maturity, believing that the gods preferred to intervene as little as possible. But now he begged and pleaded for them to give him something, anything, to save his life. He asked for wise Lutho, for graceful Tututika, for warlike Fithowéo, for compassionate Rufizo, for fierce Kana and deliberate Rapa, for proud Kiji, and even for unpredictable Tazu—if only the shark-toothed god would end his life and thus his torment. . . .

But the gods did not answer, as he had known they would not.

They were not present here in the wild ocean beyond the Wall of Storms. He was all alone, more alone than any man of Dara had ever been.

He collapsed at the edge of the raft and howled, a sound that was not a cry of sorrow, but something more primal, an urge connected to the first noise made by all of us as we come into this world from our mothers' wombs. His lips and tongue were so parched that all he could do was to moan and howl incoherently, unable to form the syllables that he no longer needed.

If he were less delirious, the noises he made might have reminded him of the song of whales and crubens.

Eventually, the noises grew fainter and then stopped.

The raft almost capsized as the sea exploded near him.

He opened his eyes, sad that he was still alive, still suffering.

A great cruben, the sovereign of the seas, surfaced barely a few dozen feet from the raft. It bobbed in the sea like a living island, and even in his near-death state, Luan Zya was awed by the magnificence of the animal.

The cruben sang, and the sound seemed to cause the bones in Luan Zya's body to vibrate in sympathy. He shivered. What was this lord of the ocean going to do?

Splash. Plop. Splash.

Three smaller creatures surfaced right against the edge of the raft, between Luan Zya and the hulk of the cruben. Measuring no longer than Luan Zya himself was tall, the scale-covered animals, miniature versions of the great cruben, gazed up at Luan Zya with curious eyes, the silvery scales on their backs shimmering in the bright sun. As Luan Zya gazed at the baby crubens, astonished, they spouted one after the other through their blowholes, and the sprays of mist drenched Luan Zya's face.

As Luan Zya wiped his eyes so he could see again, he could hear the rumbling laughter of the great cruben.

The baby crubens raised themselves out of the water, swaying back and forth on their tails, and chirped at him. The single horns on their foreheads, each only about the length of Luan Zya's forearm, waved through the air like short swords. One of them bent and pointed the horn at the pile of coconuts on the raft.

Dumbfounded, Luan Zya picked up one of the coconuts and crawled over to the edge of the raft, and as the baby crubens backed up, chirping excitedly, he dropped it into the water.

The baby crubens dove out of sight; the great cruben remained drifting not too far away, the gentle motion of its fins causing slow waves to beat against the raft.

Then the water exploded as one of the baby crubens shot up from the depths and struck the coconut with its horn. The coconut sprang into the air, rising some ten, fifteen yards before falling back down, but just as it was about to hit the surface, a second baby cruben surfaced and struck it with its horn as well. The coconut arced away from the raft in a long, graceful flight, only to be struck by the third baby cruben as it leapt out of the sea, and the coconut flew at Luan

Zya, who grabbed it with both hands more out of instinct than calculation.

Warm, fragrant juice gushed from three holes in the shell, and Luan Zya sealed his lips around them, hungrily gulping down the life-saving liquid.

The baby crubens played the game with Luan Zya for another quarter of an hour, opening a half-dozen more coconuts for him to drink his fill.

"Thank you." Luan Zya knelt on the edge of the raft and touched his forehead to the water.

The baby crubens bobbed up and down in the water, squeaking and chirping. Then, with a long and low moan, the great cruben began to swim away, its giant tail slapping against the surface thunderously. The baby crubens followed their parent like three reef rocks being towed by a moving island until the pod finally disappeared from sight.

Luan Zya felt the wetness on his face. He wiped his eyes and looked up: It had begun to rain.

The presence of coconuts suggested that land was nearby. Luan Zya strained for signs of it. He wished that he had some way of raising himself into the air: a kite, a balloon, a small airship.

One especially scalding noon, he looked south and saw a sight that made his heart stop for a beat. In the shimmering air just above the horizon, he could make out, just barely, a city with tall towers and gleaming domes, and there seemed to be streets filled with the wriggling motion of people and vehicles.

He fought to leave the current, tacking and pulling his sail this way and that, rowing through the water with broken spars from the kite, even considering jumping into the water to make a desperate swim for it. But the current was too strong and the kite-raft barely deviated from its course.

He jumped and shouted, wishing that he had a signaling rocket to draw the attention of the distant inhabitants of this strange country.

Fire, he thought desperately. He had never wanted anything as much as he wanted fire at that moment.

The city wavered, and then, vanished.

He stood on the unsteady surface of the raft and looked at the empty horizon, confused and angry. He had seen the city with his own eyes, but where had it gone?

A moment's reflection made him realize that he had likely been fooled by a Tututika's Impression. These were mirages seen sometimes in deserts and over the sea, when the image of a distant object below the horizon was reflected by a trick of air and light to appear in the vision of weary travelers. It was an illusion, but there was a real source, a source that lay just below the horizon.

If only he could get high enough or send a signal.

He gazed up at the sun, and then again at the distant horizon. Light rays had been bent to give him a glimpse of land that lay just out of reach.

What could bend light?

He recalled the Curved Mirrors invented by his father that had kept the shores of Haan safe from Mapidéré's invading fleets using nothing but the power of the sun. An idea took shape in his mind.

Half stumbling, half crawling, he made his way over to the cocoon of the kite, which he had dragged out of the water some time ago so that the two halves, like the shell of a split nut, could be used to store fresh water.

He pried the glass loose from one of the portholes and looked at it. Circular in shape, it was flat and clear.

Picking up a handful of coarse sand scraped out of the belly of a fish he was drying on the raft, he scattered it over the surface of the glass. Then, dipping a piece of rough dogfish skin in the sea to wet it, he began to polish the glass, feeling and hearing the satisfying sound of glass being ground away. He turned it a quarter of a circle in his hands and continued to grind.

He worked without stop, taking a break only now and then to eat and drink. The edge of the disk of glass in his hand gradually grew thinner and the surfaces took on a convex shape. Over time, he shifted from rough sand to fine sand, and then to using just the dogfish skin. The flat disk gradually transformed into a lens under his insistent motion.

After a few days of this laborious work, he was finally satisfied as he glanced at the magnified, distorted world through the lens. He broke one of the bamboo spars he had been using as an oar into small, short sticks and piled them on a platform made from one half of the hard jujube cocoon, which would no longer hold water because the porthole had been pried out. Stuffing some dried coconut husks under the bamboo sticks as kindling, he was ready to light a fire.

He held up his lens and moved it until the projected image of the sun shrank into a tiny dot on the kindling. He waited. After a few seconds, smoke rose from the pile.

He whooped with delight, and carefully, keeping his hands steady, he waited until the smoke grew thick and a tiny tongue of flame flickered to life. Putting the lens aside, he bent down and blew on the flame gently, trying to keep it alive, to nurture it.

After a while, when the fire was big enough, he tossed torn strips of silk onto the flames. The silk burned slowly and generated a lot of smoke. He hoped that he was still close enough to land that the smoke would draw the attention of fishermen and merchants, and perhaps someone would come to investigate in a boat.

He kept the smoke signal alive for most of the day, using the fire to cook fish when he was hungry. The fire meant that even the fish whose flesh was full of tiny bones could now be eaten, as grilling the fish over the fire softened the bones and made it possible to chew the fish whole and swallow. Though he enjoyed the taste of cooked food, no ships appeared over the horizon.

In the end, he was forced to conclude that the hope he had harbored was false. He had no idea how far the land in the mirage really was, and maybe the people there did not possess ships capable of coming out so far.

But at least he had a way to make fire, and that was something.

He was immensely cheered: The knowledge he had gained in his travels through Dara was still worth something. Though he was far from home, the sun and the sea still worked as before. A lens still bent light, and fire could be made by harnessing the power of the sun. He could still improve his lot through diligence and ingenuity. Though the gods could not hear his prayers, the universe was knowable.

The fire eventually went out, but hope had returned to his heart.

After the episodes of delirium earlier, Luan no longer knew precisely how long he had been on the endless sea. The new constellations in the sky made it impossible for him to tell the seasons; the persistently hot and humid days were very different from those of Dara.

The raft was now drifting east. To deal with the sweltering weather, Luan Zya turned his thick outer robe into a blanket to sleep on. The thin under-robe he wore was now grimy, tattered, and barely covered his body, so he stripped it off and walked around the raft nude. To provide some measure of protection against the sun, he made hats and shawls for himself out of fish skin and pieces of the kite itself. His hair and beard grew out, snow white in color, and sometimes when he looked at his reflection in the sea he couldn't even recognize himself.

He dared not burn more of the raft, and so he had to painstakingly gather bits of driftwood and seaweed and dry them for fuel. He thought the presence of driftwood indicated that land was nearby, but the current never brought him within sight of any landmass or ship.

And then, one day, he realized that the current had slowed down and turned north. He tried to steer with the sail again, and the raft actually made progress against the languorous flow.

He was free, on his own.

For the entirety of the time he had ridden this current, Luan had sought to escape it. But now it seemed as if he was saying good-bye to an old friend. He hesitated for a moment, looking at *Gitré Üthu*, with his rough maps of the course he had taken and the new stars he had seen.

Even if there is nothing but the endless ocean out there, it's better to die sailing my own course.

He pointed his raft east and did not look back at the current.

The sores on his body scarred over and broke open again, and he always felt weak. He could feel his teeth growing loose in their sockets and his eyesight failing—his diet wasn't giving him all the nourishment he needed, and exposure to the elements was giving him no chance at true recovery. After continuing east for weeks, he decided to shift to a more northerly course to seek a more temperate climate. The stars once again became familiar, though the view of the ocean still didn't change.

Tazu, I can see why you are the way you are, he thought. *The sea would drive even the gods mad.*

Day after day, he peered into the distance and saw only water and more water. The fishes he caught now were yet again different from those in Dara as well as the ones he had seen in the current, and he continued to record them in *Gitré Üthu* with diligence. At night he dreamed feverish dreams, and he argued with the gods about the nature of the world.

Tututika, is there beauty in a society of one? Could there be imperfection when the world consists of only one soul?

Fithowéo, do you think there can be warfare between the self and the self?

The weather turned chilly, and the wind now consistently blew to the north and east. He wrapped himself in the tattered remains of his heavy robe, and draped clumps of seaweed over his tent to make it more difficult for the cold breeze to find openings. After some more weeks, the temperature had dropped to the point where his teeth began to chatter, and he wasn't sure if he preferred the hellish heat of the southern regions or this.

Then came the day he beheld a sight that he at first thought was yet another mirage: tiny dots hovering on the horizon, circling.

Birds.

He looked at the ocean around him, and noticed floating vegetation:

vines and twigs and leaves that didn't appear to belong to the sea. Where had they come from?

He steered straight toward the birds, trying to hold back his excitement lest he be disappointed once more. By the time evening fell, a thick fog had descended over everything. He wrapped himself in his robe, now so decayed as to more resemble a shawl, and, as he slept, dreamed of landing on unknown shores, where immortals dressed in rich and colorful silks welcomed him with a lavish celebration.

He woke up, and there it was: a coastline that loomed across the entire horizon, a flat, tan expanse dotted with bits of green. Luan stood up on the swaying raft, clad only in his fish-skin cap and tattered robe, unable to believe his eyes. He had found land.

As he guided the kite-raft toward the shore, he saw a few small dwellings, white in color and shaped like mushrooms, clustered on land a short distance from the surf. A few small boats of a design Luan had never seen before rested on the beach. Shaped like shallow bowls, they appeared to be woven from grass, and a few air-filled bladders tied to the rims provided additional flotation.

The raft caught on something underwater and stopped. Luan Zya crawled off and splashed into the shallow water. The cold shocked his body, and the feeling of solid land under his feet felt unnatural after so much time spent on the ocean; his wobbly legs would not allow him to stand, and he had to support himself on his knees and hands. A wave crashed over him, drenching him in ice-cold water, and he almost fainted from the shock. He saw that some men and women, pale-skinned and light-haired, had emerged from the mushroom-shaped tents to gaze at him in wonder.

"Before the sea, all men are brothers," he croaked, and then collapsed against the beach.

CHAPTER FORTY-FIVE

AN INTERLUDE

RUI: THE SECOND MONTH IN THE TWELFTH YEAR
OF THE REIGN OF FOUR PLACID SEAS.

The wintry sea was calm outside the port of Kriphi, but the sky was overcast and faint flashes of lightning could be seen deep within the clouds. As the sun gradually set, the underwater wreckage of city-ships seemed to take on various shapes in the failing light: a giant turtle, a grinning shark, a school of glimmering carp, even massive birds that had somehow abandoned the rarefied air for a far denser medium.

- *Where have you been, Old Turtle?*
- *Away at the edge of the world, to probe at the Wall of Storms again.*
- *What did you find?*
- *Terror of the unknown; I still could not pass through.*
- *You know we aren't supposed to cross it, brother. Our mother told us that Moäno created it to mark Dara apart.*
- *But the world beyond has come to Dara, as well as new gods.*
- *We have not felt the power of these new gods yet; perhaps they are still weak from their journey.*

In the last rays of the setting sun, the great shadow of the turtle seemed to shake its head.

- I fear that the Wall of Storms is a barrier that only the mortals may pass through, but not the gods.

The underwater shadows held still, as though the gods were shocked to hear this unimagined horror.

But Tazu, as always, was the first to break the morose mood.

- You're missing a great story—your favorite mortal has been on quite an adventure.

- Did I miss much?

- They're just getting to the good part.

- Lutho, why didn't you follow your protégé beyond the Wall when he broke through three years ago?

- I tried to help him as much as I could, but I felt my power weaken as I tried to reach beyond that barrier. Our power comes from these islands, and we cannot leave our home without becoming . . . mortal.

- But maybe that means . . . the gods of these strangers also could not leave their home. The Lyucu have left their gods behind, their prayers unheard.

The gods pondered this as they continued to listen to the tale unfolding in the halls of the Palace of Kriphi, like patrons nursing drinks by the firelight of a pub as the storyteller continued his performance.

Zomi sat between the two stretchers, one hand holding the hand of her father, the other the hand of her teacher. The two men were now asleep, their pain temporarily dulled by medicine.

"Is there any hope?" she asked.

The army doctor furrowed his brows, neither nodding nor shaking his head. "They have been severely tortured," he said. "I'm surprised that . . . they're alive at all."

Zomi nodded numbly.

On the ground before her lay *Gitré Üthu*, whose pages had told a tale that she hardly dared to believe.

"Rest, Father," she murmured. "Rest, Teacher."

Behind her, the generals and advisers and soldiers waited for her to read more.

CHAPTER FORTY-SIX

PRINCE AND PRINCESS OF UKYU

IN THE COUNTRY OF STRANGERS:
TWO YEARS EARLIER.

Luan woke up in a tent, lying on a bed of furs and covered by another fur. The dim interior of the tent was redolent with the musk of animals, strong but not unpleasant. Light came through a single central opening in the top, which also served as the chimney for the smoke from the cooking fire, over which a pot made of animal skins bubbled.

An old woman came to him and held a bowl to his mouth, feeding him something that smelled of fermented milk. He was famished. The sour taste was strong but also felt nourishing. He swallowed and swallowed, and fell back asleep before he finished.

He dreamed that his stomach became a battlefield. Currents of lava and ice fought for dominance inside him, hissing and steaming. He woke up vomiting, and he could feel that he had soiled himself. The old woman and several other figures came to attend to him, and he tried to croak out an apology, but was too weak to get out more than a mumble.

When he woke up again, he felt even weaker, but his stomach had finally settled. This time, the herders gave him something different, a soup or stew made of meat and vegetables. He tried to eat slowly this time, to give his body time to adjust to the new foods.

He finished one bowl and they fed him another, and this time, he felt strong enough to try to hold the bowl—made out of the seedpod of some plant chopped in half—himself. While he drank, the family spoke around him. Though he could not understand their language, he did pick out a word that sounded like "Dara."

They know about my home? He couldn't understand how that could be. But then exhaustion and sleep overtook him again.

He was jolted awake. Looking around, he grew alarmed. There were vertical bars all around him, made of white animal bones, and above him was a roof of animal skins. The sensation of being lifted and set down made him feel like he was in the sea again. He struggled to sit up, and what he saw took his breath away.

He was inside a cage, and his feet were tied to the bars of his prison with strong cords of sinew. But he didn't even bother to struggle to free himself.

The cage, and he, were airborne. He was on the back of some great beast with wings that slowly beat through the air like the oars of an Imperial airship. A neck extended before him like the thick vines of the jungles of Arulugi or the rearing form of a giant python, and terminated in an antlered head shaped like a deer's, though many times larger.

Somehow, the massive beast seemed familiar. But how could that be? He was sure he had never come across any description of such a creature in his travels.

Then it struck him. They looked exactly like the strange winged and antlered beasts he had seen on the wreckage pieces that had inspired his voyage.

His heart pounded with the thrill of discovery, of having stepped through a dream into a new world.

He examined the bones in the cage he was imprisoned in—long, large, hollow-sounding—and suspected that they came from the same kind of animal as he was riding on.

The great beast flew at a height of perhaps a few hundred yards above ground, similar to the cruising altitude of an Imperial airship. Far below, Luan could see an endless, flat, tan landscape dotted with clumps of brush and grass. Herds of animals—they resembled cattle, but far shaggier and somewhat bigger—roamed beneath him. And each herd was accompanied by two or three beasts like the one he rode on. They waddled alongside the herds, their wings folded, carrying herdsmen who looked up at his mount as it flew overhead. Far in the distance, he saw the slate-gray ocean, dotted here and there with a few of the small bowl-shaped grass ships bobbing over the waves.

There were guards all around the cage, maybe half a dozen of them, secured in harnesses or saddles attached to the back of their mount. Some were men, and some were women, but they all wore simple clothing made of fur and woven grass, and wielded war clubs and axes made of bones and stones, or slingshots made from antlers and sinew. Sensing that he was awake, a few turned to look at him with curious eyes.

Recalling that the herders who had rescued him seemed to know the name of Dara, he thought he would try to see if they knew his language.

"What country is this?" he asked. "Which people inhabit these shores?"

There was no response. The guards looked at him, their expressions unfathomable.

It was useless to try to ask questions when he had so little information. He had to bide his time and understand his situation better.

The universe is knowable.

About an hour later, the beast carrying him landed next to a cluster of mushroom-shaped tents, panting heavily. Another winged and antlered beast, similar in size but freshly rested, strode over to stand opposite his.

One of the guards, the one who rode at the base of the beast's neck and was evidently the pilot, let out a series of loud whistles.

The beast lowered its head while keeping its neck stiff and straight, like a drawbridge. Luan saw the other beast mirroring the same motion until the two heads met in the center, their necks perfectly parallel with the ground. The two heads nuzzled against each other and moaned, and then they held still.

The guards unlashed the cage from the harness on the beast's back, heaved it over their shoulders, and stepped onto the beast's neck. Luan gripped the bars of his cage tightly as it swayed, certain that someone would lose their balance on the knobby vertebrae of the beasts and cause the cage to tumble down to the ground.

But the guards carried the cage across the living bridge formed by the necks of the two beasts as steadily as the palanquin carriers of Dara might have borne a passenger across a city moat. They secured the cage to the back of the new beast and buckled themselves into new harnesses and saddles.

Luan had already learned something. These beasts, though powerful, did not appear to be capable of sustaining flight for long. That probably explained why the herdsmen he had seen earlier had kept their mounts waddling awkwardly along the ground instead of hovering in the air.

His suspicion was confirmed as his new ride also landed after an hour, and the process of transfer was repeated. He reached for *Gitré Üthu* out of habit to record his observations and speculations about the novel flying beasts, and only then did he realize that the book was no longer with him. An intense pain racked him, as though a part of himself had been cut away—and that was true, in a manner of speaking. The book had been his sole companion during the long voyage across the ocean, the mirror of his delirium and the ledger of his dreams. Now that the kite-raft was gone, *Gitré Üthu* was the only witness left to all that he had experienced.

After switching through twelve beasts in this manner, they finally arrived at a massive settlement, a city made up of thousands of mushroom-shaped tents, many of them far larger than the ones he had seen so far.

In the center of the city was an especially massive tent that dwarfed the others, with a diameter that rivaled the Grand Examination Hall back in Pan. The flying beast landed, and Luan saw that in front of the tent was a tall bone pole, from whose crown several furry long tails flapped like banners. Luan was shocked to see two metal helmets—the first signs of metal he had seen anywhere in this new land—also dangling and flapping from the tip of the flagpole. The helmets were familiar to him, being constructed in the style of the old Xana Empire, and he could see that inside the helmets were the mummified remains of two heads.

Something writhed in the depths of Luan Zya's mind, the beginning of a vague answer that could explain some of the riddles around him.

The beast touched its head to the ground to form a long, gentle slope with its neck, and the guards untied Luan's feet, took him out of the cage, and then walked him down this makeshift flight of stairs.

One of the guards went inside the large tent, and after a while, she emerged and said something to the other guards. Together, they guided Luan to a small structure next to the large tent: a circular hut whose walls were made from a bone palisade covered with a layer of woven plant fiber and mud and whose roof was made of animal skin.

Inside, the only illumination came from a small opening in the roof and a small fire under the smoke-hole to keep the enclosure warm. Besides a stack of dry animal dung meant as fuel for the fire and a large seedpod-bowl that was likely intended for his night soil, the hut was bare save for a pile of pelts and furs, very clean, and he figured that he was supposed to use them as bedding. He could not find anything hard or sharp, no instruments that could be used as a weapon.

The guard closed the door behind him, and he heard the sound of something heavy being moved outside. When he tried the door again, he found that it was blocked from the outside.

Still weak from his ordeal, he lay down in his prison and went to sleep.

Several times a day, whatever blocked the door from the outside was rolled aside and someone came in to bring him food and to empty the night soil bowl. As blinding sunlight pierced the murk inside the cell, Luan shielded his eyes and tried to speak to whoever came in. They never answered him.

The food they served him was plain but filling: a hard cake that seemed to be made from pulverized dried meat, animal fat, and berries; a kind of flatbread that tasted of flour made from nuts; and plenty of water to drink in skin pouches. He could tell that this was the kind of food that could be prepared in large quantities and then stored away to be doled out over time to a large population, the kind of food that would be favored by armies or nomadic peoples on the move.

I'm being fed the same thing as the rest of the tribe, he thought. *At least they aren't mistreating me.*

Then, on the fifth day, the door to the hut opened, but no one came in.

After his eyes had adjusted to the bright light, Luan decided that he would go to the door to see what was going on.

A semicircle of guards stood a few paces away, but Luan's attention was drawn to the two young figures kneeling right before the door to the hut. Both were about twenty years old, one a man and the other a woman. The quality of the furs they wore and the delicate bone-and-teeth jewels they wore in their hair told Luan that they were nobles.

He noticed that they were kneeling in the position called *mipa rari* in Dara.

Could it be?

He knelt down also in formal *mipa rari* in the door of the hut.

"Luan Zya," he said. He enunciated each syllable carefully and pointed at himself. Then he swept his hands out to the two young people kneeling opposite him.

"Forgive us, Honored Master," they said together.

The accent was unfamiliar, but Luan's face twitched uncontrollably and his vision grew blurred as he again heard, after having given up hope that he would ever do so, the speech of Dara.

"Welcome to Ukyu, the country of the Lyucu," said the young man who introduced himself as Cudyu Roatan, the king's son. "You're in Taten, the capital of our humble land."

"Our father is away to put down a rebellion," said the young woman, who called herself Vadyu Roatan, the king's daughter. "We apologize for the terrible ways you've been treated. The guards didn't know you were an honored guest from Dara, a land we have always admired."

They were sitting in the grand tent that Luan had seen when he had first been brought to the tent-city. The cavernous interior was thickly carpeted by furs, and clusters of low tables and partitions made from bone and animal hide marked out areas for dining, sleeping, sitting, holding court, and other functions that Luan could not begin to guess. The small table between them held plates full of fragrant roasted meat, skull-bowls filled with rich stew, and bone cups full of the intoxicating fermented milk drink the Lyucu called kyoffir.

As he sipped at his stew, Luan thought back to the way the family who had rescued him whispered the word "Dara" in his presence, but it was possible that he had been wrong during his fever-induced delirium. There were too many questions for him to focus on such small details.

He decided to get to the point right away. "How did you come to know of Dara? And how did you learn its speech?"

The prince and princess looked at each other and seemed to converse with their eyes.

"That is a long story," said the prince, as he turned back to look at Luan.

"It might be easier to show you rather than tell you," said the princess.

Sitting in a saddle and strapped into a harness this time, Luan Zya soared above the land and the sea as Vadyu piloted the winged beast—which she called a garinafin—in the saddle in front of him. This garinafin was much smaller than the ones that had carried him here, and Luan could feel every stroke of the powerful wings as the princess guided her mount along the coastline.

"Do you recognize those ships?" Vadyu asked.

Luan could hardly miss what she was talking about. There, anchored in the bay below him, were more than twenty massive ships, each as big as a small city. They were fitting tributes to the memory of a man who had dreamed of connecting the Islands of Dara with tunnels under the sea and whose projects were all monumental in scale, almost beyond mortal comprehension.

"So Emperor Mapidéré's expedition to the immortals came here," murmured Luan.

"More than twenty years ago!" Vadyu shouted to make herself heard above the sound of the rushing wind. "Before I was even born."

Then, as they circled over the legendary fleet of city-ships that now bore silent witness to the grandness of Mapidéré's vision, Vadyu told him a story that had changed her world.

For decades, perhaps centuries, the people of the scrublands lived simple lives as nomadic herders of cattle, relying on the winged garinafins to guard the herds as well as to provide companionship and transportation. Life was unchanging but also satisfying.

Then, one day, like a vision from an old creation myth, a fleet of ships as large as floating islands appeared on the horizon.

The coming of the people of Dara turned the world of the Lyucu upside down. The visitors showed the Lyucu how narrow their world had been, how devoid of all the joys and refinements associated with high civilization: machinery, art, literature, manners, true beauty.

It was as if, before the coming of the people of Dara, the Lyucu had been mere worms slithering in the grass, without an understanding of how falcons could soar and take in at a glance a world grander than the accumulated experience of thousands of generations of worms.

The people of Dara were excellent teachers, and the Lyucu and their honored guests lived in harmony for many years. This was how both Vadyu and Cudyu had learned the language of Dara, because they had caring and skilled teachers.

But then, one day, a calamity struck. All the visitors from Dara fell sick from some unknown plague, and every single one of them died within a few days despite heroic efforts from the Lyucu to save their teachers and friends.

"There, you can see the graves," said Vadyu as she guided the garina-fin into a low sweep along the ground next to the coast.

Luan glanced down and saw neat rows of thousands of grave markers made of bone. Each mound was about the size of a small hut in Dara. He was struck silent by the sight. What horror Vadyu and her people must have experienced as their foreign friends died in such an incomprehensible manner.

"We grieved for years," said Vadyu. "And Father vowed to find a way to honor the final wishes of the visitors of Dara: to have their bodies interred in the soil of their homeland."

Luan nodded. Kon Fiji had taught that the souls of the dead could not find rest until they had returned to the land of their birth. This was why the people of Dara had always expended extraordinary effort to bring the dead home, and why mass graves in foreign lands for dead soldiers had caused so much sorrow for the people during the rebellion and the Chrysanthemum-Dandelion War.

But Luan also noticed something odd. The graves and markers were so uniform in shape and color that it seemed as if they had been constructed by some predefined plan. Would a mass cemetery built in response to an unexpected plague look so neat, so . . . *new*?

"We honor the people of Dara in every way we can," Vadyu said. "Admiral Krita, who led the expedition to these shores, still watches over us, as do the eyes of his wife, a Lyucu woman who fell in love with him. We have preserved their heads after the custom of our people, and they are displayed at the top of the flagstaff in front of the grand tent of Taten."

Luan nodded. This explained the two metal helmets and the mummified remains he had seen dangling from the top of the flagpole. Yet something about Vadyu's explanation bothered him. The way those heads had been displayed seemed to be a kind of warning, a celebration of cruel barbarism—but maybe he was just being too narrow-minded. The people of Lyucu had their own culture and customs, and he warned himself not to force his own preconceived ideas onto a new world.

~ ~ ~ ~

Back in Taten, Luan Zya was installed in a tent that the prince and princess of the Lyucu shared. As they explained it, since he was clearly a learned man from Dara, he was fit to be their teacher as well and should live with them.

"Here is your book," said Cudyu. Reverently, he held *Gitré Üthu* in both hands and presented it to Luan. "You must be an extremely learned man to have such a thick tome with you."

"We've preserved the city-ships as best as we are able," said Vadyu. "If only we could find a way to help guide the lost souls of the honored guests from Dara back to their home. Alas, we lack the knowledge of the master navigators of Dara."

"While the guests from Dara were alive, they tried to find their way home many times," said Cudyu. "Father always gave them whatever help they needed. But none of the fleets they launched to find a way home ever succeeded . . . and some never came back, except as wreckage that washed ashore after many years."

"Do you have records of Emperor Mapidéré's expedition and details about the subsequent explorations?" asked Luan. He couldn't help himself. The prospect of such a puzzle was too tempting, and if he could solve the puzzle, not only would the bodies of the members of Mapidéré's expedition be brought back to Dara, he would also be able to go home.

Cudyu and Vadyu looked at each other again, and Cudyu excused himself and left.

"From the visitors of Dara, we learned about an impenetrable Wall of Storms that surrounds the Islands," said Vadyu. "Is it true?"

Luan nodded. "It is. I got through it by sheer luck."

"You'd have to sail through it again to return home, wouldn't you?"

"Something I've been thinking a lot about."

"Whatever you need, you just have to ask. It's the least we can do after all the people of Dara have done for us."

Luan nodded. He was feeling more than a little overwhelmed by the care of the prince and princess for the welfare of people from a faraway land. They were demonstrating, far more skillfully than many philosophers of Dara, the ideals behind Kon Fiji's dictum that strangers should be honored as the gods.

Cudyu returned with a pile of scrolls and volumes and maps. "These are the logs left by Admiral Krita of his voyage to Ukyu, as well as the prelaunch plans of later exploratory missions."

"Do you have records of when and where the wreckage of these exploratory missions were discovered?"

"Yes." Cudyu showed Luan where to look.

Luan was amazed by how quickly and neatly Cudyu had assembled so much material. It was as if everything had been set aside ahead of time, just waiting for him to ask for them. . . .

He shook his head. He was acting paranoid and suspicious, a bad habit from his time in Dara, where politics and plots seemed to infuse every interaction with those in power. This was a different land and there were different rules. He would not insult the prince and princess who tried to honor the memory of strangers who had come across the sea and become their friends.

This was a fresh world of wonders, of new sights and new paths. After being alone for so long on the endless sea, the succor of human contact was too sweet for him not to savor it. The inquisitive and respectful prince and princess awakened the teacher in him, who always craved the stimulation of conversing with fresh, young minds. The joy of exploration and discovery was intoxicating, and he could not resist the lure of testing his mettle against an intricate new puzzle.

And yet, the ever-cautious Luan could not fully suppress his own nagging doubt. He decided to take precautions.

For days Luan kept himself at his task. He pored over tables of figures and scratched out computations in a tray of sand; he compared the maps from Admiral Krita's logs with the maps he had drawn in *Gitré Üthu*; he examined Krita's observations of the Wall of Storms and matched them against his own; he correlated records of the winds and tides and times of sunrise and sunset; he pulled out dates and times, arranged and rearranged them, and drew connections between them and made inferences; he seized on every detail in the records that seemed significant or unusual; he built models and made leaps of logic.

Cudyu and Vadyu left him alone to his work, but they kept him supplied with nourishing food and refreshing drink. When they sensed that he needed a break, they took him on sightseeing tours of the surrounding country on garinafin-back, and they humbly asked him to share his theories and thoughts.

The prince and princess were ideal students, Luan realized, and he enjoyed the stimulation of talking with them. Scholarship required the sharpening of bright minds against other bright minds, and Luan was reminded in conversing with these two of his time drifting around Dara in a balloon with Zomi.

Then, one night, Luan Zya put down the bone pen he had been using to write in the tray of sand. He had solved the puzzle of how to get back to Dara.

The universe is knowable. Patterns could be discerned and made useful.

He wanted to shout with joy, but it was so late that Cudyu and Vadyu had already gone to bed. He would have to wait until morning to share his discoveries.

But he was too excited to sleep, and so he decided to take a walk. The guards at the door of the tent nodded at him as he passed. The prince and princess had accompanied Luan everywhere the last few days, and the guards now treated him with great respect.

The light of the moon gilded the scrublands with a silver sheen. The tent-city of Taten appeared like the palaces on the moon in old sagas. Luan made a slow circuit of the grand tent, admiring the workmanship—the Lyucu were a people as different from Dara as it was possible to imagine, and yet love of beauty and the care for doing one's work well seemed universal.

Luan Zya was now behind the grand tent. He saw a strange mound, in the side of which was a door made of a grid of bones.

A cold hand seemed to clench around Luan Zya's heart. He couldn't explain why he felt such dread.

As though seized by a will other than his own, Luan went up and opened the grid. It was pitch-black inside. He took a tentative step forward—

—and he tumbled down a long, sloping tunnel. He shouted for help, but the darkness swallowed his cries.

Air knocked out of him, Luan had to lie still on the ground for a while to recover. He was in an underground cave that reeked of rotting food and human waste. It was cold. The only light and fresh air came from the tunnel he had tumbled through.

CHAPTER FORTY-SEVEN

MAPIDÉRÉ'S EXPEDITION

IN THE COUNTRY OF STRANGERS:
TWO YEARS EARLIER.

He heard something, or *somethings*, scurrying away in the darkness.

A rat? Or something far worse?

But he kept calm and called out, "Who's there?"

The murk seemed to swallow his voice. There was no reply except more sounds of scurrying. Luan peered into the darkness, and he could see several vague shapes, each about the size of a man, huddled on the far side of the cave. He couldn't be sure, but he thought they resembled miniature garinafins.

He waited until his eyes gradually adjusted to the darkness, and he found his initial impression to be correct. About half a dozen juvenile garinafins were huddled in a corner, their necks leashed with thick cables made of hide, which were tethered to the walls of the cave.

Are they being punished?

But there was another figure in the darkness, shaped like a man, not a beast.

"I came in here by mistake," he said tentatively, and took a step toward the man. He wished he knew the language of these people. "I mean you no harm."

"Are you from Dara?" a voice asked. It sounded raspy, hesitant, as though the owner was no longer used to speaking aloud. But the accent was not like that of Cudyu and Vadyu—it was redolent with the harmonies of home. "Have you been sent here by Emperor Mapidéré?"

Luan took another step forward, his heart pounding with excitement. *Could it be? Were Cudyu and Vadyu wrong about everyone having died?*

He realized that the figure in the cave was shackled to the wall with thick cables as well. Confusion seized his mind. *Why?*

"No . . ." He took a deep breath and fought to keep himself calm. "I'm Luan Zya, a man of Haan. Emperor Mapidéré has crossed the River-on-Which-Nothing-Floats a long time ago."

"The emperor is dead?" The voice was colored in equal measure by disbelief and awe.

"He is," confirmed Luan Zya. "Did you come on his expedition to the land of the immortals? How did you survive? Why are you here? What is your name?"

"I did . . . though to answer all your questions would require a very long story. I'm Oga Kidosu, once a fisherman of Dasu and now the pékyu's disgraced storyteller. Tell me how you came to be here."

And so, in that dank, cold cellar, two men connected by the life of Zomi Kidosu shared their tales.

Luan told Oga of the sad fate of his sons during the wars of the rebellion, and he spoke to him of the remarkable young woman his daughter had grown up to be. He described the resilient expression on Aki Kidosu's face and the strength in her every simple word and resolute motion. He recounted for Oga the hot-air balloon rides he had taken with Zomi over Dara, and he tried to re-enact, as best as he could, the young woman's performance at the Palace Examination.

"Surely you are spinning tall tales!" exclaimed Oga. "Pearl of Fire! What a lovely formal name—how it must fit her. Even as a baby she was fiery and stubborn. And my daughter a *cashima*? A *firoa*? A scholar who dared to speak to the Emperor of Dara without averting her eyes?"

"She was all those things, and more."

With so little time and so much to tell, his account was necessarily abbreviated, and he had to assure Oga repeatedly that he would help fill in the details later.

Oga wept and wept, with joy at hearing news of his wife, with grief at the deaths of his sons, with pride at the achievements of his daughter.

And then it was Oga's turn to tell his story.

Like all true stories, it was a mix of legends and facts, of myths imagined and deeds done, of the heart of darkness and the crown of light, of experiences borne and gaps filled, of things seen and visions that could only be authenticated by the mind's eye.

He spoke of a storm that capsized his small boat twenty-two years ago; of hanging on for days to a piece of wreckage, hungry, thirsty, terrorized by sharks, and delirious from the harsh sun and the relentless waves; of finally letting go of the wreckage so that he could seek the solace of death; of opening his mouth to suck in lungfuls of water; of being lifted out of the water on the back of a sea turtle, friend of those lost at sea; of being carried, half-dreaming, half-asleep, across the waves until coming into sight of the fleet of city-ships; of sailors on the decks cheering at him as at an omen; of being taken aboard and being fed and watered and clothed and given a bunk to sleep in.

"Everybody in the fleet was so excited and full of confidence. They thought Lutho, the hope of drowning men, had sent me as a sign of further good fortune. They had had calm seas and speedy winds that carried them north for days—"

"I was wondering about that!" interrupted Luan Zya. "I saw no record of any storm shortly after departure in the logs of Admiral Krita, and I thought that odd."

"It *was* strange. No one remembered any storm. I couldn't explain it."

Luan pondered this. It appeared that the storm that everyone thought had devastated the fleet had been but a trick of the gods, most likely Tazu.

"We sailed straight north, and the wind was so strong behind us that I would have sworn that we were flying. We had no trouble until we came to the Wall of Storms—"

Luan shuddered as he remembered his own encounter with that awe-inspiring sight.

"—and we were certain that we were doomed. We tried everything to pull back; everybody—sailors, marines, cooks, maids, seamstresses, even Admiral Hujin Krita himself—manned the oars, and the city-ships flexed and shuddered as we fought against the sea.

"But it was no use. The winds would not relent, and the fleet was pushed, bit by bit, into the way of certain death. So many men and women jumped into the sea in desperation, thinking they would try swimming back to the Islands of Dara rather than sailing into the maw of the Wall. Even the prince himself, Emperor Mapidéré's son, grew so terrified of the storm that he leapt into the ocean and was never seen again.

"Eventually, exhausted, the rest of us gave up and waited for the storms to smash us and bring us to the undersea palace of Tazu.

"But somehow, as we accelerated toward the Wall, the cyclones and twisters parted ways and opened a path between them. The fleet sailed through like a caravan going through a valley formed with towering waves! Admiral Krita said it was a sign that even the forces of nature had to obey the edicts of Emperor Mapidéré. . . ."

After passing through the Wall, Oga recounted, the fleet encountered a powerful current.

Unlike Luan's tiny kite-raft, the city-ships under Admiral Krita's command were able to escape the current's pull after a great deal of struggle: The sails were filled with a cooperating wind, and everyone aboard helped with rowing. The fleet then continued due north.

However, after many days voyaging in the endless ocean, the weather grew chilly and icebergs appeared in the water. These were not the conditions described in the ancient sources consulted by Krita and Métu in their research into the Land of the Immortals, and it seemed that if the city-ships continued along the same course, they risked being caught in ice.

Krita made the bold conjecture that the ancient sources had perhaps been mistaken and that they were meant to follow the current. The fleet turned around, and after reaching the current again, allowed it to seize the fleet.

Eventually, as the current carried them on a wide, looping course—west, south, east, and north again—and slowed down, Krita decided to depart from it.

But whereas Luan chose to head east after leaving the current, Admiral Krita had directed the fleet to go west, in hopes of returning to Dara. However, the fleet eventually ran into the Wall of Storms again, some distance to the east of Wolf's Paw by the guesses of the navigators. It seemed that the Wall of Storms surrounded all of Dara.

Krita ordered the fleet to head back east, and crossed the current again. Eventually, the city-ships landed in this terra incognita, much as Luan had.

They were on an island many times larger than even the Big Island of Dara, Oga explained. Perhaps it was akin to the legendary lost continent spoken of in ancient Ano sagas. The coast extended north until it turned into the land of permanent ice, and extended south until it became impassable desert. To the east the land ran on and on, eventually running up against mountain ranges that were so high that the tops of the mountains pierced the clouds and were permanently encased in ice. In the flat scrubland that made up most of the rest of this continent, scattered tribes made a living herding long-haired cattle.

Though Oga's account of the lives and histories of the people of the scrublands was necessarily abbreviated and limited, Luan would eventually come to fill in the holes with many more details.

Over the eons, the tribes roamed over the land, following the ebb and flow of rivers whose courses shifted with each spring melt and winter freeze. After the grazing herd wore out a patch of land, they moved on to new pastures, giving the old grounds a chance to recover.

The tribes were small and their lives always on the edge of disaster. Their survival and the survival of the herds depended on a balance between drought and flooding. Even in good times, the plains were filled with predators with sharp claws and sharper teeth: massive horrid wolves who hunted in packs, tusked tigers who stalked the watering holes, and giant flightless birds with swordlike beaks who could kill a long-haired calf with a single, well-placed thrust.

Gradually, some of the tribes learned to tame the garinafins, gigantic beasts with barrel-shaped bodies, serpentine necks, antlered heads, and taloned, birdlike feet capable of flight for short periods of time as well as breathing fire. The winged creatures, ridden by skilled warriors, could protect the herds from predators and scout out faraway pastures and water sources, and the lives of the tribes came to shape them and be shaped by them.

As the scrubland lacked large trees, garinafin and cattle bones and skin were the preferred construction material for shelter, clothing, weapons, and everything else the people needed. Those living near the coast sometimes took to the sea to fish on coracles—shallow, keelless circular boats made from woven grass or animal hide—but the vast majority of the tribes lived nomadic lives on the backs of the garinafins.

The garinafins were fiery tempered and required years of bonding between pilot and mount to be reliable, and as riding and herding were skills needed and learned by all the members of the tribes of the plains, men and women were equally likely to become skilled pilots.

Life on the plains had always been brutal and hard. The numbers of cattle and people that could be supported by the scrub and grass was limited, and competition for fresh pastures was fierce. As long as people could remember, there had always been small skirmishes between the tribes, and incessant reprisals and revenge killings a fact of life.

But the addition of the garinafins transformed the nature of these conflicts. The flying beasts and their riders allowed a tribe to project power far beyond the territory it directly occupied. The milk of the garinafins was especially rich and nourishing, and warriors could subsist on nothing but garinafin's milk for days, fighting far from home. Whichever tribe had more garinafins was almost certain to come out ahead in any conflict.

Small, traditional skirmishes thus grew into increasingly large-scale wars, and eventually raids between dozens of warriors turned into massive battles between thousands, involving clashing armies on the plains as well as hundreds of garinafins soaring and diving overhead.

Over time, the scattered tribes of the scrubland were unified under two great chiefs, called pékyus. The unified tribes of the north called themselves the Lyucu, and named their land Ukyu; those in the south called themselves the Agon, and named their land Gondé.

For centuries, the Lyucu and the Agon were locked in a stalemate punctuated by occasional, but bloody and indecisive, border skirmishes. However, during the decades immediately before the arrival of the expedition from Dara, the Agon gradually came to dominate both Ukyu and Gondé with an advantage in the number of garinafins. After a series of massacres in which tens of thousands of Lyucu were slaughtered, the Lyucu chieftains rebelled against their king, Pékyu Toluroru, and forced him to acknowledge the suzerainty of the Agon. To show the sincerity of the Lyucu chieftains and Toluroru, the prince of the Lyucu, Tenryo Roatan, was given to the Agon as a hostage.

"The Agon would come to regret this decision," said Oga. "Had the boy not been raised as a hostage among them, you and I would also not be conversing today in this underground prison."

CHAPTER FORTY-EIGHT

THE LYUCU AND AGON

UKYU AND GONDÉ, THE LAND OF THE LYUCU

AND AGON: A LONG TIME AGO.

Tenryo was born to one of Pékyu Toluroru's youngest wives, a thane's daughter who was known more for her skill as a carver of garina-fin bones than for her prowess on the back of a garinafin. That his mother lacked the support of the warriors of her tribe meant that the young prince was never one of his father's favorites. It made perfect sense then that when Pékyu Toluroru Roatan of Ukyu surrendered to Pékyu Nobo Aragoz of Gondé, the young boy, barely ten years old, was chosen as the hostage to be sent south to the great camp of the Agon as a sign of the Lyucu's obeisance.

The young boy was treated well by his hosts and captors. Raised alongside Pékyu Nobo's sons and daughters, he was even given the same instructions in wrestling, wielding the war club, riding the long-haired bull, and piloting the garinafin. The hope was that as he would grow up among the Agon, he would come to view them as a second family; then, after he reached maturity and returned to the Lyucu—a younger brother or sister or cousin having been sent to replace him as hostage—he would act as an advocate for the interests of the Agon among Pékyu Toluroru's thanes and thus help preserve the peace. Nobo even had the thought of marrying one of his daughters to the young man when he came of age to further cement their bond.

The Agon exacted a heavy price on the surrendered Lyucu tribes: They had to yield up the best pastures and pay yearly tribute to the conquerors in the form of cattle, slaves, and garinafin hides and bones. Anger seethed as Pékyu Toluroru's thanes enforced the terms of the surrender on their own people with little mercy.

Yet, for years afterward, the peace bought so dearly with blood held as the Lyucu tribes seemed content to suffer in silence and did not seek vengeance. Pékyu Nobo's thanes congratulated their chief on the success of having broken the stubborn will of their savage enemies.

However, in the year Tenryo turned sixteen, Toluroru Roatan rebelled. Starting years earlier, he had slowly and secretly diverted a trickle from the supply of tribute that was supposed to be paid to the Agon, managing to amass an army of three hundred garinafins and thousands of riders in the foothills of the mountains far to the east, out of sight of Agon spies. A surprise attack on Agon herdsmen in territories that had traditionally belonged to the Lyucu turned into a great success as Lyucu slaves—some of them married to Agon spouses—rose up against their masters to join the rebellion. The slaughter was brutal as many mothers and fathers bashed in the heads of their Agon wives and husbands in sleep and strangled their half-Agon children, their hatred for their ancient foe as hot as the breath of the garinafin.

"As Cudyufin and Nalyufin are my witness," declared Pékyu Toluroru, invoking the names of the goddesses of the fiery sun and the icy moon, "we will cleanse this land of the stench of the Agon with blood." Any liberated Lyucu slaves who refused to kill their half-Agon children were declared traitors and publicly executed.

News of the rebellion was brought to Pékyu Nobo, and Tenryo, the young hostage, was taken in front of the Agon king.

"Your father doesn't seem to care about your well-being," said the old man.

Tenryo held his tongue. What Nobo said was obviously true; his father had decided that he could be sacrificed. That was always the danger a hostage assumed.

"I have treated you like my own son," said Nobo, and his eyes were dim with genuine sorrow. He sighed. "But you must pay for the misdeeds of your father, just as Aluro, the Lady of a Thousand Streams, freezes in winter to atone for the errors of the All-Father. In consideration of our time together, I will not shame you by spilling your blood in the Eye of Cudyufin, the Well of Daylight."

What he meant was that Tenryo would be tied up and wrapped in a sheet of garinafin skin and then placed on the open plain, where a herd of long-haired cattle would be driven over him and trample him to death. As his blood would never be exposed to sunlight, the goddess Cudyufin would not see that he died without a fight. This was considered the most merciful means of execution among the Lyucu and Agon alike, a death with some honor for those who were not lucky enough to perish in war.

"I ask only that you have my brother Diaman carry out the order," Tenryo said. Diaman was one of Nobo's sons, and he and Tenryo were such good friends that they called each other brother.

"Of course," said Pékyu Nobo. He thought it was a sign of the young prince's nobility that he did not beg or plead for his life, but submitted to it with dignity. Asking for Diaman to carry out the order further endeared him to the old king. To take the life of another was a great honor, even if it was bloodless. Though Diaman was fierce and brave, he had not had a chance to prove himself on the battlefield due to the long peace with the Lyucu. For Tenryo to offer his own life as a way to give Diaman a taste of what it meant to kill was a selfless act of love for his brother.

"You have the grace of a true prince," said Nobo. "Liluroto, the All-Father, will prepare a special place for you by his side in the afterlife. How I wish you were truly my son and we did not have to do this."

Tenryo nodded and said nothing.

$\backsim\ \sim\ \backsim\ \sim$

On the day of the execution, Diaman escorted Tenryo to the open plains some distance from the main camp. This was an important location for the Agon for it was here, many years ago, that Nobo Aragoz, still a young man, had first vowed to bring the Lyucu to submit and unite all the tribes of the plains, to stop the endless cycles of slaughter.

The two young men—barely more than boys really—gazed at the commotion in the distance, each lost in his own thoughts. Pékyu Nobo's warriors were preparing to march on the impudent Toluroru and his rebel Lyucu. Thousands of men and women were preparing for war: striking camp; packing up the bone poles and skin tents; loading the bundles onto the backs of long-haired cattle and garinafins; sharpening the stone blades embedded in bone clubs; and praying to the All-Father and Diasa, his bright-eyed club-maiden, for glory on the battlefield.

"I am truly sorry that it has come to this," whispered Diaman. He remembered the times Tenryo and he had wrestled as boys, the times they had helped each other as they first learned to ride the garinafins, the times they had disobeyed Pékyu Nobo and gotten in trouble— Diaman had almost forgotten that Tenryo was the son of his father's foe, a hostage. He had grown close to him; he would pay for that now.

"Don't be foolish," said Tenryo. He smiled. "If our positions were reversed, I wouldn't be sorry at all. What can be a better gift than giving my life to someone I admire so much? You'll be a great leader one day, my brother."

Diaman thought Tenryo was very brave. Even at a moment like this he was trying to make his friend feel better.

"Prepare the shroud," Diaman ordered. Several warriors came over, carrying a large section of the thin, membranous skin cut from the wings of a garinafin. They also brought over a length of sinew that would be used to bind Tenryo's wrists and ankles.

"Would you grant me a last favor?" asked Tenryo.

"Anything, brother."

"When I was younger and had trouble sleeping, I needed to hold on to a baby blanket made from the soft skin of a long-haired calf.

Could you use that to wrap me instead? I'm afraid that . . . I might embarrass myself at the last minute if I don't have some way to calm down."

"Of course," said Diaman. He sent the guards to exchange the garinafin wing leather for a blanket made of calfskin.

"And remember the pair of horns we got as boys that we used as weapons?"

Diaman chuckled. When Tenryo had first come to live with him and the other children of Nobo, he and Tenryo had played with a pair of yearling cattle horns as though they were war clubs. Those early fights were how they had become friends.

"I'd like those with me as a last memory of our time together."

Diaman nodded, trying to blink back his tears. He asked the guards to fetch those childhood mementos from his tent and handed them to his old friend.

"I have to tie you myself," said Diaman. This was what would make the kill his, the act that would mark this the day he turned from a boy to a man.

Tenryo held out his hands and said nothing. Diaman could see that his hands weren't even trembling. He bound Tenryo's wrists and ankles loosely, not willing to use too much force to break the skin of his friend and thus ruin the point of the execution: to not spill blood in sunlight. He saw Tenryo whispering *thank you* to him silently.

"Good-bye, brother," said Diaman.

"Good-bye, brother," said Tenryo.

And then the guards wrapped him in the calfskin blanket, lay him over their shoulders, and carried him into the middle of the open field. A herd of cattle was brought over and lined up to face the lonely bundle in the middle of the field.

Diaman whistled and summoned his mount, a young, strong-spirited garinafin named Kidia, who was only about fifteen feet tall from the ground to neck. Such juvenile garinafins were good for training and scouting missions, as well as camp security, leaving the full-grown beasts for frontline warfare. The garinafin folded her wings and knelt, and the Agon prince climbed on. Then he waited until the guards had jogged away from the bundle. He took a deep breath.

So this is what it feels like to kill a man.

He squeezed his knees around the base of Kidia's neck, and the young beast leapt into the air, spreading her wings impatiently. Diaman directed the beast to rise up about thirty yards into the air, turn around, and dive at the herd.

As planned, the herd stampeded, rushing at the lonesome bundle in the distance with thundering hooves. Diaman tapped the base of the neck of the garinafin lightly with his bone trumpet, telling her to land slowly. Since a garinafin's power of flight was limited, there was no point in wasting its energy uselessly.

In a minute, the herd had charged over the spot where Tenryo lay. Diaman looked at the unmoving bundle, and his heart was full of sorrow and pain—and, he couldn't deny it, a measure of excitement. The deed had been done.

It was now his job to go up and unwrap the bundle, to be sure that his friend was dead. He couldn't bear the thought of seeing the crushed bones, the trampled limbs and broken skull. But he had to. If he failed to carry through the ritual, his friend's calm acceptance of death would mean nothing.

He urged Kidia to approach the bundle. One waddling step. Another. He tapped against the garinafin's neck to make her kneel and climbed down. He was now standing next to the motionless bundle. He retrieved the war axe strapped to his back—in case Tenryo had survived the stampede, he would have to deliver the killing blow personally and rob him of an honorable death. Though that was an unlikely outcome, his hand shook.

Strange, the yearling horns had somehow been attached to the outside of the bundle with Tenryo trapped inside, giving it the appearance of a calf dozing in the grass.

Diaman steeled himself for the unpleasant task ahead. He was alone, his guards hundreds of yards away. This was his duty: To gaze upon the face of the man who had died because of his action was a crucial part of growing up on the scrublands, an essential rite of passage for a warrior and especially the son of a great pékyu. He took a deep breath, bent down, and reached for the calfskin.

But before his hands had even touched the bundle, it began to unroll by itself. Diaman was so startled that he stumbled.

Tenryo emerged from the skin; his hands and ankles were free, and he was completely unharmed.

"How—" Diaman's question was choked off with a gasp as Tenryo stabbed a thin, long dagger made from the sharpened ear bone of a garinafin into his throat.

Diaman collapsed, and before the stunned guards could react, Tenryo had grabbed his war axe, climbed onto the back of Diaman's garinafin, and strapped himself into the saddle. The war axe, a prized possession that had been in the Aragoz family for generations, had a handle that was fashioned from the rib of the garinafin that had been the mount of Togo Aragoz, the first pékyu of the Agon in the mists of ancient history, and a blade that was made from one of the talons of the same beast. The bone handle, after rubbing against the calloused hands of dozens of Aragoz warriors, was smooth as the pebbles found on the bottom of a creek and glinted pure white, and the blade itself had smashed through the skulls and torn through the torsos of countless men and women. Named Langiaboto, which in the language of the tribes of the scrubland meant "self-reliance," it was a weapon that had always been wielded by the heirs of the House of Aragoz.

Tenryo kicked Kidia hard under the neck, causing the beast to moan angrily and shoot straight into the air, her massive wings flapping arrhythmically. Tenryo stabbed the bone knife into the soft folds of skin at the base of Kidia's neck and whispered into this makeshift speaking tube. The beast circled over the corpse of her old master a few times. Shuddering and hissing, she seemed to come to some decision.

The garinafin rose higher into the air and headed north with powerful wing strokes, leaving the Agon guards scrambling to tend to the body of their dead prince and to figure out what had happened.

~ ~ ~ ~

Tenryo Roatan journeyed north to the ancestral homeland of the Lyucu on the back of his new mount. It was not an easy journey. As a juvenile, Kidia's stamina was even less than full-sized garinafins. Whenever she got tired, he had to find a dried riverbed or a butte with an overhanging cliff where the young beast could be hidden from the view of pursuing garinafins. They took to flying during the night and sleeping during the day, and Tenryo spent hours at sunset and dawn cautiously scampering over the scrubland to collect feed for Kidia so that she would not have to reveal herself.

His plan, though one conceived in desperation, had been carried out with perfection. He had counted on his friend's compassion to give his hands and feet enough freedom to escape from the loose binding. He had also gambled on simulating the appearance of a sleeping newborn calf with the skin and horns to avoid being trampled by the long-haired cattle herd. Most of all, he had manipulated Pékyu Nobo Aragoz into appointing Diaman as his executioner because of Diaman's mount, Kidia.

The garinafins were highly social and intelligent creatures who lived in family groups, and like the elephants of Dara, they had never been domesticated in the true sense. While some pilots connected with their mounts with real bonds of friendship, such relationships took years to build and were not conducive to fielding massive flying armies where pilots and riders died in large numbers and their mounts had to be transferred to new pilots at a moment's notice.

Pékyu Nobo Aragoz of the Agon, the uniter of a thousand tribes, had achieved his victory over the Lyucu by fielding much larger garinafin herds than was believed possible. He had achieved this feat by inventing a new model for pilots and flying beasts. Instead of allowing each pilot to cultivate a personal relationship with their mount from the birth of the creature, he reconceived the garinafins as being in enforced servitude to the riders. To ensure that the beasts would accept any Agon pilot and carry out their order and serve the army loyally, garinafins who were in the prime of life and suitable for warfare were sent to the front lines while their aged parents and young children were imprisoned back home and threatened with harm.

"Like these baby garinafins around us in this underground cell," said Luan Zya. He looked at the frightened beasts chained to the walls of the cell. They appeared emaciated and passive, kept deliberately in a state of near starvation and frailty.

Oga Kidosu nodded. "That's right. They usually picked the smallest and youngest, the runts of the litter, and kept them in holding cells like this one. This cell is rigged with a mechanism so that the entire place can be collapsed at a command from the pékyu, and these children would be buried alive. There are cells like this throughout Taten, the Lyucu capital tent-city, and they guarantee that the Lyucu army's war garinafins would not dare to rebel against their masters."

Luan Zya's heart clenched at the thought. "This is great evil."

"Tenryo Roatan, as a hostage himself, understood the psychology of the enslaved garinafins of the Agon very well."

"So well that he has apparently re-created it for his own advantage here," said Luan.

"Control of the garinafins is now the foundation of both the cultures of the Lyucu and the Agon."

"So how did Tenryo convince the garinafin Kidia to rebel?"

Unusual among the garinafins in Pékyu Nobo's army, Kidia was an orphan. Her grandparents, parents, and elder siblings had all died in battle, and she was too young to be mated. Adolescent garinafins in her situation were considered untrustworthy and, in the normal course, would be slaughtered for meat, leather, and bones. But Diaman had taken a liking to the beast when she was still a baby and pleaded for her life. As a shackled hostage to ensure the loyalty of her parents, Kidia had demonstrated unusual docility, and so Pékyu Nobo, in a moment of weakness, had indulged his young son and let the creature live.

Tenryo had learned to ride Kidia along with Diaman and always thought of her as timid. But one day, while no one else was around, he secretly observed the young garinafin stealing and breaking one of Diaman's favorite antler slingshots and surreptitiously dropping it in the tent of one of Diaman's grooms, who were charged with caring for the young prince's garinafins. When the prince couldn't find the slingshot, Pékyu Nobo had publicly chastised him, and when the humiliated Diaman eventually discovered the broken slingshot in the tent of his groom, he had the man whipped to within an inch of his life.

Puzzled by this series of events, Tenryo made some discreet inquiries and discovered that the groom had once been a guard for baby garinafins kept as hostages and had a reputation for being quite sadistic. Kidia, in fact, had been one of his charges.

Tenryo understood then that the seemingly docile beast was really a kindred soul—they both put on the disguise of harmless servility while harboring cold thoughts of vengeance and hot ambition. He retrieved the broken slingshot and came to Kidia at night, and, as the startled beast watched, mimed a re-enactment of Kidia's crime.

As Kidia's eyes narrowed and her neck tensed, Tenryo stood his ground and looked into her eyes. "We are allies," he whispered, hoping against hope that the unusually intelligent beast would understand. Then, as the beast watched, he broke the slingshot into even more pieces and buried them in a pile of garinafin dung that the grooms had not yet had a chance to remove.

Next to the pile of dung was a tent that belonged to the man Diaman had whipped. He had been assigned the duty to clean garinafin dung as punishment, but he had already fallen asleep after seeking solace in kyoffir.

In the pale moonlight, Kidia and Tenryo looked at each other, and Tenryo grinned. Kidia snorted and went back to sleep while Tenryo stole away as quietly as a plains mole sliding back into its tunnel.

The next day, after the discovery of the pieces of the slingshot in the dung heap, the unfortunate groom was executed by garinafin breath for this act of petty vengeance and dishonor to the prince.

Thereafter, there was an understanding between Kidia and Tenryo; they simply waited for the right opportunity.

When Tenryo leapt onto the young garinafin's back after murdering his friend, Kidia understood that her moment to return the favor had come. As the young garinafin circled over Diaman's body, Tenryo murmured into the speaking tube his desire to one day carry out justice against the people who had enslaved Kidia and her family. He knew that the garinafin, no matter how smart she was, could not possibly understand his speech to that degree, but his confident tone was enough for Kidia to decide to throw in her lot with him.

When Kidia landed in the camps of the Lyucu with Tenryo on her back, no one was more surprised to see him than Pékyu Toluroru Roatan, his father. The crafty rebel leader had not expected his young son to have the courage and skill necessary to survive his Agon captors, and he had been fully prepared to sacrifice the child. But the legend of Tenryo's daring escape soon spread like wildfire over the scrublands, and Toluroru had no choice but to elevate Tenryo to the position of a prominent thane and give him the command of his own army.

Toluroru's surprise rebellion against the Agon proceeded well, and soon the Lyucu had recovered most of their ancestral moiety of the scrublands from their erstwhile conquerors. But warfare was an expensive affair and could not be carried out indefinitely in the scrublands, where harsh winter storms and unpredictable summer droughts made survival the first priority and forced the tribes to continuously seek out new pastures as they migrated across the land. The two nations of Lyucu and Agon, each unable to overcome the other, eventually conceded that they had to, once again, coexist peacefully.

Tenryo seemed content with his new position as a respected, though still not favored, child of Pékyu Toluroru. It was clear that he would not succeed his aged father as Pékyu of Lyucu—that honor belonged to one of his siblings who had grown up by the side of the pékyu and were thus more trusted and loved, but until the death of his father and the inevitable succession wars that would follow, his place at least seemed secure. He was expected to idle his time away as just another one of dozens of princes and princesses, leading the tribes and cattle herds under his charge to roam over the vast scrubland, searching for better pastures and enjoying his privilege.

But Tenryo did *not* remain idle. He devoted his energy to training the warriors under his command for a new way of making war.

The concept of a professional army did not exist among either the Agon or the Lyucu. Most of the men and women of the tribes were herders during times of peace, and picked up war clubs and axes and mounted the garinafins for fighting only when war flared up. Tenryo broke with tradition by drafting a son or daughter from each of the families in the tribes given to him to lead and keeping them in constant training.

To support such a standing army, he increased the annual tribute the tribes were required to pay, and he led raids on Agon tribes—and sometimes even Lyucu tribes led by other princes or princesses—for cattle and slaves, though he always took care to raid far from his home territories and disguised his raiders so that they could not be traced back to him.

The traditional tactics of warfare among the scrubland tribes relied on individual courage with little coordination, but Tenryo drilled his army in coordination and obedience. He devised new fighting techniques for the garinafin riders and pushed his army to refine them through practice. Instead of each garinafin fighting and flying and breathing fire as the pilot directed on his or her own initiative, Tenryo taught the pilots to guide their mounts to fly in formation, to compensate for each other's blind spots, and to reserve fire so that the garinafins could unleash their limited fire breath in coordinated volleys for maximal damage.

As well, he standardized the war parties riding on the backs of the garinafins. Instead of a haphazard collection of riders mostly taken from members of the same family who fought with whatever weapons they found convenient, each garinafin would have a crew of between six and two dozen. Besides the pilot, there would be look-outs, responsible for paying attention behind and to the sides of the pilot to detect new threats; shield men, responsible for protecting the pilot; and warriors with slingshots and war clubs who would focus on attacking the pilots of enemy garinafins from a distance or leaping across onto other garinafins at close range to engage in mêlée war-fare. To facilitate these techniques, he standardized the type of net-ting draped across the backs of the garinafins as well as the saddles and harnesses.

He also devised ways for foot warriors to coordinate better with the garinafins. Sometimes the garinafins would drive the enemy toward lines of warriors on the ground so that they functioned like the mortar and pestle that the tribes used to grind up the tough nuts collected from thornbushes and annihilate the enemy between them. At other times, if his garinafins were outnumbered, he would have them feint and draw the fire of the enemy garinafins until they had used up all their charge and had to land from exhaustion, where warriors lying in ambush would overwhelm them and slaughter their riders on the ground.

He also confiscated the best weapons from every family and equipped his standing army with them. No longer would his warriors simply fight with whatever war club or slingshot they had inherited from their fathers and mothers.

"Those who are good at herding may not always be good at fight-ing," he said. "We should no more make warriors herd cattle than we should force cattle-whisperers into fighting."

When some questioned him on his unproven new organization, he replied that he was inspired by the grass-cutter ants whose large mounds dotted the scrubland. These ants chopped up blades of grass and bush leaves and carried them back into their nest, where they fermented them in underground chambers to grow a mushroom—considered a delicacy also by the people of the scrubland—that they relied on as food. These ants followed a strict hierarchical order: There was a queen who was in charge of the colony, workers who gathered the materials for the mushroom gardens and tended them, and fighters who, with their outsized mandibles, specialized in warring against rival colonies and slaughtered the enemy workers and queens and enslaved their juveniles.

"Should we not organize ourselves as intelligently as the ants do?" Tenryo asked those thanes who objected to his new innovations because they seemed against the unspoken rule that had held sway over the scrublands from time immemorial: Every family was equal to every other, and every man and woman should be able to live in peace as well as fight wars. But Tenryo held fast to his new professional army and ignored all criticisms.

Above all, he trained his warriors in the ways of absolute obedience to his command. Over and over, he told them that they should carry out his orders without hesitation; just like an ant colony, there was only one source of authority in his army, and everyone had to do what he demanded of them without hesitation.

To carry out such concentrated authority, he established a system of flag signals. Always he carried with him a collection of small war clubs affixed with the white tails taken from small plains foxes in winter. From the back of his mount, he would toss these clubs at specific targets, and wherever they landed, his warriors were directed to focus all their efforts on attacking that target without hesitation.

In other words, Tenryo had invented a new profession for the tribes of the Lyucu: soldiering.

One day, after having drilled his soldiers in yet another complex set of maneuvers, Tenryo dismounted from Kidia and walked back toward his tent. Kidia, who was now a full-grown garinafin almost a hundred feet in length from head to tail, knelt down to enjoy fresh feed and some well-deserved rest.

But after Tenryo had walked about a hundred paces away, just as his soldiers were dismounting from their own garinafins and preparing to rest after a long day of hard practice, Tenryo turned around and tossed one of the flag clubs at Kidia herself.

Everyone knew that Kidia was more like a companion than a mere mount for Tenryo. The garinafin had rescued him from certain death at the hands of the Agon, and she was so favored that Tenryo only drank Kidia's milk.

No one made a move.

"What are you waiting for?" Tenryo shouted. "Have you forgotten all your training?"

Kidia gazed at Tenryo, her black eyes showing surprise, anger, and then finally fear. She started to beat her wings in an attempt to take off, but Tenryo had ridden her hard that day, and she couldn't summon the strength for flight or to breath fire.

"Attack! Now!" Tenryo shouted again.

The other garinafin riders shuddered and scrambled to obey. They mounted their beasts and took off, diving at the riderless Kidia. The foot soldiers followed their training and formed a protective formation around Tenryo, raising their garinafin-hide shields to defend their lord against a final, desperate assault.

Kidia died within minutes, her body singed and torn to bloody pieces by a coordinated assault from dozens of garinafins.

Tenryo gathered all the pilots of the garinafins and the squad leaders of his foot soldiers, and ordered one in five executed as an example of the consequences of not following his orders with alacrity. The families of the executed men and women were made into slaves and distributed to the other pilots and squad leaders.

"Never question my orders," he said. "Never."

Then he knelt down before the carcass of Kidia and whispered, "I'm sorry, old friend. But unless I tested them with someone I loved, they'd never be as obedient as I need them. I will carry out my promise to you and avenge you and your family. May the All-Father and his faithful servant, Péa of the Winged Beasts, grant you eternal rest in the silver pasture in the heavens."

Conflict with the Agon flared up again; both sides raided each other across the ever-shifting border between Ukyu and Gondé.

Tenryo's army gained a reputation as the most powerful fighting force on the scrublands. In border skirmishes against the Agon, they won victory after victory, and people began to whisper that perhaps Tenryo really was the best candidate to succeed his father as pékyu after all.

Pékyu Toluroru summoned Tenryo to his own encampment for a meeting. There was no explanation for what the old pékyu wished to discuss, but rumors spread that Toluroru was unhappy with the way Tenryo had kept most of the prizes from his raiding for his own tribes instead of turning them over to the great pékyu for equitable distribution to all the tribes. Some of Tenryo's thanes advised the young man not to go, and instead wait out the crest of his father's displeasure.

"It is a son's duty to attend to his father," Tenryo said, "regardless of the consequences. Even if the father demands his son to go to the enemy and be a hostage, what right does he have to refuse the order of the man who gave him life?"

On the day of the meeting, Tenryo left his honor guard at the periphery of the great pékyu's encampment and approached the central Great Tent by himself. Although the great pékyu had many more men and women under his command milling about the encampment, the discipline and ferocity of Tenryo's own soldiers and garinafins, lined up in neat ranks some distance away, impressed all the tribes who had gathered to witness this meeting between father and son.

Pékyu Toluroru stood outside the door to his tent. He looked old and frail, and smiled kindly at his son, this son that he had once been willing to sacrifice. As Tenryo approached, he could dimly see through the flap of the Great Tent many warriors assembled within. Some of them had their hands on the handles of their war clubs; others had unsheathed their bone daggers. Far in the back, in the dim light of the interior, Tenryo saw the figures of some of his brothers and sisters, the ones favored by his father.

About a hundred paces from the door of the tent, Tenryo stopped.

"Father, what do you have to say to me?"

"Come into the tent, my beloved son, and we'll share some kyoffir. We haven't been spending nearly enough time together."

"Why are your warriors acting as if they're preparing for the visit of an enemy instead of a beloved son?"

Pékyu Toluroru's face didn't change. "Nonsense. Come into the tent and sit down. We should not be shouting at each other from so far away. Why do you regard your own father with such suspicion?"

Tenryo took Langiaboto, the battle axe he had taken from his childhood companion Diaman Aragoz, off his back. He had tied a fox tail to the end of the handle. Spinning in place to add momentum to his outstretched arm, he heaved it at his father. Everyone in the encampment followed the axe's graceful arc of flight across the space between them.

And as one, Tenryo's garinafin riders took to the air, while his foot soldiers rushed ahead to join their lord. Toluroru stumbled back and Langiaboto landed with a loud thud at the foot of the old chief, whose face held a look of utter disbelief. But before he could give any order, tongues of flames descended from the sky. The old chief was incinerated instantly, and the Great Tent engulfed in a fiery inferno.

The garinafins circled overhead while Tenryo's guards surrounded him, looking fearlessly at all the stunned men and women in the encampment.

The only sounds that could be heard were the crackle of fire and the screams of those trapped within the Great Tent.

And then, a shout began among the crowd. "The pékyu is dead! Long live Pékyu Tenryo Roatan!"

And this was how Tenryo Roatan became the Great Pékyu of the Lyucu, and a new era arrived for both the lands of Ukyu and Gondé.

"Pékyu Tenryo is a ruthless and dangerous man," said Luan Zya.

"He is. Though the stories about him have grown ever more elaborate, turning into legends full of embellishment, yet it is undeniable that he is a leader of unsurpassed vision."

    ~ ~ ~ ~

After securing his position as the leader of the Lyucu, Tenryo turned his attention to waging war against the Agon in earnest. By fighting only with a dedicated professional force using his new tactics and employing the rest of the population for support, he was able to overcome the much larger numbers of the Agon.

The day came when Pékyu Nobo knelt before him.

"When I lived in your home as a hostage, did you ever think such a day would come?" asked Tenryo.

Nobo shook his head. "Such is the way of fortune. The All-Father favors who He will. You have the allegiance of the Agon. I pledge that in my lifetime we will no longer wage war against you." There was no shame in submitting to the stronger. Such was the way of the scrubland.

Tenryo laughed. "Do you think I'm so foolish as to repeat the mistake you made? If I leave you and yours alive, who knows what will happen in ten years? In twenty? Shall I wait until I am infirm only to kneel before one of your children in a repeat of today's scene?"

Nobo looked up at him, his face pleading. "Do you intend to massacre us even though we have surrendered? The All-Father will not contemplate such an act of senseless evil."

"Do not invoke the name of the All-Father," said Tenryo. "Do not blame your failure on the All-Father, just as I do not attribute my success to Him. It is only the weak who think that the gods care about the affairs of men; the strong know that they make their own path in this world, and the gods always favor those who triumph."

Nobo looked up at him, shocked by these words of sacrilege.

Tenryo's guards, who surrounded the pair, looked on impassively. They showed no reaction to Tenryo's speech because the pékyu had not told them to attack anyone. Like an ant colony, their mission was simply to obey. Until Tenryo made up his mind and told them what to do, all they needed to do was to wait and listen.

"When my father sent me to you so that my life could guarantee his safety, where was the All-Father? When I spilled the blood of your son to save my life, where was the All-Father? When I committed patricide to seize the reins of power, where was the All-Father? Every winter, hundreds of men and women die because of lack of food or shelter; where are the All-Father and His son, the Merciful Toryoana of Healing Hands? Every summer, families starve as their cattle fail to make it across the parched landscape to the next watering hole; where are the All-Father and His daughter, Aluro of a Thousand Streams? In battle, both your warriors and mine invoke the names of the All-Father and Diasa, His club-maiden, to aid their cause; who do you think they listen to?"

Nobo said nothing. These were ancient questions that he had never dared to ponder, trusting that the shamans would have the right answers.

"The All-Father, the Every-Mother, and their children do not care, no more than you or I care about the fate of the ants when we dig into their nests for a meal of mushrooms. I can only conclude that there is no good or evil in the eyes of the gods. All that they care about is success or failure. If I am mighty, I am good. If I am weak, I am evil. That is all."

He stepped up to the figure of Nobo and crushed his skull with a single blow from Langiaboto, the Self-Reliant.

All the sons and daughters of the House of Aragoz were made to kneel in a row before the Agon Great Tent, and Tenryo walked down the row, smashing their skulls one after another. This was the most humiliating and disgraceful way to die, as the men and women could not resist, and blood spilled and soaked into the grass under the bright rays of the sun, the Eye of Cudyufin, ensuring that their souls would be forever marked with the brand of shame.

The Agon chieftains and their families were given to the Lyucu nobles as slaves, and the Agon common herders were forced to leave their home territories and move to the least desirable pastures close to the mountains in the east, the deserts in the south, or the ice fields in the north.

But the name of Tenryo was celebrated among the Lyucu. He

was the greatest hero of them all, having delivered them vengeance against the hated Agon. And he had brought them a life of relative peace and prosperity.

He had understood the will of the gods better than any shaman.

"That was when we arrived," said Oga.

CHAPTER FORTY-NINE

THE DREAM OF
THE CITY-SHIPS

UKYU AND GONDÉ, THE LAND OF THE LYUCU
AND AGON: TWENTY-ONE YEARS BEFORE LUAN'S
ARRIVAL IN UKYU AND GONDÉ.

News of the sighting of the strange fleet off the coast caused much consternation among Tenryo's thanes.

"Their ships are thousands of times bigger and more powerful than the small coracles we can construct," said one of the advisers. "These strangers pose a danger. We should attack them as soon as they land." She stood up and ululated, emphasizing her point by raising her war club in the air.

Many of the other nobles voiced their agreement with this opinion as they stood up and banged their war clubs against the bone poles that held up the tent.

But Tenryo ordered the assembled thanes to sit back down. "It is precisely because they may be powerful that we must not act rashly. We shall be as wily as the horrid wolves who blend into the thornbushes before a hunt."

He ordered the garinafins moved miles away from the anticipated landing site of the strange fleet of giant ships. He made it clear that the strangers must never see any of the flying beasts until he directed otherwise.

Then he gave the strangest order of them all: Those with tents constructed from new material should disassemble them and send the hides and poles away. The only dwellings left near the landing site should appear as decrepit and worn down as possible.

The thanes were confused by these commands but did not question them. They were used to obeying the pékyu.

Led by the pékyu himself, the Lyucu welcomed the people from across the sea as honored guests. Long strips of cattle hide were laid out on the beach, and trenchers of meat and cheese and berries and nuts were brought out, along with gourds and skull-cups filled with fragrant kyoffir. The Lyucu stood well back from the surf, giving the visitors plenty of space to land.

The massive mountain-ships dropped anchor some distance away in shallow water and let down small pinnaces that carried visitors onto the beach. Pékyu Tenryo and his thanes gawped at these exotic new people: *Look at how dark some of them are! Have they been sunburnt until their skin refused to heal? And why are so many of them so fat? Do they not work or fight? And look at the shapes of their eyes and noses and foreheads—who knew people could look like that?!*

The visitors pulled their leaf-shaped pinnaces onto the sand and huddled around them tensely. They drew odd-looking weapons and examined the Lyucu, their postures full of fear and suspicion.

Pékyu Tenryo noted with interest how their long daggers—almost as long as war clubs—glinted and dazzled in the sun as though they were made from the reflective surfaces of placid lakes; he observed how some of them carried crescent-shaped clubs with a single string that resembled the curved lyres used by singing bards—though he suspected these were also weapons, perhaps used in conjunction with the bundles of sharp-tipped sticks they carried on their backs; he paid attention to the fact that everyone who was on the beach appeared to be a man—where were the women?—and how luxurious the objects owned by these new people were: Everything seemed to be made from the shiny, waterlike material; some kind of fabric that resembled mist or cloud made substantial; or wood.

So much wood! Pékyu Tenryo could not recall ever seeing so much wood in his entire life as existed in a single mountain-ship. Tall trees did not grow in large numbers on the scrublands; the Lyucu used the short, gnarled branches of wind-bowed bushes as firewood, and the occasional copses of real trees found next to waterholes were reserved for making luxury goods like carved cradleboards, ceremonial bowls, and statues of the gods. One had to journey many days to the east, to the foothills of the massive mountain ranges, to see a real forest. To use wood in such quantity and with such carelessness confirmed the strangers to be incredibly powerful.

He held up his hands to indicate that they were free of weapons, and led the thanes of Lyucu in a slow procession toward the people from across the sea.

After their yearlong voyage, the men of Dara who stumbled ashore were half-starved and grateful for solid land.

But they couldn't relax yet; this land wasn't uninhabited.

Warily, Admiral Krita and his advisers inspected the approaching natives. Their clothes, made of animal skin and woven grass, appeared dirty and crude; the weapons they left behind in a pile, made of bone and stone, looked primitive; their women were dressed just like their men and looked almost as ugly; the dwellings above the beach looked small and unimpressive; there didn't appear to be fields of cultivation or any signs of industry around the area.

And the postures of the natives, led by their empty-handed chief, appeared submissive and humble. Krita could also see a feast laid out on the beach, filled with food that made his mouth water.

Whoever these people were, they didn't appear to be immortals.

Krita relaxed, and told his men to stand down and put away their weapons.

The men of Dara might have thought of themselves as refugees desperately in need of baths and food that wasn't rotten or stale, but the delicious feast prepared by the Lyucu and the ingratiating manner of their hosts made them feel like kings, or perhaps even semi-immortals. To be sure, the fermented milk drink called kyoffir made them want to throw up, but no one was expecting everything to be perfect.

"This is a gentle and harmless people," declared Admiral Krita. And he let it be known to all his followers—just under ten thousand men and women who had survived the arduous journey—that they were free to relax and enjoy the feast.

"Dara! Dara!" they shouted while pointing at themselves. The natives seemed dim-witted, given their incomprehensible jabber, and they hoped that shouting would help.

"Savages," said Admiral Krita. He sighed, sorry that he had not found the land of the immortals after all. Mapidéré's expedition would just have to make the best of a bad situation.

The rest of the expedition—craftsmen, servants, maids, families of the captains and officers—came onshore as well since the coast was declared safe.

The honored guests of Dara were given everything they asked for: food, fresh water, daily entertainment, even native servants and guides for Admiral Krita and his staff. All conversation had to be conducted by miming and gestures and exaggerated expressions, but that was sufficient for the men of Dara to make their desires known.

To be sure, whenever the guests wanted to explore the surrounding countryside, the Lyucu hosts smiled with confusion at their requests and instead offered more food and that strong fermented milk drink, which the guests did not really enjoy as it upset their stomachs. But considering how primitive these people were, the men of Dara weren't all that keen on seeing more tents full of half-dressed savages or more stinking herds of long-haired cattle.

It was clear that these barbarians didn't know anything about immortals. The expedition members, surrounded daily by admiring glances and expressions of amazement, began to feel as if they were the lords of all creation.

They became ever more arrogant toward their hosts, demanding more food, service, and the company of women—whether willing or not. When a few of Krita's men acted out their base instincts on some of the native women—Mapidéré's expedition was mostly staffed by men—the insulted women, one of whom was a Lyucu chieftain, reacted with anger and brought their friends and followers to demand justice with clubs and axes drawn.

Krita decided that a show of force was necessary, and, instead of retreating to the city-ships with the offending members of the expedition, he ordered the marines to stand their ground and do whatever was necessary to defend the Dara camp.

The result was a one-sided slaughter. The Lyucu had never fought against metal weapons or bows and arrows, and seventeen Lyucu warriors lay dead at the end of the skirmish while only one of Krita's men was injured. Still, Krita was keenly aware of how vastly outnumbered his side was, and he ordered everyone to retreat onto the city-ships and prepare to set sail if the situation deteriorated further.

But Pékyu Tenryo came personally to apologize, kneeling on the beach and begging for Krita to return. Thinking that he had impressed the barbaric chief with that display of force, Krita agreed, over the objection of some of his more cautious advisers.

"These people do not even know the use of metal," Krita said contemptuously. "What risk do they really pose? They must be terrified of us! In a way, we *have* found paradise—we are the immortals here, almost like gods to these people!"

In truth, the Lyucu did know about metal, but it was a resource that they rarely had access to except in the form of occasional lumps found lying on the scrubland, supposedly the remnants of fallen stars. Only the most powerful Lyucu chieftains and the pékyu himself had crude metal jewelry formed by hammering these lumps into various decorative shapes.

Krita now demanded that the Lyucu acknowledge the suzerainty of Dara and Emperor Mapidéré, with himself as the emperor's personal representative. The pékyu readily acquiesced and treated Krita as his lord and master.

The Lyucu thanes were outraged and stared at their king in disbelief, but Pékyu Tenryo's authority was such that not a single person objected.

Next, Krita demanded that the Lyucu supply his troops with feminine company—the lack of which was the cause of the unpleasantness in the first place. Again, the pékyu immediately agreed and ordered several of his female chieftains and their daughters to undertake the task personally.

Once again, Tenryo's thanes were shocked by the servile behavior of their chief, but once again they obeyed him without question.

The will of this people has been broken, thought Krita. *A little demonstration of force goes a long way with savages.* In some ways, he even admired the flexibility of Pékyu Tenryo. His people were confronted by a race whose might they could not match, and the barbarian king had chosen wisely to submit rather than to resist uselessly.

The Lyucu began to fall sick. The strange new disease was not like anything the tribes had experienced before. People coughed, boils appeared on their skins, and many died. Every family mourned because every family lost someone.

But the visitors from Dara seemed immune from the plague.

Many began to whisper that this was a punishment from the All-Father and Every-Mother for Pékyu Tenryo's craven behavior.

Pékyu Tenryo executed those who spread such rumors. He reminded his thanes that he had guided them to victory over the Agon, and he would lead them on a new path that, in time, they would come to understand.

Eventually, people stopped dying. "We have become more like them," said Tenryo. And it was not clear if he meant it as a lament or a celebration.

ᔇ ᔁ ᔇ ᔁ

"The story you've told me so far is nothing like what I've heard from the Lyucu," said Luan.

"You'll soon understand why," said Oga.

To further ingratiate himself with his new masters, Tenryo followed the men from Dara around like a lapdog, trying to anticipate their needs and giving them everything they might desire.

The Lyucu warriors gazed at their king with utter contempt, but he seemed to pay them no heed.

Since just nodding and smiling all the time bored the "Lords of Dara"—the moniker began as a joke among Krita's officers, but they rather liked the way it sounded, even though none of them were important enough back home to rank among true nobles—Tenryo peppered them with questions conveyed by gestures and exaggerated facial expressions. He mimed that he wanted to hear stories about how the great city-ships were built, and he promised to be delighted and awed if his masters would show him how the ships actually sailed.

Admiral Krita decided to take advantage of their new faithful servants by squeezing everything possible out of them. With elaborate pictures and lots of pointing and shouting, Krita and his captains managed to explain to Tenryo that they needed lumber to repair the city-ships after weathering the long voyage. They had noticed the absence of suitable trees in the country and, though not very hopeful, decided to try to see if the barbarian chief had any ideas.

Tenryo nodded and bowed and smiled. Secretly, he dispatched teams of garinafins and riders to the distant mountains in the east to collect lumber. This was not something the tribes had ever done, and many expressed doubts about the wisdom of breaking with tradition, but Tenryo would not be persuaded.

When the teams returned after weeks of strenuous labor, Tenryo had the chopped trees dropped into the sea so that the tides carried them in like so much flotsam, and then he made a big production of waking Krita up in the middle of night, literally jumping up and down and joyously proclaiming his delight.

Although Krita was irritated to be woken up from his dreams, he was delighted to find so many excellent logs piled up on the moonlit beach. By now, Tenryo had picked up enough broken bits of Dara vernacular that Krita finally understood that the ecstatic barbarian chief was celebrating the fact that the gods of Dara had delivered the wood as a miracle. Though Krita had never been particularly religious, drifting over the sea for almost a year without knowing whether he was going to live or die had a way of changing attitudes. He piously thanked the gods and now viewed Pékyu Tenryo, who had delivered the exciting news, as some sort of exotic native good-luck charm.

Up to this point, Krita and his captains had taken care to keep the natives away from the city-ships in order not to reveal too much information about themselves. However, good-luck charms were harmless, beloved, and trusted, and Hujin Krita now brushed aside urgings of caution from his advisers and allowed the barbarians, especially the good-looking women, to come aboard the city-ships to better serve their Dara masters and lovers.

He began to forget where he was, so much did he enjoy the hospitality of these rather primitive, but innocent, savages.

Tenryo and a group of high-ranked thanes now seemed to spend every waking moment with Admiral Krita and his officers, admiring their clothes, their bowls and eating sticks, their jewelry and musical instruments. Aboard the city-ships, Tenryo and his nobles acted like children delighted by a magic wonderland, and they begged Krita and his retinue to teach them the language of Dara and the uses of the wondrous machines and gadgets around them.

The women who had been assigned the duty of caring for these Lords of Dara—several of them high-ranking thanes—took to their task with special zeal, and were solicitous of their men's pleasure in every manner. They were impressed by almost anything and everything the men of Dara did and eagerly learned to adopt the customs and artifice of Dara—makeup, courtly dance, coquettish looks—

—much to the annoyance of the wives of Dara who had accompanied their officer husbands on this expedition. They suggested to the men, pointedly, that the giggles of awe in the bedrooms and the enthusiastic screams of joy everywhere else emitted by these barbarian women were perhaps not completely believable.

"Why is it implausible that the native women would fall in love with the Lords of Dara?" scoffed Admiral Krita when these complaints came to his attention. "When these barbarian girls are properly cleaned up, they look quite fetching! Surely the love of beauty and admiration for nobility are universal among the weaker sex. These poor girls! All their lives they've only known smelly, savage barbarian men who don't know anything about refined manners, romantic poetry, or the delicate arts of love that are the fruits of civilization. They've only worn rough fur instead of smooth silk; they've only drunk revolting fermented milk instead of fragrant, rose-scented tea; they've only known a terrible life in which they're forced to herd cattle and fight off thieves along with the men, instead of a life of gentle leisure suitable for proper ladies. If I were one of these women, I'd fall for me too!"

Of course, when some of the women of Dara requested that Lyucu men be assigned to them—surely when these savage men were cleaned up, their lives spent in rough and hard labor in fresh air and open sun ought to have produced fetching bodies too?—Admiral Krita denied the demands immediately as incompatible with the teachings of Kon Fiji and other sages.

Undaunted by ridicule or loss of face even when he knew only a few phrases, Tenryo made rapid progress in learning the vernacular of Dara, but when Krita and his officers asked to study the language of the Lyucu, Tenryo explained (in halting, awkward, but ever-improving Dara speech) that as the Lyucu were so far behind Dara in refinement and civilized progress, he did not wish to sully the superior intellect of his lords with the primitive speech of the people of the scrubland.

As the Lyucu helped Admiral Krita repair his ships and resupply them for an eventual journey back to Dara, Tenryo proposed that progress would be sped up if the craftsmen and engineers of Dara would take on Lyucu apprentices to perform less skilled work. This was readily assented to, and the shipwrights, carpenters, and smiths of the exploration fleet worked with crews of Lyucu apprentices, teaching them their art. After the city-ships were mostly repaired, Tenryo discovered yet another supply of lumber in a cove not far from where the city-ships were anchored.

"The gods know that the honored Lords of Dara will surely depart one day to continue the magnificent task of finding the immortals. Perhaps they think it would be useful for the Lyucu to help you construct more ships to prepare for unknown dangers in the sea? . . . Though it is of course difficult to see what dangers could not be overcome by the Lords of Dara, surely almost like the immortals themselves."

Cradled and caressed and kissed by four beautiful Lyucu thanes with long blond tresses, Krita approved Tenryo's request to have the shipwrights teach the Lyucu how to build ships after the fashion of Dara. They wouldn't be city-ships—the shipwrights explained that they lacked the equipment and shipyard facilities to undertake such a massive project—but they would be sturdy, seaworthy ships far better than the coracles of the Lyucu.

Truth be told, Admiral Krita had little appetite to brave the seas again. After the terrors of the long journey to Ukyu, he really wanted nothing more than this happy life where all his needs were taken care of by Pékyu Tenryo and he could spend almost every hour in the company of a string of lovely, exotic mistresses whose athletic bodies showed him heights of pleasure he had never imagined. Once in a while he thought of his old friend Ronaza Métu, and felt a twinge of guilt as he suspected that Emperor Mapidéré had already carried out his threat against him. But if that was so, wasn't it even more incumbent on him to enjoy this life for both of them?

Most of his senior staff agreed. Their Lyucu mistresses demonstrated great curiosity about everything having to do with Dara—a natural reaction of barbarians confronted by a superior civilization—and the men rather enjoyed playing the role of fonts of wisdom, regaling their companions in bed with all kinds of lectures about the history, geography, science, and politics of Dara. To the delight of many of these Lords of Dara, the women seemed especially impressed with tales of the martial prowess of their homeland, and asked the men to explain in detail the brilliant field tactics of these legendary generals and to demonstrate the proper way to use the terrible, fancy weapons of Dara. They giggled coquettishly—the way the Lords of Dara had taught them—while watching these men huff and puff through weapons drills, cooing appreciatively when one of the men over-exerted himself and had to take a break from swinging a steel sword or drawing a heavy bow.

The women seemed rather disappointed when bladesmiths and fletchers explained that they could not make more steel swords and bronze arrowheads unless they discovered easily mined sources of metal. The ingots carried by the city-ships would only suffice for a few replacements. It struck some of the men as a bit unseemly that women would be so interested in weapons, but the Lords of Dara blamed the wild nature of barbaric life for such unfeminine behavior.

Even though Krita refused to permit any of the Dara women on his expedition—hired by the fleet as servants, cooks, seamstresses, sailmakers, fisherwomen, and so on, as well as the families of the senior command staff—from "enjoying" the company of the Lyucu men, this was a prohibition that grew increasingly hard to enforce over time as the Lyucu and expedition members mingled freely. The Lyucu lovers Dara women took on were equally curious about that distant, magical land, where words could be frozen into marks on paper and where wind and water could be commanded to push wheels and sails and do useful work.

The stories the Dara women told their lovers, of course, had a distinctly different flavor than the stories told by the men—for one thing, Admiral Krita and his command staff appeared much less heroic in these stories than in their own tellings. The women shared with Lyucu men the sort of knowledge that these "Lords of Dara" were unfamiliar with—the actual lives of ordinary families, practical geography, and how the real Lords of Dara appeared to those whose lives were decidedly less grand.

As the days went on, Admiral Krita and his senior staff grew even more indolent and more reluctant to leave their comfortable position as quasi-kings of Lyucu, worshipped by everyone from Pékyu Tenryo down. Luckily, the pékyu kept on coming up with new reasons for them to tarry.

Perhaps the Lords of Dara would like to make more metal weapons with Lyucu aid? Or how about teaching and training Lyucu sailors to help when the expedition fleet decides to resume its journey? Maybe the Lyucu craftsmen, some of whom are now fairly skilled under the tutelage of Dara masters, could help re-create some of the wonders the Lords of Dara have spoken of in their homeland?

Admiral Krita nodded. "An excellent plan, Pékyu Tenryo! If only Emperor Mapidéré knew that he had such a faithful servant across the seas!"

Pékyu Tenryo bowed so deeply that Krita could not see his face.

Krita became more tyrannical and whimsical in his demands. He no longer referred to himself as the personal representative of Mapidéré, but demanded that the Lyucu address him as the emperor himself.

Some members of his expedition, especially the scholars, became uneasy.

"It is not right that we should treat this people, who have welcomed us, as though they're our slaves," they pleaded with him. "This is hardly the behavior of a truly civilized people. If they deal with us as brothers, we should deal with them the same."

Krita scoffed at these objections. In his imagination, he was a miniature version of Emperor Mapidéré, fated to rule over this benighted, though docile, people. The gods of Dara had given him a gift: this new domain that was his to mold and sculpt. He would lift this people out of ignorance and give them the benefits of civilization.

Unlike the savages of Tan Adü, who resisted being cultivated and reined in by the wisdom of Dara, these savages of the new world were eminently teachable. He began to dream of his descendants ruling over this people far into the future, and he started to plan for a palace—it would be grand and circular (for wasn't a circle the height of perfection, like himself?), made out of the highest quality wood, even if this land seemed to have so little supply of it—as well as which of his many mistresses he would make into the lucky consorts he would install into this pleasure dome.

Then, one morning, Krita woke up and found his hands and feet bound. His two favorite Lyucu mistresses, Nolon and Kya, stood at the foot of his bed, holding his sword and bow.

"What sort of joke is this?" asked Krita.

But Nolon, who had always been so submissive, smiled coldly at him. "We've learned all we need from you." There was something odd about the way she spoke in the vernacular of Dara: There was no trace of coquettishness in it at all.

"What are you talking about?" Krita struggled against his bounds and found the strong sinews to give not an inch. "Untie me immediately! When Tenryo finds out about this, he's going to kill everyone in your families, you damned whore—"

Kya, who had never once before thwarted his will, stepped up and slapped him hard across the face, silencing him immediately. "Pékyu Tenryo gave the order this morning. As of this moment, all your commanders have been trussed up just like you, and Lyucu warriors are boarding every ship and taking over. The only people who'll be killed are your followers who refuse to surrender."

It wasn't until they had dragged him out of the cabin, loaded him onto a pinnace, and marched him onto land so that he could join the other captured "Lords of Dara" that Krita's disbelief was dispelled.

He and his senior command staff hung their heads in shame, finally realizing that they had all been taken in by the wily and patient barbarian king.

By the time the sun had completely risen, almost all the city-ships of the expedition fleet had been captured. Most of the captains and senior officers had been incapacitated by their Lyucu lovers in sleep, and of the few who had awakened in time to try to put up some sort of resistance, the Lyucu women overcame them easily, as they had seen the men's fighting techniques in great detail and worked out countermoves ahead of time.

Using the officers as hostages, the women had forced the sailors and marines to drop down rope ladders and welcome aboard the Lyucu warriors who rowed out to the anchored ships in coracles and pinnaces. The Dara encampment onshore, of course, had been overrun before dawn.

Of the fifty city-ships in the expedition fleet, only two had captains who refused to give in and commanded their crews to resist to the utmost. They were killed, but the sailors were able to overwhelm the Lyucu women and lift anchor in an attempt to escape from this sudden turn of events.

They barely managed to get about a mile away before the great garinafins rose over the horizon and fell on them like Mingén falcons diving for fish. Soon, the two ships were nothing more than two burning wrecks, and sailors who hadn't been incinerated were crying desperately for rescue in the churning sea, begging to surrender to the Lyucu.

An astonished Krita finally understood how utterly foolish he had been.

The former Lords of Dara were packed into underground cellars while Pékyu Tenryo gathered his warriors to announce his plans.

"This is a gift from the All-Father, brothers and sisters," declared Tenryo. "It is the best gift from Him since the time He created the lands of Ukyu and Gondé, since He placed us and the Agon in this world to test our faith.

"Our land is beautiful—who can deny the thrill of watching a sunset from the back of a soaring garinafin?—but it is also harsh and difficult. All of you have known grandmothers and grandfathers choosing to stay behind to die in times of drought so that the tribe could move on without being burdened with their needs. All of you have known mothers forced to decide which child to feed when there is not enough for all and she must maintain her strength for the migration. All of you have seen fathers beat their chests in despair when a pack of horrid wolves, a plague, or even a flash flood wipes out the family's herd, their livelihood. The scrubland is unforgiving, and we live ever at the mercy of forces beyond our ken or control.

"And the wars. Who can forget the wars? The wars between the Agon and the Lyucu are still fresh in our memories, but long before our peoples had coalesced into nations, the tribes have fought each other, as did families. I doubt there has been a single day in the history of this land when it was completely at peace. How many men and women have lost their lives in the struggle for survival? It was either kill or be killed because this land, though vast, can provide but for so few.

"It was not always so. Late at night, next to the fire pits and after everyone has had their fill of kyoffir, the elders tell stories of our past. We know from these old tales, the waystones of our spirit, that long ago our ancestors lived in a land that was lush and green, a paradise. There, the rivers flowed with honey and milk, and the bushes were heavy with soft, juicy berries, not the hard nuts that break teeth. In that land, the cattle calved each spring without fail, and there were no wolves to steal from us. Our ancestors dined on plenty and every parent could have as many children as they wished, not having to worry about how many they could keep alive. War was unknown because there was enough for everyone, from the oldest grandmother who had lost all her teeth, to the mewling babe yet to chew her first piece of fatty marrow.

"Our ancestors then angered the All-Father somehow. The stories of the different tribes do not agree on this. Some say that it was because they stole the special kyoffir that the All-Father kept for his immortal children, the purified spirits who dwell in the mountains and clouds and whom we worship. Some say that it was because they had become slothful and arrogant due to their life of leisure and ease, and they disobeyed the All-Father's command to keep the celestial herd well-watered and fed. Some say that it was because they had forgotten the virtues instilled in them by the All-Father and fell to greed and internecine strife.

"Whatever the reason, the All-Father cast us out of paradise and placed us here so that our lives may be hard and our faith sharpened by suffering.

"But now we have learned something new and momentous. The All-Father has prepared another land for us, a new paradise called Dara. Have you heard the stories the savages of Dara tell? Over there, the rivers overflow with delicious wine—kyoffir made from fruit!—and fat fish practically leap out of the water onto your plates. The fields are so green and lush that they could feed all of us and our cattle and garinafins even if we were as numerous as the stars in the sky! Families there may have a dozen children, a dozen! And the old die peacefully in sleep while the young honor their memories by multiplying and being fruitful. Luxury greets you everywhere you look: shiny metal poking out of the ground; great, sky-clawing trees arrayed in dense forests; sparkling jewels dangling from every ear and neck like ripe berries.

"That is the land that we should live in.

"'But Pékyu Tenryo,' I hear some of you say. 'That land is already inhabited.'

"That's right. But look at what manner of inhabitants they are: arrogant, soft, lazy, devoid of virtue. They arrived at our shores as terrified refugees who had almost run out of food and water. We took them in as honored guests, shared our food and kyoffir with them, offered them all they needed.

"And for this hospitality, how have they repaid us? They acted as though they belonged to the race of immortal spirits, though they knew perfectly well that they were but ordinary mortals like you or me. They deliberately infected us with sicknesses previously unknown in this land . . . please forgive me for my tears, but who can forget the piteous cries of fathers holding their disease-stricken daughters or the howls of sons cradling the bodies of their illness-ravished mothers? Barbaric in their customs—consider how they degrade their women!—they dared to call us savages and insulted our women, many of them thanes and chiefs, as well as the wives, mothers, sisters, and daughters of our men. They slaughtered our warriors with better weapons and think that makes them superior—but the measure of a warrior is in her spirit, not her tool.

"So we bided our time; we hid our strengths to lure them into revealing their weaknesses; we pretended to submit so that we could observe them up close and learn their secrets. What have we learned?

"They have no concept of honor and lie constantly to make themselves appear greater and more powerful. Effete and stupid, they understand only the language of violence—they thought they could intimidate us with their metal swords and vibrating bows, and yet when our garinafin riders appeared, all they could do was to cower in fear without even putting up a real fight. Though we followed the custom of the scrublands and opened our tents and hearts to strangers, sharing all that we possessed with them, they sought only to dominate and enslave us.

"No, the All-Father could not have meant for such a barbarous race to possess paradise. Rather, He sent these savages to us as a message, telling us that He has prepared a new home for us already filled with slaves.

"Do you not see how these indolent, arrogant men sound so similar to the fallen ancestors in our ancient tales? They have squandered their fortune, wallowing like greedy calves in muddy puddles, not knowing that winter is around the corner. We are the instruments of the All-Father, meant to cleanse that land of these ingrates. We are the punishment for their sins. We're the divine scourge.

"Brothers and sisters, we have a mission. We shall conquer Dara and enslave these people until their spirits are purified of the diseases they call civilization, until we have redeemed paradise for the All-Father's favorite children."

And the scrublands were filled with the ululating war cries of a thousand warriors calling for blood, for cosmic justice and sacred war.

And so the Lords of Dara overnight became the captives of the Lyucu, and a nightmarish stage of existence began for them. The prisoners were forced to divulge every bit of information that could be useful to their new masters in planning their invasion of the Dara homeland.

Although the technologies brought by the city-ships were interesting, Pékyu Tenryo quickly decided that most of them were not practical for adoption by the Lyucu. Ukyu and Gondé were simply too different from the Islands of Dara, and it was no more sensible for the Lyucu to adopt the way of life of Dara than it would be for a desert cactus to be transplanted to the glaciers of the far north. The bronze and steel swords wielded by Krita and his officers were certainly stronger than bone axes and clubs, but Lyucu had no known source of iron or copper, and the supply brought by the city-ships would be quickly exhausted. Likewise, the scrublands lacked the wood to supply fletchers with arrow shafts, and stone arrowheads would be no better than slingshots.

Pékyu Tenryo did not think it wise to adopt a new mode of warfare that relied on weapons that the Lyucu could not replenish, and so he decided to focus on learning as much as he could about the fighting techniques of the Islands of Dara so that they could be countered.

An arena with walls made from garinafin bones was constructed— using the slave labor of the men of Dara, of course—and afterward Krita and his men were forced to spend their days inside the arena fighting against the warriors of Lyucu from sunup to sundown, so that Tenryo could study how the men of Dara waged war.

From Cocru sword dances to Faça infantry formations, the pékyu studied everything and carefully noted the weaknesses of each technique. Officers and soldiers were coerced to describe past battles in excruciating detail so that the general patterns of Dara military thinking could be discerned.

Krita eventually suffered a wound that became infected in one of these meaningless mock battles—an infection that the doctors who had come along on the expedition could not cure as they lacked the herbs native to Dara. As Krita lay in a feverish delirium before death, he could be heard to mutter words of love for Nolon and Kya, the Lyucu thanes who had beguiled him and then captured him, as well as prayers to the gods for Dara to take him to the land of immortals.

The women and other noncombatants—craftsmen and craftswomen, traders, navigators, sailors, cooks, maids, doctors—from Dara were not spared either. They were made to fill in details of Dara society that the Lyucu had not already learned: how roads were constructed; how villages were organized; how Imperial power was wielded by Mapidéré in Pan and how the ordinary people felt its effects. Tenryo understood that he would have to conquer a much larger population with a small force, and even with the advantage provided by the garinafin riders, controlling such a population required some understanding of the motivations and patterns of life, which had to be exploited to benefit an occupying force.

Oga presented a special case. At first, upon being informed that he was a fisherman, Tenryo decided that Oga's knowledge was of limited use. Fishing was not an important source of food for most Lyucu, and the species of fish common in Dara were different from the common species near the coast of Ukyu and Gondé, with Dara fishing techniques often inapplicable. Oga was thus assigned the most menial tasks.

But Tenryo's thanes then noticed that Oga was the center of attention for gatherings of captives. After a long day's hard labor, he entertained them with lively tales and kept their spirits up. Some thanes became suspicious of Oga, fearing that he might become the leader of a secret revolt.

Tenryo decided that he would listen to Oga's stories himself. For several nights in a row, disguised as a simple Lyucu slave overseer, he sat on the very edge of the crowd of captives from Dara gathered around the fire, listening to Oga's performances.

Oga's tales were not mere retellings of legends from Dara; instead, he spun embellished tales of their journey here to Ukyu and Gondé. Though he was unlettered, he had a natural storyteller's gift for craft and invention. He spoke of the wonder of the Wall of Storms, of pods of whales and crubens at sea, of the immortals who lived amongst the spinning stars, of fantastical creatures and princes who inhabited new lands. He had even picked up bits of the Lyucu tongue and learned some of their stories, which he wove into fantastic tapestries of savage daring and dauntless cunning.

Tenryo was mesmerized. Oga was a man who had somehow managed to marry the sophistication of Dara's storytellers with the raw materials gathered from a new land. He was telling Dara-style epics using the setting and values of the land of his captivity.

And so the great pékyu ordered Oga into his own service. "You will accompany me everywhere I go and see everything I see. Like your court historians who wrote down the deeds of the Lords of Dara, you will be my biographer, the architect of my living monument, a story to instruct a thousand ages."

Of course, every captive from Dara was also used to teach the Lyucu their language. Pékyu Tenryo's young children were brought up to speak it—it was essential to understand the thoughts of a foreign people if the Lyucu were to rule over them.

As the captives exhausted their store of useful information, pressure intensified. Torture became routine, and the daily drills in the arena became more relentless. Some of the captives died from disease or injuries, and others took their own lives. Even in death, however, their suffering did not end. Their children—whether born to marriages among the captives or from couplings between the Lyucu and their slaves—were enslaved in their place. The cursed blood of Dara doomed them to the same fate as their parents, though a few of the mixed-blood children were raised as full members of the Lyucu tribes if their mothers or fathers were powerful thanes.

Two years after landing, nine out of ten of the men and women who had arrived in Ukyu in the city-ships were dead.

The first light of dawn filtered through the bars at the top of the tunnel,
dimly illuminating the inside of the dark cell.

"I cannot imagine how much you have suffered in the ensuing nineteen
years," said Luan Zya. Not a single thing Cudyu and Vadyu had told him
was true. He hoped against hope that the old man's survival meant that the
Lyucu had abandoned their mad quest to sail across the ocean to wage war.

"Has it already been nineteen years?" muttered Oga Kidosu. "So many
friends . . . maimed, beaten, then dead. So many times I've wanted to die,
but I wanted to see home one last time. . . ."

To conquer Dara, first the Lyucu had to find a way back to it.

Pékyu Tenryo understood that the path Krita's fleet had followed,
which depended on the strong oceanic current, was a dead end. Even
the city-ships could not do much against the powerful pull of the
current, and sailing "upriver," as it were, seemed an impossible dream.
Tenryo thus dedicated himself to the task of figuring out a new way
back to Dara.

By carefully examining the navigational logs of the city-ships and
skilled application of torture to the Dara navigators—who had been
spared so far for this purpose—Tenryo was able to obtain an approxi-
mate idea of the location of the Islands of Dara. Ever cautious, he
decided to send out a small scouting expedition whose only goal was
to confirm the location of the Islands.

Instead of using the captured city-ships, which he intended to use
to transport his invasion force, Tenryo built a small exploratory fleet
based on traditional Lyucu seafaring designs enhanced with the knowledge of Dara shipwrights.

Though the Lyucu and the Agon were both nomadic peoples
living on the backs of garinafins across the scrubland, some tribes
had settled along the coast and were skilled with navigating the sea
in more advanced craft than the small coracles that Luan Zya had
seen. Some of these craft were constructed out of multiple circular coracle hulls connected together with a bone-lattice frame, and

garinafin hide, which was both waterproof and fire-resistant, was then stretched over it to form a platform. Animal bladders filled with air were then attached to the lattice to provide additional flotation. These keelless craft were very shallow-drafting by design, but they were surprisingly stable on the sea, though they did not have anywhere near the capacity of the city-ships and transporting any garinafins was out of the question.

A fleet of these Lyucu ships, augmented with a few Dara-style ships constructed by the Lyucu as learning projects while Admiral Krita was still alive, were dispatched and sailed due west to try to find the Islands of Dara. The Lyucu had never sailed that far into the ocean, believing that the ocean extended in that direction as a featureless, endless expanse. Most voyages by Lyucu ships in the past had been coastal, transporting goods for trade or warriors for raids. But now that they knew there was land beneath the horizon, the men and women aboard were eager and expectant.

Only one of the ships returned, more than a year later, with news that the path west was impassable. The fleet had managed to cross the ocean current in its slow-moving portion, just as recorded in Krita's logs; it had then come into sight of the Wall of Storms, also reported by Krita.

The survivors spoke of a curtain made of cyclones that rose from the sea to the sky. For months, the ships sailed north and south in the hopes of locating an opening, but none could be found. Frustrated, the fleet commander ordered the ships to try to brave the cyclones head-on, but the storms were so furious that all the other Lyucu ships had perished, and this one barely escaped in time. Thereafter, one of the cyclones had left the wall and seemed to gain a will of its own as it pursued the surviving ship for days like a cat toying with a mouse. It was only by pure luck that the ship managed to escape and return to tell the tale.

The pékyu had to give up his dream, the terrified survivors explained, for paradise seemed to be guarded by furious demons of the sea and the air.

But Tenryo did not give up. He had the survivors executed for cowardice and disobedience—he had told them to find a passage to the Islands of Dara, not to come crawling back with excuses for why it couldn't be done.

A second fleet was dispatched to complete the task that the first could not finish.

"Absolute obedience!" thundered Pékyu Tenryo. "Remember that."

This fleet suffered a fate even worse than its predecessor, for not a single ship returned after a year. Some of Tenryo's most trusted thanes grumbled that the pékyu's uncompromising style of command probably taught the members of the second fleet that it was better to leave and find some uninhabited island to live out the rest of their days than to face certain death, either at the Wall of Storms or at the hands of the pékyu.

The pékyu had to accept that his plan to conquer Dara was but an unfulfillable dream and spoke no more of it.

The surviving captives were distributed to the tribes as ordinary slaves, and the Lyucu resumed their nomadic life across the scrubland, visions of paradise seemingly forgotten. The fleet of city-ships remained anchored next to the shore, guarded by a detachment of the Lyucu army along with about a dozen garinafins. From time to time, the Agon, who had been forced into parts of the scrubland with the harshest conditions, revolted, and Tenryo would lead expeditions to put down these rebellions. But for the most part, life seemed to return to its familiar rhythm for most of the people of the scrubland.

And then, five years after the second fleet had left, pieces of wreckage washed ashore on the coast of Ukyu and Gondé. The designs carved into the bone spars proved beyond a doubt that they came from the second fleet.

However, although the fleet had departed from Ukyu and sailed northwest, the wreckage came in from the southeast.

"That was the clue that solved the mystery of the current for me," said Luan.
"Clue?"

Luan explained that Cudyu and Vadyu had asked him to find a way back to Dara, and he had gone over the records they showed him in great detail. The direction and timing of the wreckage had led to the breakthrough.

"It is a circle," he muttered. "The great oceanic current moves in a circle."

"That was Pêkyu Tenryo's conclusion as well," said Oga Kidosu. "The current that had carried us here is like a serpent that had swallowed its tail. Had Admiral Krita continued to follow the current even as it slowed down near the coast of Ukyu, we would have been carried back to the Islands of Dara."

"Zomi, your daughter, and I might have found pieces of the wreckage from the same fleet," Luan said. And he told Oga about the incredible vision Zomi had seen as a young child and how his own interest in exploring far to the north had been kindled by the mysterious artifacts carved with stylized designs of the garinafins.

"So Mapidéré's expedition inspired Pêkyu Tenryo's fleets, which brought you here in a roundabout way," marveled Oga Kidosu. "What an amazing series of coincidences."

"As roundabout as the great oceanic current that connects us all," said Luan Zya. "Perhaps fate is made up of such coincidences when we gaze back at the path of our lives."

Oga shook his head and chuckled. "I'm not much of a philosopher. What I can tell you is that the wreckage of that second fleet made Pêkyu Tenryo think that there was a northwest passage to Dara. The invasion fleet would have to sail to the northwest, pick up the current again, and follow it until arriving in Dara. Pêkyu Tenryo's dream of the grand conquest of paradise was revived.

"He sent out a third fleet to ascertain the route, this time with strict orders not to take unnecessary risks so that useful information could be obtained. This expedition returned in a year with reports that the current did indeed bring them north of Dara, where the coracles had to struggle mightily to depart from its pull.

"But the Wall of Storms was also there—"

"—as both of us well know," interrupted Luan Zya with a light chuckle.

"The storms that made up the wall there moved chaotically and threatened to destroy all ships that approached. Though this third expedition tarried *for over three months near the Wall, they could not find a way through. It was likely another rash attempt to break through the Wall by force that had caused the demise of the second expedition.*

"From the far-flung tribes over the scrubland, Pēkyu Tenryo rounded up the survivors of Admiral Krita's fleet and imprisoned all of us."

"Because the pēkyu wanted to find out your secret for passing through the Wall of Storms?" Luan asked.

Oga nodded wearily. "No matter how many times we tried to explain that we had passed through the Wall purely as a matter of luck, without any knowledge of how it worked, the pēkyu refused to believe us. The tortures were relentless, and some of the prisoners, unable to tolerate the pain, made up answers.

"These supposed navigation tricks, of course, were proven to be false during subsequent expeditions, and so the men responsible were executed.

"For years, I had been composing the epic of Pēkyu Tenryo—you have been hearing snippets of it. It was a way to survive, and I was fascinated by Tenryo, hoping that I could mitigate against his life of brutality and conquest with a fictionalized account that sought virtue, much as Tututika was said to hold up magical mirrors to men and women that showed them as better than they were, thereby driving them to improve themselves.

"But I could no longer hold my tongue in the face of such horror. I composed a new chapter that showed him exactly as he was: a man who thought he was dreaming a grand dream but who only bestowed nightmares upon all. The pēkyu was enraged, and I was dismissed from his presence and tossed here to meditate upon the errors of my ways. I have lost count of the days spent in this sunless dungeon.

"I'm the very last survivor of those who came from Dara, and as you can see, I do not think I will last much longer."

Luan Zya closed his eyes and reviewed his entire experience since coming to shore. Everything had been a lie.

The Lyucu had likely figured out that he was a scholar of some skill based on Gitré Üthu and the remnants of his kite-raft, and then concocted an elaborate ruse. They had constructed the mass graves and manufactured an alternative history of the relationship between Dara and the Lyucu. Taking advantage of his instincts as a teacher and his vulnerability in the wake of his harrowing journey, Cudyu and Vadyu had deceived him into helping them figure out a way to lead a fleet back to the Islands of Dara.

Instead of delivering the bodies of the dead members of Krita's expedition, the fleet would carry an invading army and bring death to tens of thousands.

Though the Lyucu already knew the oceanic current went around in a circle, they did not reveal that fact to Luan. That was probably a test to see if Luan really was skilled or merely someone who thought highly of himself without possessing real knowledge, like so many of the "Lords of Dara."

The puzzle they couldn't figure out was how to get through the Wall of Storms, and that was the real task they had given Luan. They wanted to make him into an accessory in the greatest calamity to ever befall Dara.

Luan shuddered. They had almost succeeded.

The Wall of Storms, like the cicadas who emerged from the earth only in certain years or eclipses of the sun and the moon, followed patterns. Over time, passages of varying length and stability would open in it. He had finally worked out a model that fit all the observed data, and using the model, it was possible to predict the next stable opening in the Wall that would allow an invasion fleet to sail through.

And he had written out the calculations in Gitré Üthu, left in the tent that he shared with Cudyu and Vadyu. He had to get back before the answer fell into the hands of the Lyucu.

As Luan rushed to climb back up the tunnel to the surface, the bone-grate door at the top slammed shut.

"Luan Zya." The voice of Prince Cudyu drifted down the tunnel. It was cold and devoid of the respect that he had always demonstrated to Luan. "Your attempt to commit treason has been uncovered."

CHAPTER FIFTY

HOMECOMING

UKYU AND GONDÉ:
TWO YEARS EARLIER.

Luan Zya's calculations yielded the date of the next stable break in the Wall of Storms to the north of Dara. In order to make that date, the invasion fleet would have to set off from Ukyu almost a year ahead of time.

This meant that preparations for the greatest invasion in the history of the people of the scrublands had to start right away.

The great city-ships had to be adapted to transport garinafins as well as Lyucu warriors, and sufficient supplies and feed had to be gathered to last a year. In the end, a total of sixty garinafins and five thousand warriors would join the expedition led by the pékyu himself, which was intended to establish a base in Dara. Tenryo's oldest son, Cudyu Roatan, would be left in charge of the kingdom. Once the base was secured and the population of Dara subjugated, more of the Lyucu tribes would be ferried over to their new home.

The success of this audacious plan hinged upon having not just a single date, but a series of future dates for when the Wall of Storms would open up a passage stable enough for the crossing of the fleet. The ships would have to make many trips between the two lands.

Despite the cleverness of Cudyu and Vadyu—nicknamed Tanvanaki—neither could make sense of the calculations of Luan Zya in *Gitré Üthu*. His incipient doubt of the sincerity of the Lyucu prince and princess had caused him to not write out every step of his derivations and to leave out crucial steps in his proofs. The final model was so complex and abstract that it was impossible to reconstruct his thought process from the few tantalizing hints left in the book in shorthand. Despite all the well-laid plans of the Lyucu, they could not, in the end, fully deceive the prime strategist of Dara.

All they had was one date, and they needed more.

Pékyu Tenryo began by trying to persuade Luan. He offered him riches beyond measure and promised to make him a powerful thane once Dara was conquered.

Luan laughed in his face.

Next, he tried torture. He had found many effective ways to apply pain, and they had always worked wonders on the soft men from Dara.

Each of Luan Zya's toenails was pulled out one by one, and Luan screamed until his throat was hoarse. His thighs were tied down to a long bone-bench and his legs then bent upward until they snapped at his knees, and Luan howled until even his guards lost color in their faces.

But when they presented *Gitré Üthu* to him with a pen, he simply shook his head.

They held his head underwater until he stopped struggling before pulling him out. They compressed his chest with heavy stones until he passed out. Afterward, the very sight of water or the stoning board made Luan tremble with terror, and he struggled vainly against his guards to escape.

Yet when they presented *Gitré Üthu* to him with a pen, he simply shook his head.

"A Lyucu warrior would not make any sound even if a garinafin's fire burned off his limbs," said a frowning Pékyu Tenryo. "But like all the pampered men of Dara, you scream and cry like a child when suffering even mild discomfort. You clearly do not possess a warrior's spirit."

"There's no shame in crying when in pain," said Luan Zya. "Neither is there dishonor in showing that you're afraid. Real courage consists of accepting pain and terror but still doing the right thing."

A furious Pékyu Tenryo vowed to flay Luan Zya alive, one thin strip of skin at a time. But Tanvanaki reminded him that they still needed the secrets hidden in Luan Zya's mind, and killing him would hardly get them closer to their goal.

"Do you have a better idea?" asked the pékyu.

"The men of Dara are very much guided by their philosophy," said Tanvanaki. "And I do have an idea that I think will work. Sometimes the most effective forms of torture do not involve the flesh at all."

Luan Zya was brought to the torture tent again on a stretcher, but this time, the one who was naked and bound to the pole was Oga Kidosu.

"If you will not do as we have asked," said Pékyu Tenryo, "we will no longer hurt you."

A Lyucu guard slashed his stone knife across Oga's chest and took off a thin slice of flesh. Oga screamed as blood oozed from the wound.

Luan's face twitched. He stared at Pékyu Tenryo and fire seemed to shoot out of his eyes.

"A stone knife is very sharp," said Pékyu Tenryo placidly. "I imagine it will take a thousand cuts before your friend dies."

Oga howled incoherently as the guard flicked his wrist again. A second wound began to ooze blood.

"After he dies," said Pékyu Tenryo, "I will choose a child born from a coupling with one of the slaves of Dara and do the same thing to him. And after he dies, I'll pick another."

Many of the visitors from Dara had had children with the Lyucu, either during the time they were treated as kings or when they were treated as slaves—the flow of power was never symmetrical in these encounters, but children, who were innocent, were nonetheless born.

Most of the mixed-blood children continued to be treated as slaves by the Lyucu.

Luan's teeth clattered as he ground them against each other; the veins on his forehead stood out and pulsed.

"You'll never be harmed again," said Pékyu Tenryo. "I intend to pamper you so that you can live as long as you can and reflect upon how many people will have to die because of you."

His words were punctuated by another scream from Oga as the guard slashed again.

Luan tried to lunge from his stretcher, but the sinew cords binding him down held. "I am *not* the one responsible!"

"Tsk-tsk," said Pékyu Tenryo. "What a hypocrite you are! Your sages speak endlessly of the value of human life and the lack of distinction between acts of commission and omission. Yet here you are, trying to pretend that you're different from the man holding the stone knife. You have the power to stop this at any moment with a simple nod; by refusing to, you might as well be the one doing the cutting."

The guard flicked his wrist rapidly three times, and the howls from Oga bled into one another and no longer sounded human.

"Stop! Stop!"

Pékyu Tenryo looked at Luan Zya, a smile on his face.

The old scholar nodded in defeat. Had he been a young man still driven by the passion to seek vengeance for injustice, he might have held steadfast to his refusal despite the heart-rending cries of tortured Oga. Had he been the young strategist who coldly counseled a king to betray his friend in order to secure a lasting peace for a people, he might have weighed the needs of millions against the suffering of a single man.

But age had worn down his logic, and he could not bear to be the instrument of torture for his friend. Sentiment makes us fools, and yet, without sentiment, we would be little better than dumb instruments wielded by the gods in their incomprehensible games.

Luan Zya produced a series of new dates for subsequent openings in the Wall of Storms. "These will work only for the northern part of the

Wall, for that is where I have records of the most observations," he explained. "And the further you go into the future, the less certain the predictions become."

To verify that Luan Zya was indeed telling the truth, Pékyu Tenryo took away the results and derivations of his calculations and asked him to redo them. He reasoned that if Luan were making up false numbers on the fly, being forced to re-create his work would reveal discrepancies.

Three times Luan Zya was asked to do this, and each time he produced the same results.

Still unconvinced, Tenryo had Luan perform various engineering calculations for how to modify the city-ships to adjust for the weight of the garinafins. After a ship modified in accordance with Luan's suggestions successfully completed a stable test voyage with garinafins aboard, the pékyu was finally satisfied that the Dara scholar seemed to have learned his lesson.

Indeed, Luan Zya became a subdued and obedient servant. As his legs healed, he hobbled around on crutches, doing whatever the pékyu demanded of him. He devised ways to alter the internal bulkheads and compartments in the city-ships to better store the feed and weapons needed for the invasion; he designed the special holds for the garinafins so that they would travel in relative comfort; he computed the best ways to distribute livestock and people across the ship so that they would weather rogue storms better.

"Why?" Oga asked him.

Luan shook his head and said nothing.

But Oga would not let it go. "I would kill myself if I were in your position. For my daughter, for all the sons and daughters of Dara."

Luan sighed. "Even if I were dead, they would still be able to get to Dara. I'm an old and weak man, and I'd like to see my homeland one more time before I die."

The invasion fleet left on an auspicious day. From the decks of the city-ships, the invading army waved at those who stayed behind. They were going to conquer paradise for the homeland.

Twenty city-ships filled with men and women, cattle, and garinafins sailed into the broad ocean current, their full sails filled with wind, looking like icebergs found in the sea far to the north. This was less than half of Mapidéré's original fleet. The rest would be saved for sending future reinforcements to Dara.

As Luan's legs healed, he gained more mobility. He spent the bulk of the voyage studying the garinafins, sketching pictures of them in *Gitré Üthu* and questioning the grooms about their habits. Pékyu Tenryo, who was on the same ship, thought of Luan's behavior as an example of his eccentricity. Even a man who was broken needed hobbies.

The city-ships sped up as the current grew stronger.

Finally, the fleet arrived at the Wall of Storms a few days ahead of schedule. The ships left the current and waited before the magnificent curtain of cyclones near the spot where Luan Zya had penetrated the Wall two years ago.

"This is the moment of truth," said Pékyu Tenryo to Luan Zya. "We'll soon find out if you really are as clever as you think you are."

Luan said nothing.

On the appointed day, everyone on the city-ships watched the storm eagerly. There seemed to be no change in the roiling waves and clouds until noon, when suddenly the zigzagging lightning bolts in the clouds began to flash in sync.

It was as if the entire curtain of cyclones had turned into a pulsing light of blinding brightness. As the lights continued to flash, the cyclones sorted themselves like combatants in heated battle who suddenly heard the order to retreat from both sides. Gradually, a thin sliver of calm sea appeared between parting curtains like the stage being revealed at the start of a folk opera.

A wild cheer arose on all the city-ships. The gamble had paid off.

Pékyu Tenryo looked at Luan Zya, whose face held a complicated expression.

"You've accomplished something amazing," said Pékyu Tenryo, and the praise was sincere. "Your name will live on in history as the first man to understand the secret of this marvel of nature."

"The universe is knowable," muttered Luan Zya, and it was hard to tell if he was joyous or sorrowful.

That night, after a wild ship-wide celebration, Pékyu Tenryo invited Luan Zya to his cabin to drink more kyoffir. The pékyu was feeling affectionate toward his pet scholar.

"You will be remembered as a hero of the Lyucu," said Pékyu Tenryo.

"And a traitor to my people," said Luan Zya.

"Don't be so morose," said Pékyu Tenryo. "The rightness and wrongness of things must be looked at from many perspectives. If you had not helped us, more grandfathers and grandmothers would have died in winters on the scrublands and many more children would remain unborn."

"Tyrants could justify anything with what-ifs."

Pékyu Tenryo laughed. "Then I'll try another tack. If your homeland is so wonderful, isn't it a sin to keep it only for yourselves? Those born in less fortunate lands deserve to enjoy its bounty as well. You've always had a restless soul, and wanderlust is what drove you to leave Dara. Why would you deny to others the freedom of movement that you view as your own birthright?"

"So you think an invasion is morally the same as a voyage of exploration?"

"I certainly saw little difference when Admiral Krita explored our land and made himself its king."

Luan Zya sighed. "You would make a good paid litigator."

Pékyu Tenryo was about to ask more about this exotic-sounding profession when he felt a sudden wave of dizziness and collapsed to the table, his skull-cup of kyoffir spilling across the leather surface.

Luan Zya got up from the table, rummaged through Pékyu Tenryo's furs for the set of keys that never left his side, and hurried out of the room.

ல ௨ ல ௨

He opened the door to the storeroom that was always kept sealed.

A strong scent of smoke and fire almost overwhelmed him.

Luan Zya did not know what was kept in this room. He only knew that the grooms always clammed up whenever the conversation drifted in this direction. It was also kept locked, and, as far as he knew, Pékyu Tenryo had the only key. Whatever was held in here was of the utmost importance to the Lyucu invasion.

He had bided his time and waited for his chance. Having fallen for Cudyu and Vadyu's trick, he had already yielded up the secret of passing through the Wall of Storms. The only way to atone for his sin was to sabotage the invaders' mission. He had already done one thing that would hopefully thwart the plans of the Lyucu to subjugate Dara, but he needed to do more to be sure.

Luan had debated between killing the pékyu as he slept, which might have led to quicker discovery of his treachery, and making his way quietly down here to sabotage the secrets in this room. In the end, he had picked the less obvious choice. The pékyu was powerful and crafty, but another thane—such as the cunning Tanvanaki—might step into his place; the contents of this room, however, might be irreplaceable. He hoped he had made the right decision.

He had gained the Lyucu's trust by seeming to comply with their wishes. He had acted the part of the weak and foolish man who could not understand that to stop evil, sometimes the innocent needed to suffer. He had allowed the pékyu to underestimate him and misjudge him. All for this chance. For this moment.

The room was packed with woven sacks holding some kind of grain, he decided. Maybe it was a potent medicine, or a food that endowed the warriors with extra strength. Whatever it was, he was going to destroy it.

But the strong, acrid smell, as though something was already burning, confused him. He was sure he had smelled it before. An image of a hot-air balloon ride taken with Zomi Kidosu, his best student, came unbidden to mind, and he wasn't sure why.

No matter, he didn't have time to investigate. There was a time for gathering knowledge, and a time to act. Lord Garu had taught him that lesson a long time ago.

He poured the jar of lamp oil he had stolen from the store all over the sacks; then he dropped the torch and watched as *poof* the room flared into conflagration.

As he hurried out of the room, he ticked through his mental checklist. *Gitré Üthu* was safely ensconced at an obscure corner in the hold, where it was unlikely to be found. In a moment of weakness, he had written a last message in it for Gin, the lover he never stopped thinking about and who he could not convince to stop the pursuit of power and honor—well, perhaps he was the foolish one. He had tried to pursue his own dream, and look where it had gotten him.

It would be good if the book survived and was eventually discovered by someone who could make sense of it, but it wasn't critical. He had nothing more to lose.

He ran to the opening of the narrow corridor that led down to this compartment and lifted the dung shovel he had grabbed on the way down. For a moment he had the illusion that he was again in the palace in Pan that had been built by Emperor Erishi, as he fought by the side of Lord Garu and everything burned around him.

He would stand here and hold off the Lyucu guards as long as he could. The longer he could keep it up, the more the mysterious material held in the storeroom behind him would burn.

"You should have invited me."

Oga Kidosu stepped into view. He was carrying two swords of Dara, kept by the thane he served as trophies.

Luan was startled. "Don't you want to see Zomi and Aki?" He accepted one of the swords from Oga and dropped the dung shovel.

"It's the duty of fathers to fight wars so that their children don't have to."

Luan smiled. "All right then, friend. Let's make this count."

The Lyucu guards came at them through the darkness, and they ululated and stabbed into the unknown.

CHAPTER FIFTY-ONE

A TRAP

RUI: THE SECOND MONTH IN THE TWELFTH YEAR
OF THE REIGN OF FOUR PLACID SEAS.

"They finally overcame us . . . the storeroom burned down . . . chained us both in the hold . . . would not kill us . . . witness the destruction of our homeland . . ."

Oga Kidosu's voice faded until, even with her ear next to his murmuring lips, she could hear nothing.

"Proud . . . daughter . . . proud . . . seen you once . . ."

The lips stopped moving. Zomi placed her head against his chest, and there was only silence.

She held his hand against her face and hot tears covered the wrinkled skin that was growing cold and stiff.

In the other stretcher, Luan Zya's hands moved. Zomi shifted over and held them. She gazed into his sightless eyes and shouted, "Teacher! I'm here!"

The hands continued to move in her grasp like slippery fish that were trying to escape. Zomi let go and watched as the hands moved through air.

She turned around and called out, "Writing wax! He's trying to say something."

Others in the grand audience hall scrambled and soon, soft wax was brought over on a tray. Zomi held the tray up and placed her teacher's hands over it. Even without his eyes, his fingers sought out the malleable wax and began to sculpt.

Zomi watched the logograms take shape on the tray, one after another. She saw that the hands were slowing down, growing sluggish. Tears flowed down her face unimpeded; she felt her heart was on the verge of breaking.

Weigh the fish, the universe is knowable.
A cruben breaches; the remora detaches.
Mewling child, cooing parent,
Grand-souled companions, brothers,
Wakeful weakness,
Empathy that encompasses the world.

To imagine new machines, to see unknown lands,
To believe the grace of kings belongs to all.
Grateful.

This was a summary of his life, the ultimate call of the wild goose departing the pond.

The last logogram took shape; the fingers stopped. And with a final, barely audible gasp, Luan Zya died.

Zomi backed up and knelt before both stretchers. She touched her forehead to the ground in the direction of Oga Kidosu.

"You are the author of my body and the mold of my spirit, Father. Though we have seen each other only twice in our lives, at the moment of my birth and the moment of your death, yet the silver streaks of our passing shall forever illuminate the vast sea of my memory."

She turned and touched her forehead to the ground in the direction of Luan Zya.

"You are the parent of my mind and the instructor of my soul, Luan Zyaji—"

Her sobbing made it impossible for her to continue.

No one objected to her use of the honorific, though it was the custom that only kings and emperors could convey such honor upon great scholars.

A detailed report was prepared and sent to Pan. Some thought it best to send *Gitré Üthu* to the emperor as well, but Than Carucono looked at the mourning figure of Zomi Kidosu, who cradled the book the way a drowning man clutched at anything that floated, and shook his head. The book was where it needed to be.

Oga Kidosu's and Luan Zya's bodies rested in the grand audience hall. After a suitable mourning period, Zomi would take both for burial in their hometowns in Dasu and Haan. Given the state of the war, however, that might take some time.

- Why didn't you whisk the body of your protégé away, Turtle-Brother, the way we took the bodies of our favorites away in their moments of apotheosis?

- Luan has always believed the universe is knowable. Making the moment of his death a mystery would be wrong.

- You have strange ideas for how to honor the mortals, Lutho.

- I've been thinking a lot about our relationship with the mortals. We may not have encountered the Lyucu gods, but have you not noticed how they've started to pray to us, giving us the names of their gods? Do you feel honored or dishonored?

Than Carucono and Zomi Kidosu debated the wisdom of the plan to bring the emperor over to Rui.

"Based on Luan Zyaji's experience, Pékyu Tenryo is a wily, clever opponent," said Zomi. "We should ascertain whether the apparent retreat is but another stratagem before committing the emperor to this path."

"But if we wait too long, it will give Tenryo a chance to regroup. The longer we wait, the more likely it is that Tenryo will strengthen his position. The right strategy is to immediately call for reinforcements and strike while the iron is hot. The emperor's presence will rally our troops and awe the barbarians, and having the emperor here will allow negotiations for the safety of Prince Timu to be conducted with alacrity."

Zomi sighed. By now, she was sufficiently experienced with the ways of the world to understand that Than Carucono's real fear was that he would be blamed if Tenryo, in desperation, decided to harm Prince Timu. He wanted Emperor Ragin here so that he would not have to face the wrath of the emperor and the empress if things went wrong. This might be wise politics, but she was sure it was the wrong strategy.

Once the messenger airship arrived in Pan, Kuni immediately began preparations for going over to Rui with the rest of the army.

"I advise strongly against such a path," said Mün Çakri. "The situation in Rui is still uncertain, and I think Zomi's concerns should be given due consideration."

"Why are you suddenly so cautious?" said Jia. Her voice took on an edge. She couldn't wait to be reunited with Timu, and the idea that Mün might be hoping to prolong the war to increase his own influence flashed through her mind.

"The marshal has always taught us that there is a time for acting, and there is a time for waiting," said Mün Çakri. "I don't trust the speedy victory and the apparent collapse of the Lyucu defenses."

"The marshal isn't fighting this war," said Kuni, an edge in his voice. "I'm going whether you come or not. My son is over there. Surely you, of all people, can understand that."

Emperor Ragin arrived in Kriphi with General Mün Çakri and a reinforcement of ten thousand men, along with more airships equipped with flamethrowers.

As the Lyucu did not trust their own airship crews—mostly manned by surrendered Imperials—not to defect, they grounded the airships they had been using as scouts in Dasu. Since the Lyucu also didn't have the training or skill to field large fleets of battle airships, they scuttled all the ships at the Mount Kiji Air Base during their retreat rather than letting them fall into Imperial hands. It would take a long time to construct more; the airships that accompanied the emperor here were the very last ones in Dara.

Mün Çakri ordered a slow and steady march by the army in pursuit of the Lyucu. Puma Yemu was put in charge of the Imperial airships, and he directed them to make hit-and-run raids against the Lyucu army. The goal of these raids wasn't to cause damage, but to draw out garinafin fire and exhaust their flight. The Lyucu responded by dividing their garinafins into groups who alternated between waddling along the ground to rest and taking off into the air to deal with Puma's harassing airships.

While the barbarian warriors slowly retreated toward the coast, forcing civilians to travel with them as human shields, the garinafins, skittish after their last disastrous battle against Imperial airships, stayed at a safe distance from the flame-tongued airships even as they rose to intercept them. The two sides thus engaged in an aerial dance, feinting and probing for weaknesses but never engaging fully.

More garinafins were sent to protect the city-ships anchored along the western coast of Rui against either airship bombardment or sneak assaults by mechanical crubens.

Pékyu Tenryo's overall plan appeared to be to get to the coast and board the city-ships. Once that was accomplished, he could either retreat to Dasu for a final stand or make a run for the open ocean.

"We have to stop him before he can reach the coast," Kuni declared, and Than Carucono took a detachment of a few hundred horsemen to try to secretly outflank the retreating mass of the Lyucu army and their abductees. A few flame-throwing Imperial airships flew at some distance from the brigade to act as decoys to draw the attention of patrolling garinafins away from the location of the horse riders. If Than could cut off the retreating Lyucu's path to the sea, the emperor's army had a chance to completely surround the Lyucu army.

Zomi Kidosu elected to join the riders of Than Carucono. The winter weather made her leg harness stiff and made walking more difficult, and riding a horse gave her more mobility. She took advantage of the opportunity to ride away from the cavalry brigade and observe the distant aerial dance of garinafins against airships. Although Luan Zyaji had taken detailed notes on the creatures in *Gitré Üthu*, she reminded herself that there was no substitute for direct observation, for weighing the fish.

The crews of the Imperial airships and the garinafin riders had by now fought each other often enough to have adjusted somewhat to each other's tactics. The airships had the advantage of being able to stay aloft indefinitely and of having flamethrowers with longer range, but the garinafins were more maneuverable and faster. As long as the airship crews remained alert and maintained careful formations that prevented blind spots, they could fend off the garinafins though they did not have the speed or agility to catch up to them.

Kidosu carefully sketched pictures of the garinafins in action and noted whether they seemed particularly protective of parts of their bodies as they fought the airships. She even took the time to examine garinafin dung heaps when they encountered them, much to the consternation of others in the cavalry brigade. She wasn't sure exactly what she was looking for, but she believed that Gin Mazoti was right: Understanding the garinafins was the key to eventually defeating them.

Occasionally, some of the civilians managed to escape the Lyucu army and ran to Than Carucono's riders for protection. There were far fewer of these escaped villagers than Carucono would have expected, and questioning of the escapees revealed that this was due to the deci-chief system set up by the traitor Ra Olu—even when given the opportunity, few of the families dared to escape because they knew that their neighbors who remained behind would have to pay for their safety. Ra Olu's system was effective at helping the Lyucu to secure their control over the population, and Carucono cursed Olu's name.

Once Than Carucono had finished questioning the escaped villagers about the morale and deployment of retreating Lyucu troops, he wanted to send them to Mün Çakri, who was leading the main army and could offer them protection. Zomi Kidosu, however, kept the escapees around longer and asked them many questions about the garinafins: how many people were assigned to feed and care for each garinafin; how much did they eat and for how many hours during the day; what exactly were their favorite foods; how often did they relieve themselves and what form did the fresh excrement take; and so on and so forth.

To Than Carucono, these questions didn't seem very useful. "Are you thinking of becoming a garinafin herder?"

Zomi Kidosu shook her head. To most people of Dara, the garinafins were monsters from nightmares, but she and her teacher both understood that even monsters were knowable.

To reach the coast, the Lyucu army and the abducted villagers had to go through Naza Pass, which was near the northern coast of Rui.

The pass was at the narrow end of a funnel-shaped valley between looming hills on both sides. The valley was about a mile in breadth at the wider end, where the village of Phada was located—the tiny hamlet had a measure of fame because this was where, during the Chrysanthemum-Dandelion War, the secret tunnel from Dasu to Rui dug by Gin Mazoti terminated.

As the tunnel had been dug only for military use, it was not suitable for commercial exploitation without significant investment, and Kuni Garu wisely thought taking up a hated project initiated by the tyrant Mapidéré would not have appealed to his subjects. The tunnel was thus soon abandoned, and over time, the crater from which Gin Mazoti's forces had emerged had been filled back in by loose stones. Few even remembered its existence except for old veterans who had fought under Marshal Mazoti in the early days.

The valley narrowed as one moved west, and by the time it reached Naza Pass, the hills had pressed in until only about a hundred yards separated them.

General Than Carucono's riders managed to get to the pass ahead of the retreating Lyucu by several days, which was plenty of time to build up impressive fortifications with stones and fallen trees.

Carucono sighed with relief. Once the fortifications were in place, even attacks by garinafins wouldn't be able to dislodge them. The five hundred riders were confident that they could hold off the much larger Lyucu force until the main army led by the emperor and Mün Çakri in pursuit of the Lyucu arrived.

Zomi looked at the fortifications, her brows furrowed.

"What's worrying you?" asked Than Carucono.

"I don't understand why the garinafins haven't found us," Zomi said. She looked up at the airships patrolling some distance off—Carucono had not wanted the airships to hover overhead, which might have tipped off the Lyucu that something was happening in Naza Pass. "They've been harassing the decoy airships the entire time we were marching down here."

"That's the point; so they wouldn't find us."

"But it was almost like they were putting on a show! Not a single garinafin patrol has come anywhere near us; it was as if they wanted to be sure that we could see that the garinafins were fooled by these airships, even though it made no sense for them to be flying away from General Çakri's main army. I think they might already know we're here."

"That's a bit paranoid."

"Doesn't it seem odd to you that they've now stopped harassing those airships?"

"Maybe the garinafins are tired and need to rest. Like you said, they've been harassing those decoy airships the whole time we've been marching."

Zomi shook her head. "They haven't been using the same garinafins to go after the airships. There are at least three different groups. While one group is keeping our airships busy, the other two groups must be recuperating."

"I'm impressed you've been tracking them that closely," said

Carucono. "But, so what? Most of the garinafins are probably busy dealing with Puma Yemu's airships escorting Mün Çakri's main army. All that matters is that we got to the pass first and set up defenses. Even if the garinafins discover us now, they wouldn't be able to remove the fortifications before the main army got here. They're doomed."

"But the plan has been working too perfectly. . . . Tenryo must know that this is the best choke point to the coast. Yet, instead of avoiding this route or trying to seize this spot first, he's still marching this way without even sending a garinafin to scout the route first. Something isn't right."

"If you think of everything as a plot within a plot within a plot," said an irritated Carucono, "you'll never commit to doing anything. If we think of the barbarians as all-knowing, then why bother fighting?"

"That's not what I meant—" Zomi protested.

"Sometimes it's best to keep things simple. The gods may have favored the barbarians by giving them these amazing mounts, but having such mounts must also have shaped the way they think about battlefield tactics. We've never impressed them except with those flame-throwing airships, and all commanders have a tendency to overplan for the last threat they faced.

"Since they don't expect our ground forces to be able to do much, the most likely explanation for your suspicion is that they don't think they need to be clever or cautious as long as they know where our airships are."

Zomi wanted to argue, but without being able to offer a plausible theory as to what the Lyucu really intended, she knew she couldn't win.

But her unease deepened.

Long before the Lyucu army came into view, the ground began to shake with the waddling footsteps of the garinafins. It sounded like a giant herd of elephants was tearing through the dark woods, or perhaps thunder was rolling across the earth.

And then, there they were: thousands of refugees being herded across the valley like cattle, stumbling, staggering, dragging children, exhausted from days spent carrying heavy bags of feed and grain and provisions for the Lyucu army. Behind them came the horde of Lyucu warriors, intermixed with the striding, oversized figures of the garinafins, their massive bulk making a startling visual contrast with the narrow confines of the valley.

Zomi's heart pounded. *Damn it. Why haven't I thought about this?* "What if they drive the civilians at us?"

"We can't let the Lyucu through."

"But these are our people! We can't just kill them."

Carucono's face looked grim. "We have to hold the line."

The Dara soldiers lined the barricades, their bows drawn taut and arrows notched.

But the Lyucu did not drive the crowd forward. Instead, the civilians were directed to sit down in front of the barricades, and the Lyucu warriors and the garinafins lined up behind them. The ranks stretched as far as the eye could see, filling the valley.

"The emperor's troops have entered the valley," said an excited Carucono, reading the flag signals from one of the airships hovering in the distance. "They are trapped!"

Kuni Garu examined the barbarian warriors lined up in front of him, searching for signs of his son.

They were now dressed in a motley combination formed from the furs and hides favored by the Lyucu as well as the silks and hemps favored in Dara. Many of the barbarian warriors had draped strands of pearls and chains of jewels and precious metal over their body, the fruits of their looting and robbery. Though lacking in the kind of discipline implied by the visual orderliness of Imperial soldiers dressed in uniforms, there was a kind of splendor in their arrogant, careless stance that reminded Kuni of his old troops, the band of bandits that had started him on the path to the Throne of Dara decades ago.

Behind them were the surrendered Imperial soldiers who had thrown in their lot with the invaders. They were shamefaced and did not dare to look at the emperor.

And still behind them, before the barricades that blocked the pass, were the civilians he had sworn to protect.

He felt old and weak. *How many more wars must I fight? How many more people must die?*

The barbarian ranks parted, and a powerful man stepped forward to face him across the space between the two armies.

"You must be Pékyu Tenryo," said Kuni.

Tenryo nodded, a wide grin across his face. "After entertaining your son as my guest for so many days, it is an honor to meet his father, Emperor Ragin."

Kuni forced his face to remain calm. That Tenryo was bringing up Timu was a good sign. It meant that he was in the mood for discussing terms. *He knows he's trapped and I have the upper hand. I just have to walk him through what he must do.*

"You have done much harm, Pékyu," said Kuni. "Dara was a land of peace before your coming, and the blood of those you have killed will stain your soul long after your death."

"I came to seek a better life for my people," said Tenryo. "I will never apologize for that."

The Lyucu warriors behind him banged their bone axes and clubs against each other, causing a terrifying din.

Kuni waited until the noise subsided. "You may have thought you were fighting for a better life for your people, but you've clearly failed."

Tenryo laughed. "I don't agree with that."

Kuni had to admire the boldness and confidence of the barbarian leader. "I know your garinafins are exhausted, which is why they're not in the air."

"Even exhausted, grounded garinafins will put up quite a fight."

"But your path to the sea is blocked, and we outnumber you four to one. In this narrow valley, how long do you think you'll last before you succumb to attrition? Those garinafins still capable of flight will not fight after the Lyucu riders are dead from our arrows, and flightless beasts may be killed by dropping stones and logs on them. You have no choice but to negotiate."

Tenryo continued to smile. "Suppose I agree with your analysis. What terms will you offer me, Emperor of Dara?"

"If you immediately put down your weapons and kill your garinafins—I don't care how—you and your people will be guaranteed safe passage back to the city-ships on the coast. Once there, you must leave the shores of Dara immediately and never return. We both know that Luan Zyaji's calculations show that there will be an opening in the Wall next year, and you may stay at the isles of the pirates until then."

"These terms don't sound generous," said Tenryo. "I don't like them."

Kuni shook his head. "These are the best terms you'll get."

"You won't change your mind even when you see your son?" asked Tenryo.

The ranks of Lyucu warriors parted, revealing the figure of Prince Timu, whose hands were bound behind him. Vadyu Roatan pressed him forward, holding a Dara-style steel sword against his neck.

Blood rushed to Kuni's face, and his heart pounded painfully against his rib cage.

Stay calm! He won't harm Timu—he knows that harming Timu would deprive him of his only negotiating chip and seal his own fate. This is just a bluff to get better terms.

"I'm not afraid, Father," shouted Timu. Murmurs of admiration rippled through the ranks of Dara soldiers.

Summoning up the same courage he had called on years ago, when the Hegemon had threatened to cook his father in front of him, Kuni forced the color of his face to return to normal. "If you harm my son, know that none of you will leave here alive."

"You sound so confident of victory," said Tenryo.

"My life is not as important as the lives of everyone in Dara!" shouted Timu. "Don't give in, Father!"

Kuni frowned. Something about the confidence of Tenryo bothered him. Kuni was a good gambler, and he could tell when someone was just bluffing in a game of cards. But Tenryo's smile . . . it was different.

And then came the rumbling behind him.

∽ ∾ ∽ ∾

The crater in the village of Phada, long neglected and forgotten, erupted.

They emerged from underground, the men and women and beasts of the Land of Ukyu. The garinafins took to the air, circling over the shocked, uplifted faces of the Dara soldiers. Behind them the Lyucu warriors moved forward, holding up shields made from garinafin skin, banging their clubs and axes rhythmically against the bone frame.

Soon, the wide end of the valley was filled. Now it was the army of Dara that was trapped inside the valley, sandwiched between Pékyu's forces at the narrow end and these new warriors at the wider.

While Tanvanaki had directed her garinafins to put on a dazzling show against the Imperial airships and kept them occupied, she had also dispatched a few of the garinafin-carrying city-ships to the coast of Dasu. From there, they had secretly moved through the tunnel under the sea back to Rui.

Tanvanaki, inspired by the lessons learned from the surprise landing by the mechanical crubens and the lore she learned from surrendered Imperial veterans, had come up with her own way to take advantage of underwater attack vectors: Lyucu reinforcements had come to Rui from under the sea, using tunnels that Kuni himself had once used to conquer Rui from Dasu.

"Would you care to offer different terms?" asked a grinning Pékyu Tenryo. "I used myself as lure, and I guess you couldn't resist!"

Kuni Garu closed his eyes in defeat. In his eagerness to rescue his son, he had ignored the warning signs. He was indeed not a commander of men at the level of Gin Mazoti.

Zomi, at the other end of the valley, cursed herself for not seeing through the wily Lyucu plot earlier.

Mün Çakri rushed up to the emperor. "*Rénga*, though we still outnumber them, the narrowness of the valley neutralizes this advantage to some degree. And now that they have so many garinafins in the air, we have no chance of overcoming their aerial advantage."

Kuni knew that Mün Çakri was trying to spare his feelings by not mentioning the biggest disadvantage of all: *He* was here. In fact, he had become the pékyu's hostage.

"What can we do?"

"The only choice is for you to board one of the airships and head for safety. All Imperial airships working together may create an opening in this trap to enable your escape. The rest of us will fight here to keep his foot soldiers occupied. You'll have to avenge us."

"That's unacceptable!"

"If you don't leave, you'll die here. If Dara is without an emperor, all the islands will fall!"

As some of the airships flew over to engage the fresh garinafins and their riders, one particularly fast ship, the Imperial transport *Grace of Kings*, began to descend toward them. Mün Çakri rallied the Dara troops to establish defensive parameters around the emperor in case the Lyucu tried to rush the position to prevent the airship from landing.

Kuni looked across the field at Timu. In his mind, he was again seeing young Timu and Théra clutching at the skirts of Jia while the city of Zudi fell around them, and he had to choose between leaving his loved ones behind so that he could fight another day or staying with them and losing forever.

The choices a king faced were not always the ones he wanted.

Grace of Kings hovered close to the ground. The gondola opened, and a rope ladder was dropped down. "Hurry, *Rénga*!" Dafiro Miro, who was at the top of the ladder, shouted.

"I'm sorry, Timu," he shouted across the field. And the scene became blurry in his eyes.

"I'm not afraid, Father!"

Kuni looked away to hide his tears. He turned to Mün Çakri. "Do not waste your life or the lives of the soldiers. Fight only as long as you must to allow my ship to escape beyond the range of pursuit."

Mün Çakri laughed. He banged his bronze sword against his shield, whose unique design featured embedded butcher's hooks as a reminder of his roots. "Lord Garu, do you think I'm really afraid of these barbarians? I will see you soon, perhaps with this Tenryo's head hooked on my shield like a pig's head."

Kuni gripped him by the arms. "I know you're a proud man, but if there's no chance of success, surrender. There's no shame in capitulating after a battle well fought. Promise me this."

Mün Çakri looked at him. "From the day I joined your gang of bandits, Kuni, I've been prepared for a moment like this. Take care of Naro and Cacaya-*tika*, and I look forward to seeing the Hegemon on the farther shore of the River-on-Which-Nothing-Floats. Maybe I'll get to yell at him again."

They embraced and then resolutely let each other go. The barbarians made no move, as if still making up their minds whether to attack.

Just as Kuni was about to start climbing into the airship, Pékyu Tenryo shouted across the field.

"Emperor Ragin! We have barely gotten to know each other. Why are you in such a hurry to leave? Don't you want to see what entertainment I've planned for you?"

"Go now! Go!" Mün shouted. But Kuni stopped on the ladder and turned to see what the barbarian chief had planned. He still didn't believe that Tenryo would truly harm Timu—as long as Timu was alive, the pékyu had leverage over Kuni.

But Tenryo wasn't threatening Timu. Tanvanaki had dragged Timu away behind the Lyucu lines, and the Lyucu ranks pulled back, leaving a blank strip of land between the two armies.

About a hundred civilians—farmers, fishermen, monks, petty merchants, and their children and aged parents—were forced into this space.

They huddled in a group, terrified.

"Mother!" Zomi screamed.

There, among the civilians trapped between two armies, was the calm figure of Aki Kidosu.

How could her mother be here? She was only a simple farmer in Dasu, miles from Rui.

Then she understood. Zomi had used the money she gained as an important adviser to Queen Gin to build her mother a big house and hire her servants, thinking that it would allow her to live a life of leisure. But her mother had not enjoyed the way all the other villagers now came to her to ask for money, and how all her friends now no longer saw her as one of them, one of the simple folk.

She had not complained to Zomi, knowing that her daughter meant well. But she had told Zomi that she was thinking of leaving Dasu to visit distant relatives in Rui. After that, Zomi had been so busy with work that she had not even realized that it meant that her mother was in Rui at the moment of the invasion.

Zomi leapt from the barricades, but Than Carucono grabbed her legs and dragged her back.

"Let me go!" Zomi struggled against his hold, clawing at his arms and hands.

Than gritted his teeth against the pain.

"You can't help her! You'll never get through all the Lyucu army between her and you."

"I don't care!"

"Sometimes we have to accept the Flow," said Than Carucono.

"I intend to keep you as my guest a little longer," shouted Tenryo. "If you really must leave, I'll have to enjoy the entertainment all by myself."

Passages from the report by Luan Zyaji came into Kuni's mind.

He understood that he was about to witness something evil, but he couldn't just avert his eyes and keep on climbing. A king had a duty to gaze upon the consequences of his decisions, he had always believed.

He stopped climbing, no matter how much Dafiro Miro, who was above him, or Mün Çakri, who was below him on the ground, urged him to keep on moving.

One of the garinafin lumbered over and crouched next to the crowd of civilians. The men and women and children shied away from the beast, but their ankles were chained together, and the panicked moves only caused them to fall down into a heap.

"Emperor, please come off that ladder," said a smiling Tenryo.

"Don't listen to him!" shouted Mün Çakri. "Go! Go!"

But Kuni hesitated. He looked at the crying, screaming men and women and children, and his hands and legs seemed stuck to the ladder.

As a young duke, Kuni had once retreated from Pan and allowed its people to be slaughtered by Mata Zyndu's army. Their screams had never ceased to haunt his dreams.

Must I add to the accusatory voices in my head?

Tenryo waved his arm decisively, and the pilot on the back of the garinafin stuck the speaking trumpet into the base of her mount's neck and shouted into it.

The beast lowered its head to the ground and closed its mouth.

"No!" screamed Kuni Garu, and he let go, falling from the ladder.

The beast snapped its mouth open, and a red glowing tongue of flames emerged from its maw and swept across the crowd before it.

Time seemed to slow down. As Kuni fell, he watched the tongue flicking across each man, woman, and child, turning each from a person into a pillar of flames. Their screams rose to a horrifying, synchronized crescendo and then abruptly ceased.

"Nooooo!" howled Zomi Kidosu. "Mother! Mother! Oh, gods!"

Than Carucono held on to her even tighter.

The scene before her was incomprehensible. Her mother, burning; her mother, dying. She had promised to give her mother a better life, and this was what she had done.

Where a hundred people had scrambled and struggled for life a moment ago, now only a hundred smoldering pyres remained. The charred but still sizzling bodies maintained the poses of the last moments of their lives: a mother shielding the body of her child, a husband interposing himself before his wife, a son and daughter trying to cover the body of their mother—all three were now fused into one smoldering corpse.

Kuni struck the ground, and Mün Çakri's arms softened the fall. The emperor's lips moved but he could not find the words. He stared at the scene of horror, benumbed.

Some Lyucu soldiers came forward and unceremoniously smothered the smoldering embers with bags of earth they carried over their shoulders. About a hundred more civilians were driven forward to stand on the crematorium, over this field of slaughter. They screamed and resisted, but the Lyucu soldiers were relentless and shackled them to stakes driven into the ground. Then the Lyucu warriors retreated, and the garinafin put its head near the ground again.

The people in the ash-filled open space screamed and cried and begged for mercy, and the soldiers of Dara were so overwhelmed by this unprecedented sight and the smell of roasting human flesh that many retched and threw up.

"Emperor, order your soldiers to drop their weapons and your airships to land and stop resisting. All your airships."

Mün Çakri gave the order for his men to attack, but they stood rooted to the ground, too shocked to move. The old general, eyes bloodred with fury, rushed straight at Tenryo himself by running through the huddled crowd.

"Hiyaaaaa!"

The pékyu chopped his arm through the air. The garinafin snapped its maw shut and snapped it open again, and a new tongue of flames flickered out, instantly incinerating the running figure of Mün Çakri and the men and women and children around him.

The fiery, dead figure of Mün Çakri continued to run at Pékyu Tenryo, as though the body was being animated by a spirit stronger than life itself. It crashed into the ranks of the Lyucu warriors standing in front of Tenryo, and four or five of the warriors were set afire by the burning body before they could stop him.

Behind him, another hundred flame pillars replaced a hundred lives.

Kuni recovered from his reverie. With tears in his eyes, he calmly ordered the soldiers of Dara to drop their weapons.

"You should have left, *Rénga*," said Dafiro Miro.

"If I leave, I don't deserve to be Emperor of Dara," said Kuni.

He ordered *Grace of Kings* and all the other airships to land.

"This is my fault," Zomi said, numbly. "I should never have left home. I should never have decided to make my talents known. My mother is dead because of me."

"If you believe that," Than Carucono said, "then you're a fool. It is the nature of evil men like Pékyu Tenryo to make his victims think that they're at fault. Do you think your mother would agree with you? Do you think Luan Zyaji would agree with you?"

Zomi stared at the chaotic scene before her. Slowly, her face settled into a look of determination.

She would have to use her talents to the utmost and avenge all those she loved.

CHAPTER FIFTY-TWO

THE MARSHAL'S DECISION

PAN: THE THIRD MONTH IN THE TWELFTH YEAR
OF THE REIGN OF FOUR PLACID SEAS.

Zomi Kidosu returned to Pan in a small messenger airship—the only one that the Lyucu allowed to depart Rui so that survivors could inform the people of Dara of the horrors they had witnessed. Emperor Ragin demanded that she be allowed to leave along with the senior officers of his army, and Zomi was grateful for the vote of confidence in her abilities.

"I will avenge my parents," she whispered to the emperor. "And I will rescue you and the prince."

The emperor nodded, but she wasn't sure if he really believed her.

She carried back to the Big Island the ashes of Mün Çakri, who was given a state funeral befitting his rank in Zudi, his hometown. Zomi also brought back her mother's ashes—mixed with the ashes of the other Dasu villagers incinerated in her vicinity—and the body of her father, and they were buried together in a quiet ceremony in a plot in the Imperial cemetery in Pan. Since Dasu was under Lyucu occupation, it was thought best to inter them here temporarily until their homeland could be liberated.

The last box in the passenger airship held the body of Luan Zyaji, who was buried in a lavish state funeral in Ginpen. All the Lords of Dara who could make the journey attended, and it was the first occasion where anybody could remember seeing Gin Mazoti cry.

Zomi also brought a message from Pékyu Tenryo demanding the immediate cessation of all resistance in Dara.

Empress Jia summoned all the governors, generals, ministers, and enfeoffed nobles to the capital to discuss a response. As the assembled advisers debated, two camps emerged.

One camp, led by Prime Minister Cogo Yelu, advocated compliance with the demands of the Lyucu.

"The safety of the emperor and Prince Timu is paramount," said Cogo.

"Surrendering Dara to the Lyucu is not what Father would want," countered Prince Phyro, who led the other camp advocating continuing war. "The Lyucu number no more than five thousand, and if each of the hundreds of thousands of the inhabitants of the Islands of Dara were to spit at the Lyucu, we would drown them! What's the matter with you, Cogo? Have you turned timid in old age? Surrendering now would sully the names of all of us and the House of Dandelion forever in history."

Anger colored Cogo's face. "It's true that we have the advantage of numbers. But after the seizure of the base at Mount Kiji and the loss of all remaining airships during the last assault, we have no realistic option against the garinafin riders."

"The garinafins are not machines, you know. They do get tired and their fire breath runs out. We can certainly overwhelm them with a sufficiently large army and navy."

"But at what cost?" Cogo asked. "How many people must die in this war of attrition you advocate to preserve the pride that you hold so dear? The emperor could have escaped but he yielded to Pékyu Tenryo so that the people of Rui would not die for his personal honor. Would you undo his grace with your brutal, barbaric tactic of human waves?"

Phyro flushed. "I of course want to lessen the loss of lives as much as possible. But have you thought through the consequences of surrender? The Lyucu have a way of life fundamentally different from ours. They will get rid of all the rice paddies, sorghum fields, apple orchards, silk plantations, water mills, and windmills, and replace them all with pastureland for their cattle. They intend to enslave the people of Dara."

"I didn't say that we would just surrender completely!" said Cogo. "As you point out, they're but few in number. They must be daunted by the prospect of having to control a population so much larger than the occupying force. It may be possible to negotiate an agreement that will cede territory to them and acknowledge their suzerainty, while also preserving for the emperor some measure of autonomy over the majority of Dara. With the passage of time, it may be possible to change the strategic balance."

"What makes you think that time is on our side? The Lyucu must surely be sending reinforcements from their homeland right now to make the next opening in the Wall of Storms. As time passes, some of the elites of Dara will find it convenient to work with the Lyucu for self-preservation and advantage, as Ra Olu has already done. Our only chance is to fight right now and to fight to the end!"

"It's easy for great lords dressed in silk and gold to speak of fighting to the end, especially when it is others who will have to pay the price."

The empress listened as the two sides argued on, neither yielding an inch; her expression was unreadable.

Jia passed by the schoolroom, where Soto Zyndu was now instructing Princess Fara in history. She stopped just beyond the doorway and listened.

"What did you think of the story about Queen Tho-zu?" asked Soto.

"I don't understand how Ologa was able to turn the people against her," said Fara. "The queen was waiting for her husband to return, so of course she was doing the right thing to say no to all the suitors. Why would anyone believe Ologa's lies?"

"It's because everyone thought the king was dead—he had been away at war for ten years, while most of the other warriors had returned. They thought Queen Tho-zu was a widow, which was why all the suitors were at the castle. They couldn't understand why she wouldn't marry any of them."

"Even if her husband was dead, her son was still alive. She was trying to preserve the kingdom for him."

"But Dacan was very young, remember, and he was also away from home. So there was another interpretation for Queen Tho-zu's refusal. Ologa hinted to the people that she wanted to hold on to the power of being regent because she enjoyed it, and in that way Ologa ruined her reputation. He accused her of being ambitious."

"Is being ambitious bad?"

"Many men think that's a bad thing in a woman."

Jia entered the room.

"Empress!" Fara stood up and ran over. But a few steps away, she remembered the protocols, stopped, and bowed in *jiri*.

Jia walked up and embraced her. "Would you leave me and Lady Soto for a moment? She'll find you later to continue the lesson."

Fara nodded and left.

Jia sat down next to Soto. The room seemed very quiet now with only the two of them in it. She remembered how noisy the place used to be when Master Zato Ruthi taught all the children in here. Phyro was now spending all his time with the generals while Théra had departed for Ginpen to study the garinafin carcasses brought back by mechanical crubens. And Timu . . .

She reminded herself that they were no longer children.

"Have you heard what they're saying about me in the streets of Pan?" asked Jia.

"I have enough to worry about without listening to the prattle of the foolish."

Jia smiled. "You don't need to spare my feelings. I heard the lesson you were giving Fara. It's timely."

Soto said nothing.

"Even Cogo Yelu looks at me strangely these days," said Jia, "as though he thinks it's possible that I'm deliberately doing nothing because I hope my husband and son would remain in the hands of the Lyucu."

Soto looked at her. "I once spoke to you of Lady Zy, whose role in history has largely been erased, though she was the force behind Lurusén's philippics against Xana aggression."

"That was what inspired me down the road to politics."

"And the alternative to erasure is misunderstanding, Jia."

"I know," said Jia. "But why does this have to be so hard? To achieve a better life for the people, why must I choose to stain my name in the annals of Dara? Why do the gods mock us so?"

Soto placed an arm around Jia's shoulders, and the empress leaned into her gratefully.

"Luan Zyaji was only half right," said Soto. "The grace of kings may belong to all, but only few are fit to take up the burden."

And Jia cried softly in the schoolroom as Soto held her.

Gin Mazoti had been moved into a guesthouse near the palace and no guards were posted. She was free to come and go as she liked, though she was without title or power—and, nominally at least, still a traitor to the throne.

She did not stray from the courtyard of her house. She received no visitors and spent her mornings instructing Aya in the art of war—with a sword and across a *cüpa* board. In the afternoons, she composed her book on military tactics.

"I may never lead an army again," she told Aya. "But perhaps it's best to leave some record of my ideas so that future generations may remember that I earned my title by talent and hard work."

One sunny day, Jia came to visit.

Gin laid out tea and dried fruits for the empress. Like the tea, her demeanor was tepid and perfectly placid, as though nothing was happening outside the courtyard of the guesthouse.

They sat down across the table from each other. For a moment, it seemed as if they were two *cüpa* players about to begin a match, but then the empress slumped in her pose in resignation.

"Marshal, I don't know what to do."

The admission of weakness clearly was not easy for her. She lowered her head, and Gin noticed the gray at her temples and the lines at the corners of her eyes. She had aged years in months.

"Sometimes there are no good choices," said Gin. "Though the sagas tell of heroes who struggle against great odds and triumph, most of the time, the odds work out the way they are supposed to."

"You were right that Kuni may be a leader of generals, but he is not a suitable commander for an army," said Jia.

"There is no shame in the emperor's defeat. Pékyu Tenryo is a tactician of great skill."

Jia hesitated for a few moments, but then made up her mind. "What if I'm willing to announce to the world that you were falsely accused by me and thus redeem your name?"

Gin stared at her. "You'd be willing to do that? Just so that I'd resume command of the forces of Dara? What about all that you've fought for? What if the enfeoffed nobles take advantage of your concession and grow in strength to threaten the House of Dandelion in the future?"

"I can't strive for distant visions of palaces on the moon when the house is on fire, Marshal. My husband and son need you now. Dara needs you."

Gin stood up and paced back and forth. Jia stared at her, trying to see signs of hope.

The marshal returned and sat down.

"No."

Jia's face fell. "Why?"

"Conditions have changed. If you clear my name now at the cost of your own, Dara will be thrown into utter chaos. And in any event, I see no chance of victory. Pékyu Tenryo is a worthy opponent, and now he has all the advantages on the board."

"Is there truly no hope?"

"I have played through the variations hundreds of times, Empress.

I can't think of a way to defeat the Lyucu and save the emperor and the prince."

"What if you do not need to save the emperor and the prince?" asked Jia.

Gin looked at her, her expression unchanged.

"Do not think I covet power," said Jia. "I know I have little credibility with you. But if you can come up with a way to drive these invaders from our shores—even if you must sacrifice Kuni and Timu—I will immediately cede to you the position of regent. When Phyro is ready in your estimation, help him be a good ruler."

Gin's expression finally shifted to one of astonishment.

"Perhaps you never believed my explanations and thought me a selfish, petty woman who relied on palace intrigue to secure the position of her son. But remember that Kuni and I were willing to die to overthrow the evil that was the Xana Empire; he would never forgive me if I saved him by putting the people of Dara under a worse yoke than Mapidéré's.

"I have always done everything I could to help the people. Believe me or not, as you will—I know only that we must not yield to the Lyucu, and I beg you to save the people of Dara, even if you must sacrifice the House of Dandelion."

She knelt up in *mipa rari* and bowed until she touched her forehead to the ground before Gin Mazoti.

Gin knelt up in *mipa rari* as well and bowed back, touching her forehead to the ground in turn. "I confess that I have mismeasured you, Jia. You're indeed a woman of capacious mind, a worthy Empress of Dara."

They both straightened, and Jia locked gazes with Gin. "You have a way, then?"

Gin shook her head. "Even disregarding the lives of the emperor and the prince, I cannot think of a way to defeat the Lyucu without sacrificing tens of thousands, perhaps even hundreds of thousands. Even the best ideas for new weapons devised by Princess Théra and Zomi Kidosu, enhanced with my input, could only sting the garinafins in a moment of surprise.

"I will have to draft every man, woman, and child, and fight a war of attrition for decades. Though I have ordered the deaths of many in my life, I cannot contemplate such a price, not even to avoid servitude.

"I'm sorry, Jia. I can see no way out other than to yield."

"Zomi!" Aya jumped up and gave her a great big hug.

"How are your studies going?" Zomi asked.

"Ma makes me practice hard every day." Aya pointed to the heavy stones in the corner. "I can lift three of those overhead at a time now. I'm sure I'll soon be able to go to war with her."

After a quick greeting, Gin Mazoti invited Zomi to stay and have lunch with her. They sat down together with Aya, much as they used to do in the palace at Nokida, when Queen Gin and her advisers would discuss the various policy matters of the kingdom.

Zomi brought out a large book and laid it on the table between them.

Gin recognized it as *Gitré Üthu*, the book that Luan Zya—now Zyaji—used to carry with him always. She had read the report of Luan Zyaji's adventures, of course, but it was different to see the original manuscript itself. With trembling hands, she opened it and began to read.

On the last page was a message that Luan had written.

It is only when one is away from home that one can see its beauty. Gin, my beloved, see you on the other side.

"What is this?" asked Aya.

"It's a book written by your father," said Gin.

"My father?" Aya didn't know how to respond as she gazed at the signature on the last page. After a while, she said, "I thought you didn't know who he was."

A complicated series of expression flitted across Gin's face.

"I lied," she finally said. "The love between us was . . . difficult."

"I wish I had known him," said Aya. "Was that why you cried at his funeral?"

"I'm sorry," said Gin. "I didn't let him know about you or tell you about him because . . . I was afraid."

"Afraid of what?"

"That you would love him more than . . . They were foolish fears, the products of vanity. I told you it was a difficult love."

Aya got up and ran away from the table.

"I didn't know my father either," said Zomi. "I'll go talk to her later."

Gin shook her head. "She's allowed to be mad at me. I was wrong. What could have been . . . We all must pay for the consequences of our actions."

After an interval of silence, Zomi asked, "Did you see anything in Zyaji's story that would help with defeating the pékyu?"

Gin shook her head. "Luan was a meticulous man, and he took excellent notes. But Pékyu Tenryo was a suspicious man, and he must have kept a close eye on Luan during the voyage back. I've thought a lot about what he wrote of the habits of the garinafins, but I don't see anything that could be used to our advantage."

"Théra is now studying the garinafin carcasses in depth, and I will go help her. It's possible we'll find a weakness heretofore unexplored."

Gin smiled. "The young are always so hopeful."

"Have you given up, Marshal?"

Gin waited a beat, then said, "The currents of life are sometimes stronger than we are, Zomi. Look at how carefully and strenuously the emperor, the empress, and your teacher all planned and fought for their lives. But sometimes fate is like that great oceanic current, which sweeps away all our plans and desires as so much debris.

"I think the Fluxists are right—there is a time to fight, and a time to yield."

The weeklong Lantern Festival was here.

Even in a time of war, life in the Islands of Dara marched on in its habitual rhythm. If anything, the celebrations seemed even more exciting than usual, as though the festival mood was made sharper by a hint of desperation.

After repeated entreaties from Aya, Gin Mazoti finally yielded and took her out to see the festivities. They went out at dusk, the best time to see the lanterns. Every shop, store, inn, and house in Pan seemed festooned with lanterns fashioned out of bamboo, paper, and silk: Some spun with the heat of the candles inside, others fluttered with the wind.

The lanterns shone in colors as varied as the new dresses and robes worn by the young men and women in the streets: bright red, dazzling gold, jade green, ocean blue. Some were painted with scenes from the ancient sagas, and as they spun, the pictures seemed to come alive, showing the Hegemon galloping on Réfiroa or Iluthan sailing away, the Queen of Écofi pining after him on the beach. Food hawkers called out the names of their wares, accompanied by scents that stirred the appetite: skewers of grilled shark steak, spiced after the fashion of Dasu; small bowls of sweet dumplings filled with sesame and coconut meat from Arulugi; sorghum flatbread baked in the traditional Cocru manner, where buyers could tell their fortune by observing the patterns left by the oven . . .

Aya wanted to try everything, and Gin happily obliged.

"Do you want to try some puffer-fish soup?" a voice asked.

Gin looked up and saw that the speaker was Soto Zyndu.

Lady Soto bowed to Gin. "Excuse my rudeness for not going into *jiri*. My hand is occupied, as you can see."

Soto was holding a small porcelain bowl. The vendor at the stall had filled it with a ladleful of hot steaming soup with noodles and a piece of translucent white flesh.

Aya looked quite interested.

"I don't think so," said Gin, pulling her back. "I've never quite understood the desire to tempt fate that way."

"If we are all to become slaves of the Lyucu, perhaps death will not be such a terrifying prospect."

Gin's face darkened. "Lady Soto, watch your tongue. This is an occasion of joy."

"Ma! I want to try it! All these people have had it and they're fine."

"Absolutely not," said Gin. She started to walk away, dragging Aya behind her.

Soto called out, "I never thought the famed Queen Gin, the emperor's marshal, would be revealed to be a coward."

Gin whipped around. With an effort, she tamped down her anger and kept her voice low. "Do not think that I don't know what you're doing. I'm not some foolish street brawler who can be goaded into a fight just because you call me a coward. Everyone who has fought with me knows that I'm not afraid to die, but I also don't believe in throwing away the lives of the soldiers under my command uselessly."

"So you are not only a coward, but also arrogant."

"What do you mean?"

"Do you think all the soldiers are your children, who need you to tell them what they should think? You are consumed with visions of draftees dying meaningless deaths, but not all men fight only because they've been told to. Come with me."

Angry and confused, Gin took Aya and followed Soto Zyndu to a carriage parked by the side of the street and got in. As soon as they sat down, the carriage started moving, slowly winding its way through the festival crowd toward the edge of the city.

Gin peeked through the curtains over the window at the families thronging the streets. The Lantern Festival was a celebration of the light and renewal of spring, when the ghosts of ancestors were supposed to join the living in harmony and joy. It was a time to be together with family, and Gin's eyes grew warm as she thought about Luan Zyaji—she wished the last time they had seen each other had gone differently. She pulled Aya close to her, and the young girl seemed to sense her mother's mood and did not squirm away as was her wont.

The carriage exited the city and eventually stopped. Gin stepped out and saw that they were at the parade ground where the emperor and his wives would observe the military parades every year in the fall, after the harvest. This time of the year the parade ground should be deserted.

But by the last light of dusk, she could see that the ground was packed with people. Their ranks were so dense and stretched out so far that she could barely see to the end.

Soto Zyndu extended a hand and invited her to ascend the dais in front of the parade ground. As though in a dream, Gin climbed up and surveyed the soldiers in front of her.

They were a varied lot. Some wore the regular uniforms of the Imperial army and flew the standard of Dara—she recognized some of the hundred-chiefs who had served under her during the Chrysanthemum-Dandelion War; some flew the flag of the rebels of Arulugi, with its blue field—inherited from the ancient flag of Amu—charged with the golden carp of Tututika; some flew the flag of her old domain, Géjira, which was parted quarterly in black and white—a reference to her prowess on the *cüpa* board—and charged with a water mill, the foundation of Géjira's industrial strength and manufacturing; some even flew the chrysanthemum flag of the Hegemon, a sight that could have been viewed as treason; there was also a group of women to the side, some old, some quite young, but all dressed in the old uniform of the Dasu women's auxiliaries, a force that Gin had founded during the Chrysanthemum-Dandelion War. . . .

From the crowd, she could pick out the standards of almost all the old Tiro states as well as fiefs that had been abolished by the emperor during Jia's campaign to weaken the founding noble families, Kuni's old generals. Never could anyone have imagined that all of them would stand side by side on the same parade ground.

"What . . ." Gin was at a loss for words.

Soto Zyndu walked up next to her on the dais. She shouted, "Men and women of Dara, what do you want?"

The crowd below the dais let out a tsunami of voices that shook the floor beneath Gin's feet.

"Fight! Fight! Fight!"

"Victory is unlikely," said Soto. "It's possible, no, probable, that all of you will die and Dara will still fall. The battle goes not always to the righteous, and evil sometimes does triumph."

"Fight! Fight! Fight!"

Soto gestured at the assembled soldiers, and a few leaders pushed through the crowd to come stand at the base of the dais.

"Why do you want to fight?" asked Gin Mazoti. "Even though you know defeat is almost certain?"

"It's more important to die free than to live as slaves," said Cano Tho of Arulugi. "The emperor may have pardoned my act of rebellion, but I will not be able to lift my head in front of Princess Kikomi on the other shore of the River-on-Which-Nothing-Floats if I did otherwise."

"The Hegemon would have fought," said Mota Kiphi of Tunoa, one of the followers of the ill-fated rebellion in Tunoa by Noda Mi and Doru Solofi. He smiled and nodded at Aya, who had once been impressed by his prowess at lifting weights. "And so will I."

"We might once have been ambitious," said Doru Solofi. "But even we understand that in front of a threat like the Lyucu, all of us must band together."

"The emperor has been exceedingly generous with us," said his onetime coconspirator, Noda Mi. "He's forgiven us for our past trespasses, and we want to pay him back with redoubled loyalty. You should do the same, Marshal!"

"My uncle was a gentle soul who trusted all strangers as brothers," said Gori Ruthi, Zato Ruthi's nephew, as he stepped forward. The grief awakened in his heart by his words was so sharp that he stumbled and almost fell, but his wife, Lady Ragi, held him up. "I will strike down the Lyucu so that we *can* trust strangers again."

"My brother once said that I chose the wrong lord," said Dafiro Miro. "I will prove him wrong."

"I have never picked up a sword in my life," said Naro Hun, widower of General Mün Çakri. "But I will give my life to avenge my husband. And should I fall as well, I hope our son will fight on in our stead."

"I'm no fighter," said Naroca Huza, onetime rival of Zomi Kidosu at the Palace Examination and one of the most prominent merchants of Géjira. "But all my wealth is at your disposal, Marshal, for even men of commerce love freedom."

Gin listened to the speeches of the leaders of the assembled multitudes, a complex set of emotions warring within her heart. Was it right to give up without a fight? Even if fighting meant certain defeat?

Soto Zyndu came to her with a sword. It was so heavy that she could only drag it along the ground. "Unsheathe this."

As though in a dream, Gin gripped the handle with both hands and pulled the sword out of its sheath. Though she was strong, it still took some effort for her to lift it so that it pointed to the sky. She was very familiar with this legendary sword, though she had never held it.

"This is Na-aroénna, the Doubt-Ender. My nephew was the last to wield it. Whenever he unsheathed it, he had no more doubt."

Gin looked at Soto. "But he lost and died, and many died with him. His lack of doubt was wrong."

Soto shook her head. "You misunderstand. On that last night at Rana Kida, Mata released all his men from the obligations they owed him as their lord. Those who fought with him until his last stand by the sea fought willingly, having no doubt that victory was impossible."

Gin was silent for a moment. "I am not the Hegemon. The storytellers do not embellish my deeds with myth and legend. I'm just an ordinary woman who knows how to make a living with a sword."

"You are much more than that," said Soto. "You have always been solicitous of the lives and thoughts of your soldiers. You abolished whippings and stockades in the army, preferring to instill discipline by rewarding initiative and providing useful training. You earned loyalty not by fear and intimidation, but by listening to the soldiers and giving them better shoes and taking care of their families. You gave the women of Dara a chance to fight for their own future. How can you be so blind now to their desires?

"It isn't the achievement of victory that makes a leader noble, but the willingness to fight for what is right in her heart even when defeat is certain. Fithowéo is the god of not just victors, but also those who fall for a just cause. Insist on seeing, even when all around you is darkness.

"All the Ano sages wrote about the unpredictability of life, and they agreed that there is nothing free of doubt in this life except the fact that we will all die. But death can come in many forms: Some are heavier than Mount Fithowéo, and some are more inconsequential than a feather in the wind. It is not your place to deny the right of each man and woman to choose how they wish to achieve that death."

"If even the gods of Dara have not shown any signs that they favor our cause, how can I know that this is the right path?" Gin asked. "I was not born with double-pupiled eyes, knowing that I was destined for greatness. I did not slaughter a great white python in the mountains and have rainbows point the way for my wife."

"There are no born heroes, and legends are just stories. Gin, you know that truth as well as I. But the world sometimes demands a man or a woman to step forward to embody the will of the many, and thus are legends and heroes born. True courage comes not from being certain and unafraid, but from doing what must be done even while being terrified and full of doubts."

Gin closed her eyes. She thought of the gang leader in her youth who had maimed children while she stood by, helpless. She thought of the men and women of Rui, chained to each other while Pékyu Tenryo calmly ordered their slaughter. Evil existed in this world; it had to be confronted.

She opened her eyes and raised Na-aroénna. The last light of the sun caught its tip as she led the crowd in a chant. The voices swelled until it seemed the very heavens shook and the first twinkling stars trembled.

"Fight! Fight! Fight!"

CHAPTER FIFTY-THREE

DISCOVERIES

Rumors spread around Dara that the Lyucu had found a permanent passage through the Wall of Storms and were sending reinforcements of hundreds more garinafins and thousands more warriors. It was said that they could conquer all of Dara within weeks. Fishermen were terrified of going out to sea lest they encounter the city-ships of the Lyucu, and everyone looked up at the sky from time to time, thinking that the barbarians could descend from the heavens at any moment.

Wealthy merchants became more reluctant to pay taxes, and the landed gentry and even some of the local administrators and lesser enfeoffed nobles began to plan for what they saw as an inevitable future. They whispered to each other, trying to ascertain what kind of deals they could strike with their soon-to-be foreign overlords to preserve advantages for themselves and their families. Some hoarded treasures, hoping that by offering them judiciously they could escape the fate of complete enslavement; some began to lecture their wives and daughters on their duties to the family, laying the groundwork for offering them to the barbarian chieftains when the right moment arrived to save their own skins; everyone stockpiled food and necessities, believing that no matter what happened, a time of hardship was about to arrive, and merchants took advantage of the general panic to profiteer.

To counter the gloomy and panicky mood, Prime Minister Cogo Yelu came up with a plan for Consort Risana and Prince Phyro to go on a tour around Dara to assure the people and rally support for the Dandelion Throne. They even cajoled King Kado out of retirement to play a minor role.

Lady Risana designed careful spectacles featuring popular actors in elaborate costumes accompanied by rousing lyrics and catchy music. At every performance, a smoky fog representing the primordial mist filled the stage as large bamboo-and-silk islands rose out of it. While actors paraded across them, enacting famous episodes from Dara's long history—from the arrival of the Ano on these islands filled with savage natives to the celebration of the founding of the Dandelion Dynasty by a united people, from the legendary heroes of the Diaspora Wars to the more recent tales of the Chrysanthemum-Dandelion War, from the most quotable Ano sages to folksy inventors, from lyrical poets to wise judges and administrators—the mist gradually spilled over the edge of the stage and enveloped the mesmerized audience, making them part of the pageantry.

The climax of every show was the arrival of Prince Phyro on the back of a mechanical cruben constructed from papier-mâché and operated by a team of men crawling underneath. The music rose to a crescendo as the prince stepped onto the soil of Rui and slew the papier-mâché garinafins on the island with powerful strokes from his sword. And then, Emperor Ragin—played by Kado Garu, who looked very much like the emperor, his younger brother—emerged from a trapdoor in the floor of the stage to thank his son and the people.

This wish-fulfilling sketch of the future, of course, was a calculated echo of Kuni's legendary cruben ride to Rui, a part of his surprise assault on Pan during the rebellion against the Xana Empire.

Then, as the prince and the emperor stood astride the carcasses of the garinafins, each holding up a severed, antlered head, a bright mirror representing the moon rose behind them and cast a magnified image across the theater to a white screen behind the audience. When the audience twisted their necks around to look behind them, they gasped as they were greeted by the sight of the eight gods of Dara smiling and nodding as the light flickered in the fragrant smoke that filled the auditorium—the magic mirrors whose secrets Théra had discovered had found a new use.

Though the propaganda message of the spectacles was transparent, they did work. History, cleansed and given a fresh coat of paint, was often far more powerful than any myth. The plays assured the population that the Dandelion Dynasty was firmly in charge; that the marshal, though she had once rebelled, had had a change of heart, and with the gracious support of the empress, was now coming up with a brilliant and devious strategy that would destroy the Lyucu and rescue the emperor and Prince Timu; that the people of Dara were the inheritors of a long and illustrious tradition of greatness; that the Lyucu, as savages who lacked strategic foresight or the benefits of civilization, were doomed to fail despite temporary gains.

After the conclusion of the spectacles, Phyro made passionate speeches exhorting the population to support the war effort: Obey the law, focus on living lives as before, punish profiteers, ignore defeatist rumors, and most important of all, pay taxes and lend money to the Imperial Treasury to help the troops. Clerks then set up tables to collect the pledges of the audience—led by the VIPs—for purchasing war bonds.

Cogo, the master of logistics, calculated that after the devastation brought to Rui and Dasu during the emperor's invasion, the Lyucu would need the entire summer and the fall harvest to recover and prepare before they could invade the Big Island. The empress did everything she could to give the marshal more time to prepare for that assault by sending messages to the Lyucu to suggest that the Dandelion Court was coming close to a decision on surrender.

Although many young men wanted to join the army as a result of the performances of Consort Risana and Prince Phyro, the marshal relied only on the ragtag troops she had met assembled on the parade ground that day. Though she had been convinced that there was meaning in fighting this hopeless war, she firmly believed in only leading men and women who were fully aware of the truth and fought out of free choice.

Though the chill between Cogo Yelu and Gin Mazoti as a result of the prime minister's role in the marshal's downfall had not dissolved, Gin did find the funds that Cogo's propaganda tour brought in helpful. She poured the money into upgrading the equipment for her small army: hiring the best bladesmiths of old Rima and mining pure sky iron to produce armor and weapons made out of expensive thousand-hammered steel; building underwater crubens that were faster and could stay underwater longer to avoid detection by flying garinafins; purchasing rare herbs that Empress Jia formulated into potent mixtures that allowed the troops to bulk up faster and recover energy with little sleep—Jia even came up with a new mixture that allowed the troops to go without sleep for days, though at the cost of some long-term damage to their bodies, but almost every single member of the volunteer force wanted to take the drug.

Most of the money, however, went to the research laboratories in Ginpen. Secret, secure facilities were quickly constructed to house the carcasses of the dead garinafins that Than Carucono's mechanical crubens had ferried back, and Cogo Yelu dispatched spies to every corner of Dara to seek out men and women of talent who might have some surprising technique for overcoming the garinafins.

The marshal didn't have much hope that such research would yield useful results—putting her hopes on that outcome would be akin to relying on the occurrence of a miracle—but she was determined to give her troops the best chance possible, even if she was convinced that the task was ultimately hopeless.

ᔐ ᔐ ᔐ ᔐ

Zomi Kidosu and Princess Théra worked alongside the surgeons, veterinarians, and anatomy specialists in Ginpen to dissect and learn the secrets of the garinafins.

They worked at a lab located inside a giant coastal cave. This facility was the brainchild of the head of the Imperial laboratories, Kita Thu, one of the Haan *pana méji* who had participated in the Palace Examination alongside Zomi Kidosu years ago. Though he had not wanted this post at the time, the instinct of the emperor and Consort Risana turned out to be correct, and over the years, Kita had grown into an able leader of scholars who was skilled at fulfilling unusual needs.

He secreted the carcasses away inside the cave as soon as they arrived and set up a system of wagons to keep them packed with ice to prevent corruption, paying the expenses out of his family's wealth even before he had Imperial funding. To most of the merchants and drivers who supplied the laboratory's needs, the facility was presented as some kind of Imperial warehouse intended to preserve seafood that could be consumed in the off-season. As the weather warmed, the wagons had to go as far as the glaciers of the Damu Mountains to harvest the ice, and the laboratory's expenses ballooned.

It was imperative that they learn what they could from the carcasses as soon as possible.

With the new war-bond funding from Pan, Kita redoubled his efforts. He expanded the cave and divided it into multiple dissection rooms so that pieces of the carcass could be studied in parallel. A system of carefully drilled holes and mirrors directed filtered sunlight to illuminate the interior of the cave, and he designed a concave frame with numerous refracting glass lenses to be placed over the dissection tables so that no shadows would block the view of the operating surgeon or dissector. To cut through the tough skin, muscle, and tendons of the giant beasts, he commissioned diamond-tipped scalpels to ensure the cuts would be smooth during the dissection process and avoid damaging the tissues needlessly with hacking and sawing. He set up several windmills on top of the cliffs above the cave, from where a series of gears and belts transferred the power down into the lab, where they operated heavy machines for lifting and moving the carcass around. Since the entire space was maintained at near-freezing temperature, everyone working inside had to dress as though it was deep winter. Except for scholars and workmen approved to work on the project, no one was allowed anywhere near the hidden laboratory: Lyucu spies and sympathizers might well attempt to sabotage the work being done here, and whatever revelations they might learn would be military secrets.

At first, the various experts were skeptical of the presence of Théra. Most thought the tales of her contributions to the suppression of the rebellion in Tunoa exaggerated, an instance of Imperial mythmaking, and more than a few grumbled that she was nothing more than a spoiled princess inserting herself among learned men to seek thrills or some sense of relevance.

It didn't help matters that Théra almost immediately insisted on the addition of two other scholars who had not been on the list of approved researchers drawn up by a select committee of the Imperial Academy Council. Çami Phithadapu was a young woman scholar from Rui who had barely placed among the *firoa* in the Imperial examinations the previous year, and Mécodé Zégate was a woman *cashima* of Haan ancestry who had grown up in Tunoa.

Both had been beneficiaries of Kuni Garu's Golden Carp Program, though even Théra didn't know that.

"Why these two in particular?" Kita Thu asked, frowning.

"Kita, you have almost no women among the researchers."

"That's because there are no qualified women candidates." Kita paused, wondering if this could be construed as an insult to the princess. He tried to be ingratiating. "Your Highness is an exception, of course, as is special adviser Zomi Kidosu."

"Although there are not nearly as many women who have passed the Imperial examinations as men, there are *some*," said Théra. "Also, since this project requires us to make novel discoveries, it's important to have a broad spectrum of opinions and views."

"Originality of thinking is a quality of the mind, not of sex," scoffed Kita Thu.

Théra persisted. "Because of their different life experiences, women may well provide fresh insights not available from traditional candidates. Unique among the examinees, Çami used her essay last year to discuss evidence of midwifery being practiced by whales, and Mécodé is well known as an expert on the history of herbal lore derived from animals' attempts at curing their own illnesses. Their interest in these traditionally neglected subjects show originality of thinking."

Kita wasn't convinced, but he relented and added the two women to the staff.

Aware of the skepticism directed at her, Théra chose to ignore the climate of mild hostility and threw herself into the work. She labored alongside the other scholars: climbing over the gigantic carcasses with rough cables and sharp hooks, never complaining about the danger; lifting and shifting massive limbs and cutting body parts without showing any sign that such physical labor was beneath her; plunging her arms deep into the blood and fat without concern until her face was spattered with gore and her body steeped in the stench of garinafin viscera. She listened to the talk of the scholars with care, and did not interrupt the discussions with her opinions.

She acted less like a princess of Dara and more like one of the apprentices or students of the scholars.

"Why do you never say anything?" asked Zomi when the two of them were by themselves. "I know you want to contribute."

Théra smiled at her. "Do you recall the legend of the Phaédo bird?"

"As told by Ra Oji?

In Damu the scarlet Phaédo sits,
For three years, snowbound, all sounds he omits.
Then, one morn he sings to call forth the sun.
Stunned, the world stands still to listen as one."

Théra nodded. "There is a time to assert your opinion, and a time to play the dutiful student. Timing is everything, in war as well as in debate—especially when one is seen as an outsider."

Zomi sighed. Théra seemed to have a far better grasp of the flow of currents of power than she did—a weakness that Luan had warned her about years ago.

Worried about Théra's health, Zomi devised a silk mask for her so that she wouldn't get sick from the garinafin gore that splashed onto her face and the fumes from the medicinal water in which they preserved detached garinafin organs. Théra was delighted, and a warmth suffused Zomi's heart as she watched the grateful princess.

"Would you mind if I asked the craftsmen to make these for everyone?" Théra asked, holding Zomi by the hand.

Zomi's face flushed. She berated herself for not thinking through how it would look if only the princess had special equipment. She concentrated on the sensation of the princess's fingers against her palm—they were rough from wielding heavy tools against tough garinafin skin, but Zomi thought they were lovely and smooth beyond measure. She nodded.

"I'll embroider some zomi berries on this one so that no one will mistake it for theirs," said Théra. "It's special; you made it."

For hours afterward Zomi caressed her own palm, trying to re-create the warmth of Théra's hand.

In contrast to the guarded reception given Princess Théra, Zomi Kidosu had everyone's respect from the get-go as the foremost *pana méji* in the Imperial examination from two sessions ago. She soon established herself as one of the leading experts on the garinafins, as she had read Luan Zyaji's accounts many times, and her own detailed notes from observing the creatures in action in Rui proved invaluable in connecting the anatomical features of the garinafins with their behavior.

Working side by side at a joint task brought Zomi and Théra even closer. As they navigated and climbed around a mountainous maze made of garinafin guts, they kept up a constant stream of chatter and laughter, as though they were strolling through a lovely garden and commenting upon the exotic flowers.

With the best minds of Dara at work, the scholars huddled inside the ice cave on the coast of Haan made steady progress toward their first goal: understanding the mystery of the garinafin's fire breath, an ability that had no equivalent in the fauna of Dara.

Once they cut through the skin and muscle of the garinafins, the scholars found a network of membranous sacs that filled the body cavity.

"These must be similar to the sacs inside the torso of the Mingén falcons," reasoned Atharo Ye, a noted Patternist scholar of Rui who had served in the court of Emperor Mapidéré as one of the Xana Empire's airship engineers. He was a descendant of the great engineer Kino Ye, who had committed sacrilege to dissect the Mingén falcons and learned the secret of the lift gas that powered the flight of the great raptors. From time to time, Atharo enjoyed puffing on a coral pipe stuffed with rich tobacco from Faça, and though the smoke lingered in the ice cave, none of the other scholars dared to object given his prominence.

"Even with hollow and light bones, as well as gigantic wings, it appears that these creatures still need the assistance of such sacs for flight," Atharo continued.

"But that means that they are as dependent on the lift gas as our airships," said an excited Çami Phithadapu, who made it a point to speak up and not let herself be intimidated by so many well-known scholars around her—a habit that irritated many of the older, established scholars. "If we can cut off their supply, the garinafins will eventually become earthbound."

Zomi shook her head. "I'm not convinced. I don't recall the Lyucu sending the beasts to Lake Dako to replenish their supply of lift gas. And there was no mention of a supply of lift gas in Master Zyaji's accounts of the lands of Ukyu and Gondé. Such an important feature surely would have drawn his interest."

"It's possible that the lift gas is far more plentiful in their land than ours, such that the Lyucu did not treat it as a rare resource or make note of it," said Atharo.

"But how were they able to sustain the supply of lift gas for so long on their voyage across the ocean?" asked Çami.

Atharo dismissed this objection with an impatient wave of his hand. "Our airships leak gas but slowly, and with careful maintenance and pooling the lift gas supply between ships, we can fly them for years before needing to refill."

"But the garinafins don't seem to be able to maintain flight for long," said Zomi. "All the evidence shows that they can fly for but a few hours at a time before needing to land. If they are reliant on stored lift gas, one would expect them to be able to stay aloft indefinitely."

"Hmm . . ." Atharo Ye had to admit that this was a rather good point. "Let me examine these sacs some more."

He located one of the sacs that was still full of gas and carefully severed it from the attached blood vessels, air tubes, and other tissue. Then he tied off the small tubes with a length of string, and, holding on to the string, let the sac go.

The sac, almost three feet across, rose into the air, pulling the string taut.

"Lighter than air, as suspected," said Atharo.

Next, he took a sharpened hollow reed and stuck it into the sac. The gas hissed out of the tube.

"Master Ye," Princess Théra interrupted. Since she rarely spoke, everyone turned to look at her. "I think it prudent to be cautious with an unknown gas. Perhaps it's best to use one of the smaller dissection—"

Atharo Ye waved at her impatiently. "I've been working with lift gas since before you were even an idea in the minds of your parents. I know very well what is safe and what is not." He closed his eyes and took a deep whiff of the escaping gas. "There's no smell at all. Pure lift gas."

He let the sac float over his head like a balloon, the hissing jet of gas from the still-leaking reed propelling it in circles like an airship. Then he took out his coral pipe filled with cured tobacco and gestured for one of the errand boys standing around to bring over a light for his pipe. Since the inside of the cave had to be kept chilled and illumination was provided by refracted and reflected sunlight, there was no lit torch or lamp around the lab. The boy had to run outside the cave and bring back a lit stick.

And just like that, the balloon over his head exploded into a fireball. As the boy yelped and jumped out of the way, the other scholars dove for cover. The fireball fell onto Atharo's head and set his hair and clothes on fire. Atharo screamed and stumbled around, bumping into the dissection table. There was no ready source of water nearby. He was going to be severely injured by the fire.

The other scholars and guards were stunned and stood around helplessly.

"Your Highness!" Mécodé Zégate, the herbalist from Tunoa, ran up to Princess Théra. "Can I have your robe?"

Théra understood at once. "Good idea!" Without hesitation, she tore off the voluminous winter robe she was wearing, and, with Mécodé's and Çami's help, covered Atharo Ye's flaming head and shoulders before pushing him to the ground. They rolled him along the ground until they were certain the flames had been extinguished.

Atharo sat up and slowly and removed Théra's robe from his head like the veil of a bride. The fire had singed off his beard and much of his hair, but the injury to his face and neck was relatively light.

"You'll be fine with an ointment of ice lilies and winter jelly," said Mécodé after examining him. "It will sting terribly for a few days, though."

"Thank you," he said, looking at Théra, Çami, and Mécodé gratefully.

Meanwhile, Zomi calmly issued orders to everyone in the cave. "Get those doors open to let in some fresh air! Don't cut open any more sacs from the garinafins, and make sure to never bring any fire in here."

At another time, the sight of three women—one of them a princess in her undergarments—rolling an elder like a log on the ground might have generated titters or gossip, but everyone in the cave understood what a brave thing Théra, Çami, and Mécodé had done.

Kidosu started to clap, and everyone else soon joined in, filling the cave with loud peals of applause.

"You have certainly taught me a lesson," said an embarrassed Atharo. "Just goes to show you that living for many years does not necessarily gain you any wisdom. How were you able to remain so calm and know what to do?"

Mécodé laughed. "Being from a poor family where I cooked for the whole household, I imagine I've spent many more hours in the kitchen than the rest of you put together. A skirt catching fire in the kitchen is a common accident, and I learned to deal with it. I imagine Çami had similar experiences."

Çami nodded. "I might have been a good student, but I was still expected to cook for my brothers and parents."

Atharo turned to Théra. "I can't imagine you learned this technique from the kitchen, however."

Théra grinned. "Not quite. When my father was a young man, his friend, Farsight Secretary Coda, was caught in a firebomb attack. My father had to figure out how to put out such a fire by separating the flames from air to save his friend. The story made quite an impression on me, and so I was able to put it into practice without much thought."

Atharo nodded. "Thank the gods you are here."

From then on, the scholars treated Théra, Çami, and Mécodé as full-fledged members of the team. When they offered opinions or observations, the others listened.

The shared trauma of losing their families to the depredations of the Lyucu and the work in the laboratory provided Zomi and Théra with a unique bond. The two took their meals together and spent hours on break discussing garinafin research, engineering principles, military tactics, and whatever else came to mind.

The investigation into the garinafins had slowed down as the scholars were mired in endless debate over the nature of the air sacs and how to reconcile them to the observed behavior of the beasts. There were too many theories and everyone was frustrated as Imperial messengers from Pan demanded updates every other day, reminding everyone of the looming war with the Lyucu.

There was a thundershower one day, and after the rain stopped, Théra convinced Zomi to take a break from their work and climb to the top of the cliffs.

"Isn't this lovely?" said Théra. The tranquil ocean was a dark turquoise. A rainbow hung in the sky as the sun peeked out behind the clouds.

Zomi smiled and pointed at the rainbow.

"What?" Théra shaded her eyes and gazed in the direction Zomi was pointing, thinking she had spied something on the horizon.

Zomi smiled and pointed at the rainbow again.

"Is this a riddle?"

Zomi smiled and pointed at the rainbow again.

"I give up. Tell me what you're trying to say."

Zomi's smile turned wistful. "My mother once told me a story about the gods and the Calendrical Dozen, and in that story Lord Lutho chose to answer every question posed to him this way. The gods are full of mysteries."

"I'd like to hear that story sometime," said Théra. "I wish I'd gotten to meet your mother."

"Both my parents were good storytellers," said Zomi. "And the story is better when told in the dialect of Dasu. I've been away from home so long I've lost my accent."

Théra put a comforting arm around Zomi as they stood side by side. "We lose much as we grow up, but we also gain much. To get to where we are hasn't been easy."

The surrounding countryside looked as fresh as though it had just been painted on a canvas: lush green fields, deep-black sandy beach, the huts and houses glinting with washed red roof tiles and bright white walls.

"A great lady once told me that gazing upon a world reborn after the rain is one of the greatest pleasures in the world," Théra said.

"It really is," said Zomi. "I'm glad I listened to you and climbed up here. Though I don't think I'd enjoy it half as much if I were here by myself."

Théra smiled. The lady had said something like that, too.

Zomi sat down to fuss with her leg harness, as the climb had loosened some of the bindings.

"That's a really amazing piece of machinery," said Théra. She sat down beside Zomi to examine how the harness flexed and magnified the movements of Zomi's weakened leg muscles.

"My teacher made this for me," said Zomi. Her eyes dimmed for a moment. "If he were here now, I bet he would have already figured out the secrets of the garinafins. We're making such slow progress that I feel like I'm letting him down."

"I don't think so," said Théra. "Luan Zyaji was a great scholar, but he wasn't a god. He was mortal like you and me. He believed the universe was knowable, and as long as we hold on to that belief and keep at it, I'm sure we'll make a breakthrough."

"How do you stay so cheerful?"

"I was taught that what we fill our hearts with has much more to do with our fates than our native talents or circumstances. I was named Dissolver of Sorrows, and I intend to live up to my name. If our situation seems hopeless, we can either give in to it and lament our fortune, or revise the script and chart ourselves a new course. We're always the heroes of our own stories."

"We're always the heroes of our own stories," Zomi repeated. She smiled for the first time in a long time.

"You know," said Théra, "you're beautiful when you smile."

Zomi bristled. She had always been sensitive about maintaining a serious demeanor to prove she belonged among the ranks of the learned. "Are you telling me to smile more?"

"Not at all," said Théra. "It makes me happy to see you happy, and I hope we'll have more moments of genuine joy together."

Zomi blushed. Few had ever commented on her appearance, given her disfigurement from that childhood experience with a lightning strike. But Théra's comment made her heart grow light.

Théra giggled. "That red-faced look isn't bad either. Did you know that you used to intimidate me? I was sure that you didn't like me, because you were so impatient every time I tried to talk to you."

Zomi laughed awkwardly. "I was arrogant and thought I knew everything. I'm sorry I used to be so rude."

"I grew up with few other children who weren't my siblings, and when I did get to spend some time with other girls my age, the difference in our statuses made it impossible to become close," Théra mused. "I'm really glad we are working on this together."

"Me too," said Zomi. She swallowed and then continued, "I never told you this, but I'm grateful that you made me see that I was being a coward when I wanted to leave court after my betrayal of the marshal."

"I only showed you what you already knew to be true in your heart," said Théra. "A real friend is a mirror who reflects the truth back to us."

"What if . . ." Zomi paused, and swallowed, looking into Théra's expectant eyes. She forced herself to go on, her heart pounding. "I want to be more than friends?"

Théra blushed as her face broke into a radiant smile. "I thought I was playing the zither to the ruminating cow, but it turns out that I was the cow who was too afraid to dance!"

"Is that a . . . yes?" asked Zomi, her heart beating wildly.

Instead of answering, Théra wrapped her arms about Zomi and pulled her into a long, lingering kiss.

The sun sparkled against the sea, and a gentle breeze caressed the revitalized world.

The voices of two young women who had heard the voices in each other's hearts, the music beneath the music, sang in perfect harmony:

How far will they go? What will they behold?
What distant shores will they touch and visit?

Before they sink and sprout and grow and bloom—
To sway over sun-dappled waves anew!

A bandaged Atharo Ye returned to the investigation with gusto. Humbly, he asked Princess Théra and Zomi to assist him.

"There are too many theories being tossed about and not enough evidence," said Atharo. "We need to do more, talk less."

Cautiously, they cut another sac from one of the dead garinafins.

"How do we measure the qualities of this gas?" asked a frowning Atharo.

Zomi grinned. "We can weigh the fish."

They inflated one of the empty sacs with the lift gas from one of the few messenger airships left under Imperial command until it was the same size as the sac from the garinafin. Then they tied various weights to the two sacs until both were buoyancy-neutral.

"The gas inside the garinafins is heavier than the gas bubbling out of Lake Dako," Atharo concluded. "That's why the other sac is able to carry a heavier weight."

"That also means that the garinafins have less lift than the Mingén falcons and our airships," said Zomi. "That explains the need for such large wings."

"It's also highly flammable, which means that it's probably the source for the fire breath," said Théra.

On a hunch, Théra asked that one of the canisters holding the gas that powered the marshal's flamethrowers be brought to the cave. The same experiment was run to compare the gas extracted from the fermented manure with the gas from one of the garinafin sacs, and they were found to have identical weight.

"But how could the garinafins have access to manure gas?" asked the puzzled scholars.

Mécodé, the expert on the effects of various herbs on animal digestion, offered a possible answer. "The fermentation process that generates the gas for the flamethrowers may be similar to what happens inside these grass-eating creatures."

Further dissection of the animals seemed to confirm the hypothesis. Like cattle and sheep, the garinafins had multichambered stomachs. It appeared that the grass had to be fermented in some of the earlier chambers, regurgitated, chewed, and swallowed again. The gas generated from the fermentation was then distributed and stored in the network of sacs found throughout the body. To prevent bloating, the gas slowly leaked out over time and had to be replenished.

"Breathing fire consumes the gas as well," speculated Zomi. "This explains why the garinafins can't fly for as long when they breathe fire. They need to replenish the gas supply by landing and eating."

"Creation certainly is full of wonders," said Atharo Ye. "The herbivores must have developed this ability as a defense mechanism. Makes me wonder what kind of other amazing creatures one might find in the lands of Ukyu and Gondé."

Seeing these fearsome creatures as cud-chewing flying cattle certainly removed some of their mystique. The scholars immediately turned to debate how to take advantage of these discoveries and generate countermeasures.

More mysteries were revealed as the dissection continued.

Although the garinafins were clearly mammals, dissection of the two carcasses—both female—revealed partially formed eggs with hard shells, suggesting that they were oviparous.

"Mammals that lay eggs!" exclaimed Atharo Ye. "I never would have believed such a thing if I hadn't seen them with my own eyes."

Looking inside the eggs yielded even more surprises.

"And unlike most egg-laying animals we know, the embryos develop at least partly inside the mother before the eggs are even laid," mused Çami, who was knowledgeable about prenatal development in domestic fowl. "We may not know a lot about the process of garinafin birth, but anyone can see that these three-winged and six-limbed monstrosities aren't normal and probably aren't viable."

"Do you think this garinafin was sick?" asked Princess Théra.

"Possible. But it's also possible that something is wrong with the environment. After all, the garinafins are in a foreign land, and they may lack some essential nourishment necessary for reproduction."

"You know, it's interesting that we haven't seen any juvenile garinafins so far," said Zomi. "We know that the Lyucu rely on having juvenile garinafins around to control their parents. If the garinafins are having trouble birthing young, then the Lyucu might be losing control of their mounts as well."

This seemed a promising prospect, but there was still too little evidence to justify optimism.

Once the preliminary work of dissecting the garinafins was done, the scholars divided into teams focusing on different areas of further research.

Since the garinafins were similar to cattle in their habits and digestive anatomy, Mécodé reasoned that perhaps they would suffer from the same digestive diseases and vulnerabilities.

"And I know just the person to ask for advice about cattle," said Théra.

She took one of the messenger airships and headed for the highlands of Faça.

Lu Matiza was happy to have her granddaughter visit, but she was much less happy to hear what she wanted.

"Why do you want to spend time with the ranch hands? If you want to know about cattle, just ask me."

"Grandma, you may know all about keeping a ranch running smoothly and ensuring that the business hums along, but what I need is practical knowledge, the sort of thing that only those who get their hands dirty can tell me."

No matter how much Lu Matiza tried to explain to Théra that it was inappropriate for a princess of Dara to live and work among the rough ranch hands—could she imagine what the gossips would say about her and about her family?—Théra would not listen to reason. She insisted that she had to learn what she needed to know from the only teacher who mattered: experience.

Lu sighed. This stubborn granddaughter reminded her exactly of young Jia.

"Your mother never listened to me either."

This piqued Théra's interest. "What about?"

"Oh, everything. I told her not to run around with the wild village children playing dangerous games during the summer; I begged her to focus more on embroidery and dance and not spend every moment digging for herbs; I had so many matchmakers storming out of the house after she mocked them. You should have heard the arguments we had."

Théra imagined a younger version of her mother resisting marriage proposals in favor of other more exciting pursuits. Considering the history of their own tense relationship, it was more than a little ironic. But the story somehow made her feel closer to Jia as well.

In the end, Grandma Lu relented. She comforted herself by recalling the fact that even though Jia had refused to obey her and Gilo and insisted on marrying Kuni Garu, things had worked out for the best in the end. Maybe it was all right to let the daughters of the Matiza family do as they liked.

And so, for a few weeks, Théra became one of Lu Matiza's ranch hands—she forbade her grandmother from revealing her real identity to her coworkers so that she could learn what was really involved in caring for cattle. Théra learned to eat dried biscuits and jerky for dinner, to drink the hot brew made from roasted chicory root to stay warm and alert, to laugh and tell bawdy jokes around a campfire, to sleep in the fields under a sky full of stars while wrapped in a cozy spring cocoon-blanket, to shovel manure into a processing pit, to drive the cattle from pasture to pasture during good weather, and to shelter them during the rainy days in barns and fill their feeding troughs with fragrant hay. With the constant exertion and a seemingly endless series of chores that had to be performed, her hands became rough and her skin tanned, and she could feel strength filling her limbs.

The ranch hands fretted about the Lyucu and shared outrageous rumors, and Théra tried to calm them without revealing who she was. It was a difficult juggling act, and she was gnawed constantly by worry that she might be too late to discover the one nugget of information that would change everything.

She learned what a marvel the ruminant stomach was and how careful one had to be in directing what went into it. One couldn't just feed whatever plant material was at hand to cattle and hope for the best. Switching from one mix of grass or hay to another had to be done gradually and carefully, lest the cattle fall sick from bloat and poisoning. What was good for people to eat was not at all good to feed to cattle. The ruminant's stomach had to be babied and the excrement of the cattle carefully examined to infer the state of the mysterious digestive process inside the cattle that turned grass and hay into milk, meat, and other by-products.

By the time she was ready to return to Ginpen with her findings, she had in mind a plan that she was rather proud of.

Zomi Kidosu, meanwhile, was consumed with the mystery of just how the garinafins turned the flammable lift gas into actual tongues of flames.

While the marshal's flamethrowers relied on a pilot light, examination of the oral cavity and the upper digestive tract of the garinafins revealed no structure capable of supporting such a thing. Neither was there any sign of metal or flint to generate a spark.

The other scholars came up with elaborate theories to explain how the beasts ignited their fire breath: Perhaps the animals' bodies contained some kind of essence that could spontaneously burst into flames; or perhaps they had learned to grind their teeth together with such force and speed as to create incendiary heat—much as travelers lost in the woods could create fire by rubbing sticks together; or maybe the eyes of the beasts could focus sunlight like the curved mirrors of old Haan into fire inside their skulls?

None of these theories found any support in the actual anatomy of the garinafins. Eventually, most of the scholars abandoned the topic as an unsolvable puzzle and turned to other—hopefully more crackable—garinafin riddles.

But Zomi could not let the mystery go. She sent out word to the farseers to gather and collect knowledge of novel ways of starting fire, hoping to learn something that would lead to a breakthrough.

CHAPTER FIFTY-FOUR

THE AID OF TAN ADÜ

TAN ADÜ: THE FOURTH MONTH IN THE TWELFTH
YEAR OF THE REIGN OF FOUR PLACID SEAS.

Dafiro Miro came to Tan Adü. It had been twenty years since he had last set foot on this southernmost of the Islands of Dara.

True to the promise he had made to Chief Kyzen in exchange for the Adüans' help with calling the crubens to the aid of the rebellion, Emperor Ragin had forbidden all his military commanders and nobles from waging war against the Adüans. During the last two decades, the only men of Dara who had come here were traders and missionaries of the various gods, and from time to time, Adüans in search of adventure would return with them to the other islands to satisfy their curiosity about the larger world.

Slowly but surely, life on Tan Adü was changing: Porcelain, lacquerware, and even silk could be found in the households of some of the Adüan chieftains, and Chief Kyzen himself had even reluctantly agreed to hire scribes from Dara to record the histories and legends of his people in writing so as to create a more secure repository than talk-story. These changes were hotly debated among the chieftains and the other members of the tribes, but the choices were being made by the tribes themselves rather than imposed under threat of conquest.

Chief Kyzen, who had become so familiar with the vernacular of Dara that he no longer needed an interpreter to converse with Emperor Ragin's emissaries, received Dafiro warmly.

"Is the All-Chief well?" asked Kyzen, a teasing smile on the corners of his lips. "When he came to me the first time, he gave me a pretty speech about overthrowing Mapidéré the tyrant. But in the end, I guess he couldn't resist the temptation to be All-Chief himself!"

Dafiro bristled at this accusation against his lord.

Kyzen laughed. "I'm only teasing. It's good to see that Kuni Garu's men are still as loyal as ever. Word of the prosperity and peace under Emperor Ragin has reached even my old ears via the nimble traders of Dara, as out of the way as this island is. There is no shame in wanting power, so long as one wishes to wield it for the benefit of the people. Besides, Kuni has always kept his promise of leaving the Adüans alone, and I appreciate that."

"The emperor is in mortal danger," said Dafiro. He proceeded to update the chief on all that had been happening in Dara after the coming of the Lyucu.

"Is it as bad as that?" asked a thoughtful Kyzen. "Do you think there's no chance you will prevail? Kuni Garu and his advisers, especially *Toru-noki*, have always been resourceful."

Dafiro shook his head. "Master Luan Zya, now honored as Zyaji, is dead, giving his life in a last attempt to stop the Lyucu. The marshal, who is the greatest war leader I have ever followed, does not speak of hope."

"And so you've come to us again for aid."

Dafiro nodded. "I convinced the marshal to let me try. If the great crubens once helped the emperor to reach the Throne of Dara—indeed, the banner of Dara still honors that episode—perhaps they will help the emperor and the people of Dara again in this dark moment."

"And why should Tan Adü be involved?"

"The Lyucu intend not just conquest, but enslavement. I have told you the savagery of their ways. The Islands of Dara shelter Tan Adü now like lips shielding teeth from a wintry blast. But if the lips are gone, will the teeth not feel the chill?"

Kyzen closed his eyes and pondered the request, slowly puffing on his horn pipe. Dafiro held his breath and waited.

Finally, Kyzen opened his eyes. "Have the gods of Dara not given you signs of their will?"

"The gods of Dara, as you know, have pledged not to interfere in the affairs of mankind, at least not directly."

"But that is an elaboration after the Diaspora Wars. They could agree to dissolve a pact as easily as to make it."

Dafiro had always wondered about the religious practices of the Adüans. "Do you pray to the same gods as we do?"

"That . . . is a surprisingly complicated question," said Chief Kyzen. "I once thought we did, but the real answer is neither yes nor no. Come with me."

Chief Kyzen took Dafiro to a large hut constructed from a bamboo-and-wood frame covered with thatching grass and reeds. The hut was airy and open, and the walls were lined with many shelves filled with statues carved from coconut, wood, and whalebone.

Dafiro looked to Chief Kyzen for more explanation.

"In the days of the Tiro states, the kings of Amu and Cocru frequently tried to conquer us. Though they never succeeded in taking this island, their raiders did rob us of the treasures we inherited from our ancestors. When some of our young went to Dara to study your arts, I asked them to go to the All-Chief and the Lords of Dara and plead for the return of these artifacts. Many had been destroyed in the intervening years, but some did make their way home."

Dafiro examined the statues more closely. They were not carved after the fashion of Dara. Some had heads so large that the torso and limbs seemed an afterthought; others melded human features with the features of sharks, whales, birds, lizards, or fish; still others bore no resemblance to humans at all, but appeared to be exotic creatures of the deep. Many of the statues were decorated with bits of coral and shells, and their broken, incomplete form showed their age.

"Were these . . . your gods?" asked Dafiro, awe infusing his voice.

"As I told you: The answer is both yes and no."

"I don't understand," said Dafiro.

"The scholars and officials who watched over the trophy archives of the ancient Tiro kings certainly thought these were our gods, and when we explained that we did not pray to the statues but only wanted them back because they had been passed down by our ancestors, the scholars of Dara were astounded."

"As am I," said Dafiro. "Do you not have stories concerning these statues?"

"There are hundreds of these statues, and even when I was a boy, the elders of the tribes did not know the names of all the statues we had kept, much less the names and tales of the statues that had been lost. Such is the nature of talk-story that some old tales are forgotten with every generation, even if new tales are also made."

"That seems . . . sad," said Dafiro.

"It's neither sad nor happy," said Chief Kyzen. "It just is. But the scholars of Dara reacted much as you did, and some of them offered to help us recover our old stories as written down in your ancient books. The Ano, while they fought the natives of these islands, also recorded their traditions."

"It's a marvelous consequence of the Ano logograms that they would allow your people to recover your past through their frozen voices," said Dafiro. He had a common man's almost mystical reverence for the logograms, though he was no great scholar, and Zomi Kidosu's proposal years ago to abolish their use in the Imperial examinations had never quite sat right with him.

"Indeed it is. The young Adüans and Dara scholars pored through your archives and learned many traditions that had been forgotten even by our elders. For example"—he pointed to a statue of a person with an oversized head and three cowrie shells embedded in the face—"I learned about the tale of the Hero-with-Three-Eyes who dived to the bottom of the sea to demand a truce between mankind and toothed whales by holding the king of the whales underwater until he capitulated."

Dafiro examined the statue with admiration, thinking wistfully that this was a tale that his brother would have enjoyed.

Chief Kyzen went on, "During this process, the young Adüans became interested in the religious traditions of their Dara hosts as well. They scanned the ancient tomes, consulted learned priests and monks, and beseeched folk witches and mediums for obscure oral knowledge. The early days of the Ano are lost in the mists of history, and there are many conflicting myths and stories purporting to speak of ancient religion. Many scholars of Dara told us that finding the truth about the past was an impossible task."

"I had no idea it was so complicated," said Dafiro.

"By comparing our stories—both those we remember and those we learned from your books—with the stories of the gods of Dara in Ano records, we made an astounding discovery."

Chief Kyzen took another puff on his pipe, enjoying the impatient look on Dafiro's face. Then he relented and continued his account.

"The early Ano sagas had several different versions of the creation myth, as well as deeds by deities with names that did not appear in later accounts. The creation myth that eventually came to dominate is the one you know well: the parting of Thasoluo from Daraméa, the creation of the Islands from her tears, and the simultaneous birth of the young gods of Dara."

Dafiro nodded, uncertain what this meant.

"This is a myth remarkably similar to our own creation story, though differing in several important respects. Our storytellers speak of the creation of the race of man from Daraméa's blood as she gave birth to the gods, a detail absent from the Ano accounts; and in our stories, Tazu was a goddess, not a god who sometimes took on the feminine aspect."

"Which version do you think is the truth?"

"That is not something mere mortals can ever find out. But I have a theory as to what happened: When the Ano first came to these shores, they brought with them their own gods, different from those you now know as the gods of Dara, who were worshipped by the natives—our ancestors."

"Their own gods!" Dafiro was so shocked that he didn't know what to think.

"Yes, the gods of the Ano had their own names, their own spheres of power, and their own stories. Some of these were recorded in the earliest sagas, but they became neglected in later ages.

"As the Ano fought and mingled with the natives, they learned about our gods and myths, and over time, came to identify their gods with ours. For example, their god of fire was melded to our goddess of the volcanoes; our trickster goddess was seen as an echo of their trickster god; our healing god was reinterpreted as their kind shepherd. Elements of the Ano homeland were transplanted onto our gods, and they prayed to them as though they were still praying to the gods of home."

As the chief explained, he pointed out various statues for Dafiro's attention: a whalebone statue of a goddess whose ample breasts were carved from coral and shaped like Mount Rapa and Mount Kana; a wood carving of a goddess who had the lower body of a shark; a figurine made from the pure white horn of a cruben whose expression of serene mercy was universally understood.

"Why would they do this?" asked Dafiro.

"Who knows? But I suspect that the gods are rooted to places they consider home, and the Ano gods were brought here in name only, not in substance. The Ano needed the presence of divinity in their lives, and the easiest solution was to pray to gods who would answer—our gods—while giving them familiar clothing and habits and viewing them as reflections of the deities they already knew."

"And the gods of Dara agreed to this?"

"The gods are mysteries, Dafiro Miro. We understand not their thoughts or desires. But I imagine being a god is not terribly different from being a king where power is concerned; both prefer the strong as followers and worshippers. If the Ano were more powerful than our ancestors, would it not make sense for the gods to favor them over us? Just as the gods direct our affairs, perhaps the mortal world also influences the celestial realm.

"What we do know is that elaborate temples to the gods of Dara were built by the conquerors, and that in these temples the gods were depicted to resemble the Ano rather than the natives of these islands. Instead of praying to statues, my ancestors shifted to praying to the sky and the sea, and as tales attached to the old statues were forgotten, our gods became more abstract, less dependent on specific representation.

"Besides taking away our land, your ancestors also took away our gods."

Dafiro was silent, too astonished by this revelation. As the statues on these shelves had been literally taken away from Chief Kyzen's people by raiders from Dara, the chief was not merely speaking metaphorically.

"So, to answer your question: Do we worship the same gods? The answer is both yes and no, because the gods have been changed by the coming of the Ano. The people of Dara, though descended from the Ano as well as the natives, see themselves as the inheritors of the Ano legacy and worship in the same manner. We, on the other hand, still honor the gods of Dara and their parents, the World Father and the Source-of-All-Waters, but we know that they favor the men of Dara more than us, the remnants of a defeated people.

"My account should perhaps also serve as a warning to you and yours, for just as the gods once favored the men of Dara, they may well shift their love to another people. That the gods haven't spoken their will is . . . interesting."

Dafiro vowed to bring Chief Kyzen's story to more learned minds than his own. Perhaps they would make sense of it. He brought the conversation back to the topic he had come to discuss.

"Let the gods do as they will. I come now to ask for your intercession on our behalf with the crubens."

Chief Kyzen's face turned somber. "The matter is not as simple as you think. The sovereigns of the sea keep their own counsel. Though the Adüans can speak to them, all we can do is plead, not command.

"The sea is vast and eternal, but men are mortal and puny. Keeping that in mind, we have always restricted our pleas to times of absolutely necessity, such as when our very lives are threatened. Centuries ago, when the kings of Cocru invaded our shores, we pled our case to the crubens, and they intervened to destroy the Cocru armada at sea. For months afterward, wreckage from those warships washed ashore."

"I had always heard that it was a divine storm that had thwarted the plans of the Cocru kings," said Dafiro.

"And we were happy not to contradict that story, for divine intervention has a deterrent effect unachievable by other means. But the crubens, though powerful beyond our comprehension, are not gods."

"The crubens must favor Tan Adü more than the men of Dara."

"For a time, we thought so as well. When Mapidéré, in his turn, launched fleets against our shores, we went to the sea to speak to the crubens again. But this time, they did nothing. Because we had been counting on their aid, we were not as prepared as we should have been, and many warriors lost their lives as we had to scramble for a plan and fight for every inch of soil until the All-Chief decided that he preferred to focus his energy elsewhere than on the poor savages of Tan Adü."

"Why did the crubens not help you that time?"

"That is a question that we have never figured out. Some of the elders believe that in our arrogance, as we took for granted the favor of the crubens, we lost our virtue. Others believe that the crubens had their own vision for the affairs of men, and wanted to test us at our moment of need."

"What do you believe, Chief Kyzen?"

Kyzen shook his head. "It is always possible to come up with some reasonable-sounding explanation after the fact, but much of life is capricious and governed by forces beyond our understanding. The secret to happiness is to plan for the worst but be ready to seize opportunities when they flash briefly like shooting stars in the night sky.

"Leaders who believe everything can be predicted and directed are most at risk of greatly harming those who depend on them, and I agreed to ask the crubens on behalf of Kuni Garu only when I was certain that he was a man who believed that all life was but an experiment."

Dafiro pondered this. "The marshal has always planned to lose, but she is also sparing no effort at surveying the heavens for shooting stars."

Kyzen laughed. "Then let us scan the sky together."

In the predawn darkness, the great whalebone trumpet carried the voice of the Adüan chief far into the sea. As Dafiro listened to the song, he was reminded of another dawn two decades ago, when he had heard the sound of the whale-trumpet for the first time. Back then, he had been a young man in search of novelty and thrills, and hoping only for a good story to share with his brother.

At the thought of his brother, he silently said a prayer. If Rat could see him from the other shore of the River-on-Which-Nothing-Floats, perhaps he would enjoy the sight of the crubens as well.

Kyzen's trumpet song went on for a long time. As Dafiro listened to the rise and fall of the instrument's somber tone, he seemed to see a vision of the Lyucu sweeping across the Islands of Dara like a tsunami, wiping away all that was beautiful and kind, the thin layer of civilization clinging to the hard, volcanic rocks like limpets sporting fragile, varicolored shells. He saw burning fields, villages, and cities, heard the screams of dying men and women, smelled the charred flesh of the thousands slaughtered, tasted the tang of blood suffusing the air. He shuddered and realized that his face was wet.

And then, just as the sun peeked over the eastern horizon and turned the sea into liquid gold, the great crubens arrived.

They breached the sea miles away, dark silhouettes arcing gracefully through the air like shadow puppets before crashing back into the sparkling water. Though they were the most massive creatures in the world, each many times greater than an Imperial warship, they moved as effortlessly as though they were made of shadows and air.

The whalebone trumpet stopped. The story had been told and the request given. Now it was just a matter of waiting for the sovereigns of the sea to respond.

The crubens approached the canoes, moving impossibly fast. The sound of their massive fluked tails slapping against the water grew like rumbling thunder.

If the crubens agreed to help the people of Dara, they would be able to destroy the city-ships of the Lyucu with no effort. And then, who knew? Would the garinafins, of the element of fire, dare to fight against the lords of the element of water? Perhaps Dara troops would be able to ride to Rui and Dasu on the backs of the crubens and conquer the Lyucu as they shivered before such a display of overwhelming power.

The crubens were so close now that the canoes rocked over the waves caused by their motion. Dafiro held on to the sides of his canoe with both hands, feeling nauseous.

A great set of flukes slapped down, and the resulting wave, like a curtain of water, hung suspended over the boat for a second, transforming everything seen through it into a watercolor painting, before crashing down and drenching everyone in the canoe. Dafiro held his breath and squeezed his eyes shut, hoping that when he opened them again he would see the crubens stopped by the canoes like living islands, waiting for the men of Dara to ride again.

But the crubens swam past the canoe, careless of their existence. The pod of crubens diminished in the distance; the waves subsided; the noises of their flukes striking the water faded and disappeared. Soon, the ocean returned to a featureless expanse, and the golden sheen of the rising sun had faded into a more mundane bright green.

"I'm sorry," said Chief Kyzen.

This time, the men of Dara were on their own.

Before he left Tan Adü, Dafiro went to visit his old friend Huluwen, who had given him his weapon, the war club named Biter.

The two embraced. They were no longer young, but the bond

between them felt as fresh as though they had said good-bye to each other only yesterday.

Huluwen was married and had several sons and daughters, and the joyous sounds of a close-knit family made Dafiro envious for a moment. He had devoted his life to the service of the Imperial household, and never started a family. Funny. He had once lectured his young brother on the importance of taking care of oneself rather than devoting one's life to the service of the great lords, but somehow, after his brother's death, he had lived according to the precepts of honor and duty. Perhaps it was a way to honor the memory of his brother, who always had a more idealistic view of loyalty.

Huluwen was not skilled in the vernacular of Dara, and so the two communicated by gestures and grunts, and the drawing of crude pictures on the ground. To entertain the children, Huluwen invited their guest to tell a story.

What story should I tell? He did not want to speak of the Lyucu again. There was enough despair in the world.

Slowly, with a combination of pictures and mimed gestures, Dafiro told the story of Ratho's death at the Hegemon's last stand. This was a story that seemed to haunt every moment of his life, and by the end, he was in tears.

The children were silent, clearly moved by the nobility of the moment. Huluwen came up to him and said, in halting Dara speech, "All men are brothers."

Dafiro nodded and said nothing. Sometimes words got in the way of feelings.

Because Dafiro's clothes were wet from the morning ride to speak with the crubens, Huluwen took him outside his hut, where the family would build a bonfire so that they could dry Dafiro's clothes and prepare roasted taro and grilled fish for lunch.

Dafiro sipped sweet arrack and watched with interest as Huluwen's daughter, Hulumara, tried to start a fire.

Instead of going to one of the nearby huts to get a piece of burning branch, Hulumara took out a section of bamboo with one sealed end and greased the inside with a bit of fish oil. Then she took up a whale's tooth that had been filed into a cylinder and tested it to see that it would fit inside the bamboo cup snugly while sliding smoothly. Finally, she placed a bit of fluffy dried moss into a hole drilled into the tip of the whale tooth, inserted the tooth halfway into the bamboo cup, and then slammed it home the rest of the way with a hard slap on the back of the tooth.

Quickly, Hulumara pulled the tooth out, and blew at the hole in the tip. The moss began to smoke and soon, a tiny flame appeared. Hulumara cupped it and set it down into the bed of kindling at the foot of the bonfire, and her siblings helped her build up the fire and begin cooking.

"How—" Dafiro was stunned. Zomi Kidosu had asked everyone to seek out novel ways of making fire, and this definitely qualified. He asked to see the strange bamboo-and-whale-tooth contraption, which he decided to call a fire tube. There was no metal or flint anywhere on either of the pieces, and he realized that since the cylindrical tooth formed a tight seal against the walls of the bamboo tube, as the tooth was slammed down, air would be trapped at the bottom of the bamboo tube and become compressed. Was that how fire started? Simply by compressing air? The very idea seemed like magic.

The meal was delicious and the drink satisfying. Dafiro gave Huluwen a set of swords made by the master smiths of old Rima—the sword he had exchanged for Biter decades ago was a rather poor piece of work, and he had always thought he had gotten the far better end of the deal. Seeing Dafiro paying so much attention to the fire tube, Huluwen presented it to him as a gift, though he wasn't sure why his friend liked such a common object so much.

The two men gripped arms as they said their good-byes. Both knew that it was likely that they would never see each other again.

Be ready to seize opportunities when they flash briefly like shooting stars in the sky.

Dafiro secured the fire tube under his clothing, making sure it would not be lost on his return journey to Dara.

CHAPTER FIFTY-FIVE

THE SILKMOTIC FORCE

DARA: THE FIFTH MONTH IN THE TWELFTH YEAR
OF THE REIGN OF FOUR PLACID SEAS.

Lady Risana and Prince Phyro's travels around Dara took them to fog-shrouded Boama, where they were scheduled to give their performance three times to allow everyone from the surrounding countryside a chance to take in the show.

Phyro had never gotten over his childish delight in street performers of all stripes. Since there was a bit of downtime before the evening show, Phyro decided to take advantage of what the metropolis had to offer by dressing as a commoner and strolling through the street markets. Boama, being quite distant from Pan, offered fresh acts that he didn't encounter in the capital.

"I'm going to send you to see Rufizo himself!" someone shouted from the middle of a crowd. "This is witchcraft!"

Phyro pushed his way through the crowd, elbowing people aside, earning him annoyed glances and not a few curses. He had gained bulk as he grew older, and he wasn't shy about wanting a good view of something exciting.

In the middle of the crowd was a street performer arguing and fighting with a burly man who had a bushy beard.

"Accusations of witchcraft should not be thrown around so lightly, good sir!" said the performer. He looked to be in his fifties, with a thin, slender build that reminded Phyro of a sandpiper. Besides a sharp chin and a hooked nose, he added to the birdlike impression with a pair of bright and lively eyes and fluttering hands that tried to shield his face from the spittle of his angry customer.

"I call it like I see it," said the burly man, whose rough accent and simple clothes showed that he was from the countryside. He grabbed the performer by the lapels of his robe, shook him until the man's eyes rolled into the back of his head and his tongue stuck out, and then tossed him to the ground.

The performer rolled a few times along the ground, and managed to climb onto his knees and hands only after lying, stunned, on the ground for a while. His indigo robe was full of colorful patches embroidered with the symbols of the gods of Dara—perhaps the intent had been to endow him with a sense of cosmopolitan mystery, of being in tune with the gods—but as it was now muddy, wrinkled, and torn in more than a few places, the effect more closely resembled an itinerant monk who couldn't make up his mind as to which god to follow.

"Rufizo save me! Civilized men use words, not fists!"

"You gave my wife such a fright! She's expecting, you idiot!"

The performer's features scrunched into a pleading, ingratiating smile. "Good master, I warned her ahead of time that she wouldn't be able to hold on to the jar, but you insisted—"

"You never mentioned that your jar would bite!" the burly man roared, and again grabbed the performer and tossed him to the ground.

The crowd laughed and urged the burly man on. This was far more entertaining than whatever act had been going on earlier.

Phyro looked over to the side and saw a woman sitting on the ground, her face pale and still trying to catch her breath. Next to her was a low table on which sat a porcelain jar on its side, a pool of water around it. This was evidently the source of the dispute.

The prince shoved more people out of the way and squatted down next to the woman. "Mistress, are you all right?"

The woman nodded, but she was clearly still shaken by her experience.

"What happened?"

"He"—she pointed to the performer, who was being tossed to the ground a third time as the crowd jeered and cheered—"offered to double anyone's money if they could hold on to the jar with one hand while touching the stopper at the top with the other hand and not drop it."

Phyro looked at the porcelain jar again. He saw that the outside of the jar was covered by a thin layer of silver that stopped halfway up the side. There was a cork stopper next to it, through the center of which poked a metal pin ending in a jujube-sized knob. From the bottom of the stopper dangled a chain, which was apparently supposed to rest on the inner surface of the jar when the stopper was in place.

"Since it seemed like easy money," the woman continued, "my husband wanted to try it. But as soon as he took a look at my husband, he offered to quadruple our money if I held the jar instead."

Phyro chuckled inside. From years of observing the street performers at work, he recognized the trick. By offering more of a payoff to her, the performer ensured that the couple would be tempted to have the wife try first. And after she failed, the husband would want to also pay, thinking that she failed only because of her lack of strength or fortitude. This guaranteed the performer more money.

"I held the jar in one hand while the man chanted some nonsensical song and danced around me, claiming to be charging the jar with 'silkmotic force.' Then he told me to grasp the knob with the other hand. I grabbed it and held on with all my strength, thinking that he was going to try to surprise me with some trick to make me let go, but instead, the jar itself bit me, my arms went numb, and I almost passed out!"

"Witchcraft! Witchcraft!" shouted the crowd as the burly man continued to visit his displeasure on the poor performer.

"What is going on here?" a voice asked outside the crowd. Phyro glanced up and saw the flag of the Boama constables. With the threat of a Lyucu invasion imminent, all the coastal cities of Dara were jumpy, and the constables were extra vigilant, keeping an eye out for troublemakers and potential Lyucu spies.

"Listen," Phyro whispered to the woman, his voice urgent. "You don't want the constables involved. With Consort Risana and Prince Phyro in town, they're going to treat every disturbance of the peace like a major crime. Even if your husband isn't at fault, they'll just throw all of you in prison until things calm down. Best if you just make peace with him and go on your way. Besides, you should go see the priests in the Temple of Rufizo as soon as possible to make sure the baby is fine after the jar bit you."

The woman, clearly frightened by the thought of being tossed in prison, nodded gratefully at Phyro. She got up, pulled her husband away from the performer, and whispered urgently in his ear.

By the time the constables shoved through the crowd, the performer and the burly man were both standing facing each other, and each was attempting to brush the mud and dirt off the clothes of the other.

"What happened here? Why were you fighting?" asked the captain of the constables.

"A minor misunderstanding," said the performer. He dipped a corner of his robe into the pool of spilled water on the table and tried to discreetly wipe away the blood oozing from a wound in one of his ears. "My act involves audience participation, and this master got a little too into it."

The constable looked suspiciously at the burly man.

"Er . . . yes. I got a bit carried away," the man said sheepishly.

"It was just a part of the act," said the performer.

"My husband and I are from outside the city," said the woman. "We just haven't seen such amazing magic tricks before. But everything is fine now."

The constable captain looked from one to the other—a third-rate street magician and a country bumpkin—and decided it wasn't worth the trouble of trying to understand what really had happened here.

"Don't let me catch you making a scene again," the captain lectured them. The couple and the performer nodded like chickens pecking for rice in the dirt. "And the rest of you"—the captain turned to the crowd—"don't loiter about. There's nothing to see here. Go on. Come on. Go! Shoo!"

The crowd reluctantly dispersed. The constables went back to their patrols, and the couple headed for the Temple of Rufizo.

"Thank you, young master," said the street performer. "If it weren't for you, that fool would have broken my nose, my arms, and who knows what else!"

"Not to mention that the constables would have confiscated your equipment," said a smiling Phyro. "And you'd have to pay a hefty bribe to get it back."

"Very true," said the smiling performer. "I see that the young master is wise to the ways of the world."

"I have always been interested in street magic."

The performer eyed him suspiciously.

Phyro laughed. "No, no. I'm no performer. I'm more of a . . . patron of the arts! I'm far more interested in promoting interesting acts than going on the stage myself."

The performer's eyes narrowed as he tried to interpret the meaning of his words. "Perhaps such patronage can be lucrative for both parties?" he suggested tentatively.

Phyro punched him playfully in the shoulder. "Exactly! You have my meaning right. I find good acts and invest to bring them a better quality of audience, and the artists share the profits with me."

"You have piqued my interest," said the performer.

"Let me take care of a few business matters first, but later tonight, how about I buy your dinner, and you tell me more about your act?"

∽ ∾ ∽ ∾

Phyro took the street magician, whose name was Miza Crun, to one of the best restaurants in Boama. After a full meal of crisp-fried carp with apple slices and wild-monkeyberry-flavored beef stew—interrupted by a cup of sweet ice in between to cleanse the palate—Miza Crun let out a satisfied burp and shared some of his secrets with his benefactor. He took out the machines from the large baskets he carried at the ends of a shoulder pole and laid them out on the table in the private suite Phyro had reserved at the restaurant.

Centuries ago, the priests of Rufizo were the first to discover that after rubbing a porcelain or glass dish with silk, the vessels attracted dust or bits of paper. Theorizing that some minute particles in the silk—or "silk motes"—had been rubbed onto the vessels (or vice versa), the priests described the attractive force as the silkmotic force.

At first, the silkmotic force was treated as a mysterious manifestation of Rufizo's universal love for humankind. Just as the lodestone's attraction for metal symbolized Fithowéo's love of warfare and weaponry, the silkmotic force reflected Rufizo's gentler, kinder aspect.

But over time, as the secret left the temples, it was the street magicians of Faça who began to experiment with and develop this new source of crowd-pleasing effects. They fashioned elaborate apparatuses and demonstrations for the entertainment of crowds, who oohed and aahed over the apparently supernatural motions.

"Come, come! Come see the wonders of paper dancers coming to life!" Miza said, and beckoned Phyro closer to one of his devices.

It was a foot-long stage made of sandalwood, upon which lay tiny dancers cut from colorful paper and decorated with logograms for good luck and prosperity. They reminded Phyro of the shadow puppets of folk operas. A two-tined fork stood at each end of the stage, supporting a glass rod over the dancers. Everything looked exquisitely made and ancient—some of the intricate carvings in the sides of the stage were worn down from decades or perhaps even centuries of handling, and the edges of the paper dancers showed the yellow tint of age.

Miza took out a silk handkerchief and rubbed it vigorously over the glass rod, and then put the handkerchief away.

As though animated with a magical spell, the tiny dancers stood up on the stage. They quivered on their feet, as though pulled up by invisible strings.

"The silkmotic charge on the glass rod pulls them up, but they're each weighed down at the feet with a bead of polished shell," explained Miza.

Miza then pumped a small bellows connected to the side of the stage with his left hand and turned a crank with his right. The dancers began to sway, flutter, bow, turn, twist, twirl . . .

"This is the veil dance, isn't it?" said an awed Phyro. "My father said he had seen it as a child."

"Yes," said Miza. "In old Faça, this was a dance reserved for the king and his most honored guests, and ordinary men and women had to make do with descriptions or a model like this one. A grid of small holes in the floor of the stage allows the wind from the bellows to propel the dancers, while this crank is connected to a paper tape punched with a pattern of holes to control the air currents, and thus, the motion of the dancers."

"That's ingenious!"

Miza smiled. "This is one of the oldest and simplest of the silkmotic machines. The particular specimen here was made by my teacher's teacher, and it's a mere parlor trick compared to later inventions. After Mapidéré made the veil dancers a public spectacle on his tours, this contraption was no longer a crowd-pleaser. I kept it only out of nostalgia."

"I can see how such a display, charming though it is, would not impress a jaded crowd who had feasted on the real thing," said Phyro. Walking slowly next to the table, he examined each of Miza's other machines. "I understand the silkmotic force began as a part of the mysteries of the worship of Rufizo?"

The wistful look on Miza's face disappeared in a flash, and he gave Phyro a sly smile. "Temple magic, like street magic, is a matter of staging. Let me show you."

He went back to his basket and found two long silk ropes. Walking to the middle of the suite, he gazed up at the beams. "This will do. Would you give me a boost?"

Phyro squatted and locked his hands together. Miza stepped onto his hands and held on to Phyro's shoulder for balance. Phyro slowly stood up, lifting Miza toward the ceiling.

"You're strong," commented Miza. "Let me guess: You are from a military family?"

"Something like that," said Phyro.

Miza didn't press. He tied the silk ropes to the beam, forming two slings that hung down. He jumped off from Phyro's hands. "All right, now please take off your shoes and lie facedown in these slings. Make sure you're comfortable."

Phyro complied. The two silk slings held him at his thighs and chest, distributing his weight evenly so that he was suspended about a foot or so from the ground. He stretched out his hands in front of him. "This feels like flying. Maybe this was how the Hegemon felt suspended from a battle kite."

Miza laughed and then took some of the paper dancers and dropped them on the ground in front of Phyro about a foot or so away from the tips of his outstretched fingers.

"Relax. I'm now going to call upon the power of Rufizo and give you the ability to command these paper men."

Miza picked up the glass rod from the paper dancers' stage and rubbed it vigorously with his silk handkerchief. Then he brought the rod close to Phyro's naked soles. "Go ahead, command the paper dancers."

Unsure what to do, Phyro stretched out his hands toward the paper dancers and waved them about. Amazingly, the paper men stood up and swayed in place as his hands moved before them.

"Imagine if we were doing this in a darkened temple sanctuary using thin ropes that cannot be seen. Imagine also some incense and smoke swirling about you so that you appear to be shrouded in mystery. Imagine the reaction of the crowd as you appear to command sparkling birds and butterflies made of thin foil to flutter about you without touching them."

Phyro nodded with a grin on his face. "That would indeed be a far more impressive demonstration. I assume that the silkmotically charged rod also charged me, thus allowing my fingers to attract the paper dancers?"

"Exactly. The silkmotic force can flow through the human body quite effectively. A better way to channel and store the silkmotic charge would involve a suspended bar of metal, which we in the trade call a prime reservoir."

Phyro climbed off the sling. "Show me."

Miza brought out a long iron rod, which terminated in a rounded knob at either end, and suspended it in the sling. "Charging such a prime reservoir is tedious with a glass rod; so we use a silkmotic generator."

He moved another of the machines over to near one end of the rod. It consisted of a wooden stand on which a glass globe was mounted in such a way that it was free to revolve about an axle. Miza attached a small metal chain to one of the knobs at the end of the suspended iron bar and dangled the other end of the chain onto the globe. Then he handed a folded bundle of silk to Phyro and started to rotate a crank to the side, making the globe spin.

"Hold the silk against the glass, please," he said.

Phyro did so. The metal chain clanked gently against the spinning surface of the globe, sounding like rain striking a tiled roof.

"This is a much more efficient way of building up the silkmotic force on the glass globe and transferring it to the prime reservoir."

After he judged the prime reservoir to be sufficiently charged, Miza stopped the spinning globe. He went about the suite, extinguishing lamps and closing up the shutters on the windows. The interior of the suite was now quite dark.

"Try moving a hand close to the prime reservoir, slowly," he said.

Phyro cautiously moved his hand closer to the metal bar. Just as his fingers were about to touch it, a spark arced across the gap like a miniature lightning, illuminating the room momentarily.

"Aw!"

Phyro jumped and waved his hand violently. He looked down at it to be sure it was uninjured. "It bit me!"

Miza laughed. "That's what happens when an object filled with silkmotic force is discharged, which means that the silk motes spill out into another object that moves close to it. Only some objects will cause the discharge, though—we call them channeling material—metals and people being the best. Other things like silk or glass—we call them damming material—do not seem to allow the motes to move about freely, which is why we support the prime reservoir with a glass stand or suspend it from silk ropes."

Phyro made a mental note of the detail and continued to play the role of the curious but idle young man of wealth. "Fascinating. Is silk the only source for this kind of force?"

"Not at all," said Miza. "Substantially the same effects may be achieved by rubbing amber with fur, or leather against glass—indeed, the combinations almost seem infinite."

"And are the motes from leather and fur different from the motes from silk? Er, in other words, is there a leathermotic force and a fur-motic force?" He was thinking of the latest letter from Théra, which described the differences between the lift gas that powered the Imperial airships and the lift gas that powered the garinafins. "Please excuse my ignorance, but the topic is of great interest."

Miza smiled and nodded. The interest from Phyro was clearly exciting to him—being able to share his learning with someone who was not going to compete with him as a street magician clearly engaged his professorial mode. "This was a topic long debated among practitioners of the art. After much research, I am of the opinion that all materials we've investigated so far generate the same force, and out of respect for tradition, we call it the silkmotic force, regardless of the source.

"However, the force does seem to come in two varieties, which may correspond to an excess of silk motes and an absence of them. We denote them the Rapa and Kana varieties after the twin goddesses, and label one type white and the other red. All you need to know is that if two objects are charged with the same variety of silkmotic force, they repel each other, but if they are charged with different varieties, they attract each other."

"Have you found any other uses for the silkmotic force besides magic tricks?"

Miza nodded proudly. "Of course! A good street performer needs variety. The best part of my show is when I cure people with the silkmotic force."

"Cure people?"

"You've already experienced what it's like to be shocked by the silk-motic force on discharge," said Miza. "But it's also possible to use your body as a prime reservoir and fill it with the silkmotic force via a generator, in which case you'll experience a tingling sensation. The silkmotic force is particularly effective against conditions like gout, epilepsy, and acute as well as chronic pains. It's a real crowd-pleaser when I play doctor."

Phyro wasn't sure just how seriously to take this part of Miza's explanation. Healing was a difficult art, and many remedies seemed to him mere superstition or just-so stories. He preferred to focus on phenomena that could be more easily verified.

Pointing to the porcelain jar that was at the heart of the dispute earlier in the market, Phyro asked, "Can you show me how this works?"

"Ah, you've come to the most interesting of my apparatuses. It's called an Ogé jar, after those islets in the east. And I have never seen any other magician with such a device."

That was apparently as much as Miza was willing to say. Clearly he considered the trade secret of great value.

Phyro didn't press. Instead, he excused himself for a moment, claiming to need to use the toilet. Instead, he went into the suite downstairs from his and knocked on the door.

The door opened, revealing Consort Risana, the smokecrafter.

"Ma, did you hear everything?" whispered Phyro.

Risana nodded. She had poked a speaking trumpet connected to a tube—one of Rin Coda's inventions—through the ceiling to rest against a crack in the floor of the suite above. With the other end, she had been keeping tabs on the discussion between Phyro and Miza.

"You really think this man has useful information?" asked Risana.

"Absolutely," said Phyro. "I'm not sure what do to with it exactly yet, but I have a hunch that Théra will figure it out."

"You are gambling this will turn out to be more than mere tricks to fool the gullible?"

"It's a calculated risk," said Phyro. Then he grinned. "There should be a little bit of Tazu in everyone's life."

Risana smiled affectionately. "You always quote your father's most outrageous lines." But then the smile faded as her husband's dangerous situation returned to her mind.

Phyro tried to steer the discussion back. "Useful or not, I still have to get the information first. Magicians tend to guard their secrets jealously, passing them on only to trusted apprentices. This is why I asked for your help."

"Why not just tell him who you are? I'm sure he would tell you what you want to know if you convinced him it could help the emperor with the war effort against the Lyucu."

Phyro shook his head like a rattle drum. "If we tell him who we are now, he would demand an outrageous sum for his knowledge. That's the sort of man he is, or at least the sort of man he thinks he is. But he really wants to do something noble, something impressive that would make him proud. We just need to . . . help him."

"I thought I was the one who was supposed to figure out what people really wanted," said Risana, chuckling. "You really are your father's son—I can't tell if you're suggesting this plot because you really think it's the right thing to do, or because you just want to drive a better bargain."

"Even patriots may be tempted by profit," said Phyro. "It's expensive to run an empire, and I've learned a few things these last few years."

ᔕ ᔕ ᔕ ᔕ

Phyro ordered a hot pot. The waiters came in and set up a small brazier, and then placed the clay pot on top. Plates of raw ingredients were left for the guests to cook to their own liking. Soon, the room was filled with the delicious scents of meats and vegetables cooking in rich broth.

"Let me have a taste," said Phyro, and clumsily, he managed to shift the clay pot in such a way that some of the soup spilled onto the coals below. Smoke quickly filled the room.

Phyro slid the window open just a crack. "My apologies. I'm sure the smoke will dissipate soon enough."

Miza coughed but nodded in assent.

Phyro watched Miza's face, praying that his mother was working her own sort of magic in the suite below.

A different sort of smoke was now coming into the room from the crack in the floor, but Miza wasn't paying attention as it blended into the smoke from the brazier.

Phyro watched as the smoke in the room took shape, solidified, and wrapped itself like a serpent around Miza.

"Tell me about the Ogé jars," Phyro prompted.

"They store the silkmotic force," said Miza.

Phyro saw that Miza's eyes had a glazed look. His mother had succeeded.

Miza popped off the stopper and showed Phyro the inside of the jar: It was also lined with a layer of silver foil that stopped about halfway up the walls. "The first jars I made held seawater, but then I found that all I needed was some channeling material on the inside. For street performances I still fill it with seawater, for effect, but we don't need to."

Miza plugged the stopper back into the jar, making sure that the chain rested against the foil at the bottom. Then he spun the crank in the silkmotic generator again to charge up the prime reservoir. Finally, he held the jar in his hand and brought the knob at the top close to the prime reservoir, generating a loud zap and bright sparks.

"Notice how the silkmotic force from the prime reservoir flowed into the Ogé jar?" asked Miza. "Would you like to hold it? Just one hand on the bottom, please."

Phyro gingerly accepted the jar, holding on to the foiled bottom with only one hand.

"Don't worry," said Miza. "The silkmotic force is stored in the porcelain—the dam between the two channeling surfaces on the outside and the inside. The jar is perfectly safe to handle, as long as you only touch the bottom."

Phyro was hardly assured. The memory of the last shock from the prime reservoir was still fresh in his mind.

"Try grasping the knob on top, which is connected to the inner surface, with your other hand," said Miza. "And try not to drop the jar." He giggled.

Phyro gritted his teeth and grabbed the knob on top of the jar with his other hand. He yelped from the resulting shock and dropped the jar like a piece of hot coal. Miza, who had been prepared, deftly caught the dropped jar with one hand.

"Sometimes these jars can keep on discharging a few more times," he said. "Handle with care."

Phyro could feel a numbness in his hand where the jar had shocked him, and his chest felt tight, as though his heart didn't have enough room to beat.

"I have to sit down," he gasped, and sat on the ground.

"Breathe, friend, breathe," said Miza. "No matter how prepared you are, the silkmotic force is so powerful that the jar will pry itself out of your hand. It's as if you can no longer control the muscles in your fingers."

Phyro finally caught his breath. "That's incredible."

Miza laughed. "So many interesting tricks can be designed around the Ogé jar. The problem with the prime reservoir and the silkmotic generator is that they're too bulky and too hard to operate in a discreet manner. Anyone can intuit the flow of the silkmotic force, and though the sparks generated are pretty, the trick loses its effectiveness because the audience can see how it's done. With these jars, however, I can charge them up ahead of time away from the crowd, and then bring them around with me. Because they look like ordinary jars, people don't suspect that they can pack such a punch. And they can hold a charge for days."

"Why are they called Ogé jars?" asked Phyro. "Did you invent them there?"

Miza hesitated. Now that the air in the room was clearing up a bit, he seemed to be becoming more inhibited as well. "I *did* get them in Ogé, but I can't claim to be the inventor."

"Oh?"

"I was in the Ogé islets during what was probably the lowest point in my life. None of my tricks were drawing much of an audience, and even in backward Ogé, where I thought the people would be less jaded than the inhabitants of the big cities, I wasn't getting good tips. It got so bad that I had to sell a lot of my equipment just to stay fed, and I knew once I started down that path, my life as a magician was over.

"In despair, I went to a shrine for Rufizo, and prayed for help.

"I fell asleep and dreamed of a handsome young doctor who came to me and showed me the design of these novel jars. He explained that these silkmotic devices could be used to treat various diseases, but they could also be used to perform magic tricks. He said that I could use them to get rich, but that I had to promise to help the people of Dara when such knowledge was needed.

"After I woke up, I constructed an Ogé jar according to the instructions in the dream, and it worked! Ever since then, I've traveled around Faça as an itinerant doctor and performer. I never did find out how a magic trick could help the people of Dara besides giving them something interesting to think about."

Phyro looked at him, hardly daring to believe his luck. Maybe the gods of Dara still cared. "I think your moment has arrived."

The evening's performance by Consort Risana and Prince Phyro was canceled.

For the rest of that evening, Prince Phyro continued to ask questions like a hungry student while Miza patiently explained the wonders of the Ogé jar: how the silkmotic forces flowing from its inner and outer surfaces were equal in strength but of opposite varieties; how connecting multiple jars together in series or parallel had a cumulative effect, resulting in either longer sparks or thicker sparks; how the size of the jar and the smoothness of the foil affected the storage capacity; how connecting two channeling rods from an Ogé jar to the legs of a dead frog made them kick and swim. . . .

The next morning, Miza was on a messenger airship bound for Ginpen.

While Lady Risana and Prince Phyro continued to travel around the islands to rally the population, Empress Jia was faced with the challenge of assuring the jittery people that the House of Dandelion was still fully in control.

Swarms of locusts appeared in the fields of Géfica, near the Imperial capital. The winged insects, forming a dense, living cloud that hovered near the ground and crawled over it, devoured everything in their path. The crops in the field were devastated, and the peasantry hid in the basements of their houses, not daring to emerge.

In the past, locust plagues were sometimes taken care of by fleets of Imperial airships spraying poisoned mist over the affected area, but now, with the airships out of commission, there seemed to be nothing that could be done except to wait for the plague to take its course.

The people of Dara whispered that this was a judgment of the gods, that it was a sign that the appearance of the Lyucu marked the end of the House of Dandelion.

"What do you want from me?" raged the empress at the statues of the gods in the Imperial shrine.

"Every sign can be interpreted in multiple ways," said the prime minister. "The key is to come up with an interpretation you like."

"If you want to have a second act," said Soto, "this is the moment to seize the story."

Empress Jia strode into the farm fields of Géfica herself. She took up a wooden winnowing shovel and swung it at the swarm. The insects attacked her, biting her arms, face, feet. She ignored the pain and continued to swat at the insects.

The ministers and generals rushed over to protect her, urging her to return to the safety of the carriage. The empress shoved them away.

"The people must eat, and I'll kill these mindless creatures one by one if that's what it takes," said the empress. "Some have mistaken my reticence as weakness. If the gods truly want the House of Dandelion to end, then let them kill me today in this field. I'm not going back."

Moved by the empress's courage, the ministers and generals also picked up shovels and forks and went at the swarming insects. Soon, the peasants cowering in their houses emerged to fight the locusts alongside the great lords.

As they swatted at the endless living tide and bore the stinging pain, more than a few in the crowd thought they must have looked quite mad, but there was also a kind of frenzy in the joy of taking action—however symbolic—that made the crowd feel invincible.

Jia no longer felt she was engaging in political theater. She felt bonded to the subjects around her as though the people of Dara were a single organism. She was buoyed by waves formed from their courage and rage. It was glorious to struggle against heaven and earth as a woman, as the Empress of Dara, as a member of the proud race descended from the Ano and the natives of these islands.

Then, from all directions of the compass, flocks of birds approached: ravens, gulls, starlings, magpies, doves, even falcons. . . . Never had Dara seen such a large flock of birds of so many species flying in unison.

They fell upon the locusts and devoured them.

Gradually, the cloud of insects shrank and then disappeared. The birds, having satiated themselves, dispersed as suddenly as they had come.

Empress Jia fell to the ground, exhausted.

The miracle of the birds was deemed to be a sign from the gods, and made many once again believe in the strength of the House of Dandelion.

But Prime Minister Cogo Yelu carefully investigated the source of the locusts and wrote a secret report to the marshal.

Marshal Mazoti surveyed the tall stack of reports in front of her from the Imperial laboratories in Ginpen and all around Dara: the dissection of the garinafin carcasses, the feeding habits of cattle, the fire tube from Tan Adü, the mysterious devices powered by the silkmotic force, the habits and history of locus swarms. . . .

Zomi Kidosu and Théra had compiled the reports into a set of suggestions, Cogo Yelu had applied his expertise in evaluating novel inventions, and Phyro, Than Carucono, and Puma Yemu had vetted them with their own field experience.

The marshal slammed her fist down on the table. She had a plan.

CHAPTER FIFTY-SIX

THE PRINCE'S FLIGHT

RUI: THE SIXTH MONTH IN THE TWELFTH YEAR OF
THE REIGN OF FOUR PLACID SEAS.

Pékyu Tenryo sent emissaries to persuade Prince Timu every day.

Many of the emissaries were *cashima* who had decided that it was easier to serve the pékyu than to labor in the fields under the lash of the Lyucu guards. The common people hated the collaborationists, which only pushed them closer to the Lyucu overlords. This was a part of Pékyu Tenryo's plan to control the conquered population by playing the elites off against the common people, and some elites against others.

Today's *cashima* was named Wira Pin, a renowned Incentivist from Dasu.

"Prince Timu, Grand Secretary Lügo Crupo once said that the wise ruler should flow with the currents of history rather than resist them."

"And I am supposed to listen to the words of Lügo Crupo, the despised adviser of the tyrant Mapidéré?" said Timu, pausing to wipe away the sweat on his brow. "Besides, if he's so wise, why did he resist the tides of history and cling to the Xana Empire?"

He went back to cutting and bundling the grass to produce hay for the garinafins. He didn't want to fall behind the other peasants, all of whom had the same quota to fill.

"Surely the wise prince does not subscribe to the notion that victors have a monopoly on the truth," said Wira. "Crupo served a lord who lost, but his wisdom is eternal."

"Collaborators with the invaders are apparently blind to irony," said Timu. "Since you are so observant of the tides, why don't you enlighten me with this wisdom I'm ignorant of?"

"The Lyucu are the scourge of the gods," said Wira Pin. "By next spring, a new fleet of Lyucu ships will come, bringing even more warriors and garinafins. Do you wish to see Dara laid waste? Do you wish to see more people die?"

"No one has to die if the Lyucu stop killing."

"The Lyucu kill only because the House of Dandelion refuses to yield. The emperor places his own weal above that of the people, which is why he has not ordered Dara to surrender."

Prince Timu stopped and glared at Wira. "The barbarians have only conquered two islands, and look at what they've done to the place. If we surrender, all of Dara will be reduced to this." He swept his arm around at the devastation around him. Many of the peasants had been forced to cut down their still-green crops as feed for the garinafins. The harvest this fall was going to be a disaster.

"The present harshness is only a temporary measure in a time of war. If Pékyu Tenryo were lord of all of Dara, the people of Dara would be his flock and charge, and he would love them as a proper shepherd."

"Because of self-interest?"

Wira nodded, an excited glint coming into his eye. "Precisely. I did not realize that the prince was so well versed in the Incentivist school of thinking."

"Let me try to formulate your argument for you," said Prince Timu. "The people of Dara will be valuable property to the pékyu, and he wouldn't want to see his property damaged. In fact, he would need good caretakers to watch over his flock. The nobles and scholars, men of learning such as yourself, would need to be given some power to help him in this task."

"Exactly!" Wira rubbed his hands. "It is so much easier to convince someone who can already see the light."

"And I, as the prince to lead the surrender to the Lyucu and to give the pékyu legitimacy as the master of Dara, can expect a life of comfort and ease."

"Your Highness has taken the words right out of my mouth."

Prince Timu nodded. "But you see, neither my father nor I can do what you ask."

"Why not? If you surrender, you will earn the eternal gratitude of the pékyu. Your family will be safe, and all this unpleasantness will be over."

"Because though my father is the emperor, he has never forgotten that the people of Dara are not his family's property." Timu went back to work, struggling to catch up to the other peasants. "The capitulation you seek isn't mine to give."

No matter what Wira Pin said after that, the prince ignored him.

"He's not going to budge," said Tanvanaki, the pékyu's daughter. "He's as stubborn as his father."

"Who would have thought that such a frail-looking weakling would have such a stout heart?" said Pékyu Tenryo, a measure of admiration seeping into his voice. "Both he and his father have exceeded my estimation."

"We could try torturing one of them in front of the other," suggested Tanvanaki. "That worked on Luan Zya."

"I doubt that will work," said the pékyu. "Remember how Kuni was willing to let his son die here and escape in his airship until I threatened to kill more people? He's bound by what he sees as his duty to his people, not mere love of his son. The prince, on the other hand, craves his father's approval so much that he will never surrender if he thinks his father will despise him for doing so."

"But why must we try to convince either of them to surrender?" asked Tanvanaki. "Victory over Dara is a certainty! They have no way to challenge our superiority in the air. These islands had been united by a lord who understood the power of the air; they'll fall to us in the same manner."

"Have you forgotten what Luan Zya did?" The pékyu glared at her. "The garinafins can't breed, and so many of the hatchlings and yearlings died on the crossing that we can barely control the adults we have. What if we lose more of the young ones and the adults become unruly?"

"A temporary setback. Our reinforcements should arrive in another year with a fresh supply of tolyusa and more garinafins. We might as well wait and conquer them by force."

"You speak with the foolishness of youth," said the pékyu. "Our warriors may be invincible on the battlefield, but they outnumber us by more than a hundredfold."

"They are still sheep while we're wolves."

"Even wolves can't kill all the sheep, and a desperate flock is capable of great feats. We already have enough trouble holding these two islands, and we must sleep at night with our clubs next to our beds. How will we ever hold all of Dara by force, even if we could conquer it? The people of Dara are wily and sly, Daughter. Do not underestimate them."

"Then what good will it do to convince the prince or the emperor to surrender?"

"The craftiness of these islanders is also their fatal weakness. If there's one quality that distinguishes them, it's that they lack our discipline. If I toss my flag at a certain target, I can be sure that every Lyucu will attack it without fail. But the people of Dara are divided, cowardly, and selfish, and cannot strive toward the same goal for long. They will each make whatever choice hurts them the least and leave someone else to suffer the consequences. The deci-chief system, which has made them spy on each other for us, is proof of that. If we can give the nobles and ministers of the emperor an excuse to *not* fight us, they will seize it—indeed, they may help us guard our human flock like loyal garinafins."

"You have a great deal of contempt for these savages, Father."

"Not contempt—understanding. We want to enjoy the wealth offered by Dara, but the source of her wealth is her people. When you wish to guide a flock, you must identify those individuals whose actions the rest of the flock follow and control these leaders. Only in this manner can a few skilled herders control a vast flock."

"The control animals you've picked out may be impossible to herd," said Tanvanaki. "We've applied pressure in every way on the old man, and the young one will yield to neither threats nor entice-ments. He speaks of virtue at every turn and quotes long-winded chapters written by their sages back at our emissaries."

"I'm about to give up," conceded the pékyu. "At least they are useful as human shields until our reinforcements arrive."

"Well," said Tanvanaki as a cold smile shaped her face. "There is still one other way that we haven't tried."

"Hey, Prince of Dara!"

Timu stopped in the field, shielded his eyes against the sun, and gazed up at the new emissary sent by Pékyu Tenryo. He was surprised to see the pékyu's daughter, the Lyucu princess. Tanvanaki was speak-ing to him from on top of Korva, her garinafin mount. The lumbering monster waddled by the side of the sorghum field like a cruben of the land, crushing crops and erasing field ridges with every taloned step and every swipe of her tail.

Oddly, Tanvanaki wasn't dressed in the crude fur-and-leather outfit favored by the Lyucu. Instead, she was dressed like a woman of Dara: silk robe, cloth shoes with wooden soles, some of her hair pinned up in a bun with a jade hairpin.

With her fair, translucent skin glowing in the sun and her strong, exotic facial features haloed by blond tresses, Timu realized that the princess was very beautiful, though he had never applied that word to her in the past.

"Your Highness," he said, and bowed.

"You may say 'Your Highness' with your lips," said Tanvanaki. "But in your heart you're calling me a barbarian, a savage, or something even worse."

"Not at all," said Timu. But he blushed.

Korva lowered her neck to the ground, and the princess stepped down the long living ramp and confidently to him, stopping only when she was about a foot away. She looked into his eyes—she was about Timu's height and didn't have to look up—and calmly said, "Liar."

Timu backed up a step. "What . . . what are you doing?"

"Don't move." She took another step forward, and as Timu's breath quickened with nervousness, she reached out and gently grabbed Timu by his chin, turning his face from side to side as she examined him. Timu's face turned bright red and he jerked his chin away from her grasp.

He could still smell her hot breath, laced with the scent of unfamiliar spices.

Tanvanaki's expression turned thoughtful as she looked up and down his body, muttering to herself the whole while, "Rather good figure . . . clear skin . . . a bit dark, but not unpleasant . . . looks like the field labor has done him some good . . ."

Timu felt extremely uncomfortable. This barbarian—*Lyucu*, Timu silently corrected himself—princess was unlike any of the young women of the court he had ever spoken to. Her boldness unsettled him, made him feel foolish.

Timu turned awkwardly away to resume his work.

"I'm not done with you yet," Tanvanaki said imperiously. "I told you to stand still."

"Your Highness should stop playing with me in this unbecoming manner," said Timu through gritted teeth. "It is not honorable to humiliate and torture a prisoner."

"Who says I'm torturing you?" said Tanvanaki. Then her lips curved into a mischievous smile. "But you would like me to play with you?"

Timu kept his lips squeezed together.

The princess took yet another step forward until her face was only inches away from his. "Do you think I'm pretty?"

Timu was stunned. This was not a question that he had ever heard a woman ask. It seemed so utterly improper; and yet, coming from her, it also seemed somehow fitting, like the fact that she wore a war club on her back, like the fact that she rode a garinafin into battle.

"I . . . uh . . . yes." Timu's face was now as scarlet as the crown of a rooster. He didn't understand why this woman was able to fluster him so. She seemed to have no shame at all, which was strange but also . . . attractive.

"Good," said the princess, nodding. "That I can tell is *not* a lie. Why do you men of Dara lie so much?"

"I haven't the faintest idea of what the princess speaks."

"I've been studying the people of Dara for a while, and you all think one thing, but say another. For example, when Zato Ruthi, your old teacher, came to meet us, he thought we were all barbarians barely better than animals, yet he pretended to treat us as honored guests. The wealthy and powerful among you want to have even more money and power, yet they say they're trying to take care of the people."

A look of anger flashed through Timu's eyes. "I'm no hypocrite."

"Aren't you? Then why do you want to watch people starve?"

"I'm trying to prevent people from starving! You've turned all these fields into grazing pastures for your garinafins and long-haired cattle. What will the people of these islands eat this winter?"

"There will be plenty of milk and meat. The grain-based diet you prefer makes us feel bloated, anyway. We aren't herbivores like you."

"You don't have enough long-haired cattle to feed everyone on Dasu and Rui! And my people can't drink garinafin milk; it makes them sick."

"Oh, so when you say 'people of these islands' you just mean *your* people, and you'd be happy to see *my* people starve. And you claim to be no hypocrite."

"But you *chose* to come here. You could have stayed where you were."

He closed his eyes, steeling himself for an angry slap or some other outrage.

But Tanvanaki looked away and her voice softened. "Did you know that until I came here, I had never seen so much green in the world?"

Timu opened his eyes and listened.

"The scrublands of my home are beautiful, but it is not an easy or forgiving land. The year I was born, a storm killed most of my father's herd, and he had to go on raids against the Agon in deep winter to keep us alive. Hundreds died in the raids, and grandmothers and grandfathers walked out into the storm to die so that they would not burden the tribe, thus saving food for the babies. My mother died fighting the Agon, and to give me and my brother milk, one of the other mothers in the tribe smothered her sons with her own hands."

Timu shuddered. The way Tanvanaki recounted this story with such calmness made it even more sickening.

"You think we're barbaric," said Tanvanaki, casting him a contemptuous look. "What do you know of barbarism, Prince of Dara? You were born in a land of plenty, and you've never known what it means to starve. You grew up in a land favored by the All-Father and Every-Mother, and you've had the leisure to develop complicated moral theories.

"Yet it is your land that has produced a tyrant like Mapidéré, who killed more men in a single battle than all the people my father has had to kill to keep his people alive. You speak of us as savages, yet your own savagery during the Chrysanthemum-Dandelion War exceeded anything we have done."

Timu struggled to come up with an answer. This girl's arguments were not like the arguments he was used to from the other emissaries of the pékyu—instead of quoting from the Ano sages, which he was skilled at countering, she . . . seemed to look at things in a new way.

"You can't compare the flight of wild geese with the dance of freshwater carp. We live here. You're invaders."

"Really? You've always lived here? I thought your ancestors took this land away from the people who used to live here."

"That was a long time ago! I—and everybody you've enslaved—was born here."

"So if you're born here, you get to decide who belongs to 'the people'? If I give birth to a son or daughter here, the child gets to call you an invader?"

"No! It's—it's—"

"I keep on hearing this idea that somehow this land belongs to you, but I don't understand it. How can land belong to anybody? The All-Father created the world, and we're all just guests in it. We migrate across the land as the wild cattle herds do. The right to exist, to eat, the only right that matters, belongs to all."

Timu heard in Tanvanaki's arguments an echo of the parable of the veil told by Zomi Kidosu.

Before birth, all of us are mere potentials. We have no control over the moment of incarnation, when we might end up as the son of an emperor or the daughter of a peasant. The veil is lifted as we come into the world, and we find ourselves holding a box that determines our fates without regard to our merit. Yet all the great philosophers have always said that our souls are equal in weight in the eyes of the World Father, Thasoluo.

There was wisdom in the words of the Lyucu princess.

"Had you presented these arguments to my father in a reasonable manner, I'm certain we could have come up with some kind of compromise," Timu said earnestly.

Tanvanaki laughed. "Really? You believe that your father would have vacated one of the islands and handed it to us? You believe he would not have extracted promises of obedience and service? You believe he would not have turned us into slaves, as Admiral Krita did? And even if he had such godlike compassion, do you think his nobles would have allowed him to give away their domain and influence? You are a fool if you believe any of that. I'm not steeped in the hypocrisy and corruption of your Dara, but even I know that life doesn't work that way."

Timu was mute. This woman had completely challenged the way he understood the world. He could no longer say that he was certain that the cause of Dara was just, a cause favored by the gods.

ഗ ന ഗ ന

And so began a friendship—or courtship, Timu wasn't sure which—that seemed completely impossible. Tanvanaki came to talk with Timu every day, lingering for hours sometimes as they walked about the fields, discussing their childhoods and arguing over the merits of their respective views of life.

Tanvanaki gave Timu a glimpse of the intricate culture of the Lyucu—the clever ways that the people of the scrublands had, over the centuries, learned to make use of every part of long-haired cattle and garinafin. The bones were turned into weapons and structural components of the tents; the fur and tough leather were made into clothing and shelter and shields; the sinews became threads and ropes; antlers, horns, and sinew mixed with scrub wood made possible the composite slingshots that provided great power despite their small size; the fat was rendered into candles and torches; the tendons and skins boiled into glue. No part of an animal was ever wasted.

As Tanvanaki told Timu the stories of her homeland and showed him the way that her people lived, adapting to the harshness of their environment, Timu began to see beneath the caricature of her people as only savage invaders.

Since Timu was a skilled musician himself, the music of the Lyucu moved him especially. Using garinafin-skin drums and bone xylophones, Tanvanaki evoked for him the sights and sounds of the vast scrublands: the pounding hooves of thousands of long-haired cattle migrating across the land, kept in line by the steady beat of garinafin wings and feet; the power and awe of sudden storms and flash floods that threatened to wipe away everything in a single deluge; a sky that seemed grander and more open than the sky of Dara, where the stars at night were not dimmed by the bright lights of teahouses and all-night gambling parlors; the long horizon that made you dizzy with the promise of endless, fresh grazing grounds.

As Tanvanaki sang to the accompaniment of her instruments, despite not understanding the lyrics, Timu could hear the powerful emotions of longing, love, resilience in the face of great adversity and danger, and boundless hope for the future. The Lyucu were like the windswept bushes that dotted the scrublands: tough, strong, willing to seize any opportunity—like a rare flood—to blossom and reinvigorate the landscape with the defiant colors of life.

The music was different from the refined and complex measures that Timu was used to on the nine-stringed silk zither or the coconut lute, but there was no doubt that the music was beautiful, no doubt that the Lyucu had a civilization, though it was as different from the civilization of Dara as a volcanic ash hare was different from a rainbow-tailed dyran.

Then, one day, Tanvanaki invited Timu to ride Korva with her.

Timu was terrified. Korva's saddle towered far above him at the base of the garinafin's neck like the crow's nest on a ship. And the way the beast imperiously stared at him with her dark, pupilless eyes made his legs weak. He wasn't even much of a horseman. The very idea of riding such a beast seemed beyond him.

"I thought your father once rode on a scaled whale, what you call a sovereign of the seas?"

"My father and I are not alike in many ways."

"Thankfully so," said Tanvanaki as she grinned at him. "Why do you think I'm taking you instead of him?"

Timu's heart pounded. Somehow, what Tanvanaki had just said to him made him giddier than a thousand compliments from the severe Master Ruthi would have. He had always felt like a disappointment to his father, but now, this lovely young woman was telling him that it was fine to be different from his father, to be his own man.

Timu did not have much experience with women. Unlike Phyro, who enjoyed flirting with the servant girls at the palace and sometimes pretended to be just a wealthy young merchant as he snuck into the indigo houses in the company of Dafiro Miro—after both Jia and Risana had discreetly explained to Phyro the necessary precautions to take to avoid a scandal to the Imperial family—Timu had never even spoken with a young woman his own age without blushing.

The attention from Tanvanaki was to him an exotic song that he did not want to end.

Tanvanaki whistled at Korva, and the garinafin, like some towering pine that was being felled, squatted down and laid her graceful, long neck along the ground. Tanvanaki lightly stroked Korva's face, and, placing one foot over the beast's jaws, began to climb up. Using the garinafin's eyelids and forehead as handholds and footholds, soon the young Lyucu princess was on top of the garinafin's elephantine head, holding on to the antlers for balance.

She turned around and ordered, "Come on up."

Hands sweating and legs trembling, Timu repeated Tanvanaki's steps. When he set his left foot above the protruding nostrils of Korva, the garinafin snorted, and Timu almost lost his grip. He scrambled up Korva's face the rest of the way, arms and legs flailing, and didn't stop until his hands were locked around the antlers.

Tanvanaki was bent over with laughter while Timu hung on to the antlers for dear life, his face crimson.

Tanvanaki gently chided her mount in the language of the Lyucu, and Korva chuckled, a rumbling, thunderous noise.

The two then headed toward the saddle at the base of the garinafin's neck as though they were walking along the top of a small mountain range. While Tanvanaki strode forward confidently, as fleet-footed as a mountain goat, Timu gingerly navigated the vertebrae in the neck of the garinafin, which stood out under the skin like weathered rock formations. Finally, the two made it to the leather-and-bone saddle.

Tanvanaki sat down, straddling her feet on each side of the neck and securing them in the stirrups. She patted the space behind her. "Sit here."

Timu obeyed. Tanvanaki twisted around and showed him how to tuck his feet into the supporting rings dangling from the saddle. Then she said, "Put your arms around my waist and hug me tightly."

The idea of taking such an intimate posture with Tanvanaki stunned Timu. He stammered, "I don't . . . don't think that's necessary."

"What, do I smell bad?" Tanvanaki lifted her left arm and sniffed.

"I bathed just this morning with osmanthus flowers and cow milk." She frowned. "Don't tell me you still believe the nonsense rumors about my people. Sure, when we first came off the city-ships, we probably did smell terrible, but that was because we barely had enough fresh water for drinking and keeping the long-haired cattle and garinafins watered."

"No, no!" Timu said, waving his hands in a gesture of denial. "You smell . . . wonderful."

When Tanvanaki visited Timu, she almost always dressed in the fashion of a refined lady of Dara, with a tight bodice that emphasized her curves, loose folds of silk that lengthened her legs and arms, and hair worn in some elaborate style that far better suited women who spent their days in boudoirs rather than on the battlefield.

Timu loved the way she looked: The contrast between her exotic foreign features and the familiar feminine styles always brought heat to his cheeks and . . . elsewhere. And as time passed, she seemed to take on more aspects of Dara femininity, like this osmanthus flower bath.

"Then what's the problem?"

"Kon Fiji . . . um . . . wrote that it's best for men and women not to touch each other unless they were married, lest impure thoughts come into their minds and keep them from the contemplation of virtue."

Tanvanaki sighed in exasperation. "This Kon Fiji sounds like an idiot. Fine. Do as you like. But if you fall from the sky, I'm not sure Korva can dive fast enough to save you."

She kicked Korva lightly at the base of the neck, and the beast responded by standing up and lifting her head until the neck was standing erect like a mast pine again. Timu immediately wrapped his arms around Tanvanaki's waist.

"You don't have to squeeze so hard!" gasped Tanvanaki. "Are you trying to crush me?"

Timu relaxed his hold slightly. The feeling of holding Tanvanaki between his arms and pressing his chest against her back was indescribably wonderful. He breathed in the osmanthus fragrance in her hair. He never wanted this moment to end.

Tanvanaki placed the speaking tube against the garinafin's neck and spoke in Lyucu, "Let's go, Korva. Keep it gentle and steady. Our guest isn't used to flying without the aid of some mechanical monstrosity."

Korva moaned her acknowledgment, and then, spreading her wings, she began to run. The pounding of the taloned feet against the ground was deafening, and the beating of the wings sounded like a typhoon. As the ground receded beneath him many times faster than the speediest horse he had ever ridden, Timu shut his eyes, not daring to look.

And then, just like that, the up-and-down rhythmic hammering of the garinafin's gait disappeared with a slight jolt, and Timu felt a smooth, gradual increase in altitude. He continued to squeeze his eyes shut and laid his cheek against Tanvanaki's back, enjoying the warmth of her body and the tickling sensation of her hair against his face.

"Look," Tanvanaki said. Her voice was low, as though she was speaking to herself more than to him. "I never get tired of this sight. This truly is a land blessed by the All-Father, the Every-Mother, and all their children."

Gingerly, Timu opened his eyes. The fields of Rui stretched out far beneath, as though they were gliding over a quilt patched together from colored cloth of many different patterns. Some of the squares were a dark, lush green, containing leafy vegetables and thick grass; others held red sorghum, ripening in late summer; still others were bare and tan, showing the cut grass and grain stalks drying to hay.

"Back home, the land is filled with swirls and curlicues, marking the patterns of the wind as they shape the bushes and scrubs in their path," said Tanvanaki. "But here, everything comes in squares and rectangles. It's like your people are afraid of the land itself and would only feel satisfied if it were confined in grids like those word-squares you draw on paper and the blocky logograms you carve."

Though he had seen Dara from the airships many times, Timu now felt that he was seeing everything for the first time, through another pair of eyes.

"You make it sound like that's a bad thing," he said. "But it's only because we cultivate the land that we can make it bountiful and feed so many. We do the same thing to the ocean, casting our nets into the water, dividing it into little squares, so that we can haul out the fruits of the sea. We may be blessed by a rich land, but we also have to work hard at it."

"I suppose you're more than just lucky. Some of the ways you make the land yield food do seem very clever, even if I can't imagine subsisting on grass like sheep or cattle."

A new idea flashed into Timu's head like a lightning bolt. "Princess Vadyu, our peoples don't have to be enemies. What if we can share this land and live side by side as neighbors, as equals? No more conquest and slaughter; no more enslavement and death?"

This must be what it feels like to be inspired, Timu thought. Master Zato Ruthi had always told him that a scholar's greatest joy was to have a brand-new idea that had never been thought before, a flash of insight that chased away the darkness of ignorance and superstition. Though he had been Master Ruthi's best student, he had never had a truly original idea until this moment.

Timu could feel Tanvanaki's waist stiffen. And for a while she was quiet as he waited, trepidation in his heart.

"I suppose it's worth a try," she said. "I don't know if my people can ever get used to the idea of tying down the land, carving it into square pieces and then living within the lines. We are used to having an open land and roaming as far as we like, whenever we like. Your way feels too much like prison."

Korva took a sudden dive, and Timu cried out in surprise as he held tighter to Tanvanaki. Korva turned and flipped in the air, rolling a few times like a cat on the floor. By the time she straightened out, blood had drained from Timu's face, and he no longer knew which way was up. Tanvanaki laughed.

"And you thought you would sit behind me stiffly because one of your silly scholars told you that was the right thing to do. Do you really enjoy the bounds of your rigid little box? This is what freedom feels like, Prince of Dara: There are no rules."

Timu couldn't answer; he was trying not to throw up. He decided he would just close his eyes and hold on to Tanvanaki. Though this woman was the daughter of a ruthless killer, at this moment, he felt that there was no one who inspired him more.

Freedom. Yes, freedom.

After flying for another hour, Korva was tired and landed somewhere near Kriphi. Tanvanaki brought Timu to her tent and treated him to a meal of roast beef and hearty stew made from nuts and organ meats. Though the Lyucu style of cooking was very different from the refined fare Timu was used to in the palace at Pan or the plain porridge and vegetables of the Rui peasantry, Timu found it satisfying after an exciting day spent in the air. He wolfed down his food hungrily while Tanvanaki looked on with a smile on her face.

Timu recognized some of the servants who brought the food and cleared the tables: prominent Rui nobles. They tried to avoid looking at him, and he felt uneasy. It didn't seem right to be sharing food with their enemy in this intimate manner.

He wiped his mouth and sat up.

"Princess Vadyu, thank you for your hospitality, but I think it's time to bring me back."

"Oh? Are you tired of my company already?"

"It's not that. . . . You're a lady of exceptional grace and beauty, but . . . but our peoples are still at war—"

"Do you only think in terms of *us* versus *them*? Do you ever just think about your own feelings?"

"What do you mean?"

Tanvanaki looked him straight in the eyes. "You like me, don't you?"

Timu blushed. Once again, the boldness of this Lyucu woman shocked and confused him. None of Kon Fiji's fables and aphorisms applied. "I—I—"

"If you want to go, you may go. But first, have some kyoffir with me."

A pouch of the strong fermented milk drink was brought out.

Timu had never tried it, but he did know that the drink upset the stomachs of most people of Dara. He was about to say no—

"Do you hate my people so much that you can't even share a drink with me? We don't offer kyoffir to anyone except those we esteem."

The way Tanvanaki looked at him, half-challenging, half-teasing, made him decide that he had to drink it. He didn't want her to think ill of him.

All life is an experiment. Isn't that what Father always says?

The smell of the drink was strong, but after the first taste, he soon got used to it. It wasn't like wine or beer, but had a bite all its own. The thick liquid was not unpleasant, and he decided to drink as much as he dared to show that he wasn't like the arrogant men of Admiral Krita's fleet. He was a fair-minded prince, a scholar with original ideas.

He finished the bowl; his head felt swollen.

"Among the Lyucu, good friends must share three bowls of kyoffir before parting," said Tanvanaki. Her face seemed to swim in and out of focus.

"Nothing would please more to be . . . than to be . . . considered the princess's good friend," said Timu. His thick tongue seemed to disobey his will.

Tanvanaki refilled the bowls and drained her bowl in one long gulp. She slammed the bowl upside down on the table and looked at him challengingly.

A storm raged inside his stomach, but Timu forced himself to drink the kyoffir.

The third bowl was even harder. By the time Timu finished, his face was flushed and as he tried to stand up, he stumbled and fell down to the floor. Tanvanaki came over to his side to support him.

"Why don't you lie down for a moment? You're not used to the kyoffir's strength."

Timu closed his eyes, enjoying the scent coming from Tanvanaki, a combination of flowers, spices, and the warmth of youth and sunlight.

Then he fell into a deep slumber.

I don't think this . . . this is right, Tanva . . . Princess Vadyu!

Don't you want to?

I . . . I do—

—Then it can't be not right.

There are proper rites that . . . must be observed—

—Shhh, I'm observing them right now.

I'm not feeling myself. I don't . . . don't think—

—Your problem is that you think too much. Let your body do the thinking for you.

No, please. Please stop. No—

—I know you don't really mean that. You say one thing with your mouth, but your body thinks another. Stop lying, Prince of Dara. Let your body express the truth.

Timu woke up, feeling utterly drained. He looked around and discovered that he was inside a large tent, lying on a soft pelt bed. He heard a rustling and looked to the side: Tanvanaki was sitting in front of a mirror, combing through her hair with an ivory comb. She had switched back to the traditional dress of the Lyucu.

Hearing the noise behind her, the princess turned around. "You're awake." Her tone was placid, a bit distant.

Timu nodded. He wasn't sure why, but he felt as though something terrible had happened. "Last night, I . . . I . . ."

The princess walked over and knelt down next to him. She examined him carefully, as though looking at something fragile and precious.

"You'd better lie back down and get some more sleep," she said. "Don't worry, the drug will wear off in another day or so. I'll come back later to see you."

"What about my work? I have to meet my quota."

"There won't be any more quotas for you," she said, and stroked his face gently. "You'll be living with me."

"I want to go back to the village where I was housed."

"Do you really? After last night? How do you think your people will see you when they learn that I've taken you to bed?"

"What—"

But the princess didn't wait for him to continue. She stood up and walked away. "I really do like you, but my father was willing to kill his friend and the garinafin that had saved his life for a better future for my people. I am my father's daughter."

Timu tried to say something, anything, but nothing came to mind as he experienced a deep sense of regret and dread.

The princess stopped at the entrance to the tent. Without turning around, she said, "The dream you had when we flew together . . . it cannot be achieved without much fire and blood. And I meant it when I served you the three bowls of kyoffir. I want you to know that."

She left. Timu stared at the flaps of the tent until they stopped moving, and then he fell back into bed, sobbing inconsolably.

She spoke to him of the wedding plans—a simple affair that would combine Lyucu and Dara elements, of the eventual coronation ceremony, of the need for him to think of the future, not the past.

At night she slept next to him, keeping him on the inside of the bed, and it was not clear if she did it to shield him from the draft coming from the tent opening or to prevent him from escape.

She did not drug him again.

Lying in the darkness, Timu replayed the events of the day of the garinafin ride. He had been attracted to her, he could not deny that. He had allowed the flame of desire to drive out reason, to incinerate the words of the Ano sages, to turn the virtue he had been so carefully guarding into something bestial, something base.

Don't you want to?

I . . . I do—

He had been weak, he knew. He had been at fault.

His father's opinion of him had been right.

He could not imagine facing his family again after what had happened. The shame would be unbearable. He was utterly alone.

"When the Lyucu want something," said Tanvanaki from next to him, "we simply take it. Do not let others tell you what you should do or want. Our lives are brief flash storms in the eternal scrublands of Time, and we honor all creation by living lustfully and passionately. Shame is a lie told to you by those who would enslave you rather than free you."

Her voice soothed him like a mug of ice plum tea in summer or a cup of warmed rice wine in winter. *Family should lift you up, not put you down,* Timu thought. *Wasn't that what the Ano sages always said?*

He turned to Tanvanaki and she had already opened her arms to welcome him.

He concentrated on his movements and the sensations coursing through his body to silence the voice of doubt, to drive out the lingering feeling of guilt.

CLASH OF
TYPHOONS

CHAPTER FIFTY-SEVEN

A PLAGUE

RUI: THE NINTH MONTH IN THE TWELFTH YEAR
OF THE REIGN OF FOUR PLACID SEAS.

Almost a year had passed since the invasion of Dasu and Rui by the Lyucu.

Small fishing boats made their way back to the harbor at Kriphi one by one, their crews looking tired and worn.

Pékyu Tenryo did not like the news they brought.

"You couldn't find a single source of tolyusa in all the Islands of Dara?" he roared in the tent. The other Lyucu thanes held their tongues. "Yesterday, yet another one of the yearlings died. The garinafin mothers are restless with child-hunger, and we won't get reinforcements until next year! How will we control the adults until then?"

"There's still no sign that the Empress of Dara intends to surrender?"

"None whatsoever. All the spies say that she's preparing for war. The woman is power-hungry and will not yield, even if we have her husband and son."

Tanvanaki followed the pacing Tenryo with her eyes. "We can still achieve victory before next year."

"Speak!"

"While our garinafins are still firmly under control, if we invade the Big Island and seize the capital, we have a chance of bringing all of Dara under heel." She put her hand on her belly. "Besides, we have a new weapon. Legitimacy matters a great deal to these people."

Tenryo looked back at her, and after a while, he nodded.

"I thought you would be happy for me," said Timu.

"Happy for you?" said Kuni Garu. He looked at the defiant face of Timu, and pain racked his heart. He had to steady himself with a hand against the wall of his prison cell.

"The start of a new life and a new family is a joyous occasion."

"But not like this, Timu. Not like this."

"This paves the way for a solution that avoids bloodshed," said Timu. "Hasn't Kon Fiji always said that war should be a last resort? The Lyucu and our people are now one family, and brother should not take up arms against brother."

"Oh, you foolish child," whispered Kuni. "You have read so many books and yet have learned so little." He gritted his teeth to prevent himself from saying something that he would regret.

The Lyucu had been pursuing a policy of deliberately impregnating as many native women as possible, Kuni knew. Almost all of these pregnancies were the result of rape. The terror, violence, and brutality of the policy were designed not only to break the spirit of the native population, but also to affirm the Lyucu claim to this land, to put down roots in it. The women warriors of the Lyucu had generally avoided becoming pregnant to preserve their own fighting readiness, and it was obvious that the Lyucu princess's bond with Timu had been coerced.

But Timu's face flushed at his restrained words. "I daresay my command of the Ano Classics is better than someone who spent more time arguing with his teacher than reading his assignments."

"You are a prince of the House of Dandelion! How could you have so little understanding of the reality of the situation? The Lyucu are using you as a pawn in their bid to—"

"You're simply angry because I have found a way to save Dara that you did not think of. The union between Tanvanaki and me will begin the healing that will ultimately bring the Lyucu together with the people of Dara. I ask you to step aside so that I can do what you cannot."

Kuni was beyond rage now. He laughed. "I can't even dignify that with a response."

"All you have to do is to write to Mother and convince her to surrender."

"Do you really wish to see all the people of Dara turned into slaves, to see all the Islands devastated like this one?"

"This is but a temporary state of affairs necessitated by Dara resistance," said Timu. "Once Dara is pacified, Pékyu Tenryo will moderate his policies. And if he will not, Tanvanaki and I will. We're the future, while you and Tenryo are the past."

"Have you learned nothing of what I've tried to teach you about the flow of power—"

"Of course I have! Just as you once seized power in order to wield it more justly, I now submit to power so that I can ameliorate its harsh bite. You and I are not so different after all, Father."

"But the Lyucu are wolves, Toto-*tika*—"

"Do not address me by that name!" Timu interrupted. "I'm no longer a child."

Kuni stared at him, as though finally seeing him for the first time.

Timu felt a twinge of regret, but words gushed from his heart like a torrent that could not be stopped. "I *have* learned from you, Father. But I learned from your actions, not your pretty words. You speak of caring for the people, yet you can't even take care of your own children. You speak of the responsibilities of power, yet all you've ever achieved is more power for yourself. You speak of the depredations of the Lyucu, yet you were responsible for many more deaths."

"This is unfair—"

But Timu would not be interrupted. "I'm going to be a father now, too, and I will never do to my child what you did to me. When the Hegemon was about to capture you in Zudi, you were willing to abandon me and Rata-*tika* just so you could escape! I remember that day as though it were yesterday."

Kuni flinched as though he had been slapped. *This is divine justice. The sins of my past have caught up to me.*

"And then you abandoned Mother to the Hegemon and allowed her to live as a prisoner for years while you used her sacrifice to build your power. At least I will never do that to the woman I love. Princess Vadyu and I will build a new Dara together on the wings of the garinafins, a world in which our child will not live in fear, doubt, or hatred rooted in ambition."

"Oh, my son," muttered Kuni. "My son."

"I have striven all my life to please you," said Timu. "And you've never been happy with me. I'm tired of waiting for your approval, Father, tired of living as your shadow.

"What is your answer to my request? Will you step aside?"

Kuni Garu shook his head and looked away from his son. Hot tears flowed down his face.

Timu left, and the door of the cell slammed shut behind him.

∽ ∾

PAN: THE NINTH MONTH IN THE TWELFTH YEAR
OF THE REIGN OF FOUR PLACID SEAS.

To the People of Dara,
   The Most Honorable Ruler of the Lands of Ukyu
and Gondé, Protector of Dara, Pékyu Tenryo, speaks to
you thus:
   Whereas the power-hungry Empress Jia has usurped the
Throne of Dara without legitimacy;

Whereas Prince Timu and Royal Princess Vadyu have
wedded and are expecting a child in the spring;

Whereas Emperor Ragin, guest of the pékyu, has abdicated
in favor of Prince Timu;

Whereas the people of Dara have long suffered under
misrule and maladministration;

Whereas the All-Father has dispatched the fiery wings of
the Lyucu to bring about a new chapter in the history of Dara;

Therefore, I, Tenryo Roatan, have decided to deliver this
ultimatum to Empress Jia. In one month, after making
proper sacrifices to the All-Father and the gods of Dara, to
wit: Cudyufin-Kana, Nalyufin-Rapa, Aluro-Tututika, Péa-
Kiji, Toryoana-Rufizo, Diasa-Fithowéo, and Péten-Lutho-
Tazu, I and the might of Lyucu will fall upon the shores of
unredeemed Dara to reclaim the throne for the legitimate
ruler of Dara, Emperor Thaké, my loyal thane, known in the
past as Timu.

All those who rally to the flag of Emperor Thaké shall
be rewarded and all who adhere to the usurper Jia shall
be punished.

—Pékyu Tenryo, Protector of Dara
As dictated to and recorded by Thaké, Emperor of Dara

The messages, packed in bottles dropped near the shores of the core islands by Lyucu boats, were read by many and immediately caused a crisis in Pan.

"Oh, my Toto-*tika*, how could you?" muttered Jia. "I should have paid more attention to your character instead of leaving you to your teacher. You've broken your father's heart. This is a betrayal that will be impossible to undo."

"Timu has always been a bit impractical in his thinking," said Théra. "Certainly he was deceived."

"I'm sure the prince had his reasons," said Consort Risana, ever hopeful. "Not everyone who collaborates with the Lyucu is necessarily a traitor; sometimes it's difficult to tell what people are really thinking based on their public performance."

At this, Jia gave a wry smile.

"The question is: Why have they decided to invade now?" asked Théra.

"Didn't we always expect them to invade after the fall harvest?" said Zomi.

"If they've made Timu into a puppet, it means they want more than military conquest," said Théra.

"So they're trying to—" Zomi started to talk but then stopped as Théra gave her a warning look.

"They're trying to destabilize Dara by inciting rebellions against me," said Empress Jia. "It's all right. There's nothing wrong with stating what's plainly in their message."

"But that plan works best if they give it more time," said Théra as she pondered the situation. "It would be more sensible for them to build up Timu's legitimacy—possibly by waiting until the child is born—and wait for reinforcements from beyond the sea when the Wall of Storms opens in spring."

"Have they suddenly grown confident in their strength?" asked Zomi. She and Théra shared a worried but also warm glance with each other.

"That's what they want us to think," said Cogo Yelu. "But I think the truth is likely the exact opposite. This might be an act of desperation."

"We have no choice but to fight," said Gin Mazoti.

"Are we ready?" asked Jia.

"The odds of victory or defeat are about even," said the marshal. "We've been preparing all summer, and I now no longer think resistance a hopeless act. But all commanders wish for more time."

"Maybe that's why they're attacking," said Jia. "They don't want to give us any more time to prepare."

"The best-made plans in the world must ultimately be put to the test of reality," said the marshal. "We've done all that we can. All the rest is chance."

But then she paused and looked at Risana. "However, Your Highness's comments on the mysterious hearts of collaborators have given me an idea."

∾ ↺

The Lyucu secured the shores of Rui and Dasu with constant airship patrols, and they caught the sudden influx of farseers from Dara. Lyucu guards brought the secret messages carried by the executed spies to Pékyu Tenryo.

Written in ornate language full of allusions to the Ano Classics and pompous quotations from Moralist treatises, the messages promised amnesty and leniency for all collaborationist Dara ministers and commanders who defected now to the cause of the empress and called for them to assassinate important Lyucu thanes and leaders, especially Pékyu Tenryo himself. Whoever succeeded would be granted dukedoms or even kingdoms.

The pékyu laughed as he read these messages and shared them with the surrendered Dara ministers and military commanders.

"Nothing confirms their desperation more than this," said the pékyu. "You all know very well how Jia treats those who served her family with loyalty. After what happened to Théca Kimo, Rin Coda, and Gin Mazoti, why would anyone believe her empty promises?"

The ministers and commanders laughed along with their new lord. Indeed, Jia's obsession with weakening the enfeoffed nobles was still fresh in their minds.

Ra Olu returned to his mansion in Kriphi—a gift from the pékyu for his service to the Lyucu—and shared the message with Lady Lon, who had been released from having to attend to the pékyu after he tired of her looks.

"This seems a very clumsy attempt," said Lady Lon. "I would

have thought the marshal too clever to try something so transparent."

"The key is not the text," said Ra Olu, "but the subtext. There is a quote from a poem by Lurusén at the end of the message:

> *Steadfast laborers paint the paddies green;*
> *Promised golden grains put the mind at ease.*
> *But hunger and danger can't be foreseen*
> *When lured by the sovereign of the seas.*
> *Keep your silos filled and sealed, prudent King,*
> *For none can know what plagues the wind may bring.*

"That's from his 'Ode to the Sea,' isn't it? What's the point of quoting that poem?"

"I'm not sure," said Ra Olu. "But I can't help but think it's the key to what the empress and the marshal have in mind."

"Could it be a gesture of defiance? Emperor Ragin once achieved his most famous victory by riding on the back of a cruben, so the reference to the sovereign of the seas may be suggesting that victory belongs to Dara ultimately."

Ra Olu shook his head. "It doesn't seem a very apt allusion. The Lyucu do not farm, and they've been destroying the agricultural base of the islands in their preparation for an invasion of the Big Island and converting the land to pasture use."

"That's true. Lurusén is the empress's favorite poet, and she wouldn't quote him without great care."

"The marshal and the empress had to know that these messages would be intercepted. So this must be a code. . . . You've always been more literary than I. What do you know about this poem?"

"Let me think. . . . Lurusén wrote it after the King of Cocru signed a treaty of nonaggression with the King of Xana, which he opposed. My father explained to me that it was a veiled political pamphlet in which Lurusén criticized the King of Cocru's shortsightedness. Though Cocru at the time was at peace and prosperous, he hinted at the oncoming storm from overseas."

"From Xana's ambition?" asked Ra Olu. "But Xana was dominating through airpower."

"True, but the political climate made it impossible to speak too openly, so he used 'sovereign of the seas' as a veiled reference to the Xana threat."

"I'm still not sure how that applies here." Ra Olu was disappointed.

"There are more layers to the poem." Lady Lon paced as she tried to recall the details of literary lessons from long ago. "I remember researching the poem in detail because I liked it, and coming upon a bit of ancient history that Lurusén also likely had in mind. Centuries ago, before the stability of the Seven States, there were many more Tiro states in Dara all fighting against each other. One of these states, Keos, was locked in a cycle of warfare with a state named Diyo. Keos was the stronger, and managed to breach the capital of Diyo, taking the King of Diyo prisoner. Only after the King of Diyo pledged fealty to the King of Keos was he allowed to go home.

"But the King of Diyo was not content to live out his days as a vassal of Keos. Secretly, he initiated a program of vengeance. He let it be known that the court of Diyo coveted a kind of oyster that grew only near the shores of Keos, and was willing to pay a high price for it. The people of Keos soon realized that they could make far more profit by diving for oysters and selling them to Diyo than by working the fields, and many in Keos abandoned their farms and headed for the sea to dive for gold.

"At the same time, the King of Diyo encouraged his own population to reclaim more land for farming and to plant varieties of rice, wheat, and sorghum with high yields. Claiming that Diyo was poor, he paid the tribute he owed Keos in kind, in the form of grain shipments. As a result, the King of Keos wasn't concerned that so much of the farmland of his domain was wasted because the tribute grain from Diyo kept everyone fed. Indeed, his subjects were growing rich from the exorbitant sums paid by Diyo for those silly oysters.

"Five years later, Diyo suddenly stopped paying tribute. The granaries of Keos were empty because the people of Keos had not been farming for several years. While the population of Keos starved, the army of Diyo swept across the border and conquered it easily. The King of Keos hung himself in shame before the army of Diyo breached the capital."

"This is a tale of the dangers of pride and arrogance, of dependence on a source of food you do not control," mused Ra Olu.

"I think Lurusén was using the tale to argue that the King of Cocru had been lured into a sense of complacency while Xana plotted Cocru's downfall," said Lady Lon. "That last line is also a veiled dig at Xana, for it was popular among the core islands at the time to describe Xana peasants, who often suffered famine, as plagues of locusts."

"Keep your silos filled and sealed . . . plagues the wind may bring . . . ," Ra Olu muttered to himself as he pondered the poem's many layers. A vague idea was starting to form in his head. "Lon, did you ever share your interpretation with anyone in the Imperial household?"

"Now that you mention it, I do remember discussing the poem with both the emperor and the empress when we visited Pan years ago. Both of them were enthusiasts for Lurusén's work and seemed to delight in novel interpretations."

Ra Olu nodded. "I think I know what the empress really meant."

He explained his theory to her.

Lady Lon looked at him. "Do you mean to do as she asks?"

Ra Olu locked gazes with her. "You and I have both done what we could not just to survive, but to live up to the ideals of the Moralist scholar who, even when captured by the enemy, never stops serving his true lord."

Lady Lon sighed. "And the empress obviously intended this message for you, as only you and I could have understood it. It's good to know that all our efforts to sneak coded intelligence to the empress through the pékyu's letters and other means have not gone unrecognized. If we survive, I'm certain the empress will be grateful."

Ra Olu shook his head. "Lon, I don't wish to give you false hope.

There is a duty placed on those who have been elevated above the base crowd by studying the words of the Ano sages. Lurusén was willing to die not for the king, but for the people of Cocru."

"And you mean to emulate him."

Ra Olu nodded resolutely. "If you renounce me now and seek a Lyucu thane who desires your beauty, it might still be possible for you to save yourself. Love makes us do strange things, Lon, but you need not die for my decision."

Lady Lon stood still, a frown on her face. "Our love has weathered torture and degradation, but my choice now isn't guided by blind romance. Lady Zy stood by her husband Lurusén and dove into the Liru River with him not for love, but for a shared ideal. I may not be her equal in talent, yet I do not think I lack her courage. I have read the same Moralist treatises as you, and there is no monopoly on virtue by those who wear the robe as opposed to the dress."

The two embraced and said no more.

With the cooling weather came the time for the High-Autumn Festival.

As the Lyucu invasion of the Big Island was imminent, security in Rui and Dasu was even tighter than usual. Local families were told to stay indoors after dark, after completing chores assigned by the Lyucu foremen, and even the traditional celebrations and banquets were canceled.

Ra Olu went to Pékyu Tenryo and asked for an exemption. "It's not a good idea to press the people too hard. If you allow some private celebrations, the people will be thankful for your generosity, and later, when many of the Lyucu warriors must leave with you to conquer the Big Island, they'll be less likely to make trouble."

"Large gatherings in public are always dangerous. They'll whisper to each other, and troublemakers will spread rumors. Besides, such celebrations take time away from their work for us."

"We can prevent that while still giving the people something to celebrate. It's our custom for families and neighbors to share a banquet of moonbread on the night of the High-Autumn Festival. If we gather a small number of people to prepare the bread ahead of time under your watch, the rest of the people can keep on working for your benefit. We can then have the bread distributed to each family so that they can celebrate privately on the night of the festival. This will prevent the spread of rumors, avoid wasteful sloth, and still mark the occasion as festive."

Pékyu Tenryo thought about the proposal and granted it. Ra Olu was always so good at coming up ways to guide these Dara sheep.

And so, as Lyucu warriors watched over the proceedings, Ra Olu and Lady Lon gathered the deci-chiefs of the various families of Rui and Dasu into Kriphi and turned them into a moonbread factory. The dough biscuits were packed with different flavored fillings—lotus seeds, taro paste, candied monkeyberries, chopped seaweed, diced bamboo shoots, and many others—as well as small slips of paper bearing simple phrases spelled out in zyndari letters. The Lyucu guards examined the slips of paper and had multiple collaborating scholars translate them to be sure they contained nothing suspicious.

All the slips contained only stock phrases wishing for good luck or clumsy attempts at praising the Great Pékyu. The Lyucu warriors laughed and shook their heads—these people truly were silly and natural-born slaves.

After the biscuits were done baking, the deci-chiefs took them back to their villages to distribute to the families under their charge. The Lyucu guards, curious about the taste of the moonbread, wanted to save some for themselves. But Ra Olu presented them with a special batch.

"Honorable Masters, these are for you to enjoy. My wife and I personally oversaw their preparation to be sure that no brazen peasant dared to spit in them or to spoil them in some other way," Ra Olu said.

"And I took out the slips of paper," said Lady Lon. "If you aren't used to eating moonbread, you might get them stuck in your throat."

"If all the savages were as thoughtful and obedient as you," one of the Lyucu thanes said, spitting bits of bread and filling in Ra Olu's face as he munched and talked, "we'd have many fewer problems."

Ra Olu didn't even bother to wipe away the spittle as he kept on smiling. "Your Honor is absolutely correct."

When the village families broke open the biscuits on the night of the High-Autumn Festival, they saw to their surprise that in addition to the inked messages on the front of the slips of paper, some of the blank backs of the paper slips were also filled with brown letters. Lady Lon had painstakingly written these messages using an eyebrow brush and fruit juice ink, which remained invisible until the heat of baking caramelized the sugar in the juices.

Families gathered around these slips of paper to read silently, and then they swallowed the slips.

∾   ∾

NORTH OF RUI AND DASU, THE TENTH MONTH
IN THE TWELFTH YEAR OF THE REIGN OF FOUR
PLACID SEAS.

The promised invasion of the Big Island was going to commence in another six days. Airships intensified their patrolling of the sea lanes south of Rui and Dasu to prevent another sneak attack by underwater boats like the one that had allowed Than Carucono's forces to gain a foothold on Rui back in the spring.

No one was watching the sea north of Rui and Dasu. After all, the captured Dara soldiers had, after much torture, confessed that they had never heard of any underwater volcano routes north of the islands.

But to the north of the islands, a small flotilla stealthily crept closer. These ships had set out from Wolf's Paw a month earlier, heading straight north until they were far out of sight of the usual shipping lanes. Then they had turned west until they were north of Rui and Dasu. The flotilla consisted of modified merchant vessels with large holds and carried little weaponry.

Their mission might be war, but they weren't warships.

Puma Yemu, master of sneak attacks and stealthy raids, had organized this mission. With funds from the marshal, he had gone to Wolf's Paw to buy merchant vessels and recruit desperadoes willing to do anything for hard cash. The cargo the ships carried would make anyone blanch.

Because Puma needed absolute secrecy, only when the ships were at sea did he reveal to his crew what they were carrying, and more than a dozen had thrown up immediately, and a few had even dived into the sea to avoid having to live with the ship's cargo for a month.

"Get dressed," Puma Yemu ordered. The moment of truth had arrived.

He lowered the fine wire mesh from on top of his helmet to drape around his face. Like a beekeeper's veil, the mesh protected his face and neck. His hands and feet were wrapped in strips of linen to prevent the exposure of any skin. A heavy canvas smock and thick leggings covered the rest of his body. The crew of the rest of the fleet were similarly dressed and lowered their protective veils as well.

"Release!"

The instruction was passed to the other ships by flag signal. Sailors held their breath as they pried open the heavy cargo doors with long bamboo poles. Then they dove to the deck and lay with their bodies curled up to make themselves as unexposed as possible.

Dark clouds emerged from the cargo holds, buzzing like an angry swarm of bees. However, the insects that made up the swarms were not bees, but locusts, each twice the size of a grown man's finger.

For weeks, they had been swarming inside the hold, feasting on the grain that the crew dumped into the hold via sieved openings daily as well as the bodies of their dead insectile comrades. They bred and multiplied in the darkness, shoving against each other, crawling over each other, making the ships hum as though they were alive.

Prime Minister Cogo Yelu had carefully bred those locusts from the eggs left behind by the destroyed swarms in Géfica. These were the largest, strongest locusts Dara had to offer, and they were hungry, very hungry.

The locusts, freed from their hold, scented the air and detected the presence of land nearby. Land, and vegetation. The swarms rose from the ships, joined together, and, like a dark thundercloud, headed south toward the fields of Rui and Dasu.

The plague of locusts descended upon Rui and Dasu like a typhoon.

Chittering, rasping, rustling, rumbling, the locusts devoured everything in their path. They swarmed over the fields—red, green, gold—and drained them of all color and shape save the tan of bare soil and skeletal, bare branches stripped of all leaves. Rice, wheat, sorghum, taro, sugarcane, grass, weed—everything was ground up by millions of mandibles and then disappeared into millions of winged stomachs.

The Lyucu warriors tried to fight the locusts at first, but what could war clubs and axes do against a beast with innumerable heads? The garinafins tried to make a stand against the storm with fire breath, but even with thousands of locusts fried in each flame wave, more kept coming. Trying to fight the locusts was like trying to fight the sea itself.

Eventually, skin blistered and blood oozing, the Lyucu warriors had to retreat into their tents and seal the flaps while the Dara peasants cowered in basements. The two islands became the domain of insects, as long-haired cattle stampeded and garinafins took off.

Overhead, flocks of birds circled in wide, placid circles as if observing a surging sea that had nothing to do with them.

On the third day, after the locusts had swept over the entire island and denuded it of all vegetation, after they had turned on each other to fill their insatiable appetites, only then did the birds finally dive down and begin the process of cleansing the islands of the insectoid plague.

Afterward, as the dazed Lyucu warriors and Dara peasants emerged from their hiding places, they saw a wasted world in which all the crop fields and grazing pastures had turned into a lifeless desert.

For some reason, while the granaries in many of the villages had been sealed tightly ahead of time and preserved their contents against the plague, the haylofts and sheds where feed for the long-haired cattle and garinafin were stored had been left open, and the locusts had mercilessly devoured the entire supply of feed for Lyucu beasts of war.

The villagers nodded at each other, finally understanding the message that had come to them in the moonbread: *Seal up your granaries with wax and clay.*

∽ ∾

RUI: THE TENTH MONTH IN THE TWELFTH YEAR
OF THE REIGN OF FOUR PLACID SEAS.

A few deci-chiefs, terrified of the consequences, revealed the truth to Pékyu Tenryo. Soon, the heads of Lady Lon and Minister Ra Olu hung from the gates of Kriphi, a warning for any who dared to engage in sabotage against the Lyucu.

"They think they would starve us with this trick," said Pékyu Tenryo, his hands shaking from anger. "I will show them what starvation truly means."

The order was given that the granaries would be opened so that the stored rice, sorghum, and wheat would be given to the garinafins and long-haired cattle as feed.

"What will we eat?" asked one of the village elders.

"You are skilled at digging food out of dirt," said Pékyu Tenryo. "So dig harder."

"You're sentencing us to death then," said the elder. "There's no time for planting another crop before the winter."

"In that case, I see plenty of pigs with two legs walking around," said Pékyu Tenryo. "I think they make excellent food. You could learn to diversify your diet."

The villagers, once they understood what the pékyu had in mind, howled with rage and despair and rushed at the guards who had come to seize the granaries. But a few more swipes of the flaming breath of the garinafins soon quelled the nascent rebellion. The villagers stood by and watched mutely as the granaries were emptied and the garinafins and long-haired cattle feasted upon the food that was meant to supply the villages over the winter.

The invasion schedule would be kept. The Lyucu would not back down from a promise made.

But then, something odd happened. The long-haired cattle fell upon the ground, groaning and foaming at the mouth, their legs twitching wildly. Many of the garinafins fell down as well, and their excrement was a thick slush and smelled foul.

"How have they been poisoned?" demanded the pékyu. Since no deci-chief would admit to the plot, the pékyu forced them to eat the grain that had been fed to the garinafins. But nothing happened to them.

∽ ∽

FAÇA: A FEW MONTHS EARLIER.

"I've heard that to get the juiciest beef, you need to feed the cattle grains," said Théra.

The other ranch hands on her grandmother's estate had accepted the new girl as one of them, and they shared bitter chicory root brew around the fire as Théra sought to understand more about their business.

"That is true. Grain-fed cattle fatten faster."

"Why aren't we feeding our cattle grains then?" asked Théra.

"Lady Lu is a shrewd businesswoman," said one of the ranch hands, an old man everyone respectfully called Old Maza. "Grass-fed cattle has a different taste. When everyone feeds their cattle grain, the unique taste of her cattle commands a better price."

"Oh." Théra nodded. She wasn't surprised that her grandmother liked to do things differently—after all, her mother's stubbornness had to come from somewhere. "Sometimes I see the cattle looking at the granary hungrily. Is it a big deal to feed them some grain once in a while, especially on rainy days? Surely grains taste much better than hay."

The ranch hands laughed uproariously, leaving Théra confused as to the source of their mirth. Eventually, Old Maza managed to hold back his laughter and tried to explain. "Girl, a cow's stomach is a delicate thing. Do you know why they chew cud?"

Théra shook her head.

"It's because grass is tough to digest. The cow has to let that sit in her stomach and ferment a bit, and then regurgitate and chew it some more. The inside of a cow's stomach is a complicated world, and even ranchers who have been doing this for generations can't explain how everything works. We do know that if you want to feed a cow grains, you've got to start to do it when they're young. If you wait till their stomachs have grown used to grass and then switch to grain all of a sudden, the cattle will get sick and can even die."

Théra nodded, thinking about the distant invaders from the north. They didn't tend the fields and had no knowledge of grains. To them, surely the grains seemed like just another kind of vegetation, and if grass weren't available, wouldn't they turn to grains meant for people as a substitute?

∽ ∾

RUI: THE TENTH MONTH IN THE TWELFTH YEAR
OF THE REIGN OF FOUR PLACID SEAS.

Pékyu Tenryo ordered work gangs composed of the peasantry of Rui and Dasu into the mountains to cut down any vegetation that had survived the locust swarm due to their elevation. Given this tougher food that more resembled their natural diet, some of the garina-fins who hadn't eaten too many grains recovered relatively quickly. However, it would take longer for the others. Pékyu Tenryo gathered the sick garinafins into one place so that they could be tended to and guarded from further sabotage by the villagers.

"Should we postpone the invasion until they recover?" asked Tanvanaki.

"No," said Pékyu Tenryo. "Our warriors already think the crafty barbarians of Dara have succeeded in their plot. The longer we delay, the lower our morale."

"It seems risky to attack without our full strength," said Tanvanaki.

"Considering the empress has no air force to speak of, we have more than enough healthy garinafins to attack the Big Island on schedule and overcome whatever resistance she can muster. And we can always send the rest later as reinforcements when they recover."

"Thank Péa-Kiji then that the thanes had the presence of mind to seal the underground cellars where the younglings are kept when the locusts struck, and we still have control over the garinafins."

Emperor Ragin paced in his prison cell.

The announcement of Pékyu Tenryo's invasion plan had jolted him, though not shocked him. He realized that he had been hoping for a miracle, even though he had not admitted it to himself.

He had been fighting for decades for an ideal, an ideal of a Dara that was more just, more fair to the common people, that balanced conflicting interests and allowed more men and women of talent to succeed. But in the end, what had he accomplished? More blood was being spilled, more people were dying because he had not planned for everything, had not foreseen everything that could go wrong.

Timu's betrayal *had* shocked him, but he could not fully blame the child for his error. How could Timu understand the full extent to which he was being taken advantage of by the Lyucu? Stuffed full of bookish ideals and rebellious anger, the young prince believed in a vision where justice could be achieved by sleeping with the enemy, where the wolf would lie down with the lamb.

He should have been more of a father to the child, but it was too late now.

He could imagine the confusion on the Big Island, now that Timu had become the puppet emperor of the pékyu—all those unsatisfied with the existing distribution of power in Dara would seize upon the occasion as an opportunity for rearrangement, for shuffling the deck to gain a better hand. He did not envy the difficult task Jia faced.

As long as he was alive, they could use his "abdication" as a way to legitimate Timu's claim. Yet if he died now, in obscurity, the Lyucu would be able to continue to lie, with his ghost as a rallying flag. He had to try to give Jia and the others a chance.

The pékyu was a calculating man, Kuni knew, not too different from himself. He tried to imagine himself in the pékyu's place. *What would I do?*

Timu is too valuable a prop to be risked, yet the fleet also needs another high-profile hostage for some battlefield theater.

He recalled a talk he had had with Jia over the dangers of battle-field injuries and what could be done to save the wounded. He closed his eyes. It was time to put that knowledge into use.

He looked and found a rusty nail in one of the window frames. He took off his left shoe and sock, and scraped the skin against the rusty nail until he had made a deep gash. He grimaced against the pain and replaced the sock and shoe.

Now he had to wait, and hope that he would be given a chance.

Twenty garinafins were deemed healthy enough to go to war. Pékyu Tenryo packed them onto eight city-ships along with three thousand Lyucu warriors. The rest would stay behind to guard Rui and Dasu with the help of surrendered Dara soldiers. Timu, or "Emperor Thaké," was nominally left in charge, but everyone, perhaps even Timu himself, understood that he was a mere figurehead.

A few of the airships captured from Emperor Ragin would accompany the fleet to act as scouts against surprise attacks by mechanical crubens while the rest would be left behind to defend Rui and Dasu.

On the morning of the day specified in the ultimatum, the fleet of city-ships and smaller escort vessels left Kriphi and sailed for the Big

Island. The elders of Rui and Dasu recalled the launches of similar invasion fleets from the Xana home islands decades ago as Emperor Mapidéré and then Emperor Ragin had sailed this same course to the Throne of Dara. Pékyu Tenryo and Emperor Thaké would follow the success of their illustrious predecessors.

The invasion of the Big Island had begun.

CHAPTER FIFTY-EIGHT

DREAM OF THE DANDELION

ZATHIN GULF: THE TENTH MONTH IN THE TWELFTH
YEAR OF THE REIGN OF FOUR PLACID SEAS.

The few airships that accompanied the Lyucu fleet sailed ahead and
to the side of the ships, and lookouts intently gazed at the surface
below, trying to spot the approach of any mechanical crubens. The
fleet took a course that avoided the known underwater volcanoes,
but Pékyu Tenryo wasn't going to take any chances.

As further insurance against a sneak attack, the flagship of the
pékyu, *Pride of Ukyu*, displayed a bright red banner charged with the
figure of a leaping blue cruben. This was the Imperial standard, and
Pékyu Tenryo wanted to make sure that any Dara ship that dared to
attack knew that they endangered the Emperor of Dara.

Empress Jia ordered Prince Phyro to stay in Pan with Consort Risana
over his strenuous objections.

"I should be at the front, fighting!"

"You're your father's only heir after Timu's error. Your safety
is paramount because you must preserve the Imperial line, and,

should the marshal and I fail, become the hope of an occupied Dara."

"And avenge you."

"No! Never let your love for your family become a hindrance to your duty to the well-being of the people. Vengeance should never be your goal, only freedom."

She turned to Consort Risana and Prime Minister Cogo Yelu. "If . . . the gods decide that I should not return, the House of Dandelion is in your hands."

Risana and Cogo both bowed.

"I am your loyal servant."

"Be well, Big Sister."

Near Ginpen, on the shore of the Zathin Gulf, Empress Jia had constructed an observation platform. This was a dais about two hundred feet on each side and about a hundred feet tall. Jia sat on top in a throne carved with leaping dyrans. Around her, the top of the dais was piled with firewood soaked in oil.

Should their stand here today fail, she intended to immolate herself in a final gesture of defiance.

Jia turned to Gin Mazoti, who stood at her side. "How do you like your new sword, Marshal?"

With some effort, Gin unsheathed Na-aroénna, the Doubt-Ender, and held it aloft with both hands. "Still getting used to it."

"As your soldiers are still getting used to our new weapons?"

Gin nodded. "Their courage is admirable. But untested weapons can't be trusted."

"I will stay here and pray for your success. Do you have any doubt?"

"I always have doubt," said Gin. "And courage, as the Hegemon proved, is not all."

"That's an improvement from before, then," said Jia. "You once told me you had no doubt that we had to yield."

Gin grinned at this. "May this sword live up to its name."

"What happened to that confident general who once told my husband that she could conquer Rui with only a thousand men?"

The marshal smiled wistfully. "Experience humbles."

Jia nodded and looked solemnly at her. "I love my husband with all my heart. I know he would be willing to die for Dara, and the same is true of my son. Do you understand?"

"In the case of Prince Timu," said Gin, "I'm not sure you're right."

Jia looked away. "Sometimes the weak need help to be strong, to do what they should do."

Gin felt a chill down her spine.

"I love my son," the empress continued. "But evil must be confronted."

The marshal gazed at the empress and, after a while, nodded.

As the Lyucu fleet approached the shore of the Big Island, Pékyu Tenryo was growing more confident by the moment.

He was going to land his army at Ginpen, sweep over land like a bolt of lightning on the backs of the garinafins, and bring Pan to her knees in a single, swift strike. Without any kind of effective airpower, the walled cities of Dara could not withstand the might of the garinafins. After all, could the marshal plant her flamethrowers everywhere?

Gazing out over the last mile or so of water that divided his fleet from land, Pékyu Tenryo let out a held breath. No Dara navy sailed from the port of Ginpen to meet his fleet; no army of Dara was lined up onshore to meet his invasion force; and there were no signs of the fabled giant war machines that Ginpen had once been famous for, like the Curved Mirrors that could set ships aflame from a distance. Likely the barbarians of Dara realized that such outdated defenses could not survive a garinafin assault.

The walls of Ginpen were bereft of defenders, and lookouts on the airships reported that the city was surprisingly quiet, with all the civilians apparently huddled in their homes. All signs pointed to the conclusion that Empress Jia's court had completely given up, and the dream of a new Lyucu homeland was at hand. Cudyu would eventually dispatch another fleet and bring more of the Lyucu to come and live in this paradise. Tenryo envisioned the Lyucu warriors living like kings, each supported by a docile herd of Dara farmers.

"I pity you, old man," said Tenryo to the supine figure of Kuni Garu. "It must be hard to see your victories come to naught, to see your accomplishments swept away by the vicissitudes of fate and the inconstancy of the gods."

Kuni remained oblivious in his slumber, turning and muttering inaudibly.

"What's that?" asked Tanvanaki, standing next to the pékyu. The other Lyucu warriors standing on deck began to point and whisper as well.

Pékyu Tenryo followed where his daughter was pointing, and at first, he wasn't sure what he was looking at: Mounds covered by bushes and beach grass seemed to be expanding, growing, rising, as though some large animals were wriggling underneath, seeking to emerge from their burrows.

"Prepare the garinafin riders," ordered the pékyu. Perhaps these farmers of Dara had not yet been completely subdued. Even a cornered rabbit would dare to kick and bite at wolves, and he wasn't going to let victory be snatched from his jaws by overconfidence.

Soldiers dressed in the finest armor of Dara surged onto the beach from hidden caves; ships carrying the bravest sailors of Dara rowed out of the port of Ginpen.

The ballooning mounds erupted, and with a sharp intake of breath, Pékyu Tenryo saw an impossible sight: six brand-new Imperial airships, larger than any they had ever seen, rising into the air.

Where did they get the lift gas?

Once Atharo Ye and Princess Théra discovered that the garinafins were powered by the same lift gas as the gas from manure fermentation used in the marshal's flamethrowers, Zomi Kidosu came up with a bold plan for creating new airships in secret.

The fermentation gas wasn't as light as the lift gas from Lake Dako on Mount Kiji, which necessitated design changes. The ships had to be made bigger to achieve the same lift capacities, and the materials used had to be lighter and the crew reduced. In underground caverns and basement workshops, the dedicated warriors and builders of Marshal Mazoti's volunteer corps toiled to bend and shape bamboo into hoops, struts, and girders, and to sew gasbags from varnished silk.

To reduce weight, the shipwrights reduced the number of internal supports for the bamboo frame, leaving as much space for the gasbags as possible. Some of the bamboo hoops and struts were reinforced with steel as the combination of materials provided more strength than either alone.

To make the most of the weaker lift gas, Atharo Ye designed the airships to have a flattened profile so that they resembled two saucers stacked face-to-face, or the body of a manta ray, rather than the traditional egg-shaped oblong. Although the new hull design was bulkier and less maneuverable, it also generated lift with forward motion, which helped the airships to stay aloft. As rowers sitting at the rim of the flattened hull wielded their massive feathered oars, the semi-rigid airships pulsated forward like jellyfish swimming through an empyrean sea.

The new Imperial ships were thus structurally weaker than their predecessors and could not weather the unpredictable conditions of long cruises as well; the marshal compensated by disguising the airships under a light covering of sand on the beach, as close to the scene of combat as possible.

The gondolas of the new airships were also shaped oddly. Instead of the sleek, sailing-ship-like profiles of the past, the new gondolas were oval in shape and far bigger, taking up almost a quarter of the bottom surface of the billowing hull and embedding a sizable portion inside the hull as well. Weight reduction was achieved by constructing most of the gondola, except the structural elements, with wicker. The crews had to be as light as possible, too, which meant once again that they were almost all women, mainly veterans of Dara's old air force and women's auxiliaries.

But as the gondolas were so light in comparison to the rest of the hull, the flight characteristics of the airships were somewhat unstable. To compensate for this, each of the airships was also equipped with a heavy ballast ball just aft of the gondolas, a large ceramic sphere suspended below the hull like a gigantic, dangling dewdrop hanging from the belly of a grasshopper.

The design seemed strangely inefficient to the shipbuilders—many of them former engineers who had retired to the Big Island to enjoy their golden years after a lifetime of service at Mount Kiji Air Base—but they reasoned that this was perhaps the best Atharo Ye could do given the constrained time frame for modifying the traditional airship design to work with a new lift gas.

The greatest weakness of the fermentation-gas-powered airships, of course, was the flammability of their lift gas. If any of the gasbags sprang a leak, even a spark would cause the entire ship to turn into a fiery bubble. There was not much the marshal could do to reduce the risk, however, as any additional armor for the ship would have increased its weight beyond the power of the weak lift gas. She had to rely on the fortunate happenstance that the Lyucu had not adopted the use of archers, especially not with fire arrows.

For the same reason, the marshal had to eschew equipping the airships with flamethrowers; instead, Mazoti would have to rely on other surprises.

Her back ached from long days spent silk-spinning,
Hands rough from nights spent boiling and reeling.
She returned from Pan with a tearstained face.
"Oh, Mama, what made your heart so heavy?"

Pick the cocoons, soak, boil, stir, reel.
Spin the wheel, sister, spin that wheel!

"My child, I saw many jade-tempered lords
And honey-voiced ladies dressed in fine silk.

How many know that they are wearing shrouds?
Or that silk makers only have hempen shawls?

Pick the cocoons, soak, boil, stir, reel.
Spin the wheel, sister, spin that wheel!

Though the song that the crew of the marshal's flagship, *Silkmotic Arrow*, chanted in unison began in the efforts of silk makers to relieve the tedium of long days in the workshops, the wheels the women now spun in the airship generated not threads or yarn, but power, power that would be stored until it was needed.

Hinged doors at the front of the gondolas dropped open as the airships readied themselves in battle configuration.

Oddly, the six airships were not all flying at the same height. Rather, four of the airships—*Spirit of Kiji*, *Heart of Tututika*, *Resolve of Fithowéo*, and *Vigor of the Twins*, all commanded by trusted captains from the old all-women Dasu air force under Gin Mazoti—hovered in the same plane to form a diamond parallel to the ground. *Silkmotic Arrow* flew above the diamond while *Moji's Vengeance*, commanded by Zomi Kidosu, flew below it.

Silk screens inside the gondolas hid most of the crews of the airships as well as the machinery they operated. Only about six women on each ship were visible from the open door at the front, holding longbows with nocked arrows.

The airships approached the Lyucu fleet as garinafins took off from the city-ships, rising to meet this unexpected challenge. Below them, Lyucu warriors scrambled around a golden canopy on the deck of the pékyu's flagship, *Pride of Ukyu*.

"That canopy must be where the pékyu is seated," said Marshal Mazoti. "Target it." In truth, she doubted that the crafty Pékyu Tenryo would be so foolish as to make himself such an obvious target. But striking the golden canopy, whatever it was hiding, would certainly enhance the morale of the Dara forces.

Dafiro Miro, who was serving as the marshal's executive officer, gave a series of quick orders to the rowers to maneuver *Silkmotic Arrow* slightly forward of the formation, and the archers at the front of the airship pointed the tips of their arrows at the distant golden canopy below.

The Lyucu warriors on the decks below jeered as they saw the few archers crouched at the opening at the front of the airship gondolas. Did the barbarians of Dara really think they would defeat the garinafins and city-ships with a few archers?

"Men of Dara," the pékyu's voice boomed from a bone trumpet installed at the top of the main mast. He was speaking from somewhere deep in the ship's hold, safely hidden from the surface. "Stand down! This is the order of your old emperor!"

As a stunned Marshal Mazoti and the rest of her crew watched, the golden canopy was whipped away to reveal a bed on which lay Kuni Garu, the Emperor of Dara.

Kuni wasn't moving.

Two of the Lyucu warriors stepped forward and lifted him from the bed, and he groaned as he twisted his face away from the light. The crews of the Imperial airships gasped.

Kuni had kept the injury in his toe hidden from the guards until it had become infected. By the time his rotting wound was finally discovered, the only option was an amputation of his gangrenous foot. But even after severing the limb, his condition did not seem to improve. The doctors the pékyu sent for declared Kuni to be on the verge of death.

Pékyu Tenryo had wanted to use Kuni as his secret weapon. He had suspected that Empress Jia might stage some last act of resistance, and he had planned to bring out his prized prisoner at the right moment as a way to grind down the morale of Dara's defenders.

Given the condition of the crippled and dying Kuni, the pékyu thought it was no longer necessary to keep him in a bone cage; rather, he left him lying on a bed under a canopy watched over by a few guards.

Even held up, Kuni appeared to remain in a deep and feverish slumber; he didn't react to the commotion around him.

Confused whispers passed through the crews of *Silkmotic Arrow* and the other airships. They were glad to see that their emperor was still alive, and most suspected that the pékyu was lying about the emperor's abdication and his orders to stand down. Nonetheless, the archers lowered their weapons.

"Target the emperor," Gin Mazoti said, her voice calm and steady.

Dafiro repeated her order and glanced at her. Though the marshal's voice betrayed no emotion, he could only imagine the turmoil that raged in her heart. Kuni Garu was the man who had lifted her out of obscurity and made her into the greatest general of Dara, but he had also stood by as she was accused of treason and stripped of her title and dignity.

She had once been willing to die for him, and now she was forced to kill him to preserve the fruits of his revolution.

Mazoti took a deep breath. This was a sacrifice that she could not avoid. As long as Kuni remained alive, her forces would not be able to fight freely. There would always be doubt among the soldiers that they were thwarting the emperor's will. Yet once she gave the order to kill Kuni, she would never be able to free herself from suspicion that she had, indeed, intended to betray him.

It was a price she had to pay to secure victory. To win, she had to give up her name and endure the judgment of history.

Mazoti steeled herself to give the order to fire.

Kuni looked around him, confused.

He was in Pan, the Harmonious City, standing in the middle of the broad expanse of Cruben Square in front of the palace. (*How can I be standing, when I've lost my foot?*) Normally the square was empty, save for children who flew kites in spring and summer and built ice statues in winter. Occasionally an Imperial airship landed in it, and nearby citizens would gather to watch.

But today the square was not empty. He was surrounded by colossal statues of the gods of Dara. The statues, each as tall as the Grand Examination Hall, were made with bronze and iron and painted with bright, lifelike colors.

Kuni remembered that Emperor Mapidéré was said to have wanted to confiscate all the weapons of Dara, all the swords and spears, all the knives and arrows, and melt them down into their constituent metals so that they could be turned into statues honoring the gods. Without weapons, there would be eternal peace in the world.

That vision had never been realized, just like Kuni's dream of a more just Dara, a Dara where a woman had as much power as a man, where a poor peasant's daughter from Dasu had as much chance to succeed as a wealthy merchant's son from Wolf's Paw, where anyone who had talent would be found and given a place to shine.

The emperor examined the statues more closely. There was something strange about them; they weren't depicting the gods in their traditional form.

Over Kiji's shoulders sat both a Mingén falcon and a garinafin; above Kana's head, her black raven hovered inside a golden globe as bright as the rays of the sun; above Rapa's head, her white raven floated inside a silver halo like the glow of the moon; Tututika's carp was swimming next to her in a maze of a thousand streams; Rufizo's white dove watched over a flock of long-haired cattle and sheep.

But the statues of Fithowéo, Lutho, and Tazu were the strangest of all. The left half of Fithowéo was male while the right half was female. The god of war carried a long, obsidian-tipped spear in the left hand and a bone-handled war club in the right. The statues of Lutho and Tazu, on the other hand, were fused together, as though the gods of calculation and of chance were but two aspects of the same deity.

What has happened? Kuni asked himself. *Who has committed such sacrilege?*

The statues of the gods and goddesses shifted and came to life.

The emperor was too stunned to move or speak.

"You don't have much time, Ragin," said Tututika, her voice at once familiar and strange. Kuni thought he could hear echoes of both the gentle streams of her homeland, the Beautiful Island, as well as something wilder and less predictable, like the flash floods of a distant plain full of scrubs and shrubs.

"Am I about to cross over the River-on-Which-Nothing-Floats?" he asked.

"Yes," replied Rapa simply, her voice as cold as the icy moon.

"I still have so much to do. Dara is under threat, Lady Rapa!"

"Everyone pleads for more time," said Kana, her voice as hot as the blazing sun, as impatient as an exploding volcano. "Mapidéré was the same way."

"The tasks of great heroes are never done," said Rufizo, the kind shepherd and healer of wounds. He waved his hand and Kuni felt some of his anxiety soothed away.

Kuni felt both pride and sorrow at this. The gods of Dara had declared him a great hero, but he was never going to complete his dream. This was the way of the world, wasn't it? No matter how carefully you planned things, fate intruded.

"Have I made the right choices?" asked Kuni Garu. "Have I been a grace of kings?" His heart pounded as he waited for the answer from the gods.

"You have lived an interesting life," said Kiji, whose voice sounded like the beating of wings, both feathered and leather. "You've soared as high as a dandelion seed riding the wind above the clouds; you've dived as deep as a cruben cruising the currents far beneath the waves."

"You betrayed reluctantly; you loved passionately; you sacrificed the affections of your children and wives; you were also a good father and husband; you defeated a tyrant; you brought peace to Dara; thousands died because of you; millions more were saved because of you; you tried to balance and accommodate competing interests; you strove to speak for those without a voice and wield power for those without influence," said Fithowéo, the blind god of war as well as the club maiden for the All-Father. "You know the world isn't perfect, but you've never ceased to believe that it could be perfected."

"Yet Dara is changing," said Lutho-Tazu, the trickster duo, wise and cunning, calculating and uncertain. "For all of us, mortal and immortal, change is the only constant. A new era requires new heroes; new pilots must guide Dara through the Wall of Storms."

Kuni knelt down before the gods. "I submit myself to the judgment of history."

"Go not gentle into the eternal storm," all the gods said together.

Kuni opened his eyes.

He had waited for this opportunity since the moment he had scraped that rusty nail into his flesh. He had planned to make himself so ill that the Lyucu would not place him in a cage, so that he would retain the element of surprise. He had wanted to free himself from being used as a bargaining chip by the Lyucu, to be near his loved ones one more time, to deliver a message.

With a sudden surge of power, Kuni pushed away the Lyucu guards holding him up and rolled along the deck until he was right on the edge. He scrambled onto the gunwale and barely stopped himself from tumbling overboard as he swayed on the narrow ledge.

The Lyucu guards shouted but none dared to approach lest Kuni let go and kill himself right in front of their eyes.

The warriors of Dara held their breath, in the air, on the ground, at sea.

It was so quiet. Even the waves seemed to lower their incessant murmur for a moment.

"People of Dara," Kuni cried out. He was using every ounce of his strength to project, and the speaking tube at the side of the ship, intended to allow the pékyu to issue orders to the rest of the fleet and connected through a system of tubes to the bone trumpet at the top of the main mast, magnified his voice, which the winds carried far and wide.

"I have sinned in my time. I have stood by as innocent men and women died for nonexistent crimes, and I have watched the helpless suffer while I saved my strength for another day. I betrayed a man as dear as my brother in the service of what I believed was a greater good, and I took petty vengeance on those who treated me ill in the past. Too often have I made decisions based on the long view, thinking that immediate sacrifices were acceptable for some ideal on the horizon."

A wave of vertigo surged through him and he had to pause. He wasn't sure if he was again standing on top of the wall of Zudi, facing down the Xana army led by Tanno Namen, or perhaps it was later, when he stood against the might of the Hegemon, struggling to see a path to a world beyond slaughter and darkness.

"Though all life is an experiment, there are moments of purity of purpose that demand no justification. Today, Dara is under threat of a dark storm that has no comparison. There is no long view that can justify enslavement and capitulation. When the only alternative is death and servitude, I believe all of us know what must be the right choice."

It wasn't possible for fathers to fight all the wars for their children. It was time for the next wave to come to shore, for the next generation to stand up and be counted.

"I name Princess Théra my successor, and Empress Jia shall be her regent until she is ready to take the reins of power. I order all of Dara to resist to the utmost until the invaders have been driven into the sea!"

Kuni was very dizzy now. The exertion had drained the last of his energy. He looked down and seemed to see the figure of Mata Zyndu smiling and waving to him from under the sea, as though he approved of his speech.

"Thank you, brother," he whispered.

Then he let go; his body plunged into the waves and did not emerge again.

Watching from a hidden observation post located in one of the shoreside caves, Théra, surrounded by a small detachment of palace guards, heard the speech and witnessed the death of her father as the surprised cry of sailors rippled from the pékyu's flagship.

She stuffed her long sleeves into her mouth and bit down hard to prevent herself from crying out in shock and grief. But she was now the Empress Regnant of Dara, and empresses did not cry.

She wished she had been allowed to ride up in one of the airships. She would wield the new weapons she and Zomi had devised and kill Pékyu Tenryo herself.

CHAPTER FIFTY-NINE

BATTLE OF ZATHIN GULF, PART I

ZATHIN GULF: THE TENTH MONTH IN THE TWELFTH
YEAR OF THE REIGN OF FOUR PLACID SEAS.

The calm before the storm broke.

The Lyucu warriors on the decks of the city-ships banged their clubs and axes against each other, creating thunderous waves of noise. The garinafins reared and dove at the airships as their riders ululated their war cries.

"Archers, fire at will!" Dafiro gave the order, and it was passed to the other airships by flag signal.

Archers crouching at the openings of the airship gondolas let fly their arrows. Most of them fell far short of the target. A few bounced harmlessly off the tough skin of the garinafins.

The garinafin riders laughed. Flamethrowers might have posed a real challenge—though Tanvanaki had taught them some tricks for how to guide the garinafins to deal with them—but it appeared that the only weapons these ships carried were puny arrows. The massive, saucer-shaped airships, gently flexing in the wind, were in reality just soft jellyfish without the ability to sting.

As he watched the arrogant faces on the approaching garinafin riders, Dafiro Miro smiled bitterly. Just as Pékyu Tenryo had repeatedly accomplished his objectives by disguising his true strength, the marshal was now doing the same thing.

On each of the airships, behind the obscuring silk screens, soldiers charged with targeting guided their secret weapons to point at the closing beasts, but none of the captains gave the order to fire. Breaths held, everyone waited for the flag signal to come from *Silkmotic Arrow*.

"Hold it . . . ," Gin Mazoti muttered. "Hold it. . . ."

Abruptly, Tanvanaki tapped hard at the back of Korva's neck, and the great garinafin swept her wings forward and hovered in place. Pékyu Tenryo had suggested that, given her pregnancy, perhaps she could direct the battle from the safety of the deck of one of the city-ships, but Tanvanaki had scoffed at the notion. Her pregnancy wasn't nearly so advanced as to hinder her freedom of movement, and she did not trust anyone else to lead the garinafins to victory against these wily opponents.

The other garinafins also pulled up and hovered a few body lengths away from the airships. The Imperial airships appeared to be so underarmed that she sensed a trap.

Better test them first.

She waved her hand, and one of the other garinafins approached the formation of Imperial airships cautiously.

"Hold it . . . ," Gin Mazoti muttered. "Hold it. . . ."

Dafiro Miro's fists were squeezed so tight that his fingernails cut into the skin of his palms.

The garinafin was within a body length of *Silkmotic Arrow* now and opened its jaws. The crew behind the silk screens tensed, ready to fire.

But no order came from the marshal.

The crew watched as the open maw of the beast loomed larger, filling the entirety of the view from the opening of the gondola. Death-dealing fire breath would issue forth at any moment.

Still, Gin Mazoti said nothing and made no gesture.

In the secret observation post, Théra pressed her hands against her mouth to prevent herself from screaming as the garinafin almost kissed the airship before swerving away at the last minute without unleashing a tongue of flames.

A volley of arrows shot out as the garinafin raced away.

Tanvanaki let out a held breath. Evidently, the Imperial airships' anemic armament could be explained by a plan to target the riders rather than the beasts with nigh-impenetrable skin.

However, having observed the Dara proficiency with projectile weapons, the riders were ready for this tactic. All of them now wore armor made from thick layers of hide. Most of the arrows flew wide of the mark due to the powerful swirling currents of air generated by the beast's massive wings. The few that did strike the riders fell off harmlessly.

The Lyucu riders watching from the other garinafins hovering at a safe distance cheered, and their celebration was joined by the warriors massed below them on the decks of the city-ships. Though the vaunted Marshal of Dara had somehow managed to find another source of lift gas, she still couldn't come up with an effective tactic against the garinafins. A Lyucu victory was assured.

"What is the marshal thinking?" muttered an anxious Théra.

Above her, in *Moji's Vengeance*, the anxious crew whispered to each other.

"Why aren't we firing?"

"What is the marshal doing?"

Zomi Kidosu, the captain, stayed calm and assured them, "The element of surprise will be with the Imperial airships but briefly. The marshal has to make sure that as many of the garinafins are within range as possible before she reveals her weapon. She's willing to sacrifice her ship if that's what it takes to maintain that fleeting advantage.

"We must wait for her orders."

လ ၼ လ ၼ

In truth, Zomi Kidosu was only half right. As she looked into the open jaws of the garinafin, Gin Mazoti gambled.

After Dafiro Miro returned from Tan Adü and showed Zomi Kidosu and the other scholars the fire rod of the Adüans, they finally understood a mysterious anatomical feature of the garinafin.

The dentition of the garinafin was generally in line with what one would expect of an herbivore. The six incisors were long and shaped like cleavers to break and chop tough grass and shrubs, and the thirty-two premolars and molars were ridged, flat, and clearly designed for grinding down the fibrous diet.

Even the ferocious upper canines were not too surprising to the anatomists. Many herbivores, such as the sludge-horse of Crescent Island, which grazed on aquatic plants, had fearsome, oversized canines for defense and territorial combat. It was conceivable the garinafin canines served similar purposes, given that the garinafins could not always summon fire breath, especially when they didn't have enough fermented gas stored up in internal sacs.

But it was the lower canines that truly baffled Zomi, Çami, Mécodé, and other scholars. If the upper canines of the garinafin reminded observers of giant daggers, then the lower canines most closely resembled scabbards. Shaped as hollow tubes, each was perfectly fitted to its upper mate, and a slit at the bottom of the tooth, near where it emerged from the gum, allowed liquid accumulated within the tooth to drain. This seemed a design destined to trap food particles and lead to tooth decay.

Indeed, the problem seemed evident to everyone who noticed that each of the upper canines showed small holes near the tip. If the beasts slept with their upper canines sheathed within the lower teeth, and bits of food and saliva were trapped at the bottom, decay would naturally start at the tips of the canines and create the pattern of honeycombed holes the scholars observed.

But with the model provided by the Tan Adü fire rods, the scholars finally realized that the unique garinafin canine teeth were actually fire starters.

Bits of dried grass became stuck in the holes in the upper canines and acted as kindling. When a garinafin wished to breathe fire, it pushed its tongue forward to plug up the drainage slit in the bottom canines, forming an airtight seal. As the garinafin snapped its jaws shut, the force and speed of the upper canines plunging into the lower canines compressed the air trapped inside the hollowed teeth, just as the fire rods of the Adüans crushed the air trapped inside their bamboo tubes.

The result was extreme heat that set fire to the tinder in the tips of the canines. When the garinafin opened its mouth and expelled a mixture of exhalation from its lungs and the flammable fermented gas from its internal sacs, the stream was lit, and that was the secret of the garinafin's fire breath. This explained why, as Zomi Kidosu and the others had often noted, the garinafins always snapped their jaws shut right before breathing fire.

Onboard *Silkmotic Arrow*, as the probing garinafin dove at the airship, Gin Mazoti had noticed that the nostrils of the approaching garinafin weren't flared, indicating that it wasn't taking a deep breath in preparation for fire breathing. What's more, while the garinafin had its jaws open, they weren't opened as wide as they'd be if it was planning to snap them shut with maximum force to generate a big spark.

In other words, all signs indicated that it was only bluffing. A test.

The marshal had certainly been gambling, but it was a calculated risk, the kind that Luan Zya and Kuni Garu both would have approved of. After all, as she wrote in her strategy book, knowing the enemy was more than half the battle.

Having ascertained that the Imperial airships really were as inept as they appeared, the garinafins moved in for the kill, confident that they could dispatch these impressive-looking but useless giants with ease. The Lyucu warriors whipped the Dara peasants who manned the city-ships' oars to urge them to work harder so that they could get to the shore faster for the storming of Ginpen.

The Dara navy that had emerged from the port of Ginpen moved to intercept. The marshal's plan was to hold the garinafins back with her airships and to prevent the Lyucu fleet from landing, giving the nimble Dara navy a chance to do as much damage to the massive city-ships as possible. The success of the plan, of course, depended entirely on the air battle overhead.

Twenty jaws opened wide as the garinafins approached the airships, their wings beating slowly and deliberately to conserve strength.

"Hold it. . . ."

Gin Mazoti's eyes were cold and steady. She put her hands on the handle of Na-aroénna, which was so heavy that it had to be held in a dedicated harness in the gondola. She missed her old sword, with which Kuni Garu had once slain a giant white python.

Could I repeat the feat of the emperor today and slay the great beasts?

She could feel the power of the machinery hidden out of sight behind her, a force that tingled her spine and made her hair stand on end.

With a grunt, she drew the Doubt-Ender from its scabbard and raised it overhead. "Box Formation, now!"

Dafiro Miro leapt to a nearby gong and struck it loudly three times to transmit the order to the rest of the crew throughout the gondola and the hull overhead, and signaling officers passed the same order to the other ships by flag signal.

Women and men aboard all the airships scrambled over the complicated internal skeleton of the massive hull, ducking beneath billowing lift gasbags to adjust rigging, turn levers, spin wheels, and perform the intricate choreography needed to operate the hidden machinery that revealed the true design of the airships.

Coordinated by a fresh round of spinning shanties, soldiers strained and pushed against the spokes of giant winches to wind thick silk cords. Slowly, the giant ceramic ballast balls hanging right aft the gondolas started to shift, changing the center of gravity of each of the airships, pitching and rolling them in midair.

Spirit of Kiji, Heart of Tututika, Resolve of Fithowéo, and *Vigor of the*

Twins—the four airships flying in diamond formation in the middle—shifted their ballast balls aft, tilting up the prows of the ships until they were standing on their ends. Rowers on the four ships worked their feathered oars furiously until the four airships backed into each other to form a box, presenting their now-vertical gondolas to the outside like miniature castles built halfway up sheer, floating cliffs of billowing silk.

Moji's Vengeance, flying below them, rose higher until its top touched the bottom edges of the floating walls to form the floor of the box.

Silkmotic Arrow, up at the top, went through an even more amazing transformation. The ballast ball was shifted until the ship had completely rolled over so that the ballast ball dangled from what used to be the upper surface of the ship, and the gondola was perched at the top. As the ship rolled, Marshal Mazoti and all the other members of the crew in the gondola moved with the tilting floor and walls until they were standing on what used to be the ceiling. Then *Silkmotic Arrow* slowly descended until its billowing hull joined the other ships to form the top of the box.

Rowers in all the airships retracted their feathered oars, which were foldable and collapsible to facilitate storage. More crew members at the rims of the saucer-shaped hulls tossed rigging across gaps to lash the ships together.

The six airships now formed a floating fortress with six gondolas pointing in every direction. This structure remedied one of the greatest weaknesses of the airships: their vulnerability to attacks from above and below, which had been taken advantage of by the highly maneuverable garinafin riders during Kuni Garu's invasion of Rui.

Then the floors of the gondolas popped off.

The Lyucu warriors on the city-ships below expected the crew of the airships to tumble out of the gondolas. However, they were disappointed because the gondolas on these airships were never designed to be anything more than decorative. Their sole function had been to conceal.

In place of the unassuming gondolas and their puny human

archers, massive crossbows that spanned the width of the entire gondola now pointed at the oncoming garinafins. The crossbows were made from a composite of layers of wood, horn, and sinew, and the strings were thick strands of twisted silk. The bows were so strong that they could only be drawn with a system of wheels, gears, and pulleys, and this was the mechanism the crews had been operating as they spun the wheels earlier while chanting.

The bolts the crossbows fired were each fifty feet long, made from the massive bamboo canes found in the cloud-fed groves of Mount Fithowéo. The foot-wide arrowheads were fashioned from thousand-hammered steel, and they glinted in the bright sunlight like the scales of a cruben. These were the airships' true teeth and claws, not the feeble arrows they had shot earlier as a distraction.

The crossbows were mounted on a mechanism that allowed them to be aimed in any direction.

Each of the gondolas had disguised a single large, circular platform suspended from an arched beam attached to the endpoints of a horizontal pole running through the center of the platform so that the platform was free to tilt up and down. A clever system of pulleys and ropes ensured that the platform always remained parallel to the ground no matter how the airships rolled or pitched.

Upon each circular platform rested a giant horizontal spoked wheel free to rotate about the central axis, and it was on this wheel that the crossbows were mounted. Some of the crew stood on the wheel to load the bolts and draw the string; others stood at the rim, ready to rotate the spoked wheel so that the crossbow could be pointed in any direction in the plane; still others stood inside the hull, ready to operate the pulleys to tilt the platform and alter the crossbow's elevation.

The garinafin riders, seeing this floating fortress reveal its secret, felt a momentary chill in their hearts.

However, Tanvanaki hesitated only a second before deciding against calling off the assault. To be sure, the bolts looked powerful, but even if they penetrated the leather and muscle of the garinafins, they would hardly be fatal unless they managed to strike the heart of the beasts—no easy feat given their speed in flight and the toughness of the animals' rib cages. Considering that the airships had time for only one volley before the garinafins were in range with their fire breath, and that the garinafins outnumbered the airships by more than three to one, the odds were decidedly against the Imperials.

However, she did tap the back of Korva's neck lightly, telling her to slow down. Placing her bone speaking tube against the spine of the garinafin, she issued a series of commands, which Korva related to the other garinafins via a series of moans and bellows.

As the garinafins approached, they divided into separate squads and swerved, heading for positions to the left, right, above and below the floating fortress. Tanvanaki was hoping that this aerial dance by the nimble garinafins would confuse and distract the crew members in charge of targeting the gigantic bolts.

But Mazoti was prepared for this. She gave the order, "Firing pattern one!" Dafiro Miro struck the gong twice in quick succession to pass the order to the other ships.

Platforms tilted, wheels spun, and every airship was now targeting a garinafin to the left of the target spotter: This minimized the chances of multiple bolts being wasted on a single garinafin and decreased the possibility of friendly fire.

With a loud twang, five long bamboo bolts blasted from the airships, heading for five garinafins. Only *Vigor of the Twins*, which was facing south, did not acquire a target as the garinafins did not completely surround the floating fortress.

Though the garinafin riders expected the bolts to do some damage, the ease with which they plunged into the tough garinafin hide and tore through thick bundles of muscle was shocking. This was the result of yet another small refinement in the construction of the arrowheads: They were diamond-tipped. Empress Jia had emptied the Imperial Treasury in Pan to supply the marshal's workshops with enough diamonds to construct these bolts, each as expensive as a baron's castle.

Time seemed to slow down.

As the bolts ripped through the bodies of the garinafins, they quickly lost energy and decelerated. The garinafins howled in pain and shuddered, their motions jerky and the riders on their backs hanging on for dear life.

But as Tanvanaki had gambled, though the bolts injured the garinafins, none of them managed to pierce the heart of a garinafin, and the wounds would not be fatal. The struck garinafins just had to curl their long serpentine necks around to pull the bolts out with their teeth.

The bolts, having now lost most of their momentum, stopped penetrating any farther into the massive beasts. The bamboo shafts flexed and something seemed to break inside them.

At that moment, the struck garinafins felt a deep, powerful jolt inside their bodies, as though some giant hand had reached in, seized their innards, and given a forceful tug. It left them with a strange sensation: not quite cold, not quite pain, but a sort of spreading numbness.

Muffled explosions.

Each of the struck garinafins seemed to bulge just slightly. The garinafins looked at their companions helplessly, their wings slowing down.

"What's wrong?" shouted Tanvanaki. But the riders on the struck garinafins looked confused. Their mounts were no longer obeying their orders, but flapped their wings laboriously and convulsively, panic evident in their dark, pupilless eyes.

And then, just like that, the five struck garinafins exploded, turning into five burning, bloody clouds—flesh, bone, leather, viscera, gore rained down upon the stunned Lyucu warriors gazing up at this fantastical display.

Théra was the first of the observers to jump up in joy as the sky turned red with the fire of the dying garinafins, and a faint mist of blood rained down around them.

"Your Highness, stay down!" one of the palace guards warned. "We don't want them to pay attention to you, especially not now, given your—"

Before he could finish or Théra could answer, the deafening cheers of the defenders on the beach washed over them like a wave.

The great bamboo bolts were the creation of Miza Crun, the street magician and itinerant healer of Boama.

Each of the hollow bamboo shafts held an Ogé jar inside, just behind the diamond-enhanced tip. Made of the thinnest glass coated with silver inside and out, the jars were intended to present the largest possible channeling surfaces to hold silkmotic power.

To imbue the embedded Ogé jars with as much silkmotic force as possible, Miza Crun designed a massive silkmotic generator whose centerpiece was a disk of glass about ten feet across—this was probably the largest piece of glass ever created in the history of Dara, and the best glassworkers of the Islands had to make multiple attempts and deal with many cracked and broken prototypes before succeeding. The disk was fixed upon an axis of ironwood and spun by a system of belts and gears powered by windmills. Rubbers made of thick layers of silk wound tightly were then pressed against the glass to generate the silkmotic force, which was channeled by thick silver chains into the Ogé jars.

Once the bolts penetrated the thick bodies of the garinafins, the bamboo bolts flexed and bent until the Ogé jars broke, causing the silkmotic force to discharge.

Tests done by Miza Crun showed that the jolt from the discharge of one of these large Ogé jars was sufficient to stop the heart of a small animal. However, unless the bolt managed to embed itself in the heart of the great garinafin, killing by silkmotic arrow alone was at best a low-probability event. Not the sort of gamble that the marshal would take.

But Zomi Kidosu, with the help of Miza Crun, had come up with an enhancement to the silkmotic arrows.

Right behind the Ogé jar in each bolt, the hollow cane of the bamboo was packed with firework powder. One of the most visually impressive effects of a silkmotic discharge was the lightning-like spark it generated. This spark, the two engineers realized, could be used to set off an explosion.

The use of firework powder bombs wasn't unknown in the annals of Dara warfare. Torulu Pering, for example, had devised floating lanterns packed with explosives and coated with tar that would stick to the hulls of airships, where they were set off by a slow-burning fuse. Other scholars had proposed adopting the design against the garinafins, but multiple difficulties aborted this plan. A tar-based attachment bomb was useless as explosions on the skin of the beasts would only cause superficial damage. A slow-burning fuse attached to a deep-penetrating bolt, on the other hand, would give the garinafin enough time to pull the shaft out.

But the silkmotic spark was the perfect trigger. Not only would the discharge shock the garinafin, temporarily paralyzing it, but it happened at the precise moment when the bomb was deeply embedded inside the garinafin.

Even so, it was hard to imagine a bamboo cane could be packed with enough firework powder to cause fatal injury. However, Atharo Ye, by now one of Dara's foremost authorities on garinafin anatomy, devised yet another way to enhance the destructive power of the silkmotic bolts.

The garinafins, he pointed out, were simply thick layers of flesh wrapped around flammable bags of fermented gas. If the explosion caused by the discharge of the Ogé jar could be channeled to the gas sacs . . .

That was why the silkmotic arrows were also made with hollow tips and packed with thin nails that, upon the explosion of the firework powder, would burrow hundreds of channels into the viscera of the struck garinafin, maximizing the chance that one of the internal gas sacs would be breached to begin a chain reaction of fiery explosions inside their bodies.

The marshal had expressed great admiration for the ingenuity of Théra's engineering team.

"Zomi deserves most of the credit," the princess said.

"How did you come up with such inventive weapons in such a short time?" asked the marshal.

"Necessity," said Zomi. Then she added, by way of explanation, "Engineering is a lot like the evolution of Ano logograms. We put existing components together to achieve a new purpose, recycle old ideas to express something new."

"That sounds like the sentiments of an old friend," said Gin.

Zomi nodded as they both thought about Luan Zyaji, who had taught Zomi to see the beauty of both engineering and Classical Ano in these terms.

"I know he would be very proud of you," said Gin.

"And he would admire what you've done," said Zomi. "Just as we've assembled a collection of odds and ends into a new weapon system, you've assembled a collection of individuals who no one thought belonged together—street magician, princess, failed rebel, renowned scholar, disgraced official, just to name a few—into a real team."

Tanvanaki watched in disbelief as five garinafins were destroyed in an instant. She immediately placed her speaking trumpet against the back of the neck of Korva and started to order a retreat.

But a long, piercing bone trumpet blast blared from the deck of *Pride of Ukyu*, far below her on the surface of the sea: It was the call for the garinafin riders to press their assault, regardless of cost.

Tanvanaki looked down, and even in the crowd milling about on the ship, she easily picked out the eyes of her father: cold, determined, and relentless.

Wherever I point, you must attack.

Tanvanaki sighed, pressed her speaking tube into Korva's neck, and ordered another assault. But once again, she told Korva to hang back.

ഌ ~ ഌ ~

Even the cheering crew on the airships had to admire the courage of the garinafin riders. Despite the death of so many of their comrades, they didn't even hesitate as they rallied their stunned mounts, swooped around, and rushed to attack the airships a second time. The airship crews had expected the Lyucu would at least be temporarily demoralized by the shocking power of the silkmotic bolts.

Only Marshal Mazoti did not find the response surprising. An immediate follow-up assault was actually very sound tactics. The machinery for launching the silkmotic bolts was so cumbersome that reloading the giant crossbow would take some time. The lull right after a volley of bolts was the perfect time to attack, when the airships would be defenseless.

But the marshal had one more trick up her sleeves.

"Gaggers, get in position!" she ordered.

Dafiro Miro banged on the gong to pass the order on to the other ships.

Crew members scrambled over the sheer, billowing cliffs of the floating fortress, climbing into arrow slits placed in strategic locations in the hulls. They waited, ready for the assault.

The garinafins were within range.

The crossbows remained empty.

The jaws of the garinafins gaped wide, ready to snap shut for the sparks that would start the fire breath.

And a barrage of arrows—shot from regular longbows—streaked at them from the arrow slits, aiming for the wide-open mouths of the garinafins.

The garinafins ignored them. From experience, the beasts knew that ordinary arrows had no effect on them. Even the inner lining of the mouths of the garinafins, who were used to a diet of thorny, tough scrubland vegetation, was practically immune to most Dara weaponry. They beat their wings even faster, the gap between them and the airships rapidly closing.

Many of the arrows struck the thick hide of the garinafins and fell off harmlessly; others struck the insides of their open maws. As the beasts had expected, they felt nothing.

But then they realized that something was wrong.

As soon as the arrows struck the hard inner lining of the garina-fin oral cavity, they began to unfold and expand. Like a stick insect unfurling itself to take on the appearance of a branch with many twigs, the arrows split into segments and struts that braced against each other, securely lodged behind the teeth of the yawning garinafins.

These collapsible bamboo caltrops were designed using the same principles that lay behind Luan Zyaji's collapsible balloon and the folding framework for the ghost airships launched from the mechanical crubens during the Imperial invasion of Rui. Once fully expanded, they made it impossible for the garinafins to close their jaws, and those who tried to bite down hard suffered such pain that their pitiable howls filled the air.

Dara soldiers and sailors observing the aerial combat cheered again as the garinafins swooped away, unable to launch their fire breaths. The bamboo caltrops were such simple devices; yet, when coupled with detailed knowledge about the garinafins, they disarmed the beasts.

Some of the garinafin riders started to climb up the long necks of their mounts in bold attempts to dislodge the caltrops manually, but the devious contraptions were designed to resist such efforts, and as the riders tried to smash through the caltrops with war clubs, the pained garinafins shook their heads angrily, and the riders were tossed off and fell to their deaths screaming.

Tanvanaki decided that she could not afford to wait. Even if the riders succeeded in removing the caltrops, which seemed unlikely and would take time, the airships would take advantage of the delay to rearm themselves. She could see that airship crews were already hurrying to winch back their gigantic crossbows and reload them.

She pressed her bone speaking tube against the back of Korva's neck and spoke an order that she thought she would never have to give:

Talons.

Korva repeated the order to the other garinafins with mournful bellows.

In traditional garinafin warfare, this was an order given only in desperation. Only a pilot whose mount had exhausted almost all supply of fermented gas and could not maintain flight or fire breath would resort to fighting with the last weapons possessed by her mount: teeth and talons—and the garinafins right now lacked even teeth.

Yet Princess Vadyu's order wasn't completely insensible. The airships, after all, were fragile constructions of silk and bamboo, lacking the tough leather and flesh that armored the garinafins. They could hardly withstand a direct strike from the powerful beasts.

Most of the garinafins were still too pain-addled to respond, but a massive brown garinafin now approached *Spirit of Kiji*, one of the airships forming a wall of the box formation, her talons leading the way as she folded her wings in a killing dive.

The airship crew tried to work even faster at winching back the crossbow. The pilot of the garinafin whistled sharply, and the other riders on the garinafin's back let loose a barrage of hard, round stones with their slingshots. Several of the crossbowers fell down, their skulls crushed by the missiles. Another screamed as her left arm hung uselessly, broken.

A few women emerged from the hull to take the place of their fallen and injured comrades, and more arrows flew from the arrow slits, but most bounced harmlessly off the riders' tough leather armor.

"Now!" the pilot shouted into the speaking tube pressed against her mount's neck.

She and the rest of her crew braced themselves against the harnesses and atop the saddles as the garinafin reared up, her powerful wings generating a wild, turbulent storm, and reached out with her left claw, slashing the sharp talons across the billowing hull of *Spirit of Kiji*.

Instantly, a massive gash appeared in the silk-and-bamboo hull. Bamboo girders snapped like toothpicks, and lift gasbags lay exposed like the swim bladders of a great fish.

"Compensate for *Kiji*'s loss of lift," Mazoti shouted from within *Silkmotic Arrow*. All the airships were connected together in this formation, and *Kiji* threatened to drag the whole formation down. "Rescue survivors if you can, but get those crossbows loaded!"

The brown garinafin continued to tear and rip at the hull of *Spirit of Kiji*. Gasbags popped like the soap bubbles blown by children in summer. Crew tumbled from the widening gash like pearls spilling out of a ripped pouch; screaming, they fell to their deaths in the raging waves below.

As the crews of the other airships scrambled to help the crew of *Spirit of Kiji* escape their dying craft and adjusted the gasbags in their own ships to maintain the stability of the overall formation, everyone held their collective breath. If a spark appeared now, all the Imperial airships would be doomed.

The garinafin ripped away the last of the gasbags on this side of the ship, and, with a triumphant series of bellows, flapped her wings and backed away. What was left of the billowing, bulky frame of *Spirit of Kiji* was now too heavy to be supported by the other ships. Slowly, the box formation began to sink toward the sea.

"We have to detach!" shouted Dafiro Miro.

Gin Mazoti nodded, her face grim. Not all the crew of *Spirit of Kiji* had been rescued, but loss of altitude was fatal to the rest of the fleet. Dafiro gave the order by banging a pattern on the gongs.

Crew members at the rims of the hulls of the other ships climbed to the very edges and cut the cables that kept *Spirit of Kiji* attached to her sister ships.

Slowly but inexorably, *Spirit of Kiji* separated from the box formation and fell toward the ocean, taking with it about a dozen crew members who had refused to abandon their places at the massive crossbow, including the captain. The desperate crews of the other airships tossed out silken ropes to the sinking hulk, hoping to rescue as many of their comrades as possible. But the crossbowers shook their heads, refusing to reach for the lines.

"Ready to fire!" Mota Kiphi, the targeting officer, reported to Captain Mué Atamu of *Spirit of Kiji*. He was one of the few men who served aboard the airship, as his extraordinary strength compensated for his relatively heavier weight.

The platform jerked wildly as the ship swung from side to side, trying to balance itself. The crossbow crew stumbled and several fell.

Captain Atamu, an old veteran of the Chrysanthemum-Dandelion War, held on to a spoke for the crossbow wheel and nodded. "Let's make this count!"

Because the few crossbowers who remained were far fewer than a full complement, turning the wheel was a slow and laborious process made possible only by Mota Kiphi's extraordinary strength. He guided and rallied his comrades until the massive crossbow was pointing at a tan garinafin with light green stripes gliding away from them.

"Stop!" shouted Mota. Then he swallowed nervously and asked, "Captain, do you think they'll remember us in the future like they remember the Hegemon?"

Captain Atamu looked at him. Mota was so young, so hopelessly in love with the idea of history. She looked at the other crossbowers, all of them looking expectantly back. The yearning in their eyes broke the old captain's heart.

She kept her voice gentle as she said to them, "Probably not. Most soldiers who die are quickly forgotten. But we don't fight to leave a name; we fight because it's the right thing to do."

"Oh," said Mota, disappointment making him slump at the wheel. "I was hoping for a song."

"Not all heroes need songs composed about them," said Captain Atamu. "It is enough that we know who we are."

Then she gave the order to fire.

The bolt leapt from the crossbow and traced a gentle arc through the air that ended in the body of the tan-and-green-striped garinafin. A loud moan. Then the sky was lit up with another fiery explosion.

The crossbowers cheered and embraced each other.

As the doomed wreckage of *Spirit of Kiji* continued to sink, the rest of the garinafins, now recovered somewhat from the pain of the caltrops stuck in their mouths, approached and took out their anger by swiping their sharp talons at individual crew members, ripping some cleanly in half and crushing others into bloody meat pies before tossing them to the ocean. Not a single crew member pled for mercy, and all died with their short swords in their hands, though they were useless against the garinafins.

The empty wreck of *Spirit of Kiji* crashed into the sea, and the small ships of the Dara navy had to scramble to get out of the way.

Heart of Tututika, *Resolve of Fithowéo*, and *Vigor of the Twins* shifted their positions to fill in the gap left by *Spirit of Kiji*. The airships, having reloaded their crossbows, fired again, and two more garinafins were struck by the bolts and disintegrated in the air.

But it was undeniable that the formation was now less formidable than before, and there were more blind angles that couldn't be covered by the silkmotic bolts.

Tanvanaki didn't hesitate to take advantage of this newly discovered weakness of the Imperial airships. She ordered the remaining garinafins, who had been focused on massacring the crew of *Spirit of Kiji*, to return to the airship cluster and attack it with their claws before the crews could reload again.

This was the moment for the marshal's last surprise.

"Plum Formation! Expose the sight lines," Mazoti shouted. "Shockers, prepare for action."

The crews of the airships carried out her orders. The great ballast balls shifted and the airships altered their positions.

Silkmotic Arrow and *Moji's Vengeance* now also stood up on their tails and moved into the same plane as *Heart of Tututika*, *Resolve of Fithowéo*, and *Vigor of the Twins*. All five ships rotated until they were standing in the air, back to back, like five swordsmen preparing to meet enemies coming from every direction, their ballast balls dangling below them.

As the garinafins approached, the thin silk skin of the airships split, ripped, and fell away from the bamboo skeleton to trail underneath the airships like the tails of kites. Deprived of the structural support of the silk skin, the frameworks wobbled and flexed even more, as though about to come apart at any moment.

What are they playing at? Tanvanaki wondered. Again she held Korva back and watched as the other garinafins approached the rippling skeletal airships, which now looked like birdcages holding clusters of eggs. Flaps of garinafin hide taken from the dissected carcasses cradled the vulnerable gasbags, apparently an attempt at some shielding against garinafin fire breath.

Incredibly, the soldiers aboard the airships stopped winching their giant crossbows. Instead, they retreated into the interior of the cagelike hull, where, working in small teams, they assembled segments of bamboo into long lances fifty feet in length tipped with bronze. Then, dividing into two columns, they raised the lances into the air and braced themselves inside the cage, along two major structural members of the hulls like two walkways. Two lances pointed forward, and two lances pointed at the back.

They were preparing to meet the onslaught of the garinafins like foot soldiers bracing with pikes against a cavalry charge, except that the riders they faced had mounts many times the size of elephants. A brutal, desperate measure that had no hope of succeeding.

The garinafins flapped their wings and dove in, their sharp talons extended.

The soldiers on the airships braced with their long lances, their expressions grim.

The battle was about to descend into a primitive mêlée contest in the air, like the ancient duels of heroes sung in the sagas.

Mazoti glanced at the thin silvery wires attached to the bronze tips of the long lances and seemed to hear deep in her heart the humming of the power beneath her feet.

The first of the garinafins loomed up against the front of the ship, its claws poised to rip the fragile frame of *Silkmotic Arrow* asunder.

"Forward Kana team, attack!" Mazoti ordered.

With a collective grunt, the lance team on the left side of the ship dashed forward, thrusting the lance through the open lattice of the hull toward the chest of the hovering garinafin.

The garinafin was prepared for this. Easily and gracefully, it grabbed the tip of the lance and shoved it to the side. Though its jaws were still blocked by the lodged bamboo caltrop, its eyes seemed to curve into a cruel smile. The giant lance wielded by the puny humans was no match for its reflexes and strength.

"Forward Rapa team, now!" Mazoti cried out.

And the column on the right side of the ship dashed forward, thrusting their lance through the open lattice of the hull at the gari-nafin.

Contemptuously, the garinafin reached out with its other claw. This attack would be deflected as easily as the first. Once it had grabbed the two lances, it intended to drag the humans out from their gondola like ants crawling along some branch and toss them to the roiling ocean below.

The claw closed on the lance.

The garinafin shuddered. Some unseen force coursed through its limbs, and the entire hovering body convulsed in the air. The riders on the garinafin felt the same jolt: It was an indescribable sensation, as though some giant skewer had pierced their bodies in an instant and frozen all their muscles.

Time once again slowed down.

The garinafin tried to let go of the lances and found that it could not. The muscles in the claws no longer obeyed its will. The force coursing through its body seemed to grow stronger, as though a million red-hot iron lances had bored into its torso and were now twisting inside.

Lines of crackling silkmotic force crisscrossed the body of the garinafin, catching it inside a web of lightning sparks. The glow from the lines of power was so bright that the soldiers closed their eyes as they hung on, willing the power they wielded to hold and destroy the massive beast in front of them.

Burning patches appeared on the garinafin's body, first on its feet, and then all over its torso. Dark columns of smoke rose. The garinafin convulsed and spasmed in midair along with its riders, puppets seized by a power that they could not understand.

With a loud pop, the garinafin's claws finally freed themselves from the lances. The lifeless body hung in the air for a second before falling, plunging straight down to the ocean below. Lines of silkmotic force still raced and crackled over its body as it splashed into the water, raising up a large wave that drenched and rocked the stunned crew observing from *Pride of Ukyu*.

CHAPTER SIXTY

BATTLE OF ZATHIN GULF, PART II

THE DAMU MOUNTAINS, A FEW MONTHS BEFORE
THE BATTLE OF ZATHIN GULF.

The ascent grew steeper, and Zomi Kidosu stopped by the side of the trail, leaning against her walking stick.

"Do you want to rest for a little while?" Princess Théra asked, concern suffusing her voice. She reached out to support Zomi under her arm.

Zomi tried to catch her breath. "I'm just not used to hiking this far without my harness. I'll be fine." She squeezed Théra's hand and gave her a quick kiss.

After weeks of silkmotic therapy, Zomi was now able to walk for the most part without her harness, relying on a walking stick only for strenuous hikes. She could feel her leg growing stronger every day with practice.

Princess Théra looked at the sky: The roiling, dark clouds in the east were fast approaching. She was worried.

"Maybe we can try this another day."

Zomi shook her head. "We need to get to the open field before the rain starts. Don't be distressed about me."

The two had been climbing the mountain for hours. Traveling without an entourage so as to draw less attention, they each carried a large canvas bag stuffed full of experimental equipment.

The mountainside was deserted. Hunters and firewood gatherers had long descended from the mountains to avoid the approaching storm. The Damu Mountains were famous for sudden thunderstorms during the summer, and it was not a laughing matter to be caught on the mountains during one: The detritus trails left by flash floods and the split trunks of trees struck by lightning provided plenty of warnings.

But the lure of lightning was precisely why they were here.

Research into weaponizing the silkmotic force had been going on for months, and everyone was growing frustrated. Despite the best efforts of Miza Crun and Atharo Ye, exploding arrows that relied on the silkmotic spark as the firing agent was the best that the engineers could do.

Several other avenues of research had not panned out. An attempt to devise a more powerful flamethrower was ruled out early on as it was simply too dangerous given the flammability of the new Imperial airships, which relied on fermented manure gas for lift. Intrigued by the Adüan fire rod, Atharo tried to see if it could be weaponized along the same lines as the silkmotic arrows. However, the resulting bolts, which relied on the fire rod instead of an Ogé jar as the detonator for firework powder, were devoid of any obvious performance benefits over the silkmotic arrows—in fact, they were worse, as the fire-rod arrows lacked the paralyzing jolt that the silkmotic arrows delivered.

"Silkmotic force, silkmotic force . . . ," Miza Crun muttered. "I'm *certain* that this is the proper direction."

The fact that a small Ogé jar charged fully by the massive silkmotic generator could let out a jolt powerful enough to kill a chicken was tantalizing. Working day and night, Miza Crun tried to squeeze more power out of his instruments of healing and entertainment so that they could become machines that killed.

The first, obvious thing to try was to create larger Ogé jars to hold more silkmotic charge. A great deal of experimentation revealed that the capacity of an Ogé jar could be increased by making the jar itself as thin as possible while making the surface area for the channeling coatings as large as possible. However, making large, thin-walled jars out of glass or porcelain proved impractical: They were too fragile to handle and transport.

The mathematician-administrator Kita Thu gave Miza Crun an idea: "While it's hard to build one large hall with a spanning dome, it is easy to make many small interconnected rooms with small domes. The total capacity of each is the same. Can the same principle not be applied to Ogé jars for the storage of silkmotic power?"

Miza Crun cursed himself for not thinking of this path earlier. Connecting multiple Ogé jars together to combine the silkmotic force stored inside each was a trick he already had some experience with. When he connected the jars end to end in a series, the intensity of the spark on discharge increased—that is, the spark could stretch across a longer gap between the two channeling rods attached to the inner and outer walls of the Ogé jars. But when he connected the jars side by side—for instance, by placing all the jars on a silver plate and then tying wires attached to the inner surfaces into a single bundle—the reservoir formed by the collection of jars generated a thicker spark, though it could not leap across as wide a gap. In other words, with the jars connected in parallel, the silkmotic force seemed to have more quantity, though it wasn't as intense.

A large reservoir of Ogé jars generated a shock powerful enough to kill a sheep or calf, though the channeling rods had to be held in such a way that the silkmotic current flowed right through the heart of the animal. It was conceivable that with enough Ogé jars, a reservoir could become powerful enough to kill a garinafin.

But calculations by Kita and Zomi revealed that such a collection of Ogé jars would be much too massive to even fit inside the hull of an Imperial airship. Besides, even if such a collection could be constructed, charging them using the single silkmotic generator would take forever. As it was, the generator had to operate continuously to create a usable supply of silkmotic arrows.

What they needed was a source of silkmotic power that would be strong enough to kill a garinafin in a single jolt and a reservoir to hold such power that wasn't so bulky or fragile as glass or porcelain Ogé jars.

Just as the scholars were about to give up, a chance experiment with Zomi Kidosu opened an unexpected path. Miza Crun suggested that Zomi try out a silkmotic bath on her left leg to see if perhaps the vitality of silkmotic force could rejuvenate it. Just as Miza had used the power of the silkmotic generator to relieve some Faça veterans of the Chrysanthemum-Dandelion War of the pain of phantom limbs, it had also done wonders for cases of paralysis and damaged nerves. If the force could even cause the legs of dead frogs to kick and swim, could it not bring life back to Zomi's disobedient left leg?

Zomi consented to the treatment. Sitting in a sitting board elevated upon blocks of resin—an excellent silkmotic dam—Zomi allowed Miza to run a silver rod attached by wire to banks of charged Ogé jars over the skin of her leg, bathing muscles and nerves long deprived of feeling in currents of silkmotic force in an effort to bring life back into them.

This was the first time Zomi had directly experienced the power of silkmotic force, and she could feel her hair stand up and the invisible force pouring into herself. Bits of paper and dust in the air swarmed around her, attracted by the power the machine poured into her body.

"Hold on to the armrests," said Miza Crun. "This will sting a bit."

Another silver channeling rod was attached to the other surface of the Ogé jars. Miza brought it over with jade gloves, and, as he touched the rod to her leg, Zomi experienced her first shock.

An invisible current coursed through her body, numbing, burning, quaking her to the very core.

The sensation of being shocked by the silkmotic force, Zomi

discovered, was like a faint echo of what she had experienced twenty years ago, when the thunderbolt had struck her and left her leg partially paralyzed.

The similarity between the appearance of the sparks generated by the silkmotic machines and lightning had long been remarked on, but until now, no one could say that the two were the same. However, as one of the few survivors of a lightning strike, Zomi knew beyond a shadow of a doubt that the power of the lightning was silkmotic force wielded by the gods.

Heavy, dark clouds loomed overhead, so oppressive and close that it seemed possible to reach out and touch them. Zomi and Théra busied themselves in the open field high up the slope of the mountain.

On the ground they had erected two winches, connected to each other by a silk belt. The first winch was connected to a large kite made of silk over a strong bamboo frame, as well as a thin iron rim around the edge for collecting charge. The string of the kite was made of silk strands twisted with silver wire. At the bottom of the string, an iron chain dangled into a large Ogé jar.

Zomi and Théra stood some distance away at the second winch, from where they could control the ascent and descent of the kite. Eyes intent on the clouds above them, they let out more of the string, causing the kite to rise higher.

"Lord Kiji," Théra fervently prayed, "please allow us to borrow your power."

As though in answer, lights flashed deep inside the clouds, but it was impossible to tell if Kiji was saying yes or no to their request.

The sky darkened as though someone had banked the fire of the sun. The world seemed to grow smaller while heaven and earth pressed closer to each other. The very air was charged with invisible lines of power.

Heavy drops of rain fell. Théra and Zomi huddled under a flat, low canopy set up next to the second winch. The sound of rain striking the roof was like the explosion of oil inside a frying pan. The kite string, laden with water, sagged.

More flashes in the clouds above.

The iron chain dangling from the kite string began to crackle, and faint sparks could be seen streaming from it into the Ogé jar.

Théra and Zomi looked at each other.

"It's true!"

"Look!"

A large stag emerged from the woods, leaping gracefully through the rain as though not bothered by it at all.

It looked at the two women with a majestic, arrogant expression. Then it walked toward the Ogé jar, still crackling with the power of the lightning.

The two women knew they were witnessing something extraordinary and did not speak.

The stag stopped by the side of the Ogé jar, placed one foot against the outside, and then bent down as though to give the still crackling chain a kiss.

And a giant spark almost two feet long leapt from the top of the jar, striking the stag in the head. The long spark was like a flower made of fire, a spiderweb woven from luminous ether, a river with tributaries filled with star matter. Zomi and Théra closed their eyes. The light was brighter than the glow of a thousand suns, and they could not gaze upon the power of the gods without being blinded.

When they opened their eyes again, the stag was gone, and only a smoking patch of ashes in the grass next to the Ogé jar in the shape of the stag convinced them that it had not been a dream.

"Thank you, Lord Fithowéo," the women whispered, knowing that they had seen a sign.

They had succeeded in bottling lightning, in capturing the power of the gods.

Théra and Zomi embraced each other, laughing, kissing, babbling incoherently. Though they were drenched and cold, the joyous heat of discovery coursed through them, irrepressible. They fell to the ground, entwining their limbs and pressing their bodies against each other as they undressed in the rain; the power that had lit up the heavens a moment ago seemed to burn through the lovers as flames of passion.

Between the heavens and the earth, there was no more fitting altar to love than that mountainside in the rain.

∽ ∾

GINPEN, A FEW MONTHS BEFORE THE BATTLE OF ZATHIN GULF.

Now that they had a source of power that was adequate to the purpose, they still needed a reservoir large enough to store the power yet compact enough to be carried in the airships.

The scholars of Ginpen and Pan worked night and day, arguing, debating, sketching plans and experimenting with novel materials. Fantastic ideas and suggestions flowed to the marshal from every laboratory, but most were too outlandish to be practical.

The answer, in the end, came from the highest and lowest places at once.

With Empress Jia practically making the entire Imperial Treasury available to support the work of the researchers, instances of graft and corruption were inevitable. Two of the palace servants were caught smuggling jewels out of the palace for private benefit.

Their method of theft was both ingenious and ancient. To reduce theft, servants who entered the Imperial Treasury had to change into special formfitting clothing without the benefit of voluminous sleeves and folds that could conceal valuable jewels. They used specially made wooden trays that were too thin to contain hidden compartments. The idea was to reduce the chances of anyone who, when faced with mountains of pearls and towers of gold nuggets, could not resist the temptation to grab and keep a few things for himself.

But wherever money was involved, theft was inevitable. *Datralu gacruca ça crunpén ki fithéücadipu ki lodü ingro ça néficaü*, or "No fish could live in perfectly clear water," as the Classical Ano saying went.

Two of the servants realized that while the clothing they wore had no pockets, there was one natural pocket with a sealable opening that was still available to them. The two servants had worked as butchers before entering the palace and were quite familiar with the capacity of the animal intestine to stretch and hold material.

And so, by practicing with marbles and coins and even chicken eggs, the two learned the art of inserting objects through the fundament and holding them within the colon for hours until they could be safely retrieved. In this manner, they stole many pearls and gold nuggets and even intricate pieces of jade from the empress.

They were finally caught, as most thieves are, because they overreached. One of the men simply stuffed too much into himself, and after the unwise choice of a large meal of stewed cabbage the night before, he gave up the secret in an explosive confession before he could get to the toilet.

The scandal, however, provided Miza Crun and the mathematical Kita Thu an inspiration.

An Ogé jar, when reduced to its essence, was nothing more than two surfaces made of channeling material separated by a thin layer of damming material. It could be in the shape of a jar, a plate, a bulb, or anything else.

Such as a long, flexible tube that could be twisted and coiled to take up as little space as possible.

The scholars turned their attention to the garinafin carcasses still being dissected inside their shoreside cave laboratory: Each garinafin's abdominal cavity contained miles of intestines, coiled and wound up into a relatively small space by volume. The inner and outer surfaces of the intestines, by Kita Thu's calculation, formed a reservoir large enough to store the silkmotic force to kill a garinafin.

But how could they coat miles of garinafin intestines with the appropriate channeling material, preferably gold?

The answer, once again, came from the world of crime. Rin Coda's farseers had many connections to the underworld economy, and the best forgers of Dara were soon brought to Ginpen to collaborate with the researchers.

The two groups made quite a sight. On one side were the renowned scholars in silk robes, their minds filled with obscure mathematical symbols and laws of nature, their spines curved after years of poring over scrolls and tablets and codices, their speech peppered with high-minded aphorisms from ancient scholars. On the other side were the forgers in their workshop smocks, their minds filled with thoughts of profit and wealth and techniques for deceit, their hands and arms scarred from years of working with heat and acid and paint in the quest of giving base materials the appearance of something far more precious, their speech spiced with thieves' cant and the grease of commerce.

Normally, these two groups would never have even shared a pot of tea, much less have much to say to each other.

But in a time of war, knowledge made interesting friendships. Soon, the scholars and the thieves were . . . well, thick as thieves. Both groups discovered that they were kindred souls interested in the pursuit of knowledge, albeit knowledge of different spheres. They complemented each other, like the Kana and Rapa varieties of the silkmotic force complemented each other, and, when put together, generated brilliance.

"I am certain that had each of you been born to scholarly families, you would have all achieved the rank of *firoa*," said Atharo Ye as raised his cup to toast the thieves at an evening banquet.

A few of the thieves flushed with fury, but Gozogi Çadé, the leader of the thieves, gestured for them to be calm. She was well respected in the community as the inventor of the technique for marking the patina of bronze replicas of ancient antiques with the warp and weft of silk wrappings that had rotted away to give them the appearance of authenticity—a very valuable and widely imitated forging technique. "I am certain that had you been born to one of our families,

Master Ye," said Gozogi as she raised her cup in return, "you would have been an inventive and adroit forger."

"Do you really think so?" asked Atharo Ye, and he blushed with pleasure. "There are so many interesting engineering problems in your field! I was thinking of an idea for how to make soapstone appear as jade that I wanted to get your opinion on."

The thieves relaxed, knowing now that Atharo's compliment was genuine, though they were speaking of forgeries. "Someday I will tell my grandchildren that I once consulted for the greatest engineer in all of Dara," said Gozogi. After a pause, she added, "I'm glad, however, that you have a job and aren't my competitor."

The thieves and scholars laughed together.

The forgers in Dara were, as one might expect, skilled at gilding base materials. They could turn a crude wooden carving into a simulacrum of the most precious artifacts made by ancient goldsmiths of Rima, and now they were charged with helping the marshal devise a way to coat the garinafin intestines with gold without destroying the thin membranes.

The scholars and the thieves together came up with the following solution. First, quicksilver was used to wash the inside and outside of the intestines to coat the surfaces with a thin layer of mercury. Next, an amalgam of gold and mercury was made by heating mercury and stirring in flakes of gold to saturation. The resulting amalgam, like molasses, was squeezed through the interior of the intestines and used to soak the outside until a layer coated the surfaces evenly, and then the intestines were brought to a gentle heat to boil away the mercury, leaving a thin, smooth surface of gold to coat the inside and outside walls.

The intestines were then cut into six long segments and coiled up: long Ogé jars with the capacity of arrays of innumerable regular Ogé jars connected in parallel, but small enough to be stored inside ceramic spheres dangling from the airships as ballast.

After they were charged in thunderstorms with the power of lightning, the coiled-up intestines were then coated in a layer of wax to further help isolate and preserve the dammed-up silkmotic force. Wires could be poked through to connect the inner and outer surfaces and draw out the Rapa or Kana variety of the force without a disastrous discharge until the moment it was needed.

∾ ∾

The scene that had played out before *Silkmotic Arrow* repeated itself in front of the other airships. Garinafin after garinafin fell from the sky, struck to death by the bottled-up power of lightning.

"Separate from Plum Formation and give general chase," ordered Gin Mazoti.

The airships separated from their defensive posture and leveled off into cruising configuration. The oars were extended, and the prey now became the predator. They went after the remaining terrified garinafins, who could not understand how their opponent had suddenly gained this fearsome new power.

Another long, mournful bone-trumpet blast sounded from the deck of *Pride of Ukyu*.

Tanvanaki angrily clenched her jaws. With only six garinafins left under her command, the two sides appeared to be evenly matched. The garinafins, however, had lost their fire breath to the bamboo caltrops and were near exhaustion, and their riders were losing faith in the wisdom of this war. On the other hand, the crews of the Imperial airships were cheering wildly at the successes of their new weapons. It was obvious who had the advantage.

But it was her duty to carry out the orders of the pékyu, to fight for the future of her people. She had to find a way to squeeze out an advantage.

Tanvanaki placed her speaking tube against the back of Korva's neck and issued a rapid series of orders that the garinafin transmitted to the others with a series of loud moans and bellows.

Five garinafins seemed to lose their will and retreated from the battle, escaping in different directions, and the Imperial airships gave chase, one after each. The garinafins appeared tired, their movements sluggish. The crews of the Imperial airships cheered and redoubled their rowing, and as they closed in on their prey, let loose silkmotic bolts at the lumbering beasts.

But the garinafins somehow always managed to dodge out of the way, and numerous silkmotic bolts were wasted.

Aboard *Silkmotic Arrow*, Gin Mazoti pondered the tactical situation. The naval fleets were almost close enough to engage each other, and some of the Dara ships were already lobbing stones from catapults at the city-ships. The Lyucu fleet, unfamiliar with such machinery, relied on their bulk to press ahead. The city-ships dwarfed the Dara ships much as elephants dwarfed packs of wolves, or crubens dwarfed schools of sharks, and even direct strikes by the catapults caused little damage.

The Dara navy needed air support. But the Imperial airships were having trouble chasing down the garinafins, and now the five airships were far from each other.

"This is a trap!" Gin Mazoti slammed her hands to the handle of Na-aroénna. "Pull back!"

Tanvanaki's mount, Korva, bellowed some more. Tanvanaki had kept her back from the air battle to survey the tactical situation from far above. She smiled. Her plan was working out perfectly.

All of a sudden, the five escaping garinafins sped up and swerved away from the pursuing airships. They looped up and around, and all five converged upon *Heart of Tututika*.

Tanvanaki had realized that the Imperial airships, when clustered together, could support each other with their silkmotic lances. By pretending to retreat, she managed to pull them apart from each other, and now she could concentrate her forces on a single Imperial airship and regain the advantage of numbers.

Soldiers aboard *Heart of Tututika* hesitated as five garinafins attacked at once, uncertain where to point their silkmotic lances. The frame of the airship twisted and crumbled under the simultaneous assault. Many of the crew tumbled from the airship and fell into the merciless ocean below, their piteous screams lingering in the air.

The garinafins had ripped open enough gasbags that *Heart of Tututika* began losing altitude. Tanvanaki called for them to pull back and focus on a different airship. As the panicked crew on the sinking *Heart of Tututika* scrambled to save their doomed ship, the silkmotic lances were brought close to each other and a long spark arced across their tips.

There was a massive explosion as the leaking gasbags caught fire. The fiery wreckage of the airship slowly drifted down to the sea, all hands lost.

"Charge the frame!" shouted Gin Mazoti as the surviving four airships once again clustered together. Her heart ached with rage and regret. No matter how often soldiers prepared in drills, the chaotic conditions of the battlefield and their lack of experience with the weapons meant that they didn't always respond appropriately to threats.

Since many of the structural elements of the frame were made from bamboo reinforced with steel, it was actually possible to charge the entire frame of the airships. As soon as a garinafin seized one of the airships' support hoops, the crew touched the silkmotic lances to the ship's frame. The garinafin grabbing on to the hoop received a massive lightning jolt that killed it on the spot.

Tanvanaki issued yet more orders, and the garinafins now dove below the airships. With the gondola floors gone and the crew standing on platforms housing the giant crossbows, Tanvanaki gambled that the platforms would be free of the deadly force that was killing her garinafins and become the vulnerable underbellies of the airships.

But the airships tossed out long chains of iron that dangled far beneath them. Like the tentacles of some aerial jellyfish, whenever pairs of charged chains touched some hovering garinafin or rider, long, massive sparks flew between them, accompanied by a boom as loud as thunder. Just like the deadly drifting jellyfish caught and disabled their fishy prey, the airships now caught and killed the straggling garinafins with their deadly chains and crackling lances.

Two surviving garinafins finally lost their will to fight, and, ignoring the orders of their pilots, fled from the battle and tried to land on the city-ships. As the pékyu cursed and shouted in anger, Lyucu warriors scrambled out of the way on the open decks as the massive, winged beasts crashed down, killing many and damaging the ships in the process.

Princess Vadyu, Flash-of-the-Garinafin, looked at the sight around her in disbelief. The sea bobbed with the carcasses of garinafins who had died from lightning strikes and the smoking remains of those who had exploded from silkmotic arrows. Of the twenty garinafins who had accompanied the invasion force, only Korva was left in the air.

Four more Imperial airships remained, and now they descended toward the fleet of city-ships, intent on dealing death to the Lyucu crew with their silkmotic tentacles.

"The gods of Dara are with us today!" they shouted in unison.

The Lyucu warriors arrayed on the wide-open decks banged their clubs against each other, fearless, but it was clear that the tide of battle had turned against the Lyucu.

"What should we do?" Korva's crew asked her. Tanvanaki had never heard their voices filled with such despair.

Tanvanaki considered the question. Korva still had fire breath, but it was impossible for one garinafin to take on four Imperial airships, especially not when they had the aid of such powerful weapons.

With a howl of rage, she kicked hard at Korva's neck and turned her to the distant ramparts of Ginpen.

"We'll burn this city to the ground and show them that the Lyucu are not afraid to die!"

ও ২ ও ২

Doru Solofi and Noda Mi stood alone in the pilothouse of *Whirlpool Runner*, the largest of the ragtag fleet of merchantmen that had been converted into auxiliary warships for the nonce.

Though the two failed rebels had pledged their lives to the cause of Dara, swearing that they wanted to redeem their stained names, the marshal had been suspicious and refused to put them in positions of power near the front, assigning them only low-level support tasks where they would be closely supervised.

Somewhat surprisingly, Doru and Noda proved themselves quite capable in their assigned roles. Noda drew upon his experience as the Hegemon's quartermaster and made sure that supplies flowed smoothly to the marshal's navy and army, and Doru blustered and intimidated the merchants into "volunteering" their ships to the Imperial war effort—Gin suspected that both also managed to skim some profit for themselves in the process, but such peccadilloes were unavoidable in a time of war.

Just before the battle, the two came to Admiral Than Carucono, asking to be put in charge of the support vessels.

"You need someone to command the civilians," said Noda Mi. "To make sure they don't panic."

"We want to do what we can for Dara!" said Doru Solofi.

"Haven't we proven ourselves?" said Noda Mi. "Emperor Ragin always said that loyalty is bred from trust."

"All the others who once took up arms against the emperor have been pardoned and given new commissions; we'll never be able to face them if we don't get our own command," said Doru Solofi.

"All we ask for is a chance," said Noda Mi. "The same way Emperor Ragin once gave us a chance."

Admiral Than Carucono pondered the question. He was perfectly aware that Doru and Noda were more interested in getting credit than in actually doing anything that risked their lives—but all the others with some command experience had demanded fighting commissions against the Lyucu, and he did need someone to corral the merchantmen and make sure they didn't get in the way of the warships. He assented to their proposal.

The main fleet of real warships had sailed out of Ginpen harbor at the start of the battle, and the auxiliary support ships were supposed to follow behind to rescue survivors and support the main fleet in whatever way that was useful.

According to the marshal's plan, if the air battle had not gone well, all vessels in the Dara fleet were supposed to engage in a suicidal, last-ditch effort against the Lyucu by ramming the city-ships. Doru Solofi had not liked that part of the plan at all, and he had tried to position as many other ships before *Whirlpool Runner* as possible, justifying the decision by arguing that in this rearguard position, he and Noda Mi could enforce discipline by catching any ships that tried to desert the scene of battle. The other merchant captains appeared to accept this explanation, proving once again to Doru Solofi that there was no shortage of gullible fools in this world.

Doru heaved a sigh of relief that events had played out otherwise. Now that the garinafins had been chased from the skies, the marshal's air force would deal a devastating strike upon the Lyucu fleet, and the ships of Than Carucono's navy would be able to mop up any final resistance. The auxiliary ships might be able to earn a share of glory just by sailing along and dispatching a few survivors (claiming that they were spies or resisting, of course). This was an easy victory, the sort he liked the most.

"Maybe we should try to sail ahead of the other ships?" Doru suggested. "If we can kill even a single Lyucu survivor, we'll have some evidence to back up our exaggerations later and maybe get our fiefs enlarged."

But Noda Mi's expression was strangely tense. "Are you content to forever remain a minor noble at the Court of Dandelion? What happened to your dream of being restored to the position of a Tiro king?"

Shocked, Doru Solofi answered tentatively, "We don't have many choices. The Court of Dandelion is strong. Our rebellion failed."

"The Lyucu are here," said Noda. "The enemy of my enemy is my friend."

Doru sucked in a breath. "You are . . . truly bold. But they won't be here for long. All the garinafins are dead except one, and the marshal will make short work of the fleet."

"You're shortsighted. By my count, there should still be many more garinafins on Rui. And you know more are on their way to Dara."

"But the pékyu will never make it back to Rui alive today."

"Not unless he gets some help. He doesn't know how to fight the marshal's airships, but we do."

Doru Solofi felt his blood turn cold as he stared at his former coconspirator. "What are you suggesting?"

"Life is all about gambles." Noda Mi's face broke into a sharklike grin. "If the Court of Dandelion wins here today, we'll be nothing more than minor foot soldiers in a war in which we did little. But if the Lyucu win because of our help, can you imagine the gratitude we'll receive?"

Doru Solofi pondered this for some time and shook his head resolutely. "I think I'm done with plots and rebellions, Noda. Kuni was generous not to hang us after all that we did, and this just seems . . . too much. I'm pretty content to be a minor noble with my head attached to my shoulders, to be honest."

"Not for long," said Noda Mi. Before Doru Solofi could react, Noda had unsheathed his short sword and plunged it into Doru's heart.

As Doru's body slumped to the floor of the pilot house, Noda wiped the sword clean and added in a low voice, "Kuni Garu always said to do the most interesting thing. On that point at least, he was right."

The Imperial airships, their feathered wings beating rhythmically, swooped down toward the Lyucu fleet of city-ships.

Below the airships, Than Carucono's fleet headed for the Lyucu fleet at a slower pace, content to let the airships strike the first blow before going in for the kill.

Noda Mi signaled for his fleet of auxiliary ships to speed up and intermingle with the warships, sometimes even overtaking them. The warship captains glanced at these merchantmen sailing next to them with frowns on their faces—clearly the move was an opportunistic attempt to grab more share of the honor of battle from the Imperial navy.

Small pinnaces were dispatched from *Whirlpool Runner* to the other ships, and messengers brought important new orders from Noda Mi to the captains. Soon, battle kites took off from the merchantmen and rose into the sky.

This was rather unusual. Battle kites were most useful for lookout duty; since the Lyucu fleet was right there in front of their eyes, such additional reconnaissance hardly seemed necessary. Still, none of the naval captains paid them much mind.

The crews of the airships waved at the lookouts riding battle kites in the air near them. The lookouts waved back. Morale was high in the sky and over the sea for the fighting men and women of Dara, while the Lyucu sailors appeared to be grimly awaiting their fate.

The lookouts hanging from the kites even held lit torches, a truly strange choice. Were they going to signal with them?

Korva swept over the buildings and streets of Ginpen, spewing fire at the windmills, multistory wooden towers, ancient lecture halls, and dome-topped laboratories. The inhabitants of the city, hiding deep in basements, remained unharmed, but the city was going to suffer a great deal of damage.

The riders on Korva's back had been poised to strike at the civilians of the city with their slingshots, and the fact that the city presented them with almost no targets left them howling and cursing.

Tanvanaki cursed repeatedly. She felt helpless. She had thought she could at least find out where the empress and her advisers were concealed and threaten them—perhaps that should have been her strategy from the start, instead of lingering to engage with the airships.

But now it appeared that even such a strategy wouldn't have helped if the leaders of Dara were hiding like turtles in their shells.

What was she going to do? Korva could not remain aloft forever, and if the Lyucu fleet were destroyed, she would have no way to get Korva back to Rui. Every choice seemed bad.

Shocked voices came from behind her; the other riders had seen something astonishing.

She glanced back at the sea, and her heart almost leapt out of her throat as she saw the Imperial airships explode, one after the other.

The crews of the airships were absorbed with the approaching Lyucu fleet and adjusting their dangling shock chains to inflict maximum damage. After the discharges needed to kill the garinafins, the power left in the ballast spheres was weaker. But it still should be sufficient to deal death by lightning to the exposed Lyucu on the decks of the city-ships.

Lookouts on the kites behind them pulled arrows from their quivers, lit them with their torches, and shot the flaming missiles at the undulating, exposed gasbags of the Imperial airships.

For her strategy, Gin Mazoti had counted on the tendency of all militaries to overgeneralize from their own experience and to rely on their known strengths. Believing the garinafins to be invincible, the Lyucu had not adopted the fighting techniques of Dara and did not add archers to the ranks of garinafin riders.

After disabling the fire-breathing ability of the garinafins, the airships had discarded the silk skin over the hulls so that the crew could wield their silkmotic lances to shock the garinafins. The exposure of the vulnerable gasbags was deemed an acceptable risk because the Lyucu did not use fire arrows, which would have made short work of the Imperial airships.

The marshal had not counted on betrayal among her own ranks.

The flaming arrows crossed the short distance between the lookouts and the airships, plunging with a hiss into the gasbags.

Within moments, the airships burst into flames and started to sink.

Soldiers screamed as their bodies were lit on fire, and many dove from the wreckage. On the decks of the city-ships, the Lyucu warriors cheered wildly, and Pékyu Tenryo laughed with joy.

The gods were indeed with them.

"Zomi! Marshal!" Princess Théra screamed from the secret observation post as she saw the distant explosions. The palace guards had to hold her back lest she run onto the beach and into the sea.

In the distance, Empress Jia sighed and asked her attendants to prepare to set the firewood piled over the dais alight as soon as the Lyucu fleet began the final push toward the undefended city of Ginpen.

"All is lost," she muttered.

Onboard *Silkmotic Arrow*, Gin Mazoti howled with rage as victory slipped from her hands.

The Imperial airships were designed with multiple clusters of lift gasbags divided by baffles made from garinafin hide to provide some measure of protection against fires. Because the lookouts had shot at them from behind, only the aft clusters were set aflame. The ships were losing altitude and pitching wildly, but they hadn't completely lost control.

"Drop the ballast ball," Mazoti ordered as she lost her footing over the tilting floor and fell down.

The ceramic ballast ball was dropped, and the ship wobbled and flexed in the wind. It was sinking much more slowly now, but still sinking. What's more, it had lost the power source for its silkmotic weapons.

The other airships followed the example of *Silkmotic Arrow*.

"We have to abandon ship," Dafiro Miro said, clinging on to a girder.

"If we abandon ship, there will be no stopping the Lyucu," said Gin Mazoti. She looked behind her and saw the confusion among the Dara fleet.

Taking advantage of his role in wrangling supplies for the navy, Noda Mi had managed to have his followers infiltrate many ships in the auxiliary fleet as well as the Imperial navy during the last few months. By now, they had established control over a significant portion of the vessels, executing confused officers, sailors, and marines who couldn't understand why their own ships were firing on the marshal.

To be sure, Noda Mi's people weren't able to control all the support ships or the warships of the Imperial navy, and Than Carucono tried to rally those still loyal to the marshal to respond. But he was hampered by the fact that he couldn't tell which ships he could trust. Deprived of central leadership, ships still loyal to the marshal milled about in confusion, and Noda's ships began to systematically surround them, breaking their oars, ramming them, and demanding their surrender.

"There's nothing we can do now," said Dafiro. "But if we survive today, we can still raise up an army in the mountains of Dara and continue to raid the Lyucu."

"The chances of victory for such a strategy are slim," said Gin. "The war might go on for years, and many more people will die. No, we must make our stand here, today."

She struggled to stand up, and as the ship burned around her, smoke cracking her voice and heated air distorting her vision, she called out to her crew.

"Soldiers of Dara, we are close enough to the surface now that if we abandon ship, many of us will survive. But Dara will be lost if the Lyucu king survives, and so I intend to crash the ship into the pékyu's flagship. You've followed me far enough. None of you need to come with me."

Nobody moved to dive off the ship; they stayed by their posts.

Gin Mazoti smiled. "I never had any doubt. Our lives are but brief respites between stormy veils cast over the eternal unknown, and we must be guided in our deeds by the inner compass of our will, not what others may think of us. Yet now that death has come to us, we shall make this a day that will live on in song and story."

The crew moved to the oars, including Gin and Dafiro. Putting their backs into the work, they started to sing as they propelled their sinking, flaming airship toward Pékyu Tenryo's flagship, *Pride of Ukyu*.

The Four Placid Seas are as wide as the years are long.
A wild goose flies over a pond, leaving behind a voice in the wind.
A man passes through this world, leaving behind a name.

Following the example of the marshal, each of the other sinking airships picked a city-ship, and the crew struggled to steer toward their targets.

The fire singed the hair of the crew, and blisters and boils appeared on their skin as the bamboo-and-steel frame popped and broke apart around them.

Their chants grew more somber and louder.

As the flaming *Silkmotic Arrow* crashed toward the pékyu's flagship, the heat from the airship washed over the deck like a tsunami wave.

Many of the Lyucu warriors dove over the sides, certain that staying meant death. But Pékyu Tenryo, wearing a helmet made from the skull of a yearling garinafin, stood steadfast on the deck, Langiaboto lifted high overhead with both hands. It was as though he was going to face down this fiery falling star all by himself.

Silkmotic Arrow crashed into *Pride of Ukyu*. The frame of the airship buckled, bent, and broke apart. Fire spread to the other clusters of gasbags, and more explosions followed, immolating most of the crew of *Silkmotic Arrow* and rocking the deck of the city-ship like an earthquake. Flaming bits of wreckage rained down around Pékyu Tenryo, and even the few Lyucu warriors still remaining by the side of their lord now dove off the sides.

Gin Mazoti and a few other crew members were fortunate to be in a section of the ship that survived the crash long enough for them to tumble from their rowing benches onto the burning deck. They rolled around on the deck to put out the fire on their bodies. As they struggled to stand up, the chief of the Lyucu attacked.

Pékyu Tenryo tore through them like a wolf through a flock of sheep. He wielded the massive war axe without any concern for his own safety. While the ship burned around him, he seemed to not feel the rising heat or the thickening smoke. With each swing of Langiaboto, he managed to crush a head or break through a rib cage.

Gin Mazoti ran back to the burning wreckage of *Silkmotic Arrow* and pulled Na-aroénna out, careless of the pain as the hot handle sizzled against her hands. Dafiro Miro took off his war club, Biter, and the sword he had inherited from his brother, Simplicity. Casting a grim look at each other, they rushed at Pékyu Tenryo.

With a few more swings of his club, Pékyu Tenryo dispatched the last of the Dara soldiers, and he turned around to face Gin Mazoti and Dafiro Miro. Fire burned around the three like a funeral pyre.

Pékyu Tenryo held Langiaboto aloft and smashed it down against the deck. The entire ship seemed to tremble.

Gin Mazoti and Dafiro Miro looked at each other and smiled.

"It is an honor to fight with you, Marshal of Dara," said Dafiro.

"The honor is entirely mine."

And they fell against each other like three crubens contesting for power in a sea of flames.

Zomi Kidosu swam hard and kicked her way to the surface. Around her, the sea was filled with burning wreckage from the airships and sinking city-ships. The Lyucu warriors, some of them badly burnt, howled with pain as they grabbed onto floating spars.

Just before *Moji's Vengeance* crashed into one of the city-ships, Zomi had ordered her crew to leap off the ship. As *Moji's Vengeance* had been heading for a cluster of ships, Zomi decided that there was no need to keep the crew aboard to steer until the very last minute.

She didn't believe in dying unnecessarily to become a part of history.

The Dara airship crew now bobbed in the sea, seeking their own places of refuge. The confusion among the Dara fleet meant that no one could be sure who was friend or foe, but everyone, Lyucu and Dara alike, was trying to avoid *Pride of Ukyu*, which was now very low in the water and could sink at any moment.

Zomi glanced on deck and saw through the fire and smoke three figures leaping and fighting. Seen through the distorting effects of the heated air, the sight seemed a scene from the tales of wandering bards come to life:

> *On one side, the rage of Dara envelops two heroes;*
> *On the other, the arrogance of Ukyu cloaks a king.*
> *Langiaboto rises, an imitation of the rearing garinafin.*
> *Simplicity and Biter cross and stand ready, two brothers now*
> *   fighting as one.*
> *Na-aroénna the Doubt-Ender swings to life, one legend serving*
> *   another.*
> *Pékyu Tenryo laughs, the prideful howl of a hungry horrid wolf.*
> *Captain Miro roars, the lowing of a loyal buffalo.*
> *The marshal's sword zings, the wild song of a defiant eagle.*
> *Lightning and thunder, tempest and flood,*
> *No force of nature can match the fury of these combatants*
> *Warring over the fates of two peoples and a thousand isles.*

With Dafiro Miro blocking and taking most of Pékyu Tenryo's forceful strikes and the marshal leaping about and swinging her heavy sword through every opening, the two sides were, for the moment, evenly matched. But it was clear that the pékyu's strength was the greater, and Na-aroénna was far too heavy for the marshal to wield effectively. Dafiro Miro stumbled a few times under the heavy blows as sparks flew from Simplicity and Biter. How much longer could the marshal and the captain last?

Zomi Kidosu gritted her teeth and swam toward *Pride of Ukyu*.

Dafiro's movements became sluggish and slow. Each strike from Langiaboto felt heavier, harder to deflect. The marshal was in even worse shape, and she seemed barely able to even lift the Doubt-Ender. In contrast, Pékyu Tenryo's movements seemed to grow only stronger and more fluid with each swing, as though he was absorbing strength from the burning air around him.

"Do you remember how we overcame Kindo Marana?" asked Gin Mazoti. She struggled to catch her breath.

Dafiro recalled the surprise attack on Rui at the beginning of the Chrysanthemum-Dandelion War, when the marshal had assigned him a most dangerous mission.

He smiled at Gin. "Of course."

Pékyu Tenryo lurched forward, and with a loud yawp, swung Langiaboto down directly at Dafiro's head. Dafiro crossed his sword and war club and blocked the strike, and sparks flew everywhere. Dafiro stumbled back.

Instead of coming to Dafiro's aid, Gin Mazoti remained where she was, her breathing labored. The tip of Na-aroénna rested against the deck; she had run out of strength.

"Your marshal is a coward," said a grinning Pékyu Tenryo. "She dares not fight me. You have wasted your life to save someone who runs away from a battle."

Dafiro said nothing. He continued to block each of Pékyu Tenryo's strikes, backing up with each strike. His arms were losing feeling; blood seeped from his palms and made the handles of his weapons slick as the power of each blow from the pékyu's war axe burst the blood vessels under the skin of his hands.

As he backed off one more step, Dafiro's back leg buckled, and with two mighty swings of Langiaboto, Tenryo knocked Dafiro's weapons out of his hands. Biter and Simplicity tumbled end over end, tracing two long arcs in the air before splashing into the sea.

The pékyu raised the axe again, bloodlust curling his lips into a wild grin.

Dafiro cried out and leapt at Pékyu Tenryo, meeting the oncoming blow of the war axe with his chest. The stone blade of the axe smashed through Dafiro's rib cage and became lodged within, and Dafiro let out a blood-choked scream and wrapped his arms and legs about Pékyu Tenryo's body. Blood erupted from his mouth and drenched Pékyu Tenryo. The two collapsed to the deck in a heap with Dafiro on top.

Gin Mazoti dashed forward, and with a mighty roar, plunged Na-aroénna through the back of Dafiro Miro and into the chest of Pékyu Tenryo.

Even with Dafiro blocking his vision, Tenryo sensed the coming thrust and managed to shift slightly to the side. The sword tip sank into his breast but did not pierce his heart.

Pékyu Tenryo laughed. "So that was your trick all along. You asked him to die to give you this chance."

"Every *cüpa* stone can be sacrificed, as long as the game is won," said Gin.

Back when she had first become the Marshal of Dasu, Gin Mazoti had whipped Dafiro Miro so that he could gain the trust of Kindo Marana. By bringing up that shared past, Gin and Dafiro were able to agree on a plan to defeat the pékyu.

"Too bad his sacrifice is worthless." Pékyu Tenryo lifted up the dead body of Dafiro Miro until he had enough room to bend his legs and brace his feet against Dafiro's chest. Gin watched with a sinking heart as she braced herself against the sword, trying to pin the pékyu to the deck, but Dafiro's body slid inexorably up the sword.

He was going to kick him off along with the marshal. Gin Mazoti would have no chance against him one-on-one.

Gin looked up, and through the smoke and fire, saw the figure of Zomi Kidosu. She was holding the broken shaft of a silkmotic arrow, still attached to the diamond-tipped head like a short spear. The firework powder in the shaft had leaked out.

Zomi and Gin locked gazes. Dafiro's body shielded the pékyu completely, and in another moment, the pékyu would be able to free himself.

The Ogé jar within the arrow required some force to break, force that could be supplied only if Zomi got a running start and struck a target head on. Dafiro's body was too close to the deck.

Gin nodded at Zomi, her face calm. *Every* cüpa *stone can be sacrificed.*

Zomi rushed forward, aiming the arrowhead like a spear.

Gin held onto Na-aroénna even tighter, and a smile appeared on her placid face.

The diamond-tipped bolt plunged right into Gin's exposed belly; her grunt was followed by the faint sound of glass smashing deep inside her body. The Ogé jar discharged.

The Marshal of Dara, the dead Captain of the Palace Guards, and the Great Pékyu froze. Bright sparkling arcs crisscrossed the three bodies connected by the Doubt-Ender.

The jolt, carried by the tip of the sword, stopped the pékyu's heart instantly, and coursed through the body of the marshal. She held on to the sword as her body went rigid until finally she was thrown off and fell backward against the deck.

Zomi scrambled over the heaving deck until she was next to the body of the marshal. She cradled the dying woman in her lap. "Marshal!"

Gin Mazoti's eyes were open, but they seemed to be looking somewhere far beyond Zomi Kidosu. "Is he . . . is he . . ."

"Yes, he's dead," said Zomi Kidosu.

"Good," said the marshal. Then she closed her eyes.

"Marshal!" Zomi gently patted her face.

Her eyes still closed, Gin muttered, "Stop, Gray Weasel, stop!"

Her voice faded, her face relaxed, and her limbs went limp.

"Marshal, Marshal!"

The Marshal of Dara was no more.

This was a woman whose body deserved to lie in state and to be given the most solemn rites of burial.

Zomi looked up through blurry eyes. All around her she could see the ships of Dara and Lyucu milling about in confusion. Leaderless, the fleets of both sides were fighting on their own, uncertain as to the tide of the battle. Billowing smoke obscured the deck of *Pride of Ukyu* from their view.

The marshal's spirit might have departed her body, but she still had to fight.

Zomi whispered an apology to Gin Mazoti and dragged her lifeless body to the prow of the ship. Half of the ship was under water now, and the prow was now the highest point. She propped Gin Mazoti up against the bowsprit, which was almost vertical, and lashed her to it securely.

She went back to the tattered canopy that had once held the sleeping figure of Emperor Ragin and retrieved the banner of Dara. She tied it to a bamboo arrow shaft, wrapped the marshal's lifeless fingers around it, and secured the shaft to her hands with a length of silk.

The cruben-on-the-sea flag flapped in the shimmery air over the burning ship.

Crawling over the debris-strewn deck, she found pieces of bamboo and sinew from slingshots that she fashioned into harnesses for the marshal's arms that would constrain and guide their movement.

She also retrieved several lengths of channeling wire from one of the broken silkmotic lances, and wrapped them around the marshal's arms. She searched for and recovered more Ogé jars from broken silkmotic arrows and connected them together in parallel.

Then, ducking down out of sight, she picked up the wires with a pair of bamboo arrow shafts as though she was wielding a giant pair of eating sticks. *Two sticks for noodles and rice,* she seemed to hear the warm voice of her tutor once more.

Wires are like noodles, right?

She whispered a prayer for her teacher to watch over her; then she touched the wires to the exposed surfaces of the array of Ogé jars.

Just like the limbs of the frogs in the laboratories that moved through the water and swam with the power of silkmotic force, the marshal's lifeless arms began to jerk and move, and, guided by the flexing harnesses, they waved the banner of Dara proudly through the air.

Again and again, Zomi touched the wires to the jars. The act felt like a violation, a desecration of the body. The smell of burning flesh filled her nostrils. She had to hold back her own nausea and continue, knowing that it was the right thing to do, that the marshal would have understood.

A breeze dissipated the smoke around the bowsprit, revealing the figure of the flag-wielding Gin Mazoti.

A lone cry rose from the deck of one of the Dara ships.

"The marshal is alive!"

"The pékyu is dead!"

Several voices joined the first, and then several more, until the wave of voices thundered from one end of the sea to the other.

Gin Mazoti, Marshal of Dara, was once again commanding the forces of Dara, even as her body began to char and smoke from the powerful currents of silkmotic force.

As the tattered banner of Dara waved through the air in the hands of Marshal Gin Mazoti, the fleet of Dara rallied. There was no doubt in the hearts of the sailors. They were being led by a god of war who had descended from a fiery ship from the heavens and killed the leader of the once-invincible Lyucu.

Neither was there doubt in the hearts of the Lyucu warriors that this was true.

Working in small squadrons of two or three, Dara ships rammed into the city-ships and support ships of the Lyucu and the traitorous ships under the command of Noda Mi.

The tide of battle was turning.

As Tanvanaki guided her mount back toward the Lyucu fleet in disarray, she noticed the observation dais on the shore of the gulf like a man-made hill. On top of it sat a solitary figure dressed in courtly finery, bedecked in glittering jewels and wrapped in flowing folds of bright red silk: *Could it be Empress Jia of Dara?*

Korva was tired and almost out of lift gas, but this was an opportunity that could not be missed. Tanvanaki gritted her teeth and gave the order for her mount to alter course and approach the dais. Either she was going to turn the empress into a pillar of ash, or she was going to force the woman to capitulate. The battle was not yet lost.

Korva reared up right before the dais, her wings thumping the air around the empress into wild turbulence, whipping the woman's long, fiery hair every which way. The woman had more than a touch of insanity about her.

"Are you Empress Jia, the usurper of the Throne of Dara?" Tanvanaki shouted from Korva's back.

"I am indeed Jia, Empress Regent of Dara."

"Yield!" said Tanvanaki.

"Or what?" asked Jia. She laughed—and it sounded like the raving cackle of a woman who had been entirely freed from reason. "My husband is dead; my son has been enslaved. But I will never yield to you because I am already dead."

Tanvanaki now noticed the smoke swirling all around the dais and the flames leaping up the sides of the towering structure. The entire dais had been prepared like a funeral pyre, and Korva had not even breathed any flames.

This is another trick, Tanvanaki realized. It made no sense that the leader of Dara, the power behind the throne of the young emperor, would sit here defenseless outside of Ginpen. It made no sense that the Empress Regent of Dara would set herself aflame. The only logical explanation was that this was not Jia at all, but some decoy madwoman intended as a lure to get her to approach the dais, which must be a trap of some sort.

"Retreat, retreat!" she shouted into the speaking tube plunged into the base of Korva's neck, and for good measure, dug her spurred heels deep into the thick hide.

Korva moaned and turned away, her wings beating with strenuous exertion as she carried Tanvanaki and her crew away from whatever crafty mechanism the wily people of Dara had hidden inside the dais.

As Empress Jia continued to laugh at the retreating Lyucu princess, attendants rushed out from their hiding spots in the bushes at the foot of the dais and desperately tried to put out the fire devouring the dais. In the end, they had to persuade Jia to leap from the top and catch her in a tarp, an escape mechanism once devised for Emperor Mapidéré.

Korva crash-landed on the deck of one of the last remaining cityships.

Noda Mi cowered at the foot of the giant beast as Korva struggled to catch her breath, her chest heaving like a living mountain. The garinafin had exhausted almost all her supply of lift gas during the attempt to burn down the city of Ginpen. She had barely managed to make it back in one piece. The Lyucu chieftains rushed over to check that Princess Vadyu was all right and to update her with the latest news. Imperiously, she waved them to silence as soon as they pointed to Noda Mi.

"Princess," said Noda Mi, kneeling and touching his forehead to the deck.

"Why have you done this?" asked Tanvanaki from the back of Korva.

"Water flows from high places to low," replied Noda Mi, "but people are always seeking to climb from low places to high."

Tanvanaki nodded. "What you've done for the Lyucu today will not be forgotten."

Then she turned to the thanes who had come to greet her. "Rescue as many survivors as you can and prepare for retreat."

"But the Imperial airships are gone!" Noda Mi protested. "And our ships outnumber theirs."

Tanvanaki shook her head. "Even if we manage to get through their fleet, we'll have to fight them on land without any air support."

"But their army number no more than a few hundred, and Ginpen itself is undefended!"

"That is surely a trick," said Tanvanaki. "I flew over Ginpen and assaulted it with Korva, but not a single fire brigade even emerged to stop the spreading fire. This can only mean that they are laying another trap for us. I won't repeat the mistake of my father's arrogance."

The somber song from the bone trumpet announced the retreat, and Lyucu thanes and warriors on the city-ships, terrified beyond measure by the deeds of the immortal Marshal Gin Mazoti, obeyed the princess's orders without question.

If Gin Mazoti could see the retreating Lyucu fleet from beyond the River-on-Which-Nothing-Floats, she would surely smile with joy. Even in death, her reputation had protected Dara.

Ginpen was burning, and it truly was undefended. Yet the empty city had frightened away the fearless Lyucu princess.

- Since both sides have invoked us, shall we come clean about who has been interfering?

As always, the mocking voice belonged to Tazu, or perhaps more accurately now, Péten-Lutho-Tazu.

None of the other gods said anything.

- I won't waste any time on the disgusting locusts, but giving mortals the gift of the silkmotic force was a bold move. Again, not strictly against the rules, but very close.

- The mortals figured out the secret for themselves. Rufizo and Kiji didn't do anything more than teach and guide. In fact, you may be said to have given them a hand yourself years ago when you struck Zomi. I do question, however, the decision to encourage Noda Mi's worst tendencies.

- If we're going to accept Lyucu sacrifices, then . . . I still can't believe that they've made us two sides of the same coin so that I have to argue with myself.

- Believe me, you can't possibly be more distressed by this than I, even though it sort of makes sense. Chance and Choice are not always so easy to distinguish.

- The people of Dara are changing, brothers and sisters. The Lyucu are not going away.

- The mortals have to figure out how to deal with this, and so do we.

- I hate it when we agree.

- I can't say I would dispute you on that point.

CHAPTER SIXTY-ONE

MESSENGER FROM AFAR

SOMEWHERE OVER THE SEA BETWEEN RUI AND THE
BIG ISLAND: THE TWELFTH MONTH IN THE TWELFTH
YEAR OF THE REIGN OF FOUR PLACID SEAS.

Two small messenger airships hovered next to each other, the doors of their gondolas wide open.

In one sat Pékyu Vadyu, also known as Tanvanaki, Ruler of Rui and Dasu, Protector of Dara, Consort of Emperor Thaké.

In the other sat Empress Jia, Regent of Dara.

The summit here in the air had been Tanvanaki's idea. Up above the surface of the sea, she was free from the worry that the crafty people of Dara might try to attack her with a mechanical cruben. Besides, both sides would be able to see far and assure themselves that no massive fleet was being readied just out of sight, ready to seize either of the leaders as a hostage.

"You're demanding tribute," said Empress Jia. Her tone was calm; the Lyucu gambit wasn't a surprise to her. After the mess Pékyu Tenryo had made of Rui and Dasu, they were without adequate supplies to feed the population through the winter.

"Think of it as trade, if that makes you feel better," said Pékyu

Vadyu. "You're paying us food and clothing in exchange for us not vanquishing you immediately like the locusts that you are."

"That's a rather empty boast, considering how poorly you did the last time you tried to carry out your threats," said the empress.

"We still have more than twenty garinafins," said Pékyu Vadyu. "And our fleet has been strengthened by Noda Mi, who's probably the only wise man who once served you. We were merciful the last time and stopped at the moment of our victory. Do you really want to press your luck?"

Jia sighed inwardly. Superficially, the Battle of Zathin Gulf was a great Dara victory, and that was how it was being spun by Prime Minister Cogo Yelu and Consort Risana. But everyone who had a full picture of the strategic situation knew that it wasn't so clear who was the winner.

Prince Phyro was agitating for war and vengeance for his father, but both Jia and Théra—now Empress Üna—understood that peace was the only realistic option for Dara at the moment. True, the Lyucu were running out of supplies, but Dara was in even worse shape: They had lost all the Imperial airships; the treasury was all but empty; nobles and merchants were grumbling about the long, drawn-out war harming their business interests; the College of Advocates was criticizing the war as not being within the core interests of the intellectually elevated classes; scholars seemed more interested in censuring Emperor Ragin's unorthodox choice of a woman as heir, which broke all their treasured traditions and beliefs, than the Lyucu threat; and worst of all, Marshal Gin Mazoti was dead, and there was no tactical mind in Dara capable of replacing her.

In addition, Kuni Garu's final decree was not witnessed by all, and there were whispers that Empress Jia was holding on to power as regent illegitimately. Empress Üna's and Emperor Thaké's competing claims to the throne generated heated arguments and debates among the literati and the noble families, and Jia knew that the apparently intellectual arguments were really disguised attempts to pressure her and Théra to grant more concessions to certain factions.

It's hard to get a free people to go to war, Jia reflected. *Too many interests to balance. Too many selfish desires to satisfy.*

"We accept your terms"—Empress Jia said—"only if you pledge not to wage war against Dara for ten years."

"Only if you continue our 'trade,'" said Pékyu Vadyu. "And the amount of grains, feed, gold, and silk shipped to us shall increase by a tenth every year."

"That's robbery!"

Pékyu Vadyu grinned. "Our reinforcements will arrive in a few more months. I can promise you that these are the best terms you'll ever get. Do not try our patience."

Next to Jia, Zomi Kidosu, now the new Imperial Farsight Secretary, whispered into Jia's ear, "The people of Rui and Dasu will starve if we don't send them the tribute the Lyucu require of us. For their sake, we have to accede."

Jia sighed in her mind. There was truth to Zomi's words. The Dara war locusts, after all, were partly responsible for the lack of provisions on Rui and Dasu.

Empress Üna had recommended Zomi for Rin Coda's old post and suggested that its responsibilities be expanded. Not only was Zomi in charge of intelligence gathering, but she was also responsible for coordinating research in the useful arts with the Imperial laboratories in Ginpen and analyzing economic and political trends so as to advise the court on looming threats. A true "farseer," as Théra put it.

Jia nodded reluctantly. She was sure that the Lyucu couldn't be trusted to keep a nonaggression treaty for ten years, but she really had little choice. "We agree to your terms," the empress declared.

"Your adviser is clearly very wise," said a smiling Pékyu Vadyu. Zomi, startled at being acknowledged, pulled back into the shadows of the gondola.

"I believe our business here is concluded," said Jia stiffly.

"Just one more thing," said Pékyu Vadyu. "As a token of your good faith, I would like you to leave behind all the jewelry you are wearing on your persons."

Jia's eyes flashed with anger. "What kind of nonsense is this?"

"Consider it an advance payment," said Tanvanaki, her tone insouciant. "I still need to convince my thanes that this peace is in our interest; a gift from you would greatly enhance my rhetoric."

Zomi and Empress Jia stared at each other.

Interesting, Zomi mouthed. *Perhaps Tanvanaki's position among her people isn't quite as secure as we thought.*

Jia nodded. *This demand for jewelry might be some kind of ritual humiliation of an opponent that will serve to shore up her support among the unruly thanes. We can play along—and find out more later with spies.*

"I will accede to this outrageous request," said the empress. "But do not view it as a gesture of submission."

"Of course not," said Tanvanaki. "I'll think of it as . . . a gift from my mother-in-law."

Gritting her teeth, the empress took off the coral pins in her bun, letting her long curly tresses fall around her face; she removed her jade earrings and cowrie shell necklace; she even took off the dandelion pins on her robe. All these she placed in a tea platter and handed over to the Lyucu pékyu on the end of a long bamboo stick that bridged the gap between their ships.

"Tell me, as a good friend should," said the pékyu, "where each piece comes from. After all, I would like to describe them accurately."

The empress complied, explaining the origin and meaning behind each item.

"And your adviser, too," said Tanvanaki. "I want everything she's wearing as well."

Startled, Zomi's hand flew to the string of zomi berries around her neck. "I wear this in memory of my teacher, Luan Zyaji—who you murdered."

"What are those beads made from?" asked Tanvanaki. "Are they corals?"

"No, these berries were discovered by him on Crescent Island, and he named them after me. Please, these have no value except sentiment. I beg of you to let me keep them."

Pékyu Vadyu laughed and shook her head. "Luan could have been a valued member of my staff. It's too bad he couldn't understand the shifting winds of power, despite his learning. Are you really willing to jeopardize a peace because you can't let go of a few berries? You'll always have your memories."

Numbly, Zomi released the string of berries from around her neck and watched as the empress handed them over to the pékyu through the air.

"My son is a foolish child, but gentle-hearted." The empress could not stop herself from saying one last thing. "Whatever political games you wish to play, please be kind to him."

"Farewell, Empress of Dara."

The doors of the gondolas closed, and the two airships departed for their respective homes.

In the gondola of the Lyucu ship, Pékyu Vadyu almost collapsed to the floor. It had taken every ounce of self-control for her not to leap across the gap between the two gondolas to seize the string of tolyusa hanging around Zomi Kidosu's neck. And the baby was kicking inside her, possibly in reaction to her stress and adding to her discomfort.

The tolyusa was a plant native to Ukyu and Gondé, and critical to the life of both the people of the scrublands and the garinafins. A spicy plant whose fragrance and flavor resembled fire, the berries were a powerful hallucinogen used in the religious ceremonies honoring the All-Father, Every-Mother, and their many children.

Even more important, the tolyusa was critical to the reproductive cycle of the garinafins. Females had to consume large quantities of tolyusa berries to give birth to healthy young. Because the berries had such powerful hallucinogenic effects and the Lyucu did not want the garinafins to give birth to many babies during the long voyage from Ukyu to Dara, Pékyu Tenryo had kept the supply of tolyusa all on his ship in a secured storeroom. That was the room that Luan Zya had burned down.

Throughout the negotiations with Empress Jia, the pékyu had struggled to present a false image of confidence and power. Because they were cut off from the tolyusa, the garinafins had not been able to give birth to new hatchlings since their arrival in Dara. The adults were growing increasingly unruly, and if a new supply couldn't be found soon, Pékyu Vadyu was going to be forced to execute some of the garinafins for safety reasons.

But now, the gods had smiled upon the Lyucu. There was tolyusa in Dara.

∽ ∾

CRESCENT ISLAND: THE FIRST MONTH IN THE
FIRST YEAR OF THE REIGN OF SEASON OF
STORMS.

The hamlet at the foot of the towering cliff was slumbering in deep winter.

Képulu and Séji were outside stuffing snow into a bucket to be boiled into water. From time to time they stopped to take in the winter landscape around them. The branches of the towering trees at the edge of the clearing were laden with snow and sagged slightly. They could see almost no signs of the fire that had devastated the land a dozen years ago.

Nature healed fast.

The sound of beating wings drew their attention. As they looked up, a great winged beast burst from the clouds—serpentine neck, leathery wings, antlered head, and cold, pupilless eyes—and headed for the cliff behind the hamlet. To their amazement, they saw tiny figures—people—riding on the back of the strange creature.

The beast swept over their heads and disappeared over the top of the cliff. The two women looked at each other and ran through the snow to report what they had seen to Elder Comi, the bucket forgotten in the snow behind them.

Taking off daily from the deck of a city-ship that hugged the northern coast of Crescent Island, the Lyucu expedition had been scouring the island for tolyusa for weeks. The riders and their mount were both growing impatient due to the lack of success. Usually they limited their flights to dawn or dusk, but with the spring hunting season just around the corner, they took risks to search for the tolyusa during broad daylight. They needed to find what they came for before the minor nobles of Dara arrived on the island in search of boar tusk trophies and interpreted their incursions into Crescent Island as an act of war.

The garinafin jerked and dove suddenly. The pilot tapped the neck of the garinafin to ask it to slow down, but the garinafin responded only by diving even faster. The riders and the pilot had no choice but to hang on tight to their harnesses as they descended at a dizzying speed.

The garinafin landed in a clearing in the woods on top of the cliff and bellowed triumphantly.

The Lyucu riders looked around them, dazed.

The garinafin was standing in the middle of what appeared to be a fresh lava flow that cut through the pure white, snow-covered clearing. The strong smell of fire and smoke only added to the impression. But a closer examination revealed that the "lava" was made from a carpet of plants whose leaves, stems, and flowers were all bright red. The tolyusa was a hardy plant that flowered in winter, and berries would come in the spring.

The Lyucu warriors climbed down from the garinafin, fell down to their knees, and wept tears of joy. In the heart of winter, they had found the hope for renewal.

"The All-Father protects us!"

"Praise be to the gods of this new land!"

Years ago, when Pékyu Tenryo had sent his exploratory expeditions to Dara, one of his ships had tried to pass through the Wall of Storms. The ship had been wrecked, but the supply of tolyusa they carried as a way to speak to the gods on the long journey had survived, washed ashore, passed through the guts of birds and animals until the seeds took root here, in the most inhospitable volcanic rock of the Islands of Dara.

∾ ∾

A fleet of small boats from the Itanti Peninsula closed in on the dome-headed whale to the east of Nokida.

This was the Year of the Whale, and winter was the season for whale hunting.

The whales, fat with blubber, migrated to the southern oceans to breed. Along the way, pods of whales passed by Wolf's Paw, the southeastern corner of the Big Island, and the Tunoa Isles. Fishermen who were brave enough to take up the harpoon and join one of the hunting fleets could look forward to a share of the rich profits to be made from blubber, meat, and whalebone, all of which fetched good prices in Dara.

The rowers on the small, slender boats, each about twenty feet long, strained in synchrony and propelled the boat to glide over the choppy sea as fast as a flying dyran. A young man stood at the prow of the boat, holding up a harpoon like a vision of Tazu.

The boat was closing in on the bobbing black figure of the whale glimpsed through the waves.

"I got it!" the young man cried, and with a grunt, heaved the harpoon. The weapon plunged into the back of the whale and the line trailing from it began to unspool at a rapid pace.

"A strike! A strike!" the crew of the whaleboat called out to the other boats. While the line continued to unspool, they reversed themselves in the boat and began to row the other way as the other boats closed in.

The largest and most desired whale to hunt was the dome-headed whale, so named for its large, bulbous forehead, which contained a large melon of wax that had been prized since ancient times as a lubricant and the base ingredient in many cosmetics. It was said that the whale was able to melt and freeze the wax in the melon as a way to adjust its buoyancy in water—a kind of watery equivalent to the gas sacs of the garinafin, perhaps.

The specimen the fleet was chasing today was a male of average size, about fifty feet in length.

When the other boats were close enough, the crews tossed over cables with hooks, which the harpoon boat's crew used to secure the boats together. Soon, the five boats in the hunting pack were strung together like a line of fish, and the cable attached to the harpoon was about to run out.

"Get ready!" the young man shouted, and sat down inside the boat to brace himself as the line ran out and the force of the whale jerked the entire line of boats almost out of the water. "Brace!" he shouted again.

The rowers in all five boats dipped their oars into the water and held on, letting the blades of the oars act as brakes. This was a contest of strength. The rowers had to place as much strain as possible on the whale while preventing it from diving and escaping.

Their goal was to tire the whale, not to kill it.

This was because the most precious material in a dome-headed whale was not the head wax, but the living amber—a soft, waxy material secreted by the whale's gut. The amber had a sweet smell that was unearthly, and it was highly prized as an ingredient in perfume, incense, medicine, and industry.

Living amber was best harvested by having the whale vomit it up. Since the living amber was far more valuable than the rest of the whale put together, the best whalers learned to tire the whales out with a long chase until they vomited up the precious material before letting them go so that they could grow more living amber for the next season. The whalers were like farmers who picked up after the goose laying the jeweled egg rather than killing it, thereby cutting off future profit.

The dome-headed whale was heading straight for the coast of the Big Island. This was rather unusual—whales typically headed for the deep sea when struck by a harpoon—but not unheard of.

But it *was* very unusual to have the whale continue to swim with such vigor half an hour after being struck. The crews on the whaleboats were rather pleased. The closer the whale came to land before vomiting from exhaustion, the less distance the crews had to row to get back to land. It was like getting a free ride.

As the whale approached the shore, it didn't even slow down.

"Is it going to beach itself?" asked one of the men.

"Just our luck to get a whale that doesn't want to live," said another, regret in his voice. The whalers who hunted the dome-headed whale tended to bond with the majestic creatures over time. Since their task was not slaughter but the extraction of a valuable resource from creatures they intended to keep alive, a suicidal whale was a cause for sorrow.

"Hold on tight!" the young man who had thrown the harpoon shouted.

Plunging through the surf, the whale slid right onto the beach, opened its toothed maw, and vomited.

Great globs of gray-black living amber cascaded onto the beach, having the consistency and appearance of lava that was just beginning to congeal. Children playing on the beach screamed in delight, knowing that this was a good haul for the whalers. They went up to the still-heaving body of the whale to examine the bounty and to see if they could perhaps help the whale by pushing it back into the sea.

The children gathered and stared at the mass of living amber. The smell was pungent, strong, a complex combination of musk, earth, camphor, and herbs.

The mess was moving.

The children screamed.

The figure of a man emerged, crawling on his hands and knees, covered in the waxy substance. He spat and coughed and retched.

"Kill the whale," he rasped.

Then he collapsed and stopped moving.

∾   ∾

The man from the belly of the whale stood before the Dandelion Throne, and as Empress Üna and Empress Jia watched, began his hesitant, halting speech.

"I am called Takval Aragoz, the son of Souliyan Aragoz, the daughter of Nobo Aragoz, last Pékyu of Agon. . . ."

He relied on simple words accompanied by many gestures, but the import of what he was saying was clear enough.

After the conquest of Gondé by Pékyu Tenryo, the Agon were scattered to the ends of the scrublands, enslaved to the tribes of the Lyucu.

Away from the fresh lakes, away from the flowing rivers, away from the meltwaters from the distant snowy mountain peaks, the Agon struggled to eke out an existence in the deserts of the south, in the harsh ice fields of the north, in the barren mountains of the east.

Such was the fate of those who lost. By the laws of the scrublands, the weak submitted to the strong.

In the year that Takval turned twelve, messengers from Pékyu Tenryo's Great Tent in Taten came to every Agon settlement and announced that each family had to supply a child to the pékyu as tribute.

Takval's mother, Souliyan, was actually the youngest daughter of Nobo Aragoz, the last Agon pékyu. She and her brother, Volyu Aragoz, had been spared in the slaughter of the Aragoz family because their mothers were slaves and Nobo had never formally acknowledged his paternity. Still, Souliyan and Volyu were treated by the surviving Agon as their only connections to their ancient glory.

But even the former First Family was not spared by Tenryo's order, and Takval Aragoz, descendant of the last pékyu, went to the capital.

There he became one of the pékyu's grooms. He cared for the garinafins, fed them, watched over the hatchlings, and shoveled their dung. He also got to know the other slaves well.

Several of the slaves were survivors of Admiral Krita's expedition. From them he learned the language of Dara and heard the tales of the wonders of that distant land. He heard about windmills and water mills, about weapons of bronze and steel, about airships that could stay aloft for weeks, and clever men who could imagine and build ships that were as large as mountains.

For most of the other slaves, these stories served as nothing more than idle entertainment in the evenings, but for Takval, they were something more. They spoke of hope.

Then, in the year he turned nineteen, Pékyu Tenryo announced that he was sending an army to conquer the glorious paradise to be found in the distant land of Dara.

Like the other slaves and Lyucu warriors and thanes who would stay behind, he stood at the shore and watched the fleet of city-ships depart. While he went through the motions of cheering with the others, in his heart he yearned to go with them. But his goal wasn't to witness Pékyu Tenryo's triumph.

Two years later, his opportunity came.

Prince Cudyu announced a second expedition to Dara to help secure the fruits of Pékyu Tenryo's conquest—there had been no news of the first expedition, but how could anyone doubt that the pékyu had succeeded?

Takval volunteered to be a rower in this second fleet. Though few Agon slaves were trusted, Takval had distinguished himself with his extraordinary devotion to the care of the pékyu's garinafins, and Prince Cudyu approved his request.

The second fleet launched on a summer morning. This time, besides warriors, garinafins, and cattle, the city-ships were also laden with families—grandmothers, grandfathers, young boys and girls and nursing babies, trusted family slaves—the Lyucu were not just going to conquer; they were also going to settle.

One morning, six months into their voyage, Takval overheard the captain talking late at night with his senior officers. Without the assistance of the clever Dara barbarian Luan Zya, the calculations for the second expedition had been off. They were running out of supplies, and the proposed solution was to toss some of the slaves overboard, starting with the Agon.

And so Takval Aragoz came up with a daring plan. Late one night, he overcame the guards of the watch on deck, stole one of the coracles carried by the city-ships, and filled it with the goods that he would use to bargain for the future of his people. Before they had discovered his treachery, he was in the water and rowing away.

By the time the morning sun rose, the fleet was out of sight. He had no idea how he was going to go through the legendary Wall of Storms, only that he had to get away, that he had to try. He drifted with the current, dreaming of the fantastic land of Dara.

Then a great dome-headed whale breached near his coracle, capsizing it. The whale swallowed him and his goods, and the rest was a long dream.

"What do you seek from us, Prince of Agon?" asked Empress Jia.

"An alliance between our peoples against our common enemy," said Takval. "A bond as tight as that between the garinafin and its pilot against the horrid wolf or the tusked tiger."

"We can fight the Lyucu on our own," said the empress. "We have triumphed over them and we will again."

"Can you triumph over another wave of garinafins, numbering in the hundreds? The Lyucu are coming, and they will bring more of the flying beasts."

"What do you offer in return?"

Takval pointed to the dozens of ovoid bodies at his feet, each about the size of a man's head. These had been found when the whalers cut open the carcass of the dome-headed whale. "These."

"What are they?"

"Garinafin eggs."

Prince Cudyu had decided that the best way to transport a large number of garinafins to Dara was to carry them in the form of eggs. Once in Dara, they could be incubated in batches and slowly incorporated into the army. This was safer and more efficient than carrying only adults and younglings.

Théra and Jia looked at each other.

Empress Üna pleaded with her eyes. *Please, Mother. Garinafins of our own will change the fortune of Dara.*

Jia leaned forward. "What is to prevent us from simply seizing them from you? After all, you have nothing more to offer."

"It took me years to learn how to care for the garinafins. Without my knowledge, the hatchlings will die and you'll never make them do your bidding."

Empress Jia narrowed her eyes. "What sort of assistance do you want from us?"

"The Wall of Storms is about to open—that's why Prince Cudyu's new fleet is coming. When it does open, I ask that Dara send a fleet to Ukyu and Gondé to help my people free themselves."

The two empresses looked at each other again.

We can't afford to start a new war, much less a war thousands of miles away on the other side of the ocean.

"And as a gesture of goodwill, we ask for a royal marriage with an Imperial princess of the House of Dandelion."

The Grand Audience Hall fell completely silent.

Théra barely stopped herself from gasping at the bold request. She looked at the young man. He was earnest and determined, his chiseled features and fair complexion and hair not unhandsome. *But marriage?*

She looked over at Zomi Kidosu, and the two spoke volumes in a single glance.

"We will get the secrets out of him, Daughter. I will feed him herbs to dissolve his will until he babbles like an idiot. Risana will trap him in smoke until he obeys every order we give him. And if neither works, we will torture him until he gladly gives us everything we ask for. There is no need for you to be troubled."

"No, Mother. If you so much as try any of these tricks, I will strip you of all power. We have seen what costs your methods impose. I, for one, am not willing to pay them."

"You are indeed stronger than your brothers," Jia muttered.

"Were you disappointed when Father named me as heir instead of Phyro? You didn't plan for that, did you?"

"No, I'm not disappointed, not exactly. Your father believed in picking the right heir to avoid the fall of Mapidéré's empire, but I have always wanted a Dara where it mattered not who was the emperor. Your strength simply makes it more complicated."

"My strength may be exactly what Dara needs."

"I am still the regent."

"Only until I am ready. I know you want the best for Dara, but there are lines I will not cross. I will solve this, my way."

The sea threshed as though at war with itself.

- Lutho, my meddling brother, I must applaud you. Keeping a mortal alive in the belly of a whale is no simple feat!

- Would you please not shout into my ear? Our heads are connected to the same torso.

- How do you justify this bit of interference?

- Saving lives from the merciless sea is something I've done since time immemorial; it's part of my charge.

- What I can't figure out is how you got the whale to swallow him in the first place. Have you figured out a way to pass through the Wall of Storms?

- Being swallowed by the whale was a matter of chance. It was only when the whale entered Dara that I could practice my art.

- *"Chance." I like the sound of that. Though I can't pass through the Wall, it delights me to know the larger world follows my rules.*

- *Or perhaps what looks like chance to us is calculation in the eyes of Moäno, the King of All Deities.*

- *You just can't let me win, even once, can you?*

And the sea roiled on, an eternal argument with itself.

∽ ∾

Masters and mistresses, lend me your ears.
Let my words sketch for you scenes of faith and courage.
I speak of a hero—queen, marshal, tactician, sage,
She might have worn a dress, but she shed no woman's tears.
Honor, betrayal, ambition, endless doubt—her deeds overcame
words,
To carve her a place among Dara's great lords.

If you loosen my tongue with drink and enliven my heart with
coin, all will be revealed in due course of time. . . .

Inside the Three-Legged Jug, the wood-burning stove warmed the air and bathed everything in a soft, hazy light. A snowstorm raged outside and ice-flowers bloomed against the glass windows.

"I don't like this storyteller," Fara seethed.

"What don't you like about him, Ada-*tika*?" asked Théra.

"He makes Auntie Gin sound like a man who reluctantly put on a dress," said Fara. "But she was proud to be who she was."

"Maybe you can tell better stories about her when you're older," said Théra. "You like to write, don't you? Maybe you'll be like Nakipo of old, whose words enthralled kings and peasants alike. I bet you can also ask Aya to help you."

After the elaborate state funeral for the marshal, Empress Jia had given Aya the title of Imperial Princess, with the same ceremonial rank as a daughter of Emperor Ragin himself, and moved her into the Imperial palace to live with Fara. However, the cynical noted that this nominal honor actually deprived her of her inheritance, as Empress Jia did not restore to her the kingdom of Géjira, her mother's old fief. One might have thought that her mother's sacrifice at the Battle of Zathin Gulf had washed away the dishonor of her betrayal, but the empress was implacable in her continuing program to reduce the power of independent fiefs.

Fara nodded resolutely, and, despite her criticism, soon became entranced by the tale of the storyteller again. He was enacting the episode of Gin Mazoti's killing of Gray Weasel, who had maimed children for profit.

"How's Takval's teaching?" Théra asked in a low voice, turning to the other woman sitting at the small table with her and Fara.

"Not bad," said Zomi. "I've taken detailed notes, but the real learning won't start until the hatchlings arrive."

The three of them were dressed in plain hempen clothes as though they were maids from some merchant's household. Fara loved hearing stories, and Théra was willing to indulge her as much as she could, while she still had the opportunity.

Around them, many of the other patrons nursing a flask of cheap wine or mug of foamy beer were in fact disguised palace guards. Indulging the young princess didn't mean that the Empress Regnant of Dara could take chances with her safety.

"Is raising garinafins really hard?" asked Théra.

"It sounds complicated," said Zomi. "The hatchlings need a lot of contact with humans, and the tolyusa—the zomi berries—help the hatchlings imprint on pilots, who are treated as part of the garinafin's family. Since we won't have adult garinafins to help train the hatchlings, the bond between pilot and mount will be especially delicate and difficult to cultivate."

The Imperial expedition to Crescent Island had returned with the news that the Lyucu had apparently gotten there first and destroyed the natural colony of zomi berries—presumably after taking enough specimens to be able to grow them back on Dasu and Rui. But the seeds brought by Takval were enough to start a new colony, and the empress was helping with their cultivation. Zomi still blamed herself for not seeing through Tanvanaki's trick, but everyone else assured her that she could not have known why the pékyu was so interested in the jewelry she and the empress wore.

"Pilots are never involved in the caging and lashing of the young-lings to get the adults to behave," Zomi continued. "It would con-fuse the garinafins. The individuals who threaten the garinafins are always different from those who bond with them."

"A combination of force and kindness," said Théra. "Sounds like a great deal of politics."

Zomi nodded and said nothing.

They both knew that the conversation was going nowhere because both were circling around the real topic, the topic that they both wanted to and didn't want to broach.

Zomi bit her lip and decided to take the plunge.

"You're really going?"

Théra held still for a second, and then turned to Fara. "Will you be all right by yourself for a bit? Zomi and I have some things to discuss."

Fara nodded absentmindedly, far too absorbed in the storyteller.

Nodding at the disguised guards around them, Théra rose and took Zomi to the tavern keepers' private residence upstairs, where they could converse just by themselves.

She turned to Zomi and said, simply, "Yes."

"Why?"

"There is no one else. Fara is far too young, and none of Uncle Kado's daughters are of marriageable age either."

"Plenty of political marriages have been arranged with young brides—and not even real princesses, either. You could have asked Empress Jia to adopt another noblewoman and make her into an Imperial princess like Aya Mazoti."

"This isn't a political marriage where the bride is just a figurehead. Whoever marries the Agon prince must lead his people with him and stop the Lyucu threat at the root. This alliance is vital for us. The Lyucu now know how to counter our airships, and the only way to defeat them, in the long term, is to possess our own garinafin force—"

"I don't mean those kinds of reasons!" Zomi's face flushed. "Do you only think in terms of politics and diplomacy? Do you really think of yourself as only a bargaining chip?"

Théra reached out and grabbed Zomi's hand. Zomi made as if to pull it out of her grasp before relenting. The two held hands and sat quietly for a while, though their hearts were hardly tranquil.

"Then come with me," said Théra.

"And watch you wed another?" asked Zomi in disbelief.

"Arrangements can be made," said Théra. "My own household dealt with such complications—conventions are just that, conventions."

For a moment, Zomi was tempted, but her rational nature would not allow her to give in: To give up the chance to change Dara as one of the most powerful officials of the Dandelion Court? To give up the chance to seek vengeance for her parents and teacher? To give up the chance to realize her dream of a more fair, more just Dara?

"I can't," she said. "No matter how much I want to, I can't. But why must you give up the throne to pursue a life in some barbaric land?"

"To hand the throne to me was my father's idea," said Théra. "But I have never liked to have my life planned out for me. As much as you wish to change the world, so much do I wish the same, but on my own terms with power obtained by my own wits, not handed to me on a platter. You ought to understand that."

"Perhaps we're both too ambitious," said Zomi wistfully, "like Luan Zyaji and the marshal."

"What we share is special," said Théra. "There will never be another like you. You hear the voice in my heart when I hum a hesitant tune. You're the mirror of my soul, Zomi, my wakeful weakness."

Zomi squeezed her hand in response, too overcome by emotion to speak.

"But our lives should be large enough to contain multitudes of loves," said Théra. "I have never liked those tales that define an entire life by a romance. Remember Luan Zyaji's poem?

"Mewling child, cooing parent,
Grand-souled companions, brothers,
Wakeful weakness,
Empathy that encompasses the world.

"Zyaji spoke of many loves in his life, only one of which was romance. He spoke of friendship, of filial devotion, of amour, of grandness of soul, of loving your work—we're defined by the web of our loves, not one grand romance."

"But Dara needs you," said Zomi. "I need you! Don't go."

"Dara will be fine with Mother and Phyro in charge, and you and Cogo Yelu to assist them. Father has done much to prepare the soil of Dara to accept a woman as ruler, and his work, though meant for me, will serve Mother well.

"I am a daughter of the House of Dandelion, and it's my destiny to seek out new lands, to see new sights, to fill my heart with the rhythm and cadence of another people's hopes and dreams. A wise lady once told me that my flower is the current-riding lotus, just as yours is the fiery Pearl of Fire. You are meant to change the landscape, to pioneer new paths, to challenge what exists with what may be envisioned. And I'm meant to seek a new home far from home, where I may bloom and create a new world. Riding the whale's way, I will go farther than any dandelion seed; I will lead a revolution."

"I have never had much patience with the passive mysticism of the Fluxists—"

"Zomi, my love, discerning and accepting the Flow of life is not passivity. I strive to dissolve the sorrows of two peoples."

After a while, Zomi nodded, but she couldn't help the tears streaming down her face. "You speak of destiny, yet what is destiny but accumulated chance made into a story in retrospect?"

"Perhaps you're right. But this is the way I want to tell my story. I love you, Zomi, but this is what I want. Respect that."

"So this is the end, then?"

Théra shook her head. "Just because we'll be apart doesn't mean that our love ends. You and I will both have many other loves, many grand romances and devotions and enlargements of the soul. But this is our first, and it will always be special. No matter how much time passes or how far apart we are, our love will remain true. We're dyrans streaking past each other in the vast deep, but our shared lightning-flash will illuminate the darkness ahead until we are embraced by the eternal storm."

Zomi wiped her eyes. "You would have done well in the Grand Examination. You composed beautifully."

"I'm named the Dissolver of Sorrows for a good reason," Théra said, her lips curling into a grin. "You look lovely even with tears, like an orchid blossoming after the rain."

Zomi's face bloomed and flushed, and she pulled Théra into a passionate, lingering kiss.

"I did pay the tavern owners to be away for the whole evening," said a panting Théra when she had a chance to catch her breath. "We have this room all to ourselves."

"You planned this?"

"Maybe."

And as the storyteller went on with his tale downstairs and the storm raged outside, the brightest thing inside the Three-Legged Jug was the incandescent glow between two bodies and two hearts.

∽ ∾

PAN: THE FOURTH MONTH IN THE FIRST YEAR OF THE REIGN OF SEASON OF STORMS.

Empress Üna's decision to depart from Dara was unprecedented, and there were no protocols to guide how it should be handled. In the end, Théra declared that she would designate Phyro as her heir and name him emperor during her absence from Dara. Until she returned to these shores, she would once again be known as Princess Théra.

After the coronation of Emperor Monadétu, formerly known as Prince Phyro, Empress Jia would remain regent, and she announced that the reign name would remain Season of Storms in recognition of the challenges still facing the empire and the fact that Empress Üna was handing over power only temporarily, at least in theory.

An empire-wide celebration was declared. Some of the most joyous celebrants were scholars who had long grumbled about the improprieties of a woman on the Dandelion Throne. For them, all was right again with the world, despite the fact that Rui and Dasu remained occupied, and another Lyucu invasion loomed on the horizon.

Empress Jia invited Consort Risana, the emperor's mother, to tea.

The empress wiped the porcelain cup, scooped powdered tea into it with a bamboo scoop, and waited until the water was just boiling in the brazier, the bubbles covering the surface like the foam blown out by fish over a quiet corner of the pond. Then she lifted the kettle off the brazier and poured the scalding water into the teacup, flexing her wrist so that the stream of hot water shot out like a concentrated beam of light.

But there was only one cup.

Risana quaked like a leaf in the wind.

"Why?" she asked.

Jia knelt up in formal *mipa rari*. "The emperor is young and brash, and he lacks Théra's political acumen. He yearns for martial glory and vengeance against the Lyucu, but the garinafin force will not be ready for another decade. We must not go to war until we can be assured of victory. He needs a firm and steady hand to restrain his impulses."

"You are that hand. I will never challenge your position as regent, Big Sister. I have not once attended formal court since the death of Kuni, and I will continue to refrain from all politics."

Jia shook her head, her face sad but resolute. "Then you're asking me to drink from this cup."

"I'm doing no such thing!"

"There cannot be two behind the throne who are perceived as the source of authority. Though Phyro has always respected me, I can't compete with a mother's love.

"Even if you do as you promise, there will be those tempted to use your name as a rallying flag. Dara has a turbulent voyage ahead of her—to keep the peace with the Lyucu until we're ready to go to war again, I will have to implement policies that may be deeply unpopular and offend the powerful. They'll come to you with tearful pleas and sweet enticements to soften your heart; they'll whisper in the emperor's ears that I am hungry for power and that he is his own man; they'll beguile you into supporting his need for independence and seduce him into looking at you for guidance instead of me.

"If you won't drink this, then it will be better for the people of Dara that I do. There will be less strife if there is only a single voice behind the throne, even if that voice isn't mine."

"You speak of hypotheticals," muttered Risana. "You speak of dangers that *may* come instead of the love and faith that *are*."

"I cannot count on love and faith," said Jia. "Those are luxuries not permitted to those responsible for the fate of millions. What we need are systems and rules to channel the flow of power, but until they're built, I must wield power myself."

"Perhaps you're simply in love with the idea of power," said Risana. "And it is Power that wields you."

"That is no doubt what some will say. They'll claim that I'm jealous of the way Kuni favored you in his later years; they'll claim that I want to arrogate to myself the authority that belongs to others; they'll call me shrill and ambitious and paint me as a harpy. But what is my reputation compared to the lives of the people of Dara? I'm content to do what is right and let others think what they will."

Risana sat still and shook her head.

Jia sighed and nodded. "I ask only that you remember what I said and do all you can to help Phyro do the right thing for the people instead of for his vanity."

She picked up the cup and placed the rim against her opened lips; she tilted the cup—

Risana slapped it out of her hand; the tea spilled across the floor.

"You were really going to do it," Risana said, incredulous.

Jia composed herself and gave her a bitter smile. "For the good of Dara, I was willing to watch my lover executed for my plots; I was willing to order my husband killed to achieve victory; and I'm willing to go to war against my son regardless of his safety. Love makes people do strange things, and I love these islands and the people who live in them. What is my life compared to the lives of all the people of Dara? Could you have made any of these decisions?"

Risana shook her head, trembling even more.

"The grace of kings does not glitter like precious gold or shine like gentle jade," said Jia. "It's forged from iron and blood."

Gradually, Risana stopped shaking. She sat up in *mipa rari*. "Big Sister, not until now have I understood you. You're a worthy Empress of Dara."

She bowed in *jiri*, and Jia returned in kind.

"Poison will require too many lies," said Risana. "It will also taint the trust Phyro has for you—though you do not care about trust, he does."

Jia nodded in acknowledgment.

"I will climb the Moon-Gazing Tower at midnight and leap from it," continued Risana, her voice steady and calm. "It will look like an accident."

Knee-walking, she retrieved the fallen teacup from the floor and wiped up the spilled tea with her sleeves before returning to the table, carefully setting the cup down next to the brazier. She smiled wryly at Jia. "We should take care to make the staging perfect—a broken support for the balustrade, a pool of spilled water near where I stand—such details are important in a performance."

Jia bowed to her again. "You will be given the title Empress of

Dara posthumously. I will ensure that the court historians honor your name in the annals of Dara."

"Do spend more time with Phyro when I'm gone," said Risana. "He may have grown up fast, but every boy misses his mother. Your presence will be a comfort to him."

"I promise," said Jia.

In her private bedchamber, Risana dismissed all her servants and maids, locked the door, and sat down on the sitting mat in the middle of the room.

She undressed and cut out the tea-soaked section of her sleeve from her dress. Slowly, meticulously, she cut the fabric into tiny strips, and then cut the strips into even smaller squares.

Her hands trembled so much that she was afraid of cutting herself.

Jia's arguments had been powerful. Risana could not imagine herself ordering soldiers to fire at the enemy when her husband was held up as a shield. She could not imagine going to war against her own son. It was true that Dara needed a firm hand to resist the tide of the Lyucu, and her quaking hands would never be enough to help Phyro, the Pearl in the Palm.

A rabbit cowered in a cage next to her. She dropped the squares of fabric into a cup, mixed it with fresh fruit slices, and slid the cup into the cage. The rabbit sniffed the food suspiciously, but then began to eat.

Risana watched the rabbit carefully. Soon, the cup was empty, and the rabbit moved away from the feeding cup and hopped around the cage, its whiskers twitching.

She could not imagine leaving Phyro behind. The boy might swagger and strut, but he was kind-hearted and gentle. Love made one do strange things, it was true. But was it strange to not want to die, to not want to leave your child behind?

The rabbit hopped around the cage, showing no signs of discomfort or pain.

The tea had not been poisoned.

Risana closed her eyes. It had all been theater. Jia was willing to drink the tea because she knew there was no danger. She had been performing to gain Risana's admiration, to gain her trust, to make her offer to remove herself from life at the court, from life altogether.

She shook even harder. She could not leave Phyro with such a woman, who thought only in terms of iron and blood. She would go to Phyro and leave the palace with him. They would disguise themselves as commoners and live in some forgotten corner of Dara, much as she had lived with her mother before she met Kuni. Jia wanted to guide Dara through the season of storms, and she and Phyro would not stand in the way.

"Mocü! Cawi!" she called out to her maids. "I need my traveling case."

"They won't be coming," a voice said behind her.

Risana whipped around and saw the figure of Empress Jia in the door.

"Your servants and maids have all been called away to receive a special bonus from the palace treasury," said Jia.

Risana opened her mouth to scream, but Jia went on, "The palace guards have blocked off all entrances to the private quarters. No one will hear you and no one is coming."

Risana stared at her, a bitter smile on her face. "I was going to leave with my son. We would hide in the most obscure valley and never emerge to bother you. I would have used smokecraft to disguise ourselves."

Jia shook her head. "You weave a romantic vision that will fool only yourself. No matter how much smoke you wrap around yourselves, the ambitious will find you and turn you into a symbol of rebellion. Phyro would never be content to live and die in obscurity when he knows he is the rightful heir to the throne. He may listen to you today, but will you be able to stop him from coming to challenge me in ten years? Meanwhile, you will have denied him the opportunity to learn how to wield power responsibly from the only one who can teach him. You will have prevented him from growing into a man who can face down Timu and Vadyu and save Dara from the looming darkness."

Risana lowered her head. "I am not like you. I cannot think as you do."

"I know. I wanted you to see the path for yourself, and you came so close to transcending your fears, so close." There was pity and compassion in Jia's voice. "That is why I have come to steel your resolve and make sure you fulfill the role that you're meant to take on, to weave a masterpiece of smokecraft that will save your son and Dara.

"The moon is particularly lovely tonight. Shall we go to the tower?"

Flickering light from a single candle; two women kneeling across from each other in a room away from prying ears.

"Let them call me a villain, so long as the lives of the people are better with me than without."

"You have a flair for grand gestures, Jia, believing that they will redeem all the messy, bloody ruins left in your path. But redemption is but a mirage so long as you persist in your methods."

"Have I finally lost you, Soto? Will you plunge Dara into civil strife?"

"For the sake of the people, I will keep your secret for now. But if you do not give up the reins of power when Phyro is ready, I swear by the Twins that I will proclaim the truth to every corner of Dara."

CHAPTER SIXTY-TWO

PARTING OF THE LOTUS SEED

KRIPHI: THE FOURTH MONTH IN THE FIRST YEAR
OF THE REIGN THAT DOES NOT YET HAVE A NAME.

Tanvanaki had come to him and asked him to choose a new reign name for himself. After all, he was supposed to be the Emperor of Dara.

It was one of the few things on which she bothered to ask for his opinion.

In truth, he knew he shouldn't be resentful. Tanvanaki had her hands full. The death of Pékyu Tenryo had created a temporary power vacuum, and several prominent thanes had made moves to challenge Tanvanaki's leadership. With a combination of guile and murder, she had barely managed to hold them off, and the other thanes had finally acquiesced to her claim as the successor to Pékyu Tenryo only after the tribute paid by Dara and the discovery of tolyusa in Dara. These were not matters in which his knowledge of the Ano Classics could help her.

And now, as he held his newborn son, he felt lost. At twenty years of age, he was barely more than a child himself. The idea that this new life depended on him, much like the fragile new union between the Lyucu and Dara, overwhelmed him.

Tanvanaki had named the boy Todyu Roatan—she did not care for the Dara custom of waiting until the age of reason to formally name a child—but Timu had taken to calling him Dyu-*tika*, and the servants, most of them Dara slaves, had followed his lead. He was pleased. It was a way in which he could feel himself making a difference, small though it was.

But with the peace now in place between Lyucu-occupied Dara and the rest of the islands, there was a chance for him to do more. His skills had always been more useful in peace than war. Tanvanaki would need his help to set up a system in which the natives of Rui and Dasu could live in harmony with their conquerors, and he would do his utmost to show his dead father that he had been right.

Dyu-*tika* mewed in his arms, and Timu soothed him with gentle cooing noises. As the baby balled his tiny fists next to his delicate chin, a powerful surge of love suffused Timu's body. Dyu-*tika* was but one of the many babies like him born during the last year and this on the islands of Rui and Dasu, products of the union between the Lyucu and the natives—however painful and violent and terrible the origins of their lives, the babies were innocent. They belonged to these islands and had a claim to these shores.

Freedom required treading new paths, required audacious leaps of faith. He was going to cast his shadow down the pages of history.

"Come," he said, summoning the scribes of his tiny court. "I have decided on a new reign name: Audacious Freedom."

∾ ᔗ

GINPEN: THE FIFTH MONTH IN THE FIRST YEAR
OF THE REIGN OF SEASON OF STORMS.

Emperor Monadétu came to the docks of Ginpen to say farewell in person.

"Big Sister—" The young emperor was so overcome with emotion that he couldn't continue.

"Hudo-*tika*," Théra had embraced him and whispered into his ear, "don't mar this happy occasion by contradicting my name. You're acting like I'm about to be sacrificed when in fact I'm going off to be a bride and the queen of a new people."

"I've lost my mother, and now I'm going to lose you. My sorrow is undissolvable."

"You're the emperor now, *Rénga*. The people look to you and expect to see hope. They need you to assure them that this alliance is the answer to the Lyucu threat. There is no moment when you're not onstage; you must not let your heart show on your face."

"I'm not like Father! I'm not like you! I was angry at first when he picked you instead of me, but now I know he was right. Timu doesn't know how to do this, and neither do I."

"Do not let what Father or I did confine your choices. I know you will plot your own course. Did you know that Father designed his crown with dangling cowrie strands so that he could veil his face as he struggled with doubt? None of us is born knowing how to wear a mask; we grow into them."

As the auspicious hour for the departure of the fleet approached, the musicians on the dock began to play: sweet silk-stringed coconut lutes, effervescent bamboo flutes, upbeat wooden rhythm sticks, lively stone echo bowls, buoyant clay ocarinas, perky gourd maracas, cheerful leather singing bellows, and—by Princess Théra's request— the majestic ringing of bronze *moaphya*. All the instrument families were represented, as though all the gods were here to celebrate with the mortals.

Théra pulled her brother into a warm embrace and whispered again. The loud music made it impossible for anyone else to over- hear. "Mother has a vision for Dara that is seductive and perhaps even right, but she has a tendency to resort to methods that poison the results. You must learn from her, but when the time comes, you must also be ready to confront her."

"Know when to do the most interesting thing, is that it?" the emperor asked.

"Exactly."

Emperor Monadétu gave his sister a last powerful squeeze with his arms before stepping back, his face now impassive. "May the gods speed your journey and bring you success in a new land, Princess of Dara."

Princess Théra turned around and walked up the gangplank to join Prince Takval, having taken her last step on the soil of Dara. She did not look back lest her tears give the lie to her name.

Back in Pan, the garinafin hatchlings had survived, and now, armed with the knowledge Prince Takval had imparted to them, the people of Dara would embark on a grand adventure to gain the trust of new allies in their war—not unlike the gingerly dance to come between the Agon and their new princess.

∾ ∾

IN THE SEA NORTH OF DASU: THE FIFTH MONTH IN THE FIRST YEAR OF THE REIGN OF SEASON OF STORMS.

Princess Théra and Prince Takval Aragoz stood on the deck of *Dissolver of Sorrows* and watched the Wall of Storms.

Nine other ships rode the waves behind *Dissolver of Sorrows*. The fleet carried Dara craftsmen, soldiers, scholars, books, seeds, tools— whatever Théra had decided would be of use in that distant land to help a people intent on achieving freedom.

"I guess we know we came on the right day," said Takval, pointing at the silhouette of the Lyucu city-ship bobbing in the distance.

"A welcoming party," said Théra.

This was the day Luan Zyaji had predicted when the Wall of Storms would open again, and the Lyucu reinforcement fleet was expected to come to Dara. The Lyucu observers on the city-ship likely did not include Pékyu Vadyu, Théra realized. She and Zomi had calculated that the pékyu would be giving birth just about now, and she wondered how Timu—"Emperor Thaké"—was handling the change of becoming a father.

"They're not coming closer to us," said Takval.

"As long as we don't make any moves toward the new fleet, they should respect the peace," said Théra. "They can't deny that we have a right to observe here in the open sea."

They were conversing in a combination of the language of Dara and of the scrublands. Théra was a quick study, and Takval was a patient teacher. As yet, there was no love between them, only the beginning of a tentative friendship that, in time, might dissolve sorrows and enlarge souls.

She was willing to open her heart and let it be filled with the story she wanted to tell about herself, and that was the most interesting thing of all, she decided.

"It's starting!" she shouted, and pointed.

The cyclones making up the breathtaking curtain began to part. Like a well-trained army going through exercises on the parade grounds, the cyclones drifted to each side, revealing a calm passage in the middle like a valley between towering mountains of water and clouds. Lightning flashed from deep within the cyclones, a fireworks show for a new era.

In the distance, they could see the small silhouettes of city-ships sailing into the passage from the other side of the curtain. Prince Cudyu's reinforcements had arrived.

"Launch the signal kites!" the princess called out.

Massive kites rose into the air from the decks of the ships in the Dara fleet. Other Dara ships below the horizon to the south would pass the signal on. Than Carucono had dispatched a flotilla of signal ships to be anchored between the Wall of Storms and the Big Island like a string of pearls so that Pan would receive the news as quickly as possible.

∾ ∽

PAN: THE FIFTH MONTH IN THE FIRST YEAR OF
THE REIGN OF SEASON OF STORMS.

Emperor Monadétu, still in mourning over the loss of both his parents within the span of a few months, urged for a secret mission conducted by mechanical crubens against the second Lyucu fleet.

"They might be able to sink one or more of the city-ships at night and leave no evidence for the Lyucu to claim that we broke the treaty," the emperor insisted.

"No," Empress Jia said.

"*I* am the emperor!" shouted Phyro. "Not you."

"You have the title," said Jia. "But the Seal of Dara is in my hand. The debate is over."

As the assembled ministers and generals watched, the young emperor got up from the throne and flipped over the table on which documents were piled. He ran from the Grand Audience Hall.

"Let us continue," said Empress Jia to the stunned officials in the hall. "The business of governance waits for no one."

For three days, the emperor locked himself in the mourning hall for Empress Risana and refused to see anyone. Courtiers could hear him cry and mumble inside. Eventually, he emerged and asked to see the empress.

"I am not ready," he said to Jia.

"Not yet," Jia said. "But do not let that fire in you burn out. Learn to govern it."

She then opened her arms and embraced the young man, who cried inconsolably.

All the ministers and generals whispered amongst themselves that Dara was indeed fortunate to have Jia as the incontestable voice behind the throne.

◌～ ～◌

IN THE SEA NORTH OF DASU: THE FIFTH MONTH IN THE
FIRST YEAR OF THE REIGN OF SEASON OF STORMS.

The city-ships were now in the middle of the valley between towering cyclones, coming closer by the minute.

"Should we get out of the way?" asked Takval.

Taking a page from the mechanical crubens, the Dara ships were designed to be able to dive underwater for brief periods to conceal themselves. Realizing that they would have to use the same passage through the Wall of Storms as the Lyucu fleet, *Dissolver of Sorrows* and her sister ships were meant to submerge as the Lyucu approached and to resurface later so that they could continue on their way. The ships weren't designed to be able to propel themselves underwater, but that wasn't necessary.

"No," said Théra. "It's already closing! Zomi was right."

Indeed, the cyclones that made up the Wall of Storms were already reversing their course. The mountains of cloud and water on either side of the passage were closing in with the Lyucu ships still trapped between them.

∽   ᔕ

PAN: A MONTH EARLIER.

Zomi Kidosu was very busy. Not only was she in charge of preparing for the princess's voyage to Ukyu and Gondé, but she also had to evaluate many proposals for new machinery and new policies that Empress Jia declared were within the bailiwick of the Imperial Farsight Secretary.

In truth, Zomi understood that some of these duties were traditionally within the purview of the prime minister. However, Empress Jia preferred to distribute the duties between her and Cogo Yelu. It was either a way to punish Cogo for the way he had zealously prosecuted Otho Krin after the unveiling of the empress's plot or a way to ensure that Cogo Yelu didn't grow complacent without someone to challenge his opinions.

"I trust systems," the empress had said to Zomi, "not individuals. You're skilled at engineering machinery; I want to see if you're as skilled at engineering the system of governance. Perhaps we will give your proposals regarding the examination system a try."

Zomi sighed. The exercise of power was a heavy responsibility. She had to learn to make a home for herself in this new role, to balance her impulses for radical changes with the wisdom of cautious gradualism. On top of it all, Théra had also asked her to remain vigilant and to assist in the shift of power from Théra's mother to her brother over time.

"Both of them will need and want your loyalty," said Théra. "You'll have to be careful."

"You know I'm no good at politics," said Zomi. "Never had any talent for it."

"Let your conscience be your guide," said Théra. "And trust in your love of the common people—they always come first. On that point, at least, everyone in the House of Dandelion is in agreement."

As the day for Théra's departure approached, Zomi tried to spend as much time with Théra as she could. Yet something about Théra's quoting of Luan Zyaji's poem gnawed at her. She returned to the poem and read it again.

Weigh the fish, the universe is knowable.
A cruben breaches; the remora detaches.
Mewling child, cooing parent,
Grand-souled companions, brothers,
Wakeful weakness,
Empathy that encompasses the world.

To imagine new machines, to see unknown lands,
To believe the grace of kings belongs to all.
Grateful.

She stared at the poem, nonplussed. She had not paid enough attention to the form of the poem at the time she first read it due to the freshness of her grief, but now, in a calmer frame of mind, the strangeness of the poem struck her.

Her teacher had a genuine love for Classical Ano forms and was an accomplished writer and poet in that ancient language. But this poem followed no Classical Ano form that she knew of. The ancient

Ano prized visual symmetry, and poems composed in Classical Ano always followed fixed patterns dictating the number of logograms per line. The poems were meant to be recited aloud as well as silently admired as visual compositions.

But each line of this poem had a different number of logograms: seven, six, four, three, two, five, zero (the blank line), eight, nine, one. Why would her teacher be so careless?

True, her teacher had written this on his deathbed, and it was possible that he had lost the ability to compose with care for visual appeal. But Zomi knew instinctively that couldn't be the real explanation.

The poem has ten lines, each line being a different numeral.

Her teacher had always instructed her on the importance of engineering as the art of assembling existing machinery to achieve a new purpose. Was he using the form of the poem to send her a message, a different message than the words of the poem indicated?

Zomi went back to the calculations in *Gitré Üthu* concerning the opening of passages in the Wall of Storms. There were too many skipped steps in his derivations for her to be able to reconstruct his work fully, but all the steps that she could follow made sense.

Her eyes were drawn to a doodle in the margin of one of the pages: rows of dots arranged in numerical order—blank space, one, two, three, four . . .

And she finally understood what her teacher had intended with the poem: It was a code. The number of logograms in each line indicated the "real number" while the position of the line in the poem was the cipher. Thus, zero mapped to seven, one mapped to six, two mapped to four, and so on.

Luan Zyaji had done what he could to obscure his method of calculation and presented false results to the Lyucu. But he had also left a key to Zomi for deciphering the false results to get at the real numbers. At the time of his death, however, he couldn't be sure that whatever information he gave to Zomi wouldn't fall into the hands of the Lyucu, and so he had embedded the key in the poem.

~ ~

IN THE SEA NORTH OF DASU: THE FIFTH MONTH
IN THE FIRST YEAR OF THE REIGN OF SEASON
OF STORMS.

As Théra and Takval watched, the Wall of Storms closed in on the city-ships.

The cipher text in *Gitré Üthu* had predicted a false opening; the real opening, according to Zomi, wouldn't happen for another ten years. It was a testament to his skill that even the false calculations pointed to a temporary opening in the Wall, completing a trap that must have taken him days to work out.

Théra imagined the terror the thousands aboard those ships must be feeling as towering mountains of water and clouds loomed over them, bolts of lightning flashing within—hopeless, numbing terror, knowing that there was no escape, that death was just seconds away. In a single moment, nature would kill more people than had died at the Battle of Zathin Gulf. Pity overwhelmed her heart, and she turned her face away.

Luan Zyaji would have his vengeance after death.

Pékyu Vadyu's forces on Rui and Dasu would still be a threat to Dara, but without Cudyu's reinforcements, there was a much better chance that Phyro and Jia would be able to deal with them.

She shook her head; she had to change the subject of her thoughts.

"I'm sorry," said Théra to Takval. "Looks like Zomi was right. There will be no path through the Wall of Storms today."

Takval was distraught. "But we can't afford to wait! In ten more years, who knows how many more of my people will die in winter storms and summer droughts?"

"We may not have to wait that long," said a smiling Théra. "Zomi gave us another way just in case this passage didn't work out."

As if in response, the sea around them roiled and exploded. Ten crubens, the majestic sovereigns of the sea, surfaced and bobbed next to the ships, dwarfing the vessels with their bulk.

Théra laughed. "Looks like the old friends of the House of Dandelion have decided to help us again."

The ability of *Dissolver of Sorrows* and her sister ships to dive beneath the sea wasn't just a means of concealment; it was a way to bypass the Wall of Storms.

Inspired by the way Prince Takval himself had come to Dara, Zomi had come up with a bold new idea. Since whales were clearly able to swim under the Wall of Storms safely, then it made sense that underwater boats could as well. Although the mechanical crubens were limited to sailing along underwater volcano ranges, a ship that could sail underwater could also take a page from the whalers and be propelled by cetaceans.

Dissolver of Sorrows and the rest of the fleet were equipped with harpoons and strong cables. The idea was to take advantage of migrating whale pods who were headed in the right direction and hitch a ride underwater. The whales would pull the boats under the Wall of Storms, at which point the lines could be disengaged and the boats resurface.

Only now, instead of having to harpoon whales, the crubens were offering to give them a hand.

Strong cables were attached to the tails of the great crubens. The ships were ready to dive.

"Incoming!" one of the lookouts shouted.

In the distance, the Wall of Storms was almost completely closed. As the city-ships of the Lyucu foundered, a single garinafin had taken off without a pilot in an attempt to escape the doomed fleet. It saw the Dara fleet and winged its way directly at them.

Observers on the city-ship sent by Pékyu Vadyu, after suffering the shock of witnessing the destruction of the Lyucu fleet, now also steered their ship toward the Dara fleet.

"Dive! Dive!"

Théra and Takval and the rest of the crew scrambled belowdecks. Hatches were closed and oar ports closed and sealed. The ballast tanks began to fill with water. The ships began to slowly sink under the waves.

"We forgot to cast off the signaling kites!" Théra said. She gazed through the underwater portholes at the turbulent water in the wake of the massive cruben flukes. "And we never got a chance to let Pan know that the second Lyucu fleet is destroyed."

"Too late to worry about that now," said Takval. "They'll figure out what happened soon enough."

Above them, the garinafin circled. The cyclones of the Wall of Storms had destroyed the city-ships, depriving it of a place to land. The garinafin—riderless, terrified, and enraged—ignored the safe haven of the approaching Lyucu city-ship, despite the bone trumpets blaring from its deck. The beast would have its vengeance on these barbarian ships.

"We have to do something," Théra said. "It takes time for the ships to dive, and the crubens are vulnerable as long as they are near the surface."

Théra and Takval climbed back up onto the deck of *Dissolver of Sorrows*.

The garinafin dove at the cruben hauling their ship. Both of them more than a hundred feet in length, the king of flying beasts was going to challenge the sovereign of the seas.

The garinafin opened its maw wide, and just as it passed above the cruben, it snapped its jaws shut and opened them again to shoot out a scorching tongue of flames.

The cruben opened its blowhole and a spray of water shot into the air, meeting the tongue of fire halfway. Fire and water contended in midair and hissing steam drifted over the sea.

The cruben escaped unscathed. The garinafin swerved away, circling around for another strafing run.

The other Dara ships were almost all underwater. But if the garinafin avoided the blowhole, it could still severely injure the cruben before *Dissolver of Sorrows* was underwater.

"We have to distract it," Théra said. "Come with me!"

How she wished they had silkmotic arrows or lances.

She and Takval took up positions next to the winch for the

signaling kite. "Battle kites are from an older time, but sometimes you have to fight with whatever is at hand."

Grabbing onto the cable, they directed the kite to swerve at the garinafin. It was just like in the old sagas, where heroes vaulted into the heavens on battle kites to duel, and their loyal retainers directed the kites to dive, swerve, and chase, creating intricate patterns in the sky as though writing in air.

The kite line cut into Théra's and Takval's palms. They gritted their teeth and held on even as blood coated the line and made it even harder to grab on. Théra tore strips from her dress so that she and Takval could wrap them around their palms and continue the fight.

The pilotless garinafin snarled at the kite and rushed at it.

Théra and Takval just barely managed to direct the kite to dive out of the way.

The enraged garinafin hovered in air and opened its maw to breath fire, the fleet below it having been forgotten.

All the other ships had disappeared safely beneath the seas.

Théra and Takval jerked the line hard, and the fire tongue from the garinafin missed the kite by inches.

Finally realizing its error, the hovering garinafin now stared at the two humans on the deck of the ship responsible for the nettlesome kite and opened its maw.

"Pull hard!" Théra screamed. And she and Takval winched the kite line hard and dragged it toward them.

The jaws of the garinafin snapped shut. When they opened again, a tongue of fire would shoot out at Théra and Takval, incinerating them where they stood.

The kite dove at the garinafin and the line caught the thin, serpentine neck as the kite made a loud buzzing noise and zoomed rapidly in tightening circles around the head of the garinafin, finally entangling itself in the antlers after tying the mouth of the garinafin shut with the trailing cable.

The garinafin struggled mightily at the end of the line, now a living kite. The winch unspooled rapidly as the cable let out.

"Let's get out of here," said Théra. The two dove back under the hatch, sealing it behind them. *Dissolver of Sorrows* continued to take on water and began to sink under the waves.

The cruben dove as well and began to pull the ship deeper under the sea for a safe traversal of the Wall of Storms. The gigantic flukes undulated gracefully in the darkening water.

The kite line jerked straight. The strong strands of silk refused to yield as the garinafin was slowly, inexorably pulled down, despite the slowing beating of its massive wings.

With a thunderous splash, the garinafin crashed into the water, its air supply choked off by the kite line.

The crew of *Dissolver of Sorrows* felt a light jerk as the kite line finally broke, leaving the death-dealing beast bobbing at the surface of the sea.

By the time the Lyucu city-ship finally arrived on the scene, all the crew could do was to butcher the garinafin carcass and retrieve useful supplies. Not a single man or beast had survived from the second Lyucu fleet. The thanes onboard mourned their comrades and did not relish the thought of reporting the news to Pékyu Vadyu back home on Rui.

Théra gazed into the murky depths of the porthole as they headed for the Wall of Storms, for the unknown, for the future.

The questioning voice was mellifluous and gentle, like a cool spring after a march through the desert.

- *You've really decided to leave in this form?*

The replying voice cracked with the weight of age and wisdom, like the back of a turtle shell.

- *I have. It's not possible to pass through the Wall of Storms as long as I remain an immortal.*

- *Giving up your divinity is a drastic step.*

- *Tazu once lived an entire lifetime as a mortal, a long time ago.*

- *That was a punishment. You're doing this voluntarily.*

- *You have to admit, it's getting a bit uncomfortable here with the Lyucu insisting that Tazu and I share the same body.*

- That's just a temporary phase. It will be sorted out.

- Maybe, but the desire to see other shores is hardly unique among the mortals. I want to gaze upon new lands, and Dissolver of Sorrows, led by your protégée, is as good an opportunity as any. I'll be just another member of the crew on this grand adventure.

- We'll miss you. No god of Dara has ever done what you're about to do.

- There's always a first time for everything.

GLOSSARY

DARA

cashima: a scholar who has passed the second level of the Imperial examinations. The Classical Ano word means "practitioner." A *cashima* is allowed to wear his or her hair in a triple scroll-bun and carry a sword. *Cashima* can also serve as clerks for magistrates and mayors.

cruben: a scaled whale with a single horn protruding from its head; symbol of Imperial power.

cüpa: a game played with black and white stones on a grid.

dyran: a flying fish, symbol of femininity and sign of good fortune. It is covered by rainbow-colored scales and has a sharp beak.

firoa: a *cashima* who places within the top one hundred in the Grand Examination is given this rank. The Classical Ano word means "a (good) match." Based on their talents, the *firoa* are either given positions in Imperial administration, assigned to work for various enfeoffed nobles, or promoted to engage in further study or research with the Imperial Academy.

géüpa: an informal sitting position where the legs are crossed and folded under the body, with each foot tucked under the opposite thigh.

jiri: a woman's bow where the hands are crossed in front of the chest in a gesture of respect.

kunikin: a large, three-legged drinking vessel.

Mingén falcon: a species of extraordinarily large falcon native to the island of Rui.

mipa rari: a formal kneeling position where the back is kept straight and weight is evenly distributed between the knees and toes.

moaphya: an ancient Ano instrument of the "metal" class, consisting of rectangular bronze slabs of various thicknesses suspended from a frame and struck with a mallet to produce different pitches.

ogé: drops of sweat.

pana méji: a scholar who has done especially well in the Grand Examination and is given the chance to participate in the Palace Examination, where the emperor himself assesses the qualities of the candidates and assigns them a rank. The Classical Ano phrase means "on the list."

pawi: animal aspects of the gods of Dara.

Rénga: honorific used to address the emperor.

thakrido: an extremely informal sitting position where one's legs are stretched out in front; used only with intimates or social inferiors.

toko dawiji: a scholar who has passed the first level of the Imperial examinations. The Classical Ano phrase means "the elevated." A *toko dawiji* is allowed to wear his or her hair in a double scroll-bun.

tunoa: grapes.

-tika: suffix expressing endearment among family members.

LYUCU

kyoffir: an alcoholic drink made from fermented garinafin milk.

garinafin: the flying, fire-breathing beast that is the core of Lyucu culture. Its body is about the size of three elephants, with a long tail, two clawed feet, a pair of great, leathery wings, and a slender, snakelike neck topped with a deerlike, antlered head.

tolyusa: a plant with hallucinogenic properties; the berries are essential for the garinafins to breed successfully.

NOTES AND ACKNOWLEDGMENTS

Much of the magic of Dara consists of what we might term "technology." I'm indebted in my thinking about this subject to W. Brian Arthur, whose book, *The Nature of Technology: What It Is and How It Evolves*, provided many of the core ideas that guided the engineer-heroes of this series.

For a wonderful introduction to the amazing inventions of the age of electrostatics, consult Michael Brian Schiffer's *Draw the Lightning Down: Benjamin Franklin and Electrical Technology in the Age of Enlightenment*. While writing this book, I shocked myself multiple times with a Wimshurst machine and multiple Leyden jars—not an experiment I recommend to readers.

Bronze mirrors that reflect embossed patterns on the *back* of the mirror onto a screen even though they appear perfectly smooth are real, and they existed during the Han Dynasty. To learn more about them, see M. V. Berry's "Oriental Magic Mirrors and the Laplacian Image," in *European Journal of Physics* 27.1, 2006 (page 109).

Slam-rod fire starters like those used by the Adüans have been used by the people of Southeast Asia and the Pacific Islands for generations. The same principle lies behind the diesel engine.

The spinning shanty sung by the crew of *Silkmotic Arrow* was adapted from "The Silk-Making Woman," by Zhang Yu, an eleventh-century poet of the Song Dynasty.

∽ ∾ ∽ ∾

Special thanks to Igor Teper, who helped me come up with the idea of using the garinafin gut as the insulator in an especially powerful Leyden jar to shock the winged beasts, and to Amal El-Mohtar, who taught me the kenning "the word-hungry animal."

As always, my beta readers gave me invaluable feedback and proffered many wonderful suggestions to improve the novel: Anatoly Belilovsky, Dario Ciriello, Anaea Lay, Usman Malik, John P. Murphy, Erica Naone, Alex Shvartsman, Carmen Yiling Yan, Florina Yezril, and Caroline Yoachim. I am deeply indebted for their help.

My editor, Joe Monti, and my agent, Russ Galen, guided me with calm and steady hands through the wall of storms that threatened to capsize this book. Joe, especially, helped me through some particularly thorny passages. Everyone at Saga Press and Simon & Schuster pitched in to make this book as good as possible, and I'm grateful for their efforts. Among the large cast are Jeannie Ng and Valerie Shea, who caught the errors in the manuscript during copyediting; Michael McCartney, Sam Weber, and Robert Lazzaretti, who provided the beautiful art design, cover, and maps; Elena Stokes, Katy Hershberger, and Aubrey Churchward, who built the publicity campaign.

Last but not least, my family played perhaps the most important role of all. My mother-in-law, Helen Tang, pitched in to help with the kids so that I could have time on the weekends to write. My wife, Lisa, was the most critical beta reader of them all, and gave me the confidence to finish what seemed an impossible task. And above all, the wonder my daughters expressed at the world was the spark that lit up the heart of this book.